Lesley Pearse was born in Rochester, Kent, but was brought up in South London. She has three daughters and a grandson. Her novels have sold over ten million copies worldwide. Lesley now lives in Bristol and writes full-time.

Also by Lesley Pearse

Tara*
Charity*
Ellie*
Camellia*
Rosie
Charlie
Never Look Back
Trust Me
Father Unknown
Till We Meet Again
Remember Me
Secrets
A Lesser Evil
Hope
Faith
Gypsy
Stolen
Belle
The Promise
Forgive Me
Survivor
Without a Trace
Dead to Me

* Also available in Arrow Books

Georgia
Lesley Pearse

arrow books

8

Arrow Books
20 Vauxhall Bridge Road
London SW1V 2SA

Arrow Books is part of the Penguin Random House group of companies
whose addresses can be found at global.penguinrandomhouse.com

Penguin
Random House
UK

Quotation on page 571 from *The Prophet* by Kahlil Gibran

First published in Great Britain by William Heinemann in 1993
First published in paperback in Great Britain by Manderin Paperbacks in 1993
First published in paperback by Arrow Books in 1998
Reissued in Great Britain by Arrow Books in 2011

www.penguin.co.uk

A CIP catalogue record for this book is available from the British Library.

ISBN 9780099557456

Typeset by SX Composing DTP, Rayleigh, Essex

Penguin Random House is committed to a sustainable future
for our business, our readers and our planet. This book is made
from Forest Stewardship Council® certified paper.

MIX
Paper from
responsible sources
FSC
www.fsc.org FSC® C018179

Printed and bound in Great Britain by Clays Ltd, St Ives plc

To my girls, Lucy, Sammy and Jo;
without your love and support
I couldn't have written it.
A big thank you too for the real Georgia
who was friend, confidante and inspiration.

Chapter 1

Clanking keys and a ponderous step woke Georgia. Her ear was so finely tuned she knew which nun was coming, even her exact position.

It was Sister Agnes. Some of the nuns moved up the stairs in one fluid movement, some panted and huffed, pausing to rest halfway, but Sister Agnes despite her bulk and age ploughed on steadily to the top, her breath wheezing faintly.

She had reached the top now, passing the long, narrow, barred window, on her way to ring the early morning bell.

Georgia sat up in bed, rubbing her eyes. A murky grey light showed up twelve iron beds, six to each side of the large room. Small mounds in each, still fast asleep.

The heavy footsteps moved away from her dormitory, down towards where the bell hung on the wall just outside the big girls' room. Another pair of feet were coming down the stairs from the floor above, this time light and bouncy, almost running as they went on down further. That would be Sister Theresa on her way to make Mother Superior's early morning tea.

A whimper made Georgia's head turn to the bed on her left. As the child stirred, so an unmistakable acrid smell of urine wafted across to her nostrils.

'Pamela!' she hissed. 'Aggie will be in here any

1

minute, run for the bathroom. I'll try and cover for you.'

The bell rang out in the uncarpeted corridor, drowning Pamela's reply and as the last echo reverberated round the convent, so heavy feet thudded towards them.

Pamela's first cry had been one of dismay to find she was wet, but her second was one of terror. Instead of shooting out of her bed, and running like a hare out of harm's way, she just cowered, small arms over her head, waiting for the beating she knew would soon come.

Georgia knew to protect Pamela she had to create a diversion. Tossing back her covers she leapt into the air.

Sister Agnes paused momentarily in the doorway in time to see Georgia's trial bounce, landing feet apart, hands clutching her pyjama trousers.

'Get down this minute!' she shouted. The child looked like a chimney-sweep. As thin as a stick in oversized striped pyjamas, her crop of black curls standing out like a wire brush.

One hand flew up to hold down the starched wimple, the other lifted her habit clear of the floor.

'How dare you?' her voice rasped as she swept down the room indignantly.

Georgia merely grinned at her, a yellow-brown face cut in two with the flash of white teeth. Another small bounce quickly followed by a stronger one, and she had flipped herself over and landed on her feet again, just yards from the exasperated nun. She had perfected this somersault only days earlier in the playroom, where she had launched herself from an old couch on to cushions in front of an enthusiastic audience. But landing on cold, hard lino had jarred her legs and back and she toppled back against the bed rail.

'Morning, Sister Agnes,' she panted, hauling the

baggy trousers back to her waist. 'Did you see how good it was?'

Sister Agnes was the oldest nun in the convent. Humourless, mean-spirited and cruel. Black hairs sprouted from her white flabby chin, a hooked nose with a jiggling wart next to it vying for attention, and sharp piggy eyes that could spot a misdemeanour almost through a wooden door.

'This is a dormitory, not a gymnasium,' she sniffed. 'You are nine, it's high time you set a good example to the younger girls.'

Instinctively the old nun knew Georgia was trying to distract her, and insolent interference was something she wouldn't tolerate. Georgia infuriated her. Not only was she scrawny with huge eyes that dominated her yellowy face, but also endless punishments and beatings couldn't wipe her ear-to-ear grin away. Despite her skinniness and her mixed blood she had managed to become the leader of the younger girls and worse still she was encouraging them all in acts of disobedience.

'I'll deal with you later,' Sister Agnes swept the dormitory with her sharp eyes. Small girls jumping into their navy blue knickers, eyes avoiding her. 'What's been going on in here?'

'There was a noise,' Georgia sidled away from the Sister, rolling her eyes round the room in pretended alarm. 'I think a bird's got in again.'

It was all she could think of on the spur of the moment. Only last summer a pigeon had found its way in and to the children's amusement Sister nearly had hysterics. The way she had sped from the room as the bird flapped around her veil was something they still giggled about.

'We heard it too,' a chorus of agreement came from three of Georgia's closest allies. As they struggled into grey skirts and jumpers, they nodded at one another, waving their hands as if to indicate the flight path.

3

Sister spun round, her hands reaching up to her veil, eyes scanning, ears straining for the sound of wings or cooing. Jennifer, the youngest child in the dormitory, stood with her thumb in her mouth, her pyjama jacket almost reaching her thin, scabby knees.

Every girl was poised expectantly, breath like smoke in the cold air, eyes alternating between the hesitant nun and Georgia. Bravery vanished as the big woman turned slowly. Each girl blanched under her inspection, fingers hastily fumbling for buttons, eyes downcast. At best she was as sour as a crab apple, angry, she was dangerous.

'Come here, girl.' Sister's voice echoed round the bare room. Her chins were quivering ominously, her face turning puce.

Georgia cast one frantic look at Pamela, hoping she had the sense to move now, then sauntered over to Sister.

Sister caught her shoulder with one hand, her other swung out and hit Georgia with her full strength across the face.

Georgia stumbled back against a bed rail catching her side with a crack. A rustle came from Pamela's bed on the other side of the room. Georgia gritted her teeth, willing Sister not to turn and catch sight of the girl. But Sister's sharp ears had picked up the sound too. She wheeled round and at the same time her nose twitched furiously. The hasty dressing was halted. Ten mouths dropped open in horror, Jennifer sucked vigorously on her thumb. Pamela just stood by her bed. Pyjamas steaming, fists covering her eyes, whimpering and shaking with fear.

She was a quiet, nervous child, still in the throes of grief from losing her mother. Straggly brown hair, a slight squint and a tendency towards fatness hadn't endeared her to anyone other than Georgia.

'Seven years old and you still wet the bed,' Sister's

4

bellow caused yet another trickle to splash on to the floor. 'You are worse than an animal, even they don't lie in their own filth!'

One claw shot out, grabbing the terrified child who didn't have the sense to run, and with the other she boxed her ears so hard that Pamela fell to the floor.

The sheer force of Sister's attack made Georgia spring forward. 'Don't you dare!' she yelled, lungeing at the black habit. She saw one heavy black shoe swing forward to kick the helpless child and she pummelled her fists against the nun's wide posterior. 'She can't help it. You only make her more frightened. Leave her alone you bully!'

The other children hopped from foot to foot on the icy lino. One of the older girls caught hold of Jennifer and began helping her to dress, anxious to get her out of the way.

Sister turned and caught Georgia by the wrists. Her face was purple now, her thin lips curling back.

'Get downstairs and fill the coal scuttles,' she roared, spittle spraying the child's face. 'You won't get away with this insolence.'

Georgia backed away to her pile of clothes. If she said another word it was quite likely Sister would lock her in the cupboard they used as a punishment cell. Bread and water only, crouching in that black hole until bedtime, without even a blanket to wrap round her. She couldn't help Pamela any further and she wanted her breakfast.

Later, as Georgia knelt in the outhouse shovelling coal, she could hear Pamela crying in the bathroom. It wasn't even screams of anger, just a wail of distress.

She could picture the scene. Sister Agnes would have her standing in a bath of cold water, scrubbing at her with a brush. Pinching, slapping and all the time lashing her with jibes about her bedwetting.

5

There'd be no breakfast for her. While the other girls ate their porridge, Pamela would be alone in the laundry, crying as she struggled to wash the sheets. Why did Aggie think punishment would make her stop doing it? Even Georgia knew Pamela couldn't help it.

'Aggie's evil,' she chanted to herself as she wielded the shovel, banging it down hard on the coal, pretending Sister Agnes was under it. 'Why doesn't someone stop her?'

Georgia was always being punished, if she dawdled coming home from school, if she talked during meals or giggled in the chapel, so much so that it hardly concerned her any longer. She learned to accept that Sister Agnes would never like her, along with accepting she was a different colour from the other girls. It even amused her when Sister called her 'Devil's spawn' it reminded her of tadpoles in the tank at school.

She had mentioned it to Sister Mary once and her laughter had banished any sinister thoughts.

'You are like a little tadpole,' her blue eyes twinkled. 'But you'll change into a beautiful woman, just you wait.'

Until she was five or six there had always been the possibility she might be adopted one day. Most Sundays couples came to St Joseph's looking for a child to love. Some old, some young, some rich with cars and fur coats, some ordinary like the other girls' mothers at school. But they all had one thing in common, they wanted pretty blonde girls with blue eyes, the younger and sweeter the better.

There had been times when Georgia tried the ploys the other girls used. Climbing on to laps, tugging at clothes, beguiling smiles, letting her eyes fill with tears, but all she ever heard was the same remark.

'She's a nice little thing, but we couldn't cope with mixed race I'm afraid.'

Georgia sighed deeply as she hauled the two heavy

coal buckets across the yard and down the stone steps into the kitchen. She was resigned to staying here until she was fifteen and found a job. At least she had school.

Most of the other girls hated school more than the convent. They were singled out as different from other children, not only by the way they were shepherded across the busy main road by one of the nuns, but by their badly fitting clothes, heavy shoes and lack-lustre hair. But to Georgia every day at school was an adventure, a chance to see the outside world, to learn about things and places, to feel normal.

She liked the pictures on the walls and growing beans in blotting paper, mixing powder paint and making puppets, the percussion band and stories. But most of all she liked Miss Powell and her music.

Miss Powell was the headmistress. She had a kind of glamour in her dark suits and white frilly blouses, her blonde wavy hair swept up at the back. But when she sat at the piano and played, that was the very best.

Hymns, sea shanties, folk songs, beautiful haunting melodies that made pictures in Georgia's head. Without Miss Powell perhaps Georgia would never have found she could sing!

Singing made her feel good. She could forget the convent and Sister Agnes, her dark skin and the people who didn't want a mixed-race child. When she sang people looked at her and listened, even her own teacher who grumbled because she didn't learn her multiplication tables looked proud of her.

'You've been given a very special gift Georgia.' Miss Powell had smiled down at her the day she picked her to be Archangel Gabriel in the school nativity play. 'I've chosen you because your voice can do justice to the beauty of Christmas. I want everyone to be as proud of you as I am.'

That afternoon in December when she had stood on the stage wrapped in a white sheet with a tinsel halo, hearing applause ringing out round the assembly hall, had been the best moment in her life.

'In the Bleak Mid-Winter' seemed so appropriate now as she rinsed the coal dust from her hands before joining the other children for breakfast. Her cheeks were icy, her hands and thighs chapped with the cold, and right now Sister Agnes was plotting her punishment.

When Sister Agnes didn't retaliate immediately after the usual Saturday breakfast of porridge and boiled eggs, Georgia put punishment out of her mind. Keeping warm outside in the playground was more important than worrying what might happen later.

St Joseph's gave the impression of being a large country house. The gravelled drive, the sweeping lawn, the walled kitchen garden and the old knarled trees were all from a more elegant period.

In fact the large house was only a stone's throw from Grove Park station in South London. Minutes away were rows of shops and a street busy with cars and buses.

Three floors, with basement and attics, it was too large to heat adequately. The once gracious drawing and dining rooms were now draughty dormitories. Only Mother Superior's sitting room held any comfort. Even the small chapel on the first floor was gradually becoming dingy through lack of maintenance.

The garden was beautiful in summer. The children ran on the grass, chasing each other around the trees. There was the smell of the flowers, the big bushes they could hide behind, and long days with little supervision.

But now in February it was torture. The wind whistled through thin gaberdine raincoats, catching sore places on bare legs, nipping at ears and fingers. If they played with the snow brushed up round the

8

playground it soon made them colder. All they could do was huddle closer to the walls. Twenty-four girls from four to twelve waiting for the bell to ring for dinner. Pale, pinched faces, gazing longingly at the steamy laundry where the older girls were privileged enough to be up to their elbows in soapy suds or sweating over hot irons.

'She'll call you in soon.' Susan Mullins a carroty-haired eleven-year-old with freckles moved closer to Georgia. 'Are you scared?'

The word had even spread to the bigger girls about Georgia's run-in with Aggie. It was almost worth being punished to see their approval. But however big and tough she felt here surrounded by admiring friends it didn't stop the need to keep going to the lavatory, or the moments of panic when she saw a nun's face at the window.

'No,' Georgia gave a wobbly grin. 'I'll get a knife and cut off her wart, then she'll bleed to death.'

The door of the playroom opened just before tea-time. Georgia was curled up on one of the old settees reading an ancient comic, younger girls were racing around the big empty room, while older girls huddled in a corner by the hot pipes.

'Georgia,' Sister Mary's voice made her jump. 'Mother Superior wants you.'

Sister Mary was the youngest of the nuns. Perhaps in her mid-thirties, but it was difficult to put an age to her. She was tall and slender, with a smooth, unlined face. She had the appearance of a china doll, dainty fair eyebrows set above eyes like summer skies, and rosy lips over small white teeth.

Yet despite Sister Mary's youth, she was tough enough to act as a mediator between them and Sister Agnes. Her rippling laughter, her understanding of children, her gentleness and soft voice gave each child a feeling of security. She had trained as a nurse. During the war she had been close to enemy lines and the older girls speculated why anyone so pretty had chosen to enter a convent instead of marrying and having children of her own.

The other girls from the middle dormitory were looking at Georgia in horror. Pamela's eyes filled up with tears, she clutched Georgia with her small podgy hands.

'It's all my fault,' she whimpered. 'You'll get a beating now, just for sticking up for me.'

'Don't worry,' Georgia said reassuringly, slipping an arm round the smaller child. 'I'm not afraid of her. Besides, I might be able to tell her how cruel Sister Agnes is to you.'

'You're so brave,' Pamela sighed, her good eye on Georgia, the other one on the window. 'I wish I could be like you.'

A statue of the Virgin Mary stood at the turn of the stairs, with a small night light in front of it. Georgia genuflected, screwing her eyes up tightly as she made a quick plea for mercy.

The wide hallway was very dark. It was oak panelled, the only natural light came from the window on the staircase, and a lone candle under a picture of the Sacred Heart. It was no use looking at the front door and considering escape. Even if she could reach the big bolt at the top she couldn't get far in the snow with only plimsoles on her feet and no coat. Instead she screwed her hands into fists, wiped her nose on her jumper sleeve and knocked at Mother Superior's door.

'Come in!' Mother Superior's faint old voice crackled from within, like ancient parchment.

Georgia turned the brass knob with two hands, opened it just a crack, and tentatively put her head inside.

Mother Superior sat by a blazing log fire, her back to the window, a small, bowed figure in an oversized winged armchair.

'Come on in, no one's going to bite you.'

To Georgia's surprise the tone was almost jovial, but then Sister Agnes was probably lurking behind the door.

Georgia slunk in, eyes down on the carpet, hands still holding the door.

'Close that door,' Mother Superior snapped. 'We don't want to freeze.'

It was the 'we' that made Georgia glance up. A lady was sitting on the settee further back from the fire, looking at her. Mother Superior was wearing the smile she usually only reserved for Christmas and visitors.

Georgia closed the door carefully, arranging the heavy wool curtain over it to keep the draughts out. She had seen this lady before once or twice at school, yet she wasn't a teacher. Had Georgia been so bad they needed outside help now, to punish her?

Mother Superior reached out one tiny, bony hand, in a gesture that said Georgia was to come closer. She was rumoured to be eighty. Whether this was true or not Georgia had no idea, but she certainly was very wrinkled; not just around her eyes, but all over her face, as if she had shrunk a foot or two and all the spare skin remained.

'Mrs Anderson is a children's officer. She's come here to talk to you.'

Georgia stood uneasily on the hearth rug, her stomach churning with fear. She knew what children's officers did, they were the ones who came and took girls away when they wouldn't behave. Yet for all that, Mrs Anderson didn't look fierce. She had that same look of authority Miss Powell had, and she sat as serenely as if she were in her own home. Her face was round and her hair cut almost like a man's, but her smile and pink cheeks were distinctly feminine.

'Hallo Georgia,' the woman got up, taking Georgia by surprise as her strong, clear voice filled the room. 'I don't suppose you remember me, but I saw you at the Christmas play.'

'You're going to take me away?' Georgia stuck out her small pointed chin defiantly. 'I didn't do anything but try and help Pamela. Sister Agnes is cruel and mean.'

The lady looked from both Georgia to Mother Superior in surprise.

Georgia was baffled now. Her entire childhood had been spent studying adults' secret looks. Whatever this lady had come for it wasn't to chastise her further.

'Now then, Georgia,' Mother Superior's tone was honeyed, the warning of punishment hidden except to the two of them. She got up unsteadily and put one hand on Georgia's shoulder, bony fingers digging in her flesh just hard enough to remind her she hadn't been brought in to reveal secrets about anyone. 'Mrs Anderson has come here today to offer you a wonderful opportunity. Don't try to be difficult.'

'Perhaps I should talk to Georgia on her own for a while?' Mrs Anderson's suggestion sounded more like a statement.

Georgia looked from one adult to the other, puzzled, but no longer frightened.

'If you think that is necessary,' the older woman replied starchly. She straightened up her small, bent frame, her bloodless lips pursed with irritation. 'I have got some important jobs to do.' She bustled towards the door, every inch of her showing disapproval.

Mrs Anderson got up, took Georgia's hand and led her back to the settee.

'She wasn't keen to go,' she said, lifting Georgia's

face up with one finger to study it. 'So I'll have to be quick.'

Georgia liked her touch. It was like her manner, confident, kindly, maybe even motherly. Her eyes were grey, with tiny specks of green, bright and unwavering, a few tiny lines around them, maybe more from laughter than old age.

There was a lovely fresh smell about her. Like sheets when they had hung outside all day in the sunshine. She was a big woman, with ample hips and a bosom that pushed out the front of her jacket, but not exactly fat. Not as elegant as Miss Powell, but she looked more friendly.

'I saw you at the school concert,' she said softly. 'I loved your voice and I couldn't forget you. When I discovered you had been here for years, I tried to find out if I could adopt you.'

Georgia's mouth dropped open in surprise.

'Apparently that isn't possible. But I still want you to be my little girl. I want you to come and live with me if you'd like to.'

It was like a dream, yet the plump, warm hand holding hers was real enough.

'You want me?' Georgia's wide mouth split into a grin which spread from ear to ear.

To her surprise Mrs Anderson's eyes seemed to be filling with tears.

'Don't cry,' Georgia leaned closer, tentatively touching the lady's face. 'I can be ready in ten minutes.'

Mrs Anderson laughed then, the sort of laugh Georgia never heard from the nuns. It was the sound of freedom, a wonderful sound that somehow embodied life outside the convent. Georgia joined in, her nose wrinkling up with merriment.

'Oh, Georgia, I knew you were my little girl when I first saw you,' she laughed, squeezing Georgia's hand still tighter. 'My goodness, you are a tonic.'

'What's a tonic?' Georgia's face was suddenly more serious.

'It's a kind of medicine you take, to make you feel better,' Mrs Anderson explained, her eyes still dancing with laughter. 'You've just banished every doubt in my mind.'

'Do you really want to take me with you?' Georgia's eyes were wary. Sister Mary and Miss Powell could be relied on but she'd never met any other adults who didn't change their minds.

'Yes, but I can't take you now. It will be tomorrow.'

Georgia thought quickly. She was sure she could trust Mrs Anderson. This wasn't one of those empty-headed ladies who came here looking for a small, cuddly plaything. She wasn't afraid of anything or anyone.

'Can you do something for me then?' Georgia asked.

'I'll try.'

'Well get someone to stop Sister Agnes. She beats Pamela for wetting the bed and she can't help it.'

'I'll do my best,' Mrs Anderson looked shocked. 'Has she ever beaten you?'

'Loads of times,' Georgia said nonchalantly. 'But I'm bigger and tougher. I can stand up for myself. Pamela can't. She's only seven and her mummy and daddy are dead.'

'But you haven't any parents either?' Mrs Anderson's voice dropped, she smoothed Georgia's cheek, then kissed her hair.

'Yes,' Georgia looked up at her proudly. 'But I've been on my own since I was born. I've learnt to cope with things, and anyway I don't wet the bed.'

Mrs Anderson seemed to find that amusing.

'Mr Anderson and myself live in a nice big house in Blackheath,' she explained. 'I'm very glad you don't wet the bed as I've bought a nice new one for you. You'll go to school nearby and we have the heath and

14

Greenwich Park just across the road. But once you have settled in with us, I'll see what I can do for your friend.'

'Have you got lots of children?' Georgia asked.

'No, I haven't any,' Mrs Anderson's mouth was twitching with merriment at Georgia's rapt expression. 'But you'll soon make new friends at school.'

'Will there be music there?' There had to be some hidden catch, but maybe Miss Powell and her piano was a small price to pay.

'There certainly will, I play the piano myself and if you like we can arrange music and singing lessons.'

Georgia's eyes lit up, her mouth fell open and if it hadn't been for the door opening again, she would have whooped with delight. But Mother Superior shuffled into the room, her wrinkled face full of suspicion.

'Have we had enough time?' her sarcasm was not wasted even on Georgia.

'We'll have all the time in the world soon,' Mrs Anderson said sweetly. She bent over to kiss Georgia, and whispered in her ear. 'When you're my little girl.'

'Run along now Georgia.' Mother Superior once more put on the expression for visitors, a smarmy smile, a patronizing tone and all the time her bony fingers fiddling with her Rosary. 'Mrs Anderson will be coming in the morning for you.'

The white tiled bathroom was full of steam. The floor was awash where less than an hour ago twenty other children had been bathed in the four large baths. Despite the steam the room was freezing, the windows rattling as a gale-force wind howled around the old convent.

Georgia wanted to dance and sing. She wanted to tell the world this was her last night. Tomorrow she would have her own room. A mother who would tuck her into bed. Someone who liked her singing and could play the piano.

Since meeting Mrs Anderson earlier on, she had been kept apart from the other children. Mother Superior had even said she was to spend the night in the isolation room at the top of the house. But no one could silence Georgia's high spirits tonight. Alone in the bathroom she stripped off the matted grey jumper, the long, ugly skirt, her flannel petticoat, liberty bodice and her navy blue baggy knickers. Forgetting the propriety of never standing naked in sight of the Lord, even the shabby old vest was tossed away.

She picked up a small towel, wrapped it round her middle like a dress, and made believe she was a grown-up lady in front of a big audience.

'In Dublin's fair city, where the maids are so pretty,' she sang at the top of her voice, dancing nimbly around the room. 'That's where I first set eyes on sweet Molly Malone.'

The door opened silently. Georgia was so engrossed in her performance, she didn't see Sister Agnes's approach, or hear the sharp intake of breath.

Crack!

Georgia jumped in the air as if she'd been stung by a wasp, dropping her towel to the floor.

Sister Agnes had one of her favourite weapons in her hand. It was merely a thin, damp towel, but in her hands it was deadly. She was poised for mischief, flicking it accurately across Georgia's naked buttocks like a whip.

'Admiring ourselves were we?' her bloated ugly face was contorted with suspicion. Already she was preparing the small towel for another blow.

'I wasn't,' the small girl retorted indignantly, jumping to one side, hands raised to ward off more blows. 'I was just singing.'

'Don't lie to me,' Sister roared, flicking the towel expertly to catch the child yet again. 'You are a wicked sinful girl with unclean thoughts. How dare you expose yourself?'

In her excitement Georgia had forgotten the incident in the dormitory, but it was clear Sister Agnes hadn't. Yet surely she wouldn't dare hurt her now, not when Mrs Anderson was coming back so soon?

'Don't you touch me,' she yelled with all the volume she could muster. 'I've got a mother now!'

'How dare you?' Sister Agnes dropped the towel and stalked towards her, her several chins quivering round her wimple with rage, beady eyes full of malice.

Georgia backed into the tiled wall, her bare toes scrabbling to get a grip on the wet floor. She was prepared now to stand her ground, not to let the old woman get the better of her.

'Don't you hit me,' she yelled defiantly, her dark eyes blazing with new-found courage. 'I'll tell her!'

'Tell her what you like. Do you think anyone will believe some half-witted nigger instead of me?'

Georgia braced herself. Time and time again Sister Agnes had thrown that word at her.

'I'm not a nigger,' her eyes filled with tears. 'That's an evil word and so are you!'

Sister stared at her for a moment, clearly surprised at any child answering her back. Georgia's darkness showed up more clearly in here, against the white walls. Naked, she looked thin to the point of malnutrition, her limbs like sticks, her head seeming too big for her body.

To Sister Agnes, the child before her was a product of the Devil. A child born out of wedlock, abandoned at a few months, proof in her eyes that the mother was a whore.

She resented the way Georgia got attention both from adults and the other children by singing and play acting. No other child at St Joseph's ever had the nerve to answer back as she did and now she had been singled out for a new home with that insolent woman who dared suggest Georgia was undernourished. Mrs Anderson wasn't even a Catholic. What right did she have to criticise the care in St Joseph's?

Georgia hadn't reckoned with Sister coming armed with her small cane. Like a snake it appeared out of the folds of Sister's habit. Some fourteen inches of thin, bendy wood, polished and smooth with years of handling.

Sister Agnes was old, fat and out of breath. But Georgia was no match for her, not now Sister was filled with righteous indignation.

Moving back, Georgia found herself trapped in the corner and she watched in horrified fascination as the old woman stooped over the bath and turned the taps on full to drown any noise. Still stooping, cane in one hand, the other on the tap, she turned slightly to look at Georgia, her lips curled into a sneer.

Georgia tried to slide along the wall. Her heart thumped and she felt as if her legs were embedded in cement.

One claw-like hand reached out and clamped on to Georgia's bony shoulder and the other hand lifted the thin cane up high.

There was a whistling noise and the cane flashed through the air, catching the child's arm, searing through the skin.

'Please don't!' Georgia yelled, dancing in pain.

'Bend over,' Sister bellowed. 'You've had this coming to you for a long time.'

'Please, Sister,' Georgia whimpered. 'I'm sorry, I didn't mean what I said.'

'Oh yes you did. You think you are special. You always have. It's about time someone took you to task, beat that proud look out of you.'

Georgia cowered further into the corner, slumping

down onto her haunches, arms raised to protect her head.

She saw one black shoe shoot out from under the habit, kicking out her legs from under her, and her bottom crashed to the floor.

The next blow caught her on the thigh. She scrabbled to get away, but made the mistake of presenting her bottom as she did so.

Again and again the cane cut into her bottom, legs and back. She screamed in terror, but it was drowned by the rush of bath water.

'Get in that bath!' Sister Agnes yelled.

Skirting round Sister, Georgia moved quickly to the other side of the bath and jumped in. The water was scalding hot, but she didn't dare cry out. It came up to her armpits and burnt into the weals left by the cane.

Georgia had no fight left. She submitted to being dragged up and scrubbed.

'Now, dry yourself and get up to bed!' Sister hissed. 'And don't take long about it.'

The door slammed behind her and Georgia groped blindly for the towel. She was shaking with cold. Her eyes stung and her body was on fire. Slowly she hauled herself out of the bath, and sunk on to a small stool. Her earlier happiness glugged down the drain with the bath water, and was replaced by tears of despair.

'Georgia?'

She blinked at the sound of Sister Mary's voice at the door.

'What is it?' Sister moved across the wet floor, arms outstretched, her face a picture of concern.

'Sis – , Sister Agnes,' Georgia stuttered.

A dry, softer towel was wrapped round her, the smaller one deftly removed and wound round her hair like a turban.

'What happened?' Sister asked, her tone gentle as always, in sharp contrast to Agnes's.

Georgia tried to explain. Another coughing fit engulfed her, this time coming in great whoops, bringing with it large quantities of fluid she had swallowed.

Sister Mary turned the child deftly onto her stomach across her own lap, patting her back until the attack stopped. Georgia could feel her soothing her wounds gently with the towel.

'What did you do?' Sister's voice was soft, yet with a touch of steel.

'I was singing and dancing, she said I was admiring myself. She called me a nigger.' Georgia sobbed.

Sister made no comment. Just lifted the child up into her arms and held her tightly against her chest, soothing her with endearments.

'Let me get you dry and into bed,' her voice shook a little. 'You've got a big day ahead of you tomorrow. Sister Agnes won't touch you again.'

Scooping up Georgia in her arms, still only wrapped in the towel, she walked swiftly up the stairs with her in the direction of the isolation room.

'Wait a moment,' she said as she dropped the child on the bed. 'I'll just go and find some pyjamas.'

The room was cosy at night. A small bedside lamp and a lighted gas fire gave the sparsely furnished room warmth that every other room in the convent lacked.

Although she hurt all over, Georgia noticed that clean clothes had been placed on the chair for the morning. A tartan kilt and a much nicer jumper than she normally got to wear. Her sobs faded to hiccups.

'Here we are,' Sister Mary bustled back into the room, a pair of pyjamas and vest over her arm.

In one hand she held a pot of ointment.

'Lay down on your tummy,' she said gently. 'This will help the soreness.'

At first Georgia winced at each soft touch, but gradually under Sister Mary's healing hands, the pain lessened. Firmly, Sister turned her and more ointment was applied to her stomach, chest and arms.

'That's better,' Sister said, picking up the vest and popping it over her head, quickly followed by the warm pyjamas. 'Now into bed with you and I'll dry your hair a bit more.'

'Why is Sister Agnes so mean?' Georgia plucked up courage to ask, as her hair was rubbed vigorously.

'I can't say anything about another Sister,' Mary said reprovingly with a twinkle in her eye. 'But you will find the world is full of all kinds of people, some nice, some plain nasty. Let's just say that maybe Sister Agnes isn't as happy inside as me.'

'Why are you happy?' Georgia twisted her head round to look Mary full in the face.

'Because God saw fit to send me here,' Sister smiled, her blue eyes twinkling. 'How else would I have met you?'

'Why is this lady taking me to her home?'

Sister laughed, showing small even white teeth in the half light. 'So many questions! I expect she liked your courage and enthusiasm, just like I do.'

'So does that mean I will be her little girl for ever?' Georgia's eyes were shining now, her sore body forgotten.

'I think so,' Sister Mary wound a curl round her finger. 'She is a strong, caring woman Georgia, you'll have a good home with her and her husband. All you have to do is be a good girl and she'll take care of everything else.'

'If I'm bad will she send me back here?' Georgia's eyes widened with fright.

'I doubt that somehow,' Sister laughed soft and low. 'I don't think she's the type to give up on anything or anyone. But don't you get any ideas about testing her will you? Even the nicest people have their breaking point.'

She pulled a comb out of her pocket and ran it through Georgia's damp hair. Georgia glanced up and saw a tear trickling down the nun's cheek.

'Why are you crying?' she whispered.

'I'm just sad to know this is the last night I'll spend with you,' Sister replied, wiping her cheek with the back of her hand. 'We've been friends a long time. I was the one who undressed you the first night you came here. You clung to me like a little monkey.'

She smiled as she remembered.

It was a wild November night when Georgia arrived with a social worker. Just twenty-one months old, plump, with a halo of jet black curls, her thumb firmly planted in her mouth, her eyes as black as night.

Whether she had been abandoned or orphaned wasn't known, just the name 'Georgia' passed on, her birth date of January 6th 1945 just an approximation.

Sister Mary had only been at St Joseph's a few weeks and she was appalled by the conditions. No toys, precious little warm clothing or bedding, children with running sores, threadworms and lice. She had been sent here because of her nursing training and youth, yet so far she had been unable to make a dent in the mountain of things wrong with the place.

She took Georgia into her arms, rocking her against her breast and watched her dark eyes beginning to droop. She knew she should insist the child was taken somewhere with proper facilities for babies, but she heard the exasperation in the social worker's voice, the complaints that every home was full, and her heart went out to the child.

It was love from that first night. Bathing, dressing, teaching and feeding, this was no longer duty, but joy. Small brown arms wrapped around her neck, damp sweet kisses, a constant reminder of everything she had given up by taking her vows.

22

But as the years passed, joy was tinged with fear. She saw Georgia's character forming, a bold clown, leader and entertainer, a child that rushed to the defence of anyone weaker and she knew Sister Agnes had the power and hate to crush it.

Mary had managed to change many things for the better in St Joseph's. Diet, hygiene and health were all improved, but still Mother Superior turned a blind eye to the sadistic cruelty of Sister Agnes, refusing to admit that women of her character had no place with children.

When she heard Mrs Anderson wished to foster Georgia, Mary felt as if her heart was being torn out. Yet at the same time she wasn't prepared to sit by and watch while Georgia's proud spirit was broken, hear her voice silenced and see her turn into a cringing, empty shell.

'Goodnight, my darling,' Sister Mary bent down over Georgia and kissed her cheek. 'Remember me in your prayers sometimes, maybe write to me when you have the time.'

'I'll come back and visit you,' Georgia said sleepily, her eyelashes dropping over her cheeks.

'Just sing for me once in a while,' Sister wiped back a tear from her cheek. 'I'll hear you wherever I am. God bless you.'

Georgia was asleep by the time she got to the door. Her dark tight curls forming a black halo on the pillow, one arm curled round her head. In that instant Sister Mary saw a glimpse of the beauty which was to come. Coffee skin with pink undertones, perfect bone structure. Features too angular for a mere child of nine, but the basic materials for a real beauty.

Silently she closed the door, pausing for one moment to compose herself.

When Mrs Anderson saw the weals on the child's body tomorrow, she knew with utter certainty that the caring woman would act fast and without mercy. Per-

Chapter 2

September 1956

'Drop me off here Daddy!' Georgia's voice had a tremor of apprehension as they turned into Kidbrooke Lane and the playing fields of the comprehensive school loomed in front of them.

It was a hot sunny morning, vivid splashes of colour in the suburban gardens, dahlias at their best as if trying to outdo one another in their brilliance.

'Don't you want me to come in with you?' Brian Anderson pulled up, turning towards Georgia in his seat.

'I'll look like a baby if you do.'

'You are our baby,' Brian chuckled. 'But I know what you mean. Some things are better tackled alone.'

'Were you scared on your first day at a big school?' Georgia leaned against his shoulder for a moment, drawing strength from the smell of starched shirt and aftershave.

'Terrified,' he admitted, patting her small hand with his big one. 'But it wasn't as bad as I expected, nothing ever is.'

'I'd better go now,' she straightened up, then leaned closer to kiss his smooth cheek. 'Do I really look all right?'

'All right! You look perfect,' he smiled, wishing he could cuddle her one more time and banish that worried frown. 'Off you go now, and don't worry about any-

25

thing, there will be hundreds of other new girls, just like you.'

Brian Anderson watched as she crossed the road and walked along the railings to the gate. Scores of other girls were filling the tree-lined avenue, peace halted now the new term had started. But Brian Anderson hardly noticed the other girls, his eyes were just on Georgia.

In two years she had changed almost beyond recognition. She was taller, her stick-like limbs had filled out with good food, the once cropped hair allowed to curl on her shoulders and her skin had lost that yellowy tinge.

The navy-blue pleated skirt swung beneath a smart new blazer and she wore her beret at a jaunty angle. Yet the sight of her childish brown legs in long grey socks and the stiff, shiny satchel on her shoulder brought an unexpected lump to his throat.

'Make them accept you Georgia,' he said softly as he put his car into gear and pulled away. 'Just the way you did me.'

Brian Anderson knew better than anyone how it felt to be different. Brought up alone with his widowed mother in the big house on Blackheath where he still lived, he understood a child's need to be just like everyone else.

His mother had meant well keeping him away from other children. She wanted to protect him from harm, wrap him in a cocoon of devotion. A small, select private school where rough games were frowned on, evenings spent reading with her by the fire, or long walks in the summer. He had allowed himself to be nudged into banking as a career. Girls, dancing, drinking or sport were things that men did who weren't gentlemen. Brian didn't consider himself weak at bowing to his mother's wishes. He was merely a loner who didn't need change, new experiences or even challenge. But sometimes he would have preferred to have had a more outgoing life.

As Brian drove down towards Lewisham across the heath he caught a glimpse of himself in the driving mirror. Sandy thinning hair, neatly combed to one side, a round, plump fresh face which had barely changed from his teens. Pale blue eyes with gingery lashes and eyebrows. A straight small nose and the kind of even white teeth which owed much to his mother's care and attention. Not a handsome man, but as his mother had always pointed out, 'Clothes maketh a man.' His suits were all hand-tailored, navy blue with a feint pin stripe for the bank, light grey for social occasions and a navy blazer for weekends and holidays.

His shirts always went to the laundry, he liked his collars stiff and starchy, his ties subdued. He had four pairs of identical black leather lace-up shoes which he rotated daily.

He looked what he was, a fifty-year-old, respectable, dependable bank manager, neat and industrious.

The traffic was heavy as Brian approached Lewisham High Street, he tutted with irritation, realizing that for the first time ever he was going to be late.

He parked his Humber in the side road close to the bank, took his briefcase from the back seat and hurriedly locked the car door.

'Good morning, Mr Anderson!'

Brian looked up at the sound of his secretary's voice.

'Good morning, Miss Bowden,' he smiled. 'I'm afraid I'm a little late. I took Georgia to her new school this morning.'

'Don't worry,' Miss Bowden didn't miss the frown lines on his forehead. 'I purposely didn't make you any appointments this morning until after ten thirty. I anticipated you might get held up.'

Miss Bowden had been his secretary for five years now. A sensible spinster in her mid-thirties, she was as dedicated to her job as Anderson himself. Her dark suit and white blouse, the sturdy flat shoes and neat brown hair were a constant reminder to the other, younger clerks that this was how a woman in banking should look.

'I just hope Coulson was on time,' Brian took up his position on the outside of the pavement, irritated still more by the amount of early shoppers pushing their way along to the market. 'It's so long since he was expected to unlock the bank, I doubt he remembers how to.'

'Of course he does,' Miss Bowden reassured her employer. 'Look, you can see yourself the lights are on.'

Anderson had no need to be at the bank before nine thirty, but old habits died hard for him, and often he was behind his desk soon after eight thirty, well before the rest of the staff arrived. It had been this sort of reliability which got him promoted to manager, and although Celia kept telling him it was time he sat back and took things easier, he still liked to be there to unlock.

'How was Georgia this morning?' Miss Bowden asked. 'Was she nervous? It's a big step going to such a huge school.'

'A little nervous, but she'll be fine once she's settled in.' Anderson's expression softened a little. 'Remind me to telephone my wife later, will you?'

'What a lovely girl she is!' Miss Bowden smiled warmly as they approached the bank door and rang the bell to be admitted. 'She's a credit to you both.'

'Well, thank you Miss Bowden,' Brian's plump face beamed at the compliment. Sometimes he felt a little overshadowed by Georgia and it was nice to know his staff at least felt he was responsible for the way she had shaped up. 'It hasn't all been easy you know, but she's been worth the disruption.'

No one knew how much he'd dreaded having a child of unknown background in his home, Celia least of all. He hid it away, just the same way he did so many things. Celia was like his mother, it was easier to go along with her wishes than argue.

Now it made him blush when he remembered the way he reported to friends and colleagues about Georgia's lacerated back on her arrival. He took all the credit for caring for her, implied he intended to move heaven and earth to get St Joseph's shut down.

He had been horrified by her injuries, but it was Celia who coped with it, not him. Why had he been so afraid that one small child would ruin their lovely peaceful home? Why had he sulked silently while Celia threw herself into her new mother role wholeheartedly?

Of course, he hadn't known then what benefits one child could bring with her. Perhaps if he'd realized he would lose his tag of 'Boring Old Anderson' overnight, he might have been less truculent. It had been like joining an exclusive club. Suddenly he was no longer exempt from conversations centred on family life. His staff took more interest in him and for the first time in his life he felt fully accepted.

Maybe it had taken a little longer to learn to be a real father than he allowed his colleagues to see, but it had its moments of wonder. Taking Georgia for walks, teaching her to ride a bike and do her sums, gave him a kick he hadn't expected. Women looked at him in a different way, stopping to speak to him. He felt powerful, a man of action, not just a sandy-haired, middle-aged man clutching a briefcase.

So maybe the magic didn't reach as far as Celia responding with any real passion to him. Neither did a half-caste child make up for one of their own. But at least Celia and himself had a common interest. She looked younger, prettier, she laughed more, cuddled up to him at nights. Maybe in time that new warmth would turn to desire.

His office smelled of fresh polish. A clean sheet of paper was in his blotter and his pens were arranged neatly on a desk tray. Soon one of the junior clerks would bring him in fresh coffee and due to Miss Bowden's thoughtfulness he had time to collect his thoughts and stop dwelling on Georgia.

Reminders were all around him. The little pen-wipe she had sewn for him last Christmas with Daddy embroidered on it. A painting of him, carefully framed by Celia. Once he would never have considered hanging a picture of a man with flame red hair on his office wall, but he secretly loved Georgia's image of him. She'd caught his hidden self, a strong-looking man playing cricket. Almost handsome in his white slacks and sweater. It was a talking point with customers, it loosened them up and made them realize he was more than just a stuffed shirt.

Finally, there was the photograph of the three of them, taken on holiday in Bournemouth. Celia in a low-cut cocktail dress, he in a dinner jacket and Georgia between them, laughing up at them, all dark curls, big eyes and dimples.

'Your coffee, Mr Anderson,' he hadn't heard Miss Bowden come in. She put his cup in front of him and placed his diary beside it. 'Don't worry about her,' she patted him gently on the shoulder. 'Georgia's a match for anyone, you know that, and don't forget to telephone your wife.'

Georgia looked up at the school as she approached the main doors, her stomach churning with fear. It was the biggest school in South London, all glass and concrete, and although she had assured both her parents some of her old friends from Junior school would be there too, the truth was that most of them had found places elsewhere.

It was easy to identify the other first-years. Like her their uniforms were brand new, they stood white-faced and anxious, biting back tears, far smaller than the girls who sauntered by shouting to their friends, throwing each other's berets into the air.

Girls, who looked like grown-up women, wearing prefect badges on their blazers directed the new girls to the main assembly hall. Georgia looked round with trepidation as teachers called out names and ordered the girls to stand in line.

The top class of the Junior school had only twenty-five children. In this hall alone there were nearer three hundred and she couldn't see one person she knew.

'Georgia Anderson.'

She put her hand up and was ushered over to a line.

The teacher who had called her name came forward smiling warmly. She was younger than Georgia had expected, probably no more than thirty, and she was very elegant. Her blonde, sleek hair was cut short and swept up at the back, and she wore a black suit with a straight skirt and a white lacy shirt. Her light-brown eyes seemed to miss nothing. She reminded Georgia of Miss Powell, the headmistress who had played the piano, and that seemed a good omen.

'My name is Miss Underwood,' she said in a crisp, well-modulated voice. 'I'll be your form teacher and I'm taking you now to your form room where I'll explain everything to you. You are in form 1B, remember that if nothing else, someone will guide you back to your class if you get lost. Follow me.'

Georgia followed the other girls in silence. As they started up the stairs she turned to the girl behind her.

'Do you know anyone here?'

'No one.' The small girl was near to tears. She hardly looked old enough to be going to a senior school, her baby blue eyes, pink cheeks and blonde pigtails looking out of place amongst the hard-faced bigger girls they'd seen strutting by.

'Neither do I, I'm Georgia Anderson. What's your name?'

'Christine Fellows,' the blonde girl whispered back. 'Do you think we'll be able to sit together?'

By morning break Georgia had tried to memorize every face. Christine had been given the desk next to her and although they hadn't been able to talk yet, at least she seemed friendly.

'Do you think we'll ever find our way round this place?' Christine sighed as they filed out of the form room for break. 'Every lesson's in a different room. What if we get lost?'

'We'd better stick together then,' Georgia giggled. 'I shouldn't think they'd punish us for getting lost in the first week!'

As they came down the last flight of stairs the number of girls converging into a large hallway had reached hundreds. Everyone was talking at once, a heaving mass of navy-blue striving to reach the doors leading out to the playground.

Christine clung on to Georgia's blazer as they reached the hall. Surrounded by taller girls pushing and shoving, they inched their way forward blindly.

The crowd cleared suddenly as they stepped outside into bright sunlight. Both girls paused, looking around for the milk.

'Another nigger in the first year!'

The remark was said loudly, with malice. Georgia's head swivelled round to see a group of girls, all around fourteen, standing by the milk crates.

Thinking the insult was intended for her she blushed scarlet, stopping in her tracks. Christine didn't appear to have heard as she walked towards the girls and lifted two bottles out of the crate.

'What's up?' she asked as she came back, giving Georgia hers.

Georgia barely heard her as she watched a small West Indian girl being pushed away from the crates by a sullen-faced big girl.

'Niggers get theirs round the corner,' she snarled at the frightened first-year. 'This is for whites only.'

The girl was brassy looking, with untidy bleached-blonde hair and her tie pulled down. Although she was actually wearing the uniform, she had done as much as was humanly possible to disguise it. Her skirt was short and tight, a wide 'waspy' belt holding it up. The sleeves of her shirt were rolled up, a heavy bust stretching the material to its limits. She wore nylons and casual shoes instead of the strong lace-ups and grey socks Georgia wore. A lovebite on her neck and a spotty, pasty face all added to her slovenly appearance.

'Do you think that's true?' Georgia whispered to Christine.

'What?'

'That coloured girls have their milk somewhere else?' She was torn between moving away into the crowd before someone noticed her colour, or joining the black girl in her defence.

'I shouldn't think so,' Christine looked puzzled. 'My sister came here. She never said.'

'They'll have to put a separate crate for me if it is,' Georgia tried to smile. 'Halfway between the two, a greyish colour.'

By the time Georgia and Christine had gone round the corner to investigate, the West Indian girl had vanished amongst hundreds of other girls, but there were no more crates and it was obvious the big girl was playing a cruel joke.

'Don't get upset about it,' Christine said. 'My sister told me all sorts of things they do to first-years. She said they held one girl's head down the toilet and flushed it.'

The day passed in a blur of new experiences. Books handed out, timetables which seemed formidable, so many new faces and names to be put to them, that Georgia forgot the incident at morning break.

Georgia parted from Christine at the school gates after arranging to meet her there the next day. Then joining a minority of girls going towards Blackheath, she turned left and crossed the road.

The sun was hot on her head and shoulders so Georgia took off her blazer and carried it. Up ahead on the corner of the road she was to turn into, a crowd of girls was gathering. Georgia quickened her pace to see what was going on.

She knew it was a fight, she could sense the tension in the air before she got there and she recognised the voice without even seeing over the other girls' heads.

'You sneaky little bastard. I'll teach you not to go telling tales!'

It was the same big girl who had stopped the West Indian from getting any milk.

Georgie sidled round the crowd, intending to go on home, but the sight before her made her stop instantly.

The big girl had the small black girl by the hair and was slapping her face backwards and forwards like someone beating a carpet.

Georgia dropped her satchel and blazer and without thinking she ran the last few feet.

'Stop it,' she grabbed hold of the bigger girl's shirt. 'She's smaller than you and she's new!'

Only as the girl paused and let go of her victim did Georgia feel a stab of fear.

'And who the fuck d'you think you are, bloody Joan of Arc?'

A roar of laughter went up from the crowd. They

were all white girls, mostly third and fourth years, three or four of them Georgia had seen with the bully at break, the rest merely going home and enjoying a little diversion.

Suddenly the tree-lined suburban street with its neat gardens seemed sinister and a long way from home. Georgia knew she'd got herself into something beyond her depth.

'I know it's none of my business,' Georgia said, more calmly than she felt. 'But it isn't right to hit someone smaller than yourself.'

The West Indian girl was backing away, her eyes rolling with fear, her face swollen from the smacking. But like Pamela that day at St Joseph's, she hadn't the sense to run.

'Don't she talk posh,' the bully smirked round at her audience. She looked back at Georgia and her mean mouth curved into a sneer. 'Oh, I get it,' she said, looking Georgia up and down. 'You've got a bit of nigger blood too!'

'Yes, I'm half black,' Georgia held her head up proudly. 'That's a darn sight better than being all white and a bully.'

'Bin taken out of the jungle by a priest and educated, have we?' The girl caught hold of Georgia's wrist before she could move away. She twisted it round and forced it behind Georgia's back, holding her in a tight grip. 'Well here we've got our own jungle, and we don't want no black bastards in it.'

'Let me go,' Georgia yelled, kicking out at the girl's shins.

Taken by surprise the girl let go. Georgia used the opportunity to run but a greasy-haired girl stood in front of her, grinning stupidly. She stood a foot taller than Georgia, her loose, sloppy mouth full of gum.

'I've got her now Bev,' she called out. 'Come and give her a pasting.'

35

Three of them were on her at once. One girl held her arms, another one caught her by the hair, and the girl they called Bev, slapped her round the face again and again.

Georgia tried to kick them, but together they were too strong for her. All she saw before Bev lifted her leg and kneed her in the stomach was the West Indian girl running up the road like a startled hare.

Winded, Georgia staggered back against a tree.

'I ain't finished with you yet,' Bev shouted at her. 'That's just a taster to show you who's boss round 'ere. Got the message?'

Doubled over with pain, Georgia heard them run off down the road, laughing loudly.

The rest of the crowd dispersed as if by magic. One moment they were all gawping inanely, the next gone.

Her parents had been a little tense about her coming to this school, now she knew why. Her face stung, the blow in her stomach had winded her and she felt sick with humiliation. By the time she collected her things and walked to the bus stop, the streets had cleared of school girls. She wanted to cry, ring up Celia to collect her, make her promise she'd find another school. Yet even as she thought these things, she knew she couldn't.

Celia was talking on the telephone as she walked in the door. She waved, then went back to her conversation. Everything was just as it always was. The sun shining in the back of the house, lighting up a vase of flowers on the kitchen table. A smell of polish, a casserole in the oven. The prints on the walls, the thick, patterned carpet, chintz covers on the chairs. A spacious, middle-class home, a thousand times nicer than the one that girl must come from.

Celia was at the telephone in a crisp blue summer dress with a white collar, carefully cut to minimize her wide hips. The kitchen table was laid with dainty china tea cups and a homemade cake. If she told her mother what had happened it would bring a cloud into this lovely home, a slur on all they had taught her.

Georgia slipped upstairs and washed her face. She was flushed, but as yet there was no bruising. Ten minutes later she came back downstairs wearing an old pink dress she'd almost grown out of.

'Hullo darling,' Celia was in the kitchen making a pot of tea. 'How did it go?'

She loved her mother so much. She couldn't bear to see hurt take the smile off her face or worry spoil even one evening together.

'It's a bit scary because it's big,' Georgia said, keeping her voice even and taking a seat with her back to the window so her mother couldn't see her clearly. 'I met a nice girl called Christine and I'm in form 1B.'

'That's good.' Celia sat down at the kitchen table, stirred the tea and poured a little milk into the two cups. She cut the large cherry cake and placed a slice on a plate for Georgia. 'That means you are actually in the Grammar stream then. What's your teacher like?'

'Nice,' Georgia said, looking down at the cake. 'Miss Underwood. She's youngish. Real elegant and sophisticated. But we'll only have her for registration and English, the rest of the time we go to other classrooms.'

'What's the matter with your face, it looks flushed?' Celia's eagle eye missed nothing.

'I ran down the road,' Georgia lied. 'I'm just hot.'

After eating the cake she went back to her room under the pretence of doing homework. Her bedroom was the prettiest she had ever been in. Decorated in pink and white, it had lots of shelves and cupboards, and Celia had even bought her a desk to do her homework on. It wasn't a large room compared with her parents' room next door, but it was on the front of the house and the window overlooked the heath across the road. Across the landing was her playroom. Even in her wildest dreams back at St Joseph's she had never envisaged a room where she would be allowed to paint, dance, dress up and do whatever she liked.

Her mother and father had taught her everything. How to speak properly and talk to people, how to dress, everything she had came from them, how could she burden them with worry about a bully?

St Joseph's had only taught her one thing that she clearly remembered. You had to stand up for yourself, or end up being bullied forever.

The next morning she braided her hair tightly.

'Why on earth are you doing that?' Celia asked in surprise. 'It looks so much better down.'

'It's a bit hot for school,' Georgia replied. 'There's so many big windows, and I sit right by one.'

There was no one guarding the milk crates at break and all day Georgia didn't even get a glimpse of Bev and her friends. She hoped that was the end of it, but she would be cautious just in case.

Once she'd said goodbye to Christine outside the school gates, she took off her blazer and beret and put them in her satchel. She rolled up her shirt sleeves and crossed the road.

She saw the four third-years cutting across the playing field. The way they scurried along, heads bent close together, made her sure they were planning to ambush her. Flinging her satchel over her shoulder she ran round the corner past the spot of yesterday's incident and paused, weighing up the area.

The wide grass verge between the pavement and the road was ideal for a soft landing, the trees good for cover. Her heart was thumping with fright, but she hid her satchel behind one tree, herself behind another, and waited.

'She must have run like the bleedin' wind.'

Georgia suppressed a nervous giggle as one of the

girls' surprised voice reached her. She didn't dare look out until they were right by her.

'Either that or she's hiding in some gateway till we've passed.' She recognized the coarse voice as Bev's, the blonde bully. 'I'll give her an extra pasting for that, the scheming black bastard,' she added maliciously.

Georgia managed a peep from behind the trunk. Three of the girls checked each garden. The girl with the greasy hair hung back slightly, as if her heart wasn't really in it. The other two were either side of Bev, copying her actions as though they had no minds of their own. One was quite attractive in a sulky, voluptuous way, with dark, long hair. The fourth girl in the group was mousey blonde, smaller than her friends with sharp features and a brace on her teeth.

Georgia waited until they were less than five feet from her, took a deep breath, screwed up her fists and stepped out in front of them.

'Looking for me?' she said, balancing on her toes.

'Yes, you little shit,' Bev was clearly taken by surprise, she blinked furiously, the late afternoon sun in her eyes.

'Planning to hit me again?' Georgia tried to keep her voice low and seemingly unruffled.

The four girls looked at one another in surprise.

'That's fine with me as long as it's fair,' Georgia said. 'One of you against me, the others mustn't join in.'

'You cheeky little bitch,' Bev spat at her. 'Who the hell do you think you are?'

'I don't think I'm anyone,' Georgia said stoutly, moving lightly on her toes like a boxer. 'I know perfectly well who I am. Georgia Anderson.'

The girl with greasy hair laughed nervously and was already moving back, away from the others.

In groups of twos and threes, other girls were turning the corner. A buzz of excitement went up, calling for others to hurry and in moments a large circle was forming round them.

Georgia was afraid now. There was nothing to stop all these girls ganging up on her. She would have to act tough to get their approval.

'Well, which one of you is going to give me the pasting?' Georgia said, looking directly at each of the ringleaders. This time the dark, attractive girl fell back. Her face growing a little pale.

Georgia focused her attention on the mousey blonde.

'You is it?' she said arrogantly, 'Or do you want to back out too?'

The girl had a look of panic in her pale eyes. She glanced round at the other two girls, who merely shrugged their shoulders, and fell back with them.

Bev stood alone now, a slight tic in her cheek as though nervous. She was big and heavy, but she didn't look quite so confident now she knew she had no back-up.

The crowd was tense, everyone waiting to see if this new kid was really foolish enough to fight.

'Looks like you and me then,' Georgia smiled charmingly, fixing her big, dark eyes on Bev's small, mean ones.

'You cocky little cow,' Bev sprang heavily at her.

Georgia waited until she was almost upon her then jumped lightly to one side. Bev stubbed her toe on the edging to the grass verge and nearly fell on her face. A roar of approval went up from the crowd and Georgia turned slightly to grin at them.

Bev recovered quickly and turned to catch Georgia again. Once again Georgia dodged. Bev's hand came out to grab her hair, but her fingers couldn't grasp the tight braids. Quick as a flash, Georgia pulled up her knee and jammed it up into Bev's stomach, kicking out at her shins as she moved back.

'Get her, Bev,' the small blonde shouted. She was

poised on her toes, clenching and unclenching her fists with blood lust in her eyes.

Bev was winded. Her face flushed like a tomato. She lunged heavily at Georgia again. This time Georgia put her foot out, caught her legs and tripped her up. Bev crashed down on to the pavement, flat on her face. Georgia stepped forward to screams of delight from the other girls.

Leaning over and catching the girl by her hair, she twisted Bev's head up and round to look at her.

'Had enough yet?' she said almost casually, as she saw a trace of blood coming from an angry red mark on the girl's forehead.

This was the danger point. If the other girls leapt in now they could beat her to a pulp.

Bev struggled to get up. Georgia waited until she was on all fours, then swiftly kicked her up the backside, sending her crashing to the pavement.

The other three girls had backed right away now, clearly terrified of being involved.

The circle of spectators moved in closer.

'Wack her, little'un,' someone shouted. 'It's about time someone stood up to her.'

Georgia sat astride Bev's back, holding the girl firmly by the hair.

'Hurts doesn't it?' she asked, teeth gritted. 'It hurts black girls too, or did you think we feel nothing?'

'Get off,' Bev called out, her voice shaky as if on the point of tears. 'We was only teasing you.'

'And I'm only teasing you,' Georgia pushed her head back down to touch the pavement. 'But I'll stop if you apologize and tell me you'll leave me alone in future.'

'Fuck off,' Bev shouted, wriggling and trying to turn under Georgia. An unpleasant smell of sweat wafted up to Georgia.

'That is very rude,' Georgia said, grinning round at her audience. 'You smell of B.O. too. Looks like I'll have to give you another taste.' She pulled sharply on the girl's hair, then crashed her head down again to the pavement.

This time Bev was sobbing.

'You'll apologize?' Georgia looked around at the crowd. 'In front of witnesses?'

'Yes,' the word came out like a groan.

'Right. Repeat after me. Bev is a bully. She is also a fat, smelly slut.'

'Bev is a bully,' the girl whimpered.

'Louder,' Georgia tightened her grip again.

'Bev is a bully,' the girl said.

'Go on!'

'She is also a fat, smelly slut.'

'Very good. I will never, or allow my friends . . .'

'I will never, or allow my friends,' Bev was crying freely now.

'To bully, or frighten anyone, especially black girls.'

Georgia waited until Bev had finished. Still sitting on Bev's back she looked across at the other three girls who cowered against the wall.

'That goes for you three too,' she said, lowering her voice to one of menace as she'd been taught in drama classes. 'I'll be watching.'

Calmly she got up, crossed over to the tree to collect her satchel, slipped her blazer out, and swaggered off towards the bus stop.

She allowed herself only one glance back.

Bev stood alone, crying and dabbing at her forehead. Her friends had vanished, the rest of the girls were standing talking in small groups.

Once on the bus she could not stop shaking. She had been lucky, if Bev hadn't been like a charging rhinoceros she would have noticed that it wasn't physical strength that beat her, but preparation and speed. If Bev or another bully caught her unawares the next time she might be the loser.

*

'Is everything all right Georgia?' Celia came up to her bedroom after tea as Georgia was doing her homework. 'You didn't seem yourself yesterday or today. Is there something you want to tell me?'

'No, Mummy,' Georgia looked up and smiled. 'I was just worried about all this homework. I don't know whether I'll have time for dancing and singing now.'

Celia sat down on the bed.

'You'll make time.' She picked up the teddy bear she'd given Georgia on her first day in the house and looked at him thoughtfully. 'Come on, the truth. I know something happened at school. Has someone bullied you?'

Georgia hadn't expected much the day she left St Joseph's in Celia's car. There was no picture in her mind of a house, or the kind of life she would lead with Mr and Mrs Anderson. She remembered the moment when the car stopped, the huge expanse of snow-covered heath on one side of the road, and the grey stone houses on the other.

'This is ours,' Celia had taken her hand again and led her up to a red front door. It seemed tiny after the convent door, little panes of coloured glass and the porch with old blue and white tiles. She had hardly noticed Mr Anderson, all she had seen and felt was warmth and comfort. Soft carpet under her feet, a big fire in the grate and the piano standing by the window.

Those first few weeks had been so exciting. New kinds of wonderful food, clothes that were brand new and toys that were all for her. Later there had been the dancing and singing lessons to give her new heights of happiness. But above all else it had been having a mother, someone who cared about her, listened and talked to her as if she was someone special.

'There was just a little trouble yesterday,' she admitted. She knew her mother too well, she wouldn't give

43

up until she got to the truth. 'But everything's okay now.'

'Someone slapped you! I knew it,' Celia stiffened, dropping the teddy bear in her hands. 'Why didn't you tell me?'

'Mum, I'm a big girl now,' Georgia laughed. 'I can stand up for myself. I talked to the girl today, it's over.'

'What was it about?'

'My posh voice, if you must know.' Georgia wasn't exactly lying, but she thought her mother could take that better than the issue of colour. She grinned cheekily. 'Maybe I'd best go back to talking like what I used to.'

'Don't you dare!' Celia smiled. 'After all the coaching I've given you!'

Chapter 3

December 1959

Georgia hurried to the church. The grass on the heath was thick with frost and the moon hung over the church spire as if endeavouring to impale itself. It was the last practice for the anthem the choir was going to sing at midnight mass on Christmas Eve.

She wore a grey duffel coat over a polo-necked white sweater and jeans, hair tied up in a pony-tail with a white ribbon, a long red scarf knotted round her neck.

Peter was waiting on the church steps. Just the sight of him made her heart beat a little faster. He was so beautiful, gold blond hair gleaming under the porch lamp, his peachy skin as clear as her own. She could hardly wait to get up close and see those forget-me-not blue eyes and his wide, soft lips.

'I thought you weren't coming.' His face broke into a relieved smile as she turned on to the church path.

'I got held up,' she said breathlessly.

Four months had passed since they'd met at a youth club debate, and since then there hadn't been one day when she hadn't thought about him. Was it possible to want someone so badly and not have the longing returned?

'Mr Grey's having kittens,' he grinned, his soft lips parting to show perfect white teeth. 'We'd better go in.'

As Georgia stepped into the church she closed her eyes for a second and inhaled deeply. She loved

45

churches. The incense, the candles, all the rich embroidery on the altar cloths, the smell of polish and flowers. Religion didn't come into it. To her it was a wonderful theatre, the choir part of a show they put on each weekend.

Flinging her coat on a pew she slipped into the choir stalls, grinning sheepishly at the others. Eight women, six men and eight scruffy little boys. On Christmas Eve they would be transformed with starched ruffles and red cassocks, but for now they were just ordinary people who liked to sing just like her.

The choir master tapped his stick on a pew.

'I'm glad you could make it Georgia,' Mr Grey's deep baritone was at odds with his stooped elderly body. His sarcasm unusual for such a gentle man. He wore a new Fair Isle cardigan in heathery shades, his pipe hanging out of one of the pockets. 'Now take it slowly. It's not a pop song, but a beautiful piece of music. I want the people in the back rows to hear you. Head up, chest out.'

It was the first time anyone in the choir had been chosen to sing a solo. She knew it was a great honour and she wanted it to be perfect.

She took a deep breath as the organ wheezed into life. The introduction filled the church with sound and Peter winked at her.

Her voice reached each corner. Pure and clear, every word annunciated in the way Mr Grey had taught her.

The choir joined her. Sopranos soaring above her contralto, the tenors and bass giving it richness and warmth.

'Very good,' Mr Grey shuffled forward up the step. He held his back as if it hurt, but his old face was alight with pleasure. 'If you sing it like that on Christmas Eve I should think Father O'Brady will get enough in the collection for his new roof. We'll do it once more, then

46

a quick run through the carols, then you can all go early.'

'You were very good tonight,' Peter walked out through the church door with her. 'I love to hear you sing.'

'Thank you.' She smiled up at him, wondering if tonight she could find the words to ask him to her party.

He was always waiting for her. He walked home with her from choir practice, talked about anything and everything, yet he had never attempted to take it further.

'Do you have to go straight home?'

His question took her by surprise. Peter was looking at his feet, he sounded as unsure of himself as she felt. 'I mean, could we go for a walk?'

'Where?' she asked, not caring where it was as long as he was with her. She felt a flush creeping up her neck. Her teeth began to chatter more from anxiety than cold.

'Over to the boating pond?'

The heath yawned in front of them. A big, empty dark space that was all theirs. A huge Christmas tree at the church steps lit up the darkness with tiny green, red, yellow and blue sparks of colour. The frosty grass scrunched beneath their feet and as they moved away from the light, so their shadows disappeared.

'You're cold?' Peter paused and looked round at her.

Her scarf was tied tightly round her neck, her breath like steam from a kettle.

'My hands are,' she said, not wanting to admit she was freezing. 'I forgot my gloves.'

He took one of her hands and felt it.

'Like ice,' he smiled. 'Put it in my pocket with mine.'

He held her hand in his pocket, running his thumb across her palm. A tiny shiver went down her spine, but this time it had nothing to do with the cold. She moved closer to him, huddling against his shoulder.

'Better now?'

'Much,' she smiled up at him. His ripe wide mouth made her feel weak inside. 'I've been meaning to ask you Peter. Would you like to come to my birthday party on January 6th?'

He didn't reply for a second, he looked straight ahead of him and she wondered if she'd asked too soon.

'I thought you'd left me out. One of the boys at school mentioned it.'

Now she felt foolish. Did he think she was only inviting him now out of politeness?

'I didn't actually invite any boys,' she blushed. 'I just asked the girls to bring a partner.'

'Does that mean I'd be your partner?'

'Yes. If you want to be.' It was too late now for flirting and pretending disinterest as Christine suggested. 'I didn't ask you before because I was afraid you'd refuse.'

She hung her head, afraid to meet his eyes.

His fingers brushed her cheek as he lifted her face up to his.

'Does that mean I can say you are my girl?'

No words came, just a nod of her head. His eyes almost closed and his hand cupped her head drawing her to him.

His lips touched hers tentatively, so light it could have been the touch of a moth's wing.

Closing her eyes she just stood there, her heart pounding, her legs shaking. One moment his other hand was still in his pocket with hers, the next he withdrew it and crushed her to him, lips covering hers.

The deserted heath, the church behind them and her home in the distance fell away. All she could feel, see and smell was Peter. A soft, warm mouth on hers, the touch of stubble against her chin, the ecstasy of being in his arms at last.

Four months of dreaming and hoping and at last the moment was here.

'Let's run?' he whispered to her, his nose rubbing against hers. 'Maybe we won't notice the cold.'

The wind caught her hair and scarf as they ran hand in hand. They were laughing like small children, racing over the crisp grass.

'I knew there was a shelter here,' he said breathlessly as they approached the silver pond. He pointed to a dark shape at one end, near a bus stop. 'It might not be so cold and at least we can sit down.'

Within seconds she was in his arms again. The soft inexperienced kisses soon becoming more adventurous and bolder.

They weren't aware of a man walking his dog, or the lone streetlamp casting a pool of golden light over a litter bin. The shelter smelled of mould and someone's abandoned chips in newspaper, but all they felt was one another's warm breath and the sweet agony of needing to get closer.

His tongue flickered over her lips, and she parted them, slipping her hands under his jacket for warmth.

She pressed closer to him, a warm, shaky feeling creeping all over her. Her breasts throbbed, she ached for him to touch them, yet was frightened that he would. Each kiss was longer than the last, tongues bolder, gaining experience with each one. Her body fitted to his, her fingers stroking, loving him. The hard boniness of his chest, the smell of soap and toothpaste. His fingers caressing her neck and the rough texture of his sweater.

'We ought to get back,' he whispered, his lips buried in her neck. 'It's nearly half past nine.'

Reality came back with a jolt. Georgia jumped up, holding her watch towards the dim yellow light. Her eyes widened with fear as she saw he was right.

'Dad will go mad,' she gasped. 'It feels as if we've only been here for minutes.'

Peter stood in front of her, buttoning up her coat and winding the scarf back round her neck.

'It's only just after our usual time,' he sounded calm and protective. 'Tell them we were talking.'

They ran then, hand in hand back across the heath, not stopping till they reached her house.

'Ask them if you can come to the pictures tomorrow,' he said, smiling down at her, both panting from the run. 'I'll come and pick you up at seven.'

'What if they say no?' she was torn between staying out with him and rushing in to make apologies.

'I'll come anyway,' he laughed, bending to kiss her once more. 'Now go on in before you catch cold.'

'Why didn't you ask me out before?' she whispered, poised to run in.

'I was afraid you'd turn me down,' he whispered back.

'You're late!' Celia said reprovingly.

Her parents were watching television by the fire. The Christmas tree lights twinkled against the dark red curtains. Celia was already in her dressing-gown, pale blue wool, with a snippet of long winceyette showing beneath, her feet in slippers. She was knitting a pair of grey socks. Brian wore the brown cardigan he always put on when he took off his office suit, yet his tie was knotted as neatly as when he left for the office earlier that day. He had a glass of brandy on the small table by his side and he looked sleepy, glasses sliding down his nose.

By day the room was almost an extension of the garden, light streaming in the French windows, bushes just outside blending with plants inside. But by night it took on a different character, shrinking in size as the heavy curtains were drawn. A snug room that somehow embodied her parents' joint personalities. Celia in the baby grand piano, the Chinese vase lamps and the warmth of the roaring fire. Brian the plump, chintz-covered armchairs and settee, the delicate water colours on the walls, the leather-bound books close to his elbow.

Georgia looked from Celia to Brian as she unwound her scarf and unbuttoned her coat.

Her father's love of order ran not only to arranging books in size, the fringe on the hearth rug brushed out flat, but also to timekeeping. Yet for once he didn't seem aware she was late.

'I'm sorry,' Georgia panted. 'I was talking to Peter.'

'Did you pluck up courage to invite him to the party?' Celia raised one eyebrow, letting her knitting droop to her lap. Georgia had spoken of this boy so often she felt she knew him almost as well as her daughter.

'Yes,' Georgia wanted to sit on her mother's knee, wrap her arms round her and tell her everything. But the child in her was gone now, left back at the church steps when Peter took her hand. 'And he asked if he could take me to the pictures tomorrow.'

'Did he now,' Celia's eyes were more green than grey in the light of the fire, twinkling like the Christmas tree lights.

'Can I go then?'

'I don't see why not,' Celia's soft pale lips curved into a smile. 'As long as he brings you straight home afterwards.'

'Just a moment,' Brian sat up sharply and took off his glasses. 'Don't I have any say in this?'

Georgia gulped. She and Celia rarely asked Brian's opinion about anything and just lately he seemed to have noticed. His face had a polished look in the soft light, faded blue eyes puckered with irritation.

'I'm sorry, Daddy,' Georgia went over to him and perched on the arm of his chair. His sandy hair was getting very thin and from her position slightly above him, she could see a bald patch as big as a half crown. She slid her arm around his neck, fondling his ears. 'Please don't be a grouch. I didn't ask you first because I was embarrassed.'

'Who is this boy?' Brian's eyes softened just enough for her to know he was at least receptive.

'Peter Radcliffe, he sings in the choir. You'd like him Daddy! He plays cricket.'

'I'll reserve my judgement until I've met him,' Brian half smiled. 'If he isn't one of those ton-up boys and he can be trusted to behave himself with you, I can't really think of any reason to say no.'

As Georgia got into bed that night she could scarcely contain her excitement. If she closed her eyes she could taste Peter's lips again, feel that strange tugging sensation inside her.

Was she in love? She had all the symptoms they mentioned in magazines. She could hardly wait till tomorrow to phone Christine and tell her Peter had finally kissed her.

She lay on her back looking at the new party dress hanging on the wardrobe. Celia had bought it just two days earlier and she couldn't wait to wear it.

It was beautiful. Red satin with a billowing underskirt of net. The bodice was tight and low cut, with just tiny cap sleeves. No one else would have a dress quite like it.

Celia smiled as she peeped into Georgia's room an hour later.

Brown arms hugging a teddy bear, face buried in the pillow. She had noticed the way Georgia looked at this boy. Guessed the big sighs and long periods of idle dreaming were because of him. Tomorrow she would want endless reassurance that he really did want to take her to the pictures!

Celia closed the door softly and went into her own bedroom. Brian was already in bed, covers up to his chin.

'What's this boy like?' he said unexpectedly.

'Very nice,' Celia said sitting down on the edge of the bed. 'Polite, rather handsome, about to do his "A" levels.'

'She's a bit young for a boyfriend,' he said.

'I don't know,' Celia climbed into bed beside him. 'Most of her friends have one. Better someone like him than some hooligan hanging around on street corners. Don't get all edgy about it Brian, teenage romances are usually shortlived.'

As she switched out the light Brian turned over and put his arm round her.

'Don't,' she said brusquely, moving away.

'I only wanted to cuddle you,' his voice sounded peeved.

'You always say that,' she brushed his arm away. 'And I'm not in the mood.'

'Are you ever?' his tone was heavy with sarcasm, and with a sigh he rolled over.

Celia lay there in the dark feeling just a little guilty. So much of their marriage was good, but she found it difficult to respond to him.

Maybe that was why she wanted Georgia to have lots of boyfriends because her own experience was so limited.

Celia Tutthill had always been a 'sensible' girl. Clothes chosen for their hard-wearing qualities rather than style, her hair cut short to save bother, swotting for her exams while others danced the night away and fell in love.

She came to this house as a lodger already set into spinsterhood at twenty-seven.

Martha Anderson and her bachelor son Brian were wrapped up in each other and for over a year the only contact she had with either of them was when they passed on the stairs.

It was only when old Mrs Anderson became ill that Celia got involved. Getting shopping for them, helping Brian in the garden, occasionally giving the old lady her medicine and helping her out to the bathroom when Brian was away on business. Martha could be a tyrant, she had kept her son on a tight rein all his life, but Celia was touched by his devotion.

Martha died suddenly one evening. One minute Brian was reading her the paper, the next she was dead, lying back on her lace-trimmed pillows, her wrinkled face suddenly younger.

It was fortunate Celia was off duty. She heard Brian cry out from across the landing and by the time she reached Martha's bedroom she found him sobbing, his head on his mother's breast.

She told herself she would stay only until he had got over his grief, then find another home. But without old Martha Anderson bullying him, Celia began to see another side of the lonely bachelor. He was capable yet sensitive, his gentleness was like a soothing balm after a day on the busy ward. She found herself looking forward to her weekends off, accepting his offers to share a meal, to go to the cinema, or even just listening to music together. When he asked her to marry him it seemed a perfect match. They both had their careers, and she could stay on in the house she'd come to love.

In her naïvety Celia hadn't fully considered what marriage meant. It came as a shock to discover that the sensitive gentleman was also sensuous and demanding.

A glimpse of stocking tops. A hint of nudity. A picture of something titillating in the paper, coupled with a drink or two would arouse him. Before she knew what was happening he was grappling with her, his mouth slobbering over her and suggesting things that made her flesh crawl.

In the new year of 1946 things came to a head. He was angry at being passed over for promotion, perhaps ashamed he'd spent the war behind a desk. But when he began to taunt her with her frigidity, blamed her for not producing a child, she felt leaving him was the answer.

While Brian was away on a course in Brighton, Celia saw it as the perfect opportunity to make the break.

'I can't go on the way things are,' she wrote. 'I blame myself because I can't respond to you the way you'd like. Perhaps I was never cut out for marriage. I care for you deeply, but I know that isn't enough. If I leave you now, maybe you will find happiness with someone else.'

But for once Brian surprised her by being unpredictable. He came home the moment he got the letter, catching her packing.

To this day she could see his face. Weak mouth quivering, eyes full of unshed tears. For once his appearance less than impeccable. He begged her to stay, insisting he wanted her on any terms.

Later that year, Brian was finally promoted to manager of the bank in Lewisham High Street and Celia gave up nursing and became a children's officer in South London. They learned to compromise. She tried harder to please Brian, he didn't press her so often. When Georgia arrived, new happiness and purpose made her more loving, at times their lovemaking was tender, if not passionate. But Brian didn't seem to understand that she found it impossible now Georgia was older. Suppose she heard them? Somehow it seemed indecent at their age!

'I want Georgia to marry for love,' Celia said to herself in the darkness. 'Just liking someone and sharing a home isn't enough for anyone.'

*

Strains of the Everly Brothers wafted down the stairs.

The door bell had been ringing constantly since eight that evening. Trudging feet, peals of laughter, shouts and giggles made them feel the playroom must now be packed to capacity.

'Do you think I ought to go up there?' Brian looked up from his book. His round, plump face seemed more irritated than anxious, but his eyes held suspicion.

'No,' Celia frowned. She had put on a new turquoise wool dress, her hair had been set that afternoon, just in case Georgia asked them to come up later. 'She won't get up to anything bad, and she knows where we are if anyone else does. This is her first grown-up party, don't spoil it for her.'

'Who said anything about spoiling it?' His look was surly. He too had put on a clean shirt and his best suit and it felt rather silly being dressed up with nowhere to go. 'But they could be necking up there. We hardly know any of them! As for that dress!'

'There's nothing much wrong with a bit of kissing,' Celia snapped. 'And she looks lovely in the dress.'

'It's too adult,' he snapped at her. 'What are you trying to turn her into?'

Georgia had come into the sitting room to show it off, her hair put up in an elaborate French plait, tiny kiss-curls on her forehead. Toffee-coloured shoulders, her waist no bigger than a handspan and small breasts peeping out of the tight bodice.

'She looks beautiful,' Celia retorted. 'I know it's sad to see her leave behind little white socks and pigtails. But she's a young woman now. We can't hold her back.'

'I don't like her seeing so much of Peter either,' Brian snapped. 'After tonight I'm clamping down. He's been here almost every day since that time he took her to the pictures.'

'Term starts again on Monday,' Celia said gently. 'He'll have homework and exams to think about. Georgia will be back to her dancing and singing lessons. What is it Brian,' she got up and went over to his chair, perching on the arm. 'You've been grumpy for days. Is it just the party? Or is there something else?'

'Nothing you'd understand.'

'Let's have a drink?' Celia ignored his cryptic reply. She got up and went over to the drinks cabinet.

'Is that a good idea?' Brian raised one eyebrow.

'Of course we can!' Celia looked over her shoulder, amused by his worried expression. 'It's our home, our daughter's birthday. I wasn't suggesting we got plastered.'

She poured herself a small gin and tonic, but gave Brian a larger one, hoping it would make him relax.

'I don't like Georgia wearing so much eye makeup,' he snapped. 'It makes her look cheap.'

'Don't be such a wet blanket,' Celia returned to her seat by the fire. Any other time she would have found his attitude rather touching, a father afraid that his little girl was turning into a woman. But now it merely irritated her.

'Put a record on,' Celia said. The overhead light was swinging with the dancing going on overhead. They couldn't actually hear the music, just the thumping vibration of the bass notes.

Brian got up slowly. He had put on some weight recently, although his good dark suit covered it well. As he bent down by the radiogram she could see he was getting a paunch which hung over his trousers. Yet even the extra pounds added something. He was actually improving with age. A few lines gave his youthful round face more character. Even the streaks of grey in his sandy hair gave him a note of distinction. Shame he had no remarkable features, his faded blue eyes were small, his nose just a fraction too wide, even his chin and mouth were weak. But he had good skin and neat straight teeth. A perfect face for a bank manager, not handsome enough for anyone to consider he might be indiscreet. Reassuring, neatly average.

'I wonder if any of the boys can "jive" as well as Georgia and Christine?' Celia wanted to lighten the mood but she was running out of ideas.

He didn't comment, just took a record out of its sleeve and dusted it carefully.

Celia was just gritting her teeth at his finicky manner when the phone rang out in the hall.

'I'll get it.' She got up, moving to the door. 'I expect it's someone's mother checking what time the party ends.'

Brian was back in his chair, drink in hand and the opening bars of 'Swan Lake' filled the room as Celia came in.

'That was the police.' The relaxed wife and mother was replaced by a stern, committed social worker. Even her voice was crisper. 'I'll have to go. A child in Stepney has been hurt by his father. The rest of the family are at risk.' She reached behind an armchair for her briefcase and looked down at her clothes as if wondering if she was suitably dressed.

'Isn't there anyone else in the world but you?'

'Not tonight it seems,' she didn't notice his sarcasm, more concerned with a five-year-old with a fractured skull. 'I don't know how long this will take. I might even have to bring the kids back here till tomorrow. I hope Georgia won't mind.'

'What about me?' Brian asked. 'Why don't you ask if I mind?'

This was the last straw. Everything revolved around Georgia, what she wanted to eat, where she wanted to go. Not once had Celia thought to consult him on anything. Now she was walking out with a hundred feet stamping on the floor above him, more concerned with some damn slum kid than her husband left on his own.

'Don't be silly,' she bent to kiss him lightly on the cheek. 'You know perfectly well I'd rather be here with you. But it's my job, just like you'd have to go out if they robbed the bank tonight.'

She was gone before he could even think of a reply.

Two boys lounged on the stairs, below them sat a couple of girls talking with their heads close together. Celia hadn't met any of them before.

'Everything all right?' she asked as they moved to let her past. 'Don't drop that on the carpet,' she looked disapprovingly at one of the boys' cigarettes dangling from his fingers.

Georgia was jiving with Christine, the red dress flaring out showing the layers of net and slim, shapely thighs. Her golden brown face, neck and shoulders glistened with perspiration, her dark eyes full of excitement. The French plait, which she'd spent hours arranging was already the worse for wear. Stray wispy curls were coming loose giving her a tempestuous look, like a gypsy dancer.

Christine had changed since the early days at Kidbrooke. Still shorter than Georgia and a little plumper, but the baby face had gone. Her blonde 'beehive' quivered as she danced. She had tossed off her high heels and her shoulders were parting company with her low-necked turquoise dress, even the elaborate Eygptian make-up was smeared.

Georgia grinned as she saw Celia peering in the door, she beckoned for her to come in.

'I can't stop,' Celia was shocked to see the room full of smoke and she was sure there were more than the twenty people her daughter had invited. Gangly lads propped up the walls, more sprawled on the floor. One girl was sitting on a boy's lap, their mouths glued together. A bunch of girls were giggling around the food table and still more were dancing. 'I've got to go out on an emergency.'

'Oh, Mum!' Georgia's mouth turned down at the corners. 'I hoped you were going to come up and meet all my friends.'

Georgia's plaintive voice cut through her professional concern as Brian's never could.

'I'm sorry, darling,' Celia tweaked Georgia's cheek. 'You know how these things are. I wanted to join you too. But I'm sure all your friends will enjoy themselves far better without me cramping their style.' She turned and smiled at Christine who offered her a sandwich.

'No thank you dear, I really must go. I may even have to bring some children with me if there's no alternative. So make sure everyone leaves at twelve and don't let them disturb the neighbours. Daddy's downstairs if you want anything.'

'Hallo, Mrs Anderson,' Peter was at her elbow. He was wearing smart grey trousers and a white shirt, the first time she had seen him in anything other than jeans. He had the same flushed, happy expression as Georgia, but mingled with concern. 'Is there anything I can do?'

Celia liked Peter the first moment she met him. It wasn't the handsome face, the clear eyes or even the obvious intelligence. There was a kind of openness about him she found refreshing. The odd remark about his parents suggested they were more interested in his earning ability than scholastic achievements, his appreciation of her home was a pointer to his own being far more humble. Yet he didn't ingratiate himself, retaining his own character and belief in himself, while he soaked up information, from food he wasn't accustomed to, to Celia's work in Stepney.

'Help Georgia to keep things under control,' she gave him a stern look, just to remind him of his place. 'Mr

Anderson's downstairs. I'll be back just as soon as possible.'

'Don't worry about us,' he glanced around the room as if already checking for trouble. 'Drive carefully won't you? It's frosty out there.'

By the time Celia had collected her coat from the bedroom, Georgia was dancing with Peter. She paused on the landing for just a second. Peter was no dancer, he shuffled awkwardly, barely in time to the music, but then her daughter's eyes were on his face, not his feet and the way Peter smiled at Georgia brought a lump to Celia's throat.

Brian felt restless. There was nothing he wanted to watch on television and the noise upstairs was getting to him. He opened the drinks cabinet again and poured himself another drink.

He was almost glad Celia had to go out, at least now he had something tangible to base his anger on.

It wasn't the party upstairs, nor even the fact he hadn't been consulted about anything that bugged him. Neither had his mood just come on him.

He was well past fifty, hair thinning, body fatter. His staff called him 'Old Anderson' as if he already had one foot in the grave and sometimes he felt so lonely he wanted to scream.

Celia was to blame. If she could arrange parties for Georgia, why couldn't she throw one or two for them? Her life was full, she had friends at her office, her clients from all walks of life, and she had Georgia.

Once she'd invited people to dinner, bought tickets for the theatre. They got invited out, they took walks together, they shared things. But lately the phone never rang except for Georgia or Celia, muffled conversations that made him feel shut out. How long was it since Celia cooked him a special meal, asked him what he'd like to do at the weekend? She only played the piano for Georgia and she cringed away from him as if he had leprosy.

What had he got for being easy-going? A job he'd been pushed into. His youth lost in caring for his mother, a house that cost a fortune to run. A child who was someone else's reject and a frigid, domineering wife.

He poured himself another drink, curling his fingers round the glass and wincing at the fire.

'I should have sold up when Mother died,' he said aloud. 'Travelled, changed my job, had some fun.' He glanced up at his parents' wedding picture on the mantelpiece as if half expecting her to reach out and box his ears for even thinking such thoughts. She looked pretty and guileless, gazing up at her uniformed husband in a classic pose of adoration. Was it becoming a war widow and bringing up her son alone that turned her into such a tyrant? She had approved of Celia, the only woman he ever heard her praise. That alone should have warned him off!

He could remember turning at the altar rail as Celia walked up the aisle on her uncle's arm, his heart almost bursting with pride.

Stout-shoed, tweed-skirted Nurse Tutthill, the plain, sensible girl who'd been there for him when he needed a friend was gone. In her place was a new Celia, curvy and feminine in a dark green, peplum-waisted costume and matching veiled hat. A soft voluptuous mouth accentuated with lipstick, shapely legs in sheer nylons, high-heeled shoes and a permanent wave.

In that moment he thought he'd got everything. Her husky voice promising to 'have and to hold', a waft of jasmine scent, and that small hand quivering as he slipped on the ring.

But just hours later in the hotel in Brighton that glow of pleasure turned to shame.

He could remember every detail of that night. The

pale green satin eiderdown, the bedside lamps with silky tassels on the shades. The shiny walnut head-board, even the smell of the starched sheets.

Maybe he was guilty of rushing things, but what man wouldn't when his fingers touched big firm breasts under silk?

'Let me put my nightie on?' she whimpered.

'You don't need clothes,' he said burying his face in her neck as his fingers fumbled to unwrap her.

On the train going to Brighton he had imagined taking her clothes off piece by piece, kissing every inch of soft flesh. Maybe he had only paid for sex before, but he thought he knew how to please women.

He turned out the light because she was embarrassed, sure that in darkness she would respond as passionately as him. But as his chest covered her naked breasts he couldn't hold back. Her skin was so silky he forgot caution, within moments he was pushing into her, squeezing her plump buttocks, whispering things he said to prostitutes.

It was only after that he realized she was icy, her face turned from him, every muscle and nerve-ending rigid with disgust. He touched her cheeks and found tears and in that moment he felt a complete failure.

'I tried to please her,' he said aloud as he reached out for the bottle of gin.

It very nearly ended after the war. No more oppor-tunities to get away and find a more amenable partner for the night. So much pent up excitement in the air as the troops came home, rebuilding all around them, yet for Brian everything stayed the same. Celia wanted a baby, he wanted promotion. A world war was fought and won against all odds, yet still he had a wife who stared blankly at the ceiling while he made love to her. Never actually refusing, but somehow that dutiful sub-servience made him feel dirty.

Perhaps he should have let her leave back then, divorce wasn't such a big deal anymore.

He felt that uncomfortable feeling of frustration now. Yesterday at the bank it had been so strong he almost went up to the West End after work. Eight hours of working alongside ten women, watching breasts jiggle as they typed. Miss Baldwin the new clerk with her tight skirts and long slender legs curling round her stool as she served customers. At the Christmas party she'd wanted to kiss him, but always he had to be aware of his position. Clerks, assistant managers, they could have affairs, but not the manager, especially one with a social worker for a wife.

'It isn't fair!' he looked up at the ceiling. The light was still quivering, but the music was softer now. All those kids up there, kissing, cuddling, their whole lives ahead of them. Was it wrong for a man of fifty to want a woman who liked lovemaking? Celia understood every wife-beater, every petty criminal, cared for the sick, the lame and the mentally unstable, why then couldn't she see what she was doing to her own husband?

Laughter on the stairs made him sit up sharply. The record had long since finished, yet he hadn't noticed. He peered at his watch. It was twenty to twelve and he'd drunk half the bottle of gin.

'She won't be back for hours,' he sighed, getting up unsteadily. 'I'd better go and see what they're doing upstairs.'

The furniture seemed to be in the wrong places. He banged against the settee, almost falling and he had trouble opening the door. It was cooler in the hall and only then did he notice he was still carrying the gin.

Christine was smooching with John on the stairs. One rounded shoulder was free of her dress, an inch of white dimpled flesh above her stocking tops showing as Brian reached the first step.

"Allo, 'allo,' he grinned. 'What 'ave we got 'ere?'

Christine jumped a few inches away from the boy, pulled down her skirt and blushed charmingly. The earlier artful hairstyle was more like a tousled bird's nest now. Blonde tendrils surrounding her mascara-smeared face. She looked like a fallen angel, her blue eyes wide with surprise.

'Hallo, Mr Anderson,' she said. 'Come to join the party?'

The boy stood up and Brian saw he had an erection.

'I thought I might liven things up,' Brian smirked at the pimply-faced boy. 'But don't let me interrupt you!'

'Can I have some of that?' Christine giggled, fluttering her eyelashes and pointing to the bottle.

'I'll give you a drop in return for a kiss!'

Christine picked up a glass just behind her and held it out to him.

Brian lunged forward at her, almost tripping. The boy caught his arm.

'Steady on!'

'I'm just a little squiffy,' Brian said, plonking a wet kiss on Christine's cheek. 'But it's my daughter's birthday so why shouldn't I be?'

He glugged some of the gin in Christine's glass, then moved on past her, leaving the pair of them whispering behind him.

They were playing that record again, the same one Georgia had played almost non-stop since Christmas Day.

'Till I kissed ya'. He'd found himself humming it in the car, singing it in the bath, but it had never sounded so good before.

He paused on the landing by the open playroom door. A small table lamp over in one corner was the only light. Four couples were shuffling round the floor, girls' heads buried in their partners' shoulders. The decorations were drooping down low over their heads, cigarette smoke swirled lazily up to the ceiling and the other twenty or so kids sat around the edges of the room locked in one another's arms.

But Brian barely noticed anyone. All he could see was Georgia in the middle of the room, Peter's mouth coming down to hers.

Her upturned caramel face glowing in the soft light, full red lips open slightly, her breasts straining against the tight red bodice.

No woman had ever looked like that for him. He felt a quiver run down his spine, a stirring inside him.

'Come on in then!' Christine was at his elbow, drawing him into the room.

Georgia barely moved. She turned, smiled at him, then looked back at Peter.

Brian felt a rush of jealousy. Next to Peter he felt dwarfed, fat and old. The golden hair, the firm resolute chin, those bright blue candid eyes all irritated him.

This boy had it all, looks, brains and now Georgia. He would never get to fifty and wonder what had happened to his life.

'Hallo Daddy,' she took Peter's hand and walked towards Brian. 'It's not twelve yet is it?' She kissed him just as she always did, one small hand touching his cheek lightly.

'Thought I'd see what you are up to,' he lurched to one side, holding the wall for support. 'Are there any spare girls for me?'

'Daddy!' Georgia frowned reprovingly. 'You've been drinking!'

'Only one or two,' he said. 'I brought some up for you too.'

She half smiled, but Peter frowned.

'Gin, Mr Anderson! Are you sure?'

Peter's sanctimonious expression irritated Brian still further.

'A man can drink in his own house,' he said sharply.

'I'd like some,' Christine was already holding her

now empty glass out to him, batting her eyelashes flirtatiously. Brian poured her a little, then himself one, and went round putting a splash in anyone's glass that was held out.

'Let's have a dance Dad,' Georgia was worried now, he had been odd and moody all over Christmas and if her mother came home and found him like this, it might turn into a row.

'That's nice, a dance with Daddy,' Brian held out his arms.

Georgia glanced around the room. She could sense everyone thought it was funny to see her straitlaced father drunk, but she was embarrassed.

He was a good dancer normally, with a fine sense of rhythm. Another time she would have been glad he wanted to join in, but she didn't like the way he clutched her to him, the fumes of alcohol on his breath, or being prevented from dancing with Peter.

'Why don't you go back downstairs,' she wheedled with him. 'The party's nearly over now and I want to be with my friends for a little longer.'

'Don't be like that,' he pouted, holding her still tighter. 'I don't get any fun.'

Christine came up beside them.

'Can I have some more gin please?' she asked. Her dress had split on her hip and creased across the stomach. She looked like a girl he picked up once in Church Street, Kensington.

'Certainly,' Brian spun round, releasing Georgia, picking up his bottle and pouring a big measure into Christine's glass. 'You dance with me Chris? Georgia doesn't like her Daddy up here.'

Georgia took the opportunity to slip away, leading Peter out to the landing.

'I'm sorry,' she said hanging her head. 'He isn't usually like this. I don't know what's got into him.'

'Just booze,' Peter smiled and took her in his arms.

'My dad's like that half the time, you don't have to apologize.'

'But he's spoilt the party,' Georgia sighed.

'Not for me he hasn't,' Peter bent his head a little and rubbed her nose with his.

Georgia lifted her lips to his and wound her arms round his neck.

She longed to be entirely alone with him, somewhere warm and comfortable where they could relax knowing no one would come in.

His kisses drove her wild. She wanted more, each touch of his hand made her tremble.

At night she lay thinking about him, imagining his hands creeping under her clothes. She would wake suddenly, hot and sticky from dreaming he was in bed with her, his naked body pressed into hers.

Again and again they kissed, each kiss more passionate than the one before. Peter leant against the wall on the landing and she pressed herself into him, savouring the male hardness taunting her through her party dress.

It was Peter who finally broke away.

'It's after twelve,' he said breathlessly. 'I don't want to go but I promised your mother. I'll have to keep in her good books if I'm ever to be allowed to be alone with you.'

'Is that what you want then?' she smiled shyly.

His face was flushed, hair falling into half-closed eyes, even his lips were swollen with kissing.

'You know I do,' he whispered, lifting her hand to his lips and nibbling at the tips of her fingers. 'I've dreamed of nothing else since that night on the heath.'

'What do you imagine?' She covered his face with tiny kisses.

'Making love to you,' he said dreamily. 'Peeling your clothes off. Exploring you.'

'We can't do that,' she looked into his deep blue eyes, tracing one finger round his lips. 'I might have a baby!'

'I'd marry you,' he said softly, burying his lips in her neck and stroking her breasts.

She loved it when he did that, she could feel her nipples growing hard and a delicious dizzy feeling creeping all over her.

'Just because I was pregnant?' she was fishing for more.

'No, because I love you,' he put one finger under her chin and lifted her face up to his. 'And so I could sleep with you and hold you for always.'

'I love you too,' she whispered, burying her face in his neck.

As they rejoined the party, her father was trying to jive with Christine.

Georgia laughed. It wasn't often she saw her father like this. A lock of hair had fallen over his face, he was biting his lips trying to concentrate and each time Christine tried to twirl round, Brian moved the wrong way. His legs were rubbery, his arms were flaying about, his jacket hanging off one shoulder.

There was a good atmosphere in the room, laughter, chatter, relaxed, almost loving, it seemed a shame they had to break it up.

'Time to go,' Peter moved first to the boys from his school.

'Not yet,' Brian said, face flushed more with drink than the dance. 'It's only just warming up.'

Peter smiled politely, but still went round getting everyone to leave. Georgia started to stack glasses on a tray.

John, Christine's boyfriend was looking anxiously at his watch, then back to Christine as she twirled round with Brian.

'I'm supposed to get her home by half twelve,' he shrugged his shoulders at Georgia. 'Her dad will blame me for getting her like that.'

'Leave her to me,' Georgia said.

Crossing the room she caught hold of Christine's arm, her father danced on alone, oblivious.

'Please go now,' she said. 'Dad's being very silly and Mum will be furious if she comes in and finds him like that. Don't encourage him any more. John's waiting for you.'

'Okay,' Christine smiled stupidly. Her eyes were like slits now, her mouth drooping and trails of mascara running down her cheeks. The split in her dress was bigger now, a bubble of white flesh peeping out and her stockings were laddered. 'Do I look drunk?'

'The walk home will sober you up,' Georgia said, wiping away the mascara with a serviette. 'I'll phone you tomorrow.'

'Lovely party,' someone shouted from the landing as Georgia bundled Christine into her coat. 'See you back at school!'

Couple after couple left till finally there was only Peter, standing just a few inches from her in the hall, his navy blue duffel coat in his hand.

'Happy birthday,' he said. His eyes were heavy with longing. His arms reached out for her, crushing her into his arms, lips hot with desire.

From upstairs music suddenly blared out, breaking the moment.

They both started, looking up at the stairs.

'I'd better stay with you,' Peter took a step towards the stairs.

'I'll be all right,' she replied, tugging on his arm. 'Go on home. Mum will be back soon. She might think we're taking advantage.'

'But what if he turns nasty?' Peter argued. 'My dad does sometimes.'

His concerned expression made her feel special. The hall light shining down on his blond hair turned him into a Greek god and in that second love overwhelmed her.

'My Dad, the boring old bank manager!' she giggled. 'Don't be daft. He'll be like a little lamb.'

'Well pack him off to bed before your mum sees him.'

'I love you,' she said softly, reaching out for him one last time.

He pulled her to him fiercely. 'How can I go away to University now?' he said softly, burying his head in her neck, nibbling and kissing. 'I want to get a job and stay here with you.'

'You may be fed up with me by then,' she said, holding his face between her two hands.

'I'll never get fed up with you,' he said.

'We'll see,' she sighed. 'Maybe a year from now you'll have forgotten my name.'

'Not in twenty years,' he shook his head, kissing the tip of her nose, his fingers in her hair. 'I love you Georgia Anderson. For ever.'

She watched as he walked across the heath. Hands in pockets, shoulders hunched in the frosty darkness. Every now and then he turned and waved again, blowing one last kiss. As he blended into the darkness Georgia closed the door.

The taste of his lips still lingered, she could smell that soapy smell, hear him saying he'd love her for ever.

Georgia went up the stairs singing.

'Never knew what I missed, until I kissed you. How did I exist until I kissed you. Oh you've got a way about you, now I can't live without you.'

Her father was still dancing on his own in the playroom. He looked ridiculous, several buttons undone on his shirt, his tie hanging off and his trousers needed hitching up.

The playroom was a mess. Many of the Christmas garlands were hanging down. Full ashtrays lay everywhere, records and sleeves strewn across the floor, along with balloons and dirty plates.

Most of the food was gone, a few sandwiches remained, covered with cigarette ash, one speared with cocktail sticks.

'That's right, sing to me,' he said, staggering towards her, arms outstretched.

'Go to bed, Daddy,' she laughed, too happy to be really cross. 'Mum will go ape when she sees you, especially if she brings kids home with her.'

'I don't give a damn about your mother,' he said, his mouth hanging open wetly.

'You don't mean that, and anyway I'm tired.' She picked up the gin bottle and held it to the light. 'Daddy! This is nearly empty!'

'Christine had quite a lot,' he said. 'She's good fun. You're getting like your mother.'

Georgia looked back at him over her shoulder. He had a peeved, sour expression on his face, like a spoilt child.

'Oh, Dad,' Georgia sighed, 'Go to bed, you're pathetic when you're drunk.'

'Pathetic am I?' Suddenly his face turned from benign and very drunk, to angry and dangerous. 'You, of course, are perfect? I saw you necking with that Peter. How far did you go when you went out of the room?'

'Don't be disgusting,' she said quietly, bending over to pick up the plates from the floor. It was tempting to go to bed and leave everything, including her father, but if her mother did bring children home they just might have to sleep in the room.

'Did he put his hand up your frock?' he lunged towards her unexpectedly and his hand went under her skirt and clamped on to her bottom.

'Stop it!' she shrieked, wheeling round and slapping his hand away. He had never said such things before and suddenly she was frightened of him.

72

'Kiss me like you kissed him,' he said, putting both hands on her shoulders.

Alarm bells were ringing in her head. Fathers didn't say or do such things. She must get away, lock herself in her bedroom, wait for her mother to come home.

'Don't be stupid,' she tried to get his arms off, but he pushed her up against the wall.

'The last thing I am is stupid.'

This wasn't her father but a stranger. His face was lungeing at her, bloated and flushed. His lips wet and sloppy, pinning her against the wall with all his four-teen stone. His mouth came down on hers and he pushed his tongue into her mouth.

It felt like a huge serpent, she gagged and pulled herself back from him, moving her head to one side.

'Daddy no!' she shouted as she struggled to get away, but he was too strong, his arms went round her, pinning hers to her side. She tried to bite his cheek but one hand came up and slapped her full across the face.

His breath came in rasps, stinking of drink as he slobbered at her neck.

'I'm going to have you,' he said thrusting his hand up under her skirt, pulling at her panties. 'You little black bitch.'

'NO, Daddy. NO!' she fought with him, nails clawing his face, legs kicking out, pummelling at him with her fists. But the more she struggled the stronger he became.

'Daddy it's me. Your daughter!' she shouted, willing her mother to walk in the door.

'You're not my daughter,' he replied huskily, his eyes gleaming with lust.

For a second he loosened his hold, fumbling at his trousers. Like a shot Georgia was off running towards the door.

He caught her in a flying tackle, knocking her down

in the open doorway, flat on her face, then leapt on top of her.

'Don't, Daddy,' she screamed, still in her heart thinking he was playing some sick, drunken joke which had got out of hand. 'Let me go!'

But she was trapped now. She couldn't reach him with her nails or fists, and she could feel his erect penis against her leg, his fingers tearing at her panties.

She was trapped, so terrified she felt paralysed, yet she waited a second, assuming he must turn her on to her back, ready to lash out at him the moment he did.

Instead he yanked her hips up towards him and thrust himself into her like a dog.

The pain was so bad her scream turned from one of terror to anguish. He caught hold of her arms by the elbow, digging his fingers into the soft flesh. Her forehead hit the floor and the force of his thrusting movements grated it on the cord carpet.

Again and again she tried to get away, but each time he got a firmer grip, first her arms, then holding her pubic hair with one hand, the other holding her shoulder. His breath burning into her back.

'Daddy, no. *Pleease* don't.' She couldn't even scream any longer. Just a pleading, tormented cry and all the while she could hear him grunting out dirty filthy things that hurt her even more than the pain of being torn in two.

He went slack suddenly.

One moment the hideous grunting noise filled her ears, the next all she could hear was her own sobbing. A draft of cold air on her legs and buttocks, alerted her that he had rolled off.

For a second she just lay there, face embedded in the carpet, too stunned to move. A groan made her lift her head.

He was lying next to her on his back, eyes closed,

74

his mouth gaping, a trickle of saliva running down his chin.

Georgia moved then, recoiling in horror as if waking to find a snake beside her.

First crawling on her knees, then as her hand came in contact with the wall, she pulled herself up, backing away, clapping her hand over her mouth as the full enormity of what had happened hit her.

He was just lying there. A crumpled, blank face the colour of raw meat. Shirt open to the waist, white flaccid chest with a sprinkling of gingery hairs. Trousers unzipped, flabby stomach oozing out, his penis like some spent reptile, brown and limp, nestling amongst the wiry foliage.

The house was silent, just the ticking of the grandfather clock in the hall below and the flapping of the 'Happy Birthday' banner Peter had hung across the chimney-breast.

A faint smell made her gag. A hot, fishy smell which seemed to come from her. As she looked down she saw a trickle of white fluid, tinged with her own blood roll down the inside of her leg and splash silently to her ankle.

Six years of happiness in this house, wiped out.

His legs were inside the darker playroom, the rest of him on the landing, bathed in bright clear light. The crisp white-painted doors, the thick carpet, all so familiar and comfortable. But nothing would ever be the same again.

Hate welled up in her like vomit.

One moment she was staring at him, the next she found herself in the kitchen, her hand reaching out for a knife.

Eight different kitchen knives. Without hesitating she took the biggest triangular one for chopping meat and holding it to her breast went back up the stairs.

No more tears now, just dry-eyed desolation. He

groaned as she stood by his side looking down at him. His eyes were still closed, one hand resting on his chest, her own black hairs stuck to it.

Holding the knife tightly with both hands she drew it up first to chest height, then closing her eyes, plunged it, right down to the part of him she hated the most.

She saw blood spurt up, heard him cry out as she withdrew the knife, ready to repeat it, but nausea washed over her and instead she turned, running back down the stairs.

Celia parked her car and looked up at the house. She was exhausted, mentally and physically. The porch light was still on, as was the hall and staircase light, but she was relieved to hear the party was over.

It had been a harrowing evening. At times she wished she'd stayed with nursing, at least there she had the satisfaction of knowing her patients would often recover.

This family were born victims. A drunken father, a half-witted mother. Five dirty, neglected children living in unspeakable filth. How many years of child guidance would they need to wipe out the horrors they'd seen? There would be no happy endings for them. The father might get a prison sentence, the children a peaceful break in a children's home for a few weeks. But before long they would be back together again. The boys turning into clones of their father, the girls merely training to become the next generation of inadequate mothers.

Celia sensed something was wrong the moment she opened the door.

Outwardly everything looked normal, but there was an atmosphere of tension, which made the hairs on her neck stand on end.

'Brian,' she called tentatively.

The door to the sitting room was open. She walked towards it, dropping her briefcase in the hall.

It was too silent. If they'd gone to bed the lights would be turned off.

Her foot touched something hard. Looking down she saw it was her kitchen knife, its grey, steel blade almost concealed in the patterned carpet.

As she bent to pick it up she saw blood-stains.

'Georgia,' she shouted, pushing the door back, almost afraid to look in.

Georgia was lying crumpled up on the settee, the fire nearly out in front of her, the Christmas tree lights highlighting the red party dress. The net of the skirt billowed round her, for one brief second she looked like a dying swan in a ballet.

Celia sped the last few feet to her child, dropping to her knees in front of her, her hands automatically feeling for a pulse, eyes scanning for injury.

Her pulse was slow, but not dangerously so. A rough, red patch on her forehead and a swelling across her cheek like a slap mark. But there was no obvious injury.

'Darling, it's Mummy.' Celia caught Georgia up in her arms. 'Tell me what's happened?'

No reply. Not a flicker of anything in those coal black eyes. No emotion, no tears, not even a trace of recognition in the blank, vacant face.

The calm nurse vanished.

'Answer me? Who did this? Where's Daddy?' She shook Georgia sharply.

There was no reply, but she sensed the child's eyes move towards the door fearfully and in the same instant saw dried blood on her hands and a splatter on her dress.

Swiftly taking off her own coat she tucked it round Georgia.

'I'll be back in two seconds,' she said breathlessly.

She saw Brian's head through the bannisters, well before she reached the top of the stairs.

'Oh my God,' she gasped, racing the last few feet to his side.

Brian was lying in a pool of blood, coming from his stomach, his hands were over it, blood trickling through his fingers.

For just one second she thought he was dead, but a faint pulse told her otherwise.

'Hold on,' she said jumping up and running to the bathroom to fetch a towel to staunch the blood.

'Which service do you require?' a disembodied voice replied to her emergency call.

'Ambulance,' she shouted. 'Quickly!'

'Someone's stabbed my husband,' she said hurriedly as she was connected, barking out the address. 'Hurry please, it's serious.'

Back again at Brian's side, she held the towel tightly against his wound. He was unconscious still, but now that help was on its way she was able to think rather than act automatically.

Her first reaction had been that someone had come into the party uninvited and the stabbing was a result of Brian asking them to leave.

But that didn't make sense! The other kids would have called for help. And why was the knife downstairs by the sitting room?

There was something very familiar about the situation. A child in shock refusing to speak. If her father had been hurt defending her she would have run for help.

Celia moved the towel away from the wound and looked closely.

His trousers were unzipped. No sign of stab marks in the material and his penis was uncovered!

She heard herself cry out. Even through the smell of

blood there were others. Body aromas, mingling with a stronger one of alcohol.

Like a shot of insulin to a diabetic, the truth came to her.

'You bastard!' she exclaimed, pushing the towel down hard again to cover him.

She got up, moving back from him in horror and disgust, an overwhelming nausea washed over her, and she clamped both hands over her mouth.

For the last ten years she had worked with the aftermath of rape and incest. She had learned to control her rage and disgust. But this wasn't a stranger, this was her husband, the man she had promised to love and cherish.

'No,' she shouted. 'You couldn't do that!'

But he had, she knew it as certainly as if she'd seen the act take place. And now she wanted to finish what Georgia had started. Her hands moved towards his throat, her thumbs were on his windpipe, fingers digging into his neck.

His eyes flickered momentarily, his lips moved as if to speak.

'No,' she stopped herself. 'It's too good for you. You'll pay for this you maggot. You'll pay!'

She forced herself to attend to him, just a nurse, going through the motions of emergency first aid. Not out of sympathy, love or any other finer motive. Just keeping him alive so he could pay the price for ruining her child's life.

She could hear the sirens coming closer. Her heart thumped painfully, her head reeling as she thought of the implications.

Georgia downstairs, still in her party dress, shocked and witless. Six years of building up her trust, over, through one man's lust.

And it was all her fault. While she was out sorting

out other families' problems, one had been festering here. She was the expert, the one who should have read the signs. Celia Anderson, the woman who knew all the answers had failed the child she loved.

Chapter 4

'Georgia! Speak to me. You can't just shut me out.'

Celia sat on the edge of the bed, leaning over to cup
Georgia's small face in her hands.

'You don't fool me!' her voice rose in exasperation.
'Dr Towle might think you have some kind of hysterical
amnesia, but I know you better.'

The pretty pink and white bedroom with its rose
sprigged curtains and bedspread, the books, games,
teddy bears, even the posters of Elvis Presley and the
Everly Brothers all seemed so very safe and cosy. Yet
Brian had made a mockery of this childhood sanctuary.

Georgia had said nothing even when the doctor
examined her. No tears, no screaming, not even angry
accusation. Just a cold, emotionless silence that terrified
Celia. Experience told her that rape cases often reacted
like this. But this wasn't a case, this was personal.

Dr Towle confirmed that Georgia had been subjected
to violent sexual intercourse. Brian's injuries and the
entire scene Celia had walked in on just a few days
earlier was surely proof enough of who was responsible, yet still the police were prevaricating.

There had been precious little sympathy for Georgia
from the police when they arrived a few moments after
the ambulance.

Inspector Forbes was a bigot. A big bully of a man,
red-faced with hair to match. A lifetime immersed in

the underworld of South London made him incapable of seeing beyond Georgia's colour. A man who'd peered down so many sewers, he'd begun to believe the whole world was one.

'But everything you say is supposition,' he retorted almost angrily when Celia had once again told him the details of what she had discovered on her return to the house. 'Why should a man in his position, knowing full well you could come home at any time, force himself onto his daughter?'

'Lust brought on by drink,' Celia burned with anger at his arrogance. She had come up against this man before and knew he loathed professional women almost as much as the blacks in his territory. She turned to the young policewoman with him, sure another woman would be sensitive enough to see the truth. 'You saw him lying there. You saw the way Georgia looked, don't tell me you agree with the inspector?'

'Why wouldn't she tell me then?' the policewoman looked nervously at her superior officer, a sure sign she didn't dare oppose him. 'I think it's more likely someone else was involved, these teenage parties can get out of hand.'

Celia heard the soft Sussex accent, noted the farmgirl complexion and knew immediately this girl had no personal experience to fall back on and even less intuition.

'You don't believe my daughter was raped by her father?' Celia wanted to slap both of them to make them see sense.

'But he isn't her father is he?' Inspector Forbes had a look of cunning in his bloodshot eyes. 'Mixed-race girls are volatile. She'd been drinking.'

'He'd been drinking,' Celia corrected the man. 'Not Georgia.'

'Then why won't she tell us?'

'She's in shock.' Celia's eyes rolled with impatience.

'Do you really expect her to sit here and tell you the whole traumatic story?'

'But the knife?' the inspector said, looking down at the weapon in his hand, dried blood sticking to its covering plastic bag. 'She could have killed him. I can't see a girl capable of wielding this, being incapable of defending herself against sex.'

'He weighs fourteen stone,' Celia said through clenched teeth. 'Georgia about eight. If she'd had the knife handy before he attacked her she might have had a chance.'

'Perhaps we'd better try again in the morning,' Forbes sighed. 'This isn't getting us anywhere. I don't see a man like Anderson being a rapist. Let's wait till I've interviewed the boyfriend. To be honest Mrs Anderson, I'm surprised at you not taking your husband's part.'

'I've never heard of anyone attempting to cut off a man's penis unless that same organ was used against them,' Celia lost control entirely, almost screaming at him.

'I do believe you are getting hysterical,' he said disdainfully. 'He has stomach wounds and his loose clothing was consistent with someone who tried to examine himself before losing consciousness.'

It was after four in the morning when they finally left the house. Georgia sedated by the doctor upstairs. Brian in hospital and there was no one she could turn to for help.

'How can they be so stupid and blind?' she cried helplessly in the kitchen, her head on the table. 'I wish I'd let him die now.'

'I know you can't bear to talk about what happened,' Celia stroked her daughter's face. 'But if you don't talk soon you'll be taken from me. You might even be charged with attempted murder. Think about it Georgia, unless Brian is charged with rape he'll walk out of that hospital a free man!'

But Georgia just lay in her bed, her eyes blank as if she were deaf and dumb.

'What are we going to do?' Celia sat in the kitchen with Peter later the same morning, her face lined and drawn. She reached out to touch his hand, the social worker at odds with the distraught mother. 'She knows exactly what's going on. She's fully conscious, she goes out to use the toilet. Yet she's eaten nothing, only drinking the water I left by her bed.'

'You're frightened they'll take her away from you?' Even after all the questioning Peter had been subjected to, he was still perceptive enough to understand Celia's fears.

He looked ill. His face was white, eyes ringed with dark circles. His chin had a rash of stubble, even his shoulders were stooped. Now he was risking more trouble by refusing to go back to school.

'I don't know how much longer I can stall the children's department,' Celia said wearily, resting her head on her hands. She looked old. Her brown hair uncombed, wearing the same old tweed skirt and jumper she'd put on the morning after the event. 'Unless she starts talking they'll almost certainly take her. I keep trying to distance myself from it, work out what I'd do if Georgia and her foster mother were clients. And I don't like the answer I keep coming up with.'

'What about him?' Peter winced as if even using Anderson's name hurt him.

'He's out of danger now,' Celia snorted with anger. 'I never thought I'd admit to such a thing, but there've been times in the past few days I hoped he'd die. She only cut his abdomen, he's got a lot of stitches, but he'll survive.'

'What's he been saying?' Peter asked.

Celia's mouth trembled.

'He claims he fell asleep in a chair, woke to see Georgia smuggling you out of her bedroom after the others had gone and that he had a row with her about it. He insists the last thing he remembers is Georgia coming at him with the knife and when he came round he was in hospital.'

'But even my parents can vouch that I got home just after half past twelve.' Peter flushed an angry shade of red. 'I left only ten minutes after the others.'

'A good lawyer would wipe him out,' Celia reassured him. 'But without Georgia's statement he can't even be charged.'

'You mean he could come home here?' Peter's face blanched in horror.

'It's his house.' Celia's greeny-grey eyes were blank with misery, her face contorted by dark thoughts.

She couldn't bring herself to tell Peter the full strength of it. Brian claimed to have caught them naked in bed together, that Peter had grabbed his clothes and made a run for it and Georgia screamed abuse at him and even threatened she would say Brian raped her if he told her mother.

At the hospital they all believed his story, but then they'd never met Georgia or Peter and Brian Anderson was charming and persuasive when he wanted to be.

'Let me try speaking to her?' Peter leaned forward earnestly. 'I might be able to get through to her.'

'I don't think she'll respond to you or any man,' Celia shook her head. 'But you can try. Just don't try to touch her that's all.'

'Georgia!' Peter whispered in the darkened room. 'Are you awake?'

There was no reply. In the gloom all Peter could make

85

out was a small lump in the bed, her dark hair sticking out of the covers like a chimney-sweep's brush.

Peter walked across the room and drew back the curtains.

It was bitterly cold outside, a dark, grey day as if all the world was suddenly monochromatic. The heath across the road was deserted, bare branches of trees looked menacingly like skeletons.

'I think it's going to snow,' he said, taking a chair just close enough to see her face.

It was crumpled, as if she'd aged ten years. Her eyes were open but they showed no signs of recognition.

'You've got to talk,' he said, keeping his voice as normal as possible. 'Maybe not to me, but to your mother. She's tearing herself apart, and she's the one who is trained for things like this.'

No movement, not so much as a flicker of an eyebrow.

'Would you like some music on?' he asked. 'I could get your record player and plug it in?'

Still nothing.

For five days he'd waited patiently for this opportunity, convinced Georgia would open up to him. But she lay there like a doll, dark eyes staring into space and now he understood why Celia was so frightened.

'School started again,' he went on. 'I haven't been though,' one hand reached out, but paused in mid air. He could feel tears pricking the back of his eyelids. 'I went to bed dreaming of you that night. I intended to come round to help you clear up in the morning. Then the police came.'

He had trusted the police until that morning. One moment he was lying in bed thinking of Georgia, the next he was bundled down the stairs into a squad car, accused of having sex with a minor.

For three hours they interrogated him. First in an

86

almost jocular 'all-boys-together' manner suggesting he had been caught by Mr Anderson with his pants down. But later it turned vicious, with insinuations about Georgia's character that left Peter bewildered.

It was only when he discovered Mr Anderson had been stabbed that the hideous truth filtered through. He remembered the way Anderson had been as he left, Georgia's insistence she would get him to bed before her mother got home. Why had he let her persuade him to leave?

Maybe it was foolhardy to take a swing at Inspector Forbes, to scream out his anger and frustration at their callous indifference to Georgia's pain, and stupidity at blaming him. But at that moment he didn't care if they locked him up forever.

There was no understanding or sympathy when he got home eight hours later. No concern that his girl had been raped, or even anger that he was being blamed. His father made lewd suggestions. His mother could see no further than Georgia's colour.

'I'll never get over the shame,' she raved. 'My son mixed up with some wog. I won't have it Peter. Don't you dare go near her again.'

Celia was the only one who shared his outrage. It was her arms he turned to for comfort instead of his own mother's, and now he hoped together they could bring Georgia out of her silence.

Peter wriggled in the small cane chair. There was still no movement from Georgia in the bed. She didn't even look round to watch him.

'I'm not going to give up,' he said petulantly. 'I shall just keep on coming until I bore you into telling me to shut my mouth. Day after day, year after year. I'll tell you what I ate for tea, what I did all day. You are my girl and I'll keep coming till you tell me to go.'

He peered at her to see if there was even a flicker of amusement.

'Right, I'll try the music,' he said, getting up and making for the door.

The playroom was much as they'd left it the night of the party. The garlands hanging down, stray balloons and records still littering the floor. Only the food, glasses and plates had been removed.

He unplugged the record player and sorted through the records, selecting only one.

Then carrying it back across the landing, he noticed the blood-stain.

Celia had obviously tried to get it out of the carpet, but still it stayed, dark and menacing against the pale, flowery design.

That animal had taken her here, only feet away from the place where Peter had held her in his arms earlier. Rage washed over him, his hands shook and he could understand only too well why Georgia had got the knife.

Taking a deep breath he pushed his way back into Georgia's room.

The record crashed down from the spigot, the arm moved across and for a second there was only a scratching noise.

'How did I exist until I kissed ya. Oh, you've got a way about ya, now I can't live without ya. Never knew what I missed until I kissed ya.'

It sounded trite and silly under the circumstances. But they'd played it over and over the night of the party.

He hummed along with it, wondering what to do next.

Leaning forward he saw a tear trickling down her cheek.

'I didn't mean to upset you,' his hand reached out to touch her, but recoiled almost immediately as he remembered her mother's warning. 'It's just it's our song isn't it?' He was sure she was going to speak now, but still she was silent.

'My feelings haven't changed,' he whispered. 'I love you.'

It was all he could do to prevent himself from sweeping her up in his arms. He wanted to hold that small crumpled body, breathe life back into that blank face, somehow he was sure the power of touch would succeed where words never could.

'Now I can't live without you.' He sang the words softly, then turned away, stumbling to the door.

Georgia lay staring at the ceiling. The soreness had faded now, though when she turned over she could still feel the bruises on her buttocks. Nothing felt right anymore. Not her own body, or even her bed. She had felt like this before, in the early morning before Celia had collected her from St Joseph's. Sister Mary's kind words had softened some of the wounds Sister Agnes had inflicted on her, just as Celia's and Peter's tenderness had, but still inside was this core of terror that nothing could make go away.

'Devil's spawn'! That was what Sister Agnes had said about her. Maybe it was her fault. Something bad within her that caused destruction and pain.

She couldn't stay here, not now. Celia and Peter might want to help, but they couldn't. What good would it do telling the police the truth? So Brian might get locked up, but what sort of hell would she have to drag Celia, Peter and herself through? And for what? It wouldn't make her forget what happened. She wouldn't even be able to stay with Celia.

Celia came in with a tray of food around lunchtime. Once again Georgia lay silently, staring into space.

'Look, dear,' Celia sounded as if she was losing

patience. 'You must be hungry, even if you don't want to speak to me. Sit up and eat this, just for me.'

The smell of the casserole made her feel nauseous. Why did Celia keep bringing food, when all she really wanted was to be left alone?

'I'll put it down here.' Celia's voice was firm and business-like as she placed the tray on the floor by Georgia's bed. 'I've got to go into the office this afternoon. You know how it is Georgia. When all's said and done the children's department will have a final say. By speaking to them now I might just get us a few weeks grace. Even the doctor has suggested you need to be taken into hospital. I can be back in a couple of hours. Will you be all right?'

Georgia nodded. The first indication she'd given her mother that she even understood what was going on around her.

Celia sat down on the bed and took one of Georgia's hands in hers.

It was that same look Georgia had seen all those years ago when Celia had taken off her clothes and found the wounds on her back. So much pity and understanding, so willing to give her anything to make things right.

'I love you darling. This evening I want you to come downstairs with me. I know why you don't want to speak,' her voice was breaking with emotion. 'But the sooner you open up to me, the sooner we can put this horrible affair behind us. Together we can find a solution.'

"Bye darling,' she said at the door. 'Eat that dinner just for me?'

In that second Georgia's resolve nearly crumbled. Celia looked so careworn, the small lines round her eyes deeper, etched with unbearable sadness. She had made an effort to look smart again. Her navy pin-striped suit with its long jacket hid the plumpness, a small brooch at the neck of her white blouse, her hair washed and brushed back from the soft cheeks. Powder and lipstick had done their best to cover the putty-coloured skin. But the apple cheeks Georgia knew so well looked sunken.

Georgia waited until she heard the front door slam and the car start up. She sat up gingerly, looking down at the tray of food. She didn't want it, but it might make Celia feel better knowing she'd eaten something.

She forced herself to eat half the meat and some of the vegetables but however hard she tried she couldn't manage the apple pie and custard.

Her legs were stiff and unsteady as she got out of bed, her face in the mirror was pale and drawn but however bad she felt she had to get dressed. She found a holdall in the cupboard on the landing and hastily packed a few warm clothes. She put on the new navy suit Celia had bought her before Christmas, which made her look older, and put her hair up in a French plait.

Finally her thick, grey overcoat, a woolly hat and scarf and a pair of sheepskin-lined boots.

Then stuffing her make-up, hairbrush and washing things in a handbag, she made her way downstairs.

The house gleamed. Celia always cleaned frantically when she was angry or anxious.

All the Christmas decorations were gone now, pine needles carefully swept away. Everything looked just the way it always did, except it could never be her home again.

Taking a sheet of paper from Celia's desk in the dining room, she sat down to write a note, her eyes filling with tears.

'Dear Mummy,' she paused, unable to see clearly through the tears, her mind suddenly blank of the right words.

'I'm sorry. I had to go. We both know it's only a

matter of days before someone takes me away and if I can't stay with you, I'd rather be alone. I'm old enough to get a job and somewhere to live. I will always love you and be grateful to you for taking me from that convent, no one could have had a better home than me.

'Please don't blame yourself for what happened and try to forget about it. Don't try to find me, it will only make things worse.'

She paused again, sobs rising up within her. There was so much she wanted to say, so many thank yous. How did you say goodbye to someone who meant so much?

'Explain to Peter for me. He must forget too and go on to university like he planned. Maybe one day we can meet again. You will never be out of my thoughts.
     I love you,
     Georgia'

Leaving the letter on the table, she lifted a ginger jar off the mantelpiece where Celia kept housekeeping money. She took twenty pounds and then returned to the desk.

'PS, I took twenty pounds as a loan. I'll send it back just as soon as I can.' She added this on the bottom of the letter, then took it into the kitchen to leave it on the table.

Picking up her bag she walked to the front door. Pausing for a moment to look back one more time.

There was snow her first day here. She remembered Celia sitting her on the stairs, taking off her shoes and rubbing her toes to warm them. Maybe the little girl who'd stared in wonder at the paintings, the thick, patterned carpets, the polished furniture and the grandfather clock had grown up, but that first impression would stay with her for ever.

She gulped back tears, opened the door resolutely and walked out, slamming it behind her.

Outside, the cold air made her shrink back into her coat. The heath had a thin coating of frost, fog concealing the walls of Greenwich Park in the distance. It would be dark in a couple of hours. She must hurry now before anyone saw her.

Peter would soon forget, whatever he said now. Brian had taught her how shallow men's love was.

Still, she paused by the church, Peter's face dancing in front of her. She could see those blue eyes fill with emotion as she sang the Christmas Anthem at midnight mass. Remember the kiss he stole as they hung up their surplices in the vestry. She hated her father for a great many reasons now, but most of all for ending something so beautiful.

Standing in Piccadilly with crowds of people milling around her, she felt numb. This was the centre of everything. The big city with its bright lights, smart shops and continuous noise. Neon lights flashing, the never-ending stream of traffic, strange smells. Men in bowler hats carrying furled umbrellas, office girls, shop assistants and shoppers.

Swan and Edgar's windows were piled high with sale goods. Around her were the shouts of newspaper men, music from a one-man-band, wafts of fried onions from a hamburger stall, and Eros in the middle directing the circus. It was the ideal place to hide in, every day of the year girls swarmed to this area to begin life away from home and most probably started with less money than she had.

At six her legs and feet were aching. She'd seen two rooms with a To Let notice, but both times she climbed the stairs to enquire she'd been told the rooms were ten pounds a day.

She was baffled. Why would a grubby little room in Soho have such a high rent?

The answer came to her on her third attempt.

A big-busted blonde girl of about thirty came to the door wearing a black negligee, a cigarette dangling from vermilion lips.

'I've come about the room,' Georgia said wearily. 'Is it still vacant?'

The girl wore false eyelashes, one was peeling off and she had traces of mascara rubbed onto her cheeks. She looked Georgia up and down, taking in the wool coat, sheepskin boots and holdall.

'You aren't a working girl,' her greyish face puckered into a frown.

'Not yet,' Georgia tried to sound bright. 'I'm going to look for a job in a café or something tomorrow.'

The blonde girl studied her for a moment. A quizzical look as if she thought someone was pulling her leg.

'Come off it love!' she laughed, but it came out like a dry cough.

'Sorry?' Georgia frowned. 'I don't understand.'

The girl just looked at her for a moment, a mixture of amusement and pity.

'You must've heard what goes on in Soho?' She took another puff on her cigarette. 'These rooms are for the girls. Know what I mean?'

Georgia's mouth fell open. 'You mean?' she couldn't bring herself to say the word.

The blonde nodded, a warmer look spreading across her face. 'Try the evening paper, or go home love. There's nothing around here for a little thing like you.'

Georgia backed away feeling foolish and just a little tainted.

'Good luck,' the girl said cheerfully. 'And watch what you are doing love!'

Earlier Georgia had welcomed the darkness. Now it seemed like a threat. She was tired, cold and her holdall was getting heavier by the minute. She bought a paper and went into a café to read it, wrapping her hands round a cup of tea to warm them.

The advertisements offered very little. Most of them were too expensive and almost all of them said 'references required'. She ringed eight which sounded possibilities, drank her tea then found a phone box.

Five of them had already been let. One was right out near Wembley and at the other two there was no reply.

Two policemen walked past as she came out of the phone box. One looked at her bag and then directly at her.

Trembling with fright, she moved off quickly, running down the narrow street, back towards Piccadilly.

The West End might have seemed exciting with the security of a friend beside her, or looking at Christmas lights from the safety of a car. But alone, in the dark it was menacing.

So many people pushing and shoving. Tramps mingling with couples out for the evening. Young office girls off to a dance, a gang of rough-looking Teddy boys shouting remarks at passing girls. Taxis, motorbikes, cars and buses, a madhouse of noise and bustle, a sinister undertone to everything. Her bag was heavy and each time someone turned to look at her Georgia sank into the shadows.

Turning again back towards Soho, she walked deliberately up one street, looking at all the notices on doors, then down the next.

There were plenty of signs.

'French Lessons, apply second floor.' 'Model first floor,' and even one saying 'Strict Instruction, ask for Mitzi.'

Girls and women stood brazenly in doorways. Tight shirts, cigarettes dangling from lips like scarlet gashes,

95

'beehive' hair do's and heavy eyeliner, clinking keys in their hands. They stared openly at Georgia as she rushed by, her heavy bag banging against her legs.

'Are you doing business?' A swarthy-looking man sidled up to her.

Shame overwhelmed her, her eyes filled with tears, all she could do was pretend she hadn't heard and carry on walking as if she had some place to go.

It was after nine and she'd been up and down each street. Almost every coffee bar she'd passed she enquired in.

Always the same answer.

'Sorry. Try the paper.'

She saw one advertisement for a room in a shop window and went round to the house immediately.

An elderly lady came to the door, opened it just a crack and peered out.

Georgia put on her most beguiling smile.

'I'm sorry to call so late. I believe you have a room to let?'

She reminded Georgia of story book grannies, white haired, wrinkled with a crocheted shawl round her shoulders. She opened the door a little wider and peered at Georgia standing on the pavement.

'No blacks!'

The door slammed shut in her face, leaving Georgia standing there mouth agape, cheeks burning at the insult.

The cold seemed to have got right into her bones, even the sheepskin boots no longer kept out the cold.

Down she went into the tube. At least there was a little warmth in the ladies' toilets. Locking herself in a cubicle she unpacked another jumper and put it on under her coat and suit.

She looked odd, shapeless under the many clothes, the woolly red hat seemed to drain even more colour from her face.

'Have you run away from home?' The toilet attendant shuffled out of her small room, wearing a flowery cross-over apron, as Georgia appeared for a second visit in an hour.

'No,' Georgia said quickly. 'I'm waiting for someone.'

'Well wait somewhere else,' she snapped. 'This is a public convenience. There's cafés up there for meeting people.'

It was too late to find anywhere now. She was too scared to go to a proper hotel and if she hung around much longer the police might pick her up.

Instead she went back into a café and bought herself a meal, taking as long as possible to eat it while she thought what she should do next.

The café overlooked a strip club. One of many she'd noticed while walking up and down. As she watched she saw men going over to the brightly-lit pictures of naked girls and some went on, down the stairs. All at once she realized she'd made a mistake coming to Soho. It was another myth, like happy families, fathers you could trust and the streets paved with gold.

Tomorrow morning she could try the flat-letting agency she'd spotted in Berwick Street. That just left tonight to get through.

Just before midnight she left the warmth of the café. She was so tired now she could hardly put one foot in front of the other.

There was nothing for it but to look for somewhere to hide, and just wait till the morning.

Earlier she had noticed some large boxes, piled out-side a dress manufacturer's workshop. It was a small cul-de-sac tucked away behind the busier streets. She made her way there now, walking quickly to keep warm.

She passed an old tramp going through a box of abandoned fruit by the market; shuddering she moved even more quickly.

Looking over her shoulder to check no one was watching, she looked in the boxes piled high against a doorway.

One of them was full of scraps of material.

Selecting the largest of the boxes, she turned it on its side, placing the opening against the wall, then moving boxes either side of it, including the one with material, she crawled in.

It wasn't large enough to lie stretched out, but curled up it was adequate. Then she reached out, taking handfuls of material until she had covered the floor with a thick layer.

Out of the wind it was much warmer, and the material soft to lie on. She wriggled out of her coat in the confined space, then using it as a blanket, her bag as a pillow, curled up to go to sleep.

A hissing sound close to her head made her wake suddenly. She lifted her head and listened.

She heard feet walking quite close. Obviously it was a man who had just relieved himself against the wall.

She cringed in disgust. In the distance she could hear music, the sound of someone dropping a bottle nearby, and shouting coming from the end of the cul-de-sac.

It was too dark to see the time, she was stiff with cold and she ached to change position and stretch out.

A cat mewed softly nearby and she heard rustlings which might possibly be a rat.

If she made any noise someone might investigate. The sort of men round here could be as bad as Brian. She turned on her back and bent her knees up, putting her hands under her head, trying hard to stay calm and not cry.

'It's only for tonight,' she said to herself. 'You'll be laughing about this in a day or two.'

To take her mind off the cold she tried to imagine a bedsitter, small and cosy with a big fire.

'I'll change my name,' she whispered to herself. 'Something glamorous.'

'Come on love, ten quid's too much,' a booming male voice made her almost jump out of her skin.

'Ten quid or nothing.' A woman with a cockney accent replied.

'What! A tenner for here in an alley?' The man's voice was slurred with drink and the couple's footsteps were coming closer.

'Take it or leave it,' the woman said defiantly. 'I can't take you anywhere now.' She sniffed loudly, she was so close Georgia could even hear her pull a handkerchief out of her pocket.

Georgia hardly dared breath. She could hear the man going through money in his pockets. She shook with fright, expecting any moment that he would sense her presence and root her out.

'I'll give you a fiver,' he said reluctantly. 'That's enough for a bleedin' kneetrembler.'

'You blokes are all the same,' the woman grumbled. 'Well, don't expect me to give you the full treatment.'

A rustle of notes, the click of a handbag clasp and the rasp of fabric.

'Give me a kiss then?' the man said. 'Don't expect me to get it up without some help.'

Georgia could hear her own heart beating. She had cramp in her leg, she was so cold she felt she might just die and the man's intentions brought her father right into the box with her.

She tried not to listen but the man's grunts penetrated even her gloved hands over her ears. Stiff joints creaked and the swishing sound of clothes being pushed aside.

They seemed to be at it forever, disgusting her so much she felt sick and faint. Sucking sounds, heavy breathing, words that made her blush with shame. Then a prolonged thumping sound, like a piece of meat being slapped against a plate.

Georgia wanted to cry. All those silly dreams she'd had of love. What was going on out there was the real world. Men weren't ruled by their hearts at all, they were just animals needing sex like food and it didn't matter to them who they shoved themselves into.

'Was it good?' she heard the man ask.

'Sure,' the woman replied, the sound of pinging elastic like gun shots in the quiet street.

She left first. Her high heels like castanets on the road, gradually fading away into the distance.

A loud belch signalled the man was still close by. She heard the flick of a lighter, the smell of a cigarette, then unsteady movements and deep breathing. He stopped, the unmistakable sound of a zipper. A rumbling fart, and the hiss of urine, followed by a deep sigh.

It was too cold to sleep again. She had pulled everything out of her bag to lay over her, and handfuls more of the material from the other box, but still she shivered.

There was no more noise from people now. But cats continually prowled, frequently jumping on her box. There were other rustlings she couldn't identify, sometimes a gnawing sound which made her eyes open with terror.

She must have slept eventually, as she came to with a start when the sound of an engine roared nearby.

Waiting a few moments, as the noise came closer and closer, she was finally brave enough to peep out round the edge of the box.

It was barely light, her breath like smoke in the cold grey dawn. At the crossroads less than a hundred yards away a dustcart had paused, four men throwing all the boxes and refuse into the back of the van.

Hastily she pushed all her belongings into her holdall, flung her coat over one arm and ran, her heart thumping like a steam engine.

She stopped for breath on the next corner and

reached for her handbag to find a hanky. It was gone. In her haste she must have left it in the box.

Dropping her holdall, she flew back. All that was left of her bed for the night was a wet patch where one of the men had urinated, and a few scraps of fabric.

A dull rumble alerted her the cart was now in the next street. She tore round the corner, catching it up and running along side.

'Please stop,' she waved her arms frantically. 'Stop!'

One of the men jumped off the back of the cart.

He was very small and stocky, a woolly brown hat perched on fair greasy hair, dressed in dark green overalls and a donkey jacket.

'What's up love?' He had a strange speech impediment, and his mouth twisted alarmingly. He was about fifty and very dirty.

'My bag,' she said breathlessly. 'I left it in a box that you've just picked up.' She pointed in the direction they'd just left.

'What sort of bag?' he frowned, looking at her dishevelled appearance, pieces of cloth in her hair.

'A handbag, it's got my money and everything.'

'Why was it in the box then?' He scratched his head through his hat.

'Because I was in there too. But I heard you coming and ran away. I didn't realize I hadn't got it until after you'd gone.'

The man looked from Georgia to the dustcart. She could see it was fitted with a crusher device, already chomping away the last of the boxes from the road they were now in.

'I can't get in there,' he said sharply. 'You should look after your stuff.'

'But all my money's in there,' she said, tears springing to her eyes.

'Can't help that,' he turned away from her.

'What shall I do?' she ran after him clutching at his sleeve.

'Go to the police,' he said wearily. 'It ain't my problem. What'cha sleeping in a box for anyway?'

He was gone before she could say anything more and Georgia felt as crushed as if she'd been in the machine herself.

It was a few moments before the full implications hit her. She went back to where she'd left her holdall and bent down in a doorway to repack it. She was so cold she was no longer shivering, and she knew she must find somewhere to get a hot drink.

A sick feeling wound its way into her stomach. She couldn't get a drink or anything now. Every penny she had in the world was in that handbag.

She saw her reflection in the glass door. She was dirty, her hair full of bits of cloth and she had nothing at all other than a few clothes.

Sinking down onto her haunches she wept. Great heaving sobs that shook her shoulders and engulfed her whole body.

Money meant everything. She couldn't get a drink, or a meal, much less a room for the night. She couldn't use a phone or get on a bus or train.

There was no difference between her and the tramp she'd seen going through the rubbish last night!

Cold and hunger had brought on a new sort of apathy by five in the evening. A day spent walking up and down Oxford Street, eyes glued to the pavement, hoping to find a shilling or so to buy a drink. She'd been in the toilets of every shop from Marshall and Snelgrove to Selfridges, lingering in a cubicle as long as she dared, trying to summon the courage to swipe a handbag or purse from one of those wealthy ladies wreathed in shopping bags.

But each time she got close something stopped her.

Sometimes an attendant watching, sometimes just a faint stirring of conscience. Eleven hours of walking and all she had to show for it was a yellow plastic comb and two halfpennies she'd found in a gutter.

For just a brief moment it seemed her luck had changed. Just off Tottenham Court Road she saw an advertisement being stuck up in a sweet shop window.

'Bedsitter to let for business person. £2 per week. 14 York Street.'

She had run there, memorising the address, so sure it was a sign from heaven that she forgot the cold and her aching feet.

'I believe you have a room to rent,' she blurted out to the man who opened the door.

He was perhaps sixty, thin and bent with yellowish skin and a big, hooked nose.

'How old are you?' He looked her up and down with sharp eyes. She felt sure he could see the creases in her clothes and the traces of fabric still clinging to her hat and coat.

'Eighteen.' She could see a steep uncarpeted staircase behind him, it looked dark and dirty and she was more than a little scared. 'I've just started a job in Oxford Street.'

'Your name?'

'Georgia.' She paused suddenly remembering she intended to change it. She looked round and noticed a small shoe shop. The sign above it was James's.

'Georgia James,' she said quickly.

The house was even worse inside than it looked from the street. Four narrow floors with uneven boards that creaked ominously. He led her further and further up, past so many brown-painted doors she lost count and finally right at the top he opened one.

Georgia gulped. Like the house itself it was long and narrow. A small window opposite the door so dirt-smeared it could have been curtained. The single bed sagged, the floor was bare linoleum, it looked as wretched as she felt.

'I'll take it,' she said, taking no more than a cursory glance at the single gas ring and chipped sink.

'A week in advance,' his hand shot out reminding her strangely of Sister Agnes. His fingernails were black and she noticed he had no teeth.

'Could I give it you on Friday?' she forced herself to smile. 'I lost my bag this morning, it had all my money in it.'

'I don't take charity cases,' he turned immediately, dismissing her. 'No advance rent, no room.'

'Please,' she caught hold of his arm. 'Please, I promise I'll pay you.'

'I wish I had a quid for everyone that's promised that,' his lips curled back. 'Go on push off. Go down the assistance if you've got no money.'

'Look, take this,' she unfastened her watch. 'Please don't throw me out.'

But there was no softening in his dark eyes.

'What do I want a cheap watch for?' his tone was contemptuous. 'Go on, push off. I can see you're trouble.'

There was nothing for it but to go on back down the stairs. He followed her in silence, Georgia pleaded silently with him to change his mind.

She turned at the door.

'If I manage to get some money now, can I come back?' She could feel prickling tears and she hated herself for pleading with him.

'Going to sell yourself?' he retorted, about to close the door.

'How dare you?' She took a step closer to him, drawing herself up and glowering at him. But before she could even get the satisfaction of giving him her opinion of his disgusting house, the door slammed and he was gone.

At half past five she found herself in Berwick Street, the sixth or seventh time she'd been through the market that day. The men were packing up now, piling boxes of apples, flinging rail after rail of dresses into vans and handcarts.

A weariness had replaced the earlier joviality. Stalls stripped down in hurried silence, the last-minute shoppers almost an intrusion. Hurricane lights softened the rubbish-strewn streets, yet drew attention to the gaunt, cold faces, highlighting abnormalities, turning every last man and woman into a Hogarth caricature.

She leaned against the lamp-post, her holdall at her feet, too weary to even go through the motions of pretending to wait for someone. Women hurried by, baskets full of shopping, rushing home to their families. Girls little older than her came tip-tapping down the street in high-heeled shoes, heads bent against the wind, perhaps planning the night ahead of them.

The notice on the club opposite beckoned her. 'Dancing girls wanted, apply within.' She'd looked furtively at the photographs of girls in nothing more than a G-string several times during the day, and now she was desperate enough to join them. Maybe it wasn't the kind of stage she'd seen in her dreams, or the kind of dancing she'd been trained for, but another night on the streets might kill her.

A crippled girl was coming up a narrow street towards the crossroads where Georgia waited, catching her attention by her strange gait, bright red hair and unusual clothes. Caught for a moment under a street lamp she had the look of a Victorian maid in her long, waisted, russet coat with a fur collar, hopping, rather than walking, one foot dragging behind her.

Despite her obvious affliction she was arresting. Glorious, shiny red hair tumbled around a small white face and her slim shoulders, somehow lighting up the whole street.

She made Georgia think of red squirrels. Not merely her colouring, or the fast hopping motion, but the nervous head movements, as if she anticipated danger. She stepped out into the road, hitching two bags of shopping up into her arms.

A car roared round a corner just a few yards behind her. The girl's head jerked round sharply, she hesitated, then tried to run. To Georgia's horror, she stumbled, falling right into the path of the oncoming car.

Instinctively Georgia waved her arms and shouted. The car swerved, going up on to the pavement, missing the girl by only inches. The driver made a rude gesture with his fist, and drove off round the corner.

The girl lay spread-eagled face down. Around her the dropped shopping bags spilled out their contents, oranges, potatoes, a bag of sugar, mingling with knitting wool and needles.

'Are you hurt?' Georgia ran over, putting her hands under the girl's shoulders and lifting her up.

'I don't think so.' The girl's voice was shaky, her face a ghastly white.

'He only missed you by inches,' Georgia said, supporting the girl with her arm. She saw a trickle of blood run down the girl's forehead, as bright as berries against her white skin. 'You'll have a big lump there tomorrow.'

She led the girl over to a wall.

'Stay there, I'll just pick up your stuff,' she said.

As she retrieved the vegetables and the knitting from the spilt milk she glanced up and noticed the girl was wearing a special built-up boot. She was leaning back against the wall panting, holding her head.

She carried the bags over to the girl.

'Do you live round here?'

The girl dabbed at her forehead with a hanky, wincing as she saw the blood.

'Over there,' she pointed to the corner where seconds earlier Georgia had stood. 'I feel funny.' Her accent wasn't a London one, the way she rolled the 'R' sounds smacked of the West Country.

'I'll help you home,' Georgia put both bags in one hand and her spare arm round the girl.

It was difficult to know if the girl was pale because of her near miss, or naturally so. She was painfully thin, her wrists and hands smaller than a child's. But as Georgia helped her along it was the limp she noticed most. She barely put any weight on her bad leg, merely dragging it along behind her, hence the hopping gait she had observed earlier.

Georgia hesitated as they came to her own bag under the lamp-post.

'Well that's something,' she said as she bent to pick it up too. 'I left a bag somewhere this morning and when I went back it was gone. Now where to?'

'Just here.' The girl pointed to a door right next to the side of the café where Georgia had smelt meat pies. She now looked faint, her colour turning from white to pale green and clearly she hardly knew what Georgia was saying. 'Can you open the door?'

Georgia took the keys from the girl's shaking hand. As she opened the door she could make out a narrow hallway with steep stairs ahead, the dank smell which wafted out suggested dirt and neglect.

'There's no light bulb,' the girl said feebly. Georgia had a feeling she was about to be sick.

'How far up is it?' she asked.

'The top,' the girl sighed.

Georgia dropped the bags on the floor, bent down and picked the girl up, hoisting her over her shoulder.

'Just hang on, I'll get you up there,' she said, feeling her way in the darkness.

Once past the bend of the stairs Georgia saw a glimmer of light ahead. The acrid smell indicated a bathroom. She slid her hand round the door and found a light switch.

It worked and gave Georgia enough light to continue up to the top.

The girl was so light it was like holding a small child, even through her thick coat Georgia could feel her bones.

There was only one door at the top. Still holding the girl Georgia unlocked the door and walked in with her.

One naked lightbulb lit up a pitiful attic room.

It was big with sloping ceilings that went from seven feet down to three on the window side. Untidy, a little dirty but the overall feeling was one of poverty.

Georgia put the girl in one of the two old armchairs, unsure whether she should go or stay. It was icy cold, yet when she glanced down at the girl she noticed beads of sweat on her forehead, mingling with the blood and the greeny tinge to her face was even more noticeable.

'You look sick,' she said, looking round frantically for something to give her. Under the sink in the corner was a plastic bucket. She picked it up and handed it to her.

The girl retched violently. Georgia averted her eyes, trying hard not to gag, and knelt down to light the gas fire.

Looking closer, the room was almost as comfortless as the one she'd seen earlier in the day. Two single old-fashioned beds, both with blankets just dumped on them like two heaps of rubbish. Armchairs with stuffing coming out of them, a table strewn with cups, plates and a sauce bottle. An old white sink was sandwiched in one corner with an ancient cooker, and a battered wardrobe with the door hanging open stood against the wall. Even the square of carpet was so old and dirty no real pattern was visible and the faded and peeling paper on the walls had patches of black mould.

Again and again the girl was sick. Georgia's empty stomach turned over as streams of vomit gushed into the bucket. She wanted to run out, away from the rancid smell, the miserable room and this odd, crippled girl.

Everything had happened so quickly, a turn of events so unexpected that for a moment she had forgotten her own predicament. But it could be an important turn, at least she might be able to have a cup of tea if she stayed.

'Let me bathe your forehead,' she said, going over to the sink and dampening a face flannel.

'I don't know how I would have managed without you.' The girl looked up at Georgia. 'You've been so kind.'

She had the biggest, greenest eyes Georgia had ever seen. As intense as traffic lights, fringed with red-brown lashes, her skin so white it was almost transparent.

'Are you feeling better now?' Georgia tried hard not to look at the brown mess in the bucket, still in the girl's hands. She bathed the wound gently, holding her breath so she wouldn't smell the vomit.

A flush of embarrassment spread across the girl's face.

'Yes,' she said weakly, trying to get up. 'But I need to empty this.'

'Let me,' Georgia said, 'I'll get the bags we left downstairs. Stay where you are.'

As Georgia made her way back down the stairs with the evil-smelling bucket, she wanted to run. There was food in the bags and probably money in the handbag. She didn't owe this girl anything, she didn't even know her name.

Nothing had prepared her for the bathroom. It was filthy. The bath was ingrained with dirt, even a spider had climbed in and died. The walls above grubby white tiles were flaking and festering with mould. The toilet was corroded with limescale, the smell catching her in the back of her throat. Cracked lino, encrusted with dirt. Even the ancient geyser hanging over the bath was daubed with more filth.

She gagged as she tipped the bucket into the toilet. Holding it at arm's length she filled it with water and swilled it round. How could anyone live in such a place? It made her think of slums her mother spoke of over in Hackney.

Leaving the bucket by the bathroom door, she went on downstairs, feeling her way in the darkness.

Her coat was still on, her belongings down here, she could be far away by the time the girl upstairs had the energy to come and look.

Looking over her shoulder back up the stairs, she rifled quickly through the girl's shopping, smelling rather than seeing. A loaf, some corned beef in grease-proof paper, eggs, cheese and bananas. She was so hungry it was all she could do not to rip the bread apart now and wolf it down.

The other bag contained some tins, potatoes and other vegetables along with the knitting.

Then there was the handbag.

It was just a cheap plastic one, with a handle so worn it could break any minute, so different from the good leather one she'd lost in the dustcart.

'Have you found the bathroom?' The girl's voice wafted down the stairs.

Georgia hesitated, her fingers on the bag clasp.

'Yes. I'm just coming,' she called back up through the darkness.

She couldn't do it. Not to a crippled girl. There had to be another way.

'It's awful down there isn't it?' The girl looked up as Georgia came in with the shopping bags and her own holdall. 'Whatever must you think?'

'In my position I can't think anything,' Georgia managed a weak smile. 'Let me make you some tea?'

'I'm Helen,' the girl turned in her chair and smiled. The greeny tinge had gone, her pixie-like face arrest-

110

ingly white against the vivid red hair, yet a faint pink tinge had come back into her cheeks. 'What's yours?'

'Georgia.' She moved over to the sink and filled the kettle, speaking over her shoulder. The sink was full of unwashed crockery and saucepans. 'Is it all right if I wash these things up?'

'What did you mean, "You couldn't afford to feel anything?"' Helen's voice had a note of anxiety. Georgia turned on the hot tap wondering how she could explain.

'Blow the geyser!' the girl said sharply. 'It'll light up then.'

Georgia blew and a sheet of flame leapt up, the water turned warm under her fingers, the first time she had been able to feel them all day.

'Come on, what did you mean?'

Georgia gulped.

'I haven't any money. I was just waiting for the club over the road to open when I saw you. I was going to ask for a job as a dancer.'

The girl got up, Georgia saw she was still shaking.

'Stay where you are.' She pushed her back into the chair. 'Have some tea before anything else.'

'But it's a strip club,' Helen said faintly. 'Are you serious?'

'Don't I look like a stripper?' Georgia tried to laugh, but she was blushing. She pulled off her woolly hat and shook her hair free.

'No you don't,' Helen retorted. 'You look about fifteen, cold and hungry. Have you run away?'

'Sort of.' She avoided further questions by noisily washing the dishes. All she could think of was drinking hot, sweet tea, maybe a slice of that bread in the bag.

Even the room didn't look so bad now. It was getting warmer, it was even growing cosy. Should she tell the girl everything? What if she turned her over to the police?

'Tell me.' Helen's voice sounded sweet and warm as she handed her a mug of tea. 'I know you don't belong around here.'

As the warm sweet liquid went down, and the heat from the fire thawed out her icy toes so she felt able to tell a version of the truth.

'I had a row with my foster father,' she said. 'I can't go back. But I lost all my money today and I don't know what to do.'

Helen reached out and touched Georgia's knee. 'Stay and have some tea with me for now. But don't go to that club, Georgia. That's a last resort.'

She got up to remove her coat and held out a hand for Georgia's too.

Helen prepared a meal then. Fried potatoes, corned beef and egg. She didn't pry further, merely chatted about general things, the market, her landlord who owned the café on the corner and the two jobs she had.

'I work on a stall in the afternoons and Saturdays,' she said. 'Then four nights a week I'm a cloakroom attendant in a nightclub.'

They sat at the table close to the fire to eat. Georgia wolfed hers down, hardly tasting it, pouring cup after cup of tea from the big brown pot.

Only when they were finished and sitting back in the armchairs did Helen bring the subject back to Georgia.

'You haven't told me why you ran away,' her green eyes watchful, but sympathetic. 'Would you like to know about my first days in London.'

Helen was certainly the strangest person Georgia had ever met. She looked so frail, yet a bright vitality shone out of the big green eyes. She claimed to have no real friends but she was as easy and comfortable to be with as Christine had been. The untidy, grubby room didn't go with her neat but old-fashioned appearance. Even the fiery, shiny hair waving over her small shoulders seemed to belong to another century where ladies had alabaster skin and kept their limbs covered at all times. She sat like a prim governess, knees and feet closely together, back straight, her boots concealed under the long brown dress, the only decoration a skimpy, cream lace collar. No one would guess that just outside her window was London's red light district.

'Did you run away too?'

'Hobbled,' Helen half smiled. 'I was seventeen, in a home for handicapped kids down in Plymouth. I knew if I didn't get out under my own steam they'd find me something they considered suitable for a cripple.'

She used the word 'cripple' like Georgia used the word 'black', getting it in first as if to protect herself.

'What's the matter with your leg?' Georgia asked.

'An injury when I was little,' Helen said lightly. 'I'm going to have an operation soon to put it right.'

'Why London?' Georgia sensed the girl wasn't keen to talk about her leg, or her background.

'Same reason as you I expect. A place to disappear, start again. When you're a kid it seems the place where dreams come true.'

'But yours didn't?' Georgia glanced around her, noting how few possessions the girl had, a feeling that it was only intended as a temporary home, yet poverty had trapped her.

'Well my dreams were a bit far-fetched,' Helen laughed. 'I thought I'd meet a millionaire, he'd whisk me off to the Ritz, you know, all that silly stuff.'

'But you found a job and a home!'

'Yes,' Helen frowned. 'Eventually, and it's not much to brag about is it? But believe me I've seen worse, especially the first few nights.'

'I slept in a cardboard box last night,' Georgia sighed. 'I thought I'd die of cold.'

'I can imagine,' Helen smiled in sympathy. 'I spent mine in St James's Park. It was summer so it wasn't so cold but I was scared witless. I didn't have a clue about anything.'

'How did you get this place then?'

Helen shook her head, blushing a little.

'That came later,' she said uneasily, as if wondering whether she should divulge everything. She looked up at Georgia defiantly. 'I let a man take me in.'

Georgia was reminded of the man who approached her the night before.

'You mean?' she couldn't actually say it.

'Not for money,' Helen shot back. 'I just accepted a bed for the night. I suppose that amounts to the same thing, but then I was desperate.'

'Was it awful?' Georgia whispered.

'Yes,' Helen winced. 'He didn't hurt me or anything, but he was weird. He made me feel so dirty. After about three days I started to get frightened. I heard him talking about me to a friend on the telephone. I think he was intending to let this chap,' she broke off blushing. 'Well, you know!'

'So what did you do?'

'I nicked his money,' Helen giggled, blushing again. 'He left his wallet behind when he went out. By the time he got back I was gone.'

'That was brave.' Georgia leaned forward in her chair, liking Helen far more for revealing she didn't intend to become a victim. 'What then?'

'Bert in the café downstairs had an advert on his window for this room. I took it and I've been here ever since.'

Georgia stared into the fire.

Already the standards she'd been taught by Celia were eroding. All day she'd contemplated theft, she was even prepared to become a dancer in a strip show. Helen's story made her feel a little better about herself, at least she wasn't the only one to fall prey to temptation.

Helen got up again, hobbled across the floor and put the kettle on again.

'Are you going to tell me about yourself?' she said gently from the sink.

Being crippled had made Helen perceptive. At twenty-one she had spent most of her life sitting quietly at the side lines of life watching others. But Georgia baffled her. It was obvious the girl had come from a good home. Her clothes were expensive, she spoke well and had beautiful manners. Yet there was deep sadness in the girl's eyes. Something more than a rich kid looking for adventure. Runaways were ten a penny in Soho. They bleated out their misfortunes, lied and conned. Never before had she met one where she felt compelled to tell her own shameful story to try and get them to open up.

'I can't tell you everything,' Georgia said in a whisper, hanging her head. 'I want to, but I can't.'

Helen just stood there, the kettle in her hand. The kid was so young, she might be a liability. For all Helen knew the police might be searching for her right now; if she had any sense she'd make some excuse to go out. Fetch her landlord and let him make the decision.

'Stay here tonight,' Helen said softly. 'Maybe tomorrow you'll find it easier.'

'Are you sure?' Georgia's head spun round to look at Helen. She could feel tears pricking her eyes at the unexpected compassion.

'Quite sure.' Helen moved nearer, passing her hand lightly over Georgia's head in just the same motherly gesture Celia used. 'You didn't hesitate to help me.'

They had more tea and biscuits. Georgia told Helen about the way she lost her money and how she'd spent the day.

'Would it really be so bad to get a job as a dancer?' she said, yawning widely.

'It would in that club,' Helen smiled. 'But you're tired and I'm afraid I'll have to ask you to make up the bed. I'm sorry the sheets aren't clean. I was going to the laundrette tomorrow.'

Georgia leapt up, grabbing the blankets and smoothing out the sheets before Helen could change her mind.

'I hope you won't mind if I use the bucket in the night?' Helen said without a trace of embarrassment after she had made a last trip to the bathroom. 'I can't go clonking downstairs, waking everyone up.'

Georgia winced, as she was reminded she too would have to go down there.

'Doesn't anyone ever clean it?' she asked on her return.

'I used to try,' Helen pulled a wry face. 'But I've given up. I go down the public baths once a week, and the other tenants are hardly ever here. My landlord keeps saying he'll do something to it, but he never does.'

Georgia hurriedly slipped out of her clothes and into her pyjamas. The bed felt damp and it was lumpy, the sheets and blankets smelled, but she was too tired to care. She put her arm under her head, nose buried in her pyjamas with the faint whiff of home and waited for Helen to put out the light.

Helen wore thick stockings under her long skirt. As she peeled them off, sitting on the side of the bed, Georgia could see how wasted her leg was. She could have put her thumb and forefinger round the ankle, the calf only slightly bigger.

Her other leg was normal, the muscles made bigger by taking the strain from the bad leg.

Earlier, out in the street Helen had reminded her of a squirrel, later that image had changed to one of a prim governess, but now as she undressed so the image changed again.

She wore a white cotton petticoat, her gleaming hair

cascading down her back, like a lady from a Pre-Raphaelite painting. Although she was too thin and her skin so pale, she was lovely in a mystical way. Her features were all small and childlike. Perfect bowed lips, green eyes sparkling under reddish-gold eyebrows and lashes. Not even a freckle as she would have expected with red hair, just pure white skin like a baby.

Georgia woke with a start, for a moment wondering where she was. It was still dark, but every now and then bright flashes of light splashed on to the walls accompanied by rumbling, banging and shouting from outside in the street.

Pulling a blanket round her, Georgia went over to the window and peered out through the dirty glass, rubbing a patch with her blanket to see better.

The stallholders were setting up. Skeleton-like stalls being hastily assembled by men in donkey jackets and woolly hats, brandishing mallets. The sound of tarpaulins being shaken, the trundle of trolley wheels and the slap of cardboard boxes hurled from vans.

Yesterday this same scene had seemed violent and brutal. The coarse jokes, the swearing and the raucous laughter had seemed like a glimpse into a madhouse as she shivered on the corner. Now it seemed jolly, almost a street party. An Indian in a red turban wheeled a rail of dresses. A woman, mummified with a scarf wound round her head and neck arranged flowers in pots. A tall thin man dancing on the spot to keep warm. Teasing banter as they pushed and shoved through the disorder, the cold air making each one of them move faster. Gleaming apples, oranges, tomatoes and bananas lay in boxes, like a feast about to be prepared.

Georgia looked at the clock. It was only seven. Although she wanted to get up she didn't think she should disturb Helen just yet. She climbed back into bed, buried her head in the pillow and went back to sleep.

She awoke again to the sound of splashing water. Helen stood at the sink, naked, washing herself as if she were alone. Sideways on she had the figure of a small boy, flat-chested, with a tiny, bony bottom and concave stomach, her thighs so slender it was a miracle she could walk at all.

Georgia closed her eyes again, afraid she might embarrass Helen, and waited for her to dress.

'Cup of tea?' Helen was now wearing an old faded dressing-gown the colour of mushy peas.

Georgia sat up and looked at the clock.

It was only eight.

'I always go out early,' Helen smiled. 'I go down to the library as soon as they open and read the papers.'

'What for?'

'To find out what's going on in the world. Besides it's warm in there, saves on heating. But I suggest you don't go far today as they may be looking for you.'

Georgia looked sharply at Helen. Could she be intending to go to the police to turn her in? Or did she mean she could stay?

Helen frowned as though she had something on her mind.

'I can't promise anything,' she said. 'Last night I wanted to invite you to stay permanently. But I'm not sure now. You're so young. We'd have to find you a job. I need time to think it over. I don't even know if I could live with another girl. But stay till tomorrow. By then we should both know if it's going to work.'

Helen's honesty touched Georgia deeply, it lit up the drab, cold room and she felt ashamed that she had doubted her intentions.

'But I've got no money,' Georgia reminded her. 'I can't help out until I get some.'

'Another day won't break the bank.' Helen limped

over and sat on the bed. 'Take the washing over to the laundrette across the street for me and tidy up. That's enough help for one day.'

She passed over a mug of tea, put some coins on the table, then under her dressing-gown she started to dress.

Her knickers looked ancient, the petticoat was worn and thin. She sat down on the bed pulling on thick brown stockings held up with a garter of thick elastic. Next a thin sweater full of holes. The brown dress she'd been wearing the day before, and over the top a thick, gold-coloured cardigan which looked hand knitted.

Georgia gulped. She thought of her drawers full of clothes back in Blackheath, dainty underwear, soft sweaters, dresses hanging on padded, scented hangers.

'You have to wrap up warm.' Helen seemed to sense Georgia's shock, turning to grin at her. 'This place is like a morgue and it's even worse on the stall.'

Pulling on her coat and a woolly hat over her ears, she left, shutting the door behind her.

Georgia sat for a moment, listening to the painful sound of the built-up boot clonking down the stairs.

Celia came sharply into focus. She could almost smell bacon frying, hear the news on the radio. Celia would be sitting at the kitchen table, drinking tea from a bone china cup as she scanned through the post.

'She'll be crying,' Georgia murmured, suddenly aware that until this moment she hadn't really considered how her mother would be feeling. 'She'll be frightened for me.'

An acute pain made her curl up into a ball. She didn't want to stay here in this dark, cold room. She wanted to be back home with Celia, fifteen was too young to be trying to fend for herself, how could she find a job alone? How was she going to manage?

But as she dug deeper into the bed, Brian's face came

back to her. She could feel his breath on her face as he lunged at her in the playroom.

'You're not my daughter.' Those were his words. Everything she remembered and loved belonged to him. The house, her clothes, the piano, even Celia belonged to him. She couldn't go back, not ever. It was over.

Slowly she lifted her head from the covers. This room wasn't hers either, for now she was dependent on a crippled girl who'd been big-hearted enough to share what little she had.

'You've got to make it work for you,' she whispered. 'Stop feeling sorry for yourself, the worst is over. Get up and get moving.'

The room was icy, but she must save the money in the gas meter. Jumping out of bed she moved the table to one side, taking the back of one of the upright chairs.

Dance exercises were the answer. She must get the blood flowing again, stretch those lazy muscles, warm herself up.

In the playroom in Blackheath, she had the record player to help her concentrate. Her own barre Brian had put up for her. She would watch each movement in the big mirror to see it was right. Back straight, eyes ahead, moving in time to the music.

She had to pretend the chair was a barre, imagine the music, forget she was wearing pyjamas and her feet were bare. Maybe she had no dancing teacher or parents now, but no one was going to stop her getting on the stage. All it took was willpower.

First one leg, up, down, up, down, repeating it till she hurt. Then the other. Knee bends, high kicks, and toe touching until she was hot with exertion.

Visions of dancing class came to her. Sixteen girls, each identical in black tights and leotards, pink ballet shoes. Hair scraped back into a tight bun, Miss Askell pounding the piano as they plié-d and jeté-d at her instruction.

Today Celia wasn't going to come for her, no flask of hot coffee while she got dressed, no hour of shopping before driving her over to her singing lesson in Greenwich. But Celia had believed in her talent enough to sacrifice each Saturday willingly. She must keep it up for Celia now.

She washed herself later in the sink, trying hard not to dwell on the sparkling bathroom she'd never see again. Then before she could get cold, she jumped into jeans and a sweater.

She filled a pillowcase with all the dirty clothes and bed linen, then made her way down the stairs, across the street.

The laundrette hadn't been open long. A woman in a blue overall was mopping the floor, she turned to look at Georgia.

'Service wash, love?' she shouted above the noise of a radio.

Georgia stared blankly at the row of machines, round glass doors standing open.

'I, I,' she stammered, blushing with embarrassment. 'What do I have to do?'

'Well are you going to work, or have you got time to watch it yourself?' the woman asked, stepping nearer.

'It's Helen's stuff,' Georgia said weakly. 'Do you know her?'

The woman's face broke into a smile, showing more gaps than teeth.

'Oh, she gets special treatment.' She reached out and took the bag from Georgia. 'I see's to it for 'er. She comes back later. She ain't ill is she?'

'No, she's fine. I'm just staying with her for a day or two,' Georgia reassured her. Already the woman had the pillowcase open, tossing the washing into two separate machines, whites in one, coloureds in another.

'That's all right then,' the woman nodded at Georgia. 'Come back around twelve, it'll be ready then.'

Back upstairs Georgia stared around her, wondering where to start.

Last night the room had looked squalid, but by day it looked far worse. The small, dirty window cut a shaft of light through the middle, but under the eaves it was still in shadow. Yet looking objectively at the room, part of the reason it looked so wretched was the way the furniture was arranged. The wardrobe so close to the window blocked the light. The beds sticking out from the wall made it seem like a dormitory. So the wallpaper was stained, and the carpet would never curl comfortingly round anyone's feet, but there was room for improvement.

Starting by the fireplace she cleared the furniture to the other side of the room by the sink. Then taking a small stiff brush she began to sweep the carpet on all fours. Again and again she went over it, until at last no more dust flew into the pan. Filling the bucket with hot soapy water she washed down the fire surround, the mantelpiece, the skirting boards and the floorboards around the carpet. Then changing the water again, she went over the surface of the carpet, being careful not to make it too wet.

By the time she had finished the whole room it was twelve. The furniture stacked by the fire, ready to rearrange. She couldn't count the number of buckets of black water that went down the drain. Her hair felt full of dust, she had tidemarks up to her elbows, but it was so satisfying.

The carpet was a red-brown. She could even see a swirly pattern now. The windows gleamed, letting in twice as much light, but most of all it smelled clean.

*

'Been up a chimney?' The woman in the laundrette grinned at her as she handed her the warm bag of washing.

'Doing a bit of spring cleaning,' Georgia said shyly. She could feel the dirt on her face and her hands were bright red from all the cleaning fluid. 'How much do I owe you?'

'Call it five bob,' the woman said. 'I dried everything real well and folded it. It's good 'Elen's got a bit of company, spends too much time on 'er own does that one.'

The market was packed with shoppers. Women from offices buying vegetables, young girls looking at clothes. Georgia kept her eyes down as she scuttled back across the street, aware of a policeman standing by the door of the café.

Was he looking for her, or merely taking a break in his beat? Her heart thumped with anxiety as she slipped in the front door. What if he asked the lady in the laundrette about her?

Upstairs again she felt safer and she had a great deal more to do before Helen got back.

Helen smelled bleach and disinfectant as she stepped into the dark hallway. Instinctively her hand went out to the light switch and to her surprise a light on the stairs came on.

She blinked. Not a sweet wrapper or bus ticket in sight. Balls of fluff and a coating of grey grit on each stair had gone. The carpet was so worn in places she could see the stair treads showing through, but it was clean!

Slowly she hauled herself up by the bannister. She was so cold she couldn't feel her toes, but for the first time ever she felt a rush of pleasure to be going home.

The open door to the bathroom beckoned her. She

paused, leaning heavily against the wall, staring in amazement.

The smell of bleach was so strong it almost choked her, but in front of her was a clean bath, basin and toilet.

Granted there was still a stain of limescale where the cold tap dripped in the bath, and nothing could be done about the chips and scratches, but the tiles were white! The window-sill was shiny, even the cracked lino was clean. The smell of stale urine was gone. They could even use the bath if they wanted to!

But there was another smell too as she went on up the stairs in a daze. An aroma of meat pie. Was she dreaming all this, or was it merely a faint memory of something from years ago?

The door opened as she turned on to the last flight of stairs. Georgia stood there, a smile of welcome on her face.

'I thought you'd never come home,' she said, taking Helen's basket from her arm. 'I've got the tea ready.'

As Helen limped into the room she stopped suddenly.

The fire was lit. Curtains drawn. The table was now under the window laid for two, saucepans and kettle rattling on the cooker.

Georgia had moved everything and it looked almost like a real home. The beds flanked the walls either side of the fire place, made up properly, each covered with the bedspreads she had never bothered to get out of the wardrobe.

'What have you done?' Helen asked, tears for no apparent reason pricking her eyelids.

She couldn't hold back the tears, she groped for the armchair and sat down heavily.

'I'm sorry,' Georgia said, as if from a long way off. 'I didn't mean to be bossy. I'll put it all back how it was tomorrow.'

'It's,' Helen couldn't speak for a moment. 'It's just such a shock.'

Only then did she really see Georgia. She wore a red sweater and jeans, kneeling down in front of her, her heart-shaped face a picture of concern, her eyes bewildered and afraid.

'I didn't mean to upset you. Please don't cry.'

Helen's mouth shook, laughter bubbling up inside her. Georgia's face was so lovely, she hadn't fully taken it in the night before.

The big, dark doleful eyes, the sooty lashes, the curly hair tied up in a pom-pom on top of her small, beautifully-shaped head. The grace in her movements, the slender hands and the soft voice. Who would have thought a girl who looked like that could be capable of cleaning a stinking toilet?

'I'm not cross,' she said weakly. 'I just didn't expect it.'

'Why are you crying then?' Georgia's voice was tentative, like a child who isn't convinced she'd really won approval.

'I've lived here for nearly four years,' Helen sniffed. 'In all that time no one has ever been up here except me. I can't remember the last time someone had a meal ready for me, or cared enough to tidy up for me. You don't know how good it feels.'

Georgia's eyes seemed to grow bigger, her wide, curvy mouth quivering.

'I wanted to show you how much I appreciated your kindness,' she said softly, reaching out and touching Helen's cheek. 'If you'll let me stay and help me find a job I'll cook and clean for you every day.'

'I thought you were such a child this morning.' Helen found herself crying again, remembering all the second thoughts she'd had during the day. 'I panicked because I thought you would want me to look after you. That's why I went out early. I even thought of going to the police and telling them you were here.'

'Why didn't you?'

'It seemed cowardly,' Helen sniffed. 'Besides, I half expected you to take the money and go. I couldn't see you wanting to stay with a cripple in a slum.'

'That isn't how I see you,' Georgia looked shocked. 'Maybe I did at first, but then you became just another girl with a bad leg, someone all alone like me with nothing but bad memories behind her. But who knows? Maybe we can have a future together.'

'Oh, Georgia,' Helen reached out for the younger girl, drawing her to her breast, an instinctive action she had never done to anyone before. 'I've got a feeling this was meant to be.'

Helen felt Georgia's tears even through her coat and in that moment she knew something shocking had happened to her, something far worse than a family row.

'What's the smell?' she said, lifting Georgia's chin up.

'Meat pies from the market.' Georgia wiped her eyes with the back of her hand. 'I bought them with the change from the laundrette. I hope that was all right?'

'I love meat pies,' Helen smiled. 'Especially when I've got company to eat them.'

Chapter 5

'Sometimes I wonder if I'll ever be warm again.' Georgia held her toes up to the fire and massaged them with her fingers.

'It's March next week, spring's nearly here,' Helen sighed in sympathy. She was stirring a pan of soup over the cooker, still wearing her coat. 'Why don't you do some exercises if it's that bad?'

'I ache too much,' Georgia growled at Helen. 'Besides you always laugh at me.'

'Sounds like a feeble excuse. What happened to your fighting spirit?'

'Died of cold.' Georgia looked round at her friend and tried to smile. She didn't want to admit she'd been sick again that morning, or about her fears.

'Did Janet get her letter from the sailor?' Helen plonked half a loaf down on the table and turned to get the teapot.

Georgia stood up, pushing her feet back into her slippers and went over to the cooker, peering into the pan.

'No, I think she's given up on him now. She made some joke about how she could always pull men, but she hadn't figured out how to keep them yet.'

Georgia prodded the soup. Her insides were bashing together with hunger, yet just the thought of vegetable soup again made her feel queasy.

127

'It's ready, pour it out will you?' Helen didn't notice Georgia's grimace as she got cups out of the cupboard.

'I can't eat this,' Georgia dropped her spoon with a clatter after a few tentative mouthfuls. She picked up a hunk of dry bread and wolfed it down.

Helen said nothing, just a slight raise of one gold eyebrow as she lifted the spoon to her lips.

'Go on, say it,' Georgia challenged, her mouth full of bread. 'I'm a spoiled brat and it's my fault there's no money left this week.'

'Did I say a word?' Helen retorted.

'You don't have to,' Georgia sniffed. She picked up her spoon and tried again.

Helen had asked her to buy belly of pork at the weekend, but she'd seen a piece of beef in the butcher's shop and bought that instead. Now she was discovering what a tight budget really meant.

'It's a good job we can get vegetables for nothing,' Helen grinned. 'I bet you won't be so daft again.'

'It's all right for you. You get a meal at the club later,' Georgia said. She had had to buy that beef, her stomach was screaming out for the sort of food Celia cooked. How was she to know how much beef cost? 'I bet you've been eating fruit all day too!'

'What is it Georgia?' Helen put down her spoon and reached across the table to touch her hand. 'There's something wrong isn't there, something more than being hungry and cold. Do you want to go home?'

'This is my home,' Georgia shovelled the soup in her mouth, barely tasting it.

Of course she wanted to go home! Day after day she dreamed of Celia's hot meals waiting for her, the clean sweet-smelling house, her warm bedroom and all the other things that home meant. But there was no way back now, this room, her job as a machinist and Helen was all she had now.

'Is it something at work then?' Helen could be so persistent. 'Is it too much for you?'

'I'm just tired and cold,' Georgia tried to smile, even though she felt a lump coming up in her throat. 'I'll go to bed early tonight.'

Helen said nothing more, just watched anxiously as Georgia finished her soup.

She hadn't believed Georgia would last a week in Soho, let alone seven. When she sent her up to Pop's workrooms to ask for a job, she hadn't expected her to even go in, let alone get the job and stick at it.

'Pop' as everyone called him in the market was a fiery Greek, his sweatshop a place you had to be desperate to work in. Four tiny rooms over his material shop, stinking of paraffin, engine oil and damp cloth. Five industrial machines and a huge steam press assaulted the ears and if you were capable of dealing with that, there was still his other employees to cope with.

Janet and Sally, two vicious-tongued women, ruled the roost, with Irene, Iris and Myrtle as their dim-witted sycophants.

Helen had spent a week in the workshop herself, before moving on to what she considered a far easier life in the market, but somehow Georgia had not only managed to master the sewing machine, but she'd also made friends with the other women.

Helen pulled two oranges out of her bag and tossed one to Georgia.

'You see I didn't stuff myself with fruit all day,' she chuckled. 'Now, in return I want all the gossip.'

Georgia was such a child. Helen saw the way her big eyes lit up with glee, grubby fingernails digging into the thick peel, tearing it off and biting into the juicy flesh like a savage.

'Iris isn't Pop's mistress,' Georgia said slurping at the fruit, juice running down her chin. 'She just kind of hints he's in love with her. I reckon she's got delusions of grandeur. She told me her boyfriend is a count!'

Iris, the cutter, was in her forties, still attractive in an overblown rose style. Flame-red hair copied slavishly from Ava Gardner, given to fox furs and the kind of glamour that related more to the war years than now.

'What did Janet have to say about that?' Helen giggled.

Georgia wiped her mouth on her sleeve, she got up quickly and turned her back on Helen, returning moments later with two pairs of socks shoved up under her jumper in a parody of the busty Janet.

'The Count of Monte Cristo?' she put her hands on her hips, imitating the tarty stance, wiggling across the room. 'Famous for his disappearing acts!'

Helen's laughter pealed round the shabby, cold room. Georgia with her slim hips in tight jeans couldn't possibly look like the woman with her blonde bird's nest hair, tight low-cut dresses and ample curves, but she'd got the essence of her as she always did with people she imitated.

'I suppose Iris went into one of her sulks?'

'Not half,' Georgia reported gleefully. 'She cut out the dresses so fast we couldn't keep up. She kept banging the shears down on the cutting table so often I thought she might stab Janet.'

'Are you keeping up with the others?' Helen fished, still convinced Georgia was hiding something. 'It must be hard when you aren't experienced like them.'

'I'm not doing too bad,' Georgia stacked up the plates and took them over to the sink. 'Pop makes allowances for me, besides Myrtle always unpicks the bits I've done wrong. You know what she's like.'

Myrtle was the sweet, uncomplaining one in the workroom. She perched in front of her machine all day like a drab little sparrow, offering very little in way of conversation. Her clothes were carefully pressed and mended but old and shabby. She rarely volunteered any information about herself, preferring to sit on the outskirts, looking in.

'Is she still with that man?'

'She must be,' Georgia looked round from the sink. 'She's got a huge bruise on her arm. I saw it when she took off her cardigan to wash before going home. I wonder why she doesn't leave him?'

'Two kids and a council flat in Hackney, that's why,' Helen said, slowly nibbling the last segment of her orange. 'I don't suppose she thinks life has anything else to offer.'

'But Janet and Sally left their husbands,' Georgia frowned. 'I can't see why anyone would stay with a man who beats you.'

'That's easy for you to say,' Helen smiled. 'You are young and pretty. What chance has Myrtle got of finding a new man?'

'I don't see why women need men. As far as I can see, they are nothing but trouble.'

Helen picked up her knitting. She had noticed how often Georgia made disparaging remarks about men. Was it the influence of Sally and Janet? Or was it part of the chain of events which led Georgia to Soho? She still wouldn't open up fully, in seven weeks all she had was a sketchy vision of a comfortable middle-class home, dancing and singing lessons, then an unexplained row which led to her leaving it. Yet she had asked Helen to get someone to post a letter in Manchester to her foster mother. Why would she even bother if she didn't care, and why did she cry out in the night so often?

'You're getting to be a right little cynic!' Helen said gently. 'To think I was hoping you'd introduce me to Mr Right!'

Helen dreamed of men constantly. At night in her cloakroom job at 'Squires' she would smile at the smart men who came in, hoping against hope one day someone would overlook her limp. Only the thought that the operation she was waiting for would be successful kept her going. It was all very well to be liked for yourself, but she wanted romance and love, a husband and children. To dance in a man's arms, to walk without a limp down the aisle, to be desired.

Georgia knew Helen guessed there was more to her than she had revealed. She yearned to open up but she was afraid. It would be like opening a door, forcing herself to look at everything all over again. It was almost over now. She no longer jumped and ran when she saw a policeman, she had even adjusted to living in this place without television, music, or dancing and singing lessons. Maybe in time she could forget Peter, stop wanting his kisses. But if she told Helen now because of her fears it would all come back, and if her period was just late, she would have burdened Helen with it all for nothing.

'We'll go out dancing when you've had the op,' Georgia smiled as if there was nothing on her mind. 'We'll make ourselves beautiful dresses and take London by storm.'

'You've got to teach me to dance first,' Helen laughed. 'Anyway, I'd better get ready to go to work. Will you do my hair for me?'

Helen couldn't imagine life now without Georgia. She filled the lonely hours before her night-time job with chatter and laughter. Sharing meals, shopping and cleaning the room was a pleasure where once there had only been a lonely void. When she came home tired from the club it felt secure to see her friend tucked up in bed and Sundays flew by with her company.

But Helen was a realist if nothing else, maybe Georgia was content to stay in now, but what would happen if she made new friends? Had it already happened? Was Georgia's troubled look because she was tired of living with a cripple who worked so many hours?

Yet if Georgia was growing weary of this place and her, it didn't show in the way she did her hair. Brushing it till it shone, coaxing curls round her fingers with an almost loving touch.

Georgia got up slowly the next morning, waiting for the expected feeling of nausea. Helen had gone out early as she did every morning, regardless of how cold it was, or how late she finished work. The gas meter had run out last night, she couldn't put the fire on, have a cup of tea or even wash in hot water. But she didn't feel sick and it was payday.

The window was frosted over on the inside. She scraped a small hole and peered out. Fridays were good. At lunchtime she could go into Sid's and have steak and kidney pie and tonight she could turn the gas fire on full and bask in front of it with a library book, knowing she could lie in tomorrow. Janet had promised to take her to a jumble sale up in Primrose Hill in the afternoon, she might find some dresses they could alter on Sunday, or if it was nice they could go for a walk in St James's Park.

She was still feeling cheerful when she arrived at work, bouncing up the stairs the way she did when she first started there.

'Well that's a good start to the day,' Pop turned round from dumping some bales of cheap tweed on the floor. 'Let's hope the good mood lasts beyond tea-break!'

Georgia grinned impudently at him, a manner she'd learned from Janet and Sally. She'd been so frightened of him, and his machines on her first day that she almost wet herself, but now she knew his gruff manner hid a kind heart she often took advantage.

Pop still had a strong Greek accent despite living in England since he was eighteen. Portly, with thinning heavily-oiled hair it was hard to see him as the slim, handsome youth he was rumoured to have been. His dark eyes had faded a little, a melancholy olive face, thick fleshy lips and a large rubbery nose made Georgia think of an old clown. Yet perhaps it was true he'd been a hit with the ladies in his prime. He did have a comfortable, easy manner with women.

'Can I make some tea now?' she fluttered her eyelashes at him. 'Our meter had run out so I couldn't have one at home.'

'You girls!' Pop shrugged his shoulders. 'One of these days I'm going to make you work like they do down at Switalski's. On to that seat at half eight, standing over you till one. Maybe then I'd be able to get myself a decent car.'

Georgia took that as agreement, sliding into the staffroom before he changed his mind.

The staffroom was a joke. It was no bigger than a cupboard, the toilet adjoining it. A shelf for the kettle, three rickety chairs and the cracked window stuffed up with old rags.

From behind her in the main workroom she could hear Pop and Iris discussing the cloth and which patterns should be used. She had been excited when she first came here, imagining she would make good clothes, but instead to her disappointment Pop specialised in making frumpy, cheap things for old ladies. Sometimes Janet and Sally would dress up in them during the lunch hour. Drab, shapeless dresses with white collars and cuffs, always in browns, dark blues and greens. Then the pair of them would do a striptease, peeling them off, more like pantomime dames than the show girls they pretended to be.

While the kettle boiled Georgia watched through the open door. Janet was threading her machine, a cigarette hanging out the corner of her mouth, her blonde hair still in curlers with a shocking-pink chiffon scarf tied round them. Next to her was Sally her close friend, leaning forward whispering something.

They were both thirty, without husbands, and three children each. They even lived in the same block of tenement flats down near Charing Cross Road. Noisy, vulgar and aggressive, the pair had seemed like dragons on Georgia's first day, yet now she viewed them almost with admiration.

Sally's raven black 'beehive' stood up an alarming six inches from her head, a slick of greasy black fringe across her forehead, with lacquered kiss-curls fixed like cement on her ruddy cheeks. Her make-up was as startling as her hair. Heavy eyeliner and several coatings of thick mascara. Lips dark red and lustrous, a beauty spot painted on her cheek. Voluptuous and wanton, she scrutinised every man who had the misfortune to come into the workshop, dark, lust-filled eyes sparkling at their embarrassment.

Sally might be the one with the startling appearance, but it was Janet who had the real character and personality. By night she worked as a stripper, something she made no secret of. She could turn the most mundane of stories into comedy, and her observations about other people were bitingly astute.

Her daytime appearance, the headscarf, shapeless sweater, crumpled skirt and no make-up, was at odds with the glamour snaps they'd all seen of her. Once the curlers were out, the warpaint and false eyelashes on, the metamorphosis from plain Janet Willoughby to exotic dancer Nicole was complete. If Pop and Sally were to be believed she bore more than a glancing likeness to Marilyn Monroe when she wiggled seductively onto the stage.

If it wasn't for the humour of these two women, Georgia might never have made it through her first week. They teased her, shouted, even swore at her, but an underlying sense of fairplay made them help and encourage her too, and when she was close to tears they had a knack of turning it to laughter.

'You dun'alf talk posh!' Janet had remarked on her first tea-break. 'Why don'cha learn us to speak proper and I'll show you how to strip?'

Georgia blushed scarlet, twisting her hands in her lap as minutes later Janet came out of the toilet wearing only a length of fabric and proceeded to do a peek-a-boo dance routine with it. She was convinced Janet was naked under the material, as first one shoulder was bared, then the other. The other women sang for her, clapping their hands and stamping their feet and as Janet dropped the fabric as a climax, Georgia covered her face with her hands.

Sally grabbed her hands away, and to Georgia's astonishment Janet was standing there wearing a pair of pink, old ladies' bloomers and two paper roses pinned to a large brassière. The sight was so unexpected and hilarious Georgia almost fell off the seat with laughter, and she'd known then she could stand working at Pop's.

'Isn't that kettle boiling yet?' Pop glanced up from the cutting table at her. Iris at his side sniffed loudly in disapproval. She was supposed to be the forewoman, but her instructions were never carried out by anyone other than Myrtle. Iris was wearing a flame-red two-piece which clashed with her red hair, a silk rose was pinned to her lapel as if she were going to a wedding.

'That's not how it was done in my day,' was her favourite whine, covering everything from Georgia making tea so early in the morning, to the way Irene swept the floor.

'When was that? Domesday?' Janet always retorted, sending Iris's heavily pan-sticked face into a vivid flush of frustration. She spoke vaguely about having a man 'in high places', alluded mysteriously to 'cocktails' after work and sometimes to 'our nest' in Brighton.

Georgia still had no clear picture about where the woman really came from. It was all snippets with no substance, even her carefully cultivated accent was a fake, as sometimes in anger she dropped it, and sounded more of a cockney than Janet or Sally.

The kettle boiled behind her and Georgia turned to make a big pot for everyone. She heard Myrtle turn on the steam press and at the same moment Irene came through the door late.

'Do you know what the time is?' Iris's high voice rose above a belch of steam. 'This isn't how it was done in my day. We thought ourselves lucky to have a job, you could be dismissed at a moment's notice for unpunctuality.'

Irene didn't answer, but by her shuffling gait coming into the staffroom to hang up her coat, Georgia knew it was one of her bad days.

Irene was not quite right in the head, as Janet put it, 'A penny short of a full quid.' No one seemed to know what exactly was wrong. She could turn up on time for a week at a stretch, neatly dressed, and chat about her elderly mother in the Oval, books she'd read, and television programmes, as normal as everyone else. But then suddenly she'd change for a few days, like today, coming in late wearing men's trousers with a huge shapeless sweater thrown over the top, her dark hair all tousled as if she hadn't brushed it, top teeth missing, lipstick up to her ears, her eyes blank. She would say the oddest things at these times, about men who followed her. Strange spirits in her house, and odder still she would profess to live in Kensington with a man called James.

But whatever she was like, she worked harder than anyone, sweeping up, pressing, sewing on buttons at twice the speed of everyone else. Sally said she was over forty, but to Georgia, the smooth, unlined face was that of a girl, only the missing teeth suggested Sally was right.

Georgia gave everyone a cup of tea and sat down at

her machine with her own. In front of her was a pile of grey wool skirts, her job was to do merely the seams, then pass them over for pressing. Later Sally would do the waistbands and zips.

'You coming to the jumble tomorrow?' Janet shouted at her over the noise of her machine. 'Our Lyndsey's gonna take the other kids to the park for a bit so we can have some peace.'

'Peace at a jumble?' Sally roared back. 'Have you warned her about the scraps you get into?'

Georgia felt suddenly dizzy as the hot tea went down in one long gulp. She sat back in her chair, wiping her brow with one hand. The paraffin stove seemed to smell much worse than usual and the hiss of the press sounded as if it was right in her ears.

The workroom was spinning. One moment Pop was standing on her right, the next on her left and the sickly smell of Iris's perfume caught her in the throat.

Weakly she got up, groping almost blindly across the room, and as her stomach churned she put her hand over her mouth and ran the rest of the way to the toilet.

'What's up with 'er?' she heard Sally shout, but her head was over the pan, vomiting as if her entire insides were coming up.

On and on it went until there was nothing left but green bile. She stood up and leaned against the toilet wall, so weak she felt she could slide to the floor.

'Ow long's this bin goin' on?' Janet's voice behind her startled Georgia.

For a moment Georgia just stared at the older woman. There was no laughter now in those dark almond eyes, no hint of malice or sneering. Just sympathy and understanding.

'About a week.'

'Does 'Elen know?'

Georgia shook her head.

'When did you last get the curse?'

138

'Just before Christmas.'

'When did you go with 'im?'

Tears came then. The sickness was going now but Janet had voiced her own fears and made it reality.

'It was my birthday, January sixth.'

'Is that why you left 'ome? Did yer ma find out?'

One moment Georgia was just hanging her head in shame, the next she was caught in Janet's soft arms. Her head on her shoulder, crying out all the fear and pain.

'It's all right little 'un,' Janet whispered, kissing her hair and stroking her back. 'We can't talk now, but I'll 'elp you, don't you fret. At lunchtime I'll come back to your place and you can tell me about it. Now dry your eyes and try to smile. We don't want that nosy Iris getting wind of it, do we?'

'Do you feel better now you've told me?' Janet said softly, as she came back into the attic room carrying two bags of fish and chips from the shop across the street.

'Sort of,' Georgia whispered.

All morning she had thought of lies to tell. She even wanted to deny she could be pregnant, but once Janet sat down beside her in the other armchair, she seemed to know the right buttons to press to make her tell the truth.

Until now, Georgia had thought it was only women like her mother who could be relied on to be this sensitive. Janet with her curlers, plucked eyebrows and hourglass figure and bawdy jokes belonged to another world, yet she'd listened carefully, then went out to buy food.

'I can take you to a doctor I know tomorrow.' Janet handed her a newspaper wrapped parcel. 'We 'ave to get it confirmed before we do anything else. He's a proper doctor, but 'e's bin struck off. If you go to an ordinary one he might just split on you. We'll make out you're sixteen anyway.'

'But,'

'I know, I know. You wants me to tell you we can wave a magic wand and make it right. I can't do that love. Let's just wait until we know for certain. It might just be the upset that's stopped your period.'

Pop sent Georgia out on an errand later in the afternoon and used the opportunity to call Janet into his office.

'What's the matter with Georgia?' he asked bluntly. 'She's been looking pasty for days. Is the job too much for her?'

He knew Janet was capable of covering up for another girl she liked, but he wasn't in the charity business.

'Just a tummy upset,' Janet distracted him with one of her sultry looks. 'She'll be fine in a day or two.'

'Is there something I ought to know about her?' Pop was sure Janet knew something, she had that sly look in her dark almond eyes.

'She needs a bit of tenderness,' Janet said, perching unasked on his cluttered desk. 'She ain't got no one but 'Elen.'

Pop sighed. His material shop downstairs was the legitimate part of his business. He ran the workshop and his market stall without declaring either to the Inland Revenue. All his employees until Georgia had been ones like Janet who could be trusted to keep their mouths shut. He didn't want any further headaches.

'Don't you worry,' Janet picked up on his fears. 'She ain't some nark, or ever likely to be. Trust 'er Pop, she's a good kid.'

As Janet went back into the workroom she smiled to herself at Pop's naïvety. He'd been married for donkey's years and had five children, the youngest Georgia's age, yet he hadn't suspected pregnancy. He might fiddle the taxman, but as an otherwise honourable man he was almost unaware of the evil some men were capable of.

Janet knew. She knew all right.

She was the same age as Georgia on VE night, just another silly little girl out dancing in the streets. The big American looked so handsome in his blue uniform, it seemed so right to go and have a drink with him.

She knew what it felt like to scream your lungs out, and she knew too, even as she was doing it, no one would come to help. The whole of England was out celebrating the end of the war and how many other simple girls lost their virginity that night?

'I 'ope she don't go the way I did,' Janet thought as she made her way back to her machine. She was lucky she didn't get pregnant, but she still hated what that man had turned her into. Off with any rich old man, taking what she could and using her body to trap them. At sixteen she saw Paris with one of them, trading her youth for nice clothes and the good life. Never mind who she hurt, as long as it wasn't her.

Yet she wasn't as tough as she thought, she still fell for Pete! Another fast-talking hustler just like herself. Just one year of wild good times, then everything turned sour. He sapped everything from her, the jewellery, the few bob she'd stashed away, he even took her looks. Why she stayed so long she never knew. Three kids, with each one she was pulled further and further down. Finally she ended up where she started, in Soho, a dirty, stinking rat hole of a flat without even a bath. He only came home in the end when he was broke, trying to push her out on the streets, anything for just one more stake. But she'd never done that. No man would make her sell herself in a doorway. Stripping was clean, taking the piss out of old wankers who couldn't get it up any other way, while she fed her kids and tried to build a new life.

'But I won't let you go that way, baby,' she whispered under her breath as she picked up the cheap tweed. 'It ain't a life, it's just survival.'

A raw wind caught Georgia's cheeks as she ran through the narrow back streets to Peabody Court.

Once away from the market it was quiet, offices closed for the weekend, too early in the morning for the night-time people to surface. Unpleasant odours seeped out of each dark alley, the many piles of vomit an indication of the previous night's revelry. Cellar trap-doors stood open, belching out a stench of beer, while the cafés competed with the delicious aroma of fresh coffee and fried bacon.

She could never be sure whether she liked or feared Soho. For all the dirt, smells and danger that seemed to lurk round each dark corner, it had a warmer side that surprised her. A friendly wave from the old man in the corner sweet shop. A wolf whistle from the boy who worked in the Bastille coffee bar and a smile from the woman on her knees scrubbing her doorstep. Helen had no fear when she walked home late at night, the big bouncers in the clubs watched out for her, even the prostitutes and strippers knew her by name and Georgia was respected as being her friend.

'Coo-ey!' The call made her look up. Janet was leaning over a small balcony on the third floor making a signal she was on her way down.

The buildings were dismal. Four storeys of soot-blackened dwellings housing sixty families. Small spiral stone staircases behind rusting prison-like bars gave more than a hint of the dark ages this place belonged to. Yet many of the windows sparkled defiantly, sporting brilliant white net curtains as if the owners wanted to prove they hadn't given up hope entirely.

Janet's high heels clattered down the last few steps,

bringing a touch of unexpected colour and glamour to the grey surroundings.

White-blonde bouffant hair, a leopardskin swagger-jacket, red lipstick and tight red skirt matching per-fectly. Now Georgia saw why she held her own against younger girls in the strip clubs, and why she'd earned the title of Soho's Marilyn Monroe.

'You look lovely,' Georgia was touched that Janet had considered taking her to a doctor enough reason to dress up. 'Your hair's so pretty!'

'I got it done last night,' Janet patted the masterpiece, and fluttered her spiky eyelashes. 'Course it's the first time you've seen me done up. Could I con anyone I was yer sister?'

'Your skin's a bit pale,' Georgia giggled despite the turmoil inside her.

'It's not far,' Janet tucked Georgia's hand under her arm and marched her quickly down to Charing Cross Road. They stopped at a door sandwiched between two record shops.

'I'm scared,' Georgia hung back. 'I don't know what to say!'

Janet took her cold face between both her gloved hands and kissed the end of her nose.

'I'll be with you. Just agree with everything I say to him. It ain't so bad.'

A bearded, tall, thin man answered the door, just as Janet was wiping her lipstick off Georgia's nose.

'Good to see you Janet,' he smiled as if he really meant it. 'Come on up, it's bitterly cold isn't it?'

His voice brought back Blackheath into sharp focus. Resonant, educated. If she closed her eyes she could almost pretend it was Doctor Towle in his spacious antiseptic surgery in the village.

Just one flight of shabby but clean stairs and they passed through a glass-panelled door.

'How's things, Roger?' Janet swaggered into the flat

as if she was no stranger to it. 'Never see you down the club anymore. Got a new lady?'

'I spend my time with good books these days,' he laughed, implying that once he had been a regular visitor, waving one hand at a huge oak bookcase full of leather bound volumes. 'And you must be Georgia,' he smiled down at her, holding out his hand.

Georgia gulped. He had such nice eyes, pale blue, the colour of baby ribbon. When he smiled he looked younger than his fifty years, an unlined, almost boyish face.

'Don't look so frightened,' he led her over to the couch and pulled out a cloth screen to put round it. 'Pop in there and take off your undies, then up on the couch. Janet will be right here with me.'

Georgia took off her coat, then hastily pulled her knickers off under her skirt. Behind the screen she could hear Janet talking softly. She gave him the date of her last period, mentioned the bouts of sickness as if she were an aunt.

She had expected someone seedier, maybe foreign, anything other than this tall, bearded man with his gentle voice and kind face.

'If she is pregnant you know I cannot condone an abortion,' she heard him say. 'I hope you didn't think I would help with that?'

'Of course not, Roger,' Janet's voice lost its cockney edge. 'She can stay with me, one more won't break the bank. We just wanted to be certain before I take her to the hospital.'

Georgia tried hard not to blush when he came back to her pulling on rubber gloves.

'Put your feet up, and let your knees fall apart,' he smiled reassurance. 'Relax. It won't hurt.'

But it did hurt, not just physically, but mentally. It brought back that other examination after the rape. One more indignity, the shame of exposing herself to a man.

Every muscle was tense as his fingers probed her. She screwed up her eyes, her toes and her fingers and wished she could just faint rather than submit to another minute of it.

His face was thoughtful as he removed his hand. He stood back and peeled the rubber gloves off as she hastily pulled her skirt down over her knees.

'Sit up now and just let me see your breasts. Are they tender or enlarged?'

'A bit,' she said, as she struggled to undo her bra.

'Hm,' he said as he peered closely at them. 'No doubt about it my dear. You are pregnant, around eight to nine weeks I'd say.'

Georgia could contain herself no longer. Tears rolled down her cheeks and she covered her face with her hands.

'I'm sorry,' he said gently, patting her shoulder. 'Ideally, every baby should be planned. But believe me, few are. In a few weeks you'll get used to the idea, in a couple of months you'll be waiting eagerly for it.'

Once out on the street, Janet steered her across the busy road to a coffee bar.

'Better now?' Janet was surprised Georgia controlled herself so quickly, remembering her manners and thanking Roger for his verdict. If she didn't know better she would assume Georgia had already come to terms with it. 'I know it wasn't the result you hoped for. But at least we know for sure.'

Janet took a booth at the far end of the coffee bar and ordered drinks for them.

Soho was full of coffee bars, by day office workers bought sandwiches in them, by night they became meeting places for the young. This one had gay red and white checked curtains, with white formica tables and a big bulbous juke box, the only customers two taxi drivers eating breakfast.

'I'd rather leave this till you've had time to think,' Janet said once the coffee was in front of them and she'd lit up a cigarette. 'But time is the one thing we're short on, so I won't go round the houses.'

She drew deeply on her cigarette.

'We could go right now to the police and tell them the whole story. They'll arrest yer dad, and with a bit of luck they might offer help with an abortion in hospital.'

'But what if they don't?' Georgia's eyes filled with fright. 'I don't know if I could bear to go through all that questioning. Besides, when Mum hears about the baby it will make her even more miserable. I can't do that!'

Janet sighed deeply. The bastard who'd done this to Georgia had filled her dreams last night. She wanted him crucified as an example to any other man who might get the idea of raping a child in his care. But however much she wanted it she was aware of the problems. Social workers would step in, the kid'd be back in care and they'd probably make her go through with the baby too.

'The other alternative is to have the baby, maybe get you into a home for unmarried mothers and have it adopted when it's born.'

Georgia stiffened. Eyes rolled in alarm, her lovely mouth tightening with hate.

'I can't have it. I loathe it already. No one could expect me to keep his child inside me, could they?'

Janet's almond eyes closed for a moment as she thought what she would have done if those Americans had left her pregnant.

'Then there's only abortion,' she sighed. 'But that's risky.'

Week after week Janet met women who had illegal abortions. Some women like her who'd already had children and couldn't afford another, sometimes they were prostitutes who'd merely slipped up. But Georgia was a child, how could she help in something which could kill her?

'How bad is risky?'

Janet looked into the dark, determined eyes and saw the same kind of stubborn pluck that had kept her going through countless hardships.

'Infection, blood poisoning, even death. I won't lie to you love, it's heavy.'

'I don't care,' Georgia brushed tears from her eyes angrily. 'Anything's better than having it.'

She put one hand on her stomach tentatively, hardly able to believe there was a tiny baby growing in there.

'It ain't a picnic,' Janet warned. 'It hurts so bad when the contractions come you'll want to die. I don't want to frighten you love, but it wouldn't be right for me not to spell it out.'

'I can stand it,' Georgia stuck out her little pointed chin defiantly.

'I hope so,' Janet said softly. 'I just hope so.'

'Tonight's the night then,' Janet whispered to Georgia at work. Three, painfully slow weeks had passed since the visit to Roger. 'Did you weaken and tell Helen?'

'No. I said I was minding your kids for you.' Georgia's face was pale but resolute. 'If I could get back home on Sunday she need never know. You know what a worry-guts she is!'

A whole week spent waiting for Janet to contact the man. Another five days while he considered whether he would do it, then another nine of being so terrified she couldn't sleep at night.

On top of that was the worry about getting the ten pounds needed, along with hiding it from Helen. No lunch, sweets, new stockings or magazines. It was lucky Pop had asked them to work overtime on several occasions for a rush job, otherwise she would have had to borrow some of it from Janet. The longest three weeks she had ever known, but now the moment was close.

What would happen if she got rushed to hospital? Would she be brave enough not to implicate Janet? And what if she did die? Would Janet go to prison for helping her?

It was raining hard as Georgia and Janet left work, for once the streets were almost empty. Neon lights from the clubs and bars were twinkling in puddles, the old yellow street lights giving St Anne's Court a Dickensian quaintness that belied the sordid activities which it was famous for.

Sally was the only other person who knew what was going to happen. She had already taken Janet's children down to her flat on the ground floor and she'd promised to look in the next morning to see how things were.

'Well, this is it,' Janet said as she opened her front door. 'Sorry about the mess. I didn't have time this morning.'

Two months earlier Georgia would have considered Janet's home a slum, but after her attic room with Helen, it looked homely. Small boxy rooms, congested with furniture. A garish, orange patterned carpet vying with a red overstuffed three piece suite. Yet despite the clothes and toys strewn about, it was clean, bright and cosy. Photographs of her children, glass ornaments and seaside souvenirs jockeyed for position on the mantelpiece, window-sill and two shelves on the walls and gave a feeling of security.

'We didn't even have a bath till last year,' Janet yelled at her as she made a cup of tea. 'I used to stand the kids in the sink. Posh ain't it?'

Georgia looked enviously at the white bathroom, almost as if she'd never seen one before. She may have improved her bathroom enough to use it, but it still made her shudder. Would there ever come a time when she and Helen could arrange their talcum powder, shampoo and face flannels like Janet had done? Or be able to invite friends round and not be embarrassed?

Georgia was in the bedroom getting herself prepared, when the abortionist arrived.

'It's time,' Janet said softly from the doorway. 'Remember what I've told you. It's embarrassing, but not painful. I'll stay with you so don't panic!'

Georgia's stomach churned as she saw the man in the bathroom. He was short and very dark with hair that grew right down the back of his hands and thick eyebrows which met in the middle.

'Call me Eric,' he smirked, not meeting her eyes. Seedy was the description that fitted him best. Clean enough, but with frayed cuffs to his shirt, and the trousers which didn't match his suit jacket were shiny with age. As he took off his jacket and rolled up his shirt sleeves, stale sweat wafted out.

Georgia could think of nothing to say. She stood awkwardly in her dressing-gown, her bare toes curling up on the cold lino as he turned to the bath and bent over.

A tubular chair was already in place, Eric was furiously whisking a bowl of bright pink soapy water. The smell of carbolic took Georgia right back to her ordeal in the bathroom at the convent. She gagged involuntarily.

The closer she looked, the less she liked him. He had a paunch that hung over his trousers and through his thin shirt she could see bumps of a string vest. How could she let this man touch her?

'I know this isn't the best way to meet people,' he said still whisking the soap. 'Try to think of me as a doctor.'

Georgia had an overwhelming desire to run away. He

had a length of rubber tubing in his hands, testing it by submerging one end in the water and squeezing a round bulb in his hand. The other end of the tube had a firm nozzle, the bright pink water was splashing into the white bath.

'Hop up on the chair,' he said, glancing round and taking her firmly by the hand. 'I expect it's been explained to you but I'll tell you once again.'

'I can't,' Georgia said suddenly as panic washed over her. She had looked at those hairy hands, knew where they were going and the thought disgusted her.

'Yes you can,' Janet said firmly behind her. 'Don't even look at Eric, sit on the edge of that chair and try to relax.'

'I don't see or feel anything,' he said unconvincingly, shrugging his shoulders. 'I'm just here to help girls in trouble.'

Between the pair of them Georgia knew she could do nothing but agree.

Clutching the dressing-gown round her she stepped into the bath and perched on the chair. Janet came forward and lifted the gown, revealing the lower part of her body. Then positioning herself by Georgia's side, she took one hand in both of hers.

'Now first I have to dilate the neck of the womb,' Eric said, already sliding two soap-covered fingers between her legs. 'When you got pregnant, that end sealed over with a thin membrane, first we have to break it, then pump the water in.'

When Roger had examined her she was embarrassed, but secure in the knowledge he was a real doctor. This man with his sweaty smell and hairy hands made her feel tainted. As he felt round inside her he kept huffing and wheezing, if it hadn't been for Janet holding her hand so tight and the desperate need for his skill, then she would have pushed him away and run for it.

Georgia turned her eyes up to the ceiling, and tried to blank out from her mind what was happening.

It didn't exactly hurt, it was more humiliating than painful. She felt a dull ache at one point, very similar to a period pain.

'That's done it,' Eric said cheerfully, withdrawing his hand and picking up the length of tubing. 'Now this end,' he lightly touched the rigid end and squirted the bulb again to see that it was working. A jet of pink soapsuds trickled across Georgia's thigh. 'This has to go right in there, then I pump the water. Janet please hold the other end under the water all the time, we mustn't risk an air bubble getting in.'

Once again his fingers felt their way in, this time with the rigid end firmly between them. He groped around for a moment or two then smiled.

'That's it, it's going in now, you'll feel an odd sensation soon.'

It seemed as if he was pushing the tube forever and the sensation he mentioned came on, making her feel slightly nauseous.

'Ready for the soap now,' he said, checking to see Janet was holding the other end down correctly. 'Here goes.'

He pumped for what seemed like minutes. The level in the bowl was going down, yet none was coming splashing out as Georgia had expected.

'That's it, job done,' he said, withdrawing the tube quickly. 'It will start working within twelve hours, if it doesn't we'll have to try again. But I'll stake my reputation on you losing the baby before morning.'

Georgia quickly covered herself as Eric left the room. She was surprised how little it had hurt and she now felt a little foolish. As she climbed out of the bath she noticed her stomach was bloated, and she was shivering, but that was the only ill effect.

She went back into the living room and found her purse.

Eric was pulling on his raincoat, refusing a cup of tea from Janet. It was obvious he wanted to get out as quickly as possible, his tools already packed in a small leather briefcase.

'Can't stop,' he said, his eyes darting about the room. 'Call it a tenner love, and remember not to spill any beans if you have to go into hospital, otherwise you might be very sorry.'

'There's no need for any threats,' Janet moved towards him, her eyes flashing. 'She's one of the girls, she knows how to behave. I'll be contacting you if it doesn't work.'

Janet closed the door behind him and thumped the wall beside it.

'What a piece of human shit!' she exploded. 'He'd sell his own granny for a shilling. He couldn't care less about his victims. I bet he gets – ' she broke off suddenly as if remembering how young Georgia was. 'Never mind that! How yer feeling?'

'Not so scared now,' Georgia smiled, a little colour coming back into her cheeks. 'I mean, I can't stop anything now can I? I just have to wait and see what happens.'

'Good for you,' Janet smiled and tickled her under the chin. 'Now let's see what I've got in the cupboard to eat, you don't look as if you've eaten for days.'

Georgia was seeing another side of Janet now as she cooked chops for their tea, folded clothes and put away toys. She was very much a mother, not the good-time girl she liked to portray at work. The lounge was very warm and it was good to watch television again, almost the same snug feeling she'd had at home in Blackheath.

'How did you come to be a stripper?' Georgia asked after they'd eaten the meal and Janet sat down with her coffee and cigarette, her slippered feet up on a pouffe.

'It started out as a bit of a lark one night,' Janet grinned wickedly. 'My old man had left me with the three kids, I was a bit down and up to my eyes in debt. A mate asked me to go down the club for a few drinks. Well, I was so cheesed off I dolled myself up and out we went.'

She paused to light another cigarette, offering one to Georgia.

'Sorry you don't do you. Anyway I got a bit pissed and when the strip act came on I fell about laughing it was so bad. The manager challenged me. "Do it better than her and I'll give you twenty quid."'

'So you did it?'

Janet grimaced, as if remembering conflicting emotions.

'Well that twenty quid meant food in the cupboard and new shoes for the kids. So I turns to him and says, "All right mate, yer on." Next thing I knew he was wheeling me up on the stage.'

'Were you any good?' Georgia was torn between shock and admiration.

'Better than the other girl!' she laughed loudly, throwing back her head. 'I felt a bit silly, me undies was a bit rough and that. But I could dance and me bum and tits hadn't sagged that much. By the time I was waving my bra round me 'ead, the whole place was in an uproar. I got called for an encore.'

'Did you get the twenty pounds?'

'Yeah, and he asked me to appear the next night. A fiver for two ten minute slots. Can you think of a quicker way to make that kind of dough?'

Georgia shook her head.

'I was planning to go to that club in Berwick Street just before I met Helen,' she admitted. 'Do you think I'd have been any good?'

'Don't you even think of it,' Janet snapped. 'I knew all the people round 'ere. I knew what to watch out for.

I make it sound glamorous, but believe me it ain't. You know what 'appens to old strippers?'

Georgia blushed.

'They end up as winos, or brass,' she said. 'I had no alternative back then when the kids was small, but I keep it in mind. I do me turn and I come 'ome. I don't mess with the guys, and I saves some of the dough for a rainy day.'

'Wouldn't you like to get married again?'

Janet snorted with laughter. 'Chance'd be a fine thing. Who wants a woman with three kids for more than a night or two? They come round, want a free meal, a quick screw and they're on their way again. It's better to have a good mate like Sal than a man who just takes.'

It was like looking in a peepshow as Janet told her things about her former life.

'I don't blame anyone but me,' Janet explained her philosophy of life. 'All the troubles I've had were my own doing. If I'd chosen a different path instead of what I thought was a short cut I'd be in clover now. I got no time for people who grizzle and whine. You make your own luck.'

It was after twelve when Janet took her into her bedroom. Next to the big double bed, a narrow single one was made up.

'You sleep in there love, and wake me up if it starts. Anything yet?'

'Nothing,' Georgia laughed. 'I don't know what to expect anyway.'

'Well the soap acts as an irritant. It starts up contractions. They feel some'at like period pains. They go on for a bit, getting stronger and stronger, then if all goes well you'll lose it. It can be messy, so put a pad on now. But don't worry about the bed, I've put a rubber sheet on it and the sheets are old ones.'

Georgia lay awake long after Janet was snoring next to her.

To help her to sleep she lapsed into her favourite game, pretending to be a famous actress in a West End musical. She imagined the crowd shouting for an encore, and herself sweeping out of the stage door into a waiting limousine. As she raised one foot to get into the car, a voice behind her made her turn.

'I knew I'd find you one day.'

She turned to see Peter standing there, his blond hair gleaming like gold under a street light, his arms open wide, waiting for her to run to him.

When she woke, for a minute she didn't know where she was, until a dull ache in her stomach reminded her. It was still dark, and Janet snored softly in the bed next to her.

Creeping out of bed silently, she fumbled for her dressing-gown and slippers and went into the lounge.

It was four o'clock, and still raining hard when she looked out of the window. Across the street four men were staggering up the steps of the Black Cat club. Two of them supported the third between them, and a fourth lurched unsteadily behind them.

Georgia perched on the arm of a chair and watched them. They paused under the club's canopy as if hoping to see a taxi. An illuminated sign was flashing on and off beside them, their faces turning red to green alternately. There was no one else about. Not so much as a light in an upstairs window or a passing car.

She turned away from the window to take some painkillers Janet had left on the table, and make some hot milk.

She turned to examine a photograph of Janet's children. It had been taken in a studio. What would happen to them if Janet didn't get rehoused in the next couple of years as she hoped? Would her daughter end up working in one of the clubs? Would the boys spend their nights in smoky billiard halls, waiting to be sucked into crime?

When all this was over she would have to think hard about her own future. Soho might be a convenient place to hide, but as Janet had pointed out so clearly, it was full of life's losers.

By six the pain was so strong she went back to bed. Every now and then the soap oozed out in spurts, the smell of carbolic making her nauseous. She lay on one side, then the other, trying to find a way to get comfortable. Between the pains she counted. At first she could get up to forty, but gradually they got closer and closer together, until they were only seconds apart.

It wasn't just in her stomach now, but in her back too. She didn't want to wake Janet yet, but it was scary lying there in the darkness.

The curtains didn't quite meet in the middle. She focused on a triangle of sky, watching as it slowly turned from black to grey. In the distance she could hear a milk float, the crates rattling as it went over bumps, and slowly the hum of traffic increased from the direction of Charing Cross Road.

It was light enough to see Janet now. Her red night-dress bunched up around her neck, one pale arm curled round her head, wheezing as she slept.

There were no gaps between the pain now, just great waves of agony that grew gradually stronger. She tried to control herself, gripping the edge of the mattress, but even biting her lips together she couldn't stop a moan rumbling out.

Janet sat up with a start.

'Oh my God,' she said, rubbing her eyes, smearing the night before's mascara all over her cheeks. 'I'd forgotten about you. How is it?'

'Bad,' Georgia said through gritted teeth. 'I've been trying not to wake you.'

'You silly mare,' Janet jumped out of bed and wrapped herself in a shabby blue dressing-gown, her hair like a ball of tangled yellow wool. 'Are you losing any blood?'

Georgia gritted her teeth as a white hot pain gripped her. This time she felt blood flowing, warm and sticky on her legs.

Janet moved over to her and pulled back the covers. She gasped as she saw the blood and hastily got two more towels.

Time and place ceased to have any meaning as pain consumed her. She was aware of Janet sitting beside her, the cooling touch of a damp flannel on her face, the soothing words of encouragement, but pain drove out thought or hope.

Janet was frightened now.

She could almost see the powerful contractions tearing at the child in front of her. Her face was contorted with the effort of not crying out. Bathed in sweat, rope-like veins on her forehead, yet still she had the iron-will not to beg for an ambulance.

It wasn't the first abortion she had helped with, but all those other girls were experienced, most had already got a child. Could she trust Georgia to tell her when she could no longer endure it?

A tapping on the door sent Janet scurrying to open it.

'Thank heavens you've come,' Janet blurted out. 'I'm scared Sal, I think she might die!'

Sally slipped in, closing the door behind her. She had left the children still in bed, intending to just check on Janet and Georgia before she went back to get them breakfast.

'Why, what's happened?' She had only a thin coat over her nightdress, hair still in curlers. Her face without her usual thick make-up was as pale as an iced bun.

157

'She ain't screaming or nothing, she's just taking it. But I don't think she can stand much more.'

Sally went whiter still when she saw Georgia. She was struggling now, tossing from side to side, her hair sticking to her head, her eyes rolling back.

'I'll get an ambulance,' she gasped. 'What shall I say?'

'Anything,' Janet almost screamed. 'Just get them here.'

As they looked back to the bed Georgia tried to sit up. Both women ran to her.

'Stay where you are,' Janet pushed her back, her hands trembling with fright. 'You can't get up!'

'Get me to the toilet,' Georgia croaked.

The two older women's eyes met. Sally nodded.

Taking one arm each they half carried Georgia across the room, out across the tiny hall into the bathroom. Janet lifted the blood stained nightdress and sat her down, holding on to her shoulders.

They could see her knuckles turn white as she gripped the seat, her head lolling to one side like a broken doll.

'I'm going to be sick,' she whispered.

Janet grabbed the waste bin, pushing it in front of her just as Georgia retched. Once again her face went purple, eyes rolled back, she bared her teeth and her neck seemed to swell before their eyes.

'Oh Gawd! She's havin' a fit!' Sally cried out. 'What do we do?'

The swollen veins in her forehead and only the whites of her eyes showing were enough to terrify the two older women but when a low roar rumbled in her throat, Sally crossed herself involuntarily.

'Push it out!' Janet cried, wringing her hands with fear and impotence. 'Push!'

Each second seemed like an hour as they waited in the icy bathroom. Janet held Georgia against her chest, sobbing now in fear. Sally knelt down in front of Georgia, eyes wide with panic.

Once again her face contorted, neck swelling, but this time her eyes opened wide and her hands gripped at the toilet seat. Her nostrils flared, teeth clenched together, and they both heard a slithering sound, quickly followed by a splash.

She slumped forward, only prevented from falling to the floor by Janet's arms.

'Was that it?' Sally jumped up, wild-eyed, black hair tossed back from her white face.

'I hope so,' Janet scooped Georgia up into her arms, lifting her as if she weighed nothing. 'You look. She's fainted. I'll get her back to bed.'

Sally came into the bedroom minutes later, she stood by the door, her face a pale green. Janet barely turned. She had Georgia back in bed now, tucking the covers round her.

'Blood always looks like pints, even when you lose a teaspoonful,' she said, more calmly than she felt. 'At least she don't seem to be in pain.'

Georgia's eyelids fluttered, then opened.

'It's over now darlin',' Janet whispered, smoothing back the girl's damp hair. 'You was a brave little soldier! How d'you feel?'

'Just, kind of odd,' she said weakly.

'Let's get you washed and into a clean bed,' Janet said. 'And Sal will make a nice cup of tea before you go back to sleep.'

Janet came back into the bedroom with a clean night-dress over her arm, but stopped by the bed, tears pricking her eyelids.

Sally had Georgia lying on a white towel, just drying her legs. Georgia's skin looked much darker now, skin shining like a light brown pebble just tossed out of the sea. Such perfection, long, slender legs, tiny waist and small jutting breasts with dark brown nipples.

But it was her face that effected Janet most. It was like a small child's when it has just woken, smooth, unlined, dark pink lips in a moist bow. Teeth and the whites of her eyes almost dazzling. Delicate bones that transported her heart-shaped face from being just pretty, to magnificence.

Janet had seen little beauty in her life. Her children's faces, flowers in the market, and a sunset once in Paris were about the only things she remembered as being truly beautiful. But as she looked down at Georgia, tears trickled down her cheeks.

'What's the matter, Jan?' Georgia's voice was croaky.

'You,' Janet retorted quickly. 'I was just thinking that you'd better not take up stripping otherwise there'll be no room for old bags like me anymore.'

Sally looked round at her friend, a smirk of understanding and affection playing on her lips.

'Come on, you silly mare,' she said. 'Get the nightie on her before the poor kid freezes. I've got to get back to those little buggers downstairs!'

Georgia slept all day till nearly nine that night. Janet checked on her constantly, and gradually relief took the place of fear. There was no sign of fever. The flow of blood had turned to a trickle and she was sleeping as quietly and soundly as a baby.

Janet was watching television around nine when she heard the door open behind her.

'What on earth!' she exclaimed.

Georgia stood there fully dressed in her jeans and the red sweater she'd arrived in. She had her shoes on and her coat in her hand.

'Where do you think you're going?' Janet demanded.

'Home,' Georgia said simply.

'Get back into bed this minute. You ain't going

anywhere.' Janet jumped to her feet. 'Never heard nothing so daft.'

'No, Jan,' Georgia said softly. 'It's time you had your children back, you've done enough. I'm all right now thanks to you. But I'm not going to impose any longer.'

'Impose?' Janet roared. 'What's that supposed to mean?'

Georgia said nothing, just came over to Janet and put her arms round her, leaning her head on her shoulder.

'I didn't realize till just now what you'd been risking,' she whispered. 'I'm so selfish sometimes. I don't think beyond me. You've been so wonderful, I'll never forget it. But your children belong here, not me.'

'But –'

Georgia lifted her head and put one finger on Janet's lips.

'I'll tell Helen I've got a tummy ache and go to bed. If anything does happen then I'll pretend it's just a bad period. It's safer that way. Our little secret.'

'You can't walk home!'

'Of course I can,' Georgia smiled. 'I'll be back at work on Monday good as new. And I've got you to thank for that.'

Georgia's colour was almost normal now, her eyelids had a faint purple tinge, but the peachy tone was back in her cheeks.

Janet shook her head. 'You're a funny kid,' she smiled reluctantly. 'Just promise me you'll put all this behind you now and try to forget.'

'I shan't ever forget you,' Georgia said hugging Janet one more time. 'Not ever.'

Chapter 6

The smell of damp wool and paraffin on top of the roar of her machine was making Georgia's head ache. Three more identical dark green dresses to be finished before six and the light was so bad she could hardly keep the seam straight in front of her.

She wriggled, trying to ease her aching back into a more comfortable position, when suddenly the electricity was cut off, plunging the workroom into silence and darkness.

'What's happened?' Georgia spun round in her seat.

There was enough light from the street lamps outside the window to see the other girls were no longer behind their machines. Irene was missing from the big steam press. Iris's scissors lay gleaming on the cutting table.

'What's going on?' Georgia called out, but the only reply was a muffled giggle from the staffroom.

She stood up, leaving the half-finished garment still in the silent machine and took one step towards them.

A faint, flickering yellow light, another giggle.

'Happy birthday to you! Happy birthday to you!' Five voices burst out from the gloom.

Now it was Georgia's turn to giggle as Pop appeared holding a cake. Sixteen candles burning and all the girls singing at the top of their lungs.

'Happy birthday, dear Georgia, happy birthday to you!'

'I thought you'd all forgotten,' Georgia's face broke into a wide smile.

The day had begun badly when Helen rushed out without remembering. Memories of all those other birthdays came flooding back. Celia waking her with a special breakfast, parcels and cards. A specially magical day where the birthday girl was treated like a princess.

When she got into work and found they too hadn't remembered, she'd resigned herself to believing that in an adult world perhaps birthdays weren't important, and she'd been too embarrassed to mention it. Not once had she suspected they were planning something.

'Forgotten?' Janet laughed. 'You reminded us enough times in the last week.'

They all stood there grinning like idiots, Iris with a bottle of sparkling wine in her hands, Sally with a plate of sausage rolls and Pop flushed with excitement.

'But how could you keep me in suspense all day?' Georgia asked. She'd had to fight back tears of disappointment when she thought they'd forgotten what day it was.

'I told them they had to,' Pop's sallow face was grotesque, lit only by the candles beneath it. He put the cake down on a machine and motioned for the lights to be put back on. 'I threatened them with the sack if they let on before five.'

'Well, you mean old thing,' Georgia thumped him playfully in the chest. 'It's okay to have birthdays as long as they don't interfere with production?'

'Come on,' Janet said, hands on hips, eyes gleaming. She had made an unusual effort with her appearance today, and now Georgia understood why. Her blonde hair was smooth for once, tied back at the nape of her neck with a ribbon, and she was wearing a black sheath dress with a white lace collar. 'One big blow, and don't forget to wish.'

It was this rag-bag group of people who had helped

her to forget the trauma of last year. Pop with his funny Greek accent, Iris's tall tales, Irene's strange moods, Myrtle's quiet shyness, and the continual vulgar banter between Janet and Sally. But as they grouped around her, their faces full of affection, Georgia wanted to cry with happiness.

Taking a deep breath, she blew the candles out. The same old wish that came to her night after night. But now she was sixteen surely it would come true?

'There's more too,' Sally grinned, her mouth red and pouting. 'But we promised Helen we'd wait for her.'

As she spoke Georgia heard the familiar clonking sound of Helen's boots on the bare wood of the stairs.

'She's coming!'

Helen paused for breath in the doorway, one hand on her side as if severely winded. Two bright pink spots of excitement on her cheeks, wearing the same old russet coat she'd worn the first time Georgia met her.

'Happy birthday,' she said, crossing the room to kiss Georgia and putting a large parcel in her lap. 'I wanted to give it to you this morning, but Janet and Sal said it would ruin their surprise.'

Georgia tore the wrapping off like a child.

It was a big, red baggy sweater, just like one Georgia had seen in Oxford Street weeks earlier. She looked up gleefully at Helen.

'You copied it, you clever darling!'

Helen blushed a becoming rose pink, her green eyes downcast with embarrassment.

'They didn't like me asking to get it out of the window,' she said in a small voice. She was never at ease with large groups of people, if Janet hadn't insisted she came to the workroom and joined in she would have waited for Georgia in their room. 'They weren't pleased when I didn't want to buy it.'

The other girls waited expectantly. Pop with an

amused smirk on his lips leant on one of the sewing machines watching silently.

Georgia pulled it over her shirt. It was the latest style, so huge it looked big enough for two, hanging right down over her bottom, the shawl neckline framing her face, the warm red complimenting her dark skin.

'It's *wooonderful*!' she whooped, jumping around the room, lifting her dark curls and admiring herself in an old cracked mirror. 'I'm going to live and die in it.' She leapt back to Helen and hugged her. 'You are the best friend in the world. How did you knit it without me seeing you?'

'Down in the library. At work in the evenings. Sometimes I even did a bit when you were asleep. It wasn't easy.'

Georgia could only hug the collar round her face and smile. It was the planned secrecy, the long hours of selfless work that made it such a special gift. A touch of the magic Celia used to weave.

'Come on, open mine,' Sally cried, almost drowned by the others who offered their presents too.

Pop stood back and smiled.

He liked to see his girls happy like this together. He didn't mind one bit that work was halted, or that soon the already untidy workshop would be strewn with wrapping paper, empty glasses and cake crumbs. He had a feeling that quite soon he would be losing Georgia. His workshop wouldn't be the same without her, but a bright young thing like her wouldn't want to sweat over a sewing machine for ever.

She had changed so much in the year she'd been with him. She'd filled out a little, grown another inch and he'd seen her change from a fearful child to a delightful woman. Georgia was never still. She filled his workroom with chatter and movement. Again and again he had to ask her to get on with her work, but it was like asking the sun not to shine. And shine she did. The ready smile, the clowning, the eagerness to know anything and everything.

He hadn't known she could sing until one day in early April when he walked up the stairs to hear her in full flight.

'Summertime' that was the song, and she sang it in a way that brought a lump to his throat.

It was lunchtime. She twirled an umbrella as though it were a parasol, a length of fabric wrapped round her. Another piece around her hair like a turban.

Sally, darkly seductive, lounged on a bale of cloth, a cigarette hanging from her scarlet lips. Janet perched on a machine, eyes shining with delight, her messy blonde head nodding in time to the beat. Iris painting her nails, glanced up now and then, not anxious to really be part of it. Irene grinned foolishly, her front teeth missing, standing hands on hips, wearing ridiculous men's trousers. And finally, quiet little Myrtle, eyes downcast, hands in her lap at her machine, drinking in every last word.

None of them were aware of him until she finished.

'Sorry, Pop,' Georgia giggled, slapping her hand over her mouth.

'I hope you intend to press that length after you take it off,' he said dourly.

Later he wondered why he hadn't told her how much he enjoyed it.

But she didn't need encouragement. She sang again, day after day, like a little canary in a cage.

The market men ribbed him all the time as spring turned to summer and the windows were wide open.

'Training nightingales up there are we? When do you become her agent and get your ten per cent?'

Pop watched as the girls gave Georgia little presents. A lamp for her room, a picture, a brightly-coloured scarf, earrings and a bracelet. He listened to her shrieks of glee, that gave equal pleasure to the giver.

He too had agonized for weeks over what he should give her. It couldn't be too expensive as the other girls would see it as favouritism. But he wanted her to know how much he appreciated her help.

Without this funny little girl his wife wouldn't be wearing a new fur coat now, and it had all started from Georgia's bossiness!

'These dresses are horrible,' she had said one day back in May, eyeing up the row of finished garments ready for the market stall. They were blue, grey, brown and beige with neat white collars, ordinary dresses for women who wanted plain everyday clothes at rock bottom prices. 'Why on earth don't you make things for younger women? Pretty ones?'

'Design me one then,' he challenged her, fully expecting her to back down.

'All right, I will,' she said, drawing a rough sketch of a scoop-necked, full-skirted dress. 'Use that gingham,' she insisted pointing to a bale of cheap cotton meant for kitchen curtains. 'Put broderie anglaise round the hem and they'll be like Brigitte Bardot dresses.'

He had humoured her by making six. But it wasn't until she tried a pink one on with a wide belt that pulled her waist into a handspan and added a can-can petticoat that he became convinced. Perhaps it was only her brown skin and tiny waist that made it look chic and expensive, but it was worth a try.

'Now get down there.' He shoved the rest of them into her arms, pointing down towards his stall in the market. 'Sell those for me today and I'll believe you.'

Her face and figure were enough to get her noticed, yet she had that bouncy enthusiasm for life that set her apart from other young girls. In less than an hour the dresses were gone, sold to little office girls who hoped they'd look as good as Georgia did in hers. Thanks to

Georgia's idea he'd had the best summer season ever and he had money put by for his expansion programme.

It was silly to think a young girl could change his life, but she had. She'd made him think big, want to reach out and grab things, just the way she did.

He was going to get a proper workshop. Employ a designer and sell his clothes everywhere. Georgia was right, the future lay with youngsters, not the staid old ladies he'd once catered for.

It was just before Christmas when the idea of Georgia's birthday present came to him. The workshop was festooned with paperchains. Cotton wool snow stuck to every window, doors decorated with large Santa Claus's, all made by Georgia out of old fabric.

Janet ushered Andreous, an old friend, into his office, bringing three glasses with her.

'Thought you'd want a seasonal drink,' she said, hands on hips, a sprig of mistletoe in her untidy hair. She winked at Andreous.

Andreous owned the Acropolis club in Greek Street and like most women, Janet fancied him.

'Who's the third glass for?' Pop asked, amused by her direct approach.

'For me,' she said, plonking a kiss on his forehead.

Pop and Andreous were like brothers, the same olive skin and dark sad eyes. But women failed to notice Andreous's thinning hair and paunch. His charm and a certain mischievous, sensuous look had ladies doting on him.

Pop rolled his eyes at his friend who laughed uproariously, patting Janet on her ample backside.

'You can have a drink if you strip for us,' Andreous said, leering at her breasts which almost popped out of her low-cut black blouse.

'I don't want to get you too excited,' Janet put on a motherly expression and patted his cheeks. 'One glimpse of my luscious body sends old men's blood pressure sky 'igh.'

'Off with you,' Pop said, his dark eyes twinkling. 'Andreous is here on business.'

He poured her a little brandy however and pushed it across his desk at her.

The idea popped into his head out of nowhere. Andreous had a club, he employed musicians and singers. Why not give it a try?

'Get Georgia to sing for us!'

She downed the drink in one gulp, and bent to kiss Andreous lightly on the lips.

'Your wish is my command,' she said in a deep throaty whisper as she wiggled out of the door.

'Who's Georgia?' Andreous asked, dark eyes alight with the prospect of a new girl to ogle.

'She's young, beautiful and I want you to just listen,' Pop said severely.

The machines all stopped seconds later. For a brief second it was silent, then a buzz of conversation started from the next room.

Pop waited, resting his head on both hands, his elbows on the desk.

Georgia started to sing, softly at first, but as she got into it so it became louder.

It was 'White Christmas', so corny and old hat Pop thought Andreous would walk out laughing.

'She usually goes in for more spirited stuff,' Pop said.

'Shush,' His friend silenced him and opened the office door so he could hear better.

Her voice rang round the old building, filling each corner with sweetness. Perfectly in tune without any accompaniment, each word crystal clear. Andreous sat looking at the floor, his ears pricked up.

'Well I'll be damned,' Andreous looked stunned as the song ended.

Pop felt a surge of excitement as Georgia burst into

the 'Christmas Alphabet'. He stood up, pushed open the small hatch on the wall that allowed him to watch the girls while they worked and beckoned to his friend.

Andreous peered in, Pop looking over his shoulder. Georgia was dancing round the workroom as she sang, a crown of tinsel on her dark curls, Christmas baubles hung on her ears. She wore a skimpy white blouse tucked into her jeans, slender brown arms waving in time to the song.

Andreous turned and grinned at his friend.

'She's gorgeous, now suppose you come clean.'

It took a little persuasion to overcome Andreous's conviction he wasn't being an old fool falling for a young pretty girl, still more to convince him Georgia could sing in front of a real audience. But all the time they talked, Georgia sang next door, gently nudging the club owner into seeing his idea was practical.

Pop wasn't an excitable man, yet his heart thumped as he waited while Georgia opened her other presents.

The envelope was in his hand, in it one of the hand-embossed invitation cards telling her that she was appearing at the Acropolis club on Sunday 15th April.

'Happy Birthday, Georgia.' He stepped forward as she sat surrounded by bits of wrapping paper, envelopes and cards. 'It's the sort of present which isn't for just today, but maybe forever.'

'Mysterious,' she laughed, taking the envelope and opening it. 'Is it a treasure hunt and this is the first clue?'

'Sort of.'

She read the card then looked up at him, her smooth brow wrinkled into a frown. 'I'm sorry I'm not with it. Am I invited to this do?'

'Yes,' he nodded gravely.

'To go with you as your guest?'

'Kind of.'

'And are the other girls coming too?'

'I hope they will.'

'Well, thank you,' she said, clearly puzzled. 'That will be lovely.'

'Did you see who is appearing that night?' He held his breath as he waited for her response.

'Georgia James,' she smiled, but it was clear she hadn't cottoned on. 'Someone with the same name as me?'

'No,' he could hardly contain himself. 'It's you who is appearing there. It's your chance to show an invited audience what you can do.'

She sat quite still. The other girls looked at one another in astonishment, not sure they had heard it right either.

'You mean I can sing in this club, with a piano and all?'

'A quartet,' he laughed. 'And you have to go along and practise a few times with them first, so they know what songs you do best.'

'So who will be there?'

'All Andreous's best customers.'

'How did you arrange this,' she said, her face pale but with the beginning of a volcano in her eyes.

'Andreous heard you sing. That's all you need to know.'

'And he didn't think I was a joke?'

'I didn't hear him laugh,' Pop said, a lump coming in to his throat as he saw her mouth curl into a wide, joyful smile. 'It's my hope this will change everything for you.'

'Oh, Pop,' Georgia hurtled into his arms. 'That's the most wonderful, exciting birthday present. I can't believe it.'

Somehow this sweet man had picked up on her dream, without her even realizing she had one. She'd talked of being an actress, a dancer, almost forgetting singing came as naturally to her as breathing.

All around her the other girls were laughing and joking, eating cake, drinking the wine. Each and every present had been carefully planned. But this one was so very special. As Pop said, 'Not just for now, but maybe forever.'

'I can't say what I feel,' she whispered, winding her arms around his neck.

'You don't have to, sweetie,' his voice was gruff with emotion. 'Just make it work for you on the night.'

'Mum's left the office,' Georgia blurted out to Janet the next morning. 'I mean she's gone for good and no one knows where.'

Even last night, with the party going on around her, Georgia had been dying to phone Celia. She had imagined the scenario, the shock, the surprise, even tears. Never once had she considered Celia might leave her job.

'Now calm down,' Janet got up and put her arms round Georgia. 'Is it that surprising she left?'

'But what do I do now?' Georgia's mouth drooped petulantly like a small child's.

'You know where Peter lives,' Janet raised one eyebrow. 'Go on over there. He's bound to know where she is!'

Eltham High Street looked different, cleaner, brighter than she remembered. No drunks or tramps, spivs or tarts like Soho. Just middle-aged ladies with shopping baskets, younger women with prams and pushchairs and men driving Fords. Even the gang of youths who stood outside Olive's coffee bar watching the girls go by looked harmless. Suit jackets over carefully pressed jeans, hair cut in the same college-boy style favoured by office workers.

Georgia checked her appearance in a shop window as one of the boys whistled at her. Her red double-breasted coat came from a jumble sale but Helen had taken in the waist and shortened it for her. Although it was a little old-fashioned she knew it suited her. Her hair hung loose over her shoulders and she had new, pointed patent-leather shoes.

As she approached Haig Road she wanted to run. It was beginning to rain and she had no umbrella.

Peter's house looked exactly the way it had when she rode passed it on her bike that first summer soon after she'd met him. A bit frowsy, litter in the bare front garden. The gate was hanging off its hinges, the front door still unpainted.

She knocked on the door, holding her breath with excitement, screwing up her eyes as she willed Peter to answer.

But instead it was a tall thin woman, a blue nylon overall over her clothes, a duster in her hand.

'Is Peter in?' Georgia smiled at the woman. She had expected Peter's mother to be shorter and fat.

'No,' she said sharply, her face tightening, her mouth a thin suspicious line.

'Oh,' Georgia felt her heart lurch, instinctively knowing she should have written rather than called. 'I'm an old friend. Georgia.'

'He's gone away,' Mrs Radcliffe stiffened visibly, already trying to close the door as if that was an end to their conversation.

'Please,' Georgia moved closer, her bright smile wiped out by the hostility, her eyes pleading now. 'Can I come in and talk?'

'What is there to talk about,' the woman looked at her with dead, cold eyes. 'He's at university. He's forgotten about you and he doesn't need any reminders.'

The woman's sharp words cut through her like a

knife. There was no resemblance to Peter. Pale washed-out brown eyes, white skin with tiny, red broken veins, thin lips and a sharp, pointed nose. Even her hair was colourless. Never golden blonde like Peter's, just dreary light brown, fading to grey at her temples.

'But let me explain,' Georgia pleaded. 'I can't find out where my mother is. You do know what happened don't you?'

'I know only one thing,' the woman's thin face loomed up close to Georgia's, small eyes full of spite. 'You ran off leaving my boy so upset he could barely take his exams. He's got over that now. He's happy with a nice girlfriend. Go away and leave him in peace.'

'Is he staying here for the holidays?' Georgia was getting desperate now. Not for one moment had she expected this.

'No, he's with his girl.' Once again the door started to close.

Georgia moved forward and held the door. 'I don't want to bother him if he's got a girlfriend,' she blurted out, tears coming to her eyes. 'But he might know where my mother is.'

'He doesn't,' she snapped, pushing Georgia's hand off the door. 'He hasn't seen her since you left. Why should he? You left him high and dry without a word. Got him into all that trouble with the police. Mud sticks you know, and you did nothing to clear his name.'

'But – ' Georgia felt sick. She hadn't even considered Peter might be blamed in some way.

'There's no "buts",' Mrs Radcliffe folded her arms across her bony chest, her narrow lips set in a straight uncompromising line. 'He's forgotten you. Now push off.'

It was that same kind of frosty prejudice she'd met when she first left home.

'Please give him my address,' Georgia pleaded. 'Tell him I don't want anything but to find Mum.'

She thought then she had brought the woman round, she hesitated for a second, letting her arms drop to her sides.

'All right,' she said grudgingly. 'But don't expect miracles. He's got enough on his plate.'

Georgia took out a notepad from her bag, quickly scribbled her address and passed it over.

'Berwick Street,' Mrs Radcliffe looked at it, then at Georgia suspiciously. 'Soho?'

'Yes. I share a flat with a friend.'

She sniffed, and put it in her pocket.

'Thank you,' Georgia could feel her face burning with shame. She knew what the woman was thinking and it hurt so badly she wanted to die.

The door was closed before she even got to the gate. Georgia stood for a moment staring up at the house, her eyes filling with tears.

She could see a few books on an upstairs window-sill. Was that his room where she'd imagined him sleeping? Why couldn't his mother have been the fat, comfortable, jolly person she expected, opening up her arms in welcome?

So he was staying with his girlfriend! He had a new life and it didn't include her. Peter's world was closed to her, as firmly as his mother had shut that door.

The rain grew heavier, but Georgia hardly noticed it as she trailed down Shooters Hill Road towards Blackheath.

This morning she had been so full of joyful expectation and now it was all gone. Celia had left her job. Peter had been blamed. Instead of solving all their problems by running away, it looked as though she added to them. Celia had told her many times about hysterical teenagers who claimed rape to cover up for staying out late, or going willingly with a man. Was that what they believed of her?

The moment she saw the old house she knew Celia

175

had long since left. The lawn in front of the house had been paved over and the railing removed. Apart from two forsythia bushes, there was nothing left of the garden. Now there was merely space for two cars, and every window sported net curtains.

Celia had never liked nets. She believed they were unnecessary, spoiling natural light, fussy and old-fashioned.

Georgia stood just a little way away from the house wondering what to do.

It was possible that Brian still lived there and the last thing she wanted to do was see him.

Instead she passed the house and called two doors away where Mrs Owen lived. She hadn't been a friend of the Andersons, just a gossipy neighbour, but if anyone knew where Celia had gone it would be her.

She rang the bell nervously.

A short, plump, middle-aged lady answered the door, wiping her hands on a tea-towel.

'Does Mrs Owen still live here?' Georgia's heart plummeted to even greater depths. She was like Mrs Owen, but smarter and several years younger.

'She's gone to visit her daughter in Australia,' the woman smiled. 'I'm her sister.' Despite her smile she looked flustered, as if caught in the middle of something.

'Oh,' Georgia frowned with disappointment.

'Can I help?' the question was one of indifferent politeness, already she was looking past Georgia out towards the heath as if wondering how long this was going to take.

'I was looking for someone who lived at number nine. Mrs Owen was friendly with her. I thought she might know where she went?'

The woman stepped forward out of her porch, glancing down the road as if to try and remember.

'Oh yes, you must mean the Andersons,' she said. 'I

never met them, but Nancy used to talk about them. They sold the house, dear. There's students living there now.'

Georgia sensed the brush off. The woman didn't want to talk, already she was retreating back into her doorway.

'Thank you,' Georgia took a step back. 'I'm sorry to have bothered you.'

'Sorry I couldn't help more,' the woman was already closing the door. 'Try the estate agents. It's Goodman and Smith, the first one you come to. They're bound to know.'

By the time Georgia got off the train at Charing Cross she was wet through and so cold her teeth were chattering.

The estate agents had given her an address, but it was Brian's.

'Terrible mess the house was in,' the pink-faced, snobby estate agent told her. 'Seems his wife left him and he went to pieces afterwards. He got us to sell off everything. He said he was going abroad.'

'But did he tell you where his wife went?' Georgia was tempted to tell him the whole story if only to get his full attention, but he was so cold and businesslike she merely pretended to be a niece.

'Rumour had it she ran off months before,' the man said haughtily. 'I believe Anderson drank, we certainly found a great deal of evidence to bear that out. We had no reason to contact Mrs Anderson, the house was his sole property.'

She took Brian's address in New Cross out of politeness, but once outside she tore it up and threw it away.

As she opened the door to her room, Helen hobbled towards her, green eyes blazing like fireworks, her pale face flushed and hot-looking. Clothes were strewn all over the place and the air thick with the smell of burnt toast.

'I've got a hospital bed at last,' she flung herself at Georgia. 'Next week. Isn't it wonderful?'

Georgia took a deep breath and tried hard to smile.

'I'm so pleased for you,' she bit back tears and held Helen tightly. 'You've waited so long.'

'I've got so much to do I don't know where to start.' Helen wriggled out of her arms, picking up things and throwing them down while all the time she trembled with excitement.

'What have you got to do?' Georgia had to laugh despite her own misery. Helen was normally so placid and quiet, it was a diversion at least from her own troubles.

'I'll have to give my notice at the club. Buy some new nighties, tell Bert I won't be here. So much.'

'Now calm down,' Georgia said, taking Helen by the shoulders firmly. 'All that will take less than half an hour.'

Helen tried to dance, hopping around on her one good leg, her smile stretching across her whole face. 'Oh, Georgia in a week or two we might be able to go out dancing. By the time you sing at the Acropolis I might be a normal girl.'

All the previous year Helen had been waiting for this bed. Twice before she had been accepted as a patient and then the operation had been cancelled just days before.

'Don't build your hopes up too high,' Georgia said slowly. 'Think the worst, just in case.'

'That's an odd thing for you to say,' Helen spun round and looked at Georgia sharply, colour draining from her face, as she remembered where Georgia had been going. 'Don't say you didn't find Peter?'

'Worse,' Georgia slumped down into a chair. 'He

doesn't care about me anymore. I think his mother hates me. Mum's vanished too.'

It was only after her abortion that Georgia had finally told Helen the whole story. It had been the opening up, the sharing of pain which had helped her to gain her old confidence. Once again Helen listened, her green eyes filling with tears and she rested her small red head on Georgia's dark one.

'What can I say?' she whispered. 'I don't really believe they don't want to see you. How could anyone turn their back on you?'

'But why didn't Mum leave an address?' Georgia sniffed. 'Surely she knew I'd want to contact her?'

'People do funny things when they're hurt,' Helen said thoughtfully. 'But even though Peter's mother sounds like a real old witch, I'm sure she will pass on your note to Peter. She probably got a shock seeing you on her doorstep.'

'I handled it all wrong,' Georgia sighed deeply. She was beyond crying now and she didn't want to spoil Helen's joy by dwelling on her own problems. 'I should have trusted Peter a year ago and written. You can't keep people in the dark and expect them to just know how you feel.'

'You haven't had much luck have you,' Helen wound a strand of Georgia's hair round her finger, her small bony arms holding Georgia tightly.

Georgia looked at Helen. The built-up brown boot was peeping out from her long skirt, her green cardigan had tiny darns where moths had eaten it and she was about to face a serious operation which might leave her lamer than before. Yet never once had Georgia heard her sniffle about having no family.

'No luck?' she forced herself to smile. 'I found you. I've got a job and a home. I've even got a chance at the Acropolis. How much more luck does anyone need?'

*

It was after twelve that night when Mrs Radcliffe pulled the address out of her overall pocket. Peter had gone to bed early, his face white and strained.

It was lucky he hadn't got home from the library ten minutes earlier, otherwise he might have caught her sending that girl packing.

Why couldn't he be like her neighbours' sons, out with the lads on a motorbike instead of mooning around waiting for her? He had a fine career ahead of him, no mother would gladly see her only son going off with some wild black girl.

'I'm doing this for your own good, son,' she muttered to herself, poking the fire up into a blaze. 'She's probably been on the game all this time. No good for you, my boy.'

She hesitated for a moment, then plunged the note into the flames before she could change her mind.

'That's it over now.' She wiped her hands on her overall and straightened up. 'You'll thank me for it one day Peter.'

Chapter 7

'You look exhausted,' Peter frowned with concern as Celia sank into a chair without even taking her coat off, an unopened letter in her hand.

It was after ten, a cold March night, yet another evening spent fruitlessly in pubs and coffee bars searching for Georgia.

'I'll make some tea, then I'd better get home,' Peter bent down to light the gas fire. 'Are you just going to stare at that?'

'It's from *him*,' Celia shuddered at the familiar neat script.

'A letter can't hurt you,' Peter came closer and put one hand on her shoulder. 'Do you want me to open it?'

She shook her head and slid one finger under the flap.

'The telephone bill,' she pursed her lips with annoyance. 'He's got a cheek, I've been gone three months!'

'No letter?' Peter asked.

'Just a curt note saying the long distance calls – ' she stopped suddenly in mid-sentence, making Peter turn his head.

'What is it?'

'A postcard too, from Georgia.'

'What!' Peter came back to her side with one bound. 'Let me see.'

Celia's hands were trembling, her eyes filling with tears. Peter snatched it from her, just the sight of her rounded, childish writing filling him with renewed hope.

'Read it to me,' Celia whispered.

'"Dear Mum, I'm safe and well. I've got a nice room, a job and new friends."' Peter gulped, glanced at Celia's radiant face, then continued. '"Don't worry about me please because everything's fine. Soon I'll be sixteen and then I can get in touch again. Give Peter my love, tell him I miss him. I love you, Georgia."'

For a moment they could only stare at one another, then Peter dropped down on to his knees beside Celia, running one finger over the few sentences as if committing them to memory.

'Manchester,' he held the card closer to the light, examining the postmark. 'But it's dated January 29th, it's almost two months old.'

'The evil swine,' Celia's face flushed with anger. 'He's sat on it for two months. How could he do that?'

'Revenge?' Peter shrugged his shoulders. 'And all the time we've been wasting our time looking in London.'

If it hadn't been for Peter's obstinate strength, Celia might have buckled under the strain weeks ago. No one else seemed concerned that an underage rape victim was out there somewhere alone. The police had given up looking for her. Even the agencies who advertised their concern had come up with nothing. Wild goose chases to places where someone had reported a girl fitting her description. A call from a hospital in North London where a girl lay in a coma, another to view a body in the Deptford morgue. Each time Celia rushed there full of hope, or dread, only to discover the only similarity was dark hair and the right age. Even the children's department had lost interest, suggesting it was high time she concentrated on other children in her care. She couldn't count the cost of phone calls, stamps or petrol, that was all incidental. What frightened her most was running out of hope. It was Peter who kept her going night after night. Meeting her to check out yet a few more clubs, pubs or bedsitter houses, never daunted by the size of the task, never flagging in enthusiasm.

Knowing Brian had raped Georgia was the worst thing that she'd ever been faced with. In the early days when Georgia lay in her bed refusing to speak, she kept that thought with her. Whatever came next had to come down on the scale of shock. Yet when she went into the kitchen and found Georgia's note saying she'd left, Celia went to pieces.

The empty bed, half-eaten meal, a holdall gone from the cupboard. When she threw herself down on the little bed and smelled her daughter on the sheets she thought her heart would break.

Even now, months later the pain was still acute. All the things she once held so dear, gone for ever.

Two grubby little rooms were her home now, sharing a bathroom with four strangers. Belmont Road in Lewisham wasn't that far from Blackheath in miles, yet it felt as if she were on another planet.

The rooms were at the top of a large house, divided into a rabbit warren of bedsitters. Cold, draughty, threadbare carpets, dirty bathrooms and continual noise from the other tenants.

It had been less than a week after Georgia left that Celia arrived home to find Brian back. He was hunched up in a chair, a blanket round him. The expression on his pale face one of a cringing dog who fully expects to be whipped.

'What on earth!' she exclaimed in horror.

'You didn't know I was coming home then?' he said,

his eyes cast down, hugging the blanket tighter around him.

If she'd had some warning of his discharge she would have made plans, at least prepared a speech to make her feelings quite plain. She wasn't prepared for the feeling of nausea that washed over her, or the terror at being alone with him.

'Look, Celia,' he said, mistaking her silence for weakness. 'I know you believe the worst of me, but it wasn't like that at all.'

'You louse,' she spat at him, pulling her coat tightly round her, wanting to walk right out again if it meant sharing the same air as him. 'Don't try to wriggle out of what you've done. Nothing will persuade me to forgive you, but don't insult my intelligence by lying!'

'I knew you'd be like this,' he said in a petulant tone, a crocodile tear dripping down his cheek. 'That girl's the liar and you are a fool if you believe her.'

'She said nothing to anyone,' Celia shook with rage. 'I saw the evidence myself remember. I know what happened as if I'd seen it on a film. You've ruined her life and I can't even bear to be in the same room as you.'

It would have been far better if she'd packed her bags and left that night. Only the certainty that Georgia would telephone kept her there a further two weeks. But two weeks was long enough for Brian to see it as compliance and she brought on herself that last ugly scene.

Looking back, that period seemed like months. Sleeping in Georgia's old room, going through old diaries and address books, hoping for a lead. She didn't speak to him, not one word. She went out daily, knocking on doors, meeting old friends of her daughter, walking the streets till exhaustion and the prospect of a telephone call drove her home.

Brian shuffled between the sitting room and the

kitchen. He cooked food when she was out, leaving the dishes.

Celia did nothing for him. She let the dishes pile up, his clothes stay where he dropped them. She bought no food, she didn't even pick up his mail.

She knew she was not behaving rationally. It would be better to scream abuse at him, hurt him as he'd hurt her. It was like an abscess that needed to be lanced. Ignoring it just prolonged the healing process, letting the poison slowly spread through both of them. But Celia remained trapped in a silent world, just as Georgia had been.

She barely noticed the house getting dirty. The dead flowers still sitting in vases and the kitchen bin full to overflowing. Brian was drinking, she couldn't avoid seeing the endless empty bottles, or miss the smell of whiskey gradually permeating round the house. She guessed that many nights he passed out in the chair downstairs, and she hoped he would drink himself to death.

Georgia was on her mind from the moment she opened her eyes in the morning till sleep finally closed them.

She could be in some awful tenement, hungry, cold, and in shock. Worse still she could have turned to someone who would betray her trust even more than Brian had.

'Let's talk?' Brian came out into the hall when he heard her key in the door one evening.

He looked old, dishevelled and desperate, with several days' growth of stubble on his chin.

Celia looked no better. She had lost weight, her once rounded rosy cheeks, sunken and grey. Hair in need of a trim, her tweed coat suddenly too large.

'We can't go on like this,' he said, one hand on his

stomach as though in pain. 'Tell me what you want of me and I'll do it.'

'Kill yourself!' All the venom she ought to have released on him earlier came gushing out. 'But you aren't even man enough to do that!'

'Don't Celia!' he begged. 'Come in the sitting room, we can't talk out here.'

She knew now it was foolish to hope he was going to make a full confession of his guilt, yet in that moment she believed he was.

A stale smell of food and body odour filled the room. She sank onto a chair as far from Brian as possible and averted her eyes from a photograph of Georgia on the mantelpiece.

Brian sat down by the fire and picked up a glass of whiskey.

'Come on then, talk,' she said. 'Start with why you had to rape a fifteen year old, then go on to what you are planning to do about it.'

'I've already told you I did no such thing,' his faded blue eyes looked hurt. 'Think about it again Celia. Why would she run away if she was innocent?'

'You liar,' Celia hissed. 'How can you sit there and continue to make yourself believe that? Do you think you're talking to some half-baked office junior?'

'If you think so little of my integrity,' his tongue flickering across his lips with nervousness, 'perhaps you'd better leave this house now.'

'I will,' she snapped back at him. 'As for your integrity, you'd better stop all that drinking before you forget yourself and go and rape some other young girl on her way home.'

'How dare you!' His face flushed with anger she'd never seen before. 'You are so self-righteous. If I'm drinking now it's because I can't bear you to think these things of me. We've been together for twenty years, yet

186

you'd let the word of some nigger brat come between us.'

'Don't Brian,' Celia got up to leave. She was sickened more by the insult to Georgia than his lies. 'I remember other pointers to your strange sexual tastes. If I have been self-righteous, it's about those. I actually believed I'd cured you!'

He leapt up, barring her way.

'Cured me?' He caught hold of her arms, whiskey-soaked breath making her wince. 'You stupid, frigid cow! All men look at dirty books, there's nothing strange in that. It's you who's weird, not me. You cheated me, made out you married me for love, but all you wanted was this house. I found that out on our so-called honeymoon!'

'Maybe that was your fault?' she said weakly.

'My fault, eh?' he squeezed her arms tightly. 'I let you have everything your own way. I even came rushing back here when you said you were leaving to keep you on any terms. No wonder we never had a child of our own, you never gave it a chance. But even then I said nothing, I even let you steam-roller me into having that kid here.'

'I did no such thing,' she retorted. 'You agreed to have Georgia quite readily.'

'I went along with it to make you happy,' he shouted, his face growing flushed. 'You call yourself a social worker, dig into other people's problems, yet you can't see ones under your own nose.'

'So you bottled up your lust to save it for her?'

She tried to push him away.

At that moment she knew he had got to a danger level. His pale eyes turned dark and a vein was ticking in his forehead.

'I didn't bottle anything up,' he snarled. 'I've had plenty of women. Pretty, tarty girls, ones that like to be fucked and they were all more fun than you.'

Celia was stunned, yet somehow she knew this much was true.

'You sicken me,' she said, attempting to shrug off his hand. 'Let me go this instant and I'll pack and get out.'

'Not so fast,' his voice deepened with menace and his fingers caught her hair, pulling her head back. 'Don't think you can walk out of here and then try to get my money or this house.'

'I don't give a damn about this house,' she screamed at him. 'I don't want anything that reminds me I brought a helpless child into a house with a pervert!'

His fist hit her cheekbone like a sledgehammer, knocking her backwards over an armchair. He reached out and pulled her back up as if she weighed nothing.

'I'll help you pack,' he hissed. 'Let's go through your clothes together, look at the thick knickers you wear, the great big ugly bras and corsets. You aren't a woman at all Celia, you are a man without a cock. I must have been mad to marry you!'

If she had ever had the slightest doubt Brian had raped Georgia it vanished that night. He was so strong and brutal, dragging her upstairs, pulling things out of her wardrobe and taunting her with everything from her sensible flat shoes to her choice of underwear.

Time and time again she tried to make a run for it. But each time he blocked her way, slapping her again and again.

In the back of her mind she could remember telling women at work how to cope with violent men, yet now it was happening to her she was unable to defend herself.

Just after eleven he eventually left her to return to the sitting room. Quickly she stuffed her clothes and personal belongings in a couple of suitcases.

'I'm leaving now,' she returned nervously to the sitting room for her handbag and car keys, poised to make a dash for it if he attempted to hit her again.

'Don't think I'll let you back in,' he said more calmly than she expected.

'There is nothing here to bring me back,' she said proudly. 'I want you to spend the rest of your life reflecting on what you've done. I hope you never have one moment of peace or happiness again.'

The rooms in Belmont Park were the cheapest she could find. The rickety old furniture didn't bother her, she could wash the soiled blankets and buy new sheets. It was only the little things she missed, photographs, her sewing basket and dainty china teacups.

It was pure spite that made her write to the head office of the bank in Lombard Street. She laid out coldly and clearly the case against Brian and allowed his employers to consider whether they could trust him amongst young girls.

It didn't stop the pain of losing Georgia, but revenge had its own kind of sweetness.

Peter made the tea and handed a cup to Celia. She had aged dramatically since the night of the party, not just more lines and grey hair, but that confident bossiness seemed to have vanished.

There had been times when he felt angry at Georgia. Not for running out on him, but for what her actions were doing to Celia. Surely she knew her mother better than to suppose she'd turn her over to the authorities?

Yet even in anger he ached for her. She was under his skin, in his head and heart. Just those few lines on a postcard made him tremble with longing. Nothing would make him give up on her, even if he had to continue his double life indefinitely.

The ugly scene with his parents soon after Georgia ran away had slammed home their prejudice and inadequacy. If it wasn't for Celia's deep understanding, he too might have been tempted to run off.

'Damn little nigger slut,' his mother shouted at him when he tried to explain how frightened and miserable he was. 'That girl's made a laughing stock of you and now you tell me you're worried about her!'

Until he met Celia Anderson he'd never thought about his own mother's shortcomings, but that night he saw them all in close-up. Not one ounce of compassion in her thin, stringy body. Jealous of anyone who had more than her, suspicious of everything. The only time she was loving was when she had a few drinks inside her, a slut and an evil gossip.

He'd tried to reason with her, standing there in the living room, the table still strewn with the leftovers of breakfast even though it was tea-time, the fire concealed by steaming washing hanging to dry.

'What makes you so bitter you have to take it out on Georgia?'

'I've worked hard all my life,' she raved, her mouth wet with spittle, eyes screwed up with hatred. 'Cleaning offices, scrubbing floors when you were little, just to pay the rent. Your father pisses away every penny he earns down the pub. I was banking on you helping us later on.'

It was the last sentence that cut him to the quick. She was afraid that somehow Georgia would prevent him getting a degree. A degree to her meant nothing more than a well-paid job at the end of it.

'You're best out of it, son,' his father said when his mother tried to drag him into it. He sat by the fire, still in mud-caked boots from the building site raising weary blue eyes towards his wife. 'My dad told me not to marry her. I wish I'd heeded his words, sometimes older people know best.'

It all came out that night like slugs leaving a trail of slime where they'd passed over a floor. His father's family were well-to-do, Josie's from a slum in Deptford.

She faked pregnancy to force Geoffrey to marry her, but the plan backfired when his parents cut him off.

Peter saw both sides of it as his parents shouted at one another. His weak but intelligent father, matched with an avaricious, cold woman. Disappointment and greed had killed any love. Geoffrey turned to the pub for friendship, Josie kept a tight rein on her son hoping he'd fulfil the expectations her husband hadn't lived up to.

It was safer to keep quiet about Georgia. He did his homework, ate his tea then made an excuse to get out to see Celia. It was ironic that his parents preferred to think he was down the snooker hall in Lewisham, rather than singing in the choir, or seeing a girl. They didn't guess he was knocking on doors, going in pubs and clubs brandishing a photo of the girl they hated.

Peter put his coat on and wrapped a scarf round his neck.

'It's Easter next week,' he said. 'Let's go to Manchester?'

Celia got up from her chair and shuffled wearily across the floor to him.

'Don't pin your hopes on finding her,' she reached up and kissed his cheek to soften her words. His eyes were shining with excitement, the way they had when Georgia first brought him home. 'It's almost as big as London!'

Celia sighed deeply as they approached Manchester.

'Why the big sigh?' Peter said softly.

'I thought you were asleep,' she smiled round at him. 'I guess I'm thinking how it looks for a forty-plus woman to be running off with a handsome young lad like you.' She had to make jokes about their predicament, she had seen the looks people gave them, wondering if he was her son, or lover. Once they got out the pictures of Georgia the looks became even odder. His parents would hit the roof if they found out he wasn't really youth hostelling. How would she feel if the situation was reversed?

Peter sat up and took the map out of the glove compartment.

'I'm happy for them to think you're my mother,' he smiled. 'But it isn't really that is it? You feel guilty.'

One of the things she liked most about Peter was his perception. He understood Georgia's reasons for running, his own parents, the emptiness inside her and no doubt if he'd talked to Brian he would almost begin to understand him too. But it was this deep understanding of other people which could be his downfall. He had to make a life of his own, he was too young and clever to give up his own needs and education.

'Will you promise me something?' She turned her eyes away from the road, reaching out to touch his hand.

He stiffened. Every muscle in his face and neck was strained, his eyes scanning the streets as they entered Manchester.

'Depends,' he smiled faintly, returning the squeeze of her hand.

He was wearing jeans, a pale blue sweater under the denim jacket and his hair was creeping over his collar.

'On what?'

'Whether you want me to abandon the search,' he said, fixing those bright blue eyes on the side of her face as if trying to read her mind.

'Not exactly,' she said choosing her words carefully. 'But I want you to promise me you will go on to university. I really do believe that Georgia will get in touch again as soon as she's sixteen. You'll only add another burden of guilt to her shoulders if you've found a job in London and not used your ability because of her.'

He frowned.

'Maybe,' he stared out the window for a moment, thinking about Celia's words. 'All right, I promise,' he said. 'But you've got to promise me something too.'

'Go on,' she half smiled.

'That you'll get yourself sorted out too,' he said earnestly. 'Georgia won't write to the old house again, she'd ring me. So there isn't a great deal of point in you hanging around waiting. You look ill, you must look after yourself for her sake. Just as you said it wouldn't do for me to put another burden on her shoulders, neither must you.'

'Fair enough,' she nodded. 'You've got a deal. After this weekend I'll rethink my life too.'

Celia doubted that Georgia was in Manchester. Runaways went to places with a connection with their past. It was a false trail to put them off the scent. But that was a good sign. It meant wherever she was, she was happy to stay there and the message on the card about her sixteenth birthday an assurance she would reappear. Could it be that she had used Manchester, knowing it had one of the universities Peter was keen to go to?

As they passed the university she saw his eyes light up, for the first time his mind on something else other than Georgia.

It had been a gruelling weekend, calling in shops, pubs and clubs showing the photographs, knocking on doors, even asking children in the street. But at least the people were friendly here, no slammed doors or rude remarks and that at least was better than London.

'You should apply here,' she said gently. 'If Georgia's around you may run into her, and anyway it's a fine place.'

'Maybe,' he said, his face breaking into that enthusiastic smile she remembered so well. 'But that won't stop me searching other places in the holidays.'

*

As the spring turned to summer Celia saw less of Peter. He was working hard for his exams and for the moment Georgia was taking second place.

Celia pretended it was the same for her. She had taken on a temporary office job which gave her more time to continue her search.

Night after night she went up to the West End of London, Chelsea and Earl's Court, wandering about, looking.

Just a glimpse of a black curly mop of hair was enough to send her heart pounding. Each brown-skinned girl was studied closely, questions asked in coffee bars until she began to think she'd spoken to half the young girls in London.

When Peter was accepted at Manchester University she was thrilled for him.

'A new start,' she said hugging him. 'You must work hard now. I'll be here when you come home for Christmas. She's bound to write to you then.'

'But you should find a better job,' he said, looking at her disapprovingly. 'It's no good telling me not to waste my talents when you are doing it too.'

'After Christmas I will,' she promised.

In October Peter left for Manchester and Celia pressed twenty pounds into his hand.

'Just a little nest egg to help you when you get there,' she said, trying not to dwell on how much she would miss him. 'Come and see me the moment you get back.'

Christmas came and went without hearing anything. She knew Peter was hanging around by the phone and watching for the postman continually and she found it almost impossible to concentrate on anything.

They both bought birthday presents and cards. Celia made a cake and iced it in readiness.

On January 6th Celia had to go to work, but all day she jumped when the phone rang in the office, fully expecting good news from Peter.

There was nothing. Not that Thursday or the Friday.

'What are we going to do now?' Peter telephoned her just before she left for home on Friday night.

'Maybe she'd been working?' Celia said. 'She could be planning it tomorrow as it's Saturday.'

'I haven't left the house,' he said wearily. 'Mum's getting really cheesed off with me. I'll have to go down to the library tomorrow morning, I've got loads of work to do.'

'Don't worry,' Celia said. 'You can't stay in for ever. If she phones and you're out, she'll ring again.'

The weekend passed without a word, and finally on the Sunday night Peter came down to Celia's flat in Lewisham around nine.

'Nothing,' he sighed, looking dejectedly at the brightly-coloured parcels on the table. 'She can't care about me anymore,' he said, flinging himself down into one of her chairs. 'It was all a dream after all.'

Celia knelt by his side and cupped his face in her hands. 'Go back to Manchester. Get involved with things up there. Who knows, a letter might come any day. Your mother will send it on.'

'But what about you?' he said, tears glistening in his eyes and his sensitive mouth dropping at the corners. 'You can't just wait here. There's no point in it.'

'I think I need a new start too,' she said softly. 'I've applied for a job with the World Health Organization. I was going to back out if Georgia came home, but perhaps I should go.'

'You should,' he said sadly. 'There's nothing to keep you here now. Where is it?'

'In Africa. I don't know whether it will be a big hospital, or a small mission somewhere out in the wilds.'

'You're very brave,' he said in a small voice. 'That's a huge step for you. I'm going to miss you so much. You will keep in touch, won't you?'

'Of course, you silly boy,' she smiled and patted his face. 'I haven't another soul I want to write to and I'm sure once I'm there I'll be clinging to you like a life raft. Now if she does get in contact make sure you write immediately.'

'Who else would I share it with?' he smiled.

Celia smiled bravely as she kissed Peter goodbye. She knew more about rape victims than Peter could ever know. It was common for them to shy away from their old life. They wanted no reminders of their pain. Georgia was a strong person, but not strong enough to come back and re-live her ordeal. Perhaps one day she would be, but as Peter so rightly pointed out Celia couldn't just brood until then.

'You must go,' she said to herself. 'Maybe helping other children will fill the void. Let Peter forget her, pack away the past and start afresh.'

She sat down at the table and opened a writing pad.

'Dear Sirs, I am writing to confirm that I wish to take up the nursing position you recently offered me. I can be ready to leave at any time.

Yours sincerely,
Celia Tutthill.'

Chapter 8

The Middlesex hospital was terrifying. From the smoke-blackened stone outside, to wards full of pain-filled faces.

Georgia looked anxiously at Helen as she climbed into her bed in the new white cotton nightdress Janet had made her. Until that morning excitement had brought a flush to her cheeks, but now she had a greeny tinge, her eyes troubled and afraid.

'I'll be round every night,' Georgia squeezed Helen's small fragile hand. 'Just think of all the fun we'll have when your leg's fixed.'

'It reminds me of the Home,' Helen whispered, glancing along the row of beds. Twenty in all, most of the patients lying still, no talking or laughter, a sense of distress in the air. 'Look at all those crutches, walking frames and wheelchairs,' she pointed over to the middle of the ward where a collection of aids was kept. 'Tell me I'll be able to walk like you when I get out?'

'Of course you will,' Georgia gulped hard. 'Just rest, and think what you are going to wear to the Acropolis!'

Georgia felt scared without Helen that evening. From down in the street were all the usual noises of car doors banging, people shouting and bursts of loud music as a club opened its doors, but up in her room it was too silent.

She hadn't fully realized till now how much they

needed one another. They had ups and downs, times when they argued and bickered. Yet their lives were intertwined. They were more than just friends, and alone she felt abandoned.

Just outside her window were other young girls meeting friends, going dancing and to parties. At only sixteen life seemed to be passing her by.

Would she ever meet a boy she wouldn't be frightened of? Why was it impossible to think of any male without holding him up in comparison to Peter?

That night as she lay staring at the ceiling, it seemed dirtier than ever. The paper was peeling off, the brown paintwork on the door scratched and puckered with age. Even the posters they'd put up didn't hide the fact the room was little more than a slum.

They had made some improvements. Newer bedspreads found at a jumble sale, a bright curtain round the hideous old sink, cushions, and a lampshade hid the naked light. But what it really needed was redecoration.

She woke early the next morning, an idea stopping her from sleeping any later.

Dressing quickly she ran downstairs to the café where Bert was in the middle of frying several breakfasts.

Bert made her think of a bloodhound. Deep lines ran down his cheeks, baggy skin round his eyes, even his eyebrows and mouth drooped. One look at his sallow face was enough to think he'd spent his entire life in misery. But Georgia knew better now, she'd heard him laughing constantly, seen him walking through the market whistling, listened to him telling his customers jokes too many times to take notice of his face. He even made jokes about his sad expression, claiming it stopped anyone asking for protection money, one look at him was enough to buy a three course meal just to cheer him up.

'Want a bit of help?' she called out gaily, squeezing

behind the counter and pouring tea for the waiting customers before he could refuse her.

Bert and Babs were an odd couple. Bert had been brought up in the café and had run it single-handedly until ten years ago when he married Babs. Now as they moved into middle-age, it had become their entire world.

A steamy, warm place in which comfort, cleanliness and style meant less than cheap, plentiful food. The customers who came in for Babs' famous steak and kidney pies didn't mind the spindly chairs or the oilcloth-covered tables. Tea came in giant china mugs, bread was cut in doorsteps and when you ordered a full breakfast you got enough to last you all day.

Bert and Babs lived in a few chaotic rooms above the café. No one would guess that this frowsy pair had the additional income of rents from their property next door.

'What's up with you?' Bert asked, amused by Georgia's bouncy appearance. 'In love, or after a free fry-up?'

Helen looked upon Bert and Babs almost as parents and both girls gave them a hand in the café when they needed it. Georgia had often thought privately that Bert could be a better landlord, but Helen never had a bad word to say about him.

Right now Georgia had plans to butter him up.

'Not love, and it's not food I'm after. I wanted to know if I could paint the room while Helen's in hospital?'

'Gor blimey, Georgie,' He wiped one hand across his sweaty brow, flipping some fried bread over with the other. Bert didn't like to spend money. 'That room's big, it'll take more than one coat.'

'I know,' she tried to look as if she really did. 'I used to help at home. Can I?'

'What colour?' He looked at her sideways, his eyes narrowed.

'White,' she said. 'With yellow paintwork.'

'Sit down love and eat this,' he said, tipping a greasy egg on to the bread and picking up a couple of crispy rashers of bacon with his fingers. 'Let me get me thinking cap on!'

Georgia wolfed down the food as if she hadn't eaten for weeks.

She watched him as she ate.

'Okay,' he said eventually, his sad, sallow face breaking into a grin. 'I'll get you the paint and brushes. But mind you do it proper like!'

'Can you get it today?'

'Blimey gal,' he groaned. Georgia had the appeal of a new puppy sometimes and he found it hard to resist. 'Ain't you gotta heart? 'Ow am I supposed to find time today?'

As Georgia came down the street at six, picking her way through the market refuse, Bert was smoking a cigarette at the door of the café. His face broke into a grin and he waved for her to come in.

''Ere you are,' he put his hand round the door and pulled out a huge tin of white paint. 'The yella's coming tomorrow. Mind you do it proper!'

It was neither as easy or as much fun as Georgia imagined. She soon discovered the paint wouldn't stick to the ceiling unless she washed it first and it was soon clear it would take far longer than she imagined.

She could only do one bit at a time, moving the furniture one way, then back another. By the time she got back from seeing Helen it was already dark and hard to see bits she had missed.

'You've got white flecks in yer 'air,' Sally laughed during the week. 'What on earth are you doing?'

'I'll tell you when it's finished,' Georgia said.

Helen was due to have the operation on Friday, and Georgia had been advised not to visit until Sunday afternoon.

On Saturday morning she got up early. The ceiling was finished now and the brilliant new whiteness was enough to spur her on. All day she worked like a slave and at twelve that night with blisters on her hands, she crawled into bed exhausted.

She woke early on Sunday. A ray of early sunshine bounced off the white walls. For a moment she just lay there looking, smiling to herself.

It looked wonderful, even with everything piled in the middle of the room. It could be an artist's studio or a nursery, so much more light and so clean she wanted to bounce up and down in the bed.

Georgia had a bath and washed her hair before going to the hospital. Her hands were red and sore but it had been worth it. Everything was back in place but it bore no resemblance to the way she'd seen the room that first night.

She wanted to attack the old furniture now. Paint the wardrobe, the table and chairs, make new curtains. When Helen came home it would be perfect.

'Hallo dear', Sister smiled a greeting as Georgia peeped nervously round the door of the ward armed with a bunch of daffodils. 'Can I have a word before you see Helen?'

Georgia had met Sister Hall when she first brought Helen in. She was very tall and thin, a sharp face, softened only by gentle brown eyes. Yet she had a gracious, kindly manner, almost as if it hurt her personally to see her patients suffering.

'How is she?' Georgia's smile faded as Sister ushered her into her office.

'I'm afraid she's feeling very sorry for herself. She's

in a lot of pain and she's not convinced her leg is any better.'

'But it is, isn't it?' Georgia felt a prickle of fear, wiping out her earlier jubilation.

'Yes, it's been more than successful, it's the nearest thing I've ever seen to a miracle. But of course she's going to need an awful lot of physiotherapy before she can walk a step.'

'You mean she can't walk at all now?' Georgia's mouth fell open in horror. Somehow she had imagined that Helen would be jumping around in a few days.

'No, of course not dear.' Sister Hall looked at Georgia as if she were simple. 'Besides she mustn't use the other leg otherwise the weak one will always be carried by the good one. Now go on in and cheer her up. But don't stay more than half an hour.'

Helen had never looked so pale or ill. If her face hadn't been surrounded by the mass of red hair she would have disappeared into the pillow.

Her leg was in traction, she looked terribly uncomfortable and her eyes were red-rimmed.

She tried to smile when she saw Georgia.

'How are you feeling?' Georgia bent to kiss her.

'Like hell,' Helen whispered, wincing at the pain. 'If I'd known it was as bad as this I would have stayed the way I was.'

'Sister says it's a miracle,' Georgia tried to sound bright.

'I don't believe that,' Helen turned her head to one side away from Georgia. 'I think they are afraid to tell me the truth.'

Pop had warned her people were often depressed after an operation, he had said it had something to do with the anaesthetic. He had advised her to disregard anything morbid Helen might say.

'Don't be silly,' Georgia forced a laugh. 'You'll feel

better in a day or two. The doctors know better than you do. Trust them Helen.'

'Easy to say,' Helen muttered.

'Sister said they'll be sending you off to a convalescent home after here. That will be like a holiday. I wish I could have a few weeks lying around.'

'You'd make a worse patient than me,' Helen said tartly. 'And don't try to patronize me Georgia, I've lived with pain most of my life and when I say this is terrible, you can believe it.'

Even though Helen never complained, Georgia was sure she was feeling sorry for herself.

'If you want to be like that I'll go home,' Georgia said, convinced she could shame her friend out of it. 'I came to see how you were and spend time with you. Not for you to jump on every word I say.'

'Please go,' Helen said, tears spilling down her cheeks. 'I expect I'll feel better in the next day or two, but right now I'm not fit company for a dog.'

'I can't go,' Georgia felt tears pricking her eyelids. 'Not when you're like this.'

Helen sighed deeply, forcing a watery smile.

'Come back tomorrow, Georgia,' she turned her head into the pillow.

Georgia bent over the bed and kissed Helen on the cheek.

'I love you,' she said softly. 'You're like a sister to me. Don't think you can get rid of me so you can feel all alone, because I'll be back tomorrow and the next day.'

She turned and walked quickly away, tears coursing down her cheeks.

It was only when she was downstairs in the street that she remembered Peter's words to her after the rape. 'I'll come day after day, till you're sick of me.' He hadn't got the chance to carry out his threat, she'd gone almost before he got home, and when she'd looked him up, he had someone else.

On both Monday and Tuesday evening Georgia went straight to the hospital from work. Helen was still very low and in a great deal of pain. Although she was pleased to see Georgia she was apathetic and touchy.

'Don't think you've got to come here every night,' she said, trying hard to smile. 'I know you must be tired and hungry.'

'But I like coming.'

That wasn't true, she hated it. The smell of the hospital made her queasy. Drips, oxygen masks, bedpans and syringes all hinted at things she didn't want to understand. She couldn't think of anything to say and even though she loved Helen, she couldn't bear to see her in pain.

'Go on home,' Helen said, turning her face away. 'I want to sleep anyway.'

Bert was just about to close up the café as Georgia got back, on an impulse Georgia put her head round the door.

'Come and see the room,' she begged him. 'Helen's been a real grouch. I'll go mad if I don't talk to someone.'

'Okay,' he smiled, guessing her request had more to do with worry about Helen than wanting to show her room off. 'Put the kettle on, we'll be up in a jiffy!'

'Blimey ducks, what a difference!' Babs gasped as she came in, quickly followed by Bert.

Big was the only way to describe her, wide hips, sagging bosom, hands and feet. Even her features were big, from her sharp eyes, her nose and a sloppy, shapeless, humorous mouth. If Georgia's features had been carved with a scalpel, Babs's had been shaped by a trowel. Yet it was an interesting, mobile face for all that, and her clothes enhanced her slovenly, yet colourful image.

Today, she wore a red jumper and a bright blue skirt, topped with a washed-out yellow pinny. Thick stockings with a hole hastily botched together, and a fraying wisp of pink petticoat trailed behind her.

'What a little palace ducks. Don't seem like the same room do it? Helen's going to be knocked out.'

Babs stood still, hands on her ample hips, her sharp eyes taking in every last detail.

'She's done this for Helen,' she thought. 'And I was the one who thought she'd be trouble when she turned up out of nowhere.'

'You've done great,' Bert cast his eyes round the room as if hoping to find something to criticise. 'Not bad for a little 'un.'

'If the singing don't work you could always take up decorating,' Babs chuckled. She put one big hand on Georgia's shoulder. 'Now tell us. 'Ow is she?'

'Still very poorly,' Georgia's face fell, a doleful look back in the big dark eyes. 'I just wish she'd look on the bright side of things. They say everything is healing well, but I don't think she believes them.'

'We was going up there Friday,' Bert said. 'I thought she was a fighter. She was always chirpy before, no matter what. If only she 'ad some family.'

'She 'as,' Babs said rather sharply. 'Everyone up the market cares, and she's got Georgia. I'll 'ave to tell her a few 'ome truths.'

'Don't be sharp with her,' Georgia turned to Babs, surprised by her tone. Babs was a mother figure to everyone. 'We just have to love her out of it. The thing I'm most worried about is that she won't be able to come to the Acropolis to see me. Not for me,' she added quickly. 'But she was dead set on having a lovely new dress and everything.'

'Well we'll just 'ave to jog her memory,' Bert said,

gazing appreciatively round the room. 'Maybe if she's got some goal in her mind she'll buck up.'

Georgia made them both some tea.

'Do you mind if I paint the wardrobe and stuff?' she asked. She wanted something more to fill up the empty hours till Helen came home. 'They look a bit scruffy now.'

'Course you can love,' Bert sank into one of the armchairs and winced as a spring shot up into his behind. 'I think we can find a better couple of chairs an' all.'

'Really?' Georgia leant over him and kissed him on the cheek impulsively.

He smiled across at his wife. 'Those green 'uns would look a treat in 'ere wouldn't they?'

Babs laughed, her wide mouth showing blackened teeth. 'I should take lessons from you in 'ow to get round my old man.'

Helen was propped up in bed on Thursday night when Georgia went in as usual. A book open on the sheet in front of her and a huge basket of flowers by her bed from the stallholders in the market. Dozens of cards were propped up everywhere.

Once again she reminded Georgia of those ladies in old paintings. Her hair showering over the shoulders of the white, almost Victorian nightdress. Her eyes were still listless, but there was a faint hint of pink in her cheeks.

'I'm never going to walk again,' she said gloomily.

'Who said so?' Georgia gasped.

'No one. I just know. They all feel sorry for me but it doesn't help.'

Georgia was torn two ways. Although Helen looked small and vulnerable in the big bed she knew her friend was tough. Should she sympathize and continue to let her wallow in self pity? Or should she be brutal to make her snap out of it?

'There's only one person who can make you walk again and that's you.'

The moment the sharp words were out she felt a deep shame, but it was too late to retract them.

'You think you are so bloody clever, don't you?' Helen sniffed. 'Everything you want comes to you. I bet you're glad I'm in here, I expect you have friends round every night, glad I'm not around to interfere.'

'Oh yes, I'm having a ball,' Georgia shot back. 'I come here straight from work, tired and hungry and go back to an empty room alone.'

'Don't give me that,' Helen pursed up her small mouth. 'I'm not stupid, even if I'm crippled, every night you've been here you can't wait to get out!'

Georgia just stared at Helen in shock.

'That's not true,' she said weakly. 'But if you're going to be like that, I will go.'

'Go on then,' Helen's cheeks were flushed. 'Go down and see Janet, she makes you laugh. Ask her to take you down the strip club.'

'All right, I will,' Georgia turned away from the bed, colour draining from her cheeks. 'If you think that little of me, then I won't come back until you ask me to. Goodbye!'

She had made some curtains during the day at work when Pop wasn't watching. They were only cheap dress cotton but colourful and bright. She had been looking forward to hanging them, but now she felt resentful and bitter.

'I don't know why I'm bothering,' she said, her voice echoing around the room. 'Heaven knows I'm doing all I can for her.'

She hung them anyway, tidied up and then crawled into bed feeling depressed and guilty.

'I shouldn't have walked out like that,' she said to herself. 'I should have told her what I had been doing.'

As Bert and Babs were going to see Helen the next evening she went home instead with Janet. She'd had enough of her own company and a bit of laughter seemed the perfect antidote.

'You did the right thing,' Janet reassured her. 'Leave her be till tomorrow, she'll have come round then. Poor kid, I expect she's feeling as bad about it as you.'

It was after eleven when she walked home, still chuckling to herself about Janet's family, when she spotted a policeman knocking on the door where she lived.

Her first reaction was to run. For the last year police had been her biggest fear and she still hadn't quite got over it.

But reason got the better of her and she crossed over to where he stood, one hand on the bell.

He was young, male, surely she could think of some way to wriggle out of any trouble.

'Can I help?' she asked, smiling brightly up into his lean face, batting her eyelashes when she realized he was nice-looking in a rather severe way. 'I live here.'

'I'm trying to find Georgia James,' he said, blushing a little under her scrutiny.

'That's me,' she said taking out her key.

'I've been asked to take you to the Middlesex Hospital,' he said. 'You have a friend – '

'Helen?' she interrupted him, no longer caring if he looked like a film star. She turned pale under the street light. 'Has she?' she paused unable to say the word.

'She's very ill,' he said gently, his brown eyes grave as he removed his helmet. 'She's been asking for you. Can you come now?'

He bundled her into a car and drove off at speed.

Georgia prayed silently as the car sped along the near empty streets.

'What time were you called?' she asked him.

'Around eight thirty,' he said, glancing across at her, seeing the big tears squeezing out from under her long lashes. 'It seems two other people had visited her earlier. She was poorly then but got worse after they left. I've been all round the neighbourhood trying to find you.'

'It's the first night I've been out other than to visit her.' Georgia was crying now. 'I was nasty to her yesterday too. Oh God, please don't let her die!'

'Now calm down,' he said soothingly. 'People often have ups and downs after ops, it doesn't necessarily mean she'll die. Besides you must go in there with a confident face, be strong for her. Is it the little redhead with the bad leg?'

'Yes, do you know her?' Somehow it was comforting to think this young policeman knew about her.

'Only by sight,' he said softly. 'Plucky little thing, always smiling even when she was frozen solid on that stall. Give her my regards won't you?'

Georgia ran like the wind once inside the hospital. Up the stairs two at a time, her hair streaming out behind her like a black flag.

It was quiet, the corridors deserted. The lights turned down for the night, bathed in a soft glow. There was none of the hustle and bustle of the day, just the odd clang of a bedpan on the sluice, and the tip-tapping sound of nurses' shoes on the polished floor.

'Sister!' she called as she turned the corner and saw a familiar back view.

Sister Hall turned at her name, and came quickly towards Georgia, her hands outstretched. The thin tall woman had concern in every line of her body.

'Oh Georgia, I'm so glad they could find you,' she said breathlessly. 'Helen's very sick I'm afraid.'

'Why?' Georgia's eyes grew huge with fright, filling up with tears. 'She was doing so well.'

The sister smoothed down her apron, her lips quivering as if unable to find the right words.

'We discovered an infection had set in earlier today, she was a bit feverish and we gave her more antibiotics. But her heart is weak too. We knew this before we operated and she fully understood the risk. Now it's her heart which is giving up.'

'Is she going to die?'

Sister put one hand on Georgia's shoulder. Her expression saying it all.

'I'm afraid so,' she whispered, he eyes glinting with tears.

Georgia just stared at the Sister.

'But she can't,' she said. 'I've painted our room and everything.'

Sister half smiled.

'I wish everyone could be cured with something so simple,' she said softly. 'Helen's a very brave girl. She has moaned to you because you were the only one she had. Go on in there now and try to comfort her. Tell her how much you care.'

Georgia had no experience with death. She stood for a moment trying to collect herself. She had faced the fact that Helen could possibly be left more crippled than she was before, but never had the possibility of her dying entered her head.

Everything about the hospital seemed strange and dreamlike. The silent, empty corridors, the yellowish night lights, the smell of antiseptic. She blinked, hoping she was merely dreaming it, and that any moment she would find herself back in bed.

Helen had been moved to a small room at the end of the ward, partitioned off with glass, curtains all round.

She was very still, ghostly pale. Her hair cascaded over the pillow like molten lava, her eyes closed, golden lashes lying on her cheeks. Arms as thin as sticks on the sheet, the long slender fingers which normally moved constantly, still and white.

Her mouth looked like a young child's, so small and innocent, perfectly shaped, lips slightly parted.

Georgia crept to the side of the bed and leaned over her friend.

'Helen,' she said softly.

Her eyes opened.

'Georgia,' she said weakly, struggling to move.

'Stay where you are,' Georgia put one restraining hand on Helen's shoulder, feeling only bone under the white nightdress. She touched Helen's face lightly with one gentle caress. 'What sort of time is this to want to see a friend?'

Helen's lips moved faintly in a flicker of amusement.

'Did you get the curtains up?'

'Yes,' Georgia took a deep breath, glad that Helen had led her into something other than her illness. 'You wait till you see our room. It's like a palace now. White walls, yellow door. I've even painted all the furniture yellow. It's like being in permanent sunshine.'

For a second Helen didn't answer. Her green eyes studied Georgia's face, as if she were trying hard to memorize it.

'You've been like sunshine to me ever since I met you,' she said at length, her voice faint and breathless.

'And you're my best and dearest friend,' Georgia said, taking Helen's small hand and holding it to her lips. 'I love you. I didn't mean what I said yesterday. I only didn't come because Bert and Babs were.'

'I know that,' Helen turned her head slightly and looked hard at Georgia. 'They told me about the room. How you did it for me. I felt so ashamed at what I said about you having friends round there.'

'It didn't matter,' Georgia felt tears threatening to run down her cheeks. 'You'll see it soon, I'll teach you to dance and we'll find ourselves a couple of rich men to take us out.'

'You do it all for me,' Helen's voice was almost a whisper. 'Become a big star in the West End, wear lovely clothes and have hundreds of admirers. I'll be watching you.'

'You'll do it with me!' Georgia tried to sound bossy and hard but it came out like a plea.

'I'm dying, Georgia,' Helen spoke softly, one thin white hand reaching up to touch her friend's face, her expression one of tenderness. 'I knew I would after the op, it was all a dream, a lovely dream of dancing and being like you. But you must carry on, make my dream a reality.'

'I can't without you,' Georgia's tears couldn't stop now. 'You are my family, everything.'

'Don't cry for me,' Helen's eyes brimmed over. 'I'm not scared or anything now, I feel peaceful and content. I'm too tired of struggling, I'm happy to be going to a place where there's no pain, no striving for anything.'

'But how will I manage without you? You are my only friend.'

'You'll make new ones. Girls who won't hold you back like I would.'

'You wouldn't hold me back,' Georgia pleaded with her, clutching Helen's hand and kissing the palm.

'It's the way it has to be,' Helen's eyes seemed like emeralds, set on white velvet. 'Just think of me going somewhere good. Everything I have is yours. In the bottom of the wardrobe is a box. There's something special for you in there.'

She made a choking sound in her throat, a flicker of pain passed across her face, her eyes closed.

Georgia put her finger on the bell. She could hear her own heart pounding with terror, but she was afraid to leave Helen even to summon help.

Sister came running in.

She moved round to the other side of the bed and felt Helen's pulse, her eyes meeting Georgia's tear-filled ones across the tiny redhead.

Helen opened her eyes again slowly.

'Sing to me?'

Helen looked at Sister with wide and troubled eyes. Sister nodded.

'I can't, not in here,' she whispered.

'Please,' Helen's eyes pleaded. 'Just let me hear you one more time?'

It was so quiet in the small room. Georgia was aware of other patients sleeping just the other side of the partition. It seemed all wrong, to sing while her dearest friend slipped away.

'Sing, Georgia,' Sister Hall whispered. 'Forget where you are.'

Georgia took a deep breath to calm herself.

'Summertime. When the living is easy.' Georgia's rich contralto voice rang out around the small room.

'The fish are jumping and the cotton is high. Your pa is rich and mama's good lookin'.' She looked down at Helen, her eyes were still glowing, yet they appeared to be getting dimmer.

'So hush little baby don't ya cry.'

Helen's face was at peace again, her eyes on Georgia, drinking in the words and the music.

'One of these days, you're gonna rise up singin', you're gonna spread your wings and fly to the sky. One of these days you gonna rise up singing. So hush little baby, don't ya cry.'

Georgia felt something in the hand in hers. Not a movement or even a flicker, but she knew without being told Helen had gone.

'No,' she cried out, leaning over to kiss her friend.

'She can't,' she looked up in anguish at the Sister.

Sister silently closed Helen's eyes and put her two

hands together on the sheet. Then she moved round the bed to embrace Georgia.

'I never saw a more beautiful and peaceful death,' she said softly, holding Georgia against her shoulder. 'Your voice and song took her where she wanted to be. Now you must be strong too. She told me about your singing, she was so very proud of you. You must let her be your inspiration. Achieve everything she wanted for you.'

Georgia refused a lift home. London's streets held no terrors for her. It wasn't strangers she had to fear. But people she knew and trusted.

Well she had no one now. Her mother, Peter, and now Helen, all gone.

The dark streets and alleys reflected her feelings. Dark, desolate, empty. Shafts of light here and there from street lamps splayed out an arc of gold light over a small area.

Her life was just like that. A patch of light and happiness, only to go a little further and she was back in the darkness, alone again.

If she had known the risk Helen was taking she would have prevented it somehow. How could Helen have been so foolish if she knew her heart was weak too?

Wearily she climbed the stairs and opened the door of her room.

As she switched on the light, the first thing she saw was the woolly, emerald green shawl Helen put round her shoulders on cold nights.

She picked it up and held it to her face, drinking in the smell of Helen it carried in it, remembering the colour of her eyes.

There was no one to see her now, here alone with all the memories of Helen she could mourn her privately.

Never again would she hear that familiar clonking

sound on the stairs. Or wake to see Helen making tea in her long, white old-fashioned nightdress, her red hair flowing over her shoulders.

So many pictures trapped in her mind like a photograph album.

Helen lying on the bed reading fashion magazines.

'Do you think I could wear my hair like this?' she'd say, holding the glorious mane on top of her head. 'When my leg is normal again I won't need to hide under all this!'

There was the picture too of Helen on the market stall. Fur collar turned up on her russet coat, blowing on her fingers to warm them. Pale cheeks turned pink with the cold wind, her hair escaping in tendrils from her woolly hat as she animatedly teased the customers.

Then there were the nights she didn't work at the club. Those were special nights when they would giggle and chat until the small hours, drinking tea and eating biscuits in bed and Helen would talk about the man she intended to marry.

'He'll have to be big and strong. Dark hair, blue eyes, a sultry look like Elvis. But he'll adore me shamelessly and buy me beautiful clothes and expensive perfume.

'We'll have two children. A boy with dark hair like him and a little girl with red. We'll have a house on Hampstead Heath with a garden full of roses.'

She sank onto Helen's bed, shawl in hands, rocking to and fro with grief, tears cascading down her cheeks. A bellow of rage started within her, filling the room with a terrible sound.

Helen would never find that perfect man, run, dance or make love. She would never know the bliss of a man's arms around her who loved her, or have those children she'd longed for.

It was after three when Georgia finally crawled into bed, her eyes swollen, her heart numb with grief.

*

'Georgia!' she could hear Babs knocking on her door and calling. 'Georgia. Pop's been on the phone and wants to know if you're all right.'

'Come in,' Georgia called out weakly. 'It's not locked.'

'What is it ducks?' Babs came bustling in bringing a smell of fried bacon with her. 'Are you ill?'

'Helen died last night.'

Babs stopped short for a moment, her big mouth dropping open. 'But we only left her at seven!' Her work-reddened hands twitched at the stained apron, her mouth sagged as if suddenly all her teeth were gone.

Georgia had forgotten how long Helen had lived in Bert and Babs's room, and that they thought of her as a daughter. Until now she had been able to feel only her own grief, forgetting she didn't have the monopoly in loving Helen.

Babs's face crumpled, tears welled up in her eyes, hands moving up to conceal them, shoulders heaving.

So often Helen and Georgia had poked fun at Babs. They laughed about the rag-bag collection of clothes she wore, the way her hair never looked clean, and the missing tooth which gave her a curious wobbly smile.

Maybe she wasn't one of the world's great beauties, but now as Georgia saw her grief, she felt ashamed.

'Her heart was weak, it just gave out. She had an infection in her leg too. She died just after midnight.'

Babs's lips shook. She rolled her eyes up to the ceiling.

'Why take 'er?' she said angrily as if addressing God personally.

"Ow did you find out?' Babs whispered, creeping nearer to Georgia across the dim room, reaching out for her hand like a life raft.

'I was with her, a policeman came here for me about eleven.'

'Oh, you poor love,' now she enfolded Georgia in her

arms, rocking her to and fro. 'I know 'ow close you were. We told 'er what you was doing. She was so ashamed she'd thought the worst of you.'

'She was so brave,' Georgia buried her face in Babs's big, soft chest, once again starting to cry. 'She said she didn't mind dying and that I had to do everything we'd talked about for her.'

'Then you must my darlin'.' Babs used that persuasive tone like Celia had, lifting her face up and dabbing at it with the corner of her apron. 'But you've gotta get up and go to work. Sooner or later you'll 'ave to.'

'I know,' Georgia buried her head in Babs's shoulder. 'But I loved her, she was my friend, sister and mother all rolled into one. I don't even know what I should do about her funeral, or anything.'

'Bert and me'll take care of that,' Babs said gently. Her voice, usually so loud, was hardly above a whisper. 'She was our Helen an' all.'

'She said I was to have everything of hers.' Georgia raised a tear-stained face. 'She said there was a box in the wardrobe.'

''Ave you looked in it?' Babs wiped at her own face with a corner of her apron.

'No,' Georgia sniffed. 'I'm kind of afraid to.'

'Well, let's do it together,' Babs said. 'Come on!'

Georgia got out of bed reluctantly. The mirror on the wardrobe door reflected back a sad waif of a girl. Tangled dark hair, red-rimmed eyes, wearing pyjamas that she'd outgrown several months before.

She found the chocolate box decorated with faded purple velvet flowers, tucked away under a pile of old jumpers.

Georgia put it on the table and drew back the curtains.

Babs was lighting the fire.

'Jesus it's cold in 'ere,' Babs said coming back to the

217

table, slapping her raw hands together, eyes glistening with tears. 'Come on, get the lid off!'

There was a letter on the top addressed to Georgia.

Georgia picked it up and looked questioningly at Babs.

'She went prepared, I'd say,' Babs smiled affectionately. 'But she was always one to think everything out.'

Under the letter were three bundles of notes with rubber bands round them.

'There's about sixty quid 'ere,' Babs said in surprise, flicking through the pound and ten shilling notes.

'There's more at the bottom, just change,' Georgia said pulling out handfuls of halfcrowns.

'Read the letter,' Babs urged.

Georgia opened it, her hands shaking.

'Dearest Georgia,

'I feel a bit silly writing this, I keep hoping that when I get out of hospital I can get this out and we both can have a good laugh about it.

'But I've had a feeling for quite some time that I might die. I've got a weak heart and I've been told about the risks. Anyway, I wanted to tell you, just in case I never got a chance to say it to your face, how much I loved you and how happy you made my last year.'

Georgia's eyes misted over, for a moment she couldn't see to read further.

'I never had a family, or a close friend. I'd got so used to being on my own that I didn't even try to make friends anymore. But then you came along, filled up my life with your presence and suddenly I felt wanted and needed.

'If I am dead when you read this I hope you'll be strong and not brood about me or feel guilty in any way.

'Without this last year with you I would have died a lonely person. You enriched my life, you gave me laughter, the joy of sharing and most of all you gave me hope.

'Carry on with your singing, fill the world with your beautiful voice. I'll be watching over you forever now. Watching to see you don't get tempted into bad things, or mix with evil people. I saw a lot of bad things while I worked at the club, gangsters, thieves, drugs and all sorts. Please be careful, don't be too trusting and watch out for men who will try to use you.

'All the money in here is for you. Buy a beautiful dress for your special night, something red, sparkly and flashy, the kind of dress we planned to wear when we were rich. You are probably amazed that I had so much. I had to be really careful when I first came to London and somehow I never got out of the habit.

'Give Bert and Babs my love, thank them for all they did for me. I thought of them as my parents. I wish them a long and happy life.

'Don't cry for me Georgia. I'm happy now and I hope you get everything you've dreamed of.

My love always,
Helen.'

Georgia read the letter and handed it to Babs.

Under the loose change were several photographs. Most were of Helen when she was a child, small, crumpled pictures of a painfully thin child with a mass of hair. There was one professional studio picture, taken before she left the home in Plymouth, her hair up, wearing a print dress with a large white lace collar. With this was a snap taken at Christmas of Helen and Georgia in the market, their arms around each other, laughing.

Georgia remembered the stallholder taking it, but she had never seen the snap until now. She held it out to Babs silently.

'Fancy her sitting and writing all this before she went.' Babs was sobbing now, great tears rolling down her cheeks. She took the picture and looked at it, lifting it to her lips.

'I'm glad you've got this, it's something to really remember her by, you both look so 'appy,' her voice shook and her lips trembled.

'I'll never forget her anyway,' Georgia said brokenly. She scooped up the pictures and the money and put them carefully back. 'Now what shall I do with all this?'

'Exactly what she said,' Babs said firmly. 'She wanted you all dolled-up for that night. You can't disappoint her.'

Chapter 9

A rush of blood to his head, a tingling down his spine made Maxwell Menzies sit up sharply as the girl's voice soared out across the Acropolis.

He hadn't wanted to come tonight. Greek family parties were almost as boring as Jewish ones. But Andreous was his brother-in-law, and Miriam had insisted.

'Summertime!'

The last time he'd heard that song was in New Orleans back in '58 and he defied anyone to surpass the fourteen-stone Negress who had turned his legs to jelly. This girl came close though, she might be young and slender, but her voice had the same depth and passion, and she was better to look at!

Max forgot his drink and Miriam's tiresome family and friends all around him, all he could see and hear was the girl in front of him.

Black curls piled upon her head, fixed with glittery combs to match the long, spangled red dress. A hint of small brown breasts nestling below the plunging neckline, and when she turned, a deep 'V' of naked brown skin made his heart thump. But it was her eyes which held him, so sad and huge, at times glistening with tears.

'This is it, Maxy,' he said to himself. 'You've found the crock of gold.'

*

Few men stood out in a crowd as Max did. It was not merely his rugged tanned face, height, wide shoulders and expensive clothes, but the sheer force of his personality.

As a young man he had flirted with boxing, but he was shrewd enough to know it would get him nothing other than cauliflower ears and a broken nose. He may not have won any titles, but it had left enough of a legend to intimidate his adversaries.

A burst of applause broke round Max as the first number ended.

'That was lovely,' Miriam put one plump, ring-laden hand on his. 'Fancy her just working in Pop's workshop!'

Max glanced across at Pop. The man's eyes were glued to the stage, a smug look of satisfaction on his usually lugubrious features. Max had barely acknowledged this invitation when it arrived several weeks earlier, much less listened to Miriam rattling on about how excited Pop and Andreous were about this girl's voice, but now he wished he'd been attentive.

She was now singing the Everly Brothers' hit, 'Till I kissed you'. It was slower than their version, plucking at his emotions in a way the original never had and as her body swayed with the music, Max found himself slipping into a dream.

The London Palladium, then Vegas and Hollywood. He could see himself in a box looking down at her, hear the applause, see the sparkle of diamonds, smell money. The time was right. American men had dominated the charts for too long. This stunning girl with her powerful voice could be the one to change everything.

Across the same table, Pop too was struggling with his emotions, but unlike Max he had no thoughts of money or power.

Helen's death sent shockwaves throughout the

market. He'd seen Georgia bent to the point of breaking with grief. He hadn't heard her laugh in weeks, her face grey with pain, every line in her body showed the depths of her feeling. Yet somehow she'd found the guts to go on and rehearse.

Right up to the moment she walked on to the stage, Pop had expected her to falter. Yet she'd picked up the microphone as if she was born to it, nodded to the band and straight into 'Summertime' as if she was merely in the workroom. Georgia had more sides than a three-penny bit. But until tonight he hadn't seen this adult and desirable woman.

Her slender body moved sensuously to the beat, eyes flashing, hips undulating in her clingy dress. He couldn't help but wonder if his wife would be quite so maternal to Georgia in future.

Glancing sideways, he saw Christina was as engrossed as the entire audience, one foot tapping, forgetting even her drink in front of her.

It was the last number of the first set. A Peggy Lee number she loved. 'Fever'.

Georgia hadn't copied the original version. Her voice was sweeter, more melodic and she sang it with just enough humour and pace to carry it off magnificently.

The audience applauded wildly.

She was just Georgia again, grinning as confidently as she did in the market. Eyes shining, beads of sweat glistening on that small brown forehead.

Then as if remembering just where she was, she bowed deeply, and ran off stage.

The girls from the workshop were practically jumping out of their seats, yelling and stamping their feet, quite forgetting where they were.

Janet had pulled out all the stops tonight. A long black dress, glittery earrings, like an actress at her première.

She wiped a tear of pride from her cheeks and grinned at the other girls.

'Our little Georgia,' she sniffed. 'I'm so bleedin' proud of her you'd think I trained her!'

'Now that girl's got class. Don't you think so darling?' Max turned to his wife.

'Oh yes,' Miriam gushed, encouraged by his dark eyes studying her so attentively. 'Couldn't you manage her?'

'That's jumping the gun a bit,' he stroked her plump arm softly. 'She might be able to sing amongst her friends, but she's still a bit raw and we don't know anything about her.'

When he married Miriam she had been as slim as Georgia, shiny dark hair with eyes to match. But like most Greek women she had turned to fat, almost as soon as the honeymoon was over. Her place was in the home, a mother and housewife, but tonight she had another purpose.

'Talk to her darling. You know how I trust your judgement about these things!'

'Oh, Maxy,' she cooed. 'What a sweet thing to say!'

Max picked up his glass of brandy and downed it in one.

Miriam could be so simple. Like a trusty dog, wagging its tail after a few kind words, forgetting how often her master stayed away from home and the women his name was linked with.

She knew how to make the best of herself though, despite her weight. Once her dark hair became grey she dyed it a dark auburn, an elaborate 'beehive' style which lengthened her round face and showed off her jewellery to advantage. The black dress she wore tonight was cleverly cut like all her expensive clothes, drawing the eye to her good points and camouflaging the bad. A low neck revealing her smooth olive shoulders and cleavage, sheer chiffon sleeves and draped empire line, hid away the damage a life of ease and plenty had caused.

'She could be the one to change our lives,' Max whispered, running one finger down her arm sensuously. 'But we don't want to get into anything blind.'

Miriam glowed at his words. He had sulked all day about coming. The best she had expected was for him to be pleasant to her family, then insist they leave before the party even got going.

She was only thirteen when her family left Greece and opened the restaurant in Greek Street. Her parents had led her to believe London would be wonderful, but all she saw in her teenage years was drudgery. Up to her elbows in greasy dishes, dark dreary rooms and a school where the other girls laughed at her accent. Pop and Andreous both worked as waiters then, and she knew her father had singled out Andreous for her.

Back in Greece she would have welcomed the handsome young man with his soft eyes and ready laughter, but in London she saw them as a trap.

At seventeen she met Max and suddenly her mind was made up. Here was a man who wanted more out of life than waiting on tables. Little Ruth her younger sister could have Andreous.

Max was a theatrical agent then. Even in his early twenties he showed signs of what was to come. Shrewd, manipulative, with an eye for the main chance. Exciting, not just the way he made her disobey her parents and slip out to meet him, but the way things happened around him.

Faced with the risk of his oldest daughter bringing shame to their family, her father finally agreed to the wedding. Andreous married Ruth and when her father died, he left them the restaurant, and Miriam a few hundred pounds.

Andreous turned the restaurant into a club and barely scraped a living out of it. But Max used Miriam's money to launch himself into the music world. He went to America and found talent, bringing them back to England and putting them on the road.

At twenty-three Max had been lean and hungry looking. But twenty years on, money, another stone in weight, he was in his prime. Sensuous, hooded eyes and fleshy lips promised passion. Thick black hair streaked with grey, detracted the eye from his Roman nose. A man who knew the effect he had on women and used it shamelessly. The handmade silk shirts, Italian shoes and his ostentatious jewellery were unnecessary adornments. No one ever forgot Max Menzies.

By the second set Georgia was getting into her stride. Her voice had a new maturity and range. Notes of caressing sweetness, mingled with shots of raw emotion that kept her audience spellbound.

'When I fall in love', had them wiping a tear from their eyes. 'The Locomotion' made their feet itch to dance, and finally when she burst into 'Wonderful World' she wrenched the last dregs of emotion from everyone.

Andreous was more than happy. His sophisticated and cool customers who rarely even acknowledged the entertainment were standing up to clap and cheer this young girl.

To think he had expected the evening to do little more than break even! They were all ordering drinks like there was no tomorrow, all because this young girl's voice had touched a sensitive spot.

Georgia mopped the sweat off her face and shoulders in the dressing room and turned to the men in the quartet.

'Thank you all so much,' she said simply. They were

packing up their instruments, obviously in a hurry to leave. 'I couldn't have got through it without you.'

She saw the exchanged glances. Four middle-aged men who'd seen everything and got credit for nothing.

'You've got what it takes,' Jack the pianist smiled. 'But a word of warning. There's a lot of sharks out there. Watch what you're doing.'

'Yes sir!' she grinned. 'But tell me how do I know the sharks from the nice fish?'

'Extravagant promises,' he turned away to pack up his music. 'Now go on, be off with you and enjoy yourself.'

'I hope we get to be together again,' Georgia couldn't find the right words to explain how much she owed her success to them.

'So do we,' Jack touched her shoulder. 'Tonight was a real pleasure.'

Greek music wafted round the club. One wall was covered in a mural of a Greek town, white houses like sugar cubes underneath a turquoise sky. Candles dripping on to bottles on every table, the vine-covered pergola round the bar all gave an impression they were far away from London.

Janet and Sally were already up on the dance floor joining two snake-hipped waiters in Greek dancing. Georgia waved to them, then went over to join Pop, Andreous and their families.

'This is my sister-in-law Miriam,' Andreous said after he'd hugged her and introduced his teenage sons, and Pop's five daughters.

'I thought you were marvellous,' Miriam said, her double chin quivering with emotion. 'I had to find a hanky at the last song. You must tell me all about yourself.'

Georgia liked Miriam. Warmth and understanding flowed out of her, reminding her just a little of her own mother. Her dark eyes twinkled, her jewellery was dazzling and before Georgia knew it she was telling her all about her room, Helen and her hopes to be a professional singer.

'You'll get there,' Miriam nodded. 'You've got all the right qualities. Your mother must be so proud of you Georgia, is she here tonight?'

'My parents are dead.'

She didn't know why she said that. Was it pique because she'd had no word from Peter or Celia? Or protecting herself from the past?

'I'm sorry darling,' Miriam leaned closer to her drowning her in expensive perfume. 'You are very young to be alone.'

But even reminders about being alone couldn't hurt her tonight. A photographer took her picture, men in evening dress kept coming up to kiss her. Women in beautiful dresses stopped by to compliment her. Finally the grey miserable feeling she'd had since Helen's death was actually fading.

'You were very good.' A deep voice behind her made her turn and look up.

For a moment Georgia couldn't reply.

He was the most handsome man she'd ever seen. Making her think of thirties filmstars. His dinner-jacket fitted perfectly, his pin-tucked shirt like the kind she'd seen in glossy magazines. Pop had a clip-on bow tie, but Max's was the real thing. He was a human black panther, sleek, just a little flashy and perhaps dangerous.

'Thank you,' she blushed.

'This is my husband, Max.' She heard Miriam speak but could barely tear her eyes from his face.

'May I?' He pulled up a chair, forcing his wife to move along. 'I expect someone will grab you any moment for a dance, but I just wanted to say how much I enjoyed your performance.'

He talked about everything and yet nothing, his hooded eyes never leaving her face. The only clear thing she remembered later was when he spoke of managing bands and artists.

It was obvious he made money out of it, just one look at the gold watch on his wrist, the shirt and suit said it all.

'Come and dance?' he said later, holding out a hand.

'I hope Miriam doesn't mind,' Georgia said as he scooped her into his arms. She felt uncomfortably aware of his big hard body against hers and she could see his wife watching them.

'She's delighted to have a chat with Andreous and Ruth', he smiled down at her, his big hand lightly touching the naked skin on her back, sending shivers down her spine. 'They all gabble away in Greek the moment I'm out of earshot. Anyway you're the star tonight.'

'I like Miriam,' she said weakly.

'And so do I,' he smiled, showing flashing white teeth. 'We've been married for twenty years. She doesn't have to worry when I dance with a beautiful girl.'

'Do you think the songs I picked were right for me?' she asked. She was very aware of the touch of his hand, his chin brushing her hair. She didn't want to be so aware of him, she wanted him to talk about her future.

'I'd like to hear you sing some good soul music,' he said, smiling down at her. 'More up-to-date stuff. But only you know the sort of music that inspires you. You are the artist, not me.'

It was after four when Georgia finally got home.

As she unzipped the red dress and hung it up she felt a sudden pang of fear. Supposing nothing did come of tonight? How could she spend another year making dresses?

Then there was Max. He'd been watching her with more than just passing interest. What she couldn't gauge was if that interest was professional, or personal.

She knew now with utter certainty that she was born to sing. If only her feelings about Max were as clean cut!

'It's Miriam Menzies on the phone,' Pop shouted out into the workroom. 'Come and take it in my office.'

Two weeks had passed since the night at the Acropolis. A small photograph of her in a music paper and then nothing. Night after night spent alone in her room staring at the red spangly dress, watching her dream fade.

Georgia came back into the workshop looking stunned.

'What did she want?' Janet switched off her machine and the others all followed suit.

'She's invited me to go shopping with her on Saturday and lunch afterwards.'

'Beats the casting couch routine,' Sally sniggered, leaning forward to listen.

'But why?' Georgia turned puzzled eyes on Janet. 'Does this mean something?'

Janet shrugged.

'She's softening you up,' Sally smirked.

'For Max?' Janet looked round sharply at her friend. 'I'd think 'e was capable of doing that 'imself. I'd be his for a gin and tonic.'

'Did she mention him?' Sally asked.

Georgia shook her head.

'Well girl,' Janet smiled. 'At least you'll get a free lunch. I bet that Miriam don't eat in Wimpy bars!'

Chapter 10

'Almost Millionaires Row,' Georgia whispered to herself as she hurried along the tree-lined Hampstead avenue. Big detached houses set in neat gardens, gleaming cars on gravel drives. Images of au pairs, tennis clubs and holidays abroad. 'Max must be stinking rich.'

The Menzies's house was mock Georgian. Double-fronted with a glossy, navy blue door and brass coach lamps.

Taking a deep breath, she walked up to the front door, the gravel scrunching under her feet, intensely aware of her shabby navy suit and run-down shoes.

A girl opened the door, smiling welcomingly.

'You must be Georgia?' she said. 'Come on in, Mrs Menzies won't be a moment.'

She was only a little older than Georgia, fair, with polished skin and an accent that suggested she could be Dutch or German. The plain black dress wasn't a uniform, but it had the same effect.

'Take a seat,' she said, ushering Georgia into the sitting room, then disappeared down the hall to the back of the house.

The room was huge. The morning sun bathed the baby grand piano in the front window, glass doors led on to the garden at the back. The sort of room her mother would have described as 'More money than taste', but Georgia was impressed.

A shaggy carpet curled round her feet. She looked around at luxurious fat couches with matching footstools, and huge exotic flower arrangements. Paintings with heavy gilt frames. A mahogany wall unit displaying family photographs encased in silver, along with a collection of porcelain figurines.

The house was silent, just the tick of a clock from the hall and birdsong from the garden. Georgia perched on the edge of a chair, taking careful note of everything, from the heavy curtains with tasselled pelmets to the imitation twin chandeliers.

Miriam swept into the room wearing a blue silk dress, she looked pretty despite her bulk, and she smelled as exotic as her choice of flowers.

'Hallo, dear,' she said, sitting down for a minute as she checked her bag, and patted her elaborate hairstyle. Georgia was pretty sure it wasn't her real colour, for the dark, burnished auburn didn't go with her dark eyes or eyebrows. It was swept up on to the top of her head, a mass of carefully arranged curls.

'I thought we'd go to Kensington,' she said as she applied a touch more lipstick. 'How do you feel now after your debut?'

Her plump hands were covered in rings, so many that Georgia wondered how she bent her fingers. Her nails were very long, painted a vivid pink to match her lips.

'I'm not sure,' Georgia felt a little awkward. 'I want something more to happen I guess.'

'It will,' Miriam stood up again, smoothing down her skirt, arranging a large, gold twisted chain round her plump neck. 'Max's meeting us for lunch, but let's forget that now. I love shopping, nothing better for giving one a boost.'

Somehow Georgia had assumed they would go by bus or tube. She hadn't considered Miriam could drive, much less whisk her into a sleek black Rover, with seats like armchairs.

Miriam attacked the shops like someone seeing food for the first time in weeks. She bought a cashmere sweater, stockings and a black cocktail dress without even checking the prices and all the time she chatted.

Greece, holidays abroad, her two teenage boys. Between bursts she fired questions at Georgia and pointed out her favourite shops.

'I don't want you to be offended,' Miriam said briskly as she whisked Georgia into the younger woman's department in Barkers, 'but I'm going to buy you something nice as a present.'

'That's very kind of you,' Georgia almost stammered. 'But I hardly know you.'

'Nonsense,' Miriam's eyes were already scanning the rails. 'I have my motives. I want Max to offer to be your manager. Now we can hardly impress him with you wearing that suit can we?'

Georgia blushed scarlet.

'Don't look like that,' Miriam wheedled, putting one plump bejewelled hand under Georgia's chin and lifting it. 'You look fine for an interview for an office job, but entertainers have to sparkle. You wouldn't think twice if I was your mother.'

'No, but –'

Miriam's nose flared.

'No buts. I'm good with clothes and I know exactly what you need.' Her tone implied there was to be no further argument. 'Now a nice dress with a jacket. Something snazzy.'

Georgia watched helplessly as Miriam pulled out garment after garment. Each one of these outfits cost more than she earned in six weeks.

'We want something that won't date,' Miriam pushed aside all the dresses with billowing net underskirts. 'And a jacket you can wear with other things.'

The assistant's arms were piled high. Black, red, blue and pink, stripes, spots and plain colours.

'We'll try all these,' she pushed Georgia into the changing room. 'I think that black and white one is right for you, but we'll see.'

To Georgia everything was perfect. The size, the colours, but she hated Miriam watching her as she stood in her greying white bra and pants.

'Put that one on again,' Miriam lifted down the one she'd mentioned earlier.

It was more sophisticated than the others. A silky low-necked dress in swirly black and white patterns, hugging Georgia's slim figure as if it was made for her. A short white jacket went over it, turning a dress that was made for dancing, into an outfit suitable for anything from church to an office.

Mirian dug one pink-nailed finger into her plump cheek and looked thoughtful.

'That's it,' she said turning to the assistant. 'Would you mind cutting off the tags? She'll wear it now.'

The embarrassment grew as Miriam whisked her down into the shoe department and insisted she had a pair of Charles Jourdan black court shoes with two inch heels.

'They're an investment,' she waved away Georgia's protest. 'If I have my way you'll be dancing all night soon. You can't do that if your feet hurt. Besides, if Max takes you on you'll soon be buying clothes much nicer than these things.'

Georgia's eyes strayed to her image as they passed a huge mirror on the way back to the ground floor.

She could easily pass for a model now. Elegant and poised. Her brown skin set off the white jacket, her hair tumbling over her shoulders stopped the outfit looking too matronly.

'What do you see?' Miriam said softly at her elbow.

'I look kind of glamorous,' Georgia giggled.

'No, you look beautiful,' Miriam smiled. 'The glamour bit we have to work on. Your nails need shaping properly, you need lessons in make-up and grooming, but if I'm right about you, one day there'll be a million young girls copying you.'

Miriam stopped by the perfume counter and sprayed her with Chanel No 5.

'The finishing touch,' she explained. 'Now let's go and meet Max. Don't tell him about the dress and shoes, this is our little secret.'

'Why?'

'You know what men are like.' Miriam wrinkled her nose. 'He'll think I'm spoiling you.'

'Is Max interested in me?' Georgia felt bold enough to ask as they crossed the busy High Street and made their way towards the parked car. Miriam puzzled her, it felt like a genuinely motherly act of kindness, yet she couldn't help suspecting a hidden motive.

'I'm not quite sure,' Miriam frowned a little. 'He was impressed by your voice, but that isn't always enough.' She paused to unlock the car boot, took Georgia's bag and put it inside with her dress bag.

'Let me tell you something about my Max,' she looked up at Georgia as she relocked it, pausing with one plump hand on the shiny paintwork. 'He's got a reputation as a hard man. You'll meet people that will tell you all sorts of bad things about him. They say he's cruel, unscrupulous, that he'd kill his granny for ten shillings.'

'Would he?' Georgia's eyes were as big as saucers.

'Maybe for a hundred pounds,' Miriam chuckled. 'But what few people will admit is, that he is the best. Maybe not the fairest, or the gentlest, but he's the best because he's tough. And if he decides he is going to make you a star, you will be.'

Miriam stepped back on the pavement and linked her arm through Georgia's.

'You won't be alone though,' she squeezed Georgia's arm. 'I'll be around too. Just remember I'm your friend. You can come to me if you have any problems.'

'I like you,' Georgia said impulsively. She could remember her mother conspiring with her about her father just like this. Somehow it made it all seem safe.

'And I like you too,' Miriam smiled.

Miriam was seething with contradictory emotions. She really did like Georgia, yet still she set her up. Soothing her with maternal advice, stimulating her greed for the 'good life'. Now she was leading the girl into the final trap, and by tea-time she would be just another of her husband's assets. Max would be pleased with her, but just this once she wished she hadn't complied with his instructions.

Harvey's in Church Street oozed quiet, expensive charm. Dark green paintwork with cream lace curtains on brass rails and windows as shiny as mirrors.

Miriam swept in leaving Georgia to follow nervously.

'Good afternoon, Mrs Menzies,' the headwaiter, a thin, whey-faced man glided towards them, a napkin over one arm. 'Mr Menzies is waiting for you.'

Georgia felt rather than saw the dark oak panelling, the cosy booths for intimate meals. All she could focus on was Max getting up from his table by the window, the width of his shoulders and a flash of white teeth.

She was out of her depth now. Foreign waiters, French menus. Even her new clothes couldn't hide the fact she had never been anywhere so grand before.

'Hullo,' he said taking Georgia's hand firmly and leading her to the table as if understanding her fears. 'Has Miriam spent all my money?'

'Only one little dress,' Miriam simpered, kissing him on the cheek.

'Do you like chicken?' Max asked once the waiter had tucked in her chair.

'Yes,' Georgia's voice was little more than a squeak.

He looked even more handsome in his light grey suit and she was sure she couldn't eat a thing, much less choose.

'Shall I order for you?' His big hand touched her briefly, like a secret message that he understood her fear. 'When I was your age I'd never eaten anywhere except at home.'

Once the meal arrived Georgia forgot her nervousness. Max told her a funny story about their son David getting lost in Barker's when he was small and how Miriam had wailed like a banshee until he was found, then amazed everyone by pulling down his trousers and smacking his bottom publicly.

'David won't ever go in there now,' Miriam added. 'He's sure someone will remember him.'

There was something very reassuring in hearing such stories, soon both Max and Miriam were just another set of loving parents and Georgia found herself reciprocating with tales about Pop's workroom.

'Miriam tells me you've no parents.' Max probed so gently she barely noticed it. 'Do you mind telling me what happened to them?'

'I don't know anything about either of them,' she said. 'The records were lost, all I had was a name. Later on I was fostered.'

'I wondered how you got to speak so nicely,' Max's thick lips spread into a wide flashing smile. 'Do you keep in touch?'

'No. They split up after I left, it's not the same anymore.'

'That's sad,' Max sighed. 'A girl of your age should have a family.'

'At least it leaves me free to do as I like,' she said quickly.

'And what is that?' Max enquired.

'Sing again as soon as possible,' Georgia dug into an ice-cream sundae with childish relish.

For a moment or two there was silence. Georgia sensed Miriam was imploring Max with her eyes, but she hardly dared look up.

Despite the couple's caring interest, Georgia knew this lunch had a real purpose. Was Max going to help her? Or had she blown it all by being too flippant?

Power seeped out of him like a strange perfume. A tiny bell was ringing at the back of her head, warning her to get advice before she made, or let anyone else make any decisions. But who could she go to? Miriam had already told her he was the best!

'I've been giving you a lot of thought,' Max spoke slowly, twisting his big gold ring around his carefully manicured finger. 'But one thing bothers me.'

'What's that?' Georgia said eagerly, wiping her mouth on a serviette.

'Your lack of experience,' he said, his thick dark eyebrows almost meeting as he frowned. 'I mean, your voice is superb, you move well and you have stage presence. But to make it in the music business you have to tour with a band putting on a complete entertainment.'

'How do I find a band?' Georgia's heart sank. She didn't know anyone other than Andreous's quartet. Was Max trying to put her off?

'Well I do have a band on my books which could be the one.' He pulled a notebook out of his pocket and studied it. 'Samson have a singer already, but he's the weak link,' he looked at Georgia again, his eyes narrowing. 'Unfortunately they are all very loyal to him. I've tried to make them part company with him before.'

'But Georgia needn't be a threat to him,' Miriam leaned forward at the table, lightly touching Georgia's hand as if to reassure her. Her dark eyes bore into her husband as if willing him to find a way round the problem. 'Why couldn't Georgia sing and Ian do the harmonies and backing vocals?'

238

'It might work,' Max beamed at his wife. 'A girl as pretty as Georgia would enhance the whole band.'

'How much work would this involve?' Georgia asked, excitement bubbling up inside her. 'I mean would I have to give up my job?'

'Certainly,' Max smiled at her naïvety. 'Once you'd met them there would be rehearsals. Then off on the road. They play six nights a week now.'

'Where?' she asked.

'All over.'

'But where would I sleep?'

'In digs while you're away,' he said with a slight touch of amusement. 'But living where you do would be handy for the London gigs.'

'Gigs?'

'That's the musician's word for a job,' he said. 'But really the first step Georgia is for you to decide whether you want me to be your manager or not.'

There was an expectant silence.

'I don't really understand what that means,' she said carefully.

'It means I arrange all your jobs, pay you, organize transportation, publicity and countless other things.'

'It means he virtually becomes your father,' Miriam's maternal, wobbly-chinned smile was reassuring. 'He looks out for you and guides you through all the problems.'

'What do you get out of it then?' Even at the risk of appearing rude and ungrateful something told her she mustn't agree too readily.

'A percentage,' he smiled, but his hooded eyes seemed a little colder now. 'Very little now, but one day when you go out for big money, I'll get my reward.'

'But how much will I get now?' Her voice dropped. 'I mean I have to pay my rent and everything.'

Max laughed then, disarming her.

'This is all hypothetical remember. I haven't got the band to agree yet. But how does fifteen a week sound?'

'Pounds?' Georgia's eyes flew open in amazement.

'Well, of course,' he replied.

Georgia stared at him. That was more than twice the amount Pop paid her!

'But what happens if the public don't like me. I don't get to make a record or anything?'

Max shrugged his shoulders.

'That's my problem,' he said. 'Do you think I got where I am today by backing losers?'

Miriam smiled, reaching forward and taking Georgia's hands.

'Grab it with both hands,' she said gently, her dark eyes full of excitement. 'Chances like this come just once. I'm sure you don't want to spend your life running up dresses?'

Georgia sat for a moment looking from one to the other.

Miriam was motherly, a woman like her wouldn't lead her into anything bad. Max might be sharp, but just to look at him was to stare success in the face.

'All right,' she smiled. 'I'd like you as a manager.'

'Welcome to our family Georgia,' Max beamed, taking her hand and shaking it firmly. 'Once I've talked to the boys in the band we'll get an agreement drawn up. Meanwhile I think champagne is called for.'

Max's big hands gripped the steering wheel to control his mounting excitement. She could really sing, she was beautiful, but best of all she was alone!

Stage-door Mamas were his bête noire. Hanging around, poking their noses in his business, demanding this and that and producing lawyers if he didn't comply.

He wouldn't even need hype this time. Georgia had the face, the body and the voice. She wasn't going to be a one hit wonder, the darling of the kids in youth clubs for two months, then dropped like a stone. No, Georgia was going to line his walls with gold records.

'A "Roller", a mansion in the country,' he said aloud, turning his driving mirror so he could see himself. 'Well Maxy, the sky's the limit this time. Straight up, no messing!'

When Max was onto something he wasted no time. After saying goodbye to his wife and Georgia he was straight off to Birmingham to see 'Samson'. They liked playing 'The Coconut Club', it was Saturday night with a day off tomorrow, all excellent reasons for them to be in a receptive mood.

Seven unambitious lads from the East End and every one of them a first class musician. They'd paid their dues in London pubs and youth clubs, all they wanted out of life was a regular wage, a bit more crumpet and someone to organize them. Too loyal to split up and join bands with a name. Too thick to realize their own potential.

Ian McShane was their leader and singer. Max had plans for him at first, his pretty-boy blond looks could have given singers like Ricky Nelson a run for their money. But despite his gentle charm, Ian was an obstinate young cuss. He wouldn't play bubble-gum music, not even for the lures that Max put out. He had an obsession about soul music and that was exactly why Max wanted Georgia to join them.

The beaten-up old van was parked outside the club. The equipment all ready inside. Max brushed past the doorman with a few words and went into the club.

Why exactly it was called The Coconut Club, eluded him, as apart from a cut-out wooden palm tree outside it had no exotic aspirations. Inside it was like a catacomb, with small cave-like seating areas leading off the dance floor. The stage was at the far end, with a long bar which reached all down one wall.

Max took a seat tucked away behind an archway. In a well-positioned mirror he could see Ian crawling around the stage checking wires, but to Max's surprise they were almost ready.

Now with the main lights on, the club looked shabby. White walls gone yellow with smoke, velvet seats with no pile left, drink-ringed tables and a sticky, dirty carpet. Yet in an hour or two it would be transformed with subdued lighting, and five or six hundred kids looking for the Saturday night dream.

'One, two, three, testing,' came the inevitable cry over the PA.

'It seems all right,' Ian shouted to the boys. 'Let's get the balance now, then we can go for a few jars.'

The usual high pitched whine. Les and Patrick tuning up and John flexing his fingers on the trumpet valves.

The organ came in, a crashing from the drums and then they started to play.

It never ceased to surprise Max that these boys could actually unpack a van full of heavy equipment, with miles of wiring, cart it into a club or pub and within half an hour create a decent sound. The drums alone looked like a Chinese jigsaw puzzle to unravel. There were endless extension leads, lights and jack plugs. Yet, at the end of the evening they would pack it all away carefully, no matter how much they'd had to drink, only to repeat the performance the next night somewhere else.

They were all in their early twenties, all too thin and unhealthy looking, not a muscle between the lot of them.

A bunch of underfed dogs, that's what they reminded him of. Mongrels with more courage and persistence than brain. All too keen to lick his hands for a titbit. On a long leash they were happy. A kick up the backside now and then to show them who was boss, then brush them up, show them off and they gave him undying loyalty.

In a year Max had learned little about them individually. At times he even had difficulty remembering their names. But then it was always Ian who spoke for them.

He was leaning lazily on the microphone. Butter-yellow hair falling into his eyes, pale skin and soft girlish mouth. It was a shame his voice wasn't that hot. He could have been a real matinée idol. He wasn't a wanker like the rest of the bunch. A bit weak, a gentleman, but a likeable lad for all that.

Rod the drummer should have been their leader. He had the height, arrogance and charisma Ian lacked. His angular, almost Red Indian features drew the eye, his glossy black hair, his lean frame were a trap for any woman under fifty. Sometimes Max had an uneasy feeling this lad was biding his time, waiting for his moment.

The others he lumped together. Anaemic looking, sharp East End faces. In their scruffy jeans and plimsolls they could be the boys he grew up with.

Sometimes when he watched the lads performing, Max wished he was in their shoes. Girls looking up adoringly, already damp with excitement. By the interval they were ripe. One drink, a little snogging and before the equipment was packed those fresh-faced girls were waiting with their knickers in their handbags. He might have the money and the flash car, he might even promise a night in a swish hotel, but he still had to take knickers off manually.

'That's it lads,' Ian called out. 'Down the pub.'

Max got up from his seat.

'Ye gods, it's the boss,' Norman leapt down from his organ and landed on the dance floor. 'Hallo Max, what brings you up here?'

Norman was an irritating little know-all, with red hair and freckles, the boy he liked least.

'To watch you,' Max said easily. 'Find out what I'm wasting my money on.'

'We're going over to the pub,' Les said. 'Are you coming?'

Les was the most easy going, possibly the dimmest of the bunch, with rounded shoulders, sallow skin and a hooked nose. Right now he had a spot on his greasy chin that flashed as vividly as a Christmas tree light.

'Why not?' Max grinned, 'I'll even do the buying!'

Once at the pub Max humoured them by listening to the same old complaints. The van that overheated, no new sheet music for Norman. Why couldn't they have new band suits, and some time off?

'Have you finished?' he said, looking from one to another, fixing them with his bright eyes. 'I didn't come all this way to have my ears bashed!'

'Go on,' Norman said. 'What is it this time? Have we used too much petrol?'

'No,' Max waited until he had their full attention. 'Have you ever wondered why you've never been approached by a record company?'

There was a nodding of heads all round. Speedy, the bass player stuck his head over Rod's shoulder and grinned inanely.

'It's not because you aren't good enough musically, but because the voice isn't there,' Max said firmly.

Max noted how Ian's face blanched, his blue eyes grew darker, his lip curled.

'Are you saying you want me replaced?'

'Not replaced, added to,' Max had to be careful not to antagonize Ian, after all he only intended them to train Georgia. 'If I could show you a girl singer who could blow the socks off everyone in the room, what would you say?'

'Do we all get to shag her in the van too?' John said dryly.

'She's not that type,' Max replied. John was better known for his irreverent humour than his classy trumpet solos. His brooding dark eyes were watching Max closely, missing nothing.

'Then she's definitely out,' Norman broke into a high-pitched shriek of laughter.

'I'm serious,' Max looked round at each of the boys, that 'Trust me because I know best' look he had perfected. 'I don't want to replace Ian. He has a big following with your girl fans, and he keeps you lot in order. But this girl will enhance everything you do. She's young, pretty and a fantastic singer, and if you've got half a brain, you'll let her rehearse with you and see what you think.'

'Can we just have a moment to talk about it?' Ian said, he looked at each of his friends in silent appeal.

'Fair enough,' Max got up from his stool. 'I'll give you ten minutes.'

He would have given anything to stay and hear what they were saying. Instead he took his drink to the other end of the bar and watched them from a distance.

'I don't like it,' Rod said immediately Max was out of earshot. His dark eyes flashed with anger. 'He's got something up his sleeve.'

'He's an arsehole,' John scowled. 'This is the first step to kicking Ian out.'

'He can't get rid of Ian,' Speedy smirked. His nickname came from his slow, lethargic attitude. But he was the only one of them that had left school with any qualifications. 'We've got a contract with him as a complete band.'

Ian flashed a look of gratitude at Speedy. He looked and acted thick because it suited him to do so, but despite appearances, he was as sharp as a razor.

'Thank, lads,' Ian said softly. 'Max is no fool. He

must have found someone special. If she's as good as he thinks she is, she may be the one to help us, too.'

'I don't want no fucking girl hanging out with us,' Norman stuck out his pointed chin defiantly. 'It'll be a drag and you know it. It's probably some tart he fancies and she'll be running back to him with stories.'

'Possibly,' Ian said. 'But on the other hand she could be what we need. Max is right. I ain't got a brilliant voice. There's nothing to separate us from a thousand other bands. Why don't we agree to an audition? Nothing more. If we hate her, if she's his bit on the side, we'll refuse. He can't make us take her.'

'But if she is good,' John surprised them by speaking up. 'Maybe we can swing it to make a record.'

'And you Rod?' Ian knew his old friend only too well, if he didn't agree at this stage, there'd be trouble later.

'It's your funeral,' Rod's slanty eyes flashed a warning message to each of them. 'Girls are trouble. We'll be fighting over who's going to screw her. She might even be Max's tart. But I'll agree to an audition. On our own, without Max sitting in. We'll discuss it further when we've heard her.'

Ian raised his hand, Max sauntered back.

'Well?' He turned back to the bar, to order another round of drinks.

'An audition, just us and her,' Ian said. 'We're not going to agree to anything till then.'

'Fair enough,' Max smiled. 'Monday week at the usual place.'

Georgia was filled with self doubt.

On Saturday everything seemed perfect. But once she got home, doubts began to crowd her mind.

How could she even think of getting up on a stage and singing with seven men she didn't know. Living with them in digs, travelling hundreds of miles. She knew nothing about men and Brian kept popping back into her head.

She thought it was over, but now alone in her room he came back. His mouth slobbering on hers, his fingers digging into her arms and thighs. If a man she trusted could do that, how much more could a strange man do?

On Monday morning Max rang her before she'd even had time to sit down and start work.

'I've talked to the boys, and they are happy for you to join them,' he said, in that clipped decisive way he had. 'I'm booking a rehearsal room for next Monday, can you make it?'

'Yes,' she said looking across the room at Pop, wondering how she could just tell him she was leaving.

'Good. I want you to come to my office today, about five thirty. I've got some records here I want you to listen to. I'll talk to you then about everything.'

Pop didn't know whether to laugh or cry when she told him her news.

'I'm happy for you, my sweet,' he said chucking her under her chin. 'This place won't be the same without you.'

'I'll be popping in to see you,' she said leaning her face against his shoulder and holding him.

'That's what I was afraid you'd say,' he teased her. 'Just don't make it too often?'

He had his reservations about Max, even if Miriam was an old friend. It was no secret he screwed every performer he got his hands on. But in the same way London had beckoned to him as a boy, the music world was calling to Georgia.

Janet listened carefully as Georgia recounted every detail of her day with the Menzies. She could see under Georgia's excitement there was something troubling her.

'Out with it!' she said as she found Georgia alone at

lunchtime in the tiny room adjoining the toilets. 'Did Max make a pass?'

'No,' Georgia giggled.

Janet sat on the broken chair and lit up a cigarette.

They were all reluctant to see Georgia leave. In Janet's case it was a protective instinct. Georgia was only a child, still limping mentally from what that man had done to her. 'Come off it, love!' she raised one eyebrow. 'I know you've got the screaming hab-dabs about something. What is it?'

'I'm just a bit worried about being alone with seven men,' Georgia giggled and looked at her hands.

Janet studied the younger girl as she sat on a bale of cloth, one leg tucked beneath her. She looked so pretty and fresh, the excitement of the phone call had put a pink glow in her cheeks, matching her gingham dress. Her hair curling over her shoulders like a doll in a toy shop. Somehow she had to give Georgia confidence, yet warn her gently too.

'You must make it clear from the start that you aren't available,' Janet said carefully. 'Men aren't all rapists. But most of them will seize any opportunity going!'

'How do I do that?' Georgia's eyes were full of fright.

'Keep your distance,' Janet puffed thoughtfully. 'Get to know them individually. Men as friends are more truthful than women I've found. Don't have a dabble with one of them unless you're sure he's the right one.'

'How do I know that?' She leaned forward to Janet, taking her hand. 'I'm scared.'

'When it's right you'll know,' Janet smiled, stroking Georgia's face. 'Pick someone gentle and caring. Mother nature will do everything else.'

'I wonder if I'll ever be as wise as you,' Georgia said wistfully.

'Wisdom comes through suffering or old age,' Janet smiled. 'Don't wish either of them on yourself.'

*

Max's office was in an elegant town house in Berkeley Square. Smart iron railings, white steps led up to gleaming mahogany double doors. Up a graceful thickly-carpeted staircase with polished wood banisters to a door marked 'Menzies Enterprises'.

A receptionist sat just inside. She barely looked up and continued to paint her nails a vivid pink.

'Yes?'

'I've an appointment with Mr Menzies,' Georgia said in a small voice.

'He's with someone,' the girl said rudely. 'Sit down and wait.'

It seemed to Georgia that she was there for hours, but at least it gave her an opportunity to look around.

Beyond the sulky, dark receptionist and her switchboard, she could see several rooms going off the corridor. In one a girl was busy typing, another girl beside her was getting the post ready.

The whole place was decorated in mossy green with white doors. Autographed photographs hung on every wall. Brenda Lee, Gene Vincent, Shirley Bassey and Jerry Lee Lewis.

A door opened further along the passage and she heard Max's voice boom out, breaking the silence.

'An audition won't be necessary I assure you,' he was saying to someone she couldn't see. 'I didn't get an office in Mayfair by selling crappy bands.'

A small man in a grey suit came scurrying back along the corridor, he looked at Georgia and nodded.

'You can go in now,' the receptionist still didn't look at Georgia. 'The far end of the corridor.'

Max was sitting behind a huge desk as Georgia looked round the door tentatively. The window behind him overlooked the square.

'Sit down,' he said, waving a cigar towards a chair and opening a desk diary.

Thick carpets, solid wood furniture and a huge cocktail bar in one corner, were even more evidence of his success.

Georgia looked up, a strange creepy sensation tickling the back of her neck.

In one corner of the room was a gold spider's web, complete with large gold spider, advancing on a gold fly.

Max put the diary down, glancing up to see what she was looking at.

'Do you like it?' he asked. 'It's real gold.'

'I think it's awful,' she said and immediately blushed scarlet at her rudeness.

'It cost a fortune,' he said in its defence, his thick lips curling a little. 'I designed it myself.'

'I'm sure it's very clever and beautifully made,' she was almost trying to apologize. 'I just don't like spiders. They give me the creeps.'

Max got up and went over to the bar.

'Like a drink?' he said, over his shoulder.

She knew he was insulted. Just the stiffness in those wide shoulders warned her.

'Just an orange juice,' she said. 'I can't stay long.' She hadn't anywhere to go. It was just something to say, but the moment the words were out of her mouth she knew that was wrong too.

He wheeled round, an angry flush across his cheeks. He reached her in two giant strides and put one great paw on her small shoulder.

'I think we have to get one thing straight,' he said gruffly. 'If I'm to spend time, trouble and money on you, I expect total commitment from you. You sing when I make bookings for you, even when your grandmother has invited you out for tea. You don't tell me you have other plans!'

Until now Georgia had thought her days of being answerable to anyone were over. But one look at Max's stern face told her this wasn't so.

His jacket was off, draped over a chair, she saw the double 'M' monogram on his silk shirt, glanced up at the gold spider, and felt a tremor of fear.

Even his face wasn't so inviting. He had dark stubble on the strong chin, his mouth looked bad-tempered and tough, every line in his big frame told her this man would be nothing like Pop.

'I'm sorry,' she said. 'I didn't mean to hurry you or anything. And I won't ever let you down.'

'Have you got a boyfriend?' his dark eyes narrowed, looking right into hers.

'No,' she said, feeling very uncomfortable.

'Well that's something. I don't want you preoccupied with any man at this stage.' He sat down again at his desk, tilting back his seat, playing with a pencil.

'I'm only serious about singing,' she said, wishing she dared to tell him it was none of his business.

'That's good,' he said, a faint smile playing at his lips. 'You see Georgia, joining a band isn't like any other job. These boys will soon be like your family. If you can't get on with them, really like them, you won't bring out the best in one another.'

'I understand that.'

'You may think you do now,' he smirked. 'Just wait until you've put up with smelling their socks. Listened to them farting in the van. Watched them snogging with girls when you are anxious to get home. That's the stuff that takes the fun out of it.'

Georgia tried hard to look serene. She was sure he was exaggerating.

'I'll cope,' she said, more confidently than she felt.

'Now for the music,' he picked up a small pile of records. 'I want you to play these until you know every word. We haven't got the music for these songs, the boys play them by ear. Make sure you really know them by next week.'

'I haven't got a record player,' she whispered.

Max looked up, surprise on his face. 'You're joking? All kids have record players!'

'I can't afford one,' she replied, wringing her hands together, wishing she was anywhere but here alone with Max.

She felt him move, coming round to sit on his desk in front of her. For a moment he said nothing, just looking down at her.

Max had that same feeling he'd had in the Acropolis. A tightening in his gut, a prickle in his heart. She looked so pretty, like a little Sunday school teacher in her pink, checked dress, her hair tied up with a ribbon. He remembered a day when he was fourteen being forced to admit he hadn't any boxing gloves for the same reason, and that prickle grew stronger.

'I've got one you can have,' he said. 'I'll go and get it and give you a lift home.'

As Max climbed the stairs to Georgia's room carrying the Dansette record player he kept in the office, he felt as if he were going back some twenty-five years.

The smell of damp, a glimpse of the hideous bathroom, the worn, dusty carpet, the poverty. It was just like the place he lived in as a child. This place was silent, as if they were alone, yet he could almost hear the sounds that had filled his childhood. Babies crying, children shouting and adults screaming at each other, mingled with a stench of boiled cabbage and toilets.

'How long have you lived here?' he asked, trying hard not to reveal his thoughts as she unlocked the door at the top of the stairs.

'Over a year. It's not so bad inside and at least it's near everything.'

She ran in ahead of him, turning on a small lamp. He understood why, she wanted to soften the bareness.

Max put the record player down. He felt huge against the low, sloping ceiling. 'You've made it nice,' was all he could say. He guessed she had painted it, wondered how she had come here, and above all whether the activities so close to this room had touched her.

'Would you like some tea?' Georgia was flushed with embarrassment, she was moving her weight from one leg to the other, hoping he'd refuse and go.

'I must get home,' he wanted to take her out to dinner, but in the mood he was in he might do or say the wrong thing. 'Shall I plug this in for you first?'

'I can do it,' she said, watching as he placed it on a spindly coffee table. 'As soon as I earn some money I'll buy another and give you this back.'

'Keep it,' he took her two hands in his, unable to control himself. 'It's a present.'

She just stood there looking at him. Her lips slightly parted, eyes like two dark pools.

'Don't be embarrassed by having nothing darling,' his voice was husky. 'I started out like this too. There's no shame in it.'

No one had ever touched him like this. He'd had dozens of young girls with less than her, and never once wanted to give them anything. Max took what he wanted. Whether it was their youth, their talent or just their virginity. A meal or a night out in a hotel was the extent of his generosity.

He wanted to kiss her so bad it hurt. Yet somehow he knew if he touched her she'd back away and maybe she'd be lost to him forever.

'It's not that,' she dropped her eyes from his. 'I've never brought a man up here before. It feels strange.'

She broke all the rules. Max understood girls who flirted and pretended to know everything, or even ones who ran a mile from being alone with him. She just stood there, still with her little soft hands in his, half child, half woman, too innocent to realize that this older man's interest in her was far from professional.

'You've no need to feel strange with me Georgia,' he

squeezed her hands then let them drop. 'I'll be going now, learn all the words, and I'll meet you at ten next Monday, outside Peter Robinson's in Oxford Street. Don't be late!'

'Thank you Max,' she smiled took a step nearer him and standing on tip-toes kissed his cheek. 'You can't imagine how lovely it will be to hear music again.'

He heard the opening chords of 'Soul Train', even before he reached the street. Max put one hand up to his cheek where she'd kissed it and paused for a moment.

This was going to be tough. She wasn't going to fall into his arms like an over-ripe peach and just this once perhaps it would be him who got hurt.

'I can't bear to leave you!' Georgia sobbed.

All week she had been in a state of hysterical excitement, but now as her last day at Pop's was almost over, she realized just how much they all meant to her.

Janet's lips quivered, Sally was chain-smoking, the other women had fussed around her all day, giving her little treats. Myrtle had even run her up a pair of warm pyjamas.

'You can always come back,' Pop said gently. 'The door will always be open for you. Good luck!'

He hadn't rebuked her all week, just long-suffering sighs at her high spirits. His sad, clown-like face was suddenly very dear to her.

'Thank you for everything,' she said, running to hug him one last time. 'I'll never forget any of you.'

Pop held her tightly, his lips quivering.

'You'll never be far from our thoughts. We'll be watching to see your name in lights.'

'None of this would have happened without you.' She lay her head on his shoulder, fresh tears filling her eyes. 'I want to sing, but I'll miss you all.'

'You'll make new friends,' he said softly against her hair. 'Not broken reeds like us lot.'

'Drop us a line when you are singing in London,' Janet's voice was husky with emotion. 'And remember all the things I've taught you about men!'

Georgia sat hunched up in Max's Jaguar, shaking with fear. In jeans and a sweater, her hair tied up in a pony tail she looked about fourteen.

'Now don't let any of them make passes at you,' Max said gruffly. 'Don't start making them tea and stuff otherwise you'll end up becoming mother to them all, and if you have any problems phone me, either at the office or home.'

'What will I wear to the gigs?' she asked.

'Miriam has all that in hand. I'll be popping in on Wednesday during the day to see you.'

The church hall was near Aldgate. Dilapidated and sad with ferns growing out of the roof, the wire-covered windows mostly broken.

As they got out of the car Georgia could hear music blasting out, surprising passers-by.

'That's good,' Max said, grinning broadly. 'They've set up. Now don't be nervous, just sing and forget about everything else.'

As Max swept her into the dingy hall she almost laughed with relief. She had imagined strong, fierce men, but all she saw were boys, weeds in jeans and sweaters, cigarettes hanging out of their lips.

'Hallo Georgia!' One of them jumped down off the stage, his pale face brightened by a wide smile. 'I'm Ian. Has Max filled you in on the music?'

'I've played the records,' she blushed. Her voice seemed to echo round the hall too loudly now the rest of them had stopped playing and just stared silently at her. 'I know all the words, I think.'

'Well, that's more than I do. I often ad lib.'

'I'll shoot off now,' Max said, backing towards the door. 'Ring me tonight at seven, Ian. We'll talk then.'

He was gone in a flash, the doors shuddering behind him.

For a moment Georgia just stood there, eyes downcast. She knew this feeling so well, just the way it had been the first day Celia left her at the new school. Play interrupted as the other kids stared at her, then moving on, forgetting her.

'Nervous?' Ian touched her shoulder lightly. 'Don't be, love, we all know what it's like. Come and meet the others.'

She knew it would take forever to remember their names. Ian with his gentle ways and angelic face stood out, and Rod the drummer for his dark brooding looks, but the others seemed so alike.

'Speedy's really called Patrick,' Ian waved his hand at the auburn-haired, fresh-faced one nursing his bass guitar. 'You'll find out why we gave him that nickname. Norman on organ, an arrogant little shit-stirrer. Les on lead guitar, thick as two short planks and finally John and Alan the brass section.'

Why did they stare so hard? Was it because Max hadn't told them about her colour?

'Let's get on with it!' Rod shouted irritably, banging on his side drum.

'We'll start with "Soul Train". Norman sat down at the organ. 'I'll play it through to refresh your memory. It might be a good idea to sing by me so you don't get thrown by the backing.'

Clammy cold hands, butterflies in her stomach and as the introduction started her face broke out in a sweat.

'I'm on the Soul Train, don't know where I'm going,' the first line came out as no more than a croak. She kept her eyes on Norman's hands dancing over the keys. The second line was easier, by the third she had forgotten her fears, throwing back her head for the chorus.

'Soul train take me with you,' she sang moving back away from Norman, microphone in hand.

The trumpet and sax were playing thrilling little riffs, Rod's drums sent out a heavy beat and she could hear Speedy and Les joining in with vocals. Tingles went down her spine, she turned to sing to them, forgetting that she'd never seen or heard of them till a few moments ago.

As the music died away she looked round.

All seven of them were staring at her.

'Did I do it wrong?' she asked turning pink with embarrassment.

'You did it as good as perfect,' Ian grinned. 'Now let's do it again and I'll do some harmonies.'

As the day wore on she had a glimpse into each personality. Rod the drummer was the most dangerous, his slanty eyes seemed to be watching her closely. He oozed raw sexuality which made her uncomfortable, when he spoke it was a mere growl. Norman knew his music. Speedy was the calming member of the band and John, Les, and Alan were the quiet ones. But the biggest surprise of the day was Ian. When Max described him as the weak link, he couldn't have been further from the truth. His sweet face, the baby-soft, yellow hair and big blue eyes, hid a committed musician. He made the decisions, knowing each member's strengths and weaknesses and he balanced them like a juggler.

'Sing from the groin,' he said at one point in the morning, making a thrusting gesture. 'This is rock not choir practice. You've got to sell yourself, not just your voice.'

'Let's go down the pub for a few jars,' John said at two, packing away his trumpet before anyone could argue. 'This is the nearest thing we'll get to a holiday for months, so let's make the most of it.'

*

'We pool our money,' Ian smirked as Georgia watched him take a brown envelope out of his pocket to pay for the drinks while the others stood watching. 'We keep a fiver each, and the rest goes in here for our rent, food, fags and beer. If there's any left at the end of the week we divide it up.'

'So what do I do?' she asked wondering if this meant she had to hand hers over too.

A wall of hostility seemed to spring up round her.

'Max didn't tell you it was only an audition?' Rod's lip curled back aggressively.

'I'm sorry.' She could have died of shame. Max had put her in an impossible position. Why couldn't he have told her the truth?

She turned and ran to the toilet, tears springing into her eyes.

'Fuck Max,' Rod said as the door banged behind her. 'He's so bloody – ' he paused, unable to find the right word.

'Right?' Speedy grinned. 'Let's face it Rod, for once he's got his head screwed on.'

'She's perfect,' John said quietly, staring at the door Georgia had rushed into. 'She's got the voice, the looks, everything.'

'She'll be trouble,' Norman's face was sharp, as if searching for an alternative argument. 'What happens when she has to share a room with us? How can we change with her around?'

'What do you think Rod?' Ian turned his lazy blue eyes on to his friend.

'I think she's brilliant.'

Ian's mouth fell open. He had expected fierce opposition, at best a bet that he could get her into bed first.

'I think she could be trouble,' Rod added quickly. 'I agree with Norman there. But more from Max than anyone. He fancies her, I saw it in his face. What we need to get straight is how she thinks of Max.'

'Let's have a vote on her anyway?' Ian scanned the boys grouped around him. He could see Rod wanted her in, John too. Alan and Les would go along with the majority.

'Hold on,' Speedy's slow voice halted them. 'I like her too, but what we've all got to think of is Ian's position. We've been together too long to split up now. If she stays we've got to integrate her right into the band, never allow her to think she's the important one. You've got to put more beef into it Ian, don't let her take over. Anyway you haven't said a word yourself.'

'I think she's our saviour,' Ian blushed. 'She's just what we need. Did you hear all of you come alive in there? She's got that magic touch to make us all reach new heights. I don't care if it's going to cause trouble. I say we take her on.'

When Georgia returned from the toilets she knew immediately they had reached a decision.

'Give us two quid,' Rod said, holding out the brown envelope. 'That'll be your contribution until pay day. We'll work out your permanent share next week.'

'You mean?' Georgia's eyes opened wide, her lips curving into a dimpled smile.

'It means you're in now baby,' Speedy drawled. 'Welcome to Samson.'

Chapter 11

'Is this it?' Georgia turned surprised eyes on Ian as he banged on a door between a Wimpy bar and a betting shop in Tottenham High Street.

'Wait till you get inside,' he grinned, eyes full of mischief. 'Welcome to de shit-house!'

The door creaked open and a small, scrawny man in a dirty collarless shirt peered out, behind him was a flight of steep stairs, up which came a warm, fetid smell of dustbins.

'You're early,' the man said. 'I haven't finished cleaning up yet.'

Georgia clutched the dress Miriam had given her to her chest, her legs turning to jelly.

'You know we like to set up early to get a balance,' Ian prodded the old man in the chest playfully. 'Now come on Sid, don't be awkward.'

Grumbling under his breath the old man tottered off down the stairs on bowed legs. Ian turned to the boys sitting in the van and waved for them to follow.

'You'll soon get used to clubs by daylight,' Ian grinned at Georgia's horrified face and putting one hand in the small of her back, pushed her gently towards the stairs. 'By the time we get back here at half nine tonight it will look different. By two thirty when we leave it will seem wonderful. That's a promise.'

An hour later Georgia sat huddled on the edge of the

stage watching the boys still putting the final touches to their equipment. All they had allowed her to carry down were the small items while they sweated profusely carting the heavy organ, speakers and amplifiers.

The basement club was a huge clammy cellar, the only seating consisted of rows of school-type benches lining the whitewashed walls. Two long strip lights lit the place, making it as inviting as a morgue. Sid was still washing the floor, or rather pushing the dirt round further with an ancient mop.

'Which one do you belong to?'

Georgia assumed Sid was talking to her, although his eyes stayed glued to the mop in his hand.

'I don't belong to anyone,' she said. 'I'm the new singer.'

'Bit young for that aren't you?' He shuffled nearer her, pushing the full bucket with one foot. 'Did they tell you what a rough-house it is?'

'Yes.' In fact it had only been mentioned on the way here when Ian gave her instructions to make for the dressing-room and stay there if trouble broke out. Georgia was more concerned with changing in a filthy, tiny hole with one forty watt bulb overhead and a mirror barely big enough to see her mouth in, than it being her sanctuary.

Now that the boys' band suits hung in there too, there was barely room for any of them. How was she going to change into that awful dress Miriam had given her, without the entire band seeing her almost naked?

'Some nights they pelt the band with glasses,' Sid said cheerfully. 'Course, they've never done it to this lot, because they like them. But you get on your toes if anything happens.'

Georgia's heart sank. She was frightened enough by just singing here, without the threat of violence too.

'Nearly there now,' Rod called down from the stage.

'We'll run through a couple of numbers, then go and find something to eat.'

Georgia couldn't imagine anyone wanting to come and spend an evening here, even though the boys insisted it was always packed to capacity. They said it was one of their favourite venues, so what must the worst ones be like? The toilets were old and grubby with no hot water. Not one glass on the bar sparkled. The seating was almost non-existent and if fire broke out they'd all be trampled to death trying to get out that one narrow staircase.

Norman began to play on the organ. A haunting little tune she remembered hearing on Radio Luxembourg while still at school.

'I'm Mr Blue, when you say you're sorry,' she forgot for a moment her anxiety and joined in, turning round to face him. 'Then show it by going out on the sly, proving your love isn't true.'

Les and Speedy immediately picked it up, leaning to the microphone and doing exaggerated backing vocals.

'Do Wah doo, Call me Mr Blue.'

Ian stood back against a speaker, his mouth twitching with mirth, as Georgia, and the three boys aped the fifties song.

'The balance seems fine,' Ian laughed aloud as they finished. 'Don't call us, we'll call you.'

The pub on the corner had been empty when they went in at seven. Now at half past eight it was getting crowded, just another reminder soon they would have to leave the comfortable bar and get back to the club.

Ian shot a glance at Georgia as though reading her mind.

'I'll go back with Georgia, you lot stay on for a bit,' he said to the others, standing up and beckoning for her to come too. Georgia flashed a look of gratitude at him. She had been dwelling on the best way to get into her dress in that dressing-room without them seeing her underwear and she still hadn't found a way of removing her bra and zipping up the hated dress without revealing something.

To Georgia with only the scantiest real knowledge of men, it seemed the boys were obsessed about sex. They described breasts in detail, the size of a girl's nipples, the weight and feel of them. Rod claimed they all masturbated at least twice a day and insisted she would get used to it. They spoke of a mysterious thing called 'muff diving' which she knew was something rude but hadn't a clue what it was. No woman under fifty was safe from their bawdy banter and not once had she heard a tender or romantic suggestion.

Only Ian was different. He too laughed along with them, even pointed out women they passed in the van, but in Georgia's presence at least he didn't swear or say anything to make her blush, and now he was intuitive enough to know she was frightened of changing with them.

'They aren't as bad as they seem,' he said as they crossed the High Street. Flynn's had bright lights over the door now and a big flashing neon sign had been switched on. It was dusk, and the street was full of groups of young people, giving the road a feeling of excitement that had been lacking earlier in the day. 'Believe it or not Georgia, they are merely trying to get you to open up. Until you do they'll keep it up.'

'What do they want me to say?' she asked as they reached the club door. A small desk had been set up at the top of the stairs, but as yet there was no one manning it. 'Do they want me to say I had five men last night?'

'No.' Ian laughed. He turned to her, brushing a strand of hair out of her eyes. 'They just want to know if there's a man in your life. Has Max come on to you. Where you come from and why you say so little.'

Silence hadn't been intentional. She had been so busy

listening to them she hadn't considered they might want to know about her. But even if she wanted to open up, how could she? One bit would lead to other bits she wanted left buried.

'There isn't a man,' she hung her head. 'I don't know what you mean about Max. I'll tell you about my past when I feel safe, and I don't talk much because you lot all do it for me!'

Ian's hand came up, with one finger he lifted her chin, leaned forward and kissed her on the nose.

'That's enough for me.'

He had the prettiest eyes she'd ever seen on a man. Saxe blue with tiny flecks of grey. Despite his blond hair, his eyelashes were thick and dark. But then there was a great deal to like about Ian. He was gentle, sensitive and his face held all the purity of a child. He was too thin, too pale. In a teeshirt and jeans he was like a rasher of bacon. Yet he had an adult quality which the other boys didn't share.

Together they went downstairs. The club looked completely different now. The strip lighting replaced by coloured spots on the walls, and the bar lit up. Only now did she appreciate that the rough wood on the bar was intentional, intended to look rustic. Even the floor didn't look dirty any longer, the smell of dustbins replaced by some kind of lavender smell.

'Sid's been spraying the place for cockroaches,' Ian sniggered.

Georgia stood up on tip-toe, peering into the gloom suspiciously.

'Not really, chump,' Ian laughed. 'It's just some kind of air freshener. Now get changed before the others get back.'

The dress was gold lurex. The top, boned and strapless, the skirt a full circle with layers of net underneath which scratched her legs unmercifully.

Georgia tried to see herself in the cracked mirror,

264

holding the dress closed with one hand. She had been struggling to zip it up for five minutes, and now music was playing out in the club she could hardly go out and search for Ian to help her.

The shape of the dress was quite nice, but any yellow or brown tones didn't bring out the right colour in her face. She looked brassy. More suited to ballroom dancing than a soul band.

'Can we come in now?' Rod's voice came through the door. 'Are you decent?'

'Yes,' she backed up against the wall holding the dress closed behind her.

'Blimey,' Rod whistled. 'Where on earth did Miriam dig that one up?'

Georgia could feel her lips quivering. She had hoped they would insist it was nice. Speedy and Alan pushed by Rod, pulling off their shirts as they went. Ian came in next.

'I can't do up the zip,' she whispered to him, turning her back to him while clutching at the top.

Ian smiled. Her small narrow back reminded him of his younger sister's, little shoulder blades sticking out like tiny wings, skin so smooth and silky he was tempted to stroke it.

'Zip it, don't kiss it,' John said behind him. 'You're supposed to be the gentleman.'

'It's horrible isn't it?' Georgia turned back to Ian once he had fastened the hook and eye on the top. 'Do I really have to wear it?'

'I can only suppose she thought it would contrast with our red suits,' Rod's deep voice chimed in. Georgia looked round and found him wearing only the scantiest of underpants barely covering a terrifying bulge. Undressed he looked like a man, broad shoulders and a sprinkling of dark hair on his chest. She blushed furiously.

'It will have to do for tonight,' Ian realized her

discomfort and distracted her. 'You'll look fine on stage.'

'You can't wear stockings,' Speedy said in his slow, almost dreamy way, gazing at her legs with a slight leer as he too removed his jeans. 'They'll all be peering up your dress all night. Take them off.'

Georgia wanted to die. Nothing had prepared her for being cooped up in this tiny airless room with seven men only half dressed. Now they expected her to remove her stockings in front of them.

'Speedy's right,' Ian said quietly. 'He could have been more tactful, but that's Speedy for you. Do your hair and stop worrying.'

'You'd have been better in red,' John had already dressed, he was putting on a black shoe-string tie. 'That colour makes you sallow.'

Georgia was on the point of tears.

'What shall I do?' she whispered.

'Put plenty of rouge on your cheeks,' Ian said. 'And finish your hair, then we'll see.'

Surreptitiously she tried to remove her stockings and suspender belt without anyone seeing.

It was a horrible feeling. If she bent forward her breasts popped out, her bare shoulders felt chilly. Suppose when she moved on stage the audience could see her knickers?

Somehow she managed to wriggle into the corner, bent over and scooped her hair up into a top knot. Miriam had suggested she wore a 'beehive', but she'd tried that already at home and all she succeeded in doing was making herself look like a tart.

'To hell with everyone,' she muttered to herself. 'I'll be me and if they don't like it, too bad.'

She stood up, pulling up the front of her dress, then turned.

Ian's face broke into a wide smile.

He could see the defiant look in her eyes. Her hair

showered over her head in a mass of bubbly little curls. He stepped forward, and with one finger released a few tiny strands by her ears, curling them round his finger.

He was already in his suit. He looked bigger, the red contrasting well with his blond hair. His black shoes gleamed with polish, shirt dazzling white and a faint whiff of woody aftershave. Georgia could see now why he had such a big following of girls.

'You need something in your hair,' he said thoughtfully. He was standing so close to her she was sure he could see right down her dress.

Georgia shamefacedly got out a gold feather plume that was with the dress and held it out.

'Who did she think she was dressing?' He shook his head in disgust. 'That makes you look like something out of the Moulin Rouge!'

'What about a flower?' Rod said, his arrogant face for once alight with interest. 'There's a vase full on the bar.'

'Go and whip a couple, red ones,' Ian said.

Rod returned in minutes with two roses.

Ian came close to Georgia and pushed them into the band holding her hair.

'That's better,' he said, standing back and smiling. 'Now put a bit more colour on your face, you might look like a clown in here, but up on the stage you'll look fine. Do you want me to do it for you?'

'Yes,' she whispered, by now so nervous she couldn't do anything.

Ian stood in front of her carefully applying the rouge. He picked up a small eyeliner brush and added a little more.

'That's better,' he said. 'Now use a lipstick brush and outline your lips in a darker colour.'

'Are you sure?' she asked. She was surprised by his knowledge, and the way he handled her like a sister was very comforting.

'Quite sure,' he said gently.

267

'I'm in a bit of a state,' she whispered, not wanting the others to overhear.

'Let me give you a cuddle?' he smiled. 'The best remedy for the collywobbles.' He put his arms round her and held her tightly, his lips close to her ear. 'I'm still nervous and I've been doing it for years. But it goes as soon as we get up there.'

'Break it up,' Rod shouted. 'I thought Max said no passes were to be made?'

'Not a pass,' Ian laughed, looking round at the others without letting go of her. 'Just a cuddle to banish nerves.'

'You nervous?' Rod sounded amazed. 'If you can come along to rehearsals when you don't know anyone, you'll sail through this.'

'Will I?' she said, still clinging to Ian.

'Of course you will,' the boys all chimed in together.

'Besides, we can get John to blast out on his horn if you can't reach the high notes,' added Norman.

Their faces touched something inside Georgia.

They were all seasoned professionals and she had been thrust on them whether they liked it or not. She was young, green as grass and she was holding them all up. Yet here they were being brotherly and kind, grouping around her offering her their support.

'Thank you,' she said simply. 'I hope I don't let you down.'

'You've got five minutes to have a pee,' Ian said with a lop-sided grin. 'Don't drop that net skirt in the bog.'

Flynn's was filling up.

Georgia couldn't bear to peer through the door as the boys were doing. She could hear raucous laughter, shouting and stamping feet, it was frightening enough just to listen, without gawping at them too. Hard, pale-faced girls with beehives and heavily made-up eyes in tight sheath dresses and stilettos. The men tough and broad-shouldered in Italian boxy jackets and winkle-pickers. They seemed an unlikely bunch to appreciate a band who didn't play top twenty hits.

Bobby Vee's song 'Rubber Ball' was playing so loudly the speakers crackled, a smell of cigarettes, beer and cheap scent taking away all the oxygen she needed.

'Never seen such a big crowd on a Thursday,' a raw-faced bouncer in an evening suit poked his head round the door. 'Looks like they all want to hear your new girl.'

'And now, the moment you've all be waiting for,' the record was halted and the club manager's voice boomed out over the microphone. 'Your favourite band, *Samson!*'

The boys pushed past Georgia, Rod blowing a kiss. Ian took her hand and squeezed it.

'We go next,' his eyes were full of understanding. 'Don't panic, let me lead you till you get into it. If you find you can't sing, just move with the backing.'

A burst of applause and Rod played a roll on the drums.

Georgia felt a cold sweat breaking out all over her and she wanted to go to the toilet again.

'You all know Ian McShane, but tonight you're in for an extra treat. Meet the lovely Georgia James, the band's new singer!'

Her legs refused to move, yet Ian was dragging her up the three steps on to the stage.

'Smile,' he said. 'Head up!'

Norman played the opening bars. Georgia saw the expectant, upturned faces lining the stage only feet from her.

Somehow she made it to the microphone. Her mouth was smiling, but her stomach churned.

She reached for the microphone, and found her mouth and throat as dry as a desert.

'Turn towards the band,' Ian whispered as he adjusted his mike. 'I'll start.'

She forced herself to turn. Rod was smiling encouragement, John and Alan moved closer to cover any mistakes with their horns.

'I'm on a soul train, don't know where I'm going,' she was mouthing the words but she could only hear Ian.

'You can do it baby,' Rod said, his eyes sympathetic. 'Just keep singing till the voice comes back.'

She managed the second line a bit better, but by the time she got to the third, her voice came out despite her terror, and the fourth followed without even thinking about it.

She twirled down, a flash of gold net around slim brown legs. Mouth wide and red, teeth gleaming white. Her voice soared over the crowd.

'I'm on the soul train and I'm coming baby to you.'

Towards the end of the first set something else had taken over. She was dancing, smiling, bending down to young men in the front row and blowing kisses. She forgot the scratchy underskirt, kicking off her shoes as she immersed herself even more into the music. Whenever she turned towards the rest of the band they were grinning like Cheshire Cats, egging her on.

Her voice found new heights, one moment deep and husky, raunchy and sexy, then sounds so pure she could hardly believe it was her.

Ian was better than he'd ever been at rehearsals. His singing was more punchy. As his head bent close to share the mike with her on some numbers, she knew he was putting his all into it.

The applause was deafening as the first set ended.

The D.J. ran on. 'Well what can I say?' he yelled, waving a hand at the departing band. 'Can that little girl sing, or what?'

As Georgia reached the dressing-room door she saw Max.

'You were great,' his dark eyes shone like jet. 'I'm knocked out!'

'I didn't know you were out there,' she was breathless, panting like a dog after a ten mile run.

'Would I miss seeing you get started?' he said. 'I even brought a photographer.' He moved closer, taking her two arms in his big hands and squeezed them.

'You were magic,' he said, his eyes burning into her. 'I've never seen the band so good.' He looked round at the boys grouped behind her and smiled broadly. 'Well done all of you. There's a reporter from *Melody Maker* out there. If I'm not much mistaken you'll get the best review of your careers this week.'

'Do we get a drink boss?' Norman as always was asking for something.

'They're set up in the back bar,' Max grinned. 'And you've earned them.

'We're privileged tonight,' Speedy drawled sardonically. 'This room's usually closed off. They only use it for card games.'

A billiard table stood in one corner, covered with a cloth, in the middle of the room a large table had nine pints of beer standing on it.

'Get a proper drink for Georgia,' Max barked out at John tossing him a note. 'And pay for that round while you're at it.'

'What'll it be?' John smirked. 'Double champagne? Gin, brandy?'

'Coke,' she grinned. 'And lots of ice.'

Georgia sat next to Ian.

'Thank you for telling me to turn round,' she said softly. 'I thought my voice had gone for good.'

'That's all right,' Ian smiled and leaned back in his

seat. 'It's an old trick, works everytime. If you can't see the punters you can forget they are there.'

It didn't seem possible she'd only known these boys for four days. Just an hour ago she had wanted to run away and forget any dreams she'd had of being a singer. Now as she looked around her she knew their futures were interlinked. She would remember their faces forever, love them for all that support and understanding.

'Her dress isn't right.' Speedy's voice rose over the others as he made sure Max listened. 'It's like something off "Come dancing", she needs something tight and sleazy.'

'I think it looks good,' Max argued, he studied Georgia with hooded eyes. 'What do you think Ian?'

'Well, Georgia would look good in a sack.' Ian leant back in his chair, his fair hair flopping over his eyes. 'But that dress is dated. It went out with Glenn Miller. I don't agree with Speedy though, she's not the sleazy type.' He paused, seeming to wake up a little, his soft lips twitching as if in silent amusement. 'I'd like to see her in something that shows her legs, so she can dance too.' He smiled and turned to Georgia. 'You held out on us there too. We had no idea you were such a good dancer.'

'I'll look into it,' Max said his eyes running over Georgia, then moving back to Ian. He was wondering if something had occurred between them. Ian wasn't usually so forceful and there was a light in the boy's eyes he hadn't seen before. 'Anyway lads, is there anyone who doesn't think Georgia did well?'

'She was brilliant,' Rod said unexpectedly. 'You've done us proud, Max.'

Georgia looked around with bright eyes. She felt fabulous, right now she could hardly wait to get back on the stage and do the rest of the performance.

The second half was even better. The audience were clapping, stamping their feet and smiling up at her.

She felt all-powerful, every nerve-ending twitching. She was no longer a frightened little sixteen-year-old. Up here she was a queen, and the audience her loyal subjects.

Thunderous applause rained down on them as they finished and the boys' faces told her it was all for her.

Back in the dressing-room the smell of sweat and socks was even worse as they changed back into their ordinary clothes.

'How are you feeling now?' Ian said softly as he unzipped her dress for her.

'On top of the world,' she laughed, clutching the top of her dress to hide her breasts.

'It's like a drug,' Ian smiled. 'Once tasted, you need it for evermore. But don't let it go to your head. Everything went well today, and the audience were great. Wait till you've done a really bad gig. When the crowd stand with their backs to you drinking, the lights fuse and the guitar strings break, and you know you've got a hundred-mile ride home in the van.'

Max looked in the dressing-room, his big, square face looking unexpectedly healthy surrounded by the boys' pallor.

'Okay boys, see you at the office at twelve tomorrow. Georgia, would you like a lift back with me?'

'But the equipment?' she said, trying to get a shirt over her top half while still holding her dress round her.

'Go on home,' Ian grinned at her. 'We can manage without you, besides, there's a bit more room in the van for us.'

She didn't want to go with Max. They would all be chatting about the gig and she wanted to be part of it. But without making herself look silly she could hardly refuse.

*

'How's it going with the boys?' Max asked as his Jaguar glided away down towards the West End. 'Any problems?'

'Everything's just great,' Georgia looked out the window, it had begun to rain and the road looked like black tar studded with diamonds of reflected light.

'Has Ian come on to you?'

Georgia's head turned sharply towards Max. Ian had said the same thing about Max. She wasn't sure what he meant at the time, but now it became clear.

'Of course not,' she retorted.

'Just asking, he seemed different tonight, that's all. I don't want you getting involved with any of them.'

'Look Max,' something snapped inside her. 'I don't mind you telling me what to do where work is concerned. But I don't see what my private life has to do with you.'

Max pulled the car over to the kerb and stopped abruptly.

'Now look here,' he said, turning in his seat and grabbing her face in one big hand. 'If I turn you into a star you won't have a private life. One whiff of scandal, one bit of gossip can ruin a career. You've got to live at close quarters with that lot and if you hop into bed with one of them they'll be trouble. I've seen it all. I know.'

She could see something in his eyes. Something deep and disturbing. He was too old for her, she didn't quite trust him, yet she wanted him to kiss her.

There was a feeling in her stomach, something primitive. Warning bells were jangling in her head, but she could only see those full red lips and feel that hand on her face.

'I feel something for you,' his voice was husky, those lips coming closer. 'I want to protect you, love you.'

Her eyes were closing. She could feel herself drowning and his lips when they touched hers were soft and teasing.

'No,' she moved back quickly, suddenly aware of his maleness.

Max straightened up. She couldn't look at him, her eyes were firmly fixed on her hands in her lap. She knew he was studying her, his elbow resting on the steering wheel.

The silence was unbearable. She wanted to make a joke, anything to get him to start the car and take her home.

'I can wait,' he said softly. 'There's something there, I know it. You're a little mystery girl Georgia. But I'll work it out in time.'

'There's no mystery,' she said, perhaps too quickly. 'You're a married man. You're too old for me. You said yourself there mustn't be even a whiff of scandal.'

He turned on the ignition and the engine purred softly.

'I'll take you home,' he said flatly. 'Forget everything, Georgia. I've never forced anyone in my life. I'm not going to start now.'

It was after nine when Georgia woke. Sunshine poured through a crack in the curtain, the sounds of the market as new and fresh as her first morning in the room.

She stretched like a cat, smiling to herself as she remembered the gig the night before.

It had been so wonderful and it was going to be repeated again and again.

She wanted to go out, stand in the sunshine and sing for joy. Get armfuls of flowers to fill the room. Buy something pretty to wear and to hell with the expense.

The boys were all in the office when she arrived.

Her hair was hanging loose over her shoulders, the pink gingham dress that Pop had given her, freshly ironed with a wide white belt and sandals.

'Well,' Max turned his attention to her, looked her up and down, noting the pink cheeks and bolder, confident stance. 'Something agrees with you!'

They were all looking at her, eight pairs of eyes, scrutinizing her.

'It's such a lovely day,' she said lamely. She had put aside Max's behaviour the night before. If she was to be a star many more men would want to kiss her. Why blame him for being the first?

Max cleared his throat. 'Sit down all of you,' he said, lighting up a fat cigar and leaning back in his chair. 'I've had *Melody Maker* on the phone this morning. They are writing a review about you for the next edition, and they want to do a special in the next week or two.'

He looked intently at each of them.

'It will be "A day in the Life of", type thing. The reporter will meet you in the morning, go with you to the gig, unload with you, set up, the whole bit. So I don't want any cock-ups, this could be the big break.'

'How will he get in the van?' Norman said. 'I'm not sitting on a reporter's lap all night.'

'He'll have his own car,' Max said impatiently. 'And a photographer with him. Ian can travel with them, he can be trusted not to tell them anything too damaging.'

The boys fell silent for a moment.

Both Ian and Rod were staring at Georgia as if they'd hardly heard Max. She wondered if Max had spoken about her before she came in.

'I've got a list of gigs for next week,' Max said, handing round some copies. 'As you will see it's mostly in the North, leaving here on Monday for Birmingham, on to Preston Tuesday, Leeds Wednesday, Hull Thursday. Travel back to London after Hull. Friday at the Marquee, Saturday at the Bag of Nails.'

'What about digs?' Ian asked, dragging his eyes away from Georgia.

'I've got those here,' Max said, handing Ian another sheet. 'The rooms are booked, go to them before the gig please, so they know you are definitely coming. Georgia, there's a possibility you'll have to share with someone,' he paused, looking at her directly, through hooded eyelids, his tongue just flickering over his lips. 'I apologize, but it was late in the day to make the bookings.'

He got up and went over to a safe. 'Your money,' he said, handing out small brown envelopes. 'And the kitty for digs and petrol.' This last envelope he handed to Ian. 'Right, Blue Boar tomorrow, have a good rest today and Sunday, you won't be getting much next week.'

He looked across at Georgia.

'I'd like a word with you please, in private. Will the rest of you wait in the office outside.'

The boys trooped out, each of them looking at Georgia, questioning looks in their eyes.

'What is it?' she asked, suddenly afraid.

'Well, dear,' he sat down and fiddled with a paper clip, his cigar burning away in a cut-glass ashtray. 'I'm sorry about the rooms. If you have to share make sure it's with Ian. He's the nearest thing to a gentleman.'

'That's all right,' she smiled.

'About last night, I was out of order and I'm sorry.'

'There's nothing to be sorry for,' she hung her head. 'Perhaps it's my fault.'

'The fault was all mine. But please let's put it aside. I don't want any bad feeling between us. You are a fine singer,' he went on, getting up from his desk and moving nearer her. He put one big hand on her hair, caressing it lightly. 'Perhaps the best I've handled, but you are very young, innocent and wet behind the ears. Now if there's anything in your past, you should tell me now, because believe me, one day it will come out.' He paused, looking closely at her, the hooded eyelids looked almost snakelike. 'I can handle anything as long as I know the truth in advance. But if you hide something from me I can't help. Do you understand?'

Georgia nodded.

'Right, now the only other thing is about your dress. Miriam is taking that gold one back to the shop to change it. But she dug this one out this morning. It's old but we kind of thought it might suit you.'

Max opened a cupboard in the wall and pulled out something white.

Georgia stood up and took it from him.

It was an exquisite dress. White silk with handkerchief points from the hip, each one decorated with tiny seed pearls.

'Go and try it on,' he smiled at her awed face. 'The last time I saw that dress was on the evening of our wedding. Miriam was as slim as you then,' he pointed to the bathroom adjoining the office. 'In there.'

It fitted as if it were made for her.

The neckline was low both back and front, skimming over her hips, then flaring out gently to the knee. As Georgia tried a twirl in front of the mirror, the skirt moved, showing glimpses of brown thigh. Although it was a style from the Twenties, somehow it was timeless.

She bounced back into the office, twirling round in front of Max. Her eyes were shining with unsuppressed glee.

'Perfect,' he smiled, putting a large hand on her shoulder to twirl her again. 'Takes me back a few years!'

For just one second she thought he was going to kiss her again. His eyes looked soft, the tip of his tongue just showing through his teeth.

'Can I show the boys?' she grinned, tossing back her hair, backing away from him.

'Of course,' he said, almost fondly. 'And wear your hair like that with it tomorrow.'

An hour later they were all in the pub around the corner. The boys were all sinking pints, but Georgia stayed with orange juice.

'So what was the secret chat for?' Norman asked, his small eyes suspicious.

'About behaving myself, not a breath of scandal,' she laughed. 'Is he serious? Will they really try to dredge up stuff about me?'

Ian took her to one side later. 'I got the same sort of chat from Max too, about you,' he said softly. 'I've got to be big brother it seems.' He leaned closer to her. 'Did something happen last night?'

'Not really,' she blushed.

'That means something did,' Ian took her hand in his, stroking it, yet hiding his action so the other boys wouldn't see. 'Look, I know he's got that fantastic charisma. He's rich, handsome and he can pull any bird he wants. But he's dangerous Georgia. You can't play games with him.'

'I didn't,' she leaned closer to Ian, needing to unburden herself. 'For a moment I was tempted. But I'm scared of men.'

She expected him to laugh. To her surprise he didn't, only squeezed her hand tighter.

'I know. I saw it the first day you were with us. I want us to be friends. Perhaps one day you'll tell me about it. When you want to, I'll be there.'

'You all stared at me when I came in the office. Why?'

'The stars in your eyes,' he laughed. 'We thought you had been in the sack with someone. But it was just the magic from last night's gig wasn't it?'

'I felt so wonderful when I woke up,' Georgia confided. 'It was like the first warm day of spring after the long winter. I'm so happy I could burst.'

'You aren't alone,' Ian looked across to the rest of the band. 'We all felt it too. We're going to make the big time together!'

'She's something else,' Norman said dreamily over his pint after Georgia had left to go shopping.

'Sings like an angel,' John said, his dark eyes smouldering. 'And moves like a whore, what more could we ask for?'

'We'll have to be careful,' Ian looked around at his friends. 'I think Max has big ideas for her, and they don't necessarily include us.'

'You mean he'll get her a recording contract and ditch us?' Rod's face clouded over.

'He's only using us to train her. But if I'm right about her, she won't want to go it alone later,' Ian had been awake most of the night, weighing up every word Max had said about Georgia. 'She's the loyal type and I don't think she's got any family. We must stick with her, be that family. I don't think she'll allow Max to ditch us then.' He looked at his hands, the soft, pale face quietly determined. 'Max fancies her like mad too, so make sure she's never alone with him.'

Rod watched Ian carefully. They had been friends from school, shared everything from footballs, bikes and later girls. He had heard his friend tossing and turning last night in bed and he suspected it was more than just concern about the band.

'Don't you feel bitter?' Rod wanted to goad Ian into admitting something. 'I mean until last night you were the front man, the one that got noticed?'

'Not at all,' Ian smiled, his dark lashes fanning over his blue eyes, a hint of pink on his round face. 'She's got everything our band needs and deserves. I'm not a brilliant singer, we all know that. But last night she made me better, took me back to the fun we used to have back in the youth club, before we got all serious.'

'You fancy her?' Speedy's auburn eyebrows rose questioningly. 'I mean we all do, but it's not like you to go ape over a girl.'

'She's special,' Ian blushed a faint pink, picking up his pint to hide in. 'But something tells me there's someone, or something else. Until I get to the bottom of that there's no chance.'

Chapter 12

1963

'I'm sick and tired of this,' Georgia flung her stage dress on the floor of the dressing-room, stamping on it in rage. 'Maybe you lot are prepared to let Max walk all over you, but I've had it!'

˙No breeze came in the small open window. Eight people trying to change their clothes in a room less than ten feet square. Cigarette smoke, socks and sweat and a sink with only cold water.

Hammersmith Odeon. The name was synonymous with success, a big concert venue where fans queued for hours to get tickets to see their favourite stars. But Samson weren't the stars, just a bottom of the bill support group and they would remain that way until Georgia complied with Max's wishes.

A year earlier Alex Rhodes, a scout from Decca, heard her sing and offered her a solo recording contract. If the man hadn't been such a creep, dismissing the band as if they were worthless, along with trying to seduce her, she might have won him round. But instead she'd lost her temper and insulted him. Now she looked around at the boys and saw what her defiance had done. Seven exhausted, pale, drawn faces, skin that reflected their bad diet and lack of fresh air.

'We can't fight back,' Ian's blue eyes were cloudy with apathy. 'We haven't a leg to stand on.'

Max tried everything to tempt the boys away from

her. A new van, long contracts on cruise ships, more pay, new suits. At Georgia's insistence all these carrots were refused. Then he resorted to straightforward punishment.

The roughest digs. Booking them in at venues so far apart the travelling time was doubled. Seven gigs a week and no extra pay.

They were trapped. If they didn't do the gigs he booked them for, he could sack them for breach of contract.

'Oh, Georgia,' Ian sighed. 'Haven't you learned yet the way it is? The guys in the record companies are all in it with Max. They've got lawyers, heavies and just about everything else on their side. They can afford to wait until we are desperate enough. They can squeeze each one of us dry, until we crack.'

'But I don't understand their motives,' Georgia wanted to scream at the boys' resignation. 'We're good together. I wouldn't be the same without you.'

The first year with the band had been pure wonder. Each gig had been a dress rehearsal for the big moment when they would cut the first record. They could laugh at the thousands of miles of motorway burned up as they huddled together dreaming of a bright future. Joke about the poor food, wages, and seedy boarding houses. It had all been preparation for the time when Max swung them a contract.

As punishment made them draw closer to one another, Max resorted to humiliation.

Bottom of the bill. The band that opened concerts with big names like Gene Vincent, Adam Faith, Ricky Nelson, Billy Fury and any other name that was flavour of the month. A warm-up band that no one took seriously.

Max knew that playing alongside big names would weaken Georgia's resolve far quicker than playing in dance halls. The support group was the one the fans chatted through, or missed by queuing for the toilet. They were so hyped up at the prospect of seeing stars, they rarely even listened to Samson. Worse still, Georgia could see at close quarters the beautiful clothes, the comfortable coaches and the money these star performers were paid, and each night of these big tours she and her band were reminded of their Cinderella role.

Below, in the theatre they could hear thousands of fans screaming, clapping, stamping their feet. Adam Faith was out there on the stage. They had prepared the audience for him, wound them up into near hysteria but already they were forgotten.

Each night in major towns they would walk out the stage door unnoticed, past the screaming girl fans waving autograph books. Back to small boarding house, fish and chips and another night in lumpy beds, while the stars drank champagne in sumptuous hotel rooms.

Disappointment and the endless travel was wearing down their loyalty to one another. Everyone of them had received offers to join another, more successful band. It was only a matter of time before the temptation of recognition, money and comfort broke down their bonds of friendship.

'He's got us by the short and curlies,' John's dark eyes were dull now, his dry humour had turned to mere sarcasm. 'Leave us Georgia. You don't have to put up with this shit.'

'John speaks for all of us,' Ian sighed wearily, leaning back against the wall. He was wearing his best dark suit, ready for the flashy end-of-tour party at the Hilton. But looking closely Georgia could see shiny marks from endless pressing, his best shoes paper thin on the soles. 'We love your loyalty Georgia. Most of us would have sold out a year ago for what Rhodes promised you.'

'I won't compromise,' Georgia gave her dress another kick. It had been mended so often she winced if anyone looked closely at her in the wings and Max wouldn't foot the bill for a new one. 'Everything I know came from you. If I do as he asks you'll never earn any more. How are you going to buy houses, get married and have families?'

She was too tired to argue any longer. If she walked out on them tonight they'd be content to go back to the old club circuit where at least they got all the adulation. She wasn't even sure why she was fighting Max now. Was it for them, for her own ego, or just to keep Ian safe?

She had learned so much in those first few heady months with the band. Schooled by them her voice grew stronger, mature and power packed. They taught her how to whip an audience into a frenzy of excitement, hold them spellbound and hungry for more. Teasing, playing with the crowd came naturally, yet even as she moved them to tears with the emotion in her voice, her own life was as empty as a dry river.

Outside of the band she had nothing. On nights when she went home alone to her room in Berwick Street she felt cut off, as if part of her was still travelling in the van, tucked in beside all those men. Without them she was like an electric guitar with no power source, and she missed both Celia and Helen to the point of distraction.

The boys taught her to live without embarrassment. She could strip off in front of them if necessary. Share a bed when it was cold. Change in the van when they were late. They zipped her into stage clothes, got her to the clubs on time. Critical yet supportive. They had rounded her out, educated her, and in return she listened to their problems, mended their clothes as they drove along and cuddled them when they were sad. They were brothers now, but they could never replace the maternal qualities of Celia or Helen.

There were fierce rows between them. Hours of frosty silence until the problem was resolved. Fights over girls nearly every week and arguments over places in the van.

But there was lots of laughter too.

So many times Georgia had walked into the dressing room and found one of the boys with a half-naked young groupie.

Hardly a night passed without one of the boys delaying their leaving by slipping out to make love to someone.

Georgia had seen it all in two years.

Squirming with embarrassment in the back seat, as a girl gave Rod a blow job while they were driving home. Averting her eyes from the girl's bobbing head, trying to pretend she didn't see it.

There was the time when John had severe diarrhoea and had an accident in the van. Les, so hopelessly drunk he kept his head out of the window from Manchester to Leeds retching violently. Norman caught in the act of making love by the woman's husband, escaping from the small council house wearing only his underpants, clutching his clothes under his arm, with a sixteen-stone bricklayer in fast pursuit.

Landladies who had threatened to call the police when the boys smuggled girls into their rooms. A Dutch cap left in the van that no one knew the owner of. Disasters on stage when Les's trousers split from waist to crutch and he didn't dare move. The driving lesson Rod gave her in the van where she'd swerved across a grassy island almost into the path of an articulated lorry. And the time Norman had jumped from the van into a field for a quick pee, and landed in a freshly-laid cowpat.

Laughter, tears, fights and the promise of fame. An addictive, heady potion that bound them together.

Yet the very first night in digs with them was almost her last.

'Is this it?' Georgia said as Norman pulled up at one of the worst hovels she'd ever seen.

It was a large crumbling house in central Birmingham. Once a substantial Victorian family home, now it was little more than a slum. The front garden was strewn with cardboard boxes, empty bottles and old carpets. Curtains hung from what looked suspiciously like string, the windows hadn't been cleaned in years.

"Fraid so,' Ian smirked. 'What did you imagine? A cottage with roses round the door? A liveried doorman?'

'No,' she said slowly, trying to quell the rising panic inside her. 'But I expected somewhere clean.'

The front door was opened by a fat, dirty looking man. He was wearing just a stained vest under his braces, his vast belly quivering like a bowl of jelly. A cigarette dangled from his lips, thinning hair hung in greasy strands down his forehead.

He didn't even speak, but turned and ambled back down the passageway that smelt of boiled cabbage and drains.

'If it's any consolation,' Ian whispered as they made their way up the grubby staircase. 'This is the "pits", nowhere else we stay is as bad as this.'

'Well let's hope we don't get to Birmingham that often,' she replied, wincing with distaste as she got a glimpse of a bathroom as bad as the one in Berwick Street when she first met Helen.

There were only two rooms, with four single beds apiece, she, Ian, John and Speedy were to share one of them. It was like a bad dream, bare lino cracked and peeling, mere hooks on the wall to hang clothes on, and a dressing table held up with a brick under one leg.

The sheets were supposedly clean, but the dirt was so ingrained she shuddered as she looked at them.

'Watch out for the bed bugs,' Speedy grinned impishly, standing in front of the smeared mirror and combing back his quiff nonchalantly, amused by her horror.

'I hope you are joking,' she shrieked.

'He is,' Ian put an arm round her shoulder, giving Speedy a sharp look. 'We've never been bitten.'

It got steadily worse. No hot water in the bathroom and the meal they were served at tea-time was disgusting.

'What is it?' she whispered to Speedy as she shuffled the greasy meat around her plate.

'Probably gorilla,' he quipped, eating his regardless.

Now she could laugh about that dining room. The violent orange roses on the wallpaper, the plastic gold Eiffel Tower and the clock shaped like a guitar. No landlord had ever been as comic as the man who plonked huge cracked mugs of strong tea down by each of them silently, stirred them with a knife, still with a cigarette dangling from the corner of his mouth.

His wife wandered in from time to time, her hair in curlers and the dirtiest apron Georgia had ever seen. She had a grey face, Georgia remembered, as if she hadn't been outdoors for twenty years, or even washed it often.

'We wasn't told about no girl coming,' she said in sullen tones. The front of her hair was a yellowy colour, as if stained with nicotine to match her fingers. 'All that Mr Menzies said was that there was an extra person.'

'I don't mind sharing with the boys,' Georgia tried to appease her.

'Just as well,' the woman snapped. 'But I don't want no funny business in this house. Girls are always trouble.'

'She probably hates another woman seeing the filth they live in,' she whispered to Rod as the woman swept out.

288

'I heard that!' The woman stuck her head back through the doorway, her grey face contorted with rage. 'Some black tart telling me my house isn't clean. I never heard nothing like it!'

Humiliation took away even the pleasure of her success that night, and later when she got into the lumpy, damp bed she felt dirty and demoralized.

Looking back it seemed ridiculous that she cried the next morning. Floods of tears just because there was no hot water or a lock on the bathroom door.

'I want to go home,' she sobbed to Ian, still wearing her thick pyjamas Myrtle had made her. 'If this is what it's going to be like, I don't want to be a singer.'

But Ian didn't laugh, or even get cross. One moment she was up there in the dreadful room, the next they were all in the van together and Rod drove them to the local public baths.

They could have made fun of her, embarrassed her still further, but that day she discovered their sensitivity and their loyalty to one another.

'Feeling better now?' Rod asked when she came out of the baths with a pink scrubbed face and still damp hair. 'We won't let Max book us in a place like that again.'

Perhaps it was inevitable she and Ian should become lovers, but at first it was just friendship borne out of mutual need. The other boys' insatiable need for sex didn't appear to be shared by Ian. While the others paired off to cruise each new town, Georgia and Ian explored together, went to the cinema, swimming or for walks.

He fitted into the hole vacated by Peter. His blond hair, blue eyes, sensitivity, warmth and compassion were all so similar. He was so easy to be with. He didn't probe at things, or make any demands. He could make her laugh, chat like another girl, yet take her side whenever the others closed ranks on her. Without her even realizing it, he was gradually taking the place of not only Peter but Helen and Celia too.

In November that first year the mild weather changed suddenly. They were on their way to Plymouth when the wind got up, buffeting the old van so hard, Norman got tired of driving and asked Rod to take over.

At Exeter it began to rain so hard the wipers couldn't remove the water fast enough from the windscreen.

'We're going to be late,' John said dourly from the back seat. 'Can't you go faster?'

'I can't fucking well see further than a yard ahead,' Rod snapped. 'If you can do better get up here.'

Stuck in the back with Ian, John and Speedy, Georgia dozed off to sleep, her head on Ian's shoulder.

'Where are we?' she asked when she woke later. It was dark now but she could see street lighting ahead of them.

'In Plymouth,' Ian said. 'We'll have to go straight to the club and set up. We haven't even got time for a cup of tea.'

She knew she had missed something while she was asleep. There was a tension in the air, as if they had been arguing.

Somehow nothing went right that night. The bad weather kept the usually large audience away. Speedy broke a string in the first number. John had a coughing fit and Norman threw a tantrum because his Hammond organ had developed a fault.

During the second set, just as they were finally getting themselves into the mood, the lights fused and the whole club was thrown into darkness.

Georgia just stood helplessly, still holding the microphone. She couldn't see anything, but the audience were shouting and screaming.

'Calm down!' she tried to shout above their noise.

'It's only the fuses.' She had visions of a mass stampede in the darkness, bodies being trampled underfoot.

The manager came on to the stage holding a torch.

'We're trying to fix it,' he shouted above the din. 'Just give us a minute.'

Staff arrived with more torches. Georgia could see them dotted around the club, trying to get everyone to sit down and wait.

'I knew it was going to be a disaster,' Norman said gloomily behind her. 'Any minute now he'll be sending them all off home and he'll blame us for overloading the circuit.'

It was after one when they finally left the club. The fuses were mended after twenty minutes of pandemonium and the show went on, but they had lost their edge.

The boarding house was 'The Gainsborough' a tall, sombre looking house of grey stone set on a corner, just behind the Lee's on Plymouth's front.

'I can't be doing with staying up to let my guests in,' Mrs Pengelly the landlady snapped at them, standing in the doorway wearing a brown plaid dressing-gown wrapped round her formidable large body.

'We're sorry,' Ian tried to charm her, explaining as best he could about the storm.

The rain was still lashing down and it was so cold Georgia's teeth were chattering. She hoped Mrs Pengelly would offer tea and perhaps even a hot water bottle, but instead she just slapped the bolts across the door behind them.

'Rooms three, four and six,' she snapped, taking three keys from a hook on the wall. 'And don't make any noise.'

Georgia and Ian got the largest and coldest room, set on a corner of the house with two large windows which rattled ominously.

'Christ it's cold in here,' Ian shivered as he pulled off

his shirt. 'There's hardly any blankets on the beds either.'

She was glad to be sharing a room. The house was creepy with the wind howling outside and she was so cold and tired she felt like crying.

When she got back from the bathroom wearing her striped pyjamas, Ian was already in the double bed, the covers pulled right up to his chin, curled up as though frozen. She prodded her narrow single bed and banged the hard pillow. It was like so many of their digs. Scratchy nylon sheets, a bedside light with no bulb and a bathroom full of notices about charges for a bath.

'What was going on in the van on the way down here?' she asked once she'd turned the light out.

'The usual,' Ian's voice sounded a long way off, almost drowned by the howling wind. 'Rod wanted to go and look up a couple of birds we used to see down here. I refused and he got a bit nasty.'

Rod had girls everywhere. He rarely stayed in digs with the rest of them, even if he didn't have a girl lined up before they arrived, he soon found one.

'Why didn't you want to?' Ian had once been as keen as the others to look up girls, but in the past few months he had become almost a hermit. 'Didn't you like her?'

'She was okay,' he sighed. 'I don't feel the need to prove myself like Rod does. He said I was turning queer.'

Rod was very cruel sometimes. He had taunted her too, suggesting there was something odd about a girl who showed no inclination to meet other men. There had been times when he made her so angry she had almost spat out her reasons for not trusting anyone enough. Yet something inside her told her it was better to keep her past firmly to herself.

'Are you cold?' Ian asked, his voice sounded sweet and warm from across the room.

'Freezing,' she said.

'Come in here with me then, this bed's quite comfy.'

Georgia got out. Her feet were like ice, her breath was like smoke in the darkness. She pulled a blanket off her bed, laid it over Ian's and hopped in beside him.

It wasn't the first time they'd shared a bed. But it was the first when there wasn't someone else in the room with them. He was good to be close to. He always smelled nice and he didn't try anything on.

Georgia curled her back up against his stomach, his arm round her middle.

'Better?' he whispered.

'Much,' she curled her feet round so they lay on his warm legs.

'I didn't want to go and see those girls because I prefer to be with you,' he said softly.

She understood everything with that one simple statement.

It was she who made the first move. She turned over and nestled her head in the crook of his arm. The warmth of his slim body was comforting, and the faint smell of aftershave stimulated long forgotten feelings.

The wind howled outside. A tree creaked somewhere down below in the garden. In the distance they could hear the sea hurtling onto the rocks. But the wild night was forgotten as he kissed her.

That gentle tugging inside her she remembered so well with Peter, warm lips tempting and teasing her, his arms round her so tightly, fear banished.

His kisses were more practised than Peter's had ever been. She felt herself moulding her body to his, aware her breathing was becoming fiercer.

One hand crept under her pyjamas jacket, stroking and soothing, slowly upwards till it reached her breast, fingers straying across her nipple.

Half of her mind was telling her to move away, to stop this now before it went any further, but the other half was responding and wanting more.

Her hand crept down towards his waist, sliding under his T-shirt. His skin was silky, she could feel his spine under her fingers, knobbly and vulnerable.

'Don't Georgia,' he whispered, trembling at her touch. 'Not if you don't mean it to go any further.'

Perhaps it was his willingness to back away which made it safe. All she could do was pull him fiercely to her and offer her lips in silent agreement.

A delicious warmth was spreading over her as his fingers became bolder and unbuttoned her pyjamas, then he moved down the bed to kiss her breasts. She held his head to her, tears filling her eyes with the beauty of it, breathing suspended as waves of sensual delight washed over her.

Slowly his hand moved down to her waist, pushing down her pyjamas, smoothing her belly in circling movements, growing lower and lower with each one. As it moved down to her legs, caressing, teasing, she could feel a strange wetness between her legs and she longed for his fingers to make their way there.

But each time she thought he was going to touch her, so he moved his hand away, to her breast or to her bottom, his lips covering hers, and teasing her with his tongue.

Her heart was pounding, breath coming loud and harsh. She grabbed his hand shamelessly and guided it to where she wanted it, groaning with delight as his fingers touched her parted lips.

She hadn't expected it to be so wonderful. Her own fingers had never felt like this. She was on fire, driven to some wonderful secret place, oblivious to anything other than those probing, gentle fingers and the heat of strange sensations washing over her.

Again and again her hands reached down to touch the bulge she could feel so close to her belly. His deep breathing would pause, she sensed he was willing her to touch it, yet she was afraid.

He moved away just slightly, his lips still on her breast, sucking at her nipples, taking his pants off with one hand. She stiffened involuntarily.

'I'm not going to hurt you,' he whispered, burying his face in her neck. 'I love you Georgia, trust me.'

Instinctively she knew this wasn't a trite remark made in the heat of passion to persuade her. Their close friendship had been building up to this moment and she was just too naïve to see it before.

He took her hand, held it for a moment to his chest, then slowly moved it down onto his belly.

'There,' he whispered as he closed her fingers round his penis. 'Is it so bad?'

There was laughter in his voice, nothing intense or scary. It wasn't even slimy as she'd expected, just hard and warm. He was kissing her again, his fingers probing deep within her and all at once she really wanted him.

'My love,' he whispered. 'You can't imagine how often I've dreamed about this!'

It was she who rushed things, pulling him on to her, digging her fingers into his back and although she braced herself for pain, there was none.

The icy room, the wind outside had all faded. Waves of pleasure, coming hard and frantic, getting faster and faster, in time to his movements. Lips reaching for the other's. His hands on her buttocks, hers caressing his back. She was beginning to drift away onto some strange fiery plane, where all sense of time and place had ceased, when he moved back from her, dropping on to her, panting furiously.

For a moment she didn't understand, her hips were still undulating under him and their bellies were hot and sticky.

'I'm sorry,' he whispered against her neck as his breathing slowly returned to normal. 'I only remembered at the last moment.'

'Remembered what?' she whispered back, feeling strangely let down, but unsure why.

'About Durex,' he said. 'I don't want to get you pregnant.'

He lay down next to her then, pulling her into his arms and kissing her deeply.

'Did it hurt?' he whispered.

'No,' she wound her fingers into his hair, her heart filled with tenderness for him. 'It was beautiful.'

'Tell me about you,' his voice was husky with emotion. 'I know something happened before. Was it rape?'

Their act of love was an anaesthetic. She found she could tell him the whole story without pain. For Helen and Janet it had been abridged, the poison left inside the wound to flare up again unexpectedly. But now as she told Ian safe in his arms, she felt the healing process begin.

'I'll make you forget,' he whispered, squeezing her to him. 'One day it will be so perfect he'll be wiped out forever.'

Georgia stroked his face, feeling the dampness round his eyes.

'I love you, Ian!' she whispered. 'You've made me whole again.'

She did love Ian. How could she not love someone as special, sensitive and caring as him? He filled a place in her life so fully she didn't need anyone else. They had the same dreams and ambitions for their music. He'd driven the demons out of her head, shown her the beauty of sexual love.

Secrecy was necessary. If Max found out they both knew he would move swiftly to put an end to it. Ian crept into her room after the others had gone to sleep, hidden hand-holding in the van, secret excursions together during afternoons in strange towns.

She saw new maturity in his angelic face. He put on a little more weight, his delicate features grew stronger.

Disappointment and hardships bound them closer together. He didn't ask for commitment, he was content just to share his days and nights with her. Never asking about his part in her future, urging her to take Max's offer. Yet why with all this perfection were there times when she despised him! What sort of person was she that she was so irritated by his sheer goodness? Why did she want to scream at him, shake him, anything to make him wake up and see things as they really were.

Her feelings for Max baffled her still further. She hated the way he was manipulating her and the boys, yet admired his single-mindedness at the same time. He was cruel, greedy, ruthless. As far apart from Ian as a predatory eagle to a chirpy robin. Sitting back in his plush office watching her struggle helplessly just like that fly in his gold spider's web. What weakness on her part made her feel that eventually he would get exactly just what he wanted? Not just a gold record or two, but maybe her body and soul!

But one thing was clear, which ever way she turned Ian would lose. Samson would flounder without her; if she stayed the pressure Max created would do the same. Had Ian really thought what would happen if she became a big star and his role was little more than a hanger-on?

'Let's go,' Speedy picked up the red stage dress and brushed it off. He shot a look of understanding at Georgia. 'There's a party to go to, remember?'

This party was the one thing the boys had been looking forward to for weeks. It would be a glitzy, star-studded event that would hit the newspapers the next morning. Girls in plenty, free food and drink. Enough to make them forget the humiliations Max had thrown at them.

'I don't fancy it,' Georgia said wearily. She was sick and tired of people for now. She wanted to be alone in her room, not getting dressed up and posing as the rising star.

'Don't be daft,' Rod said brightly. 'You can't not turn up. We're all ready to go.' Rod looked like a star himself, in black leather trousers and a ruffled shirt, his hair cut in the new 'Beatles' style.

'You all go,' she said firmly. 'Have a great time, get drunk and screw as many birds as you can find. I'm going home.'

Ian was looking at her, one eyebrow raised. A 'does that mean you want me to come home with you' face.

'You go too Ian,' she said turning away from him so she couldn't see the sad look she knew would come into those beautiful blue eyes.

He followed her out the door, catching hold of her bare arm and squeezing it.

'Have I done something?' he said, his eyes soft like a puppy's.

For a moment she weakened. His long dark lashes framing his eyes, a perfect straight nose and that soft vulnerable mouth. He was perfection, not just his angelic beauty but the depth of his love and understanding for her.

'No, of course not,' she lifted a hand to his face, stroking it tenderly. 'I just can't cope tonight. I'd only spoil it for all of you. Get drunk and be silly and you can tell me all about it tomorrow night. We've got a week off remember? Maybe we can go somewhere together.'

'I love you,' he took her face in both his hands, regardless of people barging along the corridor.

His kiss was sweet and lingering. She felt the dressing-room door open behind them and someone look out, but she no longer cared.

'I love you too,' she whispered. 'Now go on and have fun.'

He was still standing by the door as she reached the end of the narrow corridor. Downstairs there were shrieks of girls' laughter, mingling with male voices and the popping of champagne corks. 'Love, love me do', the Beatles' song was playing at full volume.

She lifted her hand and blew him a kiss. She could see his soft lips curved into a smile, brushing back his floppy fair hair impatiently from his eyes. Tomorrow she had to come to a firm decision about him, it wasn't fair to take his love yet give him no real commitment in return.

Outside in Hammersmith Broadway she slipped unnoticed through the huge crowd of fans waiting for the big stars to make their appearance. It was a hot night, only just getting dark, the traffic as heavy as if it were six in the evening instead of ten thirty. No one noticed the slim dark girl in a pink dress pushing her way through the crowd.

She would catch a tube to Piccadilly, wander about the way she used to do with Helen. Tomorrow she would go in and see Pop and the girls. By then she'd be feeling her old self again. It was just exhaustion that made her feel so prickly.

It was almost twelve as she approached Berwick Street. Nothing had changed here. It was as dirty, smelly and full of noise as always, but just seeing her front door made her more cheerful.

Bert had surprised her in the last year. He'd spent money on the house, turning the lower rooms into a suite of offices, and she was the only tenant left. What had once been the small landing outside her room was now a tiny bathroom just for her, only a shower, basin and toilet, but it was bright and new. A fitted carpet had been laid. Not only in her room but up the stairs too. The old cooker and sink had been replaced with a smart fitted sink, a baby belling cooker and a fridge. She knew Bert had made these improvements not for her, but as an investment. When she moved out he would treble the rent, or even sell the entire place at a huge profit. But at least she had no need to feel ashamed of where she lived now.

'Georgia! What are you playing at?'

She had been so deep in her thoughts she hadn't spotted the new maroon MK 10 Jaguar parked outside. Max was sitting behind the wheel, his arm resting on the open window, wearing a white dinner jacket.

He could have passed for a film star as he leapt out of his car. His tanned, rugged face, the white jacket gleaming under the street light, his wide shoulders, animal grace and his sensuous features were enough to make any woman stop and stare.

'Why aren't you at the party?' he asked.

'I couldn't face it,' she sighed. 'Don't get at me Max. I'm not in the mood.'

'I didn't come here to get at you,' he snapped. 'I was concerned about you. I was in the audience tonight and I thought you lacked your usual sparkle. Then the boys said you'd gone off alone. What's wrong?'

'I'm just pissed off,' she snapped back at him, getting out her key and putting it in the door. 'Don't say I'm not even allowed an off day or I'll spit at you.'

His big hand covered hers on the lock.

'Come and have something to eat with me?' His voice was softer, almost understanding. She could feel his body close to hers and for some reason it felt comforting. 'I'll take you somewhere nice and quiet, feed you up and let you relax. I didn't come to fight with you.'

'I want to go to bed,' she said weakly. In fact she was very hungry and she knew the only food she had was a tin of baked beans.

'You don't,' he insisted. 'I know perfectly well you

didn't get up till two o'clock today. You may be tired and fed up, but you aren't sleepy. Now hop in the car and we'll go somewhere.'

She hadn't the will to argue further. Perhaps it was time she talked to him instead of ducking the issue. Maybe if she told him about how bad things were he might stop persecuting the band.

He drove silently up the narrow road to Oxford Street, then turned up towards Marble Arch.

'Don't even think of taking me to the party,' she said quickly.

'Not all roads lead to Park Lane,' he grinned. 'Though what on earth you've got against a bash like that I'll never know.'

'Girls getting goosed in corners. Loud-mouthed louts making fools of themselves and all the PR birds falling over themselves to get one of the stars into bed,' she said bitterly. 'I can live without that.'

'You sound like an old lady,' Max smiled. 'Could it be you wouldn't be the centre of attention?'

'I'm just tired!'

He was right of course, when had she ever wanted to pass up a party before? Adam Faith was fun, he wasn't such a big shot, and if the PR girls were a pain, at least all the other performers agreed with her. 'But we can't go on like this Max, it isn't fair and you know it. Our band is far better than any of the others. We deserve more than bottom of the bill.'

Max didn't answer. They were passing the Hilton's glass frontage, awash with golden light. A Rolls Royce drew up outside and the doorman rushed forward to welcome the occupant.

'Petula Clark,' Max waved one big hand, his gold watch gleaming on a thick wrist. 'One day you'll have a car like that Georgia. Just stop being so stubborn and listen to reason.

He took her to a small restaurant in Chelsea, ushering her through the main area to a floodlit garden beyond.

'It's too nice to be indoors tonight,' he smiled at Georgia's rapt face. She looked like a little girl tonight, in that pink cotton dress and her hair in a pony-tail. Surrounded as he was by predatory secretaries who hid behind masks of make-up, her innocence and straight talking was a tonic. 'The food's good here too.'

It reminded Georgia of places she'd seen on films. Honeysuckle covered walls, urns of bright petunias and pansies with little stone statues half hidden beneath the foliage.

They were the only people eating outside, soft music wafted out as they ate French onion soup and Max kept filling up her wine glass.

'It's like being on holiday,' she grinned. Max could be so charming when he wanted to be. She hadn't eaten anything more than fry-ups and hamburgers for weeks and from inside the restaurant she could smell sizzling steaks being grilled.

'Come away for a few days with me,' he said unexpectedly. 'We could catch a flight tomorrow to Spain. You could have this every night.'

For a moment she could just see a golden beach, turquoise sea and palms waving in a soft breeze. She could feel the sun on her shoulders, the sand between her toes.

'No strings,' he smiled, sensing her temptation. 'Separate rooms. Just time to talk and relax.'

'I couldn't,' she reluctantly pulled herself back to reality, Ian's face full of hurt. 'Besides I haven't any clothes.'

'We could buy anything you need,' he leaned closer across the table, putting one big hand over hers. 'Of course you can come. What's stopping you?'

'The boys,' she merely whispered it. 'They'd think I'd sold out.'

'Would you come if I said I'd allow you to make a record with them?'

Georgia felt her stomach turn over. Was this black-mail, teasing, or merely trying to find out her price?

'Are you serious?'

He was such a good-looking man. His face in the soft floodlights had a golden glow, his dark, hooded eyes so sexy she felt she wanted to reach out and touch him even if he was the enemy.

The waiter interrupted the moment by clearing away their soup bowls. It gave her time to collect herself.

Would the thought of making a record absolve her from being alone in Spain with Max? Would Ian believe nothing happened?

'Of course I'm serious,' he looked at her through half closed eyes, a faint smile twitching his lips.

'What would Miriam say about this?' By turning the tables on him she was giving herself time to think.

'I'd tell her and the boys we were going to see a promoter,' he said too glibly. He hadn't really planned anything tonight. It had all tumbled into his head when he saw her sad, troubled expression. He wanted her. He had from the moment he clapped eyes on her, her combination of girlish sweetness and the tough rock singer was enough to give any man a hard on. But for now he was content to woo her.

'I can't make up my mind just like that,' she said weakly, tempted now to the point where she was almost agreeing.

'There's plenty of time,' he smiled, sensing she was almost his. 'I'm serious Georgia. I can't fight you any longer this way. I can't swing a recording contract for the band, but if they came up with the right song, written by themselves, we could insist they got equal billing. After the first hit, Decca might review the situation.'

The steaks arrived with a huge bowl of salad. Georgia's mind was still churning over his idea. Was this another ploy to weaken her resolve? Could she hold him to it, get a real promise before they even talked seriously about getting on a plane?

The lack of contract for the boys wasn't important. If her first record was a hit, there would be enough exposure to launch them in their own right. They would have the shared royalties and her debt to them would be paid in full.

The steak was perfect, succulent and tender. The wine was giving her a rosy glow and the smell of honeysuckle filled her nostrils.

Max was talking about one of his new bands. Georgia smiled as if she was listening carefully, but all the time her mind was on Ian.

He was the stumbling block. Samson for all their talent couldn't survive without a strong singer. They would have to replace him or lose all credibility. How could she even think of putting Ian in such a precarious position?

The steaks were followed by strawberries and cream in huge glass goblets. Max filled up her glass yet again, then sat back and lit up a cigar.

'You're worried about Ian?' he said, looking at her with half-closed eyes. 'How long has it been going on?'

He hadn't been certain before. Secret looks between the pair of them, the lack of complaints about sharing rooms. Jokes from the other boys. Nothing definite to point to involvement with the lad, but he could see that look of concern in her eyes and he knew it wasn't for the rest of the band.

'Eighteen months,' she sighed. It was too late for lies. Why should she cover it up anyway?

Max crossed his legs, tilting back his chair. The floodlights reflecting on the foliage around him had turned his face green. He looked sinister now. Calculating and mean.

'What made you get involved with him?' he snapped. 'He's a nice enough lad, but by God Georgia, couldn't you look ahead and see the problems?'

'I could say the same about you,' she retorted. 'You've got a wife you don't seem to consider. Did you look ahead and see that coming?'

'Leave Miriam out of this,' his mouth turned mean and bad tempered. 'We're talking about your future. I told you that lad was the weak link. He's useless as a singer and if you stay together he'll be a millstone round your neck. If it had been Rod I could have understood it, or Speedy. They've got a future. Ian's got nothing.'

He painted the scene she'd seen so often at the back of her mind. Ian waiting patiently at home while she got all the glory, how long would it be before his role was nothing more than a lap dog?

'Don't you dare speak about Ian like that,' Georgia stood up, her chair tumbling over behind her. 'You may be my manager. But I won't stand by and let you belittle him.'

'Sit down darling,' he reached out for her hand. 'People are looking!'

Out of the corner of her eye she could see heads turning, middle-class socialites looking down their noses at her cheap cotton dress and assuming she was a pick-up.

'I don't give a shit,' she snarled. 'You've got no idea how much of Samson is Ian have you? Without his ideas and drive they would never have got off the ground. If you had any sense you'd be looking for another slot to fit him into, on the management side, instead of trying to get rid of him.'

A wave of red-hot anger was washing over her. This was the man who was responsible for all the problems, yet for a moment she'd been tempted to conspire with him!

'It won't be me who gets rid of him,' Max arched one eyebrow. 'The lure of fame and wealth does many things to people.'

'You should know,' she snarled. 'You wrote the dirty tricks book didn't you?'

She turned and ran then, straight through the restaurant, pushing aside a waiter, tears streaming down her cheeks, out into the street.

'Is the young lady coming back, Mr Menzies?' The waiter approached tentatively, his thin body bending in supplication.

'I doubt it,' Max snapped. 'Just get me a large brandy.'

Chapter 13

As Georgia rushed headlong towards Sloane Square, angry with herself for being foolish enough to believe she and Max had anything to discuss, the boys were just leaving the Hilton.

'We'd better get a cab,' John wobbled unsteadily along the pavement.

They were all drunk. Ian so bad he could barely walk, lost in a silent world of his own.

'We can't all get in one,' Rod said, slurring his words. 'Perhaps we ought to walk anyway.'

Speedy turned at a high-pitched shriek from behind them. A public relations girl from Decca was tottering towards them. Earlier in the evening her blonde hair had been piled up on her head in elaborate curls, now it was dishevelled, falling over her face.

'Take me home Speedy,' she called out.

'One down,' Rod murmured, pausing against a car showroom window and pressing his face against the glass. A gleaming red Mercedes was turning round slowly on a revolving platform, it made him feel even drunker.

Ian swayed, white-faced, eyes half closed a few feet from Rod. John and Alan were sitting on the kerb. Les was throwing up noisily behind a parked car.

Speedy and the girl crossed the road towards Knightsbridge. The tall blonde girl's white dress was so tight she could only hobble, she trailed a pink feather boa over her shoulder, unaware it was touching the pavement behind her. The pair of them had linked arms and it was hard to see which one was holding the other up.

'He won't be much good to her when they get back,' Rod said to nobody in particular. 'But then I think he's already given her one in the toilets.'

It had been a wonderful party. Scores of girls milling around, convinced Rod was every bit as much of a star as Adam Faith, Billy Fury and all the others. One tart had given him a wank under the table and he could have pulled anyone he wanted if he'd put his mind to it.

But Ian was bugging him. He hadn't said or done anything other than drink himself stupid, and he knew it was all to do with Georgia.

'Where's Norman?' he asked, lurching forward towards where John and Alan sat hunched mindlessly on the kerb.

'Gone off with some girl,' John turned bloodshot eyes on Rod. 'Can you get it together to flag down a cab?'

Ian was usually the one that rounded them all up after nights like these, but one glance at his blank face was enough to know he was the one who needed looking after.

'All right,' Rod lurched into the road and put up his hand.

A taxi came seconds later.

'Where to mate?' A raw-boned face under a flat cap looked out suspiciously.

'Ladbroke Square,' Rod said. 'Just a minute while I get my mates.'

'Don't any of you throw up in the back otherwise I'll rub your noses in it,' the taxi driver said sharply. 'And open the bloody windows, the fumes are enough to make me sick.'

Rod paid the driver as the others almost fell out the taxi. Les rushed back to the gutter, and once again vomited.

The house was in darkness. Timed switches on the wall turned themselves off even before they climbed slowly to the first landing. A smell of curry came from behind the door of a Jamaican family. Their flat was right at the top of the house. Three large rooms on the fourth floor and another up a flight of steep narrow steps to the attic.

Rod put his arm round Ian, supporting him as they made their way up. Alan and John had already reached the top now. Les was hauling himself up by the banisters like an old man.

'What's been eating you tonight?' Rod asked Ian as they finally got in the front door.

'Georgia,' Ian said stupidly, his mouth drooping. 'She's only staying with the band because of me and I can't bear it any longer.'

'Come on now mate,' Rod eased Ian back into an armchair. The whole flat was filthy. He would have to find some bird to come and sort it out. Clothes in heaps, records all over the floor, piled up ashtrays, half eaten food going mouldy on plates left there weeks ago, and at least two dozen empty beer bottles.

The flat was a mixture of tastes. Speedy's collection of old books. Ian's posters and records of blues and soul artists. Rod himself was responsible for the red warning road lamps, picked up on another drunken binge. There were nude girl posters. A Salvador Dali print and a bull-fighting poster personalized with Norman's name. A black and red pair of knickers had been on the table lamp so long no one could even remember who they belonged to. A messy, tasteless place, but it was a storehouse of good memories.

Alan was lurching up the steep stairs that led to the attic. His new grey leather jacket was stained with drink and he'd burned a hole in his one good pair of black trousers. His small, boyish face grinned inanely, his blond hair brushed down on his forehead made him look like a medieval page boy. He didn't even realize he was making for the wrong room. The attic belonged to Rod and Ian, but Rod couldn't be bothered to turf him out. Les was in the bathroom being sick yet again and John was attempting to make some coffee.

'Get some in here sharpish.' Rod called out. He turned back to Ian and crouched down beside him. Even drunk, Ian was as immaculate as when he arrived at the party. Tie neatly knotted, shirt crisp and fresh. Even his hair was perfect, baby soft, shining pale yellow in the murky light.

Rod knew Ian loved Georgia. He'd even been jealous at first, hurt that anyone could come between him and his best friend. But Ian was level-headed. He had maintained all his old enthusiasm in the band, perhaps even increasing it. What had happened to make him react like this now?

'Don't worry about it,' Rod felt a pang of sympathy for his friend. If a girl made him miserable, he just went out and found another, but Ian was different. 'Why don't we give her the elbow? Insist we want to go it alone that way she won't have to feel bad about us?'

'Don't be such a fucking idiot,' Ian seemed to sober up suddenly, his blue eyes flashing ice cold. 'Do you really think I could fill Georgia's shoes as singer?'

'We did all right before she joined us!' Rod said evenly.

'We didn't know what a good singer could do then, did we?' Ian slumped back in his seat, eyes closing. 'You'd be looking to me to make it right. The audience would wonder why you had a wanker like me up front. I'm stuck in the bloody middle holding you both back. That's the reason she won't go. She's afraid for me.'

'Aren't you forgetting we all used to sing before she

joined us?' Rod had never seen Ian like this before. 'Mick Jagger's voice ain't so hot, and what about the Beatles? All we have to do is use a bit of strategy. Stop feeling sorry for yourself mate. Georgia loves you, anyone would think she wanted to dump you!'

'Maybe she does!' Ian's head slumped down towards his chest. He looked defeated and old. 'Aren't I more like a brother to her? You can love someone, and be "in love" with them, the two aren't necessarily the same. She loves all of us. That's the bloody trouble.'

'Of course she loves you,' Rod said firmly. He sat down on the arm of the chair and hugged his friend awkwardly. 'After all it's you she sleeps with!'

Rod wasn't one for soul searching. A girl to him was a diversion, nothing more. They all had their attractions, once he'd played them out, he moved on. He couldn't really understand why other men agonized over feelings, it was such a waste of energy.

'You don't know anything about her,' Ian sniffed. 'Her father raped her when she was only fifteen. That's why there was never any blokes in her life until me. If any of you had been the one to press the right buttons you might be the one sharing her bed now.'

Rod was too drunk to think that one out, or even be shocked.

'It's you she loves, you prat,' Rod hauled him up by the shoulders. 'You was always mates, right from the start and she ain't the type to use anyone. All you gotta do is to push her out on her own, 'cos she's too damned stubborn to do it herself.'

'Then why didn't she come with me to the party tonight?'

'I expect she knew we'd all end up rat-arsed like this,' Rod grinned. John was swaying behind him with three cups of coffee. 'Now drink that and piss off to bed. And stop seeing problems where there aren't any.'

Ian seemed to pull himself together a little after his coffee.

'I shouldn't have told you about Georgia,' he said as he went on up the steep stairs to the attic. 'I only told you because I know you're a real human being under that flashy exterior. You won't let on to anyone?'

'You're a wanker when you're pissed,' Rod called after him. 'Any more crap from you and I'll tell her what a feeble little prat you can be.'

Rod woke up, a faint smell of something in his nostrils.

For a moment he couldn't quite place where he was, he had cramp in his legs from lying curled up on the couch and as he moved he fell on to the floor knocking over the half drunk coffee.

'Shit,' he exclaimed. It had splattered his new shirt and it would stain if he didn't see to it.

Standing up, he looked around.

There was a smell, and a strange noise, a kind of faint roaring above him. His head felt as if it were full of cotton wool, his stomach was churning. Yet he was sure he wasn't imagining that smell.

'Fire!' he yelled, running out the door and leaping up the stairs to the attic, three at a time. The door was closed, smoke billowing under it and as he opened it another cloud of it hit him in the face. Beyond the smoke were flames. Licking up by the window, fanned by the draught from the door.

He closed the door quickly, leaped down the stairs again and rushed into the other bedroom.

'John, Les,' he shouted, shaking their arms. 'Fire! Ring the fucking fire brigade. Alan and Ian are in there burning alive!'

John was up immediately. Dark eyes gleaming in the dark. He grabbed his trousers and ran for the door.

'Les, for fuck's sake wake up,' Rod screamed now. 'Fire. Get out now!'

He stopped only long enough to grap a heap of blankets, his heart thumping like a steam hammer.

Running into the bathroom he turned the taps on full, then dunked the blankets in, hauled one out and carrying it dripping in his arms he made his way up the stairs again.

'Get the other tenants out, Les,' he shouted back down the stairs as Les lumbered out. His sallow, long face stared stupidly, dark hair hanging over one eye. He wore only a pair of jeans, feet bare, his sunken chest and spindly arms almost pitiful. 'Get going!'

The smoke made him choke as he opened the door and the heat of the flames made him recoil momentarily. Putting the blanket over his head he got down on all fours and began to crawl across the floor.

The bed closest to the window was well and truly alight, flames licking over it, but the black smoke prevented him from seeing anything. The curtains had caught, taking the fire to the other bed, and he could just make out the outline of a body, flames just flicking out like evil fingers to consume it.

He threw the blanket over the body, standing just for a moment choking with the fumes. Then grabbing the body by the feet he hauled it away from the bed.

There was a thud as it hit the floor, but it was too late to be cautious. Blinded by the black smoke he hauled it back across the floor, towards the door.

It was Alan. His face blackened by smoke, burns on his arms and legs, his fair hair almost completely gone on one side of his head, sharp little features so familiar, but different seen black.

John was coming back in the front door.

'Bring me more blankets!' Rod shouted. 'In the bath.'

Rod stood coughing on the landing. His hands were burned but that was unimportant. Somehow he had to get Ian out of there too.

'Don't go in again,' John flung him blankets, rushing

313

up to look at Alan lying inert on the landing bending over him to feel for a pulse. 'The floor might go. Wait for the fire brigade.'

'Try giving him the kiss of life,' Rod hissed. 'I'm going back.' He dropped down to his knees, one blanket over him, dragging the other behind him, as at last the sound of sirens wailed down the street.

'Up the top,' Les directed the firemen at the front door. He had sobered up the moment he knew what had happened, but now he wished he'd had the presence of mind to grab shoes. He had cut his foot on a piece of broken glass and blood was pouring out.

'You stay here lad,' the big fireman pushed him aside. 'Who else is in there?'

'Three of my mates,' Les tried to follow but was pushed back. 'No, four, John went back into help.'

The two first fire engines were quickly joined by another two making a 'V' shape in the road. Firemen rushed in one after another, hauling hoses behind them.

Outside a crowd was gathering, more stood behind the railings of the communal gardens in the centre of the square. Old women in nightdresses. Children in pyjamas, men wearing nothing but a pair of trousers like himself.

'How did it start?' A fireman tugged at Les's arm as he stared up at the house. Flames were flickering on the roof now, turning the dark sky purple. Thick black choking smoke wafted down, almost concealing the ladder from the fire engine and the man on it wielding a high-pressure hose. Another two fire engines came roaring into the square, the men leaping out even before the engine stopped.

'I don't know,' Les was crying now, tears splashing down over his cheeks, a dew drop gathering on his hooked nose. 'We'd been to a party. We were all drunk. Perhaps it was a cigarette.'

John came out first, quickly followed by two firemen carrying a body on a stretcher.

Les broke through the cordoned-off area and ran to John.

'Who is it?' he asked. 'Where's Rod?'

'That's Alan,' John's dark eyes were filled with tears. He reached out for Les like a child, burying his head on his shoulder. 'Rod went back to try and get Ian. I think he's copped it too.'

'Is Alan dead?' He could hardly bear to ask.

'Yes, overcome by the fumes before the fire reached him. I tried to revive him, but I didn't know how. Rod risked everything, for nothing.'

It was like some hideous nightmare. John and Les stood bare-chested, huddled together. Windows opened, more people drifted onto the square in their nightclothes, all around them were whispers, pointing them out and giving other neighbours their opinion as to who was still inside.

Two firemen came out again with a stretcher. Their faces black, the whites of their eyes showing clearly in contrast, under their helmets.

'Who is it?' John cried out.

'The one who went in to rescue them. He's in a bad way.' The firemen handed over the stretcher to the ambulance. 'But he's alive.'

'And Ian?' They both knew the answer, but they had to ask.

'He didn't stand a chance,' Another fireman came out of the doorway, he moved closer to them putting one big gloved hand on John's shoulder. 'He was dead before your friend even got in there. I'm sorry.'

Georgia jumped violently as the doorbell rang. For a moment she ignored it, thinking it was for one of the offices downstairs. Again and again it rang, and slowly she got out of bed to look out the window.

Sunday mornings were the only time the street was quiet. Empty of stalls, the only litter from drunken revellers the night before.

'Who is it?' she called down, peering out over the window-sill.

'It's John,' an ashen face turned up to her. He was wearing nothing over his bare chest but an old cardigan. 'There's been a fire!'

She threw a key down to him, then hastily pulled on jeans and a shirt. She was just pushing her feet into a pair of plimsolls when John came through the door.

'Ian and Alan are both dead,' he said sinking into her arms like a child. 'Our flat's gone, and Rod's seriously hurt.'

For a moment Georgia just held John staring vacantly at a poster of poppies on her wall.

'Ian, dead?' she whispered.

She made him coffee, putting in lots of sugar, and found him a shirt of Ian's left in her wardrobe. She was shaking, yet she couldn't cry. She knew she was behaving like a mere neighbour, not like someone who'd just been told her lover was dead. All the time she kept thinking it was a dream, that any minute she'd wake up and find she was alone.

But John was very real. He was icy cold to the touch. Bristles of beard showed through on his chin. His feet were bare and his eyes were full of tears, why couldn't she share them?

'Let me find you something to put on your feet,' she said. 'Ian left some shoes here.'

'Georgia, have you heard a word?' John shouted at her. 'Ian and Alan are dead, Rod maybe too by now and you worry about my feet?'

He grabbed her in his arms, holding her so tightly she could barely breathe, sobbing on her shoulder like a two-year-old. She could see Ian standing in the corridor at the Odeon last night, his hand lifted to

316

return her kiss. All at once the reality hit her. She saw flames licking around that slender body, reaching out for his blond silky hair.

John held her against his shoulder, patting her back as they sobbed together. 'My two best mates just wiped out and I never even said goodbye to either of them.'

It was just half past seven in the morning when John woke her and as the day slowly passed there was no end to the misery. Rod had been taken to Hammersmith hospital. Alan's body was already in the morgue and Ian's charred remains followed later. Les's foot was so badly cut it needed stitching and John, after rushing across London to find Georgia, had sunk into shock, barely speaking. Alan and he had been like brothers from the age of six, their whole adult life had been spent together, even most of their possessions were shared. Now he was gone, and the next closest friend, Ian, with him.

'Can you tell me about Rod?' Georgia asked the nurses who scurried by, averting their eyes from the two boys still with smoke smuts on their faces sitting there shoeless and silent.

'He's holding his own,' was all they would say. 'It's too soon to know yet.'

Later, Speedy arrived at the hospital. He had gone home around ten in the morning to find the house still faintly smoking, the whole top floor caved in. He at least was calm enough to find John and Les other clothes and shoes from a nearby friend and to insist they washed and combed their hair.

Norman's whereabouts were still unknown. Soon the parents of Ian, Alan and Rod would be wanting to talk to John and Les, but neither was capable of anything more than nodding and shaking their heads.

Max came striding down the corridor around noon. He had been out when John had phoned him early that morning and Georgia suspected he had probably stayed out all night. He had stubble on his chin, his eyes bloodshot.

'How did it happen?' he demanded of John, even though he could see the boy was hardly able to speak.

'They don't know,' Georgia spoke up. 'They think Ian must have been smoking in bed and dropped it on the floor. What are we going to do?'

She waited for Max to say something harsh, but to her surprise his eyes filled with tears.

'It's not fair,' he said, turning away so they couldn't see his face. 'So much to look forward to, snatched away in their prime.'

Georgia stood up, putting one hand on his arm, the other wiped away his tears with her hanky. His shoulders were slumped, his full lips quivering.

'We've got to pray Rod will make it,' she said.

'Speedy,' Max straightened up, getting back his self control. He sniffed, wiping one big hand across his eyes. 'Take John and Les to my house, get Miriam to put them to bed and call a doctor to give them something. Will you stay here with me Georgia?'

She nodded.

The clock hands moved so slowly. Each doctor who passed the waiting room made them straighten up and hope it was news. The police called to say that Rod's parents were away on holiday in Devon, but they were passing the information over to the police there. Alan's widowed mother had been informed as had Ian's family.

'None of them were close to their families,' Max said softly. 'Alan's mother rejected him when her husband was killed in an accident when he was thirteen. Ian put up a show of caring about his, but I never knew any of them come to gigs or anything. Yet I still don't know how I'm going to face them.'

'If only I'd taken Ian home with me last night,' Georgia

blurted out. 'He wanted to come Max, but I insisted he went to the party. It's all my fault.'

'Of course it isn't,' Max put his arm round her and cradled her to him. This was a side she'd never seen of him before and it touched her deeply. 'It could have happened at any time. If someone's number comes up, that's it. Can you imagine how low I feel now after what we were talking about last night?'

All at once Georgia felt tears welling up inside her. The same terrible loneliness she'd felt that night when Helen died. She put her head on Max's chest and sobbed and sobbed.

'I wish I could find the right words,' he said softly stroking her hair. 'You don't deserve any of this, baby. I'll find a way to make it up to you.'

The door of the waiting room opened. A young woman doctor with pale brown hair and kind eyes was smiling.

'He's going to be all right,' she said. 'We had some trouble with his breathing. But it's stabilized now.'

'You mean he's not going to die?' Georgia sat up straight, wiping her eyes with the back of her hand.

'Far from it,' the doctor laughed softly. 'He's got a few burns, but nothing too serious. He was a brave lad by all accounts. He won't be running for any buses for some time. I doubt he'll ever want a cigarette in his life again and of course the shock of seeing his two friends burned to death will take some getting over. But go along and see him for yourself.'

'I'll wait here,' Max touched her shoulder. 'It's you he'll want to see. I'll wait till he's stronger.'

Georgia peeped round the door of the small side ward. There were three beds, but the others were empty. Rod was propped up on pillows, a drip in his arm, his face an angry shade of red. Both arms and his head were swathed in bandages.

319

'How are you feeling?' she asked, standing tentatively at the end of the bed.

'Sore,' he whispered, his voice unexpectedly croaky. 'I tried to save them,' a big tear rolled down his cheek.

'You were wonderfully brave,' Georgia came closer, wanting to hug him but afraid of hurting him. 'You couldn't have done any more.'

'I should have gone up and got Alan out of my bed,' Rod said. 'I might have seen the cigarette then.'

'I should have taken Ian home with me,' she wiped a tear from her cheek.

She pulled a chair up close to his bed, laying her head on the covers. Without another word the burden of shared guilt passed from one to another.

'He told me he loved you,' Rod's eyes opened wider, wincing as if they hurt. 'Make a deal with Decca now, Georgia. It's what he wanted.'

'I don't want to sing again ever,' she whispered, unable to hold back her tears.

'You must,' he croaked. 'Wherever Ian and Alan are they'll be waiting for it. Right now I don't believe I'll ever be able to play again either, or even want to, without them. But if I can manage it, so can you.'

She looked up and saw tears streaming down his face.

'Don't Rod,' she got up and reached out tentatively to wipe them away.

'Kiss me,' Rod whispered.

Georgia moved forward and put her lips on his.

'I feel better already,' he tried hard to smile. 'One of these days I'll give you a real one and see what that does for you.'

She smiled at his brave attempt at flirtation, and patted his bandaged hand gently.

'You can have all the kisses you want if you just get better. I think you must be the bravest man I ever met.'

Chapter 14

'The time's right to cut a record Georgia,' Max sat in his office looking at her under hooded eyelids. 'You've had all that publicity. If we don't get it out now we'll lose the benefit.'

'Do you have to be so ghoulish?' She leapt to her feet, eyes blazing at his callousness. 'Rod still can't hold drumsticks. John can hardly eat for grief. We've lost our saxophone player. Your timing stinks.'

Max ignored her outburst. A fortnight had passed and it was time to crack the whip again.

'I'm talking about you,' he said calmly. 'You cutting a record, not the boys.'

'Don't start that again,' she stared at him coldly. 'Surely they can come in on it with me after what's happened?'

Max studied Georgia. She had lost weight, her hair was dull and lank, she even had a couple of spots on her chin, her skin the colour of porridge. He didn't want to be cruel, but he knew if he gave her too much time she might never get back to work.

'They can work as your backing group,' he said sharply. 'But that's all. I've got plans to find them a new male singer. Someone raunchy who'll get the girls screaming. I've also put the word out I want a new song for you.'

'Why can't we record something we've written?'

Georgia stuck out her lip. She was actually glad Max was going to find Samson a new singer. New blood was needed in the band and she knew Speedy, Rod and Norman hungered for stardom in their own right.

'Because I want a big dramatic number with strings and a full orchestra,' he smirked. 'I don't want some drippy bit of bubblegum music.'

'But what if we came up with the right song?'

'Don't make me laugh,' he snapped. 'I'll listen to anything you come up with of course, but don't waste my time Georgia.'

Georgia wasn't surprised by Max's apparent heartlessness. He alone was behaving characteristically. In a strange way it was more comforting than fan letters and the endless sympathy poured on the band by people who scarcely knew Ian and Alan.

She had written the words of a song already, sitting alone in her room after the double funeral. Now with Max pushing her she might just find the strength to show the boys.

It had been such a beautiful funeral. A ray of sunshine shone through the high window at the crematorium, and rested on the two pine coffins side by side, each with a wreath of red roses. The chapel was packed to the doors with fans, old school friends, relatives and more than a sprinkling of musicians.

All the papers had covered the story, perhaps only because Adam Faith, Billy Fury, Helen Shapiro and Marty Wilde were there. But it meant a great deal to all of the band to see these stars take time off in their busy lives to pay their last respects.

So many bouquets of flowers and wreaths lined the entrance to the chapel and spilled out on to the forecourt. Some had sheets of music wound into them, some were just simple bunches brought along by unknown fans. The bright colours and the perfume belied the seriousness of the occasion. Few of the mourners wore dark clothes either, as if knowing the boys would prefer them to come the way they remembered them.

Georgia wore a simple black dress with a white collar. She knew Ian would have told her she looked like a missionary and urged her to wear red, but she was afraid his mother would misinterpret her actions.

Speedy and Les accompanied Norman with their guitars while Georgia sang 'Morning has Broken.'

Up till that morning she had thought she couldn't sing, but it was Rod who convinced her. The bandages were off his head now, but his hands were still covered. His face was peeling like a bad case of sunburn, but he said he was well enough to attend the funeral.

'You will sing,' he said, raising one singed eyebrow, at her protest. 'They would have wanted you to. It isn't your feelings that count, but theirs.'

Put like that she could do nothing but agree, but when she stood up by the pulpit, she nearly lost her nerve.

'Turn your back away from the audience,' she could almost hear Ian's whisper on stage at the first gig. 'If you can't see them, it's okay.'

She had turned to the altar to sing, looking up at the window high above. She concentrated on the patch of blue sky so much like Ian's eyes, and as Norman played the introduction and she filled her lungs with air, so her voice came back, filling the small chapel.

During the prayers her thoughts were all with Ian and Alan. She could see them squabbling in the changing rooms over a bar of chocolate. Jumping fully clothed in the river at Oxford, sleepy in the back of the van. Laughing over a book of corny jokes. Alan was the one she knew least about. He hadn't been flashy like Rod, or even famous for his dry humour like John. He had none of Norman's know-all tendencies, Les's dimness, or Speedy's sloth to make him exceptional. Just a bright little cockney, happy to be privileged enough to play in a band, and his saxophone spoke for him.

But Ian. There were a million memories there. The way he wrapped his arms around her when he went to sleep, the kisses first thing in the morning. Day after day of love-filled hours. He'd taught her how to trust again. How to project her voice and wring the last emotion out of a song. One day she'd replace the lover, but her friend would always be in her head and heart.

When Rod got up to speak on behalf of all of them, Georgia found it hard to hold back the tears. She wasn't used to seeing him in a formal dark suit, his hair slicked back from his face, and neither was she accustomed to seeing pain in his eyes.

As he left the altar steps he put his hands over his eyes, his shoulders bowed with the weight of his sorrow. His red peeling face, his bandaged hands were a testimony of his courage. At that moment Georgia understood why Ian had stood by Rod even when he was arrogant, selfish and sarcastic. Had he always known that Rod would be prepared to give his own life to try and save a friend?

It was late that evening, alone in her room that Georgia's grief and guilt finally surfaced and spilled out. She had been trying to write down her thoughts in a poem, but nothing came to her.

All she could see was the boys, standing in a group by the gates of the crematorium. They were lost without Ian to tell them what to do. Home, belongings and two of their members, gone. Broken by grief, tormented by the guilty feeling that they could have prevented the accident. Lost like a ship without a rudder.

Norman's carroty hair caught the sunshine as he bowed it towards John to comfort him. Speedy had been in control earlier, talking to both Ian and Alan's mothers, but even he now seemed to have lost several inches in height, his shoulders hunched up in his borrowed suit. Les was deathly pale, his dark hair had lost its shine, his hooked nose almost like a beak, eyes glued to the path beneath him. Rod towered above them, straight-backed, but red-eyed, trying in vain to take Ian's place.

'Why didn't you insist I came to the party? If you'd just stood up to me for once I might not have been so angry.' She put her hands over her eyes and wept. 'I almost went away with Max and now we've run out of time.'

She didn't know how long she sat by her window crying, but once it was all spent it was dark and Berwick Street was coming to life again as the neon lights were switched on.

As she undressed, words started to come. 'There's no time baby. It's all slipped away.' She could almost feel Ian's presence in the room, forcing her to pick up her pencil and write it down.

'Do you know what sort of first record Max wants me to make?' she asked the boys a few days after her talk with Max. She had asked them all round for a meal, hoping that by bringing them together again, a little of the old spirit might return.

She had cooked enough spaghetti for an army and a saucepan full of sauce, there were four bottles of wine and a bowl of trifle in the fridge, but none of them seemed interested in either food or drink.

John was staying with his parents in Dagenham. Les with his girlfriend in Wapping. Norman with his granny and Rod and Speedy had found one room together in Fulham. Their equipment was in the van and unless someone pulled them together it would stay there.

'Some big, powerful ballad,' Rod said gloomily, he sat on the floor his back against her bed. His jeans had a hole in the knee and his dark hair needed washing.

'That's right,' Georgia frowned. She wanted to provoke an argument, even at the risk of seeming uncaring. Anything was worth a try rather than this apathy. 'Of course, that's one of Max's objections to you. He thinks you are incapable of writing that type of song.'

'He's never given us a chance,' Norman, sprawled on her bed, lifted his head, eyes sharp with indignation.

'Well get to it,' Georgia snapped. 'Prove him wrong.'

'What's the point?' Speedy sighed. He at least had managed to buy a new pair of trousers and a black polo neck sweater, but his auburn hair needed washing too. 'He won't let us get near the studio with you.'

'He will you know,' Georgia smiled round at them. 'He said I could use you as backing. He even said he would listen to anything we wrote. If we could come up with the right song, written by us. You would all get royalties and publicity.'

Speedy's eyes lit up, his mouth curled up at the corners. 'Not a bad idea, but it'd have to be good.'

Georgia looked round at each of them. Five sad faces. Boys who once thought only of the next gig, or the girl in the next town. What would it take to get them all back in one flat again, and bring back their sparkle?

'I've written some words,' she spoke casually, careful not to be too forceful. 'Shall I read them to you?'

Rod nodded. He was sitting up again now. His face had turned from red to brown at last. He still had one bandage on his right hand, but the rest of his burns were healing well.

'Go on then.'

She reached up to a shelf and pulled down a notebook.

'It's called "No time",' she said softly.

> There's no time baby.
> It's all slipped away,
> I thought we had forever,

Now there's only a day.
I dream of your kisses,
I see only your eyes,
We have no tomorrows,
Only goodbyes.
There's no time baby.
All we have is now.
There's no time baby,
This is the last bow.

'It's a bit morbid.' John spoke up, the first remark he'd made all evening. 'I mean I could just see Ian and you together.'

'We can't forget what's happened,' she said gently. John troubled her the most, his dark eyes had lost their lustre, he was thinner than ever, his skin a putty colour. For years he had shared everything with Alan and now memories haunted him. 'All dramatic songs are sad. Don't you think we need that memory for us to write something worthwhile?'

'It's not bad Georgia,' Norman surprised her. 'I can sort of make out a melody.'

'Let's thrash it out together,' Rod's deep voice seemed to fill the room. 'If nothing else it's a challenge.'

Georgia hardly dared breathe while they thought it over. The notebook was passed from one to the other, already they looked brighter. She could somehow imagine her words padded out. Speedy and Norman had the ability to find a strong, beautiful melody. John could write the arrangements for brass. Les could be trusted to play a fantastic lead guitar, it only needed Rod to step forward and take command.

'Let's open the wine,' Rod said, getting up and stretching. 'We'll have to find somewhere to rehearse and while we're at it, we'd better look for a new pad.'

*

'Where have you been?' Max was red with anger when Georgia walked into his office a fortnight later.

'Resting, rehearsing, helping the boys get themselves organized again,' she sat down without being asked. 'You should have helped them with a flat.'

'Don't come all that holier than thou crap with me,' Max stood up and took a threatening step towards her. 'I paid for the funeral. They've been on full wages. I even gave them extra money for new clothes.'

'Where's the money from the "Benefit" gone?' she asked.

Some of the musicians at the funeral had played a gig to raise money for the boys. A cheque for over two hundred pounds had been handed over to Max, but he hadn't passed it on.

'I've got it here,' Max's lip was curling back, but she knew his anger was because he had been caught out. 'I was intending to give it to them today.'

'Don't forget,' her pointed chin stuck out defiantly. 'Because I know you got an insurance payout to cover everything else you've spent.'

She had been into the office during the week while Max was out. Deirdre on reception had slipped out for a sandwich and Georgia used the time to snoop. Max had been doodling on his blotter. An insurance policy lay next to it and it hadn't taken her more than two minutes to read it, then slip back out before Deirdre even knew she'd been there. Max wasn't out of pocket at all. He was making claims for broken engagements, equipment and possibly claims on the boys' lives.

'Now look here,' he blustered.

'No, you look here,' she said more bravely than she felt. 'You owe the boys. I want you to come and listen to something we've written. Can you arrange a gig at the Marquee so we can try it out on an appreciative audience too?'

'I don't know,' he shook his head. 'I've got a song

lined up myself, you don't need the boys. I'll get them a singer and sort them out.'

'Do as I say or I'll start talking too loudly,' she spoke softly, yet with enough menace to make him understand she meant it. 'The boys need to feel wanted right now. I need them too. Or have you forgotten my feelings?'

He hesitated.

She could see a rope-like vein quivering on his forehead. She really didn't know why she liked him. He was slippery and heartless. Yet there was something strong about him that was attractive and compelling, neither could she forget his gentleness on that awful day at the hospital.

'Okay,' he sighed deeply. 'I'll arrange it. But don't think you can hold a gun to my head, young lady. If the song's no good, that's it.'

Georgia got up and walked round his desk. She dropped a kiss on his surprised face.

'That's for saying yes,' she smiled down at him. 'And this is to make sure you listen when you come.' She bent over and kissed his lips gently, just lingering long enough so his hands came up to hold her, then jumped nimbly away out of reach.

As she backed towards the door, she glanced up at the gold spider's web. More and more she felt like that poor fly. Another year and she would probably be in the spider's jaws.

Max folded his arms on his desk and lay his head down on them. He could never quite analyse his feelings about Georgia. If he wasn't such a cynic he could call it love. Any other girl singer who had worked for him had been in his bed before her first week was up. Yet somehow he'd never fathomed out a way to get Georgia. She couldn't be persuaded by flattery. Presents would merely be laughed at. She certainly wouldn't respond to just grabbing her. Yet she'd nearly agreed to come away with him.

He couldn't admit, even to himself that his first reaction to hearing about Ian's death had been almost pleasure. With Ian out of the running Georgia could be his, he could run her life the way he had always intended to.

But the pleasure had been hollow. Even he, tough as he was, cared for Ian, and Georgia's stricken face those first few days had cut him to the quick.

'I should never have put her with that band,' he murmured, sitting up again, tipping back his chair and putting his feet up on his desk. 'I should have dangled her the carrot of a recording contract. Bought her new clothes and set her up in a flat.'

Yet Ian and the other boys had produced something in her he couldn't have managed alone. She kept her girlish breathless charm, while learning poise and timing. Her voice had gone from good to incredible and maybe Ian was responsible for adding that extra emotion. Everything was right for launching her. The tragedy of the boys' deaths was still in the public's mind.

Like the phoenix she could soar out of the flames into stardom, and all he had to do was sit back and watch the money come rolling in.

Reminded of something, Max frowned and opened his desk drawer. The letter had come for her this morning, yet something had stopped him from giving it to her.

He turned it around thoughtfully in his hands. A blue envelope. Postmarked Manchester. The writing bold and masculine. It was probably only a fan letter, but there was no harm in checking.

Taking a small silver dagger from his desk tray, he slid it under the flap carefully, in case he had to stick it down again later. He drew out the single sheet of paper and spread it out on his desk.

'Dearest Georgia,

I had almost given up hope of finding you. When you didn't contact me on your birthday three years ago I drew the conclusion that you didn't want me to. I understand after what happened that you wanted to sever all connections with your past. But just when I'd finally reconciled myself to a life without you, I read the story about the fire and the two boys burned to death.

I might never have given it a second thought, but one of my friends up here had seen the band, and went on to tell me about the girl singer. He didn't remember her name, just how she looked, and of course I began to wonder. Then in the story about the funeral I saw the name Georgia. I've never heard of anyone else called that. Could there really be another Georgia who sings like an angel, dark-skinned with long curly hair and eyes like giant pansies? I doubt it somehow! It didn't require much detective work to find your manager's address and here I am writing with my heart thumping wondering how you'll receive this letter.

Even if you have no further interest in me, please write back and tell me if Celia managed to find you? I kept in touch with her up till last Christmas, then gradually she stopped writing. She went to Africa to nurse, moving on several times. I guessed she stopped because she felt it was unhealthy for us both, but it has occurred to me she may now be reunited with you and you stopped her.

Please let me know how things are with you. I won't pester you, or bring back unwelcome reminders. I just need to know you are happy. Of course I'd like to think that you still hold a small torch for me, but I'm realistic if nothing else. I'm so sorry about your friends, it was a terrible tragedy. God bless you.

My love Peter'

There was a depth of passion in this letter that disturbed Max. Whoever this man was he came from a time before Georgia joined the band.

'A childhood sweetheart?' he mused. 'And who is this Celia?'

Georgia had always been evasive about her past. The way she spoke, her education all hinted at a good home. Yet girls who came from good homes didn't normally turn their backs on them.

'After what happened!' Max skimmed through the letter again. 'What could have happened?'

Could she have been in trouble for seeing this boy? But if so who was Celia? An older sister? An aunt?

Max pondered for some time. If he showed this to Georgia now, in her already disturbed state she might do anything. If she'd hidden from this young man once, she might have good reason to bolt again. Just a glance at the content of the letter and the bold handwriting was enough to know this wasn't some dim, uneducated lout. She was getting ideas above her station already; aided and abetted by intelligent friends she could break away from Max altogether.

He got up and went over to a typewriter on a small table. Taking a plain sheet of paper out of the drawer he inserted it, sat down and began to type.

'Dear Mr Radcliffe,

Miss James thanks you for your letter and has asked me to reply for her.

Although she appreciates your concern, she feels she has nothing further to say to you. Her career as a singer is all important to her and leaves no time for socializing. She wishes me to assure you she is well and happy in her chosen career, and sincerely hopes you are too.

Yours sincerely,

Deirdre Richards.

P.P. Georgia James.

Max pulled the letter out of the machine, signed it with a flourish, folded it and put it in an envelope.

'Maybe that will dent his pride enough to leave her alone,' he said to himself. He picked up Peter's letter, screwed it up and tossed it into the bin.

The Marquee club seen by daylight had little to recommend it. A tiny stage, a plain wooden floor, the only seating further back in a cavern-like room by the bar. But then the people who flocked to the Marquee came to hear music, and they knew this club could be relied on to have the best.

Norman played 'No time' through alone.

Georgia stood back in the shadows by the bar listening. She and Norman were alone now. The equipment was ready on the stage for tonight's gig, the rest of the boys were out getting sandwiches. A tingle ran down her spine, a rush of affection for Norman as she watched him crouched over his keyboard. This wasn't something he was playing under duress. He was putting his heart and soul into it, and it was good.

It cried out for strings, a full orchestra, but already it was a powerful melody, the kind that lingered in the mind long after it was finished. It could be a classic in the making.

Norman just sat on his stool as he finished, he looked like a small elf with his red hair and sharp features, chin stuck forward, deep in thought.

'It's brilliant,' Georgia clapped and ran over to him.

'I'm pleased with it,' he blushed, for once less cocky. 'But wait till we get Speedy on bass and Les's throbbing

333

lead. Up till now I've only been able to play it through on piano, but I know they are going to amaze you too.'

'Oh Norman.' Impulsively she jumped up on the stage and threw her arms round him. 'It's beautiful.'

'Ian helped me,' his head drooped as if embarrassed at saying such a thing. 'I felt his presence, almost as if he were humming it to me. You remember the way he used to?'

Georgia nodded. It had been odd that Ian who could play nothing more than 'chopsticks' on a piano had been able to invent melodies in his head.

'God, I miss him,' Norman's eyes filled up with tears. 'I wish I could take back all the snidy things I said to him over the years.'

'He wouldn't have had you any other way.' Georgia leaned over Norman and kissed his cheek. 'Now play it again and I'll sing.'

After several false starts they got it together. Georgia's voice soared out across the empty club, lost in the beauty of Norman's melody.

A loud clapping came from the front door as they finished. Georgia spun round to see Jack Fellows, the club owner, leaning against the wall.

Tall, stringy and untidy, Jack looked more like a struggling artist than the successful businessman he really was. His hair hung well past his ears, thinning on top. He had a long, pointed nose and a wide, smiling mouth that gave an indication to his inner nature. The Marquee was more than just a money spinner to him. He would rather have talented unknown bands playing than compromise an inch. But his high ideals had paid off, for his customers knew that any night in his club would be memorable, and the bands knew if Jack booked them, they were worth something.

'That's a beautiful song,' he said, his thin face alight with enthusiasm. 'Did you write it?'

'A joint effort,' Norman grinned. 'We're hoping Georgia might be able to record it.'

'If Max approves?' He raised one bushy eyebrow. 'The man's a complete Philistine if he doesn't.'

Georgia bounced down Wardour Street just before nine. For the first time since Ian's death she felt the cloud hanging over her was moving back. In tight white jeans, a red T-shirt and boots she felt right. The Marquee was home ground, she didn't have to squeeze into the changing room and pour herself into something swish. She could just turn up, sing her heart out, then go home. No one dressed up for the Marquee, students, beatniks, office people and manual workers flocked there for music, and tonight she was going to give them something special.

'Remember, we're not warming up for another band tonight,' she reminded the boys as they waited off stage for Jack to turn off the records and introduce them. She could see John standing alone, twiddling the valves of his trumpet, the first time he had ever played publicly without Alan beside him. 'You can do it John,' she reached out her arms to hug him. 'I feel the same about walking on without Ian, but we'll get through it.'

She could hear Jack out there on the stage. A joke with the audience about the price of beer, a word or two to remind them of Samson's recent loss of two members. She didn't have to look behind the worn curtains to know the club was packed to capacity, every face upturned, waiting for them.

Rod leapt on first, going straight to his stool and performing a dramatic drum roll. Norman was next, quickly followed by Les and Speedy and they launched into the opening number 'Soul Train'.

Georgia took John's hand in hers, leading him just as Ian had once led her, out into the spotlights.

She had to be better than her best tonight. She missed

Ian's close harmonies, and Alan's sax, but putting that aside she sang first for the band. She put a new wildness in her dancing, strutting, teasing, bending to the audience till she knew the boys were on form again.

John surprised her. He and Alan had tended to fall back on one another, staying together to play, never taking a lead. Now he moved forward, legs apart, blowing like she'd never heard him before, eyes closed, chest fully expanded, bringing out notes of such passion and sweetness, it was as if Alan's spirit had entered him.

When the first set ended to wild applause Georgia was drenched in sweat.

'You were something else tonight,' Rod grinned as she stripped off her T-shirt in the changing room and mopped at herself with a towel. 'When are we going to do the new number?'

'Last,' Speedy said pulling open a can of coke and resting it for one moment on his sweat-covered forehead. 'If we do it too early it might kill the mood. Keep to our usual routine, then "He's no good" followed by "No time", and let's hope we all remember our parts.'

Max came in just after the second set started. He stood by the side of the stage speaking to Jack Fellows giving the band no more than a cursory glance.

Georgia had relaxed sufficiently to notice there were fans in the audience from back when they played in London roadhouses and clubs a year before. She rewarded their loyalty by singing for them rather than Max, bending to touch outstretched hands, blowing kisses and finding the strength she thought she had lost in their smiling faces.

'He's no good, he's no good, baby he's no good,' she sang cheekily to Max. Pulling off her hair ribbon and throwing it into the audience and tossing her mane of hair round her shoulders.

'Finally,' Georgia mopped her brow to thunderous

applause. 'We're going to do a totally new number we wrote ourselves. It's a breakaway from our usual stuff, but we hope you like it.'

The introduction started. She saw Max turn to look in surprise as Norman played the haunting first few bars. Tingles went down her spine, she tapped her feet to the beat and filled her lungs.

As the song went on, so Georgia drowned in it. She was singing to Ian all the things she wished she'd said while he was with her. And to Max too, to remind him she was her own person.

She knew without a shadow of a doubt it was the finest singing she'd ever done. Even if the audience walked out, her own ears had told her the truth.

The applause was simply deafening. On and on it went with calls for more. They left the stage once but had to go back and do another number.

When it was finally over Max came forward.

'So that's it?' He had the oddest expression, surprise, delight, mixed with a tiny amount of pique.

'Yes,' Georgia smiled up at him. 'What do you think?'

Her heart was in her mouth. If he turned her down now she had nothing more to offer.

'A gold record,' he said, a smile stretching from ear to ear. 'You wrote it?'

'I did the words, the boys did the rest,' she said simply, surprised that for once he wasn't hiding his enthusiasm behind criticism.

'I'll get the studio booked for next week,' he said, putting one big hand on her shoulder and gripping it. 'This is it baby. I feel it in my water.'

Chapter 15

'That's it then!' Max's voice crackled abrasively in their ear phones. Through the glass screen they could see him gesticulating wildly, as if he didn't believe his voice could really reach them. 'As they say on the movies, "that's a wrap".'

Georgia took off her head phones and wiped the perspiration from her forehead.

She was too tired to even think of celebrating. Nine hours of being stuck in a soundproof room, technicians staring at her through the glass as if she were a goldfish. This was an entirely new ball game to playing live.

Mixing, loop tapes and umpteen different tracks. Session men who'd filed in, played their parts then left. She had imagined they would just perform together over and over until it was perfect. She hadn't expected the separate instruments to be added, or harmonies put on afterwards. It was confusing, frustrating, and the constant stopping and starting irritating. But then Max had insisted they produced master tapes perfect enough for the disc to be cut from, a half-hearted demo tape just wasn't good enough.

The boys had come to the studio that morning dressed as if it were another gig. Rod in velvet trousers and a flowered shirt. Norman in a smart new green jacket. But now they looked like wilted flowers, hot and sweaty, hair sticking damply to their heads.

Steven Albright, the producer was waiting for her, the boys grouped round him in the ante-room, waiting for his opinion.

Steven had the look of an overgrown schoolboy. Not what they expected from a man in his thirties with four gold records already under his belt. Six foot tall, painfully thin, with greasy hair dangling over his thick specs. Even his clothes had a charity shop look about them. A city shirt with stiff collar, an old, stained school tie and suit jacket, then in contrast a faded pair of jeans and desert boots.

It was difficult to have confidence in someone who blinked owlishly behind his glasses and silently chewed a pencil. But he surprised them, not only was he alert to every last note, he had imagination, flair and a complete knowledge of many instruments.

'Time to play the finished article,' he smiled warmly, his plummy, Old Etonian accent somehow reassuring. 'You look tired Georgia, but you did very well.'

He sat down at the controls and the introduction started.

The finished result was perfect. It was the sort of song that would be played last at every dance up and down the country. Bodies entwined, arms round each other's necks. A song for lovers everywhere.

'It's good,' Steven turned off the tape as the last notes faded away. Like Max he was sparing with his praise. All day he had pushed them. They had seen him angry, frustrated, disinterested, even bored on occasions, but now at last his dark eyes shone with excitement and exhilaration. 'You can all be very proud of it. I'd say it will make it.'

Somehow that simple statement meant more than gushing praise and for the first time all day, not one of them came back with a flippant remark.

'You can all clear off now.' To Max it was business as usual. He had come in and out several times during the day, listening half-heartedly, flashing his gold watch and leaving again just as quickly.

'You've got gigs in the Midlands for the next week. Put all this out of your minds and get on with playing.'

Max had seemed preoccupied since the funeral. Georgia couldn't help wondering if he'd found another band who excited him more than Samson. She'd spotted brochures for new vans on his desk and receipts for band suits which she was sure weren't for them. Also there were three new girls in the office who barely acknowledged her. Was she being paranoid? Or was Max about to pull another stroke?

The next week or two was as if they'd gone back in time. If it hadn't been for the pressure of wondering what was happening in Decca's offices, and Ian and Alan's absence, they could have been back to the carefree days before Max put them on the cinema tours. Their re-appearance at dancehalls was enthusiastically received, old fans coming forward to show their pleasure at seeing them again.

But Georgia hadn't reckoned with all the old memories. She could handle it by day, wandering around town with John or Rod, even performing in places she associated with Ian. But by night when she crept into a cold, often damp bed, Ian's face came back to her.

She missed his jokes and chatter, all the little things he helped her with. The other boys were clumsy at zipping up dresses and putting make-up on her when there was no mirror handy. She missed him singing with her, complimenting her, spurring each other on. But it was making love that dominated her thoughts at night. She would torment herself remembering the way he stroked her. The thought of his kisses made her hot and damp. She longed for the blissful glow that followed making love, and waking early to find him aroused and holding her.

When she lost Peter there had always been the hope he would return. Even when Helen died she had been able to comfort herself with the thought that she had left pain and poverty behind. But there was no sense to Ian's death. It wasn't right that he missed by just a few weeks the one thing he had aimed at all his life. And neither was it fair that everyone she loved was snatched from her so cruelly.

'You can always count on me,' Rod said one evening as they made their way up the staircase to their rooms. 'My body's free anytime.'

Georgia stopped and turned to look at him. Two years ago she would have found his arrogance insulting. But now she saw it as a gesture of comfort and perception.

The boarding house was just like all the countless others they stayed in. Shabby, flowered wallpaper, worn at shoulder height with the hundreds of people that had gone up and down rubbing against it. Candlewick bedspreads, nylon sheets and plastic flowers.

She saw Rod then as other women saw him. His strange dark slanty eyes, high cheek-bones and thin, almost cruel lips. Raw sexuality seeped out of him, his height, coupled with wide shoulders, narrow hips and his shiny blue black straight hair gave the picture of a primitive savage.

'Things aren't that bad,' she grinned.

'No?' his eyes laughed at her.

'I miss him so much it hurts,' she said softly. 'But it isn't just sex I miss.'

'I didn't think it was,' he said, his hand reaching out and stroking her cheek. 'But sometimes another body can be very comforting.'

With one finger he traced round her lips. She felt goosebumps come up all over her and she couldn't move away.

'I could make you forget at least for tonight,' he whispered. 'It doesn't have to be forever.'

She felt a tug in her stomach, a tingle of desire.

'I'm not brave enough to chance it,' she took a step back from him and hesitated, looking down at him two steps beneath her. His eyes were half closed, narrow lips apart showing white teeth. For a moment she almost went back to him.

'One day,' he smiled. 'Just for laughs!'

That night she thought of Rod's hands on her breasts. His tanned chest above her, skilful fingers playing with her and it was all she could do not to cry out.

As she let herself into her flat on their return to London, she found a note from Max summoning her to his office the next morning.

There was little hope of falling asleep after the note. Could this be the stroke she suspected? Or could it be that her dreams were finally about to be realized?

'Go on in,' Deirdre on reception smiled a welcome as Georgia leapt up the stairs on the stroke of ten. 'He's waiting for you.'

This in itself was a good sign. Max frequently kept her waiting for hours.

Max looked relaxed as she walked in the door. A pale lemon shirt open at the neck, sleeves rolled up revealing thick, brown arms. His chair was tilted back and he puffed on a cigar as if day-dreaming.

'Hallo darling,' he stubbed out the cigar, leaping to his feet, reaching her in two giant strides and pecking her cheek. 'Sorry I couldn't give you more warning. I've been rushed off my feet.'

'How are things going?' she asked, taking a seat by his desk, noticing many changes in the room.

Two years earlier Max had perhaps ten or so bands on his books. Now it looked as if he had expanded overnight. A new filing cabinet stood with drawers open. Stacks of contracts lay on his desk, glossy photographs of groups unknown to her scattered everywhere.

'I've got some excellent news for you,' he returned to his desk, picking up a gold fountain pen from his blotter, shaking it, then signing a letter in front of him with a flourish.

'They want it?' Georgia felt a rush of adrenalin to her head.

'Yup. They are anxious to get the disc cut and released for the first week in September.'

'I can't wait to tell the boys,' Georgia felt a bubble of glee rise up inside her.

'The contract is just for you.'

She stared at him, mouth agape. He had that cold look in his eyes she knew so well. Had he actually managed to outmanoeuvre her despite everything?

'Don't look like that,' he snapped at her. 'Their names will be on the recording as backing and co-writers, they'll get their royalties.'

'You've got something up your sleeve.' She stood up, leaning towards him over the desk, dark eyes blazing. 'Are you trying to tell me this is the end of the line for us together?'

'Georgia, darling,' he shrugged his shoulders, spreading his hands wide. 'I'm only thinking of you. The Palladium, the Albert Hall, that's where you're heading. You'll need an orchestra, not a bunch of dance hall musicians.'

'But before we get there we'll still be playing in clubs and stuff,' she said desperately. 'I need them Max!'

'Of course you do, for now.' He moved round the desk and caught hold of her arms. 'As from tomorrow when you sign with Decca you pay them just as you would a session musician.'

'Whaaat!' Georgia stared at Max in horror. 'You mean I've got to tell them I'm their boss now?'

'Just a re-arrangement of finances. I'll still be the one organizing everything. Financially this is far better for you. When you give interviews, television game shows etc, it means that money is all yours, and rightly so, you'll be the one working your butt off.'

'But – '

Max interrupted her. 'Look here Georgia, I'm getting a little tired of this game. Hasn't it ever occurred to you the boys might want a change of direction? I'll get them a new singer. If they deserve it they'll get their own recording contract. Stop bloody well harping on about them.'

'What time is it tomorrow?' she asked weakly. 'We've got to leave for the gig at twelve.'

'Ten thirty. You can catch the train afterwards,' he grinned as if he was giving her a treat. 'The boys left this morning to pick up some new speakers. Soon you won't be travelling with them anyway. It will be limousines for you. Gold stars on the door of the changing room. Now clear off and buy yourself a smart outfit for tomorrow.'

He had sent them away from town on purpose to avoid any last minute rebellion, now he was opening his wallet and pulling out fifty pounds.

'Something outstanding,' he said. 'I don't want them to think I kept you short.'

Georgia knew how Judas felt as he pocketed his thirty pieces of silver.

Decca's offices were only a stone's throw from her room in Berwick Street.

For the last two years Georgia had looked through the big glass doors every time she passed by, dreaming of this very day.

The dream had come true, but why did she feel so empty?

Max had been brusque with her when they met earlier. More interested in getting into the boardroom than speaking to her.

She had been left to sit outside, he hadn't even remarked on her outfit.

Was this how it would be from now on? Alone all the time, watching out for people ready to stab her in the back? Once she would have been thrilled to be given fifty pounds to spend on clothes. All the boys would have come with her to choose them. Yet the boys were off buying speakers while she was signing away her future without them.

Was the outfit she'd chosen right? A white knee length dress, with a diamond cutout showing her brown abdomen, and new white shoes. She could see herself mirrored in a chrome plant stand. Her hair in soft ringlets, a white ribbon nestling amongst the curls. Was an impression of innocence the right look? Ian would have insisted on something red and dramatic!

For a place that employed hundreds of people, it was eerily quiet. The faint tapping of a typewriter in the distance, the occasional ringing of telephones, and a buzz of conversation from the boardroom where Max had gone.

A thick green carpet curled over her shoes. The seats were brown leather, big and comfortable. Huge plants stood in tubs and a brass-topped coffee table held a selection of quality magazines. It was more like a posh dental surgery than a place that dealt with music.

'Would you like to come in now Georgia?' The blonde iceberg of a secretary was holding the door open, a false, rather cynical smile on her china doll face.

Beyond the secretary's notebook, Georgia could see at least ten business men wreathed in cigarette smoke around a boardroom table. All at once she was more nervous than when she went on stage. Her palms were sticky and her stomach turned over.

'This is Georgia,' Max stood up and pulled out a chair for her, his smile a contrived attempt at a fatherly one.

She sat down, thrown by the lack of interest in the men's faces.

'Hallo Georgia.' A short fat man with small dark eyes held out his plump hand. 'I'm Jack Levy. Might I say on behalf of all of us, how much we have enjoyed hearing you sing. You're a girl with an exciting future.'

Georgia knew he was the top man at Decca. She had expected someone larger, not a nearly bald man with a wrinkled sallow face, a nose so huge it looked like a beak and gold-rimmed spectacles. He looked more like a banker than a maker of stars.

She glanced around the table.

Alex Rhodes was there, avoiding her eyes. She had heard he had an administrative position now, perhaps that's why he had abandoned the tweed jacket and corduroys. His sandy head was bent over some papers, as if trying to forget this was the girl he couldn't lure away from her band all those months ago. Had he put Max up to the cinema tours? Had he hoped one day she'd come crawling to him?

Maybe she wasn't exactly crawling, but it didn't feel like triumph either.

Max's lawyer John Cohen she knew slightly. But here he blended in with all the others. They were all the same. Dark men, all of them greying at the temples. Not one of them less than forty, papers spread out in front of them. All with the same dark suits, gold watches, rings and cufflinks glinting, as if showing their allegiance to the same club. Not one look of interest or admiration. Tense faces as they approached yet another business deal.

'We are offering you a three year contract,' Jack Levy went on. 'Under this contract we have the right to choose and oppose any songs which are offered to you. Though of course your opinion will be sought in this matter.

'You may not work for any other record company during your contract with us. Also, work that is outside our field, a film for instance, would be vetted carefully before we agreed to it.'

He looked at her carefully over the top of his glasses, a shaft of sunlight played on his balding head and his nose seemed to grow larger.

'Do you understand?'

Georgia nodded. These men were planning to take over her life. Once she'd signed with them she was just another pawn to be pushed anyway that suited them.

'I want you to read through the contract,' he said more gently. 'It may seem difficult in parts, legal jargon does sound odd to someone who isn't used to it. But if there's anything you don't understand, please ask.'

He handed her a document.

Georgia had no idea what she was supposed to look out for. It seemed fairly straightforward, mainly revolving around her inability to do anything without their permission.

Then her eyes caught an interesting section about immorality.

'What does this mean?' she asked, pointing to the section.

'Well, my dear,' he smiled condescendingly, his eyes so small behind his thick glasses they looked like currants. 'We understand that young people sometimes get led astray when they find themselves in your position. However, an established company like ourselves do not like scandal.

'Should one of our clients get involved in something which could have a damaging effect on ourselves, we have the right to cancel their contract.'

'What sort of scandal?' All the men were looking at

her now, perhaps wondering if she had anything to hide.

He shrugged. 'Something criminal maybe. Drugs. Not turning up for performances continually. Loose behaviour.' He gave her a half smile as if implying she would never do any of these things.

'I see, and is there a clause in here which protects me if, say, you didn't act in my best interests?' She wasn't going to let them think she was a pushover.

'Why should that be necessary?' Jack Levy looked shocked.

Georgia could see he was another Max, he had the same expression on his face Max wore when confronted with his deviousness.

He looked round the room and laughed. 'Do you think all these people would be gathered here today if they didn't intend to look out for you?'

Georgia had a feeling they were rather more interested in the money aspect than her soul, but she thought it prudent to keep that to herself.

She continued to read the document, although most of it went over her head.

'It seems okay,' she said at length.

'Of course it is,' Max laughed, sucking on his huge cigar. 'We know what we're doing.'

Georgia had always imagined the signing of a record contract would be in a party atmosphere, with champagne, streamers and smiling faces.

Instead she signed her name in chilly silence. It was witnessed by the secretary who ushered her into the room and then signed by Jack Levy and one of his colleagues. The men all shovelled their papers into their briefcases and got up to leave, barely glancing at her.

'Is that it, Mr Levy?' she asked as they all filed out.

'That's the boring part,' he said, smiling in a more pleasant manner. 'Now come with me and I'll show you a little more of our operation.'

*

It wasn't until she was on the train that what was really happening finally sank in.

She was going to be a star. Making a lot of money for Decca, Max and the lawyers. Soon she would be able to move to a smarter home. Employ a cleaning lady, even a cook if she wanted one. She could have proper driving lessons and buy a car. She would be invited to smart parties and buy all the clothes she wanted. People would want her autograph.

She ought to have been dancing with happiness, yet somehow she felt cheated.

'I've let you down,' she blurted out to the boys as she made her way into the changing room of The Purple Pussy Cat. 'I signed a contract with Decca this morning.'

All the way on the train she had wondered how to tell them. Should she pretend she was happy with everything? Insist their rights were protected? Assure them that everything would remain the same?

'So that's why he let us get the speakers at last,' Rod sighed deeply. 'I wondered why he'd suddenly become so generous. He just wanted us out of the way.'

Speedy was watching Georgia. He saw how pale she looked, her hands shaking.

'It's all right Georgia,' he slipped his arm round her shoulder. 'We're happy for you. We didn't expect a contract too.'

'I did,' Norman's voice chipped in, his small face alight with pique. 'I worked my balls off with that song. Now she'll get all the credit.'

Georgia burst into tears and ran from the room.

'You arsehole,' Speedy exploded with rage. 'What did you have to say that for? The poor kid is already eaten up with anxiety about us. Haven't you learned anything about her in two years?'

'Speedy's right,' Rod sprawled on a bench, a faintly amused expression on his handsome face. 'Georgia's incapable of being selfish, which is more than I can say

349

for myself. Max has beaten her down, the same as he's done to us countless times. But when it comes right down to it she deserves all the success coming to her.'

'I don't begrudge her it,' Norman was sullen now, his lower lip stuck out like a sulky child. 'I just wonder where it leaves us.'

'With a friend in important places,' Speedy snapped. 'Now for God's sake make it up with her. Show some pleasure that she's got what she worked so hard for. That's what real friends do.'

On September 1st, 'No Time' was released. Two days later it was on Juke Box Jury.

They were all together in the boys' new flat in Paddington. Later that night they would be playing at the Bag O' Nails in Soho, but Max had rung them while they were setting up the equipment to let them know he had managed to pull strings to get it on.

Georgia had no television, so they had leapt in the van and rushed back to Paddington. Now the programme was starting Georgia was biting her nails.

'Stop that,' Rod smacked at her hand. 'If you nibble each time it gets on the air you'll be up to your elbows in a few weeks.'

Their old flat had been grubby and untidy, but it had been a home. This new flat might be tidy, with almost new furniture but it was soulless, like the boarding houses they spent so much time in. No clutter, no personal touches, just another reminder how much they had all lost.

'Memphis Tennessee' was the first record played, a catchy number, guaranteed to hit the top twenty immediately. They listened impatiently while the jury deliberated and finally voted it a good song but one they doubted would make it.

'They haven't a clue,' Speedy said in amazement. 'Does our future really lie with people like them?'

The next record was a ballad called 'Blue Nights', so dull and banal Rod pretended he had fallen asleep.

'That's what I call a good song,' one of the jury enthused. 'Great backing, a little slow,' said another, 'But it will be a hit.'

'They won't like ours, I know they won't,' Georgia said, sitting on the edge of her seat.

As David Jacobs introduced 'No Time', Georgia thought she saw him wince. It made no difference that the introduction still gave her goosebumps of pleasure, his impassive shiny face seemed to hold more than a trace of irritation.

The jury however leaned forward in their seats to listen. The youngest man had his eyes shut, resting his face in his hands.

'Look they love it, they're all spellbound,' John shrieked.

To their surprise, the dreamy-eyed man said he loved it yet doubted it would be a hit. But the other three gave it a resounding thumbs up.

'There you are,' Rod said triumphantly. 'Aren't I always right about everything?'

Max left no stone unturned. He invited reporters to drop in on their London gigs. Copies of the record found their way on to every important desk in the music world. Bribes were passed out to give it plays on the radio.

The first week after its release was the worst. Rod reported it played first late at night, then again the next morning, but then nothing.

Anxiety that it might not even make it into the top fifty was quickly dispelled by Max who was suddenly booking them into London clubs only and appearing nightly with photographers, behaving as if Georgia was the only person in his life.

'I'm taking you to a party tonight,' he announced

during the break at The Scene in Windmill Street. 'Nip off home and get changed the minute you've finished here. I want you all glammed up.'

It was on the tip of her tongue to protest she was too tired, but a look of excitement in Max's eyes hinted this was one party she couldn't miss.

'Where is it?' she asked instead, remembering both Norman and Rod had dates later that night and all she had to look forward to was a new book.

'Kensington,' Max had that kind of smug grin which meant it would be very swish. 'It's important, so don't let me down.'

'Is that it?' Georgia saw big wrought-iron gates with the huge house beyond ablaze with lights. Loud music was wafting out, people dancing in front of one of the windows and scores of others sitting on the steps leading up to the front door.

They had turned off from Kensington High Street just minutes before, but with Holland Park lying in darkness next to this house, they could have been right out in the countryside.

'Don't be scared.' Max patted her knee. 'It's the home of Louise Wainwright the heiress. She collects stars like others collect stamps or matchboxes, but she's a good sort.'

Even with Max's arm firmly round her shoulders, Georgia felt tongue-tied with nerves as they walked into the hall.

Max's cream suit looked just a little ostentatious under a crystal chandelier. Shouldn't she have worn a proper cocktail dress instead of her new white outfit?

She had seen glimpses of houses like this back in Blackheath. Antique furniture, Oriental rugs, art that had been collected over centuries, not snapped up from some shop in Chelsea.

'Maxy, darling!' A bony woman with bulbous frog-eyes and a flame-red, poker-straight bob, rushed to them. 'You've managed to bring Georgia, you absolute angel.'

She inclined one angular cheek to Max, drowning them both in 'Joy' perfume, then reached out for Georgia, enveloping her in a bony hug. Behind her on a wide sweeping staircase Georgia saw Vogue's top model, Bonnie Jackson in a long chiffon pink dress, her blonde hair caught up with a single rose.

'This is Louise Wainwright,' Max said, winking at Georgia, suggesting silently she made out she had squeezed in the time for parties between other pressing engagements.

'Thank you so much for inviting me,' Georgia stammered, feeling distinctly underdressed next to this formidable woman in her Dior emerald green evening dress. Diamonds glistened on her ears, more on her fingers.

'My darling,' Louise gushed. 'It's my pleasure to meet you at last. All London's talking about you and your record.' She touched Georgia's hair lightly, her frog eyes nearly leaping out of her face. 'I didn't expect such devastating beauty. But come on in and meet everyone.'

With a glass of champagne in her hand, Georgia found her nervousness leaving her. The huge drawing room with doors open on to a floodlit garden beyond was too crowded to feel conspicuous. Some of the guests might have pedigrees going back to the Armada, others had forged their way out of far humbler homes than her own, but they all seemed to be linked by a common theme, they were people who were on the way up.

A disc jockey modelling his patter on Alan Freeman kept the sounds coming and with Louise Wainwright holding her elbow she was whisked round to meet everyone.

'Bill Johnson, the photographer,' Louise said breathlessly, as she introduced her to a gaunt-faced man in black leather. 'I expect you know his pictures, he did that wonderful spread in *Queen* a few weeks ago.'

Georgia didn't know, but she smiled, shook his hand and Louise whisked her on to her next protégé.

Actors, models, debutantes and professional men. People from the advertising world, still more entrepreneurs doing everything from running art galleries to boutiques in King's Road.

By her third glass of champagne Georgia was doing the 'twist' with a red haired architect called Ivan. Louise had told her he won an award for an office block in the City, but he was more interested in talking about Georgia.

'Get into films,' he said as if he knew all about it. 'That's where the real money lies. Demand to go to Hollywood, you'll be bigger than Doris Day.'

The entire party was like a film set. The backdrop was the gracious, high-ceilinged room, with its paintings and exquisite furniture. Jewellery glittered and jingled, perfume assaulted the nose. Outrageous dresses on perfect bodies. Dinner jackets and bow ties. Braying 'Sloane' accents mingled with cockney and Liverpool. One minute she was just another singer hoping for a break, now suddenly she found herself amongst kindred spirits.

She spotted Michael Caine's blond hair and glasses across the crowded room, dancing with an equally tall languorous brunette. His friend Terence Stamp was said to be there too but she didn't see him.

Dance after dance. Friendly chatter as if she had always been part of this exclusive club, shared jokes and invitations to everything from dinner to a country house weekend.

'No Time' was played while she was in the dining room helping herself to food. She giggled with embarrassment as heads turned towards her, and Max caught her eye.

'This is what it's all about.' He came up behind her and whispered in her ear. 'By tomorrow you'll be the name on everyone's lips.'

As Georgia sipped yet another drink she contemplated whether she would ever be rich enough to have even a small house of her own.

Apart from the drawing room, and the dining room she'd only had glimpses of the other rooms in this huge place. A library lined with old books, a sumptuous sitting room with silk-lined walls and matching peachy-coloured armchairs. Upstairs there were at least six bedrooms and there was another floor above that and a basement too. What would you do with all that space? Would you end up like Louise, throwing parties all the time just to fill it?

'I think this had better be the last one,' Max's deep voice came from just behind Georgia as he handed her yet another glass of champagne, an hour later.

'Who says?' Georgia giggled. They hadn't been together for more than a few minutes at one time all night, yet she'd been aware of his presence. Even amongst all these dynamic people he was still a man to catch the eye. His shoulders broader, his tan deeper than most. The expensive cut of his cream suit, the animal grace. 'Have you been watching me?'

She was on a real high, not just drunk. Everything really was going to happen for her at last. It was as if she were standing at a doorway, looking in on a whole new world and all it took was one more step to be part of it.

'Of course I've been watching you,' Max said, taking her elbow and steering her towards the drawing room to dance. 'Everyone has, and I don't want you to get so drunk you make yourself look silly.'

355

Georgia leaned against his big chest. She was already a little wobbly but it felt good.

'I'm proud of you,' Max said putting his arms round her. 'I don't think I've ever felt so proud of anything. Come and dance with me. You've danced with everyone else.'

She looked up at Max's rugged face, felt his arms around her and his words of praise ringing in her ears, gratitude overwhelmed her. The sharp practice, the bullying were all forgotten. This was the man who had believed in her. Without him she would still be back at Pop's on the sewing machine.

The wild dancing had slowed to smooching. Small groups of people sat on the stairs, in corners, even in the garden to talk.

Max held her close, his lips against her hair. The heat of his body, the sweet music and the slow dancing made her feel almost unbearably happy.

'The summer's nearly over,' Max said softly in her ear. 'How about those few days in Spain now while we wait for the record to reach number one?'

She giggled softly.

'Why the giggle?' he asked putting one hand under her chin and lifting her face up to his. 'I just thought you needed a rest.'

His dark eyes weren't probing into her as they often did, they were soft and loving, his lips wide and smiling showing his white even teeth.

It was two years since that night when he'd kissed her, but it was a memory she hadn't forgotten. A strange and wonderful feeling was creeping over her, like she was being sucked into something she couldn't and didn't have to fight any longer. His hands were holding her so firmly, fingers just running down her spine, making her knees turn to jelly.

His eyes closed as his lips came down to meet hers, one hand moving up to caress her cheek. This time there was no fear, just a sense of something stronger than both of them and that this was the moment they'd been waiting for.

She felt his tongue first, flickering round her lips, sending out messages to each nerve-ending. Sensual, light touches that set her body on fire.

The music seemed to be engulfing her, as if written specially for them and slowly his mouth covered hers.

Never before had a mere kiss been so intimate. It was everything, blocking out the other guests. It wasn't just a kiss but making love. She could feel her nipples growing hard, dampness seeping from her and at the same time she could feel his hardness pressing into her belly.

Inside she was trembling, her arms were reaching out to draw him closer, her tongue thrusting against his. Her fingers caressing his ears, neck and cheek, wanting him, now.

She had no idea how long they stayed wrapped in each other's arms. It was no longer teasing or tempting, but a need to possess so strong there was no question of backing away.

'I've wanted you for so long baby,' he whispered against her neck, licking and stroking until her legs almost buckled under her. 'I want to kiss every inch of that beautiful body, I want it to sing for me.'

Georgia didn't remember Max suggesting they left, or even walking out the door. It was as if they floated out, one moment in a music-filled room, the next in the front garden, the smell of roses and damp earth mingling with the smell of their bodies.

It was hard to break away even to get in the car. Before Max turned on the ignition he had to pause to kiss her again.

Golden light from a street lamp bathed them as his big hands cupped her breasts. She found her hands reaching for buttons on his shirt, wanting to touch flesh so badly it hurt.

She didn't ask where he was taking her, it didn't matter. Her pulse was racing, her limbs ached for him, if he had pulled into the side of the road that would have been enough.

He drove only a few streets away and stopped, turning to her and taking her in his arms again, his mouth devouring hers.

When he released her and opened his car door, only then did she notice they were outside a block of Victorian flats with railings and marble steps up to plate glass doors.

Like a child she took his hand trustingly. She leaned closer to him as he unlocked the door and his arm encircled her and drew her inside.

Up a wide staircase with olive green carpet and delicate silk wall coverings. On past polished wood doors with brass numbers, the sort of place she imagined snooty ladies and gentlemen living.

On the second floor Max pulled out another key, he drew her closer and opened the door.

A glimpse of honey coloured carpet stretching up a long narrow hall, gilt wall lights and hessian-covered walls.

He kissed her again, kicking the door shut behind them, then scooping her up into his arms, he carried her into the dark bedroom.

'Watch this,' he whispered. She couldn't see much, just his hand reaching out for something in front of them. She heard him flick a switch and the room was filled with soft light.

It was a huge room dominated by a giant bed with a suede headboard. As he touched another switch, so gold velvet curtains slowly closed over the big window and sweet music filled the air.

'What do you think of that?' he looked down at her in his arms. His expression was almost boyish, showing off his latest toy, but rather than spoiling the moment she loved him for it.

'Amazing,' she smiled, unable to look at anything other than him. His big, rugged face looked softer now, his lips so red, eyes full of fire. 'But just kiss me again?'

He lowered her to the floor as he kissed her, his fingers already unzipping her dress, slowly peeling it from her shoulders, letting it drop to her waist.

'Even more beautiful than I imagined,' he whispered, touching her breasts reverently. 'I've always loved you Georgia.'

The satin bedspread caressed her back. He kissed her feet as he took off her shoes, slowly licked her thighs as he moved slowly upwards to peel off her panties.

Only when Max stood up to tear off his own clothes did she realize something wasn't quite right. Her eyes didn't focus as they should, her breathing felt odd. The music seemed to be right inside her head and her heart was pounding with more than just desire. She was no stranger to drink, it was something else entirely. But she was helpless, a fire seemed to be raging within her, she wanted him so badly it burned.

Naked, Max seemed even bigger. Wide muscular shoulders, tanned dark brown with a matt of black hair on his chest. His stomach was flat and taut with muscle and as he pulled off silk shorts, his penis rose up alarmingly large.

'You're so perfect,' he said moving beside her and bending to kiss her small pink-tipped breasts, his tongue flickering over her nipples. 'I'm going to love you tonight like you've never been before.'

Love-making with Ian had been sweet and tender, his hands gentle but unsurprising. With Max it was like being on a whirlwind of pleasure, one moment rough and demanding, the next so sensitive she wanted to cry. One moment his arms were crushing her, the next

359

he moved away using only his tongue to tease her into rapture.

Again and again he brought her almost to the point of orgasm, then he'd pause, almost laughing at the way she tossed her head on the pillows and clawed at him for more. One moment he was on top of her, his hands holding her buttocks, driving himself into her, then suddenly he would roll over, taking her with him, lifting her gently, his lips back on her breasts.

It was naughty and delicious, rough and passionate, beautiful and gentle all at once. Georgia saw his red pointed tongue slithering down her body and she felt as if a pit of fire was about to consume her.

'Make me come,' she heard herself cry out, catching his head between her hands and pushing him down onto her.

Bliss so exquisite she could only claw at the bed-spread, writhing under his tongue. 'Harder, harder,' she shouted. 'It's wonderful!'

She was out of control now, carried away to a plane where only sensation mattered, all sense of reality gone. A million fireworks were going off inside her, she could hear brass bands.

Her hands reached down to Max to draw him into her arms, but instead he knelt up beside her as she lay trembling.

She opened her eyes to find the room was spinning. Max was grinning down at her, tiny curls had crept round his face, lascivious red mouth and hairy chest made her think of a satyr.

'Don't,' she said involuntarily. She couldn't say what it was that disturbed her, but she wanted a more tender look, more words of love.

'Don't what?' He reached over to a drawer beside the bed, pulling out a packet of Durex. The ease he bit off the packet with his teeth and the speed with which he slid the rubber on his erect penis was further proof of how often he seduced girls.

'I'm going to fuck you senseless now,' he whispered hoarsely as he scooped her up and turned her on to her stomach. Before she could protest he was pushing his way into her from behind, gripping her like a dog with a bitch.

'Please don't, not like that,' she called out. Memories she'd thought she'd buried for ever were rushing back. But Max was oblivious.

She tried to wriggle away but he grabbed her round the middle so tight she felt nauseous, his breath rasping on her back.

She was no longer on a satin-covered bed with a man who'd taken her on a brief trip to heaven.

It was her father. Forcing his way into her, humiliating, degrading and hurting her. She could smell the smoky room, the drink on his breath. Feel the carpet beneath her, the prickle of her net petticoats against her thighs, even hear the filthy things he was saying.

'No,' she whimpered. 'Please don't.'

She heard his breathing getting louder, grunts of animal joy, and finally he shuddered to a halt, slithering onto the bed beside her like a deflated balloon.

For a moment Georgia just lay on her stomach, face buried in the pillow. She wanted to cry, but no tears came.

'Come here for a cuddle.' His voice wounded her further, she could hear the tenderness in it. He didn't even know he'd hurt her.

The room looked hideously vulgar now, all gold and ivory. This was his lair. Satin, mirrors, even the electronic devices to operate the curtains and music. Every last thing designed to impress and seduce silly drunken girls. She could see his silk shirt lying on the floor, the double 'M' monogram in gold thread glinting in the light.

'What's up?' he asked, turning heavily towards her, one hand on her arm.

What could she say? Was it possible to explain to any man that one moment she'd been almost fainting with desire, the next he made her remember a rapist?

'Georgia,' his voice was soft as he realized something was very wrong. 'Tell me what it is? What did I do?'

'I don't like it like that,' she whispered. 'Didn't you hear me telling you to stop?'

He sat up then, moving round to look at her. The face looking down at her was stricken with remorse.

'I didn't hear you. I'm so sorry.'

The anger at him faded, replaced by a sick feeling about herself. He wasn't to blame, she was. What on earth had possessed her to even kiss him, let alone come here with him?

'It's all right,' she whispered back. 'Get into bed, I'm just going to the bathroom.'

He moved then pulling back the gold satin covers to reveal black satin sheets.

'It's just down the passage,' he said softly, crawling into bed. 'Come back quickly and we'll talk.'

She could see the sleepiness in his eyes. His face looked lined now, revealing his age. She pulled the covers up round him and dropped a chaste kiss on his forehead. As she reached the door she looked back.

His eyes were closed already, his hand snaking up to turn down the lights and music. Bending down she picked up her clothes and boots and backed out of the door.

The bathroom gleamed with opulent bad taste. Mirrored walls, soft lighting. A bath big enough for four people sunk into the floor. The basin set into white marble with gold taps, a purple carpet with matching sets of towels hanging on thick gold rails. Erotic pen sketches were framed in gilt, a naked male statue in one corner.

When she opened a drawer under the washbasin there was even more evidence of who Max entertained in this place. A variety of cosmetics, even a vaginal douche.

For a moment she wanted to be sick. She was one of his groupies now. For two years she'd laughed at these vacuous, wide-eyed dolly birds. Not one memorable, designed like paper tissues to be used and thrown out. Yet mindless as they were, surely none of them had been foolish enough to think it was love that motivated Max?

Ten minutes later, Georgia stole back up the corridor towards the front door fully-dressed, her shoes in her hand.

Glancing to her left, she could see Max lying on his back, mouth open, snoring softly. She opened the door and let herself out silently.

As the cool night touched her flaming face she knew with certainty she had been drugged. Her legs were unsteady, her heart beating too fast, throat dry. Some of that could be explained by the champagne, but not the strange way things looked, the brightness of colours, or her losing her inhibitions so suddenly.

She could blame Max for that perhaps. He was a practised seducer who would use anything at his disposal. But the rest of it was all her fault, and somehow she would have to live with that, and the repercussions later.

Chapter 16

Georgia heard the doorbell ring but ignored it. It was nearly four in the afternoon, and she was certain it was Max.

'I can't face him,' she whispered to herself.

The door bell rang again.

Her window was open, a soft warm breeze wafting in, the street below was silent, the way it always was on Sundays.

'Georgia!' She heard a voice. 'Come on, open up.'

Not Max but Rod. She didn't want to talk to him either, but he spotted her peering over the window-sill.

Slowly she went downstairs. It had been nearly five in the morning when she got home. The drug she'd been given let her walk all the way home without noticing the distance, but it hadn't numbed the shame of what had happened, or allowed her to sleep. How was she going to face Max again?

'Being a recluse, eh?' Rod grinned at her. He looked like an Apache warrior as the afternoon sun caught his high cheek bones and made his blue-black hair gleam. Even his faded denim shirt and jeans fitted the image. 'So how was the party?'

Rod's dark eyes skimmed round Georgia's room. It was unnaturally clean and tidy, as if she'd been cleaning all day, the smell of polish and disinfectant worse than a hospital. Her eyelids had a faint mauve tinge, the way she always looked when she'd been up all night worrying. Even her hairstyle, two childish fat plaits either side of her face was a sure sign she was insecure.

'Someone's upset you,' he said with sharp perception, noting the blue-checked shirt she wore over her jeans was Ian's. 'Come on, tell me everything.'

'The party was wonderful,' she said in a small voice, going over to the window and staring out rather than face his probing eyes. 'I'm just kind of hungover.'

She couldn't tell a man who shared Max's attitude to women how things were.

'You're hurting,' he said softly, coming up behind her, sliding his arms round her waist and putting his chin on her shoulder. 'Is it missing Ian, or something more?'

His brotherly hug brought tears to her eyes. She wanted to tell him the truth, but she couldn't.

'I'm fine, really,' she sniffed. 'I just did something last night I regret. Don't try and get me to tell you. I couldn't explain.'

It was odd how Ian's death had changed Rod. Two years ago she wouldn't have dared to be alone with him. But the tragedy had revealed more than his courage. Underneath the arrogance and sardonic wit, he had a deep insight into human behaviour.

For a moment he said nothing, just increased the pressure of his hug.

'Don't waste time with regrets,' he said softly. 'I can imagine what happened, you met a man who sweet-talked you, now you feel like a tart.'

Georgia turned her head, nuzzling her cheek against his.

'That's about the strength of it,' she sighed. Perhaps he wouldn't be so understanding if she told him it was Max, but at least in principle he knew the full story.

'I do it all the time,' Rod gave a hollow little chuckle. 'I don't learn. But you will, you aren't as thick as me.

The only advice I can give you is to tell the man the truth. Don't turn one mistake into a series of them as I usually do.'

'You mean you regret things sometimes?' Georgia's dark eyes grew wide with surprise.

She could remember all the times the band had picked him up from girls flats, the cocky way he swaggered out, his ribald comments, never a look back at the pale sad face at the window.

'Yeah,' he moved away from her and filled up the kettle. 'The ones that wanted more than I could give them.'

'Have you ever thought it was love?' she said. 'You know, when everything seems so perfect, then – ' she stopped short, unsure she should say more.

'Lots of times,' he smiled and took two mugs out of the cupboard. 'But you mean when you realize right in the middle of it, that it's a mistake?'

She nodded.

'That's a bummer,' he laughed cheerfully, almost dispelling her gloom. 'I usually tell them I was attracted to them because they reminded me of a girl I lost, but I can't go through with it now I know what a fine person they are.'

Georgia giggled. 'Does it work?'

'Rarely, they usually go so chilly on me I have to leave,' he pulled a woebegone face.

'Oh Rod,' she was really laughing now. 'I'm glad you came round, you've made me feel much happier.'

'Well, take Ian's old shirt off,' he said as he made coffee. 'Put something snazzy on and we'll go and see a film. Regret's a mug's game.'

Delivery vans woke her early on Monday morning. She got out of bed and put the kettle on, but only then did she realize she had no milk left.

Slipping on a pair of jeans, and the first sweater that came to hand, she ran down the stairs.

There was a cold, crisp autumn feeling in the air. Even though the sun was shining it was too low in the sky to reach her side of the street as it did in the summer.

'Good morning Georgia.'

She stopped and looked around. The market men were always calling out to her. But this voice didn't belong to a cockney barrow boy.

Two men were pushing their way through the stalls towards her. Both had cameras slung round their necks, but she didn't make the connection immediately.

'Good morning,' she replied, aware several stallholders had stopped work to watch. 'How do you know my name?'

One was in his thirties, neatly-combed brown hair, wearing a tweed jacket, a pleasant open face that invited trust. The other was older, fat-faced and balding, wearing a beige three-quarter-length raincoat.

'Don't tell me you didn't know your record reached number forty on Saturday?' the younger one said, smiling as though amused by her surprise. 'Surely we aren't the first reporters to track you down?' As he spoke he lifted his camera and took a picture of her.

'Yes. No,' she was flustered, aware her hair was uncombed and her sweater had a hole in the elbow. 'I mean, yes you are the first, and no I didn't know it had reached the charts.'

'They reckon it could be number one in a couple of weeks,' the older man said. 'It could topple the Beatles. How do you feel about that?'

'Thrilled.' She didn't actually feel anything, in fact she was sure it was some kind of hoax. If she'd known they were hanging around her door she wouldn't have come out at all. 'What paper are you from?'

'The *Mirror*,' the older man's hand shot forward to

grasp hers. 'Dave Barnet's the name, could I buy you some breakfast and have a little chat?'

The younger man lifted his camera again, she turned to him waving her hand to stop him, suddenly anxious.

'Couldn't you have phoned or something? Are you from the *Mirror* too?'

'No, I'm from the *Evening News*,' the younger put down his camera and advanced on her. 'Giles Wentworth. I tried to telephone yesterday, but you aren't on the phone here. This must be just a temporary place?'

He was gazing around the market, noting the pile of empty boxes and refuse by her door. His tone was warm, yet she bristled at the implication behind his words.

'No,' she said, running her hand through her hair, wondering if she should be charming, or send them away quickly. 'I like it here. It's where I belong.'

'You were born here then?' the older man chimed in.

'No, in the East End.' She saw the pit yawning before her. She would have to get a grip on herself, make a sensible background for herself before she said something she might regret later. 'Now look, I'm surprised and flattered by your interest,' she batted her eyelashes at the younger reporter. 'But it's too early for questions or pictures. I haven't even had a cup of tea yet this morning. Why don't you phone my manager Max Menzies and he'll arrange a proper interview?'

The market men were getting really interested now. They pressed in closer and from out of their depths came ribald comments and encouragement.

'Give 'em a song Georgia!'

'Tell 'em 'ow hard you've worked love!'

'They seem to be your friends,' Giles Wentworth looked almost nervous at the crowd gathering around him. 'Could you pose with them for me?'

She never knew whose arms came up and lifted her

off her feet, one moment she was vertical, the next horizontal lying in the men's arms supported by four of them.

A click of the shutter, someone tickled her and another picture caught her laughing.

'Just tell me Georgia,' the older man moved closer as the men released her. 'Is "No Time" in memory of Ian and Alan?'

She was flustered. She should have thought all this out before. One wrong statement now and she could be damned forever.

'Not exactly, though the words came to me after their funeral.' Was that the right thing to say? She hadn't wanted anyone to dwell on Ian and Alan's death, and after the evening with Max she felt she'd betrayed Ian.

'You were in love with Ian McShane,' the younger man said. It wasn't a question, more a statement he wanted confirmed. 'It must have been a terrible blow?'

'The worst kind,' Georgia felt tears rise in her eyes. 'But you must excuse me now. I've got an appointment later on this morning.'

An hour later as she showered and washed her hair, the significance of the two reporters sank in. This was what she could expect now, people popping up at all times, trying to catch her unawares. Even though she didn't want to see Max, she had to. Like Rod said, regrets were a mug's game!

'Why did you run out on me?' Max sat at his desk twiddling a paperclip. Thick dark stubble covered his lower face. If he wasn't wearing a different suit and tie she would have thought he hadn't been home since the party.

Rod had made her feel better yesterday. The news of the record making the charts suggested at last things were about to blast off. She had to find the right words, make Max realize that Saturday night was something behind them both.

'It was all a mistake,' Georgia blushed, it sounded so cruel. 'Someone slipped something in my drink.'

To her surprise Max grinned, showing his white even teeth.

'Well, that's a flattering thing to say. I take it you mean letting me make love to you was the mistake, not walking out the door?'

For a second she thought Max was relieved at her attitude, that he'd thought it over and decided it was a non-starter.

'I shouldn't have let it happen,' she hung her head. 'You're married and my manager, you're even old enough to be my father. It would be best if we buried and forgot it.'

'You don't claim it was rape then?'

Georgia's eyes flew wide open, she stiffened visibly.

'What did I say?' Max got up and came round the desk towards her.

'N – nothing,' she stammered.

Max shook his head, a faint glimpse of amusement in his eyes. He perched on the desk just inches from her, staring at her hard.

'I can't forget,' he said softly. 'You can play hard to get if you like. The terrified virgin if that's how you feel. But I know you enjoyed it, whether or not someone slipped something in your drink. I know I'm too old for you, but there's always been a spark of something between us, even you can't deny that.'

'All right, maybe there was,' Georgia looked up defiantly. 'But it's something I don't want to repeat. If it had been right I would have been happy about it. All I feel now is misery and shame.'

'You certainly know how to flatter a guy,' Max folded his arms, his mouth turning down at the corners. 'I can't say I won't try again because I want you Georgia,

370

any way, any how. But if you want breathing space, you've got it. Can I be fairer than that?'

'I want Saturday night to be wiped from your memory and mine,' she said in a whisper. 'I want us back where we were, business only. If you can't handle that then I'm sorry.'

She couldn't look up at him. She knew he was hurt, yet if he felt so badly why didn't he come round to her flat the next day, or even ask how she got home?

'Is this all you came here for?' his tone was icy now, and she remembered all those secretaries and office girls who'd been sacked once he'd lost interest in them.

'Not exactly.' She had to remember he needed her. She must be adult even if she felt like weeping inside. He wasn't going to grind her down like he did everyone else who crossed him. 'There were two reporters outside my door this morning. They said the record's at number forty. I thought we ought to talk about both things.'

'Did you now,' Max sneered, not even a flicker of affection in his eyes. 'I suppose you realized the old man has some uses?'

'Fuck off Max,' she snapped, getting to her feet. 'I've done my best to be straight with you. If you don't want to be my manager then I'll find someone else. Don't try and make me crawl to you, because I'll start to hate you.'

He caught hold of her wrist, digging his fingernails into her flesh.

'Getting a bit above ourselves?' he hissed. His breath stank of cigars and uncleaned teeth. Georgia recoiled in disgust.

'I learned that from you,' she snapped. 'Now either we talk about what we say to the press or I go out and say whatever I feel like. It's up to you!'

He dropped her wrist immediately, stood up and backed away, returning to his seat behind his desk. She could see a vein throbbing in his forehead and she guessed he was trying to control himself.

'Let's pretend Saturday night ended with the gig at the Scene,' he said slowly, looking down at his big hands clenched on his blotter in front of him. 'I won't bring it up again, I'm just your manager.'

It was a hollow victory to see him like this. Part of her wanted to rush round the desk and hug him, to reassure him he wasn't old and ugly, that he would always have a place in her life. But she didn't dare. Max would take it as a sign of weakness.

'So is it true? The record is number forty?' she said, sitting down again.

'Yes.' He sighed deeply, as if struggling to control conflicting emotions. 'I heard last night, and came over to your place to celebrate with you. But you were out.'

'I see.' She wasn't going to apologize, or explain where she was. 'I take it you found someone else to celebrate with?'

He half smiled then, rubbing one hand round his bristly chin.

'You could say that.'

'Well I suggest you get in that bathroom and shave.' Her tone was brisk and unsympathetic. 'I'll sit here and write a profile of myself while you're gone.'

Max looked at her for a moment, then threw back his head and laughed. It echoed round the big office, shaking the framed photographs of Bill Hayley and Jerry Lee Lewis.

Georgia was stunned, but at least his laughter was better than morbid self-pity.

'You can be a right little bitch sometimes,' he said, still spluttering with laughter. 'But you've certainly got a head on your shoulders.' He pushed a sheet of paper towards her and his gold pen. 'When I've made myself presentable we'll talk photographs and press releases. You'll need new clothes and somewhere better to live.

Berwick Street might have been handy when your face was just another pretty unknown one. But by the time the *Evening News* has printed something tonight you'll have fans and weirdos camping on your doorstep. With you alone at night in that house, anything could happen.'

Max stayed in the bathroom for over half an hour. When he came back into the office he found Georgia resting her head on folded arms on his desk. The litter bin beside her was piled up high with screwed up pieces of paper.

'Have you done it?' He came round behind the desk and looked down at what she'd written.

'You've said nothing about yourself!' he exclaimed. 'Orphaned during the war. Left school without any qualifications, spent some time as a machinist before getting a first chance to sing at the Acropolis club in Greek Street.' He flung the paper down angrily. 'You'll have to come up with a bit more meat than that!'

'There is nothing else,' she grinned up at him. 'We'll just have to be mysterious.'

Max sat down heavily on his chair, loosening his tie and undoing his top button, a waft of Moustache aftershave reached Georgia's nose.

'I wish I could believe you,' his eyes narrowed with suspicion. 'What is it you're hiding?'

'Nothing.' Georgia stood up and stalked across the office to the window, keeping her back to him. 'I just don't think my childhood can possibly interest anyone. Who cares anyway what school I went to, or whether I was happy. It's now that counts. Let them ask me what I'm interested in, what books I've read, or who influenced me. That's enough for any fan surely?'

'Just think, Rod,' Georgia said later that evening as together they pored over a copy of the *Evening News*, in the dressing-room at the Marquee. 'In a couple of weeks we might be eating at the Ritz!'

Max's phone had rung constantly all day with press wanting to know more about her. The paper in front of them proved the public was hungry for information.

She liked the picture of her in the arms of the stallholders in Berwick Street, but she wasn't exactly sure about the rest.

'Berwick Street beauty tipped for the top,' was the headline.

'Georgia James races up the charts with her record "No Time". Two years ago Georgia was selling frocks in Berwick Street on a market stall, now she's on her way to stardom with a heart-stopping ballad written by herself and her band Samson. Two of the boys in the band died in a fire earlier this year and the song is dedicated to their memory.'

'Shit,' Rod exploded. 'Why did you say that?'

'I didn't exactly,' Georgia said. 'Neither did I say I sold dresses.'

Maybe the article was corny. Yet she couldn't help raise a smile about her love for Soho and the market.

'They've made me sound like a cockney sparrow,' she giggled. 'Look at what Bert in the café said!'

'"She's got a knockout voice. Of course she'll go all the way to the top, we never doubted it round here. She's a lovely girl and we're all very proud of her,"' she read, wiping a tear from her eye. 'Bless him.'

That night people were turned away from the Marquee. Inside it was packed so tight with fans the temperature rose to the nineties. No dancing for the fans now, just pressed up together, hundreds of people clamouring to see her, prepared to face the discomfort just to hear her before she moved on to bigger venues.

The next day it was the *Mirror*'s turn, taking it a stage further with pictures of her against piles of fruit, her door in the background. Another one of her on stage in

Miriam's old white dress, belting out a song, head thrown back, hair like a storm.

They re-capped on the tragedy of Ian and Alan's death and the star-studded benefit concert that followed it.

'No time', seemed almost prophetic now. There was no time to visit her old friends, no time to catch her breath. She had caught the public's imagination and as the week passed, so the record flew up the charts.

Menzies Enterprises was besieged with callers. Club owners wanted to book the band while they could still afford them. Magazines wanted profiles. Radio and television producers offered guest appearances and fans stood outside hoping for a glimpse of her.

But to Georgia it became real when people turned to stare at her in the street and bolder ones came up to her and asked outright for her autograph.

Two days after the reporters found her home, Georgia was whisked off by Max to The Sunderland, a small hotel close to Sloane Square, leaving most of her belongings behind in Berwick Street.

'We'll carry on paying the rent,' Max said as he closed the door behind them. 'Let the public think you're still here for the time being.'

No more long hours of lying in bed catching up from the gig the night before. No afternoons spent wandering around new towns or listening to records with the boys. Max would ring first thing in the morning to arrange her day, every minute planned to give her the maximum publicity.

Whether she was buying clothes, or eating a meal, somehow the press were always there. Cameras zooming in on her, microphones poised to catch even the most trivial of remarks. She had to learn to think before speaking, to keep her guard up at all times.

It was exciting, yet frightening. Like that drug, it distorted her feelings, one moment she was high as a kite, the next strangely alone.

Max was in his element as 'No Time' approached number one. He didn't miss a trick. Sending men ahead to gigs to erect crash barriers for crowd control, creating mass hysteria himself. Press releases were timed to keep her image high, and almost every day there was a picture of her in one of the papers.

At each performance the crowds got steadily larger. Queues stretched down the roads outside for hours before, and as she arrived in a limousine with blacked out windows the fans would surge forward, hands reaching out to touch her.

Georgia was amused yet frightened by Max's ploys. She understood that he had to promote her with everything within his power to make sure he got a return on his investment, but there was something vaguely dishonest about the flashy way he approached it.

Once it had been hard to get him to watch an entire set, but now he never missed one. He strutted around in his expensive clothes and gold jewellery, opening magnums of champagne. He ordered people around as if he were the star, with a retinue of vacant-looking girls posing as personal assistants clinging to him.

Suddenly everything had to be the best. A luxury coach, to get the band to gigs. A couple of tough-looking men to act as 'minders.' A permanent photographer. Hairdresser and make-up artist. Public relations girls, a woman to look after their stage clothes, and roadies to unload and set up the equipment. Hotels were booked for them, dinners, parties and press conferences. It was a circus, with Max as the ringmaster. He didn't consult the band about anything. But who was paying for it all?

The big black Daimler cruised almost silently down the Strand. Georgia wriggled forward in her seat, her heart thumping with excitement.

Just three hours ago she had heard 'No Time' was

376

finally at number one, pushing the Beatles off their perch. Tonight she was going to a party at London's Savoy Hotel, where she was to be the guest of honour.

'I used to come down here late at night with my friend,' she confided to the chauffeur. 'We used to watch all the rich people and pretend we were rich too.'

It was New Year's Eve, she remembered most distinctly. Helen with the fur collar of her coat turned up against the cold wind, her hair like gold under the street lights, shivering as they stood in a doorway to watch a stream of cars like this one, disgorging women in furs and silk dresses at the hotel.

'You never guessed one day it would be you?' The man chuckled, surprised by the star's childish confession.

'Not even in my wildest dreams,' Georgia laughed softly, breath hot on his neck, her perfume filling his nostrils. 'I wish Helen was with me now. She died before I got my first singing job.'

'Are you nervous?'

Robert Wells was over fifty. He'd been working for this company for almost ten years and in that time he'd driven more famous people than he could count. Actors, opera singers, lords, members of Parliament and film stars, but never once had he driven anyone so pent up with excitement.

'Terrified,' she admitted. 'Do you think I look all right?'

He glanced into the mirror. All he could see clearly were her sparkling eyes, but he could remember the way she looked as she walked out of the hotel.

A long red clingy dress, dark curls tumbling over her bare shoulders, and a face so lovely he could hardly drag his eyes from it.

'All right?' he laughed softly. 'You look fabulous. You'll knock 'em all dead!'

Robert slowed the car, ready to turn into the forecourt. The Savoy had never looked more beautiful. Floodlights had turned it into a golden temple framed by a black velvet sky. Gleaming plate glass doors, beyond, white marble, rich carpets and chandeliers. A perfect setting for this enchantress.

Georgia smoothed down her dress, spreading her fingers out to check she hadn't chipped the matching nail varnish. She could see Rod waiting for her by the door and she wondered if he was as nervous as her.

He looked so handsome. A white suit straight out of a Hollywood film, his black hair sleek and shiny, restyled with a middle parting, accentuating his Red Indian looks.

The car cruised slowly to a halt. A liveried doorman leapt forward to open her door. A group of fans pushed against the security men who tried to contain them.

'Have a great time.' Robert turned round from his driving seat to look at Georgia one more time. 'I'll be back to pick you up later.'

'Well, you look the business,' Rod said softly, taking her arm and leading her towards the open door.

'I could say the same about you,' Georgia touched his bow tie lightly. 'Thank you for waiting out here for me, I'm scared stiff.'

Ahead of them as they walked up the few heavily-carpeted stairs, Georgia could see the ballroom. It was already very crowded, the soft music almost unheard under the barrage of chatter and clink of glasses.

'I never thought we'd end up anywhere as posh as this,' Georgia giggled to Rod, pointing up to a chandelier above them. 'That's the real thing, not like the kind Max has in his hall. Don't any of you get too drunk and show us up!'

There was a hush as they walked in, people turned and stared at her and in that instant, Georgia felt a charge of something strange.

It lasted only a second. A glass of champagne was

put in her hand, and all at once there were people clamouring to speak to her.

'Congratulations on reaching number one. I'm so thrilled to meet you at last. I just love the song.' The flattery wrapped her in a warm blanket. These sophisticated people in evening clothes, dripping with jewels seemed to know so much about her. Every one of them looked important.

Across the crowded room she could see John and Norman with two leggy, blonde girls. Les looked almost handsome in a grey suit, as a red-haired woman talked to him earnestly. Speedy's auburn hair caught under the lights, complemented his grey velvet jacket and his dancing partner could have been a model.

Yet for all the glamour, there were no friends in the crowd. Where were all the other stars she'd met on tours? People who she could really talk to. Charming as most of the guests were, Georgia felt a little out of her depth. Lawyers, promoters, club owners, business men and their wives, surely if this party was thrown for her, real friends should have been invited too.

'Georgia,' Max pushed his way through the crowd, took her hands and kissed both of them. He wore a dark dinner jacket with a plum-coloured cummerbund. 'You look gorgeous!'

With him was a tubby smaller man, reptilian eyes flickered behind gold-rimmed spectacles, his large forehead glistened with perspiration.

With one arm round her Max introduced them.

'This is Al Green from Memphis, he flew over this afternoon to meet you.'

The name 'Al Green' was one Max often brought up in conversation. Georgia understood he was responsible for the glut of American pop stars that dominated the charts. He arranged tours for everyone from Elvis Presley downwards.

'Hi there.' The man put a podgy hand into hers, his

thin lips barely moved and she could see no pupils in his dark eyes. 'You're quite a girl Georgia. We've been hearing your name even back in Memphis. This is one helluva party honey.'

'I've heard a lot about you, too,' she smiled politely. 'How nice of you to come all this way just to meet me.'

She didn't like him. It was ridiculous to feel something so strong when she'd only spoken a few words to him. Maybe it was just those eyes, how could anyone feel anything but repulsion for a reptile?

'I don't know whether I'd have come if you hadn't been footing the bill,' he laughed, double chin wobbling, taking out a flamboyant red handkerchief and wiping his shiny brow. 'But now I'm here, I'm just loving it.'

Georgia looked round for Max, only to see his back view retreating into the crowd.

For a moment she just stared at the man. His dinner jacket was midnight blue, as he moved she caught a glimpse of silver lining. It was vulgar, even for someone in show business, the mark of a man who had no taste.

'Me footing the bill?' She could feel her heart thumping just that little bit harder. Something smelled fishy, and she was going to get to the bottom of it.

'Well, Max is your manager,' he licked his thin lips focusing on her cleavage. 'Don't that mean the same thing honey?'

What was it Max had said right at the outset? 'I lay out all the money, and when you start earning that's when I'll get it back.'

All those chauffeur driven cars, champagne, new clothes, photographs, hairdressing. Everything was being logged down against money she was earning. But why should she pick up the tab for a party that was supposed to be for her? Or pay to fly this jerk over to meet her?

'You and Max are lining up an American tour?' The

man must have got his wires crossed. Maybe Max just implied the expenses would be met by him to try and impress Al.

'Sure thing, honey,' he drawled. 'I'm gonna take a look see round this little island, get myself a piece of the action.'

'How do you think I'll go down in the States?' she smiled sweetly. 'Has the record reached the charts there yet?'

'It's been played honey,' he shot her a scathing look. 'But what our kids want is good old rock and roll.'

All at once Georgia understood. Max was offering free seats on the gravy train. This man wasn't interested in her. It was an excuse to get his podgy hands on some British rock and roll bands, kids with stars in their eyes and no experience. The pair of them were intending to expand their interests, using her earnings to finance it.

'Where are you staying?' she asked through clenched teeth.

'Here, honey,' he drawled. 'Max booked me into a suite overlooking the Thames.'

He couldn't even pronounce Thames correctly, making an awful th sound.

'It was nice to meet you,' she lied. 'I must go and talk to the band now. Goodbye.'

Her earlier euphoria vanished. Already the vultures were gathering and if she didn't keep one jump ahead, she might end up with nothing.

Slipping out unnoticed to the reception desk, using the excuse she wanted to know who to thank personally for the evening, she discovered the whole event had been booked by Menzies Enterprises.

Champagne by the truck load. Smoked salmon, caviar, breast of chicken, roast beef, fresh cream gateaux, mountains of salad, all paid for by her. She was the guest of honour and the mug who'd paid for it.

Now she understood why none of her friends had

been invited. It wasn't to celebrate her success. Just another way for Max to climb further up the ladder. She was just another trophy he'd won, and tonight he was displaying her publicly.

As the prattle of high-pitched snobby voices washed over Georgia, she felt murderous.

That feeling she'd had when she first walked in! She knew what it was now. Everyone here had the same motive as Al Green. They weren't interested in her talent, just how they could get a slice of the action.

Soon these people would be involving Max in further deals. Films, tours, advertisements, public appearances. Money flowing backwards and forwards, but somehow never reaching her bank account.

She hadn't had a penny yet. Everything spent had been charged to Max's office. She didn't begrudge the boys new clothes, they deserved them. Norman's green mohair suit must have cost a hundred pounds, John's leather jacket another fifty, that was mere chicken feed to the amount of food and drink being consumed. Deirdre the receptionist from Max's office in a sparkly dress costing probably twice as much as her own. Miriam across the room with a pair of diamond earrings she kept touching protectively. Max no doubt had a new car in the garage.

Was the man who owned the limousine company dancing with the Sloaney woman from the King's Road boutique? Could the fat man with bow legs be the printer? The tall man with the beard a director of the musical equipment store? They were leeches who would suck her blood until she was dry, then spit her out and look for another victim.

'Wonderful party darling.'

Georgia smiled at the elegant redhead who sailed past her on Jack Levy's arm. She owned a string of secretarial agencies in Oxford Street and by Monday morning she would have a list of new contacts.

'Don't let anyone know you've cottoned on,' she whispered to herself as she slipped into a toilet to compose herself. 'Just stay cool and observe. They'll soon find out you aren't quite as dumb as you look!'

It was easy to play the role of the little innocent. The glass in her hand was just water with ice and lemon, no one guarded their tongues when faced with a girl they thought was tipsy. Listening, watching, observing, remembering names and filing them away for another time.

It was late, almost one o'clock when she overheard something interesting.

She had stopped by the buffet, helping herself to some chicken and salad. Standing just a foot or two beside her were two men. One of them she knew slightly. He was the lawyer from Decca who had been there when she signed her contract. Slim, dark haired, an accent like cut glass which belied his swarthy Mediterranean looks. The other man was smaller, sandy haired and stout. But by the way he was speaking she suspected he was a lawyer too.

'I knew he'd be trouble when he said he had Riox acting for him,' the man from Decca said. 'Damn me if the little guttersnipe didn't start asking all kinds of questions.'

She guessed the men were talking about a singer called Ricky Delaney. A tough Liverpool rock singer that Max had attempted to handle and then abandoned because of his wild behaviour. Or at least that was what Max claimed!

Was this Riox a new manager on the scene?

'I've heard the name,' the stout man replied frowning as if trying to put a face to the name. 'Is his office in Chancery Lane?'

Georgia sidled closer, pretending to be engrossed in the food.

'The Strand,' the Decca man was swaying slightly as

383

if he'd drunk too much. 'Old established law firm. Riox's got a bee in his bonnet about protecting the interests of young entertainers. Sharp as a razor.'

'Eton man?' the stout man asked.

'Rugby I believe. Strange fellow. French father, mother, one of the Asprey family. One has to admire his integrity, but there's such a thing as loyalty to one's peers.'

'Did you have a good time?' Robert the chauffeur was waiting for her, the car gliding silently towards the steps at just a wave from one of the porters.

'It was interesting,' she said slowly as she sank back into the comfortable leather seat.

Robert glanced over his shoulder. The spark had gone from her, she wasn't tired, or drunk, just kind of sad.

'Not your sort of people?' He had a desire to ask her if she wanted to ride in the front with him, but that would be too impertinent.

'No,' her voice was faint, like a child about to cry. 'And I've got a feeling I'll need to watch my back from now on.'

Georgia sat before Simon Riox's desk and wondered if somehow she'd got it wrong.

He was only a junior partner in the law firm of Hollins, Burke and Gibson, too young, too lanky to be the formidable lawyer she'd imagined. His brown hair threatened to stand up in spikes, dark-rimmed glasses reminded her absurdly of Buddy Holly. Behind the thick glass his dark eyes were as soft as a spaniel's.

'Of course I know who you are,' he laughed softly at her suggestion he wouldn't.

His voice at least was the kind she expected, deep, resonant, entirely at odds with his almost feminine small features. She could see now he was older than he looked, at least thirty-five. 'What I'd like to know is how you heard about me. I'm not a visible attraction like yourself.'

'Eavesdropping,' she admitted. 'I heard a lawyer complaining you had too much integrity.'

She had tried four different lawyers' offices in the Strand before she found him and now as she sat in the small oak-panelled office she was beginning to lose her nerve.

She had put on a red trouser suit because it made her feel strong and decisive, but in this formal place it looked too loud.

'I find that very flattering,' his eyes never left hers and all at once she knew she could open up to him. 'I expect you feel nervous Georgia, let me order some tea, then you can tell me what's troubling you. If I can help, I will. I'm sure I hardly need tell you anything you tell me is in the strictest confidence.'

'I haven't had any money yet,' she said simply. 'I found out last night I was footing the bill for a party at the Savoy, and flying over men from the States who aim to fill their pockets at my expense.'

He listened carefully to the whole story, looking at her over his thick glasses from time to time, writing copious notes in a thin, spidery hand.

'Don't be put off by my notetaking,' he said at length. 'I actually have an excellent memory, but writing it down helps cement it in here,' he tapped his forehead with a pencil.

'I felt used last night,' she rung her hands in her lap. 'Humiliated even. I mean can you imagine thinking you are the one they've all come to see, and then discovering almost every guest is on the make?'

'I understand your feelings,' Riox smiled sympathetically. 'This kind of thing happens all the time, it's all show, glitz and promotion. Max was probably astute in throwing this party. Perhaps he even had good reason to oil the wheels in America. But he should have discussed it with you. Made it clear it was ultimately your expense.'

'But that Al Green wasn't even interested in me. I just paid for a free holiday for him!'

'I wish you'd come to me before you signed the contract with Decca. I could have acted for you independently, protected you from sharp business practice,' he sighed deeply, as if afraid he was too late to help. 'I despise people who prey on young talent and grow rich while they wear out their protégé.'

'Is it too late to change things?'

'The contract with Decca is rock hard.' He flicked through the copy she'd brought with her. 'But it's a fair one. However, your contract with Max Menzies is another story.'

'Really?'

Riox smirked, almost as if he relished a challenge.

'Less than three months to go. He slipped up there, but maybe he was too busy thinking about Decca's contract. This will be a good lever to make changes. To make sure you get what you've earned. For goodness sake when he suggests you sign another, consult me first.'

'Do you think it would be better to find a new manager then?'

'Not necessarily.' Riox had a look of cunning in his eyes. 'Max Menzies may be too sharp, but he is the undisputed king of promotion. If you got yourself a gentler character, the chances are Max would outwit him, just for spite. There is only one way to beat him, and that is by being just as sharp yourself.'

'What should I do?'

Simon Riox weighed up the girl in front of him and he liked what he saw. He had heard her record soon after it was released, liked it so much he actually bought a copy, and since then he had watched her shoot to overnight success.

Perhaps it was merely the blanket coverage in the press that had put him off her a little. Somehow he had formed the opinion she was just another vacuous pop star who would burn herself out with the high life. Now he could see beyond the beautiful face and passionate voice. She was highly intelligent, brave and resourceful. How many girls of her age would balk at throwing a Savoy party surrounded by all those socialites fawning at her? Indeed how many would stay sober and work out what was happening?

'I was going to say I'll handle it all for you,' he smiled at her, suddenly boyish and mischievous. 'But I can see you are a woman of action. Go to him now, tell him you discovered last night's bun fight was at your expense. Demand to see his books and tell him I'm your lawyer. That is, if you want me to be?'

'Yes, please,' she said softly. There was strength in him, she felt it now, flowing across his desk to her.

'I'll write to him today. I'll outline how we expect your affairs to be managed in future. If you need advice on handling your money I can do that for you too.'

'I'm so glad I came,' she breathed a deep sigh of relief, as she got to her feet. 'I felt murderous last night, but now I feel calm.'

'I'm glad to hear it. A murdering pop star makes too many ripples,' he laughed, standing up and pushing back his chair. 'I think you'll find he will play reasonably fair from now on,' he said as he shook her hand. 'He'll probably be hiving off a bit, but a man like that is so practised at deceit even an auditor would have a job to catch him out. I'll do a little double checking from time to time. Just so he knows he can't be greedy. Ring me if you have any further problems.'

Georgia was fired up now. She caught a taxi straight to Berkeley Square and ran up the stairs two at a time.

Without waiting for Deirdre to invent some reason

she couldn't see Max, she barged down the corridor and straight into his office.

'What is it?' Max looked up from his desk, surprise and some irritation showing in his face. 'I'm busy.'

'So am I,' she said sharply, slamming the door behind her. 'But neither of us is so busy we can ignore what's going on.'

Max sighed deeply and pushed his papers away.

'Five minutes,' he said. 'That's all I can spare.'

She sat down opposite him and crossed her legs.

There was never a time when she wasn't struck by his looks. The broad shoulders, the dark handsome face, gold jewellery, handmade suits, silk shirts and Italian shoes all added to the image of a man to be obeyed and feared. But she wasn't going to let him get the better of her this time.

'Has it ever occurred to you that you work for me? Not the other way around?'

Max's hooded eyes shot open, they were as dark as her own, for a moment stunned by her statement.

'What?'

'You heard.' She held herself in check. Not for one moment must she falter, or the chance might never come again. 'You're treating me like an idiot Max, and I won't stand for it any longer. I'm your best client. The golden goose if you like.'

'Georgia darling,' he gave her his widest, most disarming smile. The one he always used while frantically thinking how he could outwit his opponent. 'What is this? What on earth do you think I'm guilty of?'

'Using my earnings to finance other deals,' she said quietly. 'Last night for example. Not only did you omit to tell me I was paying for it, but Mr Green seems to believe I'm in the English holiday business.'

'Now come on Georgia,' Max stood up threateningly. 'Have I ever kept you short? Don't you trust my judgement to make a shrewd move?'

'A sharp move,' she corrected him. 'I wouldn't have paid to entertain that load of wankers. I'm the one with a number one hit. I don't need all that. You did it for your own ego, at my expense. I want to see your books. I want every penny accounted for. You can have your percentage, and I want the rest.'

'But Georgia, you already owe me. I've been keeping you on full wages for over two years even when you didn't bring in a penny.'

'Bullshit,' she exclaimed. 'I've done my sums. You've been on to a nice little earner from the day I started with Samson.'

'But expenses have to come out of that,' he said smarmily. 'What's this all about Georgia? Do you want money for a new frock?'

'No. I want what's mine,' she put her hands on her hips, glaring at him defiantly. 'The books Max, the ones you keep each week. I'm entitled to see them.'

'Who's put you up to this?' He turned his back on her, moving over to the window.

'No one. Are you surprised I have a brain as well as a voice?'

'I never doubted you had a brain.' She knew Max was struggling to find a good excuse for his behaviour. 'You don't know the business like I do. Even a singer as good as you needs promotion.'

'Thousands of pounds are being made out of me each day,' she snapped, striding across to him and grabbing his arm to turn him. 'Every gig, every personal appearance brings in a fortune. I hired you to manage my career. Not my money. Like I said. You work for me.'

'How dare you?' His dark eyes flashed. She saw his hand clench into a fist.

'Don't even think of hitting me,' she hissed. 'You've done some shabby things in your life I'm sure. But don't add hitting women to them. All I want out of you is straightness. Itemized accounts showing every penny

I've earned, and every penny you claim you've spent on me. Then we'll come to the point where you hand over the rest.'

'But you must understand that the money coming in now is paying back all I spent on you earlier,' he said with a snake-like smile. 'New equipment, the van, the band's suits.'

'Bollocks,' she retorted. 'You might have spent money on Samson, but not on me.'

She waited just a moment or two for the implications of this statement to filter into his mind.

'I'm on my own! Right?' she snapped. 'You diddled the boys out of a shared contract with me. When did I ever sign anything to take over their expenses?'

'Come on, play fair,' his mouth opened and closed like a goldfish. 'You were part of that band!'

'You didn't think so when you wanted me away from them. The only equipment I need is in here,' she touched her throat lightly with one red talon.

'Who put you up to this?' his eyes narrowed.

'No one. But I have found myself a lawyer just in case you're tempted to try and wriggle out of it. Simon Riox.'

She knew as she saw the colour drain from his face that Riox really was the best.

'I understand my contract with you has only another three months to run,' she added airily.

Max stared at her. For the first time ever she saw indecision in his eyes. He looked hunted.

'Don't be like this Georgia. Aren't you forgetting that I was the man who believed in you two years ago, gave you a chance and supported you?'

'I haven't forgotten anything,' she said softly. 'But let's clear the air Max. You knew you were on to a good thing, the moment you met me. You didn't do it for love, or charity. Just money. That's okay. It's a good pure motive. But during that time you've thrown a great deal of shit at me and I'm just calling time if you like.'

'You wouldn't find another manager!' It wasn't a question, more a statement of belief in himself.

'Not if you play straight. I like your strength and singlemindedness. But from now on there are new ground rules. I will not pay for this office, the legions of girls who work for you, yachts, gold toilet seats or villas in the South of France. I'll foot the bill for last night, but not for that cocksucking Yank's holiday and suite at the Savoy.'

'But – ' he spluttered.

'But nothing. I'm telling you that I don't need or want any of the hangers on. As from today I select who stays and who goes. I pay the boys, a couple of roadies and perhaps I'll find a wardrobe mistress I like.'

'I only took people on to make life easier for you,' he was almost whining now. 'Some thanks I get for it.'

'I can appreciate that,' she snapped. 'But from now on I want to have people around me I have chosen. I didn't wear myself out for two years, just to watch other people take over my life!'

'And if I agree?' He looked deflated, for the first time since she had met him, unsure of himself.

'You can continue to be my manager,' she smiled charmingly. 'I'm sure you don't want to kill the golden goose, not when it may lay a golden egg each month or so for years. But if not I'll start legal proceedings.'

'Look Georgia,' he shrugged his shoulders, 'I'm not a crook. Most of the money hasn't even come in yet. I'm not a fool either. But you are young, and inexperienced with large sums of money.'

'True,' she cut in on him. 'But unless you hand it over I'll never learn. By next Friday I want accounts and a cheque. If not you know what to expect. Have I made myself clear?'

Chapter 17

1965

Max pulled the girl closer to him, thrusting one big hand up her skirt and pulling at her lace panties.

'Oh Max,' she sighed against his chest. 'You're so big. I don't know if I'm ready for this.'

'Of course you are baby,' he buried his face in her blonde hair. 'Come and sit on my knee and show me those lovely titties.'

A room that overlooked the Thames, pale green brocade settees, a drinks table laden with bottles, fruit piled up like a feast in a cut glass bowl. Through open double doors he could see a huge bed beyond, turned down in readiness for them, soft lamps illuminating it invitingly.

But Max's heart wasn't in it. Georgia had even spoiled this for him. Once he would have taken this dumb little dollybird on the office floor. Screwed her senseless in ten minutes and been off to a meeting within half an hour. Now for some reason he'd spent over fifty quid on a meal and champagne and even booked the pair of them into the same suite Al Green had stayed in.

Jenny pulled up her skirt and sat straddled across his lap. Once a glimpse of smooth white thigh above stocking tops was enough to give him a hard on in two seconds flat, but now the sight of white panties with dark blonde hair curling round the lace wasn't even giving him a twinge.

'Look what Jenny's got for you,' she said in that idiotic baby voice. She unbuttoned her prim secretary's blouse to reveal breasts like two melons. 'Does Maxy want to hold them?'

Max took hold of her breasts roughly, pulling them free of the restraining push-up bra. He tweaked her big pink nipples and waited for the expected sigh.

'Oh Maxy, kiss them,' she said, pushing herself up against his face.

Once this was his idea of heaven. A willing sexy girl, pretty as paint, with knockers that made every man in the room turn round to look. Why did he still dream of small breasts, ones with tiny brown nipples that reminded him of the wild strawberries he used to find hop picking in Kent?

He was merely going through the motions, sucking at her tits, sticking his fingers up round her pants and hoping he'd get hard enough not to disgrace himself.

But he felt nothing. No passion, not even disgust. She could be an inflatable doll, bland, obedient and perfectly formed.

'Suck me!' He pushed her down on to the floor between his legs, unzipping his fly and pulling her head to him. He would be all right in a moment, just stick it in that big red mouth, feel that drooling tongue and he'd forget Georgia.

'I will if you lick me too,' she said already pushing his silk shorts aside. With one hand she released her skirt and wriggled out of her pants, leaving only her blouse, the suspender belt and stockings.

'Let me see how good you are at it first,' he said drawing her head towards him. 'If you're a good girl I'll suck you all night.'

This girl wanted what they all wanted. Only an hour ago she had informed him she had a good voice. She really believed that if she went to bed with him then he'd be getting her a recording contract within a week.

Didn't the silly bitch know London was full of girls who thought they could sing?

'Is that good?' she asked, running her tongue down his cock. It was lucky he was so well hung. She hardly noticed it was still flaccid. He'd have to turn his mind on to something else. Make up some fantasy with three negro girls pandering to his every whim.

'Wonderful,' he groaned, looking down at that triangle of damp hair in front of him. She was fingering herself and that usually turned him on a treat. 'Make yourself come for Maxy, darling,' he sighed. 'Be a rude little girl. I like that.'

It was beginning to work. The combination of her mouth and watching those fingers sliding in and out of that damp fanny made his cock rise up. He'd wait until it was right up then pause to take one of those pills in his pocket. Then he'd give her something to think about.

It was after two now. Max glanced at the clock by the bed wishing he could come and get it over and done with. That guy in the bar downstairs knew what he was doing giving him these pills, they really did keep you going. But he'd fucked little Jenny in every position he could think of and now she was almost asleep.

'Sit on my face,' he ordered her. 'I'm going to wank myself off while I suck you.'

That was better. He could close his eyes, taste that damp hot pussy and make believe it was Georgia. Her waist was as tiny, even if her skin wasn't as smooth, as long as she didn't try to drag his hands up to those great melons again.

'I love you Maxy.'

Why did they always have to say that? They didn't mean it anymore than he did. There was only one woman he loved and she didn't want him.

'Think of those long, brown legs,' he told himself.

'That juicy pussy. She wanted you more than any other girl that night. You'll get her yet.'

His strokes were getting frantic. He willed Jenny not to speak and spoil the illusion. He was tired of being told what a wonderful lover he was. He wanted a girl who hadn't experienced any of this before.

He came then, quivering, shaking, his mouth biting into that hot, furry mound.

'I came again,' she sighed, rubbing herself all down his chest. 'That's twelve times.'

'No, you didn't,' he said rolling over to get away from her. 'Why do women make such preposterous claims? Twice maybe, that's enough for anyone.'

She was hurt now, sitting up in bed with her blonde hair falling over those huge breasts, arms clamped around her knees, ready to cry.

'You don't really like me,' she said, full lips turning down at the corners. One of her false eyelashes was coming loose and she had mascara streaked down her cheek.

'Of course I do.' Max reached up from his position on his side, half-heartedly fondling her leg. 'Now cuddle down and go to sleep. It's late.'

She fell asleep almost at once. Max heaved himself up on to the pillows and looked down at her. She looked about sixteen now. She said she was twenty-two but the truth was probably eighteen. Once a girl like her could have kept him interested for weeks. Silky blonde hair, eyes like a couple of cornflowers all wrapped up in a cool presentation which didn't give a hint of how sexy she was.

He was sorry now he had treated her badly, he liked his women to fall asleep smiling.

What was happening to him? Once he wouldn't have given a shit whether he'd been a brute, or the world's greatest lover. Women liked a combination of the two, Miriam always told him that.

'Poor Miriam,' he murmured softly.

Max loved his wife. Perhaps he had never been 'in' love with her, but he cared deeply. She was a good woman, warm, comfortable and caring. Did she notice he stopped making love to her around the same time he met Georgia?

He had thought he had it all that night Georgia let him take her to his flat. A number one hit in the bag, money pouring in and the girl of his dreams at his side.

Sex didn't really come into it. He would have held her all night without making any demands and he still didn't understand why she'd suddenly frozen on him.

But even after she'd said she wanted it forgotten, Max hadn't given up hope. Georgia wasn't the type to give herself to a man without really caring.

Then there was that damn party at the Savoy. Of course he was using her money, that's what the game was all about. But the way she attacked him was ridiculous.

Now she had Simon Riox in her court and between them they'd sewn him up so tight he could barely manage to buy a new car.

If she just let him direct her to the places he'd negotiated deals, that would be something. But no, she didn't let him get a look in.

'A thousand pounds that bird in Sloane Street offered me for getting Georgia to wear her clothes,' he muttered. 'The fucking bitch wouldn't even walk through the door of the boutique. She's even made some private deal with a chauffeur to ferry her about, that's another five hundred down the Swanney.'

The contract with the stage management team was torn up before it was even signed. Now she had two great hulks who were so protective to her Max couldn't get near enough to even smell her. She even had the men at Decca eating out of her hand.

Her could overlook all that. After all he was making a

fortune from her straight. It was the ideas she might give other entertainers that bothered him. If everyone ran their affairs themselves there would be no more room for men like Max.

'First Love' had been even bigger than 'No Time' and that bouncy, snappy 'Dancing with you,' would still be played in clubs when he was getting his pension. Now he heard she'd written another winner, rumour had it Jack Levy had been heard singing it in his office, yet Georgia hadn't even mentioned it to her manager.

That was what hurt the most. Somewhere along the line Georgia had stopped needing him. She really believed he knew nothing about music, she didn't want to confide in him. She didn't even care if he was in the audience.

Take his idea of booking the Albert Hall with a full orchestra just after she got her first hit. She laughed at that!

'Don't be silly Max,' she said, standing there with her hands on her hips in a pair of jeans so tight it took his breath away. 'It would alienate my fans. It's too soon. I don't want them to think I've sold out already. Book me into places the kids can dance in. Let's carry on with soul music and rock. When I've made my first long player that's the time to lure the listening people in.'

Didn't she know he wanted her to be more than just a pop star? He wanted her in cabaret in Las Vegas, chatting on the Johnny Carson show, then moving on to making a big musical. She could be Carmen!

Why did she have to make such a big thing about her band too? How could he separate them now without causing ripples? She pushed each one of them forward, made sure everyone knew what a stud Rod was, or that Speedy was the thinker in the band. They were supposed to be faceless men in the background. She'd managed to make each one of them a star in his own right. Les even claimed she was going to pay for him to have his nose fixed!

How the hell could Max push them back into line after she'd spoilt them all?

Was there anything left up his sleeve to pull out?

'More long tours,' he murmured, banging the pillow and lying down beside Jenny. 'That should knock the stuffing out of her, piss the boys off. I can get a few backhanders again and fiddle the expenses. In a year or two she'll be dying to sing at the Albert Hall.'

Max smiled to himself as he slipped off his suit jacket and opened his office window. In his briefcase he had enough cash to buy himself the new 'Roller'. A white one this time with red upholstery and his double 'M' on the doors in gold.

The second LP was already the top selling album for '65. He had five gold records on his wall, and any day he would be getting the sixth.

Where did she get the inspiration from to write such brilliant songs? Every one fresh and new, the latest 'Devil Man' he liked to think was about him, but she only laughed when he suggested it.

August in London was usually impossible, but right now it looked wonderful.

'Strange how things work out,' he said aloud, posing in front of the mirror. That masseur in King's private health club in Pall Mall was doing him a power of good, he'd tightened up his muscles, made him look ten years younger. 'I send them off to Europe thinking they'll soon be urging me to bring them back home, and what do they do? Make it fucking well work for all of us!'

Sell-out concerts in every major city, promoters ringing Max offering him anything to book a return date. That was where this new wedge had come from. Five thousand pounds, slipped under the table. Riox, Georgia and the taxman couldn't trace it.

'They've been working their arses off,' Max chuckled, opening his silver cigar box and lifting one out. He paused to smell it, savouring the moment before lighting it. 'Yet somehow they found time to write enough material for an LP and a string of new singles.'

A tap on the door surprised him. He wasn't expecting any visitors today and Deirdre always used the intercom.

'Come in!'

'I'm sorry to disturb you.' It was Deirdre, her dark hair dyed a deep auburn and cut into a ridiculous copy of Cilla Black's. 'There's a man in reception and he won't leave.'

'Who? What does he want?' Max's earlier feeling of well-being fizzled away. 'You know I don't see anyone without an appointment.'

There were times he wanted to get rid of this girl. He never had fancied her and she was far too thick with Georgia. But at least she wasn't hysterical like most of them.

'I told him that. He say's he'll just sit there and wait until you are free. He says it's personal.'

'Do I know him?'

'I don't think so.' Deirdre was hopping from leg to leg, her mouth twitching with nervousness. 'He's different from the usual boys we get in here. He's kind of stern.'

'I'll give him stern,' Max snapped. 'What's this creep's name?'

'Peter Radcliffe,' she said softly. 'He isn't a creep Max, he's got a kind of,' she paused.

'Peter Radcliffe?' The name came back to Max, as sharp and clear as if he'd heard it earlier today. 'All right, I'll see him.'

'You will?' Her brown eyes opened wide in surprise, mouth dropping open.

'Why not?' Max regained his composure quickly. 'I

don't know him from Adam, but I can't have people cluttering the reception area all day. If he's selling something you'll be for it.'

The cigar was still unlit in his hand. Max grabbed his jacket from the back of the chair, put it back on, returning to his desk just as the knock came at his door.

'Come in,' he lowered his voice to a growl, opened a file and bent his head over it as the door opened. 'I don't know who the hell you are, but you've got five minutes.'

'I'm Peter Radcliffe, sir. An old friend of Georgia's.'

Max looked up. The voice was deep and well rounded, just a trace of a London accent, but the face in front of him gave him a jolt.

That day as he wrote the fake letter back to Manchester, he had imagined some weedy academic with acne and greasy hair. This lad was like a Greek god, blond hair, blue eyes with the deepest golden tan Max had seen away from St Tropez. Big shoulders almost bursting out of a washed-out denim shirt, jeans that fitted so snugly round his narrow hips he could be a male model.

'Georgia is away on tour,' Max said picking up the cigar and lighting it. 'But even if she were in London I doubt she would see you. Every day we get people claiming to be old friend of hers.'

'I understand that sir,' the boy had no trace of belligerence in his voice or face. 'But I do believe she would like to see me. I can't believe she's changed that much.'

'Sit down. What did you say your name was again?' Max waved his cigar at a spare chair by his desk, tilted his chair back and narrowed his eyes.

'Radcliffe, Peter.' He sat down, his arms bent slightly, resting his fists on his knees and leaning forward.

'Tell me where you know Georgia from?' Max said.

The lad was looking unswervingly into his eyes, he wasn't sure he liked that much honesty.

'We were sweethearts,' Peter said. 'That sounds a bit trite I know, but it's the best explanation. She ran away from home.'

'When was this?' Max wanted to know what happened, and where, but he'd have to take it one step at a time.'

'January 1960,' Peter said. 'She was fifteen then, I was seventeen. She sent her mother a postcard saying she'd be in touch when she was sixteen. But we heard nothing more.'

'Well, there we are,' Max shrugged his shoulders. 'It's an open and shut case. She didn't want to know.'

'But I think she did,' Peter insisted. 'Her mother moved and the only address she knew was mine.'

'Mother?' She's an orphan!' Max said quickly.

'That's right,' Peter half smiled. 'I should have said foster mother. Anyway Celia moved on. I suspect Georgia called at my house and my parents never told me.'

'Now why would they do that?'

'Because she has mixed blood.' Peter raised one perfect golden eyebrow. 'They thought she would mess up my career.'

'Which is?' Max had a sinking feeling this lad was going to be more difficult than he imagined.

'Teaching,' Peter replied.

Max felt a bubble of pleasure. Thank goodness he wasn't a lawyer. Any man with looks like his who wanted to spend his life with kids couldn't be dangerous.

'But if all this happened five years ago why are you concerning yourself with her now? Aren't you just jumping on the band wagon?'

'Her mother and I looked everywhere for her.' Peter didn't turn a hair at Max's suggestion. Pride and truth shone out of his handsome face. 'Until I read about the fire and a friend described Georgia James to me I was in the dark, assuming she had forgotten me. I wrote to this office then and I received a letter back making it quite clear she had no time for me.'

'But why persist then?' Max puffed on his cigar, blowing the smoke up to the ceiling.

'One of the tracks on her LP.'

Max gulped. He knew immediately what the boy meant. He had listened to the track himself so many times, wondering where the inspiration came from. Yet until now it hadn't clicked.

'We were so young, we thought we had it all,' Peter said slowly. 'Nights of crying for you, are you out there crying too?'

'Don't be daft man,' Max chuckled. 'It's just a love song. They all have the same theme.'

'Do they all mention kisses in the hall, a glimpse of blonde hair, waving goodnight in frosty air?'

'You know the lyrics better than I do,' Max raised one eyebrow. 'But even I could work those words around to any number of old loves. Anyone could.'

Peter reached behind him and pulled a cutting out of his back pocket.

'This is from *Honey* magazine,' he held it steady and Max knew he intended to read it to him. 'An interview. "Do your lyrics have special significance, or do you write about general feelings?" That was the journalist's question. Georgia replies, "Mostly it's general, but now and then it's like a secret message to someone. 'The girl with red hair' is an old friend of mine who died. 'No Time', was for Ian and Alan. 'Crying' for someone very special."' Peter folded the paper and put it back in the pocket of his denim shirt buttoning it deliberately as he calmly stared at Max.

'That doesn't mean it's you!' Max retorted, feeling

just a little hot under the collar. How come he hadn't read this interview?

'No?' Peter looked up at Max. 'Why does she go on to say "It was someone who coloured my idea of love, when I was very young. Someone I lost and still hope I'll find again." Does that sound general?'

Max gulped. He could see now why Georgia had been attracted to Ian. He was a watered down, punier version of this lad. Everything made sense now. The way she turned down dates, kept herself at arm's length. If only the women in his life had been so constant!

'Let me tell you something in confidence,' Max leaned forward in his chair, trying hard to be chummy and pleasant, yet he knew he was going to assassinate Georgia's character.

'We keep it well under wraps, but Georgia has had many love affairs. Every one to her is special for a week or two, then she moves on. Ian McShane is the only man she ever moped about, and if he'd lived it would have ended the same way as all the rest.' He wanted to add more, imply the girl was a bitch and a whore, but somehow he knew Peter Radcliffe might just get angry. 'Forget her Peter, she's not the girl she was any longer. Singing and making money is what drives Georgia these days. Stay with the beautiful memories you've got, don't try to see her and find yourself disillusioned.'

'I'm not a kid,' Peter leaned forward, eyes flashing dangerously. 'I haven't sat on the sidelines of life pining for her. While she's been setting the world alight, I've done my share too. Of course there've been other men in her life. There've been women in mine too. I'm not some jerk with a broken heart.'

Max noted the muscles straining the denim shirt. He hadn't got those just lifting books!

'I didn't think you were a jerk,' Max said carefully. 'But I've been very close to Georgia for a long time. I know her as if she was my daughter. To be honest she can be a pretty cold, calculating girl.'

'Has she talked about her childhood?'

Max had a feeling he was being tested and he felt trapped.

'Which incident?'

'Why a fifteen-year-old felt running away from home was the only option?'

Max tried to bluff it out. 'Oh, the row! She regrets that now.'

Peter sat back in his chair. 'Just as I thought,' a cynical smile played on his lips. 'If Georgia was really close to you, she would have told you.'

'Don't be a smart arse with me boy!' Max half stood up, clenching the edge of his desk. 'Come on, out with it!'

'No,' Peter's lips moved into a straight determined line. 'I didn't come here to blab her secrets. Just tell her I called.'

Max's heart thumped. This boy had the missing bit of the jigsaw and he wanted it.

'Why don't we go down to the pub?' Max said. 'It's hot in here and I could do with a pint.'

'It won't work Mr Menzies,' Peter looked right into his eyes. 'I'm not about to spill the beans, even with eight pints inside me. All I ask is that you give her my address.'

'Sure,' Max pushed a pad and pencil across his desk. What was it about her that inspired such integrity? Riox couldn't be bought, or the boys in Samson, and now this guy?

Peter stood up, flicking back his golden hair in a weary gesture and picked up the pencil.

'Don't hold your breath,' Max said flippantly. 'The way things are going with Rod, she might just be married by then.'

He saw the lad's neck swell, and a tinge of pink colour rose to his tanned cheeks.

'Just give it to her sir.' The 'sir' sounded more of a threat than respect. 'I'll be away till October, but if I haven't heard anything by Christmas I'll be back to check up on you.'

It was as if the sun had suddenly been blotted out. In the past few months Max had regained Georgia's affection. He'd helped her buy her first car, even gone with her to choose furniture for her flat. Granted he hadn't got beyond giving her the odd cuddle, but at least she looked on him as a father if nothing else.

Perhaps it was because he played it straight with her about that flat. He'd wanted her to buy something ritzy, not the top floor in a block full of old Brigadiers and snooty blue rinses. But when she took him to see it he could see she had her heart set on it.

It was huge if nothing else, with a nice view of the Thames from the balcony. But the old lady who'd died hadn't had any repairs done for years. The kitchen was something out of the dark ages, the Regency striped wallpaper was almost peeling off the walls.

'But can't you just see it Max?' she wheedled. 'The lounge all painted yellow, white carpets and huge comfy settees. I can get someone in to do all the work.'

She had magic eyes that day, she'd even managed to make him enthusiastic. It took him back to the thrill of buying his own first home.

Of course she didn't let him get anyone in he knew. A poncy woman from Sloane Street drew up all the plans. Swedish pine in the kitchen, a bathroom designed to look like a tropical jungle. All Max got to do was oversee the workmen and make sure it was all done to Georgia's plans while she was away.

Yet she knew immediately she arrived home that he had put in some work for her. She didn't miss a thing. The row of little yellow duck soaps in the bathroom.

The tubs of flowers on the balcony, food in the fridge, even a hot water bottle to air the new bed.

The woman from Sloane Street had laughed at his idea of hundreds of red roses, or a silver champagne bucket. But he had to admit the freesias and the Nottingham lace bedspread she did approve of him buying, were more Georgia's style.

'Let me cook you and Miriam a meal,' she said, bouncing around the place like a puppy when she saw the finished work. 'You've been an absolute angel Max, without you I bet it wouldn't be so perfect.'

He had to settle for the meal. He would rather have sat in her tub amongst the palm trees with that ridiculous monkey grinning down at him, seeing those small breasts again and carrying her later into that pink and ivory bedroom. But instead he had to listen to Miriam advising her on the best places to buy bedlinen and china, and eat over-cooked roast beef.

Miriam leaving him should have made everything right, yet for some strange reason he felt gutted. She went home to Greece for a holiday and the next thing a letter came saying she was staying there permanently.

'I think I'll always love you,' she said in her letter. 'But I want more than being your hostess and housekeeper. I want to sit in the sun with a man who needs me, grow old with a man who desires me. I didn't come out here looking for that, but I found him, here in the village which has always been my real home. Be happy for me Maxy. Find someone for yourself that makes you feel like this too. I hope we can always be friends.'

Why wasn't he rushing around like a man with two cocks? He could have it all now. Georgia was so concerned she was even inviting him over for drinks and meals. He was top unattached male on every hostess's list. So why did he get a lump in his throat thinking about Miriam with her fat Greek? What made him keep recalling the way she looked on their wedding night?

Guilty conscience maybe? Afraid that if Peter Radcliffe did find a way to Georgia he'd be snookered? She might not care about the guy any longer, but she sure as hell wouldn't like Max playing God. If she wrote him out of her life too, he'd be finished.

Chapter 18

'Something wrong, Georgia?' Rod shook his head like a dog, spraying her with water. 'Don't you want a swim? You've been quiet all day.'

Georgia pushed her sunglasses up on to her head, dropped her book to the ground and smiled up at him.

'Just thinking,' she reached out for her suntan oil and rubbed a little into her legs, stomach and arms. She could see now how tanned she was getting, her skin had turned from coffee coloured to a rich dark brown, her white bikini standing out in vivid contrast. 'I was just thinking about how lucky we've been. Even if we don't get time to appreciate it.'

Three days earlier they were playing in Paris and with over a week before their next gig they had flown down to Barcelona to catch a few days of sunshine and sea.

Rod dropped his towel on to the ground beside her, picked up a bottle of water and guzzled it down before replying.

'Thousands of miles of travelling, more success than we ever dreamed of, fame, money, the works. And now this place.'

The villa they were staying at belonged to the family of a saxophone player who had joined them for many of the European gigs. Set amongst pine trees, above a deserted stretch of beach, it was the closest Georgia had ever seen to paradise.

Seen from the road it looked like a dilapidated fortress, peeling shutters firmly shut against the strong sun, a neglected, abandoned home. A huge old door creaked open as if protesting against visitors, but once inside, it was obvious it had been cared for with love, its outer neglect protecting it from unwanted intruders.

Designed in a traditional Spanish style, the villa was built round a central courtyard, complete with fountain, palm trees and a vine-covered pergola. A Moorish influence was strong, with vivid blue and yellow tiled steps to the upper floor, white stone walls and wrought-iron balconies. Purple bougainvillaea and scarlet hibiscus, scrambled up the walls. Urns full of bright orange lilies, geraniums and daisies filled each nook and cranny. Everything was simple, cool marble floors, heavy dark furniture, brightly coloured, scattered rugs and huge cushions, walls painted dazzling white. Yet for all its simplicity it was comfortable and inviting. Tiled bathrooms adjoined each of the spacious, airy bedrooms, a kitchen with every modern device to make their stay a happy one.

Two local women came in daily to clean, bringing with them fresh bread, salad, fruit and eggs. They scuttled about their work, heads down, clearly intimidated by five half naked young men with only one woman. Georgia's attempts at making herself understood were met by laughter and a torrent of fast Spanish.

The other boys had left yesterday to drive into Lloret further along the coast. Two days of swimming alone in clear turquoise sea, sunbathing without admirers and drinking the local wine had been enough for them. They wanted excitement which really meant girls and right now Georgia was hoping they wouldn't bring them back here.

'Perhaps you should have gone with the boys?' She turned over on to her stomach, resting her chin on her hands. 'I wouldn't have minded being on my own.'

'I can live without the fleshpots for a while,' Rod laughed softly, dropping down on to his towel and leaning back with the sun on his face. 'I don't mind you being silent, it's nice. Just unexpected that's all, after last night.'

They had sat out on the terrace overlooking the sea. Watching the sun like a huge fiery orange slowly dip into the sea. Talking about their childhood, revealing things to each other that once were taboo.

Rod was different without the other boys around. He dropped his sarcasm, his cynical approach to life, and when he began to admit what a failure he felt as a child, Georgia understood what had made him the way he was.

'I thought it was my fault because my Dad left. Somehow I was responsible for the lack of money, the slum we lived in and Mum's bad temper. When she started to go out all the time drinking, I kept quiet, never admitting how much I wanted her home with me. She caught me once cuddling and sniffing her nightdress, she accused me of being weird. She never understood it was because I missed her, that her perfume kind of made me feel safe.'

He told her that he worried because he was too skinny. That he saved up to buy a bullworker and hid it in the wardrobe. He spoke of men that came late at night, his mother laughing one minute, crying the next. The insecurity with the lovers who didn't leave.

'Some were nice,' Rod grinned. 'Took me to Southend or to the football, but I was afraid to like them in case they left too. But mostly they were mean types. They hit me when Mum wasn't around, resented me as much as I loathed them.'

'Did you ever tell her how you felt?'

'You can't tell Mum anything. She's either on a high when she laughs at everything, or so low she's practically suicidal,' Rod grimaced. 'If I went out she said I didn't care about her, if I stayed in she said I was spoiling her chances. I couldn't win with her.'

'How do you feel about her now?' Georgia asked.

'Embarrassed more than anything,' his dark eyes looked thoughtful. 'She's so flashy and empty-headed. I haven't got anything in common with her, but because I'm making money she pretends I mean everything to her.'

Georgia remembered her from the boys' funeral. Bleached blonde hair piled up in elaborate curls, wearing a black dress so low cut and tight it had embarrassed everyone. Not for one moment had she looked distressed at the boys' deaths. Her dark flirtatious eyes had merely wandered off to the more famous people present. She hadn't even shown any real pride in Rod's bravery at trying to save Ian and Alan.

'It's because of her you don't like women much,' Georgia said softly. 'I mean, you pull so many girls, but you don't choose them for company do you?'

'I guess that's right,' he laughed. 'Except for you I can't ever remember telling a girl the truth. I put on an act about everything. I don't feel anything inside for them. It's like there's a basic function missing.'

'Emotion,' she said. 'But you do feel that Rod. You felt it when Ian and Alan died, it comes out in music. It's there all right, you just haven't had anyone tap the right keys.'

'We're a lot alike,' he said ruefully as they moved back towards the house once the wind turned chilly. 'Tell me why you don't trust anyone enough to give love another stab. You can't still be mourning for Ian?'

They lit a log fire in the huge old hearth, sitting on cushions close to the blaze, opening yet another bottle of wine.

'I don't think Ian has anything to do with it,' she said at length after staring into the blazing logs, thinking about Rod's question. 'I'll always miss him, just the same way I miss Helen, my old friend. But I was never convinced we were made for each other.'

'The other guy?' Rod looked round at her and lightly touched her hand. 'Ian told me there was someone before.'

'Maybe,' she said. 'I keep telling myself it's stupid to hold a torch for someone who doesn't give a toss for me. But it isn't only him either, there's my mother too.'

Rod listened carefully as she told him the whole story about running away from home.

'Why hasn't she come forward?' she asked him. 'I mean my records have sold in just about every corner of the globe. How can she have missed seeing my picture or read things in the papers? It must be that she changed her mind about me, decided I was to blame. What other reason could there be for her silence?'

'You're in a position now to do something about it,' he said thoughtfully, gazing into the fire, poking it viciously. 'You've got enough money and connections to get her found. Why don't you? At least that way you'd know for sure.'

'I'm scared too,' she whispered. 'Everyone I've ever cared about deeply has gone. Sometimes I think I'm some sort of jinx. Peter, Celia, Helen and Ian. Even my real parents abandoned me. On top of all that I'm afraid if I dig too deeply I might just meet up with Brian, my foster father again.'

'Maybe that's the real hurdle you need to overcome,' he said. 'That man can't hurt you again. By facing him you might be better for it.'

Rod's high cheek-bones stood out in sharp relief lit only by the fire, his black hair shining like a raven. A primitive face, like so many of the Spanish men, the whites of his eyes and teeth contrasting brilliantly against his dark skin.

'I know it sounds daft,' she said reluctantly. 'But recently I've had a feeling he's watching me.'

'That is daft,' Rod laughed, throwing back his hair. 'You've hardly stayed still long enough for us to watch you, let alone him.'

'I don't mean he's actually watching me in the flesh,' she explained. 'More a feeling he's observing me from a distance, noting everything about me, biding his time, if you like.'

The reason she'd been silent all day was not from dwelling on the past, their lack of time to enjoy things, or even the thought of Brian watching her. It was Rod. She had a feeling something was starting up, something she couldn't fight, avoid, or protect herself from. Since Ian's death they had grown close. But last night there had been a brief fiery spark of something more. Should she quash it now? Save any further heartache, or take the initiative and worry about the results later?

This morning she'd woken without any solution, and silence had seemed the only way out, just as it had the morning after Brian raped her. By doing nothing and saying nothing she was preventing either steps back, or forward.

They had raked out the fire. Turned out the lights and walked together up the tiled stairs to the rooms above.

The moon shone down into the courtyard, reflecting clearly in the pool around the fountain and picking up the white of a towel left lying on a chair. Enough light to see the gallery on which they stood, wrought-iron railings going right round into a rectangle, dark wood doors invisible against the white stone walls, like yawning holes in a piece of cheese.

'Back in Stepney I never thought I'd ever see a palm

tree,' Rod said softly. 'The moon looks as if it's hanging on it like a Christmas tree bauble.'

It was beautiful. A star-sprinkled sky and the moon lighting up the feathery fronds of the tree.

Rod stood with her at the balcony, two pairs of hands so close on the railing, their sides just touching.

'Whatever happens I'll remember this forever,' he said, so softly it was almost a whisper.

She could feel a current flowing between them, like two magnets so close they wanted to jump across the void. But instinctively she moved a step away to prevent it.

Had Rod's words meant that he knew something was going to happen? That this was the moment when it started? Or did he mean that seeing the moon and the palm tree was the first time he'd been aware of the beauty of his surroundings?

'Come with me for a swim?' Rod jumped up, dipping his hand in the pool round the fountain and splashing some on Georgia's hot back.

'You swine,' she laughed, rolling over on to her back and rubbing the cold water off on the sunbed.

'Please?' he said softly, a soft boyish plead in his eyes.

He was tanned almost as dark as Georgia now. His black brief trunks almost disappearing against his skin. His body had filled out remarkably in the last year, good food and a little exercise had given him broader shoulders and muscles in his arms. Slim hips, straight firm legs and a narrow waist coupled with his six foot height was enough to make any girl turn her head and look. But for Georgia it was his smooth olive glistening skin that attracted her and a face which reminded her of Red Indians. Such high cheek-bones, dark narrow eyes which could turn from laughter to anger in a second. A straight, proud nose and thin, stern lips.

Even his hair completed the picture. It was much longer now, almost touching his shoulders, straight, sleek with blue black lights. Sometimes she wanted to put a band round his forehead and turn him from just Rod to a warrior.

'All right,' she sighed, pulling the band from her hair and tossing it down. 'I'm just about frying anyway.'

They walked through the arched wrought-iron gates that led on to the patio where they'd sat last night, the tiles warm under their bare feet. There were steps hewn in rocks down to the beach, smooth, as if polished daily by someone they never saw. A small green lizard ran across in front of them, disappearing into a crack in the ground silently.

It was five in the afternoon, the desperate, sweaty heat at noon replaced by gentle soft warmth. A breeze was getting up, whipping little white horses on to the beach.

The nearest house was nearly a mile away, but here they were able to feel as if they were the only two people left in the world.

'It's like heaven,' Rod said, pausing at the bottom of the steps. The last one had a big jump to the beach and he held out his hand to her.

She saw her hand go out to him. Only seconds in reality but it seemed like a lifetime before his fingers closed over hers. That spark again as skin touched skin, and she jumped, right into his arms.

For a moment they just stood together, his arms were round her, chests just touching. Her eyes were on line with his naked shoulders, the sea just visible beyond. Her hands rested on his hips. She dared not look up, not yet.

His hand moved so slowly up from her waist, over her shoulder blades, pausing on her shoulder lightly.

Fingers creeping up her neck, his thumb cupping round her chin, lifting her face to his.

415

Rod's eyes were closed, his mouth curved into a smile, just the tiniest glint of white teeth before he bent his head to hers.

Coarse sand between her toes, more blowing up her legs, the breeze taking his hair and hers, bonding them together.

A kiss that made her think of drowning. Sweet, peaceful on the surface, yet already an undercurrent rising to pull her down. His hand was holding her head, the other arm so firmly round her there was no escape, even if she'd wanted it.

She didn't know how long that kiss lasted. It was frantic, deep, world shattering. Strings inside her only vaguely remembered were being tugged and all the time her hands were caressing his smooth skin, pressing herself closer.

'Oh Georgia,' he whispered at length, taking her face in both his hands and holding her away from him a little. 'Is this for real?'

They held each other as they walked to the sea, hands touching waists; the unexpected nakedness of their skin so available made it seem harder to touch.

The sea was warm. They entered it as one person, walking until it came up to their waists. Only then did Rod turn to her to hold her and kiss her again.

A swim apart, then back together again, hands searching for each other, lips drawn back like an addict for a drug.

Salty kisses, hair flapping like seaweed against their faces, skin that had lost the smooth warmth from the sun.

'Let's go back now,' Rod said, taking her hand and walking up the beach.

A shower stood just inside the courtyard. They stood under it together, blasted by the icy water and Rod unfastened the top of her bikini, letting it drop to their feet. Next the pants, one tie on each hip until she stood naked under the jet of water, reaching out for his trunks to push them down his legs.

The towels lying in the sun were hot to the touch. Rod wrapped one round her, pressing himself against her, rubbing her back, flicking back the strands of wet hair from her face, kissing her again and again until she could see nothing but him.

A mattress still lay under the pergola where Georgia had retreated at midday to cool off. Rod led her there now, half carrying her, his lips on her neck and shoulders, breath hot and sweet.

Dappled sunshine filtered through the grapevine above them, the wind rustling the palm trees. Rod's lips were on her breasts, her whole body arching towards him.

Ian had been gentle and sensitive. Max rough, experienced and compelling, but Rod was so sensuous she wanted to scream out how much he was pleasing her.

Stroking, biting, kissing and probing. He made her feel like a woman and she could barely wait for him to enter her. Surprise at the hardness and length of him. Shock that he could immerse himself so far into the act of love he barely knew it was her. His mouth devoured hers, his tongue fierce and yet loving. His hands on her buttocks squeezing, kneading, a steady rhythm that sent shock waves pulsating through every nerve-ending.

Georgia could feel her heart thumping, it was joyous and wonderful, mixed with a fear that it would be over too soon.

Perhaps Rod sensed it. He moved back from her, playing with her with his fingers, bringing her to the edge of an abyss again and again. She could stand it no longer. Grabbing his buttocks in her hands she pulled him to her, forcing him back inside her, head tossing from side to side, then reaching back to his mouth to kiss and bite him.

When she came it was like a roller-coaster in pitch darkness, stars shooting past her, falling, then rising each time higher and higher. A hot feeling, burning, sucking her into oblivion.

Georgia lay with her eyes closed, holding his head against her shoulder, fingers wound into his hair. Words of love were on her lips, but she was afraid he would laugh at her.

How many times had she come upon him, during or just after lovemaking? In dressing rooms, hotels, even in the van. The girls would look like she felt now, but Rod's eyes were always cold and calculating. He was just a tom-cat with no finer feelings, he rarely even tried to protect his girls, often he made a sarcastic remark about them.

She felt him move away from her, taking his weight on his arms. Slowly she opened her eyes, fully expecting him to be looking around for a cigarette or a drink, already bored.

But instead he was looking down at her, narrow almost slanted eyes brimming with tears.

'You are the most perfect woman in the world,' he whispered.

No words were necessary. She lifted her arms and reached for him pulling his face down to her again.

'I'd like to stay here forever,' he said later that evening as he cooked her an omelette.

Georgia sat on a high stool at the breakfast bar. She had put on a red cotton housecoat with nothing underneath. He wore only a pair of faded denim shorts, his bare chest gleaming under the light above the cooker.

'You wouldn't,' she said. 'We've got no sounds, no car, there's not even a bar for miles. What would we do all day?'

'Play house,' he grinned. 'Make love all the time, go

for walks, swim. I never thought I'd see the day when I dreaded the lads coming home.'

'We've got tonight,' she said softly. 'They won't come back now.'

'Let's pray they get arrested,' he said turning the omelette onto a plate. 'We won't answer the phone, we'll just let them languish in gaol.'

'We'd better be careful,' Georgia blushed at the need to discuss something like contraception in such a tender moment. 'I don't want to get pregnant.'

Rod pulled a packet out of his pocket.

'I'm a regular boy scout,' he grinned. 'Sorry I didn't have them with me this afternoon, but I didn't expect to be seduced. Let's just hope it isn't too late!'

They ate by candlelight close to the fire. The wind had got up, shaking the palm tree and rattling the iron gates that led to the beach. The empty plates were left on the table, while Rod fed her black grapes picked from the vine in the courtyard. They drank more wine, made love again, and dozed by the fire.

Georgia woke first the next morning. Sunshine was creeping through the slats in the blinds, making stripes on Rod's face and chest.

Ian had always slept curled up, one hand around his face like a small child, but Rod looked like a man. Flat on his back, arms and legs sprawled out, his angular face could have been carved from a piece of mahogany.

Her cheeks, chin and lips felt tender from the dark bristles which had sprouted up overnight on his chin. Her arms, thighs and breasts felt bruised and pummelled, but her heart was singing.

No remorse, no fear, guilt or worry. Every moment of last night was one to savour. She was happy.

When the phone rang later that morning Georgia stiffened. Jokes about the boys getting arrested were one thing, but she knew when Speedy and Norman went on the rampage it could happen.

'How's it going?' Rod said quite casually, leaning nonchalantly against the wall blowing kisses at her. 'What are we doing? Nothing much, just going down to the beach. When are you coming back?'

Silence while he listened.

'Do we want to go to a party tonight?' Rod shouted out to Georgia. She could see him shaking his head, not quite tough enough to admit to his friends he didn't want to go. 'The usual stuff, loads of crumpet, booze and loose living.' Georgia shook her head. Rod grinned cheerfully.

'No I don't think we'll bother. It's nice doing nothing. No, we don't care about the car. We'll get a taxi if we want to go anywhere.'

Again a silence as Rod listened.

'Okay we'll meet you at the airport. We can pack your stuff for you and call a cab. Just don't miss the plane, blockhead or Max will castrate you.'

He put the phone down and leapt out to where Georgia sat in the courtyard.

'Our prayers were answered. They don't want to come back here. They were feeling guilty because I was missing all the fun.'

She had never seen this side of Rod before. The boy in him that had been stamped out perhaps by his own mother. His eyes sparkled, his thin lips fuller. Once Rod would have refused to even make tea he was so full of arrogant chauvinistic ideas. Yet since they'd been alone he had cooked, washed up, even washed her hair and dried it. Now he was choosing to be alone with her, instead of rushing off to join more hedonistic pursuits.

'So what's going on?' Georgia smiled. 'Let me guess. They've pulled some birds?'

'Partly. Speedy got chatted up by an older woman

with pots of money. She's a French film star, living in a fabulous Hollywood-style place along the coast from Lloret. Anyway they all went back there with her for drinks and she invited a bunch of English people she knows round, and it's turned into a mini orgy of sex, drugs and rock and roll.'

'Drugs!' Georgia's eyes flew open.

'Only cannabis I think,' Rod said airily. 'Anyway they want to stay there. Speedy said this place was too isolated and the road so awful he didn't fancy driving back to pick us up. I think he was relieved when I said we didn't want to join them, perhaps he was scared I'd nick his tart.'

'Would you?' she laughed.

'I'd be too frightened someone might nick you.'

Three days more of loving and being loved. An unspoken knowledge that maybe once they got back on the plane everything could change. Long hours walking along the beach, swimming, lazing and talking. No dressing up, nor fans interrupting the peace. In a capsule where gigs, money and other people couldn't touch them.

Again and again Georgia looked for signs of his boredom. She had never known him able to even stay in one room for longer than an hour, he liked noise and confusion.

But there were no signs. When he flopped down on the beach he was totally relaxed, reaching out for her hand as if to reassure himself she was still with him. He told her more stories about his early youth, of meeting Ian and the others. Yet he never spoke of the future.

Hours and hours of lovemaking, made sweeter with the ending being so uncertain. But finally the last morning came and Georgia woke to find Rod standing by the bed with a cup of tea in his hand.

'Time to go,' he said. 'I packed the boys' things and booked a cab. We've got just an hour to say goodbye.'

'Is that it then?' she asked. His face was full of something she couldn't quite define. Sadness certainly, but something more.

'You know how it will be when we get back,' he sat down beside her and put the tea into her hand. 'The fans will be there, the press. We'll revert to our usual ways.'

'My usual ways would include you,' she whispered. 'Do you think I'll change with the click of a camera?'

'No girl, you won't, but I will. The old flash Harry bit will come back. I'll be chatting up birds because it's the way I am. You'll get pissy and before we know it will turn ugly.'

Somehow she knew he wasn't telling her he didn't care, rather that he cared too much to hurt her.

'Are you always going to run from everything?' she asked. 'Because that's what it is Rod, running.'

'No my sweet,' he turned and took her by the shoulders. 'I could try and trap you now, get a commitment from you and you'd stick to it whatever happened. But I know I'm not the one for you, not deep down where it counts.'

'Was all this for nothing then?' She reached up and traced his tanned cheek-bones, ran one finger round his thin lips.

'I wouldn't call it nothing,' he said looking right into her eyes. 'We've given each other something special in these few days, not just our bodies. You've made me realize I can feel love. I've freed you from that bogey man of a father. Perhaps you don't know it yet, but I have.'

He took her down to the beach later, kissed her again in the same spot where it all started and together they looked back up at the villa.

It was just nine in the morning, the sun barely rising

above the palm tree. Through the iron gates they could see the cool courtyard with its splashes of purple, red and orange flowers. The white walls of the house almost a symbol of the peace they felt. The bedroom where they'd done so much of their lovemaking had the shutters wide open. The sheets white against the dark wood of the heavy oak bed.

'We're too much alike,' he said softly. 'We could get lost in a power struggle. We both need gentler people to complement us.'

She knew he was right, but it hurt so much. Here alone they could be everything to each other, but once the real world stepped in between them, with jealousy, greed and vanity it couldn't be the same.

'So we leave it here?' she whispered.

'Yes baby,' his lips were against her hair, she felt his shoulders quiver and knew he was crying.

Chapter 19

January 1966

'Fasten your seat belt sir,' the red-haired stewardess leaned over to touch the black man's hand lightly. He had slept for almost the entire flight from New York and now they were landing.

'Sure was fast,' he opened his eyes and sat up sleepily. 'Don't seem mor'an hour since I got on. I hope that's England down there?'

'It is,' she smiled, more at his delightful Southern drawl than his little joke. 'Good old wet, cold London. Is it your first visit?'

'First time in such comfort, ma'am,' he smiled showing gleaming white teeth. 'I was here last during the War.'

'Well you're gonna find a few changes,' she said. 'The only thing the same is the weather.'

'Sleeping Beauty's awake at last.' Sonia buckled herself into her own seat and smirked at Muriel her dark-haired friend on the seat next to her. 'If only they all slept like that our job would be easier.'

'Did you find out about him?' Muriel enquired. It had been an uneventful flight and they had spent much of the time playing guessing games with each other about the passengers. The sleeping black man was the most intriguing because he'd given nothing away about himself.

'I reckon he's going to see a woman. But I could hardly ask him, could I?'

Most of the passengers were business men. Smart, seasoned travellers who either drank themselves into a stupor to relieve the boredom of the long flight, or put on their glasses and studied files and papers as if they were still in their office. No mystery with any of them, some of them flew backwards and forwards across the Atlantic like commuters.

There was a young couple near the rear of the plane who they guessed were newly married. The way they held hands, dozed on each other's shoulders and wrapped themselves up in each other was a sure sign. There were three younger men, travelling alone. Students, judging by their desert boots, jeans and thick sweaters, presumably running short of money as they only accepted free drinks.

Two blue-rinsed American ladies visiting their offspring in England. Five middle-aged couples who'd spent Christmas in New York. But it was the odd balls on the flight who gained the girls' real interest.

Could that nasty little weed from Dallas be a dealer in pornography? Was the woman in a shabby coat with the huge frightened eyes a runaway nun? And was the group of couples from Philadelphia really on a church mission? Wasn't it more likely they had heard about swinging London and they just wanted a slice of the action?

The black man had a magnetic presence. Something that invited curious glances. Although he had spoken to no one, they sensed this was from being caught up in his own thoughts rather than unfriendliness. His clothes were old, but they had style. A leather officer's flying jacket with a fur collar, dark green cord trousers and a checked, warm-looking shirt, faded around the collar. Just the confident way he moved, looked and spoke gave a feeling that he was someone special, even if he had no money.

They knew from his passport that he was from New Orleans, that he was forty-three, a musician and his name was Samuel Cameron. If he hadn't fallen asleep they would have got to the bottom of it.

'Such a good-looking man,' Muriel leaned closer to Sonia, dark eyes full of mischief. 'Just look at that face!'

He was sitting in an aisle seat, his head lolling over to one side as if he was about to go back to sleep. Rich goldeny-brown skin with high cheek-bones and long curling eyelashes. His nose was straight, almost Roman, lips wide and fleshy as might be expected with his dark skin, yet shapely and well defined. Even his ears were perfect, like two small shells flat against his beautifully shaped head.

'I could go for him,' Sonia said. 'That black treacle voice gives me goose pimples.'

'I'm more interested in his body,' Muriel giggled. She loved the way his hair was cut in a close crop, his broad shoulders and his muscular thighs. 'You know what they say about black men!'

'Well it's too late now,' Sonia sighed. 'We should have kept him awake right from the start.'

Samuel Cameron wasn't just tired. He was exhausted. Greyhound bus from New Orleans to New York, then two days of partying with old friends before catching the plane. It had seemed a good idea to avoid the expense of a New York hotel. But now he wasn't so sure. Men he hadn't seen since his de-mob, musicians he'd promised he'd look up when he was in town. Twenty years of catching up, packed into forty-eight hours.

They all believed landing a six week residence in Ronnie Scott's club in London was the big break he hoped for. But now in the early morning, tired and needing a bath and a shave, Sam had misgivings.

The money was little better than back home. By the time he'd sent something back for the kids and found himself somewhere to live there would be precious little left.

Yet he had to take a gamble. The war had changed nothing in the South. Still the same old prejudices. The whites got the good jobs, the decent homes. Which was worse, to leave his kids with his sister to chase a dream? Or to let those kids see him stay for their sakes and grow old and embittered?

'Damn you Ellie for taking off,' he thought as through a gap in the clouds he caught a glimpse of London. 'If you'd been a proper mother we could have worked something out between us. But then you never cared for the kids.'

He ought to have known a barfly like Eleanor wouldn't settle for diapers and strollers instead of dancing all night and pretty clothes. Yet he managed to turn a blind eye to the way she neglected Jasmine and Junior, put up with her sulking, and worked longer hours to bring in more money. He didn't guess she was running off to meet this white guy. If it hadn't been for that freak storm and a cancelled gig, he wouldn't have found out his kids were alone at home, night after night.

'I have to get out,' that was her explanation. 'The kids drive me crazy and you don't love me enough.'

That was the last night he spent with her. He could see her now as she threw herself into his arms begging forgiveness. The red satin dress she said her sister had lent her, damp from the rain, clinging to her curvy little body, her black hair a shower of tiny tight curls glistening with water. He'd believed her that night, loved her hard and long, promising to try harder to make her happy.

But the next evening when he got back from work, she was gone, taking everything worth selling and the savings from the box under the bed. She didn't even leave a note for her children.

It was left to the neighbours to fill him in about the man from Vegas who promised her a job as a dancer. And he had to tell his children Ellie wouldn't be coming back.

Five years of trying to be mother and father. Finding babysitters so he could work. But Jasmine was ten now, Junior twelve, old enough to understand he wasn't deserting them for ever as Ellie had done. Just trying something new which might make a whole new life for all of them.

There were far more people in the arrivals lounge than he expected so early in the morning. Women rushing forward to hug their husbands. Children's faces alight with expectation. A feeling of pent up excitement in the air, shrieks of laughter, questions, perhaps the inevitble row brewing.

Sam stood still for a moment, his kitbag on one shoulder, his tenor saxophone in his right hand. Everyone had someone, except him.

'Sam, over here.'

He could hear Clive's voice yet he couldn't see him. His eyes prickled with affection for the man who had not only arranged his contract, but also made the time to meet his flight.

'Sam! Good to see you.'

Clive was pushing through the crowd, a wide grin spread over his small face. 'I thought you'd missed the flight, everyone else got off ages ago. What kept you?'

Sam's friend was smaller, paler than he remembered. His dark hair thinner, the moustache tinged with grey. But the grin was the same, pale brown eyes dancing with excitement, his mouth stretching from ear to ear.

'Customs, what else!' Sam shrugged his shoulders.

'Only black guy on the flight. So it goes without saying they'd pull me.'

For a moment Sam felt unsure of himself. He had remembered Clive in old jeans and a sweat-soaked T-shirt. He hadn't expected the dapper grey pin-striped suit and neat polished shoes. Was this really the man who had dared to penetrate Harlem just to see and hear his jazz idols play?

'Did they find anything interesting?' Clive took his sax from him, and squeezed his arm, the nearest thing he could get to hugging the man.

'Just a pair of smelly socks I'd forgotten about under the sax,' Sam laughed. 'It sure is good to see you Clive. I've been havin' more than a touch of the colly-wobbles.'

It was strange to find their roles reversed. Three years earlier in the Ghetto club in Harlem, Sam had been the big man who saved the drunken Englishman from being rolled if not murdered. He had seen the raised eyebrows as the white fool flashed a wad of notes, and he found himself suddenly protective, just because the man had an accent that plucked at some forgotten chord.

Pulling a knife and bundling Clive out the club could have backfired on him badly, but fortunately by the time Clive sobered up, with his money still in his pocket, he was astute enough to understand Sam's motives.

Now it was Clive's turn to be protective, leading Sam to his world.

That night in Harlem he thought Clive was a jerk. A white man who wished he was black, hung up on all the old jazz legends. But that was before he found out the guy was sincere, knew about music even if he did play the shittiest trombone he'd ever heard. And the guy had a big heart.

'You got collywobbles?' Clive laughed heartily.

429

'You've got a contract, your air fare paid. You'll be knockin' em dead in Soho tomorrow.'

It hadn't seemed much to take Clive back to New Orleans with him. What else could he do with such a likeable jerk, hell bent on his own destruction? The man had a wife and kids at home in England. Someone had to straighten him out, let him hear some good music and get him on the plane home.

He didn't expect the guy to keep in touch. Clive was from the white middle classes with a high-flying job in the motor trade. He had money, good connections and education. Why would a man like that want to befriend an itinerant musician who lived in a cold water, one bedroom apartment with two kids to slow him down?

Perhaps it was music that sowed the seeds of real friendship, but an understanding of each other made it grow. Clive had his problems. Sam had his and somehow as they shared them, they began to care.

'What the heck!' Sam stopped and stared. Just outside the doors of the arrivals lounge was a vast crowd of kids, shouting and hollering, pushing and shoving. For a moment it reminded him of a riot scene he'd witnessed in Alabama, except most of these kids were white.

Policemen stood by, forty or fifty of them. The helmets and blue serge uniforms just the same as he remembered all those years before. Around twenty of them had linked arms to form a human fence, but the kids were still pushing to get through.

'Georgia! Georgia!' they chanted. Girls, some no older than thirteen or fourteen, in white socks and school scarves, faces contorted in their screaming.

'What's goin' on Clive?'

'Shit.' Clive caught hold of Sam's arm, blushing furiously. 'I'd forgotten.'

'Forgotten what? Is it a riot?'

'Georgia, the singer. She's leaving with her band for

the States. We may as well go back and get a drink at the bar, we won't get a taxi now.'

It was impossible to talk over the babble of noise from outside. Each time they started to speak, the doors would burst open and fans would rush in looking for another vantage point to get closer to their idol.

There was something hysterical about so many youngsters waiting for a celebrity Sam had never heard of. A sad reminder that he was too old and cynical now for such foolishness. A whole generation born and raised since he was last in England.

'So who is this Georgia? I thought it was only the Beatles who got this kind of scene?' Sam laughed as he saw one girl trip another and she landed on her face, her short skirt flying up, revealing a pert bottom in white panties. 'I'd like to thank the person who's giving me this free show.'

'Georgia James. Don't tell me you haven't heard of her?' Clive's face registered surprise. 'She's had five or six top twenty hits.'

'I don't listen to that pop shit,' Sam grinned. 'Is she any good?'

'Brilliant,' Clive's pale face took on that look of worship he'd once kept for giants like Duke Ellington. 'Beautiful girl with a voice that makes your toes curl up. She's one of the greats, buddy. Pop star or not.'

They sensed the arrival of the limousine even before they caught a glimpse of the gleaming black car. It started with a roar, a surging forward that made Sam leap to his feet despite his natural inclination to stay where he was. With long strides he made it to the window, forgetting even his kitbag and instrument left lying by the bar.

He was tall enough at six feet three to see over the heads of the fans, but even so he jumped up on a chair to see better.

The police had made a chain along each side of the

car. More police were holding open the doors, and still more waited inside the departure lounge.

By now there were thousands of fans, elbowing each other, fighting to get to the front. Screaming at the top of their lungs, waving autograph books, handkerchiefs, scarves, even hats.

A policeman rushed forward to open the car door. Sam saw first a long, slim, brown leg in white boots snake out of the car, then the other, and his eyes travelled upwards.

She was beautiful! Coffee coloured like the mulattos in New Orleans. Long black curly hair with a white fur pill box hat perched at a rakish angle that matched her short white fur coat.

She said something to the crowd. Dark eyes dancing with pleasure at seeing them, but a hefty man with shoulders like a barn door was grabbing her arm and urging her to get inside the airport.

Georgia looked up and Sam caught her eye, just for the briefest moment. Her hand flickered at him, and she was gone, dragged inside to the comparative safety of the airport.

'Wow,' Sam jumped down. Clive had joined him, but his short stature had stopped him from seeing anything. 'She was something else, man.'

'If you'd been here two weeks earlier you might have got to play with her,' Clive laughed at the animated expression on Sam's dark face. 'She often pops into Ronnie Scott's. She used to live in Soho and from what I hear there isn't one musician who wouldn't cut off his balls to play for her.'

'I sure wouldn't go that far,' Sam smiled. 'But I'll have to check her out.'

'I've found you a pad,' Clive said later in the taxi. 'I'd have liked you to stay with me and the wife, but Surbiton's too far out of London.'

Was Anne, Clive's wife as enthusiastic about this Yank arriving in England? Clive had come to the States that time because his marriage was on the rocks. Maybe Sam was the man who sent her husband back, but as he remembered, sometimes women's minds worked differently to men's.

'That's swell of you,' Sam sighed with relief. He didn't want to impose on Clive anymore than he had to. 'How much does it cost?'

'Just a fiver a week will do,' Clive said. 'It belongs to a mate of mine. He's away on business right now. It's just a place he takes his chicks to. But don't have any wild parties there and upset anyone.'

Sam was too immersed in looking at London to reply.

There was nothing he could pinpoint to reassure himself this really was England. Somehow he hadn't expected streams of traffic, or tower blocks of apartments and offices. The only real point of reference was the biting cold.

Funny little houses in rows. Millions of them as far as he could see. The big red double-decker buses and all those small chunky cars. The England Sam had imprinted on his mind was full of small green fields, thatched cottages and gardens full of flowers. Bars where old men played darts and dominoes. Women with scarves tied round their heads queueing up for rations. Little boys who asked the Americans for chewing gum and chocolate.

London had meant Katy. Begging a lift in a jeep, or jumping on a train, barely noticing the bombed houses, or the narrow streets. Leave, to most of his friends had meant drinking, dancing and parties. To Sam it had been his girl in his arms.

'Has it changed much?' Clive asked. It was strange to be with Sam again. Perhaps he'd built up the friendship to more than it really was. Maybe it was a mistake encouraging him to come over. Was that coldness on the other man's face, or just memories of something he'd never opened up about?

'I guess so,' Sam looked round at Clive, his mouth straight and severe. 'But then I didn't know this part of London. Bayswater was one bit I knew. Soho and Whitechapel. But most of the time I was out at Lakenheath. Ask me again when I've seen them.'

'I expect you went to the service men's club in Bayswater?' Clive needed to find some common ground. 'The Douglas House?'

'That's right!' Sam grinned suddenly, happier memories chasing away the blues. 'Is it still there?'

'Still there,' Clive chuckled, pulling out some cigarettes and offering Sam one. 'Packed with G.I.s on paydays. Maybe we can get up there one night. Georgie Fame and the Blue Flames play there.'

'Mockingbird Hill!' Sam's eyes twinkled. 'I thought they were black guys when I first heard that song. Couldn't believe my eyes when I saw he was a little white guy.'

'I think Georgie Fame would take that as a compliment,' Clive laughed.

Clive had been on the verge of cracking up when he went to the States. He was successful, he had a lovely wife, home and three kids, but he wasn't happy. It was like he had a self-destruct button attached to his chest. He wanted some excuse to push it, and blast away all the shit in his life. Sales managers, targets, social climbing, he'd had enough of all that. He wanted something more, something meaningful. He wanted to listen to music, fall in love with a wild woman, break out and be different.

If he hadn't met Sam he probably would never have got home again. His idealistic dream was already tarnished. He heard all the great jazz he hungered for. Yet the free spirits he'd expected were as trapped as himself. They had problems too, drugs, drink and poverty.

Sam put it all into perspective for him. Showed him the real America you didn't get on package holidays. The hospitality, the hypocrisy. Scenery he'd only ever dreamed of, poverty he wished he could forget. A country that had so much richness and beauty, but with an underlying core of greed and corruption.

'You've already got the things that are important man,' Sam said. 'Go home to your wife and kids, learn to be happy with what you've got. Don't go crying for the moon.'

Clive knew when he said goodbye to Sam at New Orleans airport that if he couldn't break away from his own life, then he would make sure Sam got his just reward. No one in England could play the sax like him. Somehow he was going to make the breaks for this big-hearted black man. He had the connections in London, and he was going to use them.

'Say, man,' Sam turned to Clive as the taxi came near to Piccadilly Circus. 'Hell, I don't know how to say this,' he paused suddenly embarrassed. 'I mean, I appreciate you setting this up. Finding me a place to stay an' all. But I don't want you to think you've gotta wet-nurse me. Okay?'

Colour had never been an issue in their friendship. But now looking out of the taxi window and seeing people who were predominantly white, Sam felt a pang of the old fear.

Clive was a true friend, but he had a white wife and kids, an important job. He didn't want to stretch that friendship so far it broke. In the States things were clearly defined. There was some sort of rough honesty in the prejudice. Here he didn't know how things stood, and he wouldn't find out for certain leaning on a white jazz buff.

'Sure.' Clive grinned. 'I know what you're trying to say Sam. You need to find your feet on your own. Call me when you want company. I'd like to think we can

435

get out to hear some bands together now and then. But I won't be on your back.'

'Thanks man,' Sam really smiled at last. 'Say, can you imagine how great it is to see all this again?'

He knew this bit of London. Eros had been boarded up then. The shops hadn't looked so gawdy. But there was the White Bear he used sometimes and down this road was surely the theatre he'd taken little Katy to?

The taxi turned outside the Dominion, swung round to the right and stopped.

'I remember this bit.' Sam got out, looking around like a kid on a Sunday school treat. 'Used to be a musical instrument shop here.'

'Over there.' Clive paid the driver and slammed the door. 'Some things don't change. They call this bit Tin Pan Alley still. 'Cept now it's all electric guitars and organs. Back in the 'fifties there were men playing pianos in some shops to sell sheet music. Now it's record shops and coffee bars.'

It was still only nine in the morning. Clive had gone to work and Sam's body clock was so mixed up he didn't know whether he wanted to eat, sleep or get drunk.

His kitbag sat on the double bed. His saxophone on a settee and this tiny place was his for the next few weeks.

One room, a tiny kitchen and bathroom off the small hall. It had that quality he remembered about England, a sturdy, comfortable feel. Smart enough with its plain dove-grey walls and dark red curtains. The oak table and chairs scratched enough for it to feel homely. Clean but not antiseptic. A place where a loner like himself could be inconspicuous. Was it Clive who stocked up that icebox with eggs, bacon and beer? Enough coffee for a month and a cupboard full of tins?

It was on the third floor above a coffee bar. The

window looked out over Charing Cross Road and there was that theatre almost winking at him.

What was the show he'd taken her to see? Darned if he could remember now. All he could see was her face shining up at him.

Such a pretty face. Small and heart-shaped, with big brown eyes under those shiny bangs. He could still feel that shiny straight hair as he ran his fingers through it, thick, sweet-smelling and so silky it drew his fingers back to it again and again.

It had been her hair he noticed first that night in Lakenheath. He was playing with the band when he saw her walk through the crowd with her friend.

All the other girls had theirs curled. Weird styles rolled up round scarves and God knows what. She was just natural in a green and white print dress, her waist so small she looked about fourteen and that thick dark hair just touching her shoulders.

She didn't exactly dance. She just stood there jigging up and down and clapping her hands. As she moved her hair swayed like a heavy silk curtain, gleaming under the mirrored ball.

He shouldn't have even looked at a white girl. He wouldn't have dared back home. But it was different then, a feeling in the air that nothing was permanent. You had to take chances, because tomorrow you might just be dead.

'Well Katy,' he said aloud as he watched the endless stream of traffic forcing itself down the narrow streets. 'What happened baby? Did you lose your nerve?'

Suddenly he couldn't stay in. London was beckoning him. He had only his tuxedo and shirt to hang up, everything else could wait.

Once out on the street he stopped to get his bearings. It was all so familiar, yet so strange. It was usually night when he came here before. Yet surely that was the tube station he'd run to once when the sirens went off?

437

Leicester Square. He knew where he was now. They went dancing here sometimes and she wore that little red costume he bought her with some sort of frill round the waist.

'Wouldn't navy blue be more sensible?' she asked, giggling as she stood there in the dress shop. 'What about the points Sam? I haven't got enough.'

The Brits were funny about their ration coupons. He'd done a deal with the woman who owned the shop. Katy wasn't so worried about the money it cost, more about not handing over the damn points.

He was into Piccadilly without even being aware he was still walking. It was smaller than he remembered. What was that song they used to sing? Something about lights going on again in Piccadilly. They didn't look much, he'd expected it more like Vegas. Perhaps it was more spectacular at night?

Regent Street. This was where the rich folks bought their clothes, wasn't it? Kind of like Fifth Avenue in New York. The girls were different to ones in the States. Kind of bolder, all that long flowing hair and big dark-ringed eyes. The short skirts were kinda neat though, women wouldn't go for those back home.

He didn't know why he got on the tube at Oxford Circus. One moment he was standing by the subway, the next walking down the stairs.

That dry, warm wind coming up from the platforms took him back. Strange dank smells that made him feel safe. No one felt safe on the New York subways. But he could remember everyone in London running to them when there was an air raid.

Platforms crowded with people. Women with picnics and knitting in baskets, small boys with a puppy or a kitten under their coat. A man with only one leg who played an accordian. Old ladies wrapped in blankets, babies crying, young girls giggling together and men who had to start work early trying hard to catch some sleep. Someone would start to sing and before long it was a party.

Perhaps that was why Sam still liked Brits so much. That ability to hold on to what was important, no matter what life chucked at them. He was sure they would have licked the Germans even without the Yanks to help them.

Sam stood holding the strap, his body swaying with the motion of the train. The stations were all so familiar as he looked at the map. Lancaster Gate, that was the station he used from the Douglas House. Marble Arch, Bond Street, then Oxford Circus. He must have taken that ride forty or fifty times. Back then, the train had been packed with servicemen. Americans and Canadians in their blue uniforms. British soldiers in khaki, Royal marines in navy blue and a smattering of sailors in bellbottoms. There was always an atmosphere of comradeship, mixed with rivalry. Showing off for the shy girls with fresh faces, passing round cigarettes and telling jokes.

Not a uniform in sight now. No conversation or jokes. Men in dark suits hugged their briefcases. Middle-aged ladies with bags bulging with shopping. Boys with their hair cut like the Beatles. Office girls with their knees neatly tucked together, eyes glued to magazines. What had happened in London that people avoided any human contact?

It was then he knew where he was going. He knew nobody else in London apart from Clive. He couldn't call into Ronnie Scott's until late tonight. What else could he do but make the trip to Whitechapel and get it out of his system?

Outside Whitechapel Station he stood helplessly. It had changed, yet he couldn't say how.

There was the old hospital across the street, blackened by smoke, as forbidding as he remembered. Surely the main road was never that wide? Where were all the tiny shops he remembered and that Yiddish theatre on the corner?

It ought to smell the same. Smoke was still coming out of chimneys, the little market was still there. But now there was spice in the air instead of fish, the roar of traffic instead of the shouts of costermongers.

Sam stood for a moment watching the scene at the small market.

Dark faces outnumbered white. Indians in turbans behind the stalls, women in saris queueing next to plump West Indians. Girls in their late teens pushed strollers, pale, harassed, with untidy hair. A heavily pregnant young woman bent over to spank a small boy, his screams unnoticed by anyone but Sam. A big white Ford drew up at the kerb, disgorging four young black men in leather jackets. An old woman in a red woolly hat was sorting through some fruit left out for the garbage men, and a burly man hopped along on crutches, one trouser leg pinned up with a safety pin.

It was good to see there were no ragged urchins standing listlessly outside the pub on the corner. None of these people looked hungry or pinched. Rosy-faced children in bright, warm clothes hung on to their mothers' hands. There was food aplenty and money to spare.

But what had happened to the cheery greetings Sam remembered? There was isolation, just the way he noticed on the tube. Men in cloth caps, their jacket shoulders worn shiny with unloading ships down at the docks, were replaced by menacing looking youths, hair cut short like convicts. Car horns instead of the jangle of trolley bus bells.

Sam sighed. It had lost something more than its slums. Despondency had taken the place of character. Maybe there was less dirt and disease, but Whitechapel as he knew it was gone.

Across the street he saw a young black man holding

a white girl's arm. In the Southern States that would be asking for trouble, yet here they passed unnoticed.

The Black Bull on the corner looked the same. White painted with black beams, the lattice windows twinkling invitingly. He had thought it was really old until Katy told him differently.

'It's just mock Tudor,' she explained as he gawped at it. When Henry the Eighth was on the throne this was all fields.'

Well fake or not, Sam liked it. Besides it stood on the corner of her street and back in '44 it had meant he was nearly there.

If it hadn't been for the Black Bull he might have thought he was mistaken. Valance Road had once been filled with tiny houses. A few gaps like broken teeth where bombs had dropped. Windows boarded up, shrapnel holes in some of the doors but it had been alive with people.

Now it was quiet. New apartment blocks in the place of all the rows of old tiny houses he remembered. Scrubby grass stretched round them. Swings for the children, seats for the elderly. Those old houses were dark, damp places, infested with rats, overcrowded as his own childhood home, yet they had a quality of welcome which was lacking now.

To his right was another empty site, this one still not cleared. Stumpy grass grew over uneven ground, but behind it he could see that creepy railway arch.

'Jack the Ripper got one of his victims here.' He could see Katy's eyes full of horror as they ran through that road one night soon after she moved here. It had been foggy, that evil yellow fog London was famous for, the kind that made every face look sinister.

He hadn't wanted her to move here. She should have stayed in Suffolk with her folks until they came round. A girl like her didn't belong in this place with its dark little alleys, the smells and the dirt. But he'd wanted to be with her so badly he didn't say any of that. London was the place where they didn't mind a girl having a black Yank. There was too much going on to dwell on tomorrow.

He remembered a hospital here. Not a big place like the one in the main street. A saint's name. Was it Peter? When did that get pulled down? It was an ugly, dark place, like a workhouse he'd seen pictures of before he came to England.

It was very cold. Sam zipped up his jacket and pulled up the fur collar. Hughes Mansions was up ahead of him. It looked different now too. Kind of forgotten. Old-fashioned compared with these new places.

When Katy lived there it was a good modern place. She took pride in telling him they were all business people who lived there and for Sam who had been brought up in a shingle shack, it was the nearest thing he'd seen to luxury.

A bathroom with a geyser to heat the hot water. Electric light, an indoor john and a proper kitchen with a boiler for the washing. Katy had a little room of her own, with roses on the walls and a satin-covered eiderdown on her bed.

Sam stopped at the gateway and stared up. It looked the same but it wasn't. Three blocks set on three sides of a square. Katy had lived in the one at the back. Five floors of red brick, stone balconies running from a central staircase. She used to wait on that landing in the summer, three floors up, just her head and shoulders visible above the stone wall.

But now there were four blocks, they seemed to press in on each other, shutting out light from the middle square.

'You looking for someone?'

Sam was startled to find a middle-aged woman standing by him. She was pushing a basket on wheels piled high with laundry. Her hair in curlers with a scarf over them, a plaid, shapeless coat with a fur collar.

'I used to know someone who lived here,' he said almost reluctantly. The expression on her tight face was one he knew meant resentment. 'It looks different now, but I can't make out why.'

'Those three are new blocks,' she said pointing to the three buildings furthest from the road. 'They may be new but they ain't as warm and dry as the old one.'

Sam could see now. They were copies, the brickwork and doorways different. Only the one on the road was an original.

'But why leave that one?' He pointed to the old one and frowned. 'It don't make sense.'

'A bomb hit two of them.'

'Bombed?' Sam felt his head reel. 'When?'

She looked at him as if he were simple-minded.

'In the war of course!'

'I meant what year. Which month,' he said quickly. His heart was pounding, a dry feeling in his throat.

'I dunno,' she turned to walk away. 'I've only lived here five years.'

She was gone before Sam could question her further. He saw her pulling her basket over the central tarmac square and disappear into a flat across the other side.

There was a sick feeling in his belly. Was that why Katy didn't reply? They moved her on somewhere and his letters never got delivered?

Sam sat down on a low wall. He was cold, colder than he'd ever been before. The sky was black and threatening above him, the four apartment blocks were dark and gloomy, yet twenty-two years ago this had been the place where dreams came true.

All those years of thinking she'd just stopped caring. Never once had it crossed his mind she might be homeless, alone or frightened. Love had turned to bitterness. He had been so engrossed in self pity it had blinded him to considering she might have had her own problems.

Sam saw an old man turn into the yard. The man paused for a second, leaning heavily on his walking stick, his shoulders bent, breath like smoke in the cold air. He looked at Sam suspiciously, old rheumy eyes watering in the cold wind.

'You waiting for someone?' His tone suggested Sam should wait somewhere else. The kind of arrogance Sam understood.

'I came to look for an old friend,' he replied, standing up and taking a step towards the man. 'One of your neighbours just told me two of the blocks were bombed.'

'You took yer time coming,' the old man said, taking a handkerchief out of his coat pocket and blowing his nose noisily. 'Twenty years ago that was.'

'Well I'm American,' Sam said. 'I got posted to Germany, then I went back to the States. Did you live here when it happened?'

The old man wobbled on his stick. The suspicious look replaced by one of interest.

'Yes son, thought I'd lost my wife and kids when I heard the news. But they was all right, it was the people in that block that copped it.' He lifted his stick and pointed to the block where Katy had lived. 'Was your friend in there?'

'Yes,' Sam felt his eyes welling up. 'When did it happen? Did many die?'

'March '45. It were one of those V.2s. No warning, nothing. Seven in the morning. Over a hundred and thirty killed.'

The sick feeling in Sam's stomach grew stronger. He swayed on his feet, closing his eyes momentarily.

'What happened to the survivors?' he whispered.

'Mostly men that had gone out to work.' The old

444

man's tone softened, seeing the pain in the black man's eyes. 'Who was it you knew?'

'She was called Katy. Small, dark-haired, shared a place with two other girls. I think it belonged to one of the girls' aunts. Number twenty-four it was.'

'Don't remember her.' It wasn't often someone wanted to talk about the old days and he was anxious to prolong the conversation. 'But my daughter might. She's in there now, getting me some dinner. Come on up and ask her.'

The old man lived on the first floor of the old block. He took the stairs slowly, clinging on to the banisters.

It was dirty now, the way these blocks never looked back when Katy lived here. Someone had written on the walls, the stairs hadn't been swept for years and there was a smell of urine.

'They was supposed to be moving us old 'uns out,' the old man held his chest and wheezed. 'But it never came about. I reckon I'll be here till the last. Eighty next month. Been here since they was built.'

'Come on Dad. What kept you?' A rosy-faced woman came out on to the landing, a flowery apron over her dark jumper and skirt. Not fat exactly, but big hips and breasts. A round, unlined face as if life had been kind to her. Calm brown eyes and a soft mouth.

'My fault, ma'am.' Sam flashed a brilliant smile at her, hoping charm would make it easier for her to talk to him. 'I kept him talking about the bombing here. He thought you might know my friend who lived in the back block.'

She smiled then, dimples showing in her pink cheeks. She had a girlish quality, even though she was in her late thirties.

'You're American? You were here during the war?'

'That's right ma'am,' he held out his hand. 'Sam Cameron. I've come over here to play at Ronnie Scott's.

445

I just wandered down here to look at the old place, and it's gone.'

'Well Sam,' she fluttered her eyelids a little at him, her hand in his was soft and warm. 'May I call you that? I'm Hilda Croft. Come in and have some coffee while Dad has his dinner. I'll see what I can remember.'

'This is real kind of you,' Sam said once he was sitting by the fire with a cup of steaming coffee in his hands. 'It's my first day back in England and here I am in a room just like the one I remember from last time.'

It was almost identical to the living room in Katy's place. A heavy old polished table covered with a cloth and a sideboard of the same wood. A small couch covered in dark red material, worn thin on the arms and two matching armchairs, placed round the fire. If it hadn't been for the big television under the window and a gas fire replacing the coal one, he could have gone back in time.

At number twenty-four there'd been a wireless in the corner. A big shiny wood one with cut out sun-ray effect. He could almost see Katy perched on the arm of the chair, twiddling with the knobs to tune it. There was a wind-up gramophone too, pictures of horses on the walls and a plaster plaque of a cottage with roses round the door. It was always warm there, even though the girls had to carry bags of coal up the stairs.

'I was only sixteen when the rocket hit.' Hilda sat down in the chair opposite him. She was wearing red fluffy slippers and her ankles were surprisingly slim. She made an impatient gesture to her father sitting at the table just behind them, half rising as if expecting him to ask her to cut up his dinner. 'I got married soon after and moved on out to Chigwell. But I know some of the people who lived in that block. What was your friend's name?'

'Katy Collins,' Sam sipped the hot coffee, curling his fingers round the cup to warm them. 'Small, dark and pretty. She lived with Doris Lessing in number twenty-four.'

'I remember Doris,' Hilda frowned. 'Big strapping girl. She was in the Fire Service.'

'That's right,' Sam's face broke into a smile. 'Can you remember Katy?'

He could see she was struggling to put a face to the name. He willed her to remember.

'She had a baby?'

'No,' Sam chuckled. 'Not Katy.'

'One of those girls did,' Hilda insisted. She frowned as if she knew she was right. 'I remember walking home with Doris once just after Christmas. She showed me the pattern for a coat she was knitting. She said her friend was about to have a baby.'

'Maybe that was Ruth?' Sam said easily. 'The other girl who lived there.'

Hilda shook her head.

'No, she was a glamour puss. She had long red hair and was always out dancing. The one that had the baby was a dressmaker. Doris told me she'd made lots of little nighties.'

A strange feeling ran down Sam's spine.

'Was she a dressmaker?' Hilda dropped her voice, aware she had hit a sensitive note.

Sam nodded. 'What happened to Doris?'

'She copped it, and the other two. Same as most of the folk did in that block,' she stopped short, covering her mouth with her hand. 'Oh Sam, I'm sorry.'

Sam's face blanched. 'Are you sure?'

'Of course I'm sure,' she lowered her eyes and twisted the ring on her finger round and round. 'I had stayed the night with my girlfriend across Mile End Road. We heard the bang, saw the smoke and dust. Someone said our flats had been hit and I ran all the way here. I knew Dad would be at work but Mum and the kids were here.'

'Were they safe?'

'Oh yes,' she closed her eyes as if reliving it. 'The rocket hit the back block, it left a crater thirty foot deep in the courtyard. The side block was almost entirely blown away too. All the windows here were broken. Some of the people were blown out of them. But Mum fell on the floor and the kids were still in bed.' She looked up at Sam again, a look of pain in those dark eyes, all flirtation gone.

'There's lots of things I've forgotten, but not about that day. They laid the dead out there as they found them. It was the worst thing I ever saw. Old ladies and men, blown out their beds. Kids blown to pieces, arms legs,' she shuddered, pausing and wiping her hand over her eyes. 'Doris, Ruth and the other girl were all together, still in their nightclothes. I can remember seeing Ruth's red hair as they put her body on a stretcher, it was hanging down over the end, almost touching the ground. So pretty.'

Tears trickled down her cheeks. Sam reached out and touched her hand.

'Don't mind me,' she sniffed. 'I wish I could say your girl wasn't there. But the three of them were all together. Doris in striped pyjamas. Ruth in a silky nightie and the other girl in between them, she had a blue dress. I even remember someone saying they must have been eating breakfast together.'

'I'm sorry I brought it back,' he said.

'It's okay,' she tried to smile. 'We got hardened somehow by it. Days and days of funerals, living in the hall across the road till it was safe to come back. We learned so much about one another, kind of shared the grief.'

'But the baby. Was that with them?' He was sure Hilda was mixing Katy up with someone else. The only evidence was Doris making a coat. That could have been for almost anyone.

'I don't remember,' she sighed deeply, frowning with concentration.

'I remember about the baby.' The old man's voice surprised them both. They turned sharply. His open mouth revealed few teeth left and some half-chewed cabbage.

'You don't remember anything,' Hilda said sternly. 'Get on with that dinner before it gets cold.'

'I do,' he retorted, putting down his knife and fork. 'They never found it until the evening of the second day. I was out there helping clear the site. A young fireman found her, he heard crying under the ground. I was there when they lifted it out.'

Sam looked at Hilda, waiting for her to snap a denial at her father. Instead she looked thoughtful.

'Dad's right,' she said slowly. 'I remember now. One of the women came tearing across the road to the church hall to tell us. There was women who'd lost their children, nearly out of their minds with grief. They all ran back to the site to see it.'

'It was a black baby,' the old man piped up again.

Hilda looked sternly at her father, then back again to Sam.

'Was it?' Sam said softly.

She didn't speak for a moment, as if trying to sort out real memories from rumours.

'Mrs Kirkpatrick, she was the old girl who acted as midwife around here, said it was, but I never saw the baby. They said she was around ten weeks old. We were all so amazed the baby wasn't dead or even hurt. She was buried alive, still in her pram, trapped under rubble.'

'Did anyone claim her?' Sam's voice was little more then a whisper. 'I mean, did this baby belong to a survivor?'

Hilda shook her head, eyes filling up with tears.

'You think she was yours?'

449

Sam couldn't reply.

A flashback took him back to that bedroom with the satin eiderdown. White curtains with red roses moving in the early morning breeze.

'I should have been careful.' He was damp with perspiration, his face pressed into her small pink-tipped breasts. His hand against Katy's face looked so dark in contrast to her white skin. 'What if I've put you in the family way?'

'I wouldn't care,' her laugh was like a caress. 'Besides, that only happens to other people.'

He remembered watching her as he dressed that last time, fastening his blue uniform slowly, anything to prolong the moment of leaving. She lay with her dark hair tangled on the pillow, dark eyes full of unshed tears.

'You will come back?' her voice wobbled. 'I'm counting on you.'

'I don't know,' Sam's voice shook as he answered Hilda. 'In her last letter she said she had a surprise for me. But I just thought she had made something for me. Why would a girl hide something like that?'

'Maybe she was frightened you'd run out on her?' Hilda sighed. 'I mean men do, don't they?'

'But we were going to get married,' Sam insisted. 'I left for Germany in April of '44. She wrote to me nearly every day. If I'd known I'd have found some way to get back. The last letter I got was dated March twenty-fifth. Then nothing.'

'It was the morning of the twenty-seventh when it happened,' Hilda said softly.

Sam just stared at Hilda. She was counting on her fingers.

'They said the baby was ten weeks old. That works right back to happening just before you left for Germany.'

The room was spinning. It was too hot. He wanted to run out denying what this woman was telling him.

Was this some sort of bad dream? Why should he believe this baby belonged to Katy anyway? Twenty years distorted everything.

'What happened to this baby?' he asked.

Hilda shook her head.

'I don't know,' she said softly. 'Mrs Kirkpatrick would have known, and my mother too, but they both died years ago. I almost wish Dad hadn't brought you up here. Perhaps it would have been better if you'd never known about any of this.'

A spotlight glinted on his saxophone as he raised it to his lips. He filled his lungs with air, fingers poised on the keys.

'Watermelon man', a fitting number for a poor black man from New Orleans. He hadn't been prepared to sit in with the band tonight, but they'd insisted.

Scores of people sitting out there in the smoky darkness waiting to see if he could truly make his horn sing and all Sam could think of was Katy.

He tried to cut out the ugly scene Hilda had described and remember Katy how she was.

The notes came out as he pictured her running to him down the lane at Lakenheath. The fields were yellow with buttercups, she was wearing a pink dress that clung to her slim legs, her arms held out to him, hair flowing back from the small heart-shaped face. Cherry lips, cheeks pink with excitement.

'I've found a place we can be together,' she shouted even before she reached him. 'I love you Sam.'

He didn't know he was putting all that into his music. It was all so real he could smell the fields, feel the sunshine on his neck and face, hear her voice.

A roar washed over him, bringing him back to the present.

451

Out beyond the stage he could see nothing but a blur of white faces and clapping hands.

So she was dead. Yet, in a way it was kinder than thinking she stopped loving him. He was back in the country that made him a man, and by that applause he knew he'd played a great solo.

He had turned a corner in his life. So Ellie had run out on him, but how could he blame her? Hadn't he ever only loved her with half a heart? He knew the truth at last about Katy and he had his children.

Maybe the baby found in the rubble wasn't his, but he couldn't rest until he found that out for certain.

'I'm counting on you.' Those were Katy's last words to him, and this time he wouldn't let her down.

Chapter 20

The headline mocked him even though he had moved away from the table where the newspaper lay. Even if he closed his eyes he could still see it.

'Our Georgia, home again in triumph.'

'How dare she smile like that after what she's put me through?' he muttered. Yet he still couldn't bring himself to screw up the paper and throw it to one side without reading further.

Moving slowly back to the table, he bent over and tried to bring the small print into focus. His glasses were broken, and he had no money left to replace them. Dirt-encrusted fingers twitched with a kind of palsy. He was cold, his chest hurt, and now this.

'Are you in there Mr Anderson?'

He heard the Irish voice at the door but ignored it. He could imagine Mrs Dooley's fat face squashed against his door as she listened, vast breasts straining her overall. Swollen purple feet incongruous in furry pink slippers.

She kept in with the landlords by acting as unpaid rent collector and stool-pigeon, while taking bribes from the black tenants upstairs to keep quiet when another friend had swelled their numbers even further.

'I know you're in there!' she called out. 'You know what will happen if you don't pay me, don't you?'

He knew all right. Those bully boys from the landlord

would come round and threaten him, maybe even throw him out on the street.

It wasn't as if the room was worth anything. A filthy hovel in Ladbroke Grove sharing the toilet with blacks and Irish. They hadn't mended the window since he fell against it, the gas meter was fixed to make money out of him and the sink was blocked up.

A sagging single bed. A sink and old black cooker. Hooks on the door to hold his only coat. Two fireside chairs, one with a broken arm. A table and two chairs. The proportions of the room were all wrong. A giant black marble fireplace. An eight foot ceiling and a long narrow sash window covered in grey net curtain, in a room twelve foot long by six foot wide. Once the room next door had been part of it, until the landlords hastily erected a thin plasterboard partition. To Brian Anderson it seemed almost coffin shaped.

Georgia's face in the paper tormented him. She was wearing a ridiculous cowboy outfit, with a Stetson, fringed jacket, indecently short skirt and even cowboy boots. They said she'd taken America by storm and London airport was besieged with fans waiting for her arrival home.

'They wouldn't like you so much if they knew what you'd done to your father!' he muttered, forcing the scissors between swollen, twisted fingers.

His room was full of her pictures. Glossy, glamour shots of her running along a beach in a red and white sarong, the wind catching her hair and holding it out behind her like a black flag. Another one and she was curled up sensuously in a white armchair, a hint of brown cleavage and those long, slim legs tucked round her. In sequinned evening dress, regal and beautiful. On stage, her hair sticking to her head with perspiration, that wide mouth open, head thrown back. Walking through fallen leaves in a park wearing jeans and a man's jacket over her shoulder, laughing as though interrupted in some private moment of fun.

He had them all. Each mention in the press. Every picture no matter how tiny. A private collection which gave him no pleasure. She was responsible for his plight and one day he would ruin her.

Sometimes he had dreams when he saw her coming for him with a knife. He would wake up sweating and shaking. But it soothed him to look at the pictures. She was the evil one, not him. He must never let himself forget that.

He picked up a thin, worn donkey-jacket and put it on. He had to go and collect his money from the post office, he couldn't risk Mrs Dooley calling the landlord again. Perhaps just one drink to warm him and stop the shakes.

The wind outside was icy. The soles of his shoes had holes in them and he had no socks left.

Was he going mad? He knew there had been a better life before. He could see himself mowing a lawn, or sitting in a sweet-smelling room listening to a piano. He imagined opening a drawer and taking out a shirt fresh from the laundry, putting gold links into the cuffs and slapping cologne on his smooth shaven face. But if he had that life once, why was it he ended up here?

Most of the time his mind was stubbornly fixed in Ladbroke Grove as if the startling memories that came to him were nothing more than something he'd seen on a film. Except for Georgia. Her face remained constant in his mind, only the details of how and why she made him suffer hazy.

Down the grey street he shuffled, eyes down in the gutter. Past dustbins spewing out on to the path. Black faces everywhere. Standing on steps gossiping, lounging on corners with malice in their dark eyes.

Where had they all come from? Surely there was a time when everyone was white?

He crossed the road at the lights, turned left and into the post office.

For once it was quiet. Only two people before him. Sometimes the queue stretched right to the door. Black women with prams, out-of-work youngsters, all the old, sick and poor people of Ladbroke Grove waiting for their state benefits.

'Have you got your book Mr Anderson?'

He liked the post office. They treated him properly here. Remembered his name and gave him respect.

He felt inside his coat and pulled out the crumpled yellow book.

'You haven't signed it.' The big woman with red hair smiled at him. She was tapping her nails on the counter with impatience, but then she was a busy woman. 'Have you got a pen?'

'Of course,' he said, feeling in his pocket again.

The snotty-nosed brats in his street called him 'The Banker'. He couldn't always remember why this was, but the pen was a clue.

He signed the book and pushed it under the grille. She counted out the notes and pushed them back to him.

'Good morning,' he said, and shuffled off to the door, his money still in his hands.

His mind was cloudy again. It was like that most days now. Like the grey net at his window had got inside his head. It stopped him from thinking or planning and each day it grew thicker. He knew he needed to buy something but what was it?

A bus stopped in front of him, then another right behind it. He was caught in the middle of a human whirlpool, trapped by women with pushchairs, old ladies with shopping baskets, young men in leather jackets and a group of school children.

He didn't see who pushed him, just a sharp thump in his chest, and the next thing he was on his back.

'Are you okay?' A male voice was speaking to him,

but he couldn't see anything but a blur of white above him.

For a moment he thought he'd just tripped, as he often did these days, yet why was he on his back instead of on his knees?

'My money,' he clawed at the air, suddenly aware his hand was empty. 'Who's taken my money?'

The man was leaning over him, touching his shoulder, but he was talking to someone else. Something about a black man who pushed him and stole his money. He was urging another man to telephone the police.

He didn't know he was crying, just a damp feeling trickling down his face.

'Poor old chap,' the man said. 'How could anyone be low enough to rob him?'

Through the grey mist he knew he must regain his dignity.

'Help me up please,' he asked. 'I can't see very well, but I'd like to get in somewhere warm.'

A hand went under his elbow and hoisted him up, he could see the man's face now. It was young, fresh and even kindly.

'Would it be too much to trouble you for a cup of tea?' Brian asked. 'I need a moment to get over the shock.'

'Of course,' the man said. He turned to someone behind him. 'I'll just take him into the café. Tell the police to come in there.' He took Brian's arm and led him into warmth. 'Sit down and I'll get you some tea.'

It was odd that the grey mist floated away suddenly. One moment confused, the next aware of everything. Just as if someone had opened curtains on a darkened room. Aware how shabby his clothes were, his dirty hands and the stubble on his chin. His tongue flickered across dry, cracked lips and he averted his eyes from a mirror on the wall.

457

He looked at least seventy. So thin, the skin on his face just hung in bags. Little hair left on the top of his head, but round his ears it sprouted out, grey/brown and greasy. His mouth appalled him most. It was sunken, his lips drooping at the corners and when he opened it his teeth were stained brown.

It wasn't tea he wanted, but whiskey. He looked across the café at the man who brought him in and wondered if he'd be good for a handout.

The man was young. Arty looking in his leather-patched tweed jacket. A long, serious face and his hair hanging over his collar. He could be a social worker or a teacher. Not someone with money.

The café was one he often had lunch in when he first came to Ladbroke Grove. They greeted him like a friend then, telling him about specials on the menu and chatting about the news. He liked the red and white tablecloths, the smell of ground coffee and baking. It reminded him of his old home.

For some reason that eluded him, they asked him to leave. Was he drunk, or perhaps they didn't like his shabby clothes? Whatever the reason was they seemed to have forgotten it now, for the two plump women behind the counter were looking at him as they spoke to his rescuer, nodding in sympathy.

The man came back, putting down two teas on the table and sat opposite Brian. He was frowning, a kind of impatient look, as if he wanted to leave hurriedly, but couldn't bring himself to.

'Are you feeling better now?' His brown eyes were gentle. A soft, generous mouth with a cleft chin. His light brown hair had a shine to it, flopping down to his eyes. 'The police will be here soon. They'll help you.'

'I didn't see anything.' Brian felt confused now, the present mingling with the past. 'I felt someone push me, then I was on the floor. Did you see who did it?'

'Two young black men,' the man frowned again. 'I

saw you just standing there. I was just going to make you put the money away and they pounced. They moved so quick I couldn't do anything.'

'Blacks!' Brian almost spat out the word. 'The place is overrun with them.'

'I picked these up for you.' The young man dug into his pocket, and pulled out Brian's payment book and a couple of photographs.

'Thanks.' Brian snatched up the book, but left the photographs on the table. Just the sight of them made his shakes come back. 'I'm sorry. I'm not well. You must excuse me.' This clarity of mind was far more painful than the grey mist and it was unreliable. He could start a conversation, think things out, then suddenly he could be thrown back to the confused man the children laughed at.

The photographs had been in his good overcoat. It wasn't until he tried to sell it that he found them. He must have had them all this time tucked into the back of his payment book.

'I saw your name is Anderson,' the young man smiled, glancing down at the pictures. 'I'm John Adams. Who's this?' Adams picked up one of the photographs. It was one of Georgia in a swimsuit, taken on the beach at Hastings the summer before she ran away. 'What a pretty girl. She looks like Georgia, the singer.'

Brian felt a hot flush creeping up his neck.

'It is Georgia. She's my daughter.'

He had often wondered what it would be like to tell someone. He expected ridicule, laughter and questions, but he didn't expect the shock he saw in this man's eyes.

His jaw dropped. He blinked hard, picked up the picture and looked again. Lowering the picture he looked right into Brian's eyes, the sort of look that meant he wanted to believe it, but couldn't.

'It's true,' Brian said. 'Look at the other one too. She's there again with my wife and I at a bank dinner and dance.'

It felt good to admit it. The hazy grey mist was lifting so quickly he could remember other things too.

Georgia sitting between them, in a light-coloured dress with a kind of ruffle round the neck, smiling at her father in dinner-jacket and bow tie. Celia, on her other side was in a chiffon, low-necked dress, a glass of wine in her hand. That night all his staff had been there, formality forgotten with Christmas coming. He'd given them little presents, shared jokes and pulled crackers.

He saw a red flush creeping up Adam's face, his eyes narrowed as he looked at the snap, going back to Brian's face, then back to the picture.

'She changed her name of course,' Brian picked up his tea and tried to control his shaking hands. 'There's things I could tell you about her.' He paused, sensing something more in the man's expression.

Not disbelief or scorn. But excitement.

'How can she be your daughter?' the man asked. 'She's black.'

'Half-caste.' Brian was surprised how easy he found to explain. 'We fostered her, gave her everything, singing and dancing lessons, nice clothes. We loved her like she was our own.'

'But – ' The man's mouth was hanging open again.

'But why am I like this if I've got a famous rich daughter?' Brian's laugh was hollow. 'Because she's a little bitch. That's why.'

John Adams wasn't a man who was shocked easily. He had grown up in Ladbroke Grove and knew many of the odd characters who lived there. Pimps, prostitutes, thieves, faded actresses, doctors who'd been struck off, he'd even met a few titled people who'd fallen on hard times. It was an area where people ended

up. A dustbin of human life. Yet if he believed everything he'd been told in pubs, listened to every old wino
who bleated out a sob story then it would be him next
for the funny farm.

He'd seen Anderson before. He knew he drank
heavily and sometimes he shouted and talked to himself. He had guessed the man wasn't as old as he
looked, and there were the rumours.

Didn't Jock down at the Bell claim he was a retired
bank manager? That a couple of years ago before he got
this far out of it, he advised him on a couple of
investments? Then there was Martha at the Black Horse,
who felt sorry for him one night and put him to bed in
her spare room. Later he'd written her a letter thanking
her and that letter had been passed round the bar.
Beautifully written in a stylish copperplate handwriting,
the type of letter that could only be written by a man
with a first-class upbringing and education.

The man lived in squalor now. His clothes were little
better than a tramp's, he was dirty, unshaven,
neglected and definitely half way round the bend. But
his accent was impeccable. He had good manners.
Despite his present appearance he could see Anderson
was the man in the photograph. Suppose it was true?
The story could make a fortune.

'Look,' John leaned closer across the table. 'I'll be
straight with you. If what you are telling me is true I
can get you enough money to make up for what those
guys took. I know you're ill. You may have even had a
bang on the head. But if you are making it up for God's
sake level with me now.'

'Can I have made that up?' Brian pushed the picture
of the family group towards him again. 'You can see
plainly that's her, even if she was only a kid then. You
can see it's me too, if you take away the fine clothes.
How else would I have that picture if it wasn't true?'

A picture five or six years old. How could it be a fake?

461

Only a practised confidence trickster could engineer something like that, and this sad old man wasn't that.

'Would you tell me everything about her?' Adams asked gently. 'I'm a writer you see.'

Calling himself a writer was stretching the truth a bit. He'd been paid for a couple of articles on local history, written a few letters to *The Times*. But he could string a few words together, and he had got a couple of mates in Fleet Street.

'All right. I will.'

Adams could only stare at the old man. He'd expected haggling, even straight, sober people asked for money up front. He remembered one of his journalist friends words. 'They either spill the beans for money, or revenge.' Revenge would pay the most!

By the time a policeman had been and taken a statement and John Adams had bought him a big breakfast, Brian was feeling better.

Adams had suggested he go home with him for a talk, he'd even suggested there might be some money in it for him. Maybe his luck was turning at last?

It was close to six o'clock when Adams showed Anderson the door. He had been tempted to ask the man to stay the night and finish what he'd started, but he was so overwhelmed by what he had heard he needed to be alone.

His feelings about Anderson had swung violently from pity to suspicion during the day, and now he wasn't sure whose side he was on.

Pity had been the major feeling when the man came out of the bathroom. He could see shame on his face, now it was scrubbed clean, further evidence that he hadn't always lived the way he did now.

'I'll get these cleaned for you and return them,' he almost whispered, touching the clean shirt and old grey

462

flannel trousers as if they'd come straight out of the window at Burton's.

'They're yours.' John hid his own discomfort by digging out a pair of black shoes which had been left behind by a friend. 'Try these for size.'

He had felt bad taking a photograph of Anderson before the transformation. Even worse putting his old clothes into a bag and tying up the top to keep as evidence to back up his story. His mind was whirling with disgust at Georgia allowing her father to get to this stage, loathing at himself for cashing in on it, and an even greater desire to get to the hard truth.

He felt more pity too when he realized just how confused the man was. He had a story all right but it came out backwards, sideways, upside down, but rarely running straight.

Adams' old tape recorder went round and round as he led Anderson through Georgia's first days at his home. He heard about her being beaten by the nuns, her injuries and the way she brought sunshine into their home. Sometimes it sounded as if she was just a toddler on arrival, sometimes far older. One moment his eyes filled with tears, the next they flashed with hate.

But when Anderson got to the bit about the party, nothing sounded right. The emotion had gone from his voice, it sounded like a story he'd rehearsed. No unnecessary detail as there had been earlier. Like a journalist's story in fact.

'My wife had to go out you see,' he kept saying. 'I stayed downstairs because I didn't want to spoil their fun. But I sensed something was going on.'

In one huge gulp he told the tale of how he saw her come out of the bedroom with her boyfriend.

'I packed the kids off sharpish,' he said. 'Then I asked her what she thought she was doing. She told me to mind my own business and I slapped her. Next thing I knew she was coming up the stairs with a knife. She lunged at me, sticking it in my stomach. When I came round I was in hospital and I'd nearly died.'

There was the scar to back it up. A vivid red slash against his white belly, the skin puckered and wrinkled around it. But even as he looked at it, he wondered why she had hit her father so low. A frenzied attack was usually in the direction of the heart.

John wanted to go back over details. There was more, he knew it, but he was afraid to stop the man in case he dried up.

He could understand Georgia running away to escape punishment. But why did his wife leave? What had been left out?

If he was to believe everything Anderson told him, the man was a victim of not only his daughter's cruelty, but his wife and employers too. Why should the bank sack him? It didn't make sense.

Anderson was an alcoholic, that much was plain. His hands shook, his eyes constantly strayed around the room as if searching for drink. But was he already one when Georgia ran away, or was she the trigger that had started his downward spiral?

John Adams understood how bitterness could warp a person. A bright kid from the wrong side of the tracks who won a scholarship to public school, only to find he was a social outcast. Later at university he worked while everyone else enjoyed themselves. He got his 'First', but they got the girls, and later the good jobs.

Why did he end up in a laboratory testing paint while others less able set the world alight? All he had to show for his hard work was a poky one-bedroomed flat, a beaten-up Ford and no savings. Maybe he too could have turned to drink to cope with disappointment.

Brian Anderson lay on his bed shivering. He'd managed to get home without going in the pub and he'd paid

Mrs Dooley what he owed, but it was a mistake to be sober in this room. The damp patches seemed to press in on him, and the sink full of weeks-old dirty dishes appalled him. He had to remain sober though; unless he did, John Adams wouldn't help him any more.

This time with Adams' help he was going to pull his life together. There was no way she could spoil things now, not like she had before.

It was November 1960 when he went up to the West End. The house in Blackheath was sold at last. The money safely in a bank until he decided what to do with it. A nice little flat in New Cross. A fresh start in a place where no one knew him.

He told his landlord he had retired early because of an old war wound. He liked the sound of that, it made him sound romantic, a man of action. He wasn't going to drink again, not the way he had in those last dreadful months when everyone, Celia, the bank, friends and neighbours had turned against him. Maybe he would leave the country if he didn't find a job that suited him, but that night as he went to the West End he was just looking for some company.

It had been some years since he last visited Soho. As he stood in Piccadilly looking at the neon lights flashing out messages and advertisements he felt charged with new life. He cut a smart figure in his new blazer, military tie and grey slacks. Somewhere in that square mile was a woman who'd share drinks and supper with him, someone to make him laugh and forget the past.

He found her sitting in the White Bear bar. Red hair curling to her shoulders and a vivid green dress that echoed her eyes.

'Is there anyone sitting here?' he said, pointing to the empty bench seat beside her.

'Feel free,' she said, moving up just slightly and crossing her long, slim legs.

He knew she was a prostitute, but that made it all the

easier. She might try to con him out of a few bob but it was better than picking up a girl on the streets.

'Hasn't it changed around here?' he said brightly. 'Last time I came in here it was packed. Don't people drink here anymore?'

'It's early yet,' she said languidly, looking at a cheap imitation of a diamond-studded bracelet watch. 'Are you from out of town?'

'No,' he laughed lightly, letting her know straightaway he understood the West End. 'South London, just came up to have a little fun for a change.'

She was probably around thirty-five, though from a distance she looked nearer twenty-five. She smelled of apple blossom perfume that took him instantly back to a girl in Birmingham once. She wasn't pretty, her face was too long and thin, her lips rather thin, but she had good breasts, pushed up to reveal deep cleavage.

The best thing about her was that she wasn't obviously a tart. She could be a secretary or shop girl waiting for her boyfriend.

Her red hair was maybe a little startling, the dress a flashy cheap one, but then that made it more exciting.

'I suppose you're waiting for someone,' he said as she picked up her glass and drank the last drop. 'Can I buy you a drink while you wait?'

'Okay,' she flashed a brilliant smile at him, which sent shivers of delight down to his toes. 'Gin and orange.'

Her name was Paula, she said she'd been a dancer and she had a flat nearby, and she was open enough to name her price immediately.

Ten months had passed since Georgia's birthday and for the first time since that day he felt like his old self. Instead of gulping down drinks in an effort to forget, he found himself slowing down, listening to Paula's chatter, enjoying the pressure of her thigh on his, his mind calm, his body relaxed.

He told her he was a retired bank manager, hinted at wealth and encouraged her natural sympathy by telling her he was a widower and their only daughter lived miles away and never visited.

'Well you aren't alone tonight, love,' she said warmly. 'Come on, drink up, let's find somewhere to dance.'

Even when she softly asked for the money up front she did it gently, winding her soft arms round him and kissing him outside the club.

'Better to get it over first,' she smiled, pressing herself against him. 'I want all the guys in there to think you are a date.'

Brian had been in the Mandrake club before. A damp basement that smelled of mould and beer. Hot, stale air wafted up as they went down the dimly lit stairs. The music came from a juke box in one corner of the room, jangling and distorted. The seats were little more than wooden benches, the floor solid concrete and apart from a few candles spluttering in Chianti bottles, the only light came from the small bar. But with a pretty woman on his arm and the promise of a night of love, it could have been the Café de Paris.

It didn't matter that each drink cost nearly a pound. Tomorrow would be soon enough to worry about money, right now he had a girl who cared about him. He was pleasantly tight, the club was warm and friendly. It had been so long since he held a woman in his arms, the smell of her perfume, the softness of her skin was like a soothing drug.

When they walked up the stairs after one, the fresh air caught them by surprise. Paula was staggering in her high heels and Brian put his arm round her.

At the end of St Anne's Court they stopped for a moment in the shadows to kiss. It was quiet now, just the distant sound of music in another bar and fainter still the traffic from Piccadilly and Shaftesbury Avenue.

She kissed beautifully, slow, deliberate and sensuous,

her tongue flickering across his, sending shudders of delight down Brian's spine. In her arms he could forget the mean streets, the glaring neon signs, the overflowing dustbins and the smell of rotting rubbish. It looked almost pretty, an old street lamp sending a golden arc of light across the road, Dickensian and quaint.

Further down the street the sound of high heels tapped out a staccato rhythm. As the footsteps came closer Brian heard a peal of laughter that made him stiffen involuntarily.

'What is it?' she whispered, her lips against his neck.

Brian didn't answer but concentrated on listening as the feet came closer.

Two pairs, one with a bouncy young step, the other older, more plodding.

'Did you see that old bloke? He must have been at least fifty.'

The woman speaking wasn't the one with the laugh that jolted him, her voice common and rough. Brian shook himself and pulled Paula closer.

'He was quite sweet though.'

This voice sounded exactly like Georgia's. He'd heard it night after night as his eyes closed with weariness and now he was hearing it again only a few yards from him.

'Shall we go now?' Paula was saying, but Brian merely held her tighter, burying his lips in her neck as he watched over her shoulder.

The two women came under the yellow arc of light, their heads close together, blond against dark.

Brian saw only the black pom-pom of hair, the big eyes that looked right into the alley where he and Paula stood and his blood ran cold.

'Don't bite me!' Paula's squeal of pain made him loosen his grip on her. 'What's your game?'

The two women had passed the end of the alley. Brian ran forward, forgetting Paula.

468

The women stopped outside a door, standing close together whispering. Hearing his footsteps they looked round.

'What's up mate?' the blonde one called out. 'Isn't one girl enough for you?'

The dark girl laughed, her hand poised to put a key in the door.

In profile Brian could see it wasn't Georgia. She was white, at least twenty-five and she had thick legs.

He backed away, feeling shaken and foolish.

Paula was standing at the end of St Anne's Court with a puzzled look on her face.

The short fur jacket she wore over her green dress hanging off her shoulders.

'What is it? You look as if you've seen a ghost.'

'I thought I had. I could have sworn that was my daughter,' he said weakly.

'That was Shirl and Denise,' she linked arms with him, urging him along. 'Nice girls don't roam around here at night. Come on, let's go back to my place.'

The small flat was just a block away. A door half hidden between two shops. They climbed up some narrow, grubby stairs and Paula opened a door on the first floor.

'You did get a shock,' she smiled and drew him in. 'I'll just light the fire and make you a drink. You've gone all pale!'

'You're very understanding,' he said, looking all around him furtively as if expecting someone to jump out on him.

It was one room, the walls and floor uneven as if the house was subsiding. A cooker and sink were curtained off in one corner, through the other door he could see a bath and toilet.

She was a hoarder. Every shelf, every surface was full of ornaments. Even the wardrobe wouldn't close because so many clothes were stuffed in there. The double bed was covered in red satin, a profusion of frilly pillows and soft toys arranged on it. Cheap prints hung over the bed, chosen for their garish colours rather than their artistic appeal. Behind the door hung a green silky dressing-gown with black lace and over one chair hung a red and black basque.

'This is cosy,' his spirits rose again as she switched on twin red lamps either side of the bed.

'Relax dear,' she said crossing the room to him. 'Take off your jacket and make yourself at home. Would you like some whiskey?'

Never before had any prostitute offered him a drink. They took their money, did the business and then expected him to go. Maybe he was already special to her? Perhaps this could be the start of something good?

She poured him a large drink, dropped a kiss on his cheek and disappeared into the bathroom.

'As they say at the movies,' she shouted through the door. 'Just slipping into something more comfortable.'

Brian took off his jacket and shoes and sat on the bed nursing his drink.

'There, I wasn't long was I?'

Paula was standing in the doorway, a black negligee open to reveal a bra, knickers, stockings and suspenders.

Her skin was very white, her thighs bulged at her stocking tops. Brian could say nothing, instead he reached out for her, putting his arms round her waist and buried his head in her breasts.

She smelt perfect, the perfume just a little too sweet and heady.

'Let me undress you?' she said, bending down to him and lifting his face up with one finger. 'You're shy aren't you?'

As her fingers reached out to unbutton his shirt he felt restored. He pulled her down onto the bed beside him and covered her face with kisses. He could feel an

470

erection starting and he knew she wouldn't insist on turning off the light.

'You're lovely,' she whispered, her tongue flickering over his, 'Let me get your things off?'

As she slid his trousers down his legs she touched him lightly on the front of his white 'Y' fronts.

'That looks very healthy,' she smiled up at him impishly, her auburn hair tumbling round her face.

Brian could hear his heart hammering. She knelt up on the bed beside him slowly unbuttoning his shirt. As she undid the cuffs she kissed both his wrists and let her lips travel up the soft insides of his arms.

'Now the pants,' she said, gripping the waistband firmly and lowering them, moving her lips down towards his penis as she pulled the pants right off his feet.

He was holding his breath now, wearing nothing but his socks and his vest. Her lips were only an inch away from his penis and her hand was poised to grasp it.

'What a lovely big one,' she whispered, looking up at him and smiling. 'I think I've just got to kiss it!'

Her tongue flicked over the end. He drew in his breath and watched her, leaning back on his elbows.

It was his favourite fantasy. A near-naked woman, about to take him in her mouth. Her breasts were full, spilling over the low cut bra, her skin very white and clear. The negligee had fallen off one shoulder and he could see a tiny sprinkling of freckles on her small shoulder.

Her tongue darted out, long and pointed, she ran it along the length of his penis one hand reaching out to cup his balls.

He could feel her breasts touching his leg and he was desperately afraid he would come before they even got started.

'Not yet,' she looked up and smiled seductively. 'First

we have to get that vest off.' She gripped it by the bottom and quickly pulled it over his head.

'Oh my God!' she gasped, moving back from him. 'What ever's happened to you?'

Her remark was like a cold shower. His penis shrank back like a tortoise into its shell.

Brian had forgotten the scar. In the past months it had become just another part of him, but seeing it through her eyes he saw how fearsome it looked.

The original gash was only an inch and a half. But during surgery they had opened it wider. It was diagonal across the fat part of his belly and as it had healed it had puckered so it looked like a pair of pursed lips.

'It's nothing,' he said too quickly. 'I fell on a knife.' He cursed himself for not remembering the old war wound story. Women had enough imagination to understand the thrust of a bayonet. She would have shuddered delicately and changed the subject.

'When?' her face was pale with fright now, the seductive look gone, replaced by morbid curiosity. 'Does it hurt?'

As if it wasn't bad enough her even remarking about it, she now reached out gingerly to touch it.

'Don't,' he slapped her hand away.

'Why not,' her eyes opened wide. 'Scars are interesting.'

Brian closed his eyes for a second.

It was Georgia again. Somehow she'd even managed to spoil this night for him.

'Don't be like that,' Paula wriggled up to lie beside him and leaned over his face to kiss him.

Brian grabbed her fiercely, thrusting his tongue into her mouth.

But he felt nothing. No reaction. She smelled too sweet, it made him feel nauseous and underneath that perfume he could smell sweat.

'Let me lick your prick again,' she said. 'You liked that.'

She moved back down the bed and once again Brian watched, holding his breath as her tongue slid out, red and pointy.

But all he could see now was the wound. Even from the angle he lay at it looked evil, like the mouth of an old crone.

When she'd done this before it was sweet and exciting, but now he felt a sense of duty in her manner.

She took his penis in her mouth, sucking at it vigorously, but still it refused to grow. Her long red nails dug into his inner thighs and then she yawned.

'Don't bother,' he said, pushing her away. 'You ruined everything anyway.'

She moved back from him, her eyes startled.

'I'm sorry,' she said perching on the bed beside him. 'I didn't mean to hurt your feelings.'

'Yes you did,' he said, getting up and reaching for his clothes. 'You women are all the same. Always got to spoil things.'

'Just a minute!' she leapt off the bed and pulled her negligee tightly around her. She stood in front of him as he pulled on his shirt. 'Who the fuck do you think you're talking to? I spent all evening with you because I liked you. I brought you back here for the same reason. I may be a tart but it doesn't stop me having feelings.'

'I paid you for a night out and sex,' he spat at her. 'I didn't expect you to pry into my private life.'

'You call asking about a scar prying?' she sneered at him. 'If you were like that to your daughter it's no wonder she ran off.'

Rage welled up inside him. He saw only the thin pale face and the expression of aversion in those cold green eyes. One moment his hands were buttoning his shirt, the next his clenched fist shot out and punched straight into her face.

'Filthy whore,' he shouted.

When he saw her backing away on to the bed, blood gushing out of her nose, he was sorry. The anger wasn't directed at her, just at Georgia. He pulled on his pants and trousers, searching for the right words to make her forget.

He moved towards her, hands outstretched. She cowered back amongst the pillows, white-faced and frightened.

'Don't you dare touch me!' The force with which she spat out the words surprised him, her eyes blazed and she scrabbled amongst the pillows behind her. 'I can defend myself you bastard!'

A glint of silver under the red light. A long curved blade, her red nails curled round an ivory handle.

'I didn't mean to hit you,' his words spilt out. 'It was just – '

The knife drove all explanations out of his head, his legs turned to jelly.

'I knew there was something weird about you,' she interrupted, getting up on to her knees, slashing out at the air between them. Her black negligee fell back, revealing her underwear and white skin. 'This could cut off your prick like a ripe banana. I'd finish what some other woman started.'

'You don't understand,' Brian shoved his feet into his shoes. He was frightened now. She looked fiendish, white-faced, bloodied nose, red hair hanging over eyes that burned almost black with rage.

'Oh, I do,' she snapped back. 'I've met dozens of perverts like you. Do you think I'm stupid just because I'm a prostitute? I know a woman made that scar and I can guess why.'

Brian backed away towards the door as she jumped down off the bed moving steadily towards him, the knife held in front of her.

'Get out you bastard,' she said through clenched

474

teeth. 'And if I ever see you up this way again I'll swing for you.'

The bottle was the only way of blanking out that night. Alone in his new flat Paula and Georgia's faces haunted him. He had to go out, down to the crowded pub until he was drunk enough to blot them out.

Some days he made an effort to forget. He washed and dressed smartly and presented himself at the labour exchange, but even there it seemed as if something was working against him. Manual work, that's all they offered. They ignored his education and qualifications, almost as if someone had been there first, whispering about him.

He wanted to make his flat a home. But daily he saw things sliding. Clothes dropped on the floor stayed there. Plates filled the sink and empty beer bottles multiplied overnight. His shirts looked grey, underwear and socks disintegrated and he never replaced them.

Bongo drums from a house behind his kept him awake. The landlord pushed notes under his door complaining of noise and smells coming from his flat. Was it before, or after he noticed how low his money was getting when he got arrested for being drunk?

There was another woman, he couldn't remember now who she was, or even where he met her, but for a time he got back on his feet. Did she help him get the night security job at Jarson's in Catford?

A period of peace. Not exactly happy, but reconciled. That hot evening in August he walked to work thinking about moving to somewhere with a garden. He even went over to the town hall to look and see what concerts were coming up. He wasn't drinking then.

There were bands he'd never heard of. Silly names that didn't give a clue to what sort of music they played.

Funny that he remembered so little about a period of

over a year, yet he could see Catford Town Hall as clearly now as if a picture was in front of him.

A rounded front, with two sets of doors going into the theatre and between them a sandwich board advertising the events. There were two teenage boys standing beside him.

'See, I told you they are coming here,' one of them pointed to the programme. 'It's next Monday.'

Brian looked to where the boy pointed.

'Who are Samson?' he asked. 'Is it jazz or a dance band?'

They looked at him and laughed. He remembered they were both smartly dressed, Italian suits with short jackets and winklepicker shoes.

'A soul band,' the smaller one replied. 'The best in England.'

'That's them, there.' The other one pointed to a poster on the wall.

The picture was of a group of young men. Sitting in front of them was Georgia.

He blinked, afraid that his eyes were deceiving him.

She had that impudent grin that belonged to no one else. Head thrown back, hair longer than he remembered, tumbling over bare shoulders. A tight black dress barely covered her breasts, eyes that held his with all that old magnetism.

It was like the knife again. But this time he could feel it turning in the wound.

'Who is she?' he whispered, turning to the boys, pleading silently with his eyes for them to say she was an American, Jamaican, anything but his daughter.

'Georgia James!' The boy looked pityingly at him, as if unable to believe he didn't already know.

The evening sun seemed to fade instantly, a cold wind whipped around him. He felt sick, giddy and threatened.

Blindly he made his way back across the road. He

heard a car horn blast out at him and he stumbled on the kerb.

That poster drew him every morning as he walked home. He had to go and look at it, even though he knew her face would prevent him from sleeping when he got back to his flat. He would buy a bottle, drink it just to fall asleep, then he'd buy another on his way to work.

He risked getting the sack on Monday evening, slipping out leaving the warehouse unattended, just to see her.

The show finished at eleven, he waited in a shop doorway just across the road from the town hall and watched the hordes of young people leaving.

Young girls in pretty summer dresses, kiss curls lacquered to their cheeks, hair backcombed up to impossible heights, stiletto heels tapping out like casta-nets on the warm summer night. Boys in jeans, some in smart suits and winklepickers, others jumping astride their motor scooters, revving them up like some sort of odd mating dance.

They were in no hurry to go home. Some ran across the street to a coffee bar. Others bought chips and stood outside eating them from the newspaper, still more wandered past him hand in hand. He could see pleasure in their faces, a world he couldn't enter. He felt old, tired and bitter.

Most of the crowd had gone now. About thirty or forty teenagers left standing outside the stage door, away from the main entrances now shut up.

A cheer alerted him. First he saw a tall, dark man come out. The waiting girls flocked round him, pressing in on all sides.

Behind them he saw Georgia. She was standing on the steps of the stage entrance wearing a white summer dress, her hair caught up with a ribbon, a few stray curls on her forehead. With the light behind her she was silhouetted in the doorway, slim and graceful.

He had hoped it wouldn't be her. A mistaken identity, just another dark girl with the same name. But as soon as her voice floated across the street he knew it was her.

'Did you enjoy the show?' she asked the waiting kids. 'Thank you for coming.' Her voice sounded as if she were whispering in his ear. He could remember a time when she sat on his lap while Celia played the piano. He could feel her soft arms round his neck, breath sweet on his cheeks.

He moved closer, crossing the road, standing beside a parked van to conceal himself.

Another young man joined them. This one blond and frail looking. The two men stood either side of Georgia as if protecting her.

Brian waited until the last piece of equipment was brought out, moving back over the road so he wouldn't be spotted. He heard their laughter, saw the familiar way they treated Georgia and as he watched so the pain in his heart seemed to get stronger.

The next day he read a review in the local paper.

'Samson's strength is Georgia,' he read, with eyes welling up with tears of impotence. 'Catford Town Hall rang to her beautiful voice capturing the enthusiastic audience with her beauty and her power. Watch this little girl, she's going all the way.'

That was the start of the collection. One tiny review cut out and pinned to the wall. But it was soon to be added to.

He began to drink heavily, his lady friend disappeared. The flat grew dirty again. His shirts needed washing. The West Indians in the houses at the back of him seemed to play their drums even louder.

When he read about the fire and the two boys who died he was glad. The band's name stopped appearing in music papers and he lost interest in buying them. The need for drink seemed to lessen and as his savings had almost gone he seriously considered moving somewhere smaller, nearer his job.

He got into a new routine at work. First the paper work, then a quick patrol round the warehouse checking doors, then back into the office for a cup of coffee to listen to Book at Bedtime on the radio.

It was cold and raining that night after the story, and he was loathe to leave the warm office for another check. He remembered twiddling the dial and finding music, settling down with his paper to do the crossword.

Violins filled the office with a melancholy sound that fitted the rain and his mood perfectly. He turned up the radio, sat back and listened.

As guitars came in, he frowned, realizing it was a pop song after all.

'There's no time, baby.'

He knew it was her the moment that voice filled the office. His hand reached out to switch off the set but somehow he couldn't do it.

Slumped over the old desk, banging his forehead with rage, hating her voice, yet loving it too. She was taunting him with failure. Sneering at him over the radio. He would never be free of her.

He could see her before him as she had been that night of her birthday. The face upturned to receive Peter's kiss, pressing herself against him. She'd shut her father out then, she hadn't wanted him to join the party and later she'd called him pathetic.

Nightmare flashes. Prickling net in his hands, strangely mixed with satiny skin. Celia showing him a small back covered with weals from a cane. Georgia standing over him with that knife and blood spurting out. More blood, this time on Celia's face and all the time Georgia was telling the world that it was too late for her father.

He didn't remember the police picking him up by Lewisham Hospital where he was lying in a gutter. Neither did he remember not locking up the warehouse. All he could remember was that song and the melody that pounded into his head long after he lay vomiting in a police cell.

After that everything became hazy. The police kept coming, questions and more questions. His landlord shouting abuse at him, some trouble with a woman downstairs. They said he'd conspired with the gang who broke in and stole thousands of pounds worth of goods. A man like him kept in Brixton prison with common criminals!

It made no difference that he was released after a few days and the case against him was quashed, the damage was done. Turned out of his flat, his mother's desk and Persian carpet taken for back rent.

A hostel for the homeless, sleeping in a cubicle alongside filthy vagrants, a spell in hospital with pneumonia and finally someone pushed him into this room in Ladbroke Grove.

National Assistance kept him now, while the girl who was responsible for his sickness made millions.

He had just cheap sherry to keep him warm while she swanned about in limousines wrapped in furs.

There was no getting away from her success. She flew in and out of England like a film star. Every word she uttered, every place she visited was recorded. Pictures of her in every shop, newspaper and magazine. Game shows on television, interviews on the radio. He knew her escorts, her clothes, beauty hints and every appearance she made. He logged it down in a little book, and when she attended a film première in the West End he waited in the shadows to see her.

She brushed past so close to him he smelt her

perfume and almost touched her hair. It was in that crowd that his glasses got broken, crushed underfoot, just the way she had crushed him.

How clever she was at skirting round the truth about her earlier life. Never at any time did she speak about her childhood. Wasn't that proof enough for anyone that she had done something shameful?

Did she know or care that her father watched her on television through the window of an electrical shop? Shivering and hungry, unable to hear her voice, only watch her dance and her lips move?

But of all the articles he read about her there was one that played on his mind above all the others.

She was posing on a white settee, bare arms wrapped round her knees, a short red dress revealing her brown thighs, hair tumbling down over her back, so shiny it looked like wet tar.

'I love simple things,' she told her interviewer. 'Bright primary colours and lots of white paint. Huge vases of fresh flowers and the sun streaming in through the windows.'

Brian thought about his old home. Walking in after a day at work to find the French windows open, the perfume of roses filling the room. Georgia on her swing, wrapped in a private world. Tea laid in the kitchen, flowers in the hall. Celia's voice calling out.

'Come in now darling, Daddy's home.'

The sun never came in his windows. The paint in his room was brown and cracked and it had never seen a vase of flowers.

He'd found her flat in Chelsea. It took him all day to walk there. A three-sided block set around a central garden. The sort of plush place aristocrats kept for the Season. He looked at the polished doors, the gleaming brass and the uniformed porter, and knew he would never get inside. He was of less importance than the youngsters who gathered there, looking up at the

481

gleaming windows, trying to guess which one of the flats was hers.

He had a pain in his stomach which wouldn't go away and sometimes when he vomited he brought up blood. Without his glasses he couldn't see clearly. His legs ached just on the walk to the post office. But if John Adams sold that story, all his troubles would be over.

Georgia would be finished.

Chapter 21

'Have you heard this man play, Max?' Georgia stood in the office, a musical paper in her hands.

'Who?' Max barely looked up. 'Do you think I've got time to listen to every musician in England?'

'Don't be grumpy with me,' she grinned, perching on the edge of his desk and waving the paper under his nose. 'Sam Cameron, the saxophone player from the States. Ronnie Scott has extended his contract, he's played to packed houses nightly. Since when didn't you take an interest in something like that?'

'Since you got back from the States and had stupid ideas about making a middle of the road album,' he snapped. 'Sometimes I don't think you've got a brain. Who in their right mind wants to buy a record full of old songs?'

'Millions of people,' she retorted. 'A far greater number than the ones who want pop.'

Georgia was tired. The long tours, the one night stands, the travelling had become impossible. Her world was up there on the stage or in a recording studio. No time for friendships or even love affairs. She had been to so many countries, yet not one had she seen in any depth. She had so much money she could buy anything, yet the simple pleasure of a day's shopping, lunch in an ordinary pub or even a night in watching the television was denied her.

At twenty-one she'd seen everything, done everything. Yet nothing. Was she going to spend all her youth pursuing nothing more than money? When did she last meet a real human being to laugh and chat with?

Bodyguards to escort her everywhere, hairdressers fussing around her, fittings for fabulous dresses she wore once then put aside. Journalists hanging on her every word. People behaved as they thought she wanted them to. They fawned on her, smothered her. Every unguarded word was recorded. How much longer could she stand it? Wasn't that why so many famous people ended up with drug and drink problems?

Her affair with Rod had changed things in so many ways. For a time it seemed impossible to stay in the same room as him. She knew he wanted her, she ached for him. But he'd been right, there was no future in it. Rod loved the high life, as soon as a gig was over he was out looking for more excitement. Her idea of a good night was a quiet dinner with people she could talk to. Compromise would have done no good, both of them would be unhappy half of the time.

But that closeness in Spain had left her hungry. How could she find that again when she was always on the move? Who could she trust enough, when half the men she met were only interested in her fortune, name and body?

She had a beautiful flat she rarely saw, a red Mercedes she hardly ever drove. Was she going to spend her life hoping for love, but never finding the time for that either?

There was a way out. To make beautiful albums for a different market. Her income would be assured, but by dropping out of the mainstream of pop she could gain time for herself. But of course Max would have none of that.

Rod and the rest of the band were restless. They wanted more now than being her backing group. She knew they were privately working on new material, an image for a band entirely different. Something that was theirs and theirs alone.

The Beatles and the Rolling Stones had paved the way. Samson wanted to do something equally innovative. She knew each one of them had experimented with drugs and it had altered their conception of sounds. They had moved in a different direction to her and they had a right to their freedom now.

The last thing Georgia wanted was to allow Max to push forward a new backing band, or even worse start booking her into cabaret work. She wanted to hold the reins herself, pick the musicians to go forward with. People she liked and trusted.

Listening to jazz in the States had started something. She had heard old classic songs revitalized and now she was burning to sing things she loved.

'Come with me tonight to Ronnie Scott's?' She bent over Max and tickled his neck playfully. 'Don't be a grouch. Aren't I still your golden goose?'

Max leaned back in his chair and smiled despite himself.

He'd met his match with this girl. However he tried he couldn't outmanoeuvre her. She took risks, she gambled on her fans' loyalty, she managed to get what she wanted every time.

Max didn't need a crystal ball to see what she was up to. She was dredging up talent to join her on this hare-brained scheme. She would do what she always did. Get something together and astound the men at Decca. But if she got her way in this, where would he stand?

It wasn't just the money now. He had enough. The one thing he couldn't face was Georgia going out of his life for good. She thought he didn't understand her, but he did. She wanted a quieter life. She needed a man to share it with. Before long someone would emerge from the woodwork and carry her off. That man might relegate him to the role of an old uncle. And that he couldn't bear.

Just the way she sat on the desk gave him goose-bumps of pleasure. The tiny mini skirt, the tight white boots and the skinny sweater might have been designed by Mary Quant but it would be Georgia who millions of young girls would copy slavishly. He had taken this girl, polished her up and promoted her. Now she was the hub of the wheel, music, fashion, all evolved round her. With her beside him Max was at the centre of the world and that's where he wanted to stay.

'Okay,' he said wearily. 'I'll go with you. But because it's the only way I can have you to myself for a night.'

It was a wicked thing to think, but sometimes he almost wished something would bring her crashing down. He would trade his fortune, his huge house and his fleet of cars just to have her dependent on him again. Sometimes he had fantasies of being her only protector. Perhaps then she'd realize how much he loved her.

Miriam and he were washed up now. The once unthinkable divorce had gone through. She'd found new happiness with a man she met in Athens. It didn't matter that there were countless young, pretty girls who adored him. He still wanted Georgia.

'Don't block me about this album?' Georgia wheedled. 'I want your support. I can't go on with this frantic pace and you know it.'

'Let's go and hear the man and then we'll see,' Max grinned. 'I suppose I should be grateful to think you care enough to want me with you.'

'There'll always be a place in my life for you,' she said softly. 'I hate you sometimes, maybe even love you a bit. But we've been together too long to part now.'

Max was important to Georgia. She took his blustering ways, his arrogance and even his bullying in her stride. He had been with her in the bad patches, and at the heights. Even that night in Kensington had its purpose, though she hadn't realized it until later. She had learned to stand up for herself, taken a little of his indestructible pride and cunning. If he'd been softer she wouldn't have all she had now. Learning to outwit him was the greatest lesson he'd given her. She knew too that it wasn't pure greed that motivated him any longer. Maybe both of them were unsure of what they were to one another, but it was something special.

Ronnie Scott's was packed, but still Max got them a table right down by the stage. Georgia wore just a plain black crêpe trouser suit, hoping no one would recognize her.

'I used to come here all the time,' Max said as he ordered them a drink. 'I don't know why I stopped coming, I've had more good times in here than I can count.'

He too was hoping Georgia could remain incognito. Jazz fans were in a world of their own and so far no one had even looked their way. Ronnie Scott maintained his distance from popular music and even though this place saw more stars in a month than anywhere else, he rarely publicised it. He hoped they would dance later, share supper or a drink. But he could never be sure of anything with this girl.

Georgia looked older tonight, her hair slicked back into a bun like a ballerina. She had lines under her eyes he hadn't noticed before and she was pale. She did need a holiday, that much was obvious, maybe if he was gentle with her, she could be persuaded to go somewhere warm with him.

How was it that not a breath of scandal had come out about her? What sort of iron will did she have to avoid dangerous relationships? The men who escorted her to parties, shows and theatre rarely got a second chance.

She was never present when the lads got out of hand. Drink, drugs and sex didn't seem to figure in her life. Or was she just careful about it like him?

There had been something between her and Rod once in Spain, but that was over before Max heard about it. He'd seen a new maturity in Rod, a more caring attitude to women, yet a touch of pain in those slanty eyes. Thank God it had fizzled out, those two together would be a recipe for disaster.

Why did he always have this feeling there was some deep well in her he hadn't managed to reach? Maybe that was the only thing needed to bring her to him?

'They're coming on!' Georgia tapped his hand. 'I can't see the saxophone player though.'

Five men in evening suits came on to the stage. Each one of them was over fifty. The man with the clarinet looked nearer seventy, he walked stiffly as if his leg hurt.

The drummer alone was black, he flashed a wide grin and played a roll on his drums, leading the quintet into a spirited version of a Glenn Miller number.

The trombone was good, the old clarinetist brilliant. The grey-haired man on the double bass was bent over his instrument as if unaware he was playing in public and the pianist one of the best she'd heard. Yet there was no real sparkle, or did she know too little of jazz to understand it?

Everyone in the audience seemed delighted. Feet were tapping, fingers rapping on tables.

As the first number ended, Georgia sensed a charge of electricity. The pianist began an introduction to a slower number, melodic and almost haunting.

From somewhere behind the stage Georgia heard the first saxophone notes, and a shudder of delight went down her spine. Rich, fruity tenor sounds, like nothing she'd heard before. She sat up, peering at the dimly lit stage. It was getting louder and she held her breath while first the saxophone appeared behind a curtain, a spotlight focusing on it.

It was a surprise to see the man playing wasn't a big man. Tall yes, but slender. His lips, hands and his entire body seemed to be playing the instrument. Never before had she seen anyone so at one with a saxophone.

She could feel herself melting inside, almost like an orgasm. His notes were so pure and delicious she barely heard or saw anyone else on the stage. Something primeval was swelling in her, her eyes filled with tears. She wanted to catch every last note and engrave it on her heart forever.

Max felt her excitement. He too was enthralled as was everyone in the audience. But Georgia looked as if she had gone off to another planet.

Her eyes that only minutes earlier had looked tired, now sparkled furiously. Her lips were parted, a glimpse of white teeth and pink tongue peeping out. She was flushed, tears rolling unnoticed down her cheeks.

Max looked back at the man. He was golden brown, hair cropped closely to his head, eyes tightly shut, dark lashes curling on his cheeks. Expanded by air his chest seemed huge, yet his hips were slim and his hands long and fine like a surgeon's. His face was too contorted by playing for him to be handsome, yet Max knew he would be.

Was her reaction purely the music, or was this something physical?

Throughout the entire set, Max tried to sit back and watch objectively. This man was undeniably the greatest saxophone player he'd ever heard. His solo sent tremors down his spine, notes that almost shimmered under the spotlights, drifting off with the cigarette smoke, filling a hunger in the belly.

It was impossible to look away. Even when he rested while others played their solos, his face drew the eye.

High cheek-bones, the straight proud nose and those

full yet delicate lips. Yet there was humour in that handsome face, the way he listened, his head on one side, picking up each note and smiling when it pleased him.

Georgia's face fell as the set ended. Sam Cameron merely nodded at the audience and hurried off with the other men without even a backward glance.

The audience was going wild. Clapping, banging glasses and shouting. Middle-class people behaving like a crowd of teenagers at a pop concert.

'I've got to make a recording with him,' was all she said, eyes as big as saucers. 'Can you arrange for me to speak to him?'

Max ordered another drink to cover his confusion. On the one hand this man and her together could be dynamite. On the other he might just lose her. If he refused to help she would do it anyway. If he was enthusiastic he would be party to whatever came of it.

One thing was clear by her expression, she liked everything about this man. They even looked like a couple, something Max had never thought about anyone before.

'I'll ring here tomorrow,' Max hedged his bets. 'From what I understand he's going home soon. So don't bank on anything.'

Max left her for a moment to talk to someone he'd spotted across the club. Georgia took a gulp of her drink and looked at the curtain behind the stage. She had seen Max's shifty look and she had so much work piled up she had no idea when she'd find time to come here again. She had to act now.

She glanced round quickly. Everyone was engrossed in talking and drinking. She walked across the front of the stage, jumped up quickly in the corner and found her way through the curtain.

Stifling a giggle she found three steps down the back

of the stage. She felt like a groupie. She had no idea of the layout in this club, but she'd find him.

'You aren't allowed back here.' A little man in overalls came out of a door and blocked her way.

'I am,' she smiled sweetly. 'I'm Georgia James and I've come to see Sam Cameron. Could you point out the dressing room?'

He faltered for a moment, but turned to one side, pointing further down the corridor. It was painted that green gloss paint they had backstage everywhere, chipped and stained, bare boards underfoot.

'In there,' he said. 'I didn't see you if anyone asks.'

She could hear a low rumble of male voices. The sound of beer pouring into a glass. She tapped on the door and waited.

The elderly clarinetist opened it. He had a pint in one hand and he peered at her short sightedly.

'Could I speak to Sam, please?' she said, feeling foolish now. Behind him she could see only legs stretched out, all the same in dark trousers and black shoes.

'It's someone for you Sam.' He turned his head back to the room and she saw the double bass player's grey head come into view. His eyes widened. He ducked back and she heard a whisper. All at once one of the pairs of legs moved.

He was taller than he looked on stage. Well over six foot, his shoulders broader without his jacket. Muscles strained his badly-pressed shirt, a button was missing and his bow tie was slightly crooked.

'I'm sorry to barge in like this,' she said nervously as she stood outside the door. 'But I had to speak to you.'

He was looking at her intently. Studying her as closely as she'd studied him earlier.

'I'm Georgia,' she said, dropping her eyes from his dark brown ones.

'I know,' he said. 'What brings you here?'

He was smiling, almost as if she was an old friend he expected. Yet she sensed shock too.

'Did you know I was out there?' She was stumped for how to approach the subject, she felt odd. Like a girl on her first date.

'No,' he said. 'But I'm glad you were.'

'Why's that?'

'Because I played good tonight. I'd have hated you to hear a bad set.'

'You were brilliant,' the words came out even before she could think what she was going to say. 'I want you to do a recording with me. I was afraid if I didn't barge in you'd leave and I wouldn't get to speak to you.' She stopped short, aware how silly she must sound to a seasoned professional like him. She could feel sweat on her forehead, she was blushing. 'I mean, that is if you'd like to.'

He didn't reply for a moment. He leaned against the door post looking down at her.

'Ma'am, I can't think of anything better,' he said. 'Just say the word and I'll be there.'

'Are you laughing at me?' She could see his mouth twitching and from the silence behind the door she knew the other men were listening. Maybe her goose-bumps were caused only by that delicious Southern accent, or was it those brown velvet eyes?

'Not laughing,' he said, his mouth breaking into a wide grin. 'Just thinking maybe there is a God up there somewhere.'

Chapter 22

Sam stood in the doorway with Georgia's address and phone number in his hand. He wanted to laugh and cry all at once.

'Well, you've got it made,' Dave the bass player came up behind him, playfully thumping him on the back. 'A year from now and you could be as big a star as her.'

Sam couldn't reply. What could any man say when he saw a dream about to come true?

Everything had been topsy-turvy since his first day in England. First grief to find Katy was dead. Guilt that a child was out there somewhere, who could be theirs. Then the unexpected spotlight turning on him, critics raving about him, real success only inches away from his grasp.

In those first few days he had imagined it would be easy to find one war orphan, but that conviction was soon dashed.

The police offered no leads. No birth was recorded at Somerset House. Bureaucracy, despair and blind alleys. Social workers who shrugged their shoulders, the young priest in Whitechapel who suggested it would be better to put it behind him. The public library had revealed more news and photographs of the disaster, but still no report of a child.

Torn between the acclaim he was getting nightly and

days spent in searching. Afraid to tell anyone but Clive what was on his mind.

He tried the local council, who referred him to the children's department and at that point he discovered all war orphans were taken to a home in Billericay in Essex.

No one had bothered to tell him the home had been pulled down years earlier, or that all the old records were destroyed in a fire. Just another pointless journey, looking for someone no one seemed interested in.

The days were ticking by. He had to slot in his search between rehearsals, interviews and keeping himself prominent so he wouldn't be forgotten. His children's future depended on him becoming a lasting success. He couldn't risk failure by turning into a recluse.

Almost at the point of giving up, he went back to the library in Stepney. They had a local history department and one of the librarians, Miss Brice, was actually enthusiastic. 'Let's study the newspapers again,' she suggested. 'We might find something interesting, a name, an event that leads us on to something else.'

Miss Brice reminded Sam of the women who helped out voluntarily during the war, manning tea stalls and organising dances for the troops. Silver grey hair, gold-rimmed spectacles and rosy, clear skin. He liked the way she used the words 'we' and 'us', it gave him the feeling she cared as much as he did.

He got really hung up on those old papers, making his way to the library almost every day, collecting scraps of information that were useless to him, but riveting all the same. He knew what was on at the movies. Men that got sent to prison, weddings, births and deaths, but nothing relating to an orphan. Time was slipping away. It was February already and he was due to leave on March 1st.

*

'Anything?' Miss Brice noticed immediately when something caught his eye.

'Just reading this about a woman who was an Army nurse taking up a position in Stepney,' he said. 'Her life reads like a novel. She had travelled in China, Africa and India, nursing, then in field hospitals during the war.'

'That'ud be Miss Hammick,' Miss Brice smiled. 'She was a regular Tartar. The kids used to shake in their shoes when she came along. She wouldn't stand for any nonsense. She ran the department like a battle campaign.'

'What department was she in then?' Sam looked up. Just the mention of children made him take notice.

'I can't remember what they called it then. She was like the forerunners of today's social workers.' Miss Brice came over to him at the table looking over his shoulder. 'She handled all sorts of things. Truants, child neglect. Unmarried mothers, family disputes. She wasn't noted for her diplomacy, but she got a lot of problems sorted while she was around here.'

'She's not here any longer then?' Sam's spark of hope died as quickly as it was fired.

'No, she retired a few years back. She must be at least seventy. But I think we may find out something more about her because they had a retirement "do" for her.'

'I've got to go now,' Sam said reluctantly. 'I've got someone to see before going on to the club. But I'll be back tomorrow.'

'I'll dig around Sam,' she assured him, making a note of it on a pad. 'This might be a real lead for us.'

When Sam met Clive later he filled him in with this news.

'Don't go building up your hopes Sam,' Clive said over a pint. 'Even if Miss Hammick knows something, this girl's grown up now. She may be married. She might not even be in England. Suppose after all that you find you aren't her dad?'

'I'm sure I am,' Sam growled. He couldn't explain why exactly, but the more he dug into the events of the bombing, the more convinced he became.

'Even if you are, she may have been brought up by white people. The shock of a black six-foot Yank may be too much.'

'No daughter of mine would have those hang-ups,' Sam laughed. 'Her mother had too much guts to create a little dim-wit.'

Whatever he said to Clive, he did have the same worry. How would Jasmine react to finding her mother years from now? And they were the same colour. The person who brought the child up was the one that counted surely? Could any girl find room for a father who left his pregnant girlfriend and never came back to look for her?

He knew Miss Brice had found something just as soon as he got in the library.

'I've got it,' she said, almost jumping with excitement. Her hazel eyes glistened behind her glasses. She twitched at her strand of beads round her neck. 'I was so excited I telephoned her last night.'

'Well ma'am, you are a surprise,' Sam chuckled. 'And they told me you Brits were cold-blooded.'

She was bursting with it, her lined face flushed salmon pink, contrasting vividly with her saxe green sweater.

'She said to send you over there. She did remember a child of the right age. Last night she needed time to think it out.'

'Where is she?' Sam said, ready to run out the door.

'Buckhurst Hill,' she said, picking up the address and telephone number and pushing it into his hands. 'Please phone me and let me know.'

'I'll do better than that,' he leaned forward and kissed her soft cheek. 'If I find her I'll bring her to see you.'

Sam straightened his jacket and rubbed his shoes on his trouser legs before pushing open the gate. It had seemed an interminable journey on the tube and he wished he had smarter clothes to see this Tartar.

It was a small bungalow, painted white with green shutters, set in a lawned garden. Everything was bare now, but it was the sort of garden he knew would be beautiful in summer. The door opened before he even reached it.

'Mr Cameron I presume?' she said.

Sam wanted to laugh. She was the type of lady he had seen in British films. Snooty, tall, grey hair cut very short and a masculine set to her features. Her body was encased in men's cord trousers, with a thick navy sweater, through the thick material he knew it was large and muscular rather than fat. Even at seventy she looked formidable.

'Pleased to meet you, ma'am,' Sam held out his hand. 'Thank you for seeing me.'

He couldn't make out what she was thinking. A woman of her age and background probably loathed black men, especially ones who impregnated young girls and left them alone to get killed.

'Come in,' she said crisply. 'Wipe your feet.'

Sam followed her down the passage. She walked straight-backed, head held high. She turned into a room and he followed.

It was a beautiful room. Big French windows looked on to the garden. A green thick carpet which seemed to make it harder to see where the garden began or ended. A stone fireplace with a roaring log fire and fat comfortable-looking chairs. He could see no television or even radio. Just hundreds of books on shelves and an artist's easel standing by the window.

'Do sit down,' she said, making a gesture to a chair. 'Last night when Miss Brice telephoned me I couldn't remember much. But I've thought it over and a little more has come back to me.'

'Where is she?' Sam leaned forward in his chair.

'I couldn't say now,' she said haughtily. 'I suggest you just listen to me and I'll tell you all I know.'

The way she barked out her orders reminded Sam of a woman he once worked for in New Orleans. She was German with an English husband, but she never let him get a word in edgewise either.

'I did take a child away from foster parents. It was in 1946 and the child was around twenty months. She had been in Billericay war orphans home, and she was coloured.'

'What was her name?'

'I can't recall her Christian name, though I do remember it was the only thing which seemed to really belong to her. She took the surname Barlow from the people who fostered her. Whether she was abandoned or the same child as was found in Hughes Mansions I can't say for certain. I wasn't working in England during the war.'

Sam frowned. Miss Hammick read his mind.

'It's no good you looking like that,' she said tersely. 'England and particularly the East End took a frightful hammering during the war. I know you Americans think you did it all, but I know better. People were buried hurriedly, records weren't kept that well. We had to conceal disasters to keep up morale.'

Sam nodded. 'I was here ma'am, I do understand, it's just painful to think a baby gets stuck in a home without anyone knowing how or why.'

'It wouldn't have happened if I'd been there then,' she said with more than a hint of pride.

'You say you took her from foster parents? To where

and why?' Was she too old to remember clearly? Was this another wild goose chase?

'She was too much of a handful for them,' Miss Hammick sniffed disdainfully. 'I can vouch for that in the one day I had her in my car. She never stopped moving.'

'What did she look like?'

Again that strange haughty look.

'Brown of course. With black curly hair. Half-caste I'd say,' she withered him with one glance. 'Anyway, I had an awful job placing her. No one knew anything about the child. Everywhere was full. I ended up at St Joseph's in Grove Park.'

'Where's that?'

'South London,' Miss Hammick sniffed again. 'Unfortunately that home has closed since. Not before time too as I believe, most of the nuns were totally unsuitable for child care.'

Sam blanched. If a woman like her thought someone was unsuitable they must have been fiends. This woman showed no emotion at all. Not even real curiosity.

'How?' he had to ask.

'Children were beaten. I dare say some of them merited it. Appalling diet, little medical attention. Had I known that then, of course I wouldn't have taken the child there. You have to understand there weren't the same standards in child care in those days. I made it my business to root out all those types of homes later on.'

'Did you see her again after that day?'

'No, I never did,' Miss Hammick spoke thoughtfully. 'When it was closed I believe most of the girls left were sent to Dr Barnardo's. But of course this child would have been thirteen or fourteen then. She might have been fostered out.'

'Is there any way I could find out?'

'Well,' she paused, as if she knew something but

wasn't sure if she should reveal it. 'I rang Downham's children's department this morning. They told me all the names of girls taken over by Barnardo's, but they had no record of a girl called Barlow.'

'Oh,' Sam's face fell. He wondered how a society could lose a child so easily.

'But I did discover the whereabouts of one of the younger nuns from St Joseph's. In fact she was there the night I handed over the baby. She is with a convent in Hampstead.'

All these names of places were confusing Sam. Was Hampstead in London?

He looked blankly at Miss Hammick.

Nuns were something he feared, he wasn't sure why. Perhaps it had something to do with one who'd beaten him as a boy.

'It's not a closed order or anything like that,' she said briskly. 'An unmarried mothers' home. From what I understand about Sister Mary you'll find her helpful and kind-hearted. It was she alone who kept any kind of standard in St Joseph's. She's still young enough to remember the details I may have forgotten.'

'Can I go there now?' he said.

'No, that wouldn't be prudent,' she said, pursing her lips. 'Write to Sister Mary giving her all the information I have given you. She'll arrange to meet you somewhere away from there.'

She paused again. 'Of course, it's very likely this child isn't yours. There is an even greater possibility that Sister Mary knows nothing of the girl's whereabouts. There were a great many war orphans. I don't know the percentage of coloured ones. But she wasn't the only one. Before you go claiming her, remember this. I'd hate to think I started something that ultimately brought disappointment.'

'I'm very grateful to you ma'am,' Sam said. He knew the interview was terminated. He was even amused that she thought it unseemly for him to go to a home for unmarried mothers. Was she protecting him, or the girls?

'We only call the Queen "Ma'am",' she said, rising to her feet. 'Miss Hammick is sufficient.'

She picked up a piece of paper from her writing desk.

'The address in Hampstead,' she said. 'I'd be pleased to hear the outcome of this quest. For both your sakes I hope it will have a happy ending.'

It was torture waiting for Sister Mary to reply. Should he have suggested a meeting place, told her more about his background? Would he find his child was one who'd been ill-treated?

On Friday morning at nine, he stumbled down the stairs hopefully, as he had each morning for four days as soon as he heard the click of the letterbox.

Endless bills for other tenants, an air letter for the woman below him. But amongst them was a blue one addressed to him. Thin, spidery writing that could only be Sister Mary, he tore it open and pulled out the single sheet.

'Dear Mr Cameron,

Thank you for your letter. I do remember the child you spoke of and I would be happy to meet you to discuss this further.

I usually go to Hampstead village on Saturday afternoons for some shopping. We could meet in the Half Moon tea shop up near the Heath. Shall we say at three thirty? I look forward to meeting you.

Yours sincerely,
Sister Mary

It was a temptation to go out and get roaring drunk, but reason got the better of him. Better to phone Miss

Brice and Clive to share his news, than to risk a hangover when he met the nun.

She was already in the tea shop when he got there. A slight, dark little figure sitting at a table by the window, her eyes downcast in front of her.

'Sister Mary?' he said, feeling too large and clumsy for such a small, quaint place.

Delicate pink and white walls, dainty lace curtains on a brass rail. Snowy white cloths and a glass cabinet at the back of the shop piled high with home-made cakes.

'Yes, Mr Cameron,' she looked up at him and took his outstretched hand. Hers was tiny, her eyes a bright blue set in a pink and white face which matched the decor.

'I imagined you old,' he said awkwardly.

'I am,' she laughed, like a trickle of water over pebbles. 'The Lord saw fit to give me a youthful face. But do sit down, I took the liberty of ordering tea.'

He could see at closer inspection she was well over fifty. Tiny lines round her eyes and mouth and her hands were veined and reddened from rough work. Her starched wimple gave her an ethereal look, enhanced by the lovely eyes.

'I don't know where to begin,' he said. 'Tell me everything you know, quickly.'

Her soft, small mouth curved into a smile. She said nothing, just looked at his face.

'Well?' Sam felt a blush creeping up his neck, but still she studied him.

'Just the way you are in such a hurry makes me sure we have the right child,' she said. 'But describe her mother please.'

Sam hadn't expected this. Once he'd had a photograph of her, but Ellie had destroyed it.

'Small, slender,' he said. 'Dark shiny hair and eyes. Her face was kinda heart-shaped. You know, with one of those little pointy chins. She had long legs and a tiny waist. And a dimple here,' he pointed to his right cheek.

'The chin and the dimple are enough,' she said. 'The rest I can see in your own face.'

A sharp pain stabbed at Sam's heart. He hadn't felt anything like that since losing Katy.

'You mean you believe she is my child?'

'I do indeed, Mr Cameron,' she smiled gravely. 'I was reminded the moment you sprang in the door. What you have told me about Katy fills in the missing part.'

'What was she called?'

'I can't tell you that for a moment,' she said. 'First you must tell me exactly what happened between you, and your circumstances now.'

It was irritating to have to explain when and how they met. Even more distressing to explain their parting and his subsequent reasons for thinking she had changed her mind. He spoke of his marriage, his other two children and all the time Sister Mary listened carefully.

When he'd finished, she poured the tea and passed a plate of hot buttered crumpets.

'Do you know where she is now?'

Sam had this terrible feeling the woman was going to give him a name but nothing more. He hadn't much time left now. How many years did it take to find a missing person?

'I know who she is,' Sister Mary said dropping her eyes from his. 'And it's because of this I feel I have to tread with caution.'

A dozen different things ran through his mind. Was she in trouble? Had she been taken by someone who'd brought her up as their own?

'So bad, huh?' he said, sipping his tea.

'Oh no,' she smiled and shook her head. 'Your

daughter is everything you could want. Beautiful, talented. But let me explain first.'

Sam listened to the story about how this woman called Celia Anderson took her away.

'I have to admit I loved that child more than any other, even if I should feel ashamed for admitting favouritism.' She smiled as if the memory was very dear to her. 'I missed her so much. She was on my mind constantly. But I was happy because she was. Sometime after her fifteenth birthday I went to Blackheath on an errand, and taking a welcome chance to see her again I stopped off at her house.'

'Did you see her?'

'No, but what I did see worried me greatly. I'd never met her foster father until that day. He came to the door wrapped in a blanket. He looked ill, and he had been drinking. I asked for Mrs Anderson and he snapped at me. He said she had left him. I asked about the girl and he flew into a rage. He pulled up his shirt and showed me a fearful scar. He claimed she had stabbed him, then run away.'

Sam just stared. Nothing had prepared him for this.

'I met Mrs Anderson on several occasions,' Sister Mary said gravely. 'She was a fine, honourable woman and I knew if she'd left that house, it was in disgust at something he had done to the girl. I believed at that time they were together somewhere. I tried to find Celia myself later on when I had given the matter more thought. Only then did I discover she'd left her job to search for the girl.'

'Why do you keep calling her the girl?' Sam said gently.

'Because her name is a household word now, and I have to be sure you can handle a reunion properly.'

'I don't know what you mean.'

'Your daughter changed her surname. She has never given anyone details of her background. Her foster father had a knife wound in here,' she touched her stomach. 'I'm not a worldly woman Mr Cameron. Yet I managed to reach an understanding of what happened in that house.'

Sam's eyes shot open wide.

'You mean,' he covered his eyes with his hand.

'Yes,' she said, softly lowering hers. 'I found out from the police that an incident had taken place.' She blushed furiously, her hand reaching for her rosary. 'No charges were ever made because she refused to speak about it. Mr Anderson claimed it was someone else and that she attacked him out of spite when he chastised her. Days later she ran away and was never found.'

'But you have found her?'

'I know who she is now, and follow her life with love, admiration and a sense of guilt that I was party to a child being placed with such a man. I believe she kept quiet in a misplaced sense of honour. Not for him so much, but her mother, and the boyfriend she had at the time.'

'The b – ' Sam stopped short, his early upbringing reminding him he couldn't say words like that in front of a nun. 'I'll swing for him.'

'You'll do no such thing,' she said firmly. 'I want you to be rational about this. Your daughter has kept that secret for six years. All her life she has thought she was an abandoned child. She doesn't even know which of her parents was black. I believe the shock of hearing you are her father could unbalance her. Fathers to her may still mean pain.'

'What would you have me do?' He felt humbled by this little woman's understanding and strength of character.

'You are well placed to get close to her,' she said. 'Try to get closer still and win her confidence. Be there for her, because she is surrounded by people who may not have her best interests at heart. God will guide you then.'

She picked up her rosary and held it between her worn red hands as if gaining strength from it.

'Your daughter is Georgia James.'

For a moment the room spun round. The girl he had seen at the airport. That beautiful mulatto with the voice of an angel.

'Are you absolutely sure of this?' he whispered. Tears were welling up in his eyes, he brushed them away almost angrily.

'Look,' she said gently, pulling out of her habit a worn old photograph of a child with short curly hair.

'This was my Georgia. I loved her as if I was her own mother. Can you tell me I'm mistaken now? She kept her real Christian name too. She dropped the Anderson because of its connections, but she couldn't change the name her mother gave her. She sang to me so often as a little girl. I recognised her voice on the radio, even without a picture of this new star. I knew her from the voice Sam, but her face confirms it.'

Sam took the picture in his hands. She was so thin, yet he could see Katy, and even Jasmine in the face before him.

'Celia Anderson sent this one to me with a Christmas card.' Another picture appeared in her hands. 'She was almost fifteen then.'

Sam gasped. The face before him now was a dark-skinned version of Katy's. Her hair was past her shoulders, the dimple in her cheek, the heart-shaped face, all served to confirm her parentage. But her eyes were his, and the chiselled cheek-bones, like looking in a mirror and seeing his own reflection.

So many times he'd stopped to look at this same face in the record shop windows, idly wondering if she would get back to sit in at Ronnie Scott's before he left to go home. He'd listened to her records on the radio, even written to his kids and suggested they buy her latest album. Now this sweet little nun was telling him it was his daughter!

'She's in the States now,' he whispered. 'I may have to go back. I've only got a contract for six weeks.'

'I checked on you, too,' she smiled. 'You've been getting some startling reviews yourself. Surely you can engineer something to keep you here till she gets back?'

'But how do I get to see her?' he whispered. 'No one gets near her from what I've read.'

'I believe in good coming out of evil,' she said simply. 'Something made you come to England, then you went to check in the East End. Did you plan to do that before you came?'

'No,' he said. 'But – '

She stopped him with a touch on the hand. 'The hand of God,' she said. 'That same hand will bring her to you. Pray for his guidance when it happens.'

Sam had Georgia's address in his hands now. His daughter had come to him, just like Sister Mary had said. If he was a man who truly believed in the power of prayer he would get down on his knees and thank Him. But right now he was going to go back on the stage, get her to come up and do a number or two with the band.

'Georgia,' he hummed the tune as he turned to go back into the dressing room. Sam remembered now, that was the number he'd been playing when he got his first glimpse of Katy back at Lakenheath.

Chapter 23

'Fever, fever when you kiss me, fever when you hold me tight.' Georgia stood under the shower, singing at the top of her lungs, wet corkscrew curls like seaweed over her slender brown back.

Six weeks ago, making the album of her dreams looked impossible, but at last all the problems had been overcome and today they were starting recording.

March's weather had mirrored what was going on around her. Meeting Sam was like an early spring day. So much promise of good things to come, an unfolding of new leaves and flowers, unexpected warmth and sunshine. Max roared in like the March wind, laying waste all her plans. The press was Jack Frost, nipping at tender shoots, threatening to kill everything.

Rows, bad feeling, criticism. Roots put down years earlier, torn up. So much opposition to something she knew was right.

Speedy and Les were heavily into drugs and behaving like a pair of deprived, vacant louts. Norman sniping at his lost opportunities. Max turning into a demented, jealous old woman. Good pianists seemed extinct, even the press turned against her. There were times when she almost backed down.

'If it hadn't been for Sam,' she said to herself as she stepped out of the shower, wrapping herself in a towel. 'You'd have cracked up.'

*

The night in Ronnie Scott's was the beginning. Up until then the album had been a hazy dream. When Sam asked her up to sing with the band in the second half she felt a little presumptuous singing the old Billie Holliday number, 'That ole Devil called Love'. Yet she found her voice had the maturity and Sam's horn inspired her. Even though Max sat glowering at her from the audience, she didn't care.

She expected Sam to play hard to get when he came round to see her the next day. With the rave reviews he was getting, he could afford to take his time and be choosy before committing himself to any band or project. But instead she found him enthusiastic, open and straightforward.

'I'm yours if you want me,' his soft dark eyes glimmered with an excitement she hadn't expected. 'My contract runs out at Scott's next week. As long as you can get my visa fixed up and pay me enough to send home for my kids, then I can stay for as long as it takes.'

Max's attitude was quite the opposite when she called at his office later the same day and outlined her plans.

'How dare you go behind my back and make arrangements? I haven't even agreed to this album,' he snapped. 'You know nothing about that guy and I suppose you rushed in there offering him the moon.'

'Not the moon,' she said simply. 'I just told him I wanted to do a recording with him. The only credentials I care about is how well he plays his horn.'

'Decca won't want to waste their time and money on an album like this,' he roared at her, purple in the face with anger. 'You're digging your own grave Georgia, it's vanity, nothing more. Stick to what you do best.'

'There's nothing more boring than an entertainer who never moves on,' she shouted back at him. 'Making this album doesn't mean I won't make any more soul or rock records. It's just stretching myself, showing a new dimension. I could reach millions of new fans.'

'The press will link your name with his,' Max snarled at her across his desk. 'Do you really think the public will be happy to see their golden girl with a big Yank nigger?'

'You evil bastard,' she hissed back at him. 'Trust you to bring everything down to gutter level. Call anyone a nigger again, and this uppity one will walk out on you.'

Of course he gave her all the rubbish about caring for her, trying to protect her. But she had hardly left his office before he was on the phone to Jack Levy, doing his best to block her.

Then the press got a whiff of what was going on, and before she could talk to the band and outline her plans they had her stitched up.

'Georgia goes it alone,' was the headline. 'No time for Samson now.'

'Georgia is to split with Samson after six years'. 'We've grown apart,' she was quoted as saying. 'I'm in a position now when I don't need or want the responsibility of a full-time band. I want to experiment with other musicians and expand my career.'

'I didn't ever say that,' she raged to Sam. 'They're making me out to be some sort of prima donna throwing off my old friends because I've outgrown them. Where did they get hold of such an idea?'

'Max?' Sam raised one eyebrow. 'He's scared, honey. He wants his little girl right under his wing. But don't take too much notice of the press. The time to worry is when they don't bother to write about you, good or bad.'

In five years there'd been many squabbles, but this time it was serious. The boys closed ranks, refusing to speak to her on the telephone, ignoring even a letter she sent them explaining her plans.

Rod and John came round after Deirdre from the office intervened and admitted she'd overheard Max talking to someone from the press. But Les, Speedy and

Norman chose to use the opportunity to make a final break from her.

There were moments she doubted her own judgement. Was it just inflated ego that made her think she could compete with singers like Aretha Franklin and Ella Fitzgerald? What if Jack Levy, Max and all the other men who had been in the business for years, were right? Suppose it was a flop, what would she do then?

But the doubts were gone now. She had swept away all the opposition to her plans. Fly or fall she was getting her chance, and she had no intention of falling.

Sam finally found a pianist in a pub in Barnes. He was a retired music teacher who played just twice a week in a jazz quartet. Harold Sweeting looked like everyone's favourite uncle. White-haired, rosy-cheeked, a jolly, roly-poly character with all the enthusiasm for music so many of the professional pianists they auditioned, lacked. He had wanted to be a concert pianist in his youth, but his wife and children had come before his own hopes and dreams. Now at sixty-five he had a lifetime of experience to fall back on, yet with a youthful exuberance that gave his playing a touch of magic.

Rod and John were joining the other session musicians too. Rod simply because he was the best drummer, and John begged to come in because he admired Sam's playing.

Perhaps it was fortunate that Speedy, Les and Norman had refused to join her. It left her free to employ strings and a classical guitarist, without feeling guilty.

All they needed now was luck!

Georgia smiled ruefully as she pulled on her jeans and dragged a red sweater over her head.

Jack Levy was cunning. He had covered himself every which way. If she didn't finish recording within a week she would be in breach of contract and he could sue her. Like Max he was running scared, knowing her agreement with Decca ran out in a few months' time. It was thinly disguised blackmail, to make sure she wasn't tempted to sign up with another company offering her a better deal. If the recording was ready in time and then went on to be a smash hit, Jack would merely laugh all the way to the bank. If it failed however, he would blame her for going against his wishes. Before long he would having her back, recording another purely commercial record.

Loyalty in this business was bought. No one really cared about talent. Half the singers who got into the top twenty were virtually manufactured, money changed hands to get them air time. Glossy promoters used hype to get their puppets noticed, and later when these one hit wonders no longer made them money, they were forgotten.

The music world was a giant ants' nest, everyone relying on the Queen to keep it fuelled. Just one slip from favour and she would be devoured by the drones and replaced.

Georgia sat down at her dressing table to dry her hair, pausing to look at a photgraph of her and Samson.

It was her favourite one, taken just a few days before Ian and Alan died in the fire. The photographer James Ogilvy had been an unknown then, a pimply-faced weed who followed stars around looking for the picture that would make his fortune. He'd been after Adam Faith that day, not the support group, but he'd taken this one while he hung around waiting.

They were in a park close to the theatre, fooling around on a climbing frame. Rod sat right at the top, the other boys made a pyramid shape and she was in the middle hanging upside down over a rail, her hair hanging down to the floor. The boys looked funny now with their short hair cuts and wide shouldered jackets, and she looked positively ridiculous in that shapeless shift dress with a long pointed collar. It had taken so long to arrange herself so the dress stayed up over her knees.

'What would you think of the boys now?' she said to Ian. He was laughing, his eyes crinkled up. Rod had just farted very noisily from his perch on the top and John was complaining it scorched his head. All eight of them had been so naïve then, trusting children who would put up with anything for a few words of praise. That day they had no idea Ian and Alan's time with them was nearly at an end, or that fame would follow so soon after.

'Would you stand by and watch Speedy and Les destroy themselves with drugs?' she asked.

She sighed and switched on the dryer. All of them, including herself, had experimented. It was as much part of the scene as groupies and drink. Purple hearts now and then to liven up the trip home or go on to a party. Smoking cannabis in the coach to relieve the boredom. But Speedy and Les had taken it a stage further since that holiday in Spain. Amphetamines to get them going, endless joints to calm them down, then out of their heads on cocaine half the night.

It was almost predictable that Les should be attracted to drugs, he was dim and he didn't have a great deal of personality. But why Speedy? He was the one with a real mind. A brilliant guitarist, handsome, charismatic and caring. What had made him prefer spending days spaced out, screwing every girl who passed his way, and every night in a West End club?

'We've all changed,' she muttered. 'Perhaps the press are right. I am getting ruthless.'

All that fighting to keep them together and now fame and money were changing each one of them. Rod keeping up appearances as a rock star, strutting around town with hair down to his shoulders, in tight red trousers and embroidered jackets, spending more money in a day than he'd once earned in two years.

John had lost his warm humour. Now he was full of astrology, meditation and every other half-chewed-over theory he happened to overhear. Norman had new friends now, society types who invited him for weekends in the country. Away from his old friends he could forget his East End origins, describe himself as a composer. He'd even been taking elocution lessons.

Even Max was unbalanced. The man she had fought with, been in awe of, and perhaps even loved had been tough and unyielding. But he'd been consistent. Now he was riddled with jealousy about Sam, terrified she would dump him. One day depressed, another fanatical. Spiteful then solicitous. He took pills for an ulcer, handfuls of vitamins to allay his advancing years and surrounded himself with dolly birds who were only interested in his money.

Sam alone remained constant. A cool breeze on a hot day. A log fire when it was cold. He could talk about anything and everything. Laugh, make fun of her, but listen when she wanted to talk.

He'd filled her life all right. But not in the grubby way Max thought.

There had been moments that night in Ronnie Scott's that it seemed like the start of a love affair. She found herself gawping at him, and found him staring right back at her.

She loved the way he looked. From the close cropped hair, the golden brown skin and doleful eyes, to his broad shoulders and narrow hips. He was a dream of a man, but not in that way.

As the days ticked past, mutual admiration turned to close friendship. He was unmaterialistic, laughed at show business hype, demanded nothing of her. One morning he could turn up at her flat with a pile of secondhand jazz records for her to listen to. The next he was out in her kitchen cooking them a meal and insisting they went out later to explore some tourist place he hadn't seen. Unpredictable, serious, funny, affectionate and cool in turn. He told her about women he fancied, his ex-wife and his children. His past gradually unfurled in a series of hilarious stories that left her hungry for more.

From G.I. to barman, truck driver to rat-catcher, he painted pictures so vivid she could see them.

'You didn't kill rats? You're making it up,' she laughed as yet another talent came to light.

'I did,' he insisted. 'Used to go round in a little van putting down poison, then round the next day to heave out the carcasses. Sometimes I even did gigs with a few bodies in the back. None of my buddies would get in it with me.'

He made light of everything. He presented his child-hood as if it had all been running barefoot through meadows, fishing and climbing trees. But as she got closer to him, she guessed it had been tough.

He spoke of the racism in the States almost as if it was a joke. No trace of self-pity, or even bitterness, only sympathy for those who were trapped by it.

'We're the lucky ones, honey,' he said. 'Up there on the stage people don't think about our colour, they only hear the music. Maybe by the time our kids are grown every black person will be valued for themselves.'

'But how can you go back to it?' she asked. 'How can you bear Jasmine and Junior to grow up under that shadow?'

'I hope I don't have to,' he said simply. 'I'd like to bring them here. Send them to good schools. England's a cool country.'

She wanted to give him the money to send for them right now. The thought of two children without either parent saddened her. She could see herself back in St Joseph's waiting while people came and looked her over, bypassing her, looking for the small, sweet blonde. It wasn't right for two children to have a father like Sam and not be with him.

But Sam was a proud man. He wanted to bring those children to a real home. But for him there would be no short cuts.

Surrounded as she was by fawning sycophants his earthy opinions counted.

'You don't have to worry about other people,' he said, when she told him her fears about the boys. 'They're grown men now. Be there for them, but don't try to hold them. You do what you know is right, and if for a while they fall off the path, then let them find their way back on to it.'

Two days of recording and everything was coming together. Perhaps the opposition to the album had made everyone stretch themselves just a little more. Sam had written all the brass arrangements and he and Steven the producer were at one in their ideas. Four tracks were already finished, another five well under way.

Session men and the technicians had frightened Georgia once, but now she understood how it all worked there was no need for fear. Each one had their role and Steven put it all together.

Harold was perfect. Every note he played sounded like a love affair. He could improvise like a jazz player, yet his classical background and knowledge of music was unsurpassed. His patience and humour made him a joy to work with.

'Come and sing with me here,' he said, drawing up another stool for Georgia by the piano. 'Just relax and feel the music.'

It was like being ten again, joining Celia at her piano with the sun streaming in through the French windows. His slim long fingers danced over the keys, his white head nodding with the beat, the warmth of his rotund body, his encouraging smiles, dispelled any nervousness. She forgot it was a glassed-in studio way below the street, the pressure of getting it all tied up in a week, or the session men who just wanted to play their bits and go home. Harold with his hand-knitted yellow waistcoat, with red and white cravat and his huge stomach bulging over his thighs was an inspiration.

On the morning of the third day they began at six. The offices upstairs silent, typewriters covered, chairs tucked under desks. The night porter unlocked the doors for them, rubbing his eyes and yawning.

'What a time to start,' he grumbled. 'I don't know how we'll get the studio cleaned. I suppose you'll still be here when I come back on tonight?'

'Sure thing,' Georgia tickled him under the chin. 'Be a darling and put on the coffee?'

Both John and Rod were better for being away from the rest of the band. Rod had dropped his cocky stance, knowing the session men, Sam and Harold had not only years on him, but a far greater knowledge of music. John hadn't mentioned meditation once so far, he was engrossed in the sound, playing far better than she'd ever heard him before. Neither of them had complained about anything, not the early starts, or Steven's continual re-takes.

She had come to trust Stephen Albright implicitly. Ever since that first recording he had produced all her records. Like her he moved with the times, never falling into the trap of making each record sound the same. He was plumper now, so his height seemed less remarkable. A half-chewed pencil, eyes tightly closed behind his thick glasses were still his trademark. But his public school speech was peppered with cockney slang, scruffy clothes replaced by designer chic, he drove a Ferrari and lived in a penthouse in Mayfair, but he was still as uncompromising about music.

Georgia was halfway through 'Summer Time' when

she saw Max's face pressed against the porthole in the studio door.

It was just after nine, and Max never normally surfaced before noon. Just one look at his bloated, angry face and the way he pummelled the glass with his fists, was enough to know something serious had happened.

'Take five, Georgia,' Stephen's voice came through her headphones from the control room. 'Max is in a paddy about something.'

Georgia sighed, taking off her earphones. As she opened the studio door Max lunged forward.

'Max wait. You can't go in there,' Stephen shouted behind him, clutching at Max's arm. He was too slight to create a real barrier between the bull-like man and Georgia, but he did his best.

'What is it?' she asked, her face furrowed with irritation. 'Can't we even get on with this without interruptions?'

'Interruption?' he roared. 'You're finished my girl, never mind interrupted.'

Georgia just stared. She had seen Max fighting mad many a time, but never quite like this. Black stubble on his chin, the shirt under his sweater looked suspiciously like pyjamas and his trousers could have been slept in. But it was his face that really unnerved her.

It was purple. Veins stood out on his forehead like ropes and he had dried spittle round his lips. Eyes blazing like a man about to kill someone.

'Calm down,' she gingerly touched his arm. 'What's the matter?'

She was aware all the technicians were at the door of the control room, and behind her she could feel Rod, John and Sam. The silence from the session musicians proved they were all listening, still in their seats, their music open in front of them on stands.

Max flicked her hand from his arm and pulled a newspaper from his back pocket.

'This,' he almost slapped her with it. 'Why didn't you tell me?'

'Calm down,' she snapped back at him. 'Why didn't I tell you what?'

'That you were wanted for attempted murder!'

Ever since her first publicity she had half expected someone to confront her with her past. So many times she had intended to take Max aside to prepare him. But even in her worst nightmares she hadn't anticipated this.

The paper felt almost hot in her hands. The face of the man she had learned to forget, staring up at her.

The studio lights seemed to burn her, the walls buckled and moved.

'Tell me it isn't true?' Max's plea seemed to come from a long way off. 'It's some sort of sick joke? It's made up?'

There was a roaring sound in her ears. She could feel the handle of the knife in her hand, see blood dripping from the blade and he was lying at her feet, fingers clutching at the wound in his white belly.

Sam instinctively knew what was in the paper, even before he got a glimpse of the headline.

Elbowing his way through the crowd in the doorway, he saw the colour drain from her face. She swayed, then crumpled to the floor.

The air was charged with emotion. Max's anger. Rod and John's shock. Stephen's eyes behind his thick glasses blinking with astonishment. The curiosity of the session men and technicians.

'Out the way,' Sam reached Georgia in two strides. He knelt down beside her, stroking back her hair from her face. 'Get some water, damn it,' he yelled at Max.

It was Rod who ran for the water. Stephen found some smelling salts and rushed over with them. The rest of the men stood in a semi-circle around them, too shocked to speak.

'All right honey,' Sam crooned softly, as he saw her eyes flicker open. 'I'm with you, baby.' He cradled her head in his arm, holding the glass to her lips.

'I knew there was something about you,' Max's voice penetrated the hushed room. 'Why the fuck didn't you tell me?'

'If you don't shut your mouth I'll shut it permanently,' Sam glowered up at Max. 'Are you so God damned dense you can't see the girl's in shock? Stop thinking about yourself and think of her.'

He rose, lifting Georgia in his arms as if she weighed nothing more than a few pounds.

'Take me home Sam,' Georgia said weakly. 'I'll tell you everything then.'

'It's me you should be telling,' Max barked at her. 'I've looked after you all these years, then you shut me out in favour of him.'

'You bastard!' Sam's lips curled back showing his teeth. 'Call yourself a human being? I've known roaches with more sensitivity than you.'

It was then Sam knew Max was in love with Georgia. It wafted out of him, mixed with jealousy, suspicion and fear.

'You can come with us,' Sam shot a warning glance at Max, holding Georgia tightly to his chest. 'But anymore outbursts and I'll wring your neck.'

It was raining hard. Still holding Georgia in his arms, Sam made a dash for Max's white Rolls Royce parked outside. He lay her on the back seat, tucking a travel rug round her. A crowd of people making their way to work, paused to watch under umbrellas, mouths gaping with surprise.

'Get going,' Sam leapt into the front seat beside Max.

The traffic was jammed solid on Oxford Street. Max's face was grim, he held the steering wheel so tightly his knuckles shone white.

For ten minutes no one spoke.

Georgia broke the silence first.

'Can I read what they've said about me?' Her hand came snaking between the front seats to reach for the paper.

Sam turned in his seat slightly to watch her. She knelt on the car floor, the paper spread out on the seat in front of her. She looked no older than sixteen in her tight little black mini-dress and long boots, hair falling over her face.

The headline read, 'Georgia wanted for attempted murder.'

Sam watched as she read the front page, shaking her head as though in disbelief, then turned the page, shuddering as she saw more pictures.

'Bad, huh?' Sam said as she sat back on the seat and silently handed him the paper. Tears were welling in her eyes, threatening to spill over and trickle down those pale, drawn cheeks.

'The worst,' she whispered, her full lips quivering. 'He's been watching me all this time.'

Sam didn't trust himself to speak. He had to read it. Pretend he knew less than Max. But inside he wanted to hold her, tell her this man was never her father. That he was the man who counted and he would take care of all this.

'Mr Brian Anderson, a sick old man living in slum-like conditions reveals that the famous singer Georgia James is none other than the foster child who tried to stab him to death several years ago.

'Yesterday in the offices of the *Mirror*, Anderson related a story that makes a lie of everything the public believes of Georgia.

'Brian Anderson and his wife Celia took Georgia from an orphanage when she was nine, to live in their beautiful home in Blackheath. They showered her with love, gave her singing and dancing lessons, bought her all the toys and clothes she'd never had.

'The Andersons were liberal people. On her fifteenth

521

birthday they allowed her to have a teenage party up in her old playroom and it was only when it got out of hand that Mr Anderson went upstairs to intervene.

'He found his daughter in the throes of making love and indications that the party was nothing more than an excuse for wild, promiscuous behaviour. In his anger Mr Anderson, like any irate father, ordered her friends out the house.

'Another girl would have felt shame. But not Georgia, instead she screamed abuse, told him she could do what she liked and then picked up a bread knife left on the party table and stabbed him in the stomach.

'As he lay close to death in hospital and the police were waiting for him to recover consciousness, Georgia ran away rather than face prosecution. She left no apology for the couple who had given her everything, instead she took all the money left in the house, and disappeared without trace. Every effort of the police to find her was unsuccessful. The Andersons spent all their savings trying to trace her which culminated in Celia having a breakdown, and Brian losing his job as a bank manager.

'While her fans have been listening to her songs of love and crediting her with sweetness, purity and sincerity, her father's life is in ruins. While she amasses great fortunes, he lives in squalor in Ladbroke Grove. Celia's heart was broken, her career and home lost and finally the long, happy marriage was over too.'

'"I still love her, even after everything she put us through," Brian Anderson wept as he told his story. "I've collected every press clipping of her, every photograph. I always believed one day she would come back to me and say she was sorry."

'Anderson's plight is a sad one. He is trapped in a vicious circle of sickness, poverty and appalling housing. He carries a childhood picture of her in his pocket.

He watches her television appearances through a shop window as he cannot afford a tv of his own.'

There were four photographs. Georgia sitting between her foster parents at a Christmas dinner. One of her in a swimsuit taken on holiday. The house in Blackheath, and finally one of the man as he was now, old, broken and sick, standing in front of a dilapidated house.

Sam felt sick as he read it. It had a ring of truth about it. If he hadn't heard Sister Mary's story and got so close to Georgia in the past weeks, he might even have believed it himself. But he wasn't concerned now with what the public thought, only what it would do to Georgia. A snakepit she would have to go back into, just to clear herself.

The car stopped at traffic lights. Across the road Sam saw a newspaper stand.

'Queen of Pop, wanted for attempted murder,' he read, and once again felt faint.

'My God,' Max exploded once again as he too saw it. His thick, bull neck flushed purple with rage. He turned his head to Georgia, eyes blazing with renewed anger. 'I take you on, I feed you, train you and you think so little of me you don't let on about this.'

'And you think so little of Georgia you prefer to believe this trash?' Sam snapped at Max with barely disguised disgust. 'I haven't known her as long as you have, but I recognize this for what it is.'

'I don't want to believe it,' Max wiped his hand across his eyes. 'But when that plopped down on my mat this morning, I thought the world had ended.'

The Thames was black. Even the Albert Bridge looked forlorn. Across the river Battersea power station's four chimneys pumped out sulphurous fumes.

'Oh shit,' Max exploded again as he drew close to Georgia's apartment block. 'Look at that lot!'

The pavements and the courtyard were blocked with

an army of people. Reporters and photographers swarmed in groups despite the rain. Men in raincoats, women in high-heels and smart suits huddled under umbrellas. A television van was parked by the entrance, the doors open and men jumping out with film equipment. Older people paused to watch from the river side of the street. Youngsters took up vantage points on walls and railings.

'We can't go in,' Max said. 'Let's go to a hotel?'

'No,' Sam put a restraining hand on the steering wheel. 'We can't run from this. Besides, Georgia needs to be in her own home. We'll just barge on through them.'

As Max stopped in the middle of the road to make a right turn, so the crowd surged forward.

'Keep down,' Sam urged Georgia. 'Put the rug over you.'

But the white Rolls was too obvious. People were running towards them, regardless of traffic.

'Barge your way in,' Sam snapped. 'Go on!'

Slowly the car inched forward, faces lunged at the windows, hands trying the doors. Max's breath was rasping as if he was having a seizure, but still he drove on, forcing the people to step aside.

Sam leapt out like a panther. He flung open the back door and reached for Georgia.

A roar went up the moment they saw her. They ran across the gardens, leaping over fences. Like hounds after the fox.

Sam held his ground, tucked his arm firmly around Georgia, brushing away reporters as if they were flies. Striding across the courtyard his face set like a bronze sculpture, almost carrying her. Max came rushing after them, his wheezy breath audible even over the shouting.

'Would you like to comment on the story about you in today's *Mirror*?' A young man with dark hair and an earnest face bounded up, running alongside them, quickly joined by the rest of the pack.

'It's a fairy story told by a very bitter man,' Georgia tried to smile, but her mouth refused to co-operate.

'Is that a denial?' another reporter shouted as cameras flashed all around her.

'Miss James will tell her side of the story when she's ready,' Sam snarled. 'You jackals! Clear off and hassle the sick man who sold you all that shit!'

They had reached the doors of the foyer. The porter moved forward to unlock the door. One reporter tried to get himself in.

'Out!' Sam put one hand on the man's collar and lifted him bodily out of the door.

Inside the block with the door locked behind them it was suddenly quiet. The wide staircase curving up round the old wrought-iron liftshaft, dark green carpet and polished mahogany doors were serenely comforting.

'They'll be climbing the drain pipes by tonight,' Max said as they waited for the lift to come. His eyes darted about as if expecting someone to crawl out of the woodwork. 'They'll dig and dig till you can't fart without them reporting it.'

'I won't let them inside.' Johnson the porter smiled at Georgia reassuringly, blocking her view of the doors so she couldn't see the crowds beyond.

He had read the story around the time the reporters began to arrive and he didn't believe a word of it. Hadn't she always had time for him and his missus? Only last Christmas she'd given him a hamper with fifty pounds tucked in a card. Some of the tenants in this place thought a porter was less than a speck of dirt. He might be close to sixty-five, with little education but he knew a good person when he met one. 'I told them it was all rubbish. I said you was a real kind girl. That man in the picture has been here before. I saw him two or three times outside. He's a loony.'

'Thank you Johnson.' Georgia touched his arm.

Even though Sam could see she was startled by the porter's revelation she was sensitive enough to understand he was offering his support. 'I'll tell you the whole story soon. But until then don't go talking to anyone will you?'

'You can rely on me miss,' he said, patting his green serge uniform as proudly as if he was one of the Horse Guards. 'No one will get beyond that door while I'm here.'

The three of them sat in a semi-circle. The phone lying off the hook. Three empty brandy glasses and a large pottery ashtray full of Sam and Max's cigarette butts lay on the glass coffee-table between them. Georgia, putty-faced with traces of mascara staining her cheeks, her fingers picking at an imaginary thread on her dress.

Sam had to close his eyes as she haltingly whispered the true story. He could feel the agony suppressed for so many years, see the scene played out before him as if he'd been hidden in the playroom.

The rain outside cast an eerie, dirty light on the vivid yellow walls, the white carpet turned grey. Daffodils in tubs on the balcony bowed their heads just as Georgia was doing. An ugliness had crept uninvited into a room once full of bright, clear colour.

Sam's fingers clenched into fists, hatred burning in his gut. She knew all the words now, understood desire and passion and what they could do to men. But what did she know at fifteen?

He wanted to move closer. To take her in his arms and comfort her as she described her first night in Soho and later her abortion. How could any girl survive that without permanent scars?

Max sat on the edge of an armchair, still red-faced, tense and angry. He reminded Sam of his sister's pressure cooker. Shaking, hissing, any moment now he would erupt unless someone could find the right words to cool him off.

'You should have told me before,' he said. 'I could have done something.'

'How could she?' Sam spoke out. 'How do you tell anyone something like that? "Say Max! I was raped when I was fifteen. I stabbed him and ran away. Make it all right for me?"' He half smiled at Max's discomfort. 'Of course you're mad, hurtin' because she didn't confide in you. But I bet there are plenty of secrets in your life you wouldn't tell?'

'If you're so fucking clever tell me what to do now then?' Max's voice was rasping and wheezy, he looked older now, tired and frightened and Sam's slow Southern drawl was making him madder.

'My gut feeling is to go out and find that creep. Beat the shit out of him until he tells the truth,' Sam said.

'We daren't touch him,' Max raised his head in alarm. 'We need legal advice.'

'A man who could rape a child in his care wants lynching,' Sam said quietly. 'You go and get legal advice Max. But if that don't work, don't bank on me sitting quietly.'

Sam wanted to be alone with Georgia. She was holding back the tears. Struggling to keep a grip on herself. He ached to tell her the truth about himself, to take over this situation as a father. But how could he blurt it out now? Another shock might just unhinge her. She was tough, but not indestructible.

Max could hardly bear to look at Sam. Nothing had been the same since he turned up. He had wormed his way closer in six weeks than he had managed in so many years. He still didn't know if they were lovers for sure, but if not what was it between them? If it wasn't for that arrogant shit, Georgia might be clinging to him now.

He was scared too. A dark terror that this was the

end of the road. He knew now why she had frozen on him that night and he also knew she really cared for that boy Peter. How long would it be before he turned up? He wasn't the type to worry about rejection, not when the girl he loved's future was at stake! Georgia might forgive a few shady deals, but she wouldn't overlook tampering with her personal life. A girl who could stick a knife in a rapist could do anything. The best thing he could do was get out of the way, lie low and just hope it would all wash over.

'Even if Georgia tells the press the true story there's gonna be lots of people who'll believe him,' Max wanted Georgia to snap at him, start a row so he could be justified in running out on her. 'People love stories like these. Maybe it would be best to just shrug it off. Just say it's rubbish and refuse to comment further?'

'Go on back to your office,' Sam snarled at him. 'You ain't doin' no good here. She needs time to think it out herself.'

Max stood up. His ulcer was playing him up, his head hurt and he resented Sam's attitude.

'I don't want you two running off half cocked and making things worse!' he said.

'How much worse can it get?' Sam's lip curled back as he looked up at Max. 'Even now they're saying she's just another no-good nigger.'

'Don't Sam,' Georgia put her hand on his arm. 'Max is only being realistic.'

'There's only one way out of this,' Sam said quietly, a touch of venom in his tone. 'To tell the whole truth. There's people out there ready to help if asked.' He was thinking of Sister Mary, but he couldn't say her name now.

'I'm going,' Max moved towards the door. 'I don't know how you expect me to sort this one!'

'You mean you can't see how you can promote rape into a money spinner,' Sam stood up, shoulders back, eyes flashing dangerously. 'Piss off Max. Don't say anything to anyone until Georgia's decided how she's going to handle it.'

Sam expected Max to retaliate, but instead he could smell fear. He noticed the man had turned pale, he seemed to shrink as he buttoned up his overcoat and kept his eyes to the floor.

'Keep the phone off the hook,' he said weakly. 'Put it back on at nine tonight. I'll phone you then.'

'Breakfast,' Sam said once he heard the lift creaking back downstairs with Max in it. 'My mother always said the brain works best on a full stomach.' He patted Georgia's shoulder. 'Eggs and ham?'

By four in the afternoon Sam was getting worried. Georgia was too silent. She had picked at food, drank every cup of coffee he put in front of her. But still she wasn't talking.

She answered his questions. She went and made a bed up for him in one of her spare bedrooms. She took a shower and washed her hair, even filed her nails. But there was no real communication.

He knew she wasn't thinking or planning. She was locked in herself. Buried in the kind of black hole he'd been in himself when he lost Katy. But telling her now that he was her father wouldn't solve anything. She had to open up that black pit where she'd buried Anderson. She had to look at it for what it was and deal with it. Telling her something good would be like putting a lid on a pan of burning fat, it might halt a fire for a while, but soon it would blow up, blasting the lid away. However much he wanted to tell her, now wasn't the time.

'Talk to me?' Sam knelt on the floor in front of her. She sat with her legs curled up under her, her head on a cushion, hair still damp in tight little ringlets. 'You look like Jasmine does when she's hurtin'. It's breaking me up.'

'I'm finished now,' she said softly. 'Overnight I'm a bad smell. Decca won't want to be involved with a scandal. My fans will hate me.'

'No honey,' Sam stroked back her hair. 'For one thing people love drama. Once the dust has settled and they know the truth, they'll admire you. You didn't allow yourself to wallow in self-pity. You didn't even allow the bastard to get away with it. You marked him for life. That's rough justice, but at the end of the day that's what everyone wants.'

'But I made everything far worse,' she said in a small voice. 'I should have told the police and Celia what really happened. Don't you think I was maybe responsible for it all?'

She had dark circles around her eyes as if she hadn't slept for days and her mouth was slack and lifeless.

He could smell guilt. She'd carried it on her shoulders the way she carried everyone's burdens. It was time she put down that burden.

'No honey. You were never responsible. A little girl learns about men through her father. She climbs on his lap naked. She might get in the tub with him. She flirts and fights with him, but no normal man feels that way about his child, however desirable she may become as she grows up. You can feel pity for him because he's a sad little pervert. Anger because he took your youth and innocence. But never guilt. All that is his.'

She cried then. Huge sobs that racked her slim body, soaking the cushion under her head and distorting her face. Sam just sat there on the floor beside her, stroking her hair, waiting for the poison to drain out.

Slowly the sobs subsided to mere hiccups. He passed her a box of tissues and waited again.

'I feel so bad, Sam,' she sat up slightly and he moved next to her, sliding his arm round her. 'I've got everything haven't I? Money, this flat, I can go anywhere, do anything. But why do I feel so empty? What have I really achieved?'

'You've given people yourself. Maybe that's why you feel so drained now. Maybe it's time you said, "Hey, this is me, not a machine. I want to have fun. Be myself."' Sam lifted her face up to his, kissing her swollen eyes. 'You've worried about others too long baby.'

'But everyone close to me gets hurt,' she whispered. 'Celia, Peter, Helen, Ian, Rod, even Max and Brian too. Now there's you. I thought I could help you and your family. Now you are right in the middle of a scandal. We'll never get that recording released, even if they let us finish it. Although my voice is a gift, it can be a curse too. If it wasn't for that I could just be an ordinary girl.'

'We all feel we've hurt people,' Sam felt a lump growing in his throat. 'Being a musician has its own kind of guilt. We follow it because we love it and sometimes it feels downright selfish.

'If I'd trained as a carpenter for as long as I have at playing my horn, I'd have a masterpiece to show the world. We put our heart and soul into each performance. Sometimes we even move people to tears, but it floats up in the sky along with the cigarette smoke and it's gone.

'An artist has the finished canvas, the writer a manuscript, a carpenter the thing he has built. But your voice and my horn, they warm people for a moment and then it's gone.'

'You mean it's worthless?' she turned a shocked face up to Sam.

'Oh, no honey, not worthless. The musicians, the artists, the dancers, we're the ones that give food for the soul. Without us the world would be a dreary, dark place with no dreams or hope. We were given that

531

talent for the same reason a rose was given its perfume, or a bird its song. Don't ever think it's worthless.'

She was silent for a time, sitting there with her head pressed into his chest and he knew the tide was turning.

'You and I are so alike,' she whispered eventually. 'Do you think this was why we were brought together?'

He nearly told her then. He could see little Katy's face in Georgia's, just the way she'd looked that last leave when he said the troops were being mobilized. She was frightened he'd be killed or wounded, yet she had smiled to reassure him.

'Don't be a hero.' She had held his face in her two hands and kissed his nose. 'I love you too much to lose you.'

It was raining hard, beating at the window. A grey miserable day that would turn into an even colder, darker night. He could remember nights like this as they went through France, fear making his skin prickle, wondering if each night might be his last. But he'd come through that unscathed. He'd even found his child after twenty years, surely he could wait another few weeks and make certain she was ready for it?

'I'm sure the Almighty has a hand in it somewhere,' he smiled. 'Now what we have to do is put our heads together and come up with a plan.'

Chapter 24

'What are we going to do?' Georgia asked sheepishly.

Two days had passed. Below in the courtyard reporters still hung around hoping for a glimpse of her, trampling on the flowers, throwing sandwich papers around, making the other tenants' lives a misery.

It was like being in a prison. Johnson the jailer, bringing up milk, bread and newspapers, passing on any information he'd heard.

Georgia spent much of the time sleeping, while Sam read, listened to music and cooked for them.

'What do you want to do?' Sam asked. It had been torture for him to just sit and wait. Every bone in his body urged him to go out amongst those hyenas in the courtyard and tell the true story. Each time he looked in on Georgia and saw her curled up asleep, avoiding any confrontation, he felt more murderous towards the man who'd done this to her.

But even in his anger he knew he must bide his time. The slander would trickle to a halt eventually, and that was the time to reap revenge on all those who had a part in it.

Georgia looked better today. She was pale still but the circles had gone from under her eyes. She wore a long pink fluffy dressing-gown, her hair tied back, yet until he saw her actually get dressed he wouldn't be convinced she was fit to tackle anyone.

'I should speak to Jack Levy,' she frowned. 'Someone's got to pay off the session men or at least give them some idea where we stand.'

'Max should have done that.' Sam felt hate rising like bile from his stomach. 'My God, Georgia he's a rat, and we can't put him down with mere poison.'

Max hadn't telephoned that first night. Instead he sent a note round the next day saying the studio was besieged with reporters and the board were having a meeting about what action they would take.

There had been no words of sympathy, not even a suggestion of concern. No telephone number for them to reach him, no promise to call round. He might just have easily said he didn't care about the outcome.

He was waiting for Georgia to find an answer. Distancing himself so if any blame came it wouldn't fall on his expensively-clothed shoulders.

'I can see to paying the men,' Sam said. Once again she was worried about others. She knew none of them could afford to wait indefinitely and she couldn't bear to think she'd let them down. 'Jack Levy should come here and see you. You can't go there cap in hand.'

'But I have to sort something out,' she sighed. 'What do you think is best?'

'Seems to me,' Sam slid an arm round her small shoulders. 'You should write the whole story as it was. Then we get it to the papers. Maybe we can even ask their help to find Celia to back you up.' Sam had lain awake at night thinking up ways of getting help. He'd even slipped out to use Johnson's phone to ring Sister Mary for her advice.

Sister Mary was anxious to go and tell the press what she knew, but like Sam she knew Georgia had to tell the story herself. Bringing Celia into it had been an idea they'd cooked up between them, hoping that the excitement of attempting to find her might break Georgia out of her apathy.

'Would they Sam?' her dark eyes gleamed with new hope.

'Of course they will!' Sam grinned. 'Do you think any newspaper wouldn't jump at that kinda scoop? But first I reckon we sit tight. Let's watch and see which rats crawl out the holes first. Find out who's on your side out there!'

'Okay,' she shrugged her shoulders, a faint smile playing on her lips. 'But first let me send a cheque to each of the men.'

It was painful to wake up each morning to find yet another slanderous story about her in the papers.

It seemed that anyone who had some minor grievance about her was prepared to slander her for financial gain.

A landlady up in Scarborough spoke of a drunken orgy in her guest house. A barman in Lancashire claimed Georgia had pushed a broken glass in another girl's face. Stories about sex in changing rooms. Drugs taken openly. Shoplifting in Scotland. Young girls procured for the band, hotel rooms vandalized.

'None of it's true!' she looked at Sam in horror. 'Why do they say these things?'

They had been drunk up in Scarborough. A girl had been slashed by a glass, but not by her. The boys were more than capable of procuring their own girls, without Georgia's help. Some of these stories had a grain of truth, distorted and embroidered, but most were pure fiction.

'Laugh at it,' Sam suggested. 'These are people who would jump on any bandwagon that came along. If the newspapers said you had a religious experience in one of those places, they'd be nominating you for sainthood.'

At first it made her cry and go back to bed. But after a day or two she became so used to it she found herself laughing at the absurdity of it all, watching for the people who cared enough about her to contradict the accusations.

Rod was the first to go to the press. He spoke passionately in Georgia's defence, explaining her loyalty to the band, her loving nature and the lengths she'd gone to for their protection.

'Me and the lads were a bit wild sometimes,' he said. 'But stick someone in front of me who says Georgia was involved, and I'll tear them to shreds.' When asked what he knew about her life before joining the band Rod got even more heated.

'Hasn't it occurred to you there's another side to this? She'll tell you when she's good and ready, as she did me. All I can say to you is use your brains, work out what would make a fifteen-year-old stab a man, then run. Ask yourself what ordeal he put her through?'

Speedy was next, interviewed late at night on television. He blamed the press for causing a rift between them, laughed at the scandal-mongering and talked affectionately about her early days with the band.

'He's straight,' Georgia said in surprise, leaning forward to the television set and peering at Speedy. His eyes were clear and unwavering, long hair trimmed, his face clean-shaven. 'Well, that's one good thing to come out of this.'

There were other people whose voices were heard. Bert and Babs from the café spoke of the way she came into their lives, the comfort and love she showed Helen, her dignity and pride.

'I don't care what rubbish people are saying,' Babs was quoted as saying. 'All of us in the market know the real Georgia. That girl's got more compassion in her than any of you will ever feel. You should be ashamed of yourselves!'

But even as that hit the papers so there was more slander from men who claimed to have slept with her in the days when the band was on the road.

'I've never even seen any of these men, let alone slept with them,' Georgia gasped as she read about three-in-a-bed scenes from Edinburgh to Penzance. 'How could they say such a thing?'

'Fantasy, honey,' Sam grinned. 'They've spent so long wishing they could do it, that now they think it's real. But just look at them. No one in their right mind would believe them.'

Ian's mother made claims that if Georgia hadn't treated her son so badly he wouldn't have got drunk and burned to death in that house. Rod's mother and stepfather backed up Mrs McShane by saying Georgia had turned their son against his family.

'I don't believe anyone could make such things up,' Georgia gasped. 'Why doesn't Max stand up for me?'

But Max was caught by a photographer at London airport, leaving for America with a blonde dolly bird simpering on his arm.

'The first I knew of this was when Anderson came forward.' Max looked furtive, embarrassed at being caught slipping away. 'I feel bitter she didn't take me into her confidence earlier, and although I know the whole story now, I'm not at liberty to say anything. I'm a business man with other clients to look out for. Georgia will handle it all in her own way.'

'What can I say?' Sam spread his hands in a gesture of 'just as I thought'. 'The man's sitting on the fence. He hasn't got the guts to stay firmly on your side. Even now he's probably planning to sell his memoirs to the highest bidder.'

If it hadn't been for the scores of letters from the most unexpected people, she might have thought everyone was as uncaring as Max and Jack Levy. Harold and his wife wrote to invite her over to dinner. Norman sent a bouquet of flowers with a note offering his apologies for ever doubting her. Other musicians, girls and technicians from Decca, and even Deirdre, Max's receptionist sent letters of support and sympathy. Flowers arrived from Andreous, Steven her producer, from an American promoter, Ronnie Scott's and from Pop and the girls in Berwick Street.

'Remember, I know the truth,' Janet wrote on a piece of bright blue paper, her spelling so bad Georgia could barely read it, her handwriting like a child's. 'If I'd had my way I would have gone to Fleet Street and told them exactly what that creep done to you. Pop says you've got your reasons for keeping quiet and if I go shooting my mouth off it might make things worse. But I want you to know we are all here for you when you want us. Who is this Sam? I hope he's good to you, if not he'll have me to reckon with.

Sal and all the others send their love, so do our kids. We play your records all the time.

Love Janet.'

'Real friends,' Georgia gulped back tears as she handed it to Sam. 'You find out the real ones when the going gets tough!'

But just when she thought they had run out of steam, Sam's face began to appear in the press. They sent someone to New Orleans to check out his home there and soon he was getting the treatment too.

'Sam Cameron has two children, left with his sister while he holes up with Georgia,' they said. They found news of a bar-room brawl he'd been in. His ex-wife was interviewed and claimed Sam not only beat her, but kept her as little more than a slave. There was a picture of his two children, both in ragged clothes and bare feet, the house behind them looked like a shack.

'I took that one myself,' Sam said, his dark eyes growing black with fury. 'They'd been out playing in some mud. I thought it was funny that they looked like

538

a pair of waifs. Everyone has a snap of their children like that.'

It was cruel the picture they had painted of him. A heartless vagabond who cared nothing for his family. Somehow by hurting Sam they had succeeded in hurting Georgia still further.

'How dare they?' she gasped. 'Oh Sam, what have I dragged you into?'

'Don't worry about me,' Sam shrugged his shoulders. 'They're scraping the barrel now.'

But the next day there were more stories. One about Georgia spending four hundred pounds on shoes in one day and another claiming she didn't wash her clothes, but threw them away.

'There can't be much else going on in England,' Georgia forced herself to laugh, even though she felt desperate. 'What are they going to dredge up next?'

'Your headmistress,' Sam chuckled, opening another paper. 'Georgia was a real leader. A strong character we all remember well. She did leave school suddenly and although I heard rumours about her father, I remained convinced she wouldn't hurt anyone unless severely provoked. I hadn't actually realized the Georgia Anderson I knew and liked so much was in fact the famous singer. Had I known I would have written and expressed my pride in her. I wish her well and I urge her to tell the true story about these events in her past.'

But the few people who stood up for her were outweighed by the hate mail that arrived daily. After seeing a sample Georgia refused to even look further, and it was Sam who sorted through it, chuckling to himself.

'You've gotta laugh,' he said in his defence. 'Just look at all this stuff. There's a woman who reckons you killed her dog, another who believes you had an affair with her husband. Even one who thinks you are the anti-Christ. The rest of them are from Rednecks who blame your colour for everything.' He shook his head in bewilderment. 'You sure stirred up a hornet's nest, honey!'

Without Sam she might have lost her mind. He somehow put it all into perspective and gave her the courage to write down the full story.

It was ten days after the news first broke that she saw a particularly cruel cartoon in one of the newspapers. A caricature of herself holding a knife over an old man, and the words 'There's no time Baby' coming in a balloon from her mouth.

She couldn't laugh now. Rage welled up in her, a desire to speak out and be heard.

'It's time Sam,' she said, wiping away tears of frustration. 'I can't stay in here another day. I'm going to the press.'

The story was ready. A sharp, impassioned account, without exaggeration or embroidery. She spoke of her happiness with the Andersons until the rape. Her feelings for both her foster parents, then the shock and torment Brian put her through. Recalling the rape and stabbing was so painful it was tempting to gloss over it. She had to dig down deep within her, make herself remember each detail. The way he had laid sprawled on the landing, the knife in her hand as she came up the stairs, the blood as it spurted out of his belly. Once she'd faced that again it was easier to put down her explanation for running away. Her first few days in Soho, the abortion later, were softened by the people who helped her.

'Want me to come too?' Sam said. He was making coffee in the kitchen, wearing just a pair of jeans, his feet and chest bare.

'No,' she said shaking her head. 'I've got to do this on my own haven't I?'

'I guess so,' he moved across the kitchen to her, putting his hands on her shoulders. 'They'll think more of you. Besides I couldn't trust myself to keep my trap shut.'

She took care over her appearance. For ten days she'd worn nothing but jeans and a sweatshirt. But now she had to look like a star.

A white leather suit fitted the bill perfectly. The skirt was short and tight, the tiny jacket trimmed with silver stars went over the briefest skimpy silver top. She washed her hair and let it dry naturally in ringlets, adding star-shaped earrings studded with diamonds and a pair of long silver boots with cuban heels.

'You look sensational,' Sam grinned up at her as she came back into the kitchen.

She faltered in the doorway for a moment.

'Stage fright?' He poured her another cup of coffee and slid it across the table.

Sitting on the edge of a chair she lifted the coffee to her lips.

'What if they still don't believe me?'

Sam's eyes crinkled up with laughter, he reached across the table and took her hand.

'Everyone who really counts already believes you, honey.'

'Do you think they will find Celia for me?' she whispered, her eyes wide with fear.

'You make them find her,' Sam said fiercely. 'Don't forget for one moment, they owe you. Now off you go. Keep your head up, take deep breaths if you're nervous. I'll be here if you need me.'

She walked round the table and leaned over on to his shoulder, pressing her lips against his neck.

'What would I have done without you, Sam?' she said softly. 'You've been mother, father and friend all in one. I can't tell you how important you are to me.'

His hand came up to caress her face and she saw his eyes were glistening with tears.

'Off with you,' he said gruffly. 'Before I say something I might regret.'

Through the glass panel on the doors she could see a
handful of reporters still patiently waiting, puffing on
cigarettes, chatting in small groups.

It had been cold and wet most of the time she had
been incarcerated in her flat, but now the sun was
shining. Daffodils almost finished, tulips about to surpass them, and the almond tree was covered in delicate
pinky-white blossom. Spring was finally here to stay.

Taking a deep breath she opened the door and
stepped out.

She wanted to laugh at the way they all jumped.
Cigarettes stubbed underfoot, sandwiches shoved into
pockets, fingers fumbling for pens, cameras lifted, every
face wiped clean with surprise.

'Good morning.' She waved the brown envelope
containing her story, holding her car keys in readiness.
'Glad to see you haven't lost interest!'

A small man darted forward. She had seen this one
before on many occasions. He reminded her of a ferret,
with his thin head, sharp nose and tiny eyes.

'Have you any news for us?' he said, as the others
quickly clustered round him.

'I'm off to the *Mirror*,' she smiled more confidently
than she felt and patted the envelope in her hand. 'The
truth's in here. As they started the whole slanderous
business, I expect them to lay it to rest too.'

'Why have you taken so long to retaliate?' A woman's
voice came through the crowd, Georgia could only see
a pair of brown eyes and a mop of untidy red hair.

'Timing,' Georgia grinned round at them. 'Giving you
enough rope to hang yourselves. The story will be out
tomorrow.' She paused to pose for the cameras. 'Go
home now. There's nothing for you here.'

The sun was glinting on her red Mercedes. She

opened the door and slipped in, winding down her window and turning her radio up loudly.

As she drove quickly out of the courtyard, she saw for once they were speechless, mouths open with shock.

It was sometime since she'd been to Holborn and she hadn't thought to check out where the building was. As she stopped at the lights, just past Gray's Inn Road, she noticed the huge modern building on her right.

Without even considering the heavy traffic going through to the West End she did a 'U' turn in the road, ignoring the other motorists who honked furiously at her and pulled up with one wheel on the kerb.

'You can't stop here.' A young policeman came forward, a frown of irritation vanishing into a smile of delight as he recognized her.

'You park it for me then,' she said dropping the keys into his hand. 'I've got important things to do.'

There were double ordinary doors up two steps or a revolving one to the side. She went through this so fast the door swung on round several times more behind her.

She got a last glimpse of the policeman staring after her, a bemused expression on his face, her keys still in his hand.

The foyer was all brown, highly-polished tiles and huge green plants in tubs. The corpulent uniformed porter looked up from his desk as she marched up to him. He knew her face was familiar, but he couldn't quite place it.

'The Editor!' she snapped. 'Where is he?'

'I'll just telephone his secretary,' he picked up the phone.

Georgia put out her hand and prevented him.

She could hear the lift coming down behind the porter, she wasn't anxious for anyone to recognize her just yet.

'Just tell me which floor,' she barked. 'Now!'

'Third, no fourth,' he stammered. 'But – '

'I'm going up there,' she said coolly. 'What's his name?'

'Phillips,' he said weakly, his hand straying to the phone again, afraid he would lose his job.

'You can warn him I'm on my way up,' she called back as she made for the stairs. 'Don't worry, I'll tell him it was all my doing!'

She was out of breath by the time she reached the fourth floor. Her face was flushed and her heart hammering nearly as loudly as her heels on the tiled corridor. She marched quickly down the corridor giving only a cursory glance into open doors where typewriters and teleprinters clattered, the girls who worked them looking up in astonishment as she passed.

His name was on the door. 'John Phillips, Editor.'

She didn't even knock, but opened the door wide and swept in.

She had expected a big man. Someone like Max in silk shirts and a fat cigar, full of bluster, a mouth like the Blackwall Tunnel. But the man behind the desk was short, thin, almost weedy, a boyish, open face. He wore corduroy trousers and a knitted tie, perhaps fifty, but he looked younger. His brown eyes blinked furiously, a small, gentle mouth opening in surprise.

'Miss James,' he jumped up, holding out his hand.

'I'm surprised you recognize me,' she snapped. 'After all the fiction you've been writing about me lately, I thought you had me mixed up with someone else.' She ignored the hand and plonked herself down in a chair, staring coolly at him.

He was disconcerted. One finger ran round the collar of his shirt, his face turning pink.

'What can I do for you?' he said weakly. 'Would you like some coffee?'

'You can print the truth,' she said, fixing her dark

eyes on his pale brown ones. She noticed he had a small mole on his cheek, one of his front teeth was slightly broken off and he'd cut himself shaving. He didn't look as if he had a woman to look after him.

'As far as we are concerned everything Mr Anderson said is the truth,' his eyes dropped from hers, tiny lines showing round his mouth.

'How much did you pay him for that garbage?'

'I, I – ,' he stammered.

She thought of how much she'd feared these people, thinking they were like gods who couldn't be beaten. Yet here was a little man in charge who couldn't even shave himself without making a hash of it.

'All right, so you don't want to tell me that,' she was calm now. She might even enjoy tearing him and his paper to shreds. 'But I have the truth here,' she put the envelope on his desk. 'All you have heard is the outpouring of a bitter man who has misled you.'

She could smell Phillips' fear. His Adam's apple was leaping up and down, one eye was beginning to twitch. As his hand reached out for the envelope she remembered Celia.

'Everything in there can be verified. I want you to find Mrs Anderson in return for that truth.'

He pulled out the six sheets of paper, flicked through them and put them down again.

'You'll read it now,' she commanded. 'Not tomorrow, next week or when it suits you. Now, while I'm here.'

'Of course,' he picked them up again, that Adam's apple threatening to get caught on his collar.

Outside the window she could see only office windows and blue sky. A pair of pigeons were canoodling on a window-sill, the male spreading his tail and fluffing out his chest. The noise of traffic just a hum, subdued by the thick glass. It was strange to just sit silently while a total stranger read a story she had hardly been able to think about, much less tell.

It was a comfortable office, with a big grey desk and plants in tubs. His desk was covered in papers, two of the other chairs were piled high with cuttings and folded newspapers. There were large glossy photographs lying around, one of her, on a pile of papers, taken as she came back from America.

She could see Phillips was moved by the story. He bent closer to it, reading it slowly and carefully. His lips quivered, his fingers fiddled with his tie nervously, occasionally he glanced up at her, as if trying to fit the star in front of him into the story in his hands.

She heard a faint sigh as he finished it. An expression of profound sadness on his youthful face.

'You write very well,' Phillips looked up at her, but he couldn't hold her steady gaze. 'Why did you wait so long to contact me?'

Shame poured out of him. He was even honest enough not to try and wriggle out of it by counter-attacking.

'I watched and waited,' she said, but to her distress she could feel tears pricking her eyelids. 'I wanted to watch every last louse crawl out of the woodwork. Have you got any idea how painful it was for me to relive that night? Do you know what you've done to me?'

'I do now,' Phillips' eyes caught hers. Sympathy and understanding, mixed with a stronger desire to set things straight. 'An apology seems futile.'

'You will apologize, by printing the truth,' she wasn't going to let him off the hook just yet. 'I expect you to use all your connections to find my foster mother too.'

He cleared his throat. Fear of a law suit flickered across his watery eyes.

'Do you understand our position? It's our obligation as a newspaper to print news as we are given it.' His voice was firm, yet there was an undeniable tone of shame in it. 'Mr Anderson's story was printed in good faith, he had photographs and evidence to support it.'

'I'm sure he did,' she said. 'He may be many things but he was always plausible. I believed in him myself until he raped me. But didn't you even think of contacting me first?'

Phillips shrugged his shoulders and waved his hands.

'That's what a scoop is all about,' he said. 'We get a story, it sells our paper.'

'Aren't you wondering why I've brought this to you?' she asked. 'I could have gone to one of your rivals, dug up dirt about how you got Anderson to sell his soul.'

'Why didn't you?' he croaked. She knew he was expecting news of lawyers. His earlier pink flush was turning a little green. She wanted to play with him, make him suffer as she had.

'Because I want your whole-hearted commitment.' She rapped one long nail on her story in front of him. 'If you succeed in clearing my name, bring that bastard to justice and find my mother, then maybe I'll just settle for a hefty donation.'

'How much?' he looked up quickly.

The sharp expression in his eyes made her think of Max. Funny how money changed people!

'You misunderstand,' she smirked. 'I have all the money I need, the donation can go to charity, one that deals with runaway kids.'

Relief poured out of him. 'That's the least I can do.'

'And you'll find my mother?'

'Any idea where she might be?' There was a glow in his eyes, as if he relished the challenge.

'No. I think she must have gone back to nursing. It must be somewhere remote or she would have read all this. I went back to Blackheath when I was sixteen, I tried to find her and Peter, but Peter's mother sent me away with a flea in my ear and Mum had left.'

He put the end of a pen in his mouth, sucking at it thoughtfully.

There was something troubling him, something in

547

her story which had tripped a wire. She could almost hear and see his brain mulling it over. Had Brian said something more which hadn't been printed?

'What is it?' she asked. 'I can see something's troubling you.'

He frowned. 'I don't know if it's important,' he looked down at her story again, then glanced back at her. 'We had a telephone call just after the story broke. A young man, he wanted your address.'

'Not another of those fictitious lovers?' she laughed lightly. 'What did he have to offer?'

'To be honest, we thought he was one of those,' Phillips looked uncomfortable. 'But the boyfriend, Peter, you mentioned – '

'It was Peter?'

Phillips heard the catch in her voice, saw her eyes widen and sensed the emotion the name evoked.

'What's his surname?'

'Radcliffe.'

Phillips' eyes closed for a moment. 'That's him. We had dozens of crank calls, so many we hardly listened to the filth they were saying, but – '

'What did he say?' Georgia was trembling now, every nerve-ending twitching. 'Tell me.'

Phillips ran a finger round his collar, beads of perspiration were glistening on his upper lip.

'Just that he was an old friend. He wanted your address or phone number.'

'Why didn't you give it to him then?'

'We never part with that kind of information.' Phillips looked shocked at the mere suggestion. 'The only reason I even remember his name was because he made no startling revelations. The girl who took the call said he was a teacher.'

'Did you take down his number or address?'

'Of course,' Phillips picked up a pen and fiddled with the point. 'We always log it down. We even tried to ring him back, but there was no reply. I think the girl suggested he could write to you care of this office.'

'And has he?' Georgia's eyes were like glowing coals.

'I don't think so, not yet.'

Georgia could feel her heart pounding, her palms sticky. The Peter she remembered wouldn't sit and read lies without doing something.

'He's still special to you?' Phillips' voice softened.

'Yes,' she dropped her eyes and blushed furiously. 'I never seem to be able to forget him. He might be married now, he certainly can't feel the same about me still. But even so.'

'You'd still like to see him again?' Phillips raised one eyebrow.

'Oh yes,' she sighed.

Phillips could hardly believe what he was seeing and hearing. All through his interview with Anderson he had sensed something wasn't quite right, he'd had to force himself to forget he was a fan of Georgia's, give the public the story, putting aside his own qualms.

He knew he had the truth now, even without checking it out. But one thing was plain, he had to make amends for his paper's part in it, and he hadn't got to the position of Editor without knowing the value of emotional reunions.

'Suppose I got him down to London?' Phillips smiled. 'Asked for his help. It would be easy for me to discover his circumstances without obligating him in anyway.'

'Could you do that?' As much as she wanted to rush down into the office further down the corridor, force them to give her Peter's address and rush there immediately, she knew that wasn't practical. The memory of his mother's chilly face was still in her mind. 'Peter when I knew him was the sort that hated injustice. That's probably the only reason he rang here.'

'I wouldn't say that,' Phillips laughed.

'You don't know him,' she said quietly. 'Look, he's

known who I was all along. If he'd still held a torch for me he would have got in touch. That means he has someone else doesn't it?'

'I can hardly believe what I'm hearing,' Phillips sat back in his chair his lips twitching with amusement. 'You've been portrayed as a cross between Lizzie Borden and Lucrezia Borgia, yet you are apprehensive about causing a few ripples in an old love's life.'

'I'll never forgive you if you turn it into a circus,' she threatened.

'I promise you no one will know about this until you say the word,' he smiled. 'And that's one helluva promise for a newspaper man!'

Georgia stood up and held out her hand. 'Ring me at nine tonight. I'll put the phone back on specially.'

He took her hand and shook it.

'Thank you for coming,' he said warmly. 'I'll get this story ready for tomorrow's paper and start the hunt for your mother. By the way,' he blushed bright pink. 'In all this I forgot to ask you. What are you going to do about Mr Anderson?'

'I'd like to kill him,' she smiled sweetly. 'But please don't quote me on that!'

Chapter 25

Georgia walked up the steps of the President Hotel, through the double glass doors and paused in the foyer.

She had butterflies in her stomach, her pulse was racing and she was no longer certain she was doing the right thing.

'He's at the President, in Bloomsbury,' Phillips said on the phone at nine. 'He wasn't keen to stay overnight. I had to twist his arm by pretending I needed more information tomorrow.'

Why hadn't she asked questions? Why hadn't she stopped to think? If Sam hadn't already left for a gig in the West End, he would have stopped her. The President wasn't even a cosy little boarding house as she'd imagined, but instead a huge, red brick Gothic hotel, the sort she hated.

She had grown accustomed to the grandeur of places like the Savoy and Claridges. The staff so well trained that they treated everyone with the same courtesy whether they were rich and famous or just stepping in to make an enquiry. But this was one that catered for international business men. The heavy red velvet drapes with ornate gold tassels, the rich red and gold carpet, the dark flocked wallpaper and the padded leather reception desk gave an impression of illicit encounters, deals and intrigue. The sort of place where the staff wouldn't balk at calling up a few journalists just to get their name in the paper.

'I should have phoned and arranged to meet him somewhere,' she thought as she approached the reception desk.

It was almost ten at night. She was attracting speculative glances from a group of middle-aged Americans in the lounge to her right, and a swarthy porter lounging by the lift. Down some stairs to her right came the sound of male laughter and clink of glasses.

Why hadn't she asked Phillips how Peter reacted to his call? An hour ago it had been enough to know he'd got the first plane out of Manchester. But lack of hesitation on his part might only mean he had a day free.

'I'd like to see Mr Radcliffe, please.'

The two women manning the reception desk were formidable fashion plates, in dark suits and candy-striped shirts. One peered at her suspiciously, glancing over the leather and wood counter at Georgia's jeans and white sweater and sniffed in disapproval.

The younger of the two opened the register, and slid one red talon down the page. Her hair was cut in geometric Mary Quant style, it swung forward over one eye, sleek and dark.

'He's in 309,' she said in a bored voice. 'Would you like me to try his room?'

'Yes please,' Georgia could see the second woman studying her closely. It was that same expression people often had when confronted with her. Her face looked familiar, but they couldn't quite place it.

'No reply,' the dark haired woman put the phone down and flicked back her hair. 'Would you like to leave a message?'

On the fast drive across town Georgia hadn't considered for one moment Peter might go out. She had merely visualized knocking on a door and Peter opening it. Now what should she do?

'Is his key there?' she asked. She could feel herself blushing and she knew the porter was now giving her bottom his undivided attention. Worse still, a man in a flashy checked suit had paused to consult a display of tourist information just to her left, and she sensed he was listening, about to offer her the kind of attention she didn't want.

The woman turned to examine the board behind the desk.

'No,' she said curtly over her shoulder. 'But that doesn't mean anything, they always forget to hand them in.'

Georgia turned away in disappointment.

'Excuse me!'

Georgia looked round. The second receptionist who had been studying her was leaning on the counter.

'Is Mr Radcliffe young, tall, with blond hair?'

'Yes,' Georgia's heart leapt, bringing a wide smile to her lips. In one bound she was back to reception, leaning on the desk. 'Do you know where he went?'

'In the bar,' the woman smiled now, revealing a warmth that hadn't been there moments before. 'I'd forgotten until you looked so disappointed. He asked me earlier if he could borrow a street map, he took it in there with him to look at it. I could page him for you?'

'I'll just go in there,' Georgia beamed at her. 'Thank you.'

As she made her way down the thickly-carpeted stairs to the bar, men's voices grew louder. A smell of cigar smoke wafted up to her and her knees were turning to jelly.

The stairs turned. In front of her she could see her reflection in yet another mirror framed by two tall imitation palms. Taller, more rounded than the night

553

she ran with Peter across the heath, but her eyes were gleaming with excitement just as they had that night.

To her left, down just five more steps lay the bar. A rich, dark red carpet, a leather front to the bar, brass feet-rails and two business men deep in conversation, was all she could see. But judging by the noise it was crowded further in.

She stopped again in the doorway. The bar stretched along the wall in front of her, three deep with men. To her right was an archway leading to a smaller room with leather Chesterfields and low tables. To her right a larger area with small polished tables and straight-backed chairs.

Few of the tables were occupied. Everyone was standing at the bar. In the main, business men in sober suits, faces flushed with drink, or was it merely the soft pinkish lighting?

Heads turned in curiosity, smirks on their lips, eyes glinting as they sensed her embarrassment at breaking into a masculine world.

Georgia gulped. She could see ginger hair, blonds, bald heads and slickly-Brylcreemed heads. But not Peter.

As she walked down the bar conversations were halted. Whispered remarks, nudges, the kind of smiles that were an overture to conversation. She didn't dare let her eyes meet anyone's.

Then she saw him.

He was leaning on the far end of the bar, deep in thought. One foot on the rail, his hand nursing a pint of beer. Golden hair caught under a light, wearing a denim jacket and a white open-necked shirt.

She had so many pictures of him trapped in her mind.

As a choir boy, in a white surplice with a ruffle round his neck, angelic and pure. The gawky schoolboy in scuffed shoes, grey slacks and a navy blazer, his cap pushed back on his head. In jeans and a sweater running with her, hand in hand across the frosty heath.

Then there was the night of her party when he told her he loved her. Eyes as blue as a summer sky, golden skin and soft lips, his hair like ripe corn.

The boy who walked her home from choir had become a man. Wide muscular shoulders strained his jacket. His square jaw, tougher with a hint of stubble. Hair longer, badly cut, streaked from palest cream to deep gold. Yet his profile hadn't changed. Straight, proud nose, curving full lips, thick eyelashes fanning those peachy cheeks.

She forgot she was standing in a room full of curious strangers. A delicious flush of excitement crept over her.

He lifted his head as if aware he was being watched. His eyes flickered across to her, then shot open in shocked surprise.

'Georgia!'

Fear of rejection forgotten, she found herself running towards him, hands outstretched, seeing only the blue eyes and a smile as wide as the Thames.

'Peter!'

For a moment it was impossible to speak. His hands were holding hers. Blue and brown eyes searching one another. Two pairs of lips smiling, unable to find the right words.

'What would you like to drink?' Peter's voice was gruff with emotion. 'Everyone's watching us,' he added in a whisper.

'Just orange juice,' she smiled. 'And I don't give a toss about them.'

He ordered her a drink, keeping a tight hold on her hand, his thumb running across her fingers as if he was checking it was real.

'Let's go over there,' he said softly, nodding to a table

over in the corner. 'You might be used to audiences but it's new to me.'

She reached the table first, sitting down quickly so she could look again at him. He was much taller, perhaps six foot two. His face had filled out. He looked fit and athletic, skin with an unmistakable glow of the outdoors. Slim-hipped in his faded jeans, but his chest and thighs powerful.

'It's all too much,' he said as he sat down. 'This morning I was having a lie-in, contemplating the marking, then the phone rang and before I knew it, I was on my way to London.'

'Marking?' Georgia frowned.

'I'm a teacher now,' he smiled, as if remembering how much time had passed. 'It was lucky it was school holidays or Phillips wouldn't have found me in.'

A stab of guilt shot through her. Phillips had said he was a teacher, yet she hadn't considered what that meant. She was like a child herself, expecting people to come running when she needed them.

'I wasn't sure you'd come,' she hung her head. 'I certainly didn't expect you here so quickly.'

'You knew he was going to ask me then?' Peter gave her an odd look, disbelief mingled with pleasure.

She had to explain how Phillips had connected the boy in her story with an earlier caller.

'You can't imagine how thrilled I was,' she said. 'I mean I thought I'd never see you again.'

'Who dictated that, "Push off, I'm not interested" letter then?'

Georgia closed her eyes. There was no point in asking what he meant, or when it was. Whatever had happened Max had to be at the bottom of it.

'I didn't know you'd written.' She reached out and touched Peter's hand, looking right into his blue eyes. 'Don't you know I would have been on the first train to see you if I had?'

'How could I know that after what happened?' his eyes were guarded. 'I just assumed you'd written me out of your life.'

It was like a fencing match. Peter thrust accusations at her, she parried with explanations.

He told her about himself and Celia waiting for a phone call or letter up to the weekend after her sixteenth birthday.

'But I went to your house, I tried to get Celia at her office. Your mother took my address and said she would give it to you. She said you weren't interested in me any longer.'

His eyes went dark with anger, his wide mouth trembled.

'I had such misgivings about going out that morning,' he said softly. 'But you just don't credit a mother with being that cruel or underhand. She seemed kind of smug when I got home. Too nice, if you know what I mean.'

He told her how close Celia had come to breaking down. Brian's drinking, the violence and fights.

'She had no choice but to leave her home,' he said, his lips trembling as he remembered. 'But we were so sure you'd write to me.'

A terrible guilt crept over Georgia. For years she'd assumed all the pain was on her side, imagining Celia and Peter had carried on with their lives almost as if nothing had happened. Now she found her sudden departure had been like a hurricane, leaving untold devastation in its wake.

'Didn't you realize what it would do to your mother?' Peter's blue eyes burned with anger. 'I saw her almost broken with grief. Not because she lost her home, or even her job, but because she couldn't bear to live without you.'

'I thought she'd understand,' Georgia's eyes filled

with tears. 'I went thinking it would be best for everyone.'

'She even understood that,' Peter's voice softened, as if Celia's memory was still very dear to him. 'I was too young then to really comprehend how shattering rape is to women. I was so screwed up with bitterness, I guess I blamed you for not writing or phoning. But Celia just went on searching and loving you.'

'Where is she now?'

'I don't know,' he shook his head. 'She went to Africa to nurse when we couldn't find you. I persuaded her to, assuming you'd get in touch with me. We wrote for over a year, but then she stopped it.'

'But why?'

Peter sighed, as if he barely understood her reasons.

'I think she was afraid for me. I was still looking for you in the holidays. My letters to her were always full of you. Several times she wrote telling me to forget you. To get on with my life, have fun and take out other girls. Not because she stopped loving you Georgia, but because she felt responsible for me too.'

'She thought you were being obsessive?' She could imagine Celia in her mind's eye, putting on her glasses, tutting to herself as she read Peter's letters, weighing up the situation and deciding to be ruthless.

'"Enough's enough," was how she put it. "Don't ever think I'm turning my back on you Peter. I just know it's unhealthy for a boy of your age to live in the past. Put Georgia and myself behind you. Look to the future."'

The quote from her mother brought her right into the crowded bar. Georgia smiled despite her sadness.

'How did you feel?'

'Relieved in one way,' he blushed, a tiny smile puckering the corners of his mouth. 'I mean it's hard to keep a broken heart when you're eighteen and surrounded by ravers.'

She could sense that he hadn't lived like a monk. A

mischievous look in his eyes, the sensual lips, an assurance which showed in his straight back and wide shoulders. But rather than hurting her, it felt almost soothing.

'So when was it you wrote? After I made the first record?'

'No, before that, when I read about the fire. Some of my mates had seen your band in Hartlepool, so they were engrossed in the story. One of them described a girl singer who sounded like you. I did some checking and wrote to Celia first. When I got no reply, I wrote to you.'

'I'm so sorry Peter. I can imagine how you felt.' She dropped her eyes from his. 'But I wonder why she didn't reply?'

'I guess she'd moved on, I mean Africa isn't like Lewisham is it? Maybe my letters just lay in the post office. Phillips is checking out the organization she worked for. If anyone can find her, it's him.'

'But she must have heard me sing?' Georgia whispered. 'My records have been played everywhere.'

'Out in the bush?' Peter raised one blond eyebrow. 'The last place she was in was over a hundred miles from even a telephone. Syringes and medicine are more important there than music.'

'I guess so,' Georgia smiled weakly.

'We'll find her,' his voice had a confident ring. 'After all, I've actually got to speak to you at last. The way Max Menzies described you, it sounded as if you had a heart of stone.'

Georgia looked at him questioningly.

'Max?'

Peter shook his head in disbelief.

'You didn't know that either? I went to his office two years ago.'

Georgia sat in stunned silence as Peter explained everything that had been said between them. Hatred for Max crept through her veins like a shot of whiskey on an empty stomach.

'But why did you come after one rejection?' she said weakly.

'Well, it's not everyone who can claim England's top star as their first love,' he laughed. 'I used to play your records, listen to the words and I got this feeling some of them were for me,' he blushed furiously. 'Daft isn't it? I expect every man who's met you thinks the same.'

'They were for you,' she said softly. Her heart leapt crazily. He did still care. Even under the bravado, the anger and bitterness, a tiny flame was still flickering. '"Crying", especially.'

Silence fell between them, so many questions as yet unasked, both waiting for the other to start again.

'Are you going to marry Sam Cameron?'

This was the last thing she expected. It jolted her into realizing just how much ground they had to cover.

'No. Of course not. He's just a friend.'

'That's a relief,' he said, his mouth twisting slightly as if this of all questions was the most important. 'I mean, he sounds heavy duty.'

'They've told almost as many lies about him as me,' she retorted quickly. 'Don't tell me you've become prejudiced too?'

'I'm like everyone else in the world Georgia,' he said quietly. 'I believe what I'm told.'

'Does that mean everything you read about me?'

He sighed. 'Some of it, I guess. I didn't want to. I kept telling myself it was all rumour and speculation, but I couldn't help thinking you must have changed.'

'Yet you rang the *Mirror* to offer help?'

'I knew the truth about Anderson, remember. I never could stand liars. But when they blanked me out, wouldn't give me your address, I was as bad as everyone else. I didn't do anything.'

The bar showed no sign of closing, even though it

was well after twelve. Some of the men at the bar were very drunk, their raucous laughter unnerving.

'Would you like to come up to my room?' He blurted it out, his eyes firmly on the table. 'I don't mean. Well you know? I just want to get to the bottom of everything.'

'So do I,' she whispered touching his hand tentatively. 'But here wouldn't be right. Come home with me?'

He didn't reply immediately, just closed his other hand over hers and squeezed it.

'Just my luck,' he smiled ruefully. 'I get a free room in a posh hotel, then I get dragged out of it by the most dangerous woman in the world.'

'You can lock up the knives if you like,' she joked. His hand over hers was making her melt inside and she wanted to kiss him so badly it hurt. 'I seem to remember my old Peter wishing he could be alone somewhere with me.'

'Don't tease me Georgia,' his voice was suddenly gruff. 'Just seeing you again has brought back so many memories. But we were only kids then. We've both moved on.'

'I don't feel as if I have.' He was overwhelmed by who she was, her money and fame. She had to convince him none of that mattered and she was still the same girl he knew. 'You've always been special to me. Come home and let's really talk.'

'But is it safe?' he said, glancing round the bar. 'Won't there be reporters about?'

'Not tonight,' she smiled. 'But they'll be round here in their droves tomorrow morning.' She stood up and held out her hand. 'Please, Peter?'

Peter looked into those dark, magnetic eyes and felt as if he were drowning. When Phillips offered him an all-expenses trip to London he almost laughed at the man. He would have walked all the way, hitchhiked,

561

even swum if there was a chance of seeing Georgia. Yet even in his wildest dreams he hadn't expected her to come here and take him off to her flat.

She was far more shapely, her little pointed chin more defiant, hair longer, and far more lustrous than he remembered. Away from him she'd grown into a woman, so desirable he could feel himself responding.

There had been many women in his life, some he'd even thought he loved for brief moments. Yet the moment Georgia stood in front of him, he understood why he had never been able to commit himself to anyone for more than a few weeks.

But he was scared now. What if her interest was only friendship? They were just kids six years ago. Was it possible to rekindle a small spark after all this time?

'I don't know how I'm going to control my kids when I get back.' He had to make jokes, anything to avoid inadvertently saying what was in his mind. They were walking up the stairs now towards the foyer. Could he take her hand again, or would she see that as a pass?

'Kids?' she stopped in her tracks. 'You got married then?'

Was he imagining it, or was that panic in her voice?

'The kids at school, silly. Do you think I would have shot down here so quickly if I had a wife and children?'

She giggled, that girlish sound he remembered so well.

'I suppose not.'

'Maybe they'll have new respect for boring old Radcliffe,' he said as he held the door open for her. 'But the Head won't be that thrilled to find his English teacher is a man with a past!'

Russell Square was deserted now. Street lights cast yellow light over the railings, highlighting daffodils planted in the grass.

'Did you ever tell anyone about me?' Georgia asked. Not once had Peter said anything that related to their relationship. How could she come out and ask if there was another girl?

'No. I wanted to, especially when you made your first record. I guess I thought no one would believe me.'

Peter stopped by her car, running his hand appreciatively over the sleek red bonnet.

'That's some car,' he grinned round at her.

'Would you like to drive it?' She took her keys out of her bag and waved them at him.

'You mean it's yours?' His eyes grew huge with surprise, his lips trembling with schoolboyish wonder.

'Well, I wouldn't suggest you drove someone else's car,' she laughed. 'You have got a licence?'

'Yes. Celia taught me. Can I really?'

As he bent to unlock the door, Georgia had to touch him. She slid her hand under the short denim jacket and ran her fingers down his spine.

He straightened up and turned to her, so close she could feel his breath on her face.

Slowly his hand came up, cupping her face, his eyes looking right into hers.

'Oh Georgia,' he groaned.

His lips moved slowly towards hers, just like the dreams she had tormented herself with so often in the early days in Berwick Street. Her heart quickened, hands reaching out to hold him, body aching to touch his.

Such a slow, deep kiss, as if the years since her birthday were just a few hours. Every nerve tingled, yet at the same time the kiss held all the practised skill of a lifetime spent with each other.

'People will think we're barmy,' he said at length, still holding her tightly, but covering her face with little kisses. He wanted to go on kissing her, tell her what was in his heart, but he was still wary of her. 'We walk out of a perfectly good hotel and stand kissing in the road.'

'Let them watch,' she said, lifting her lips to his. 'I hope they're green with envy.'

'I don't know which is best, kissing you or the thought of driving that car,' he whispered, holding her so close she could feel every line of his body. 'But I know we can't do both at once.'

'And to think I was frightened of a rival in Manchester,' she playfully tapped his face. 'Come on then, drive!'

'I haven't told you where I live,' she said as he took a road down towards Blackfriars.

'I found that out today,' he turned to her and half smiled. 'I was torn between going straight home tomorrow or bearding you in your den.'

'Which had you decided on then?'

'I hadn't,' he grinned sheepishly. 'My friends back in Manchester would never let me forget it if I didn't see you. But then I reckoned it would be worse for my ego if you said "thank you and goodnight."'

'You didn't used to care what people thought,' she said. 'And I don't remember you having much ego either.'

'I'm not the pure, idealistic boy you remember,' he said, glancing round at her. 'I've done things you wouldn't like, used people for my own ends. Maybe that's why I don't feel so angry with Max Menzies. I can identify a little with him.'

'That's daft,' Georgia said briskly. 'You're nothing like him.'

'Think about it,' he said quietly. 'We both wanted to escape our backgrounds. I used books, Max used his looks and wits.'

'You'd never be as corrupt as him!' she said in horror. 'Besides how do you know so much about him?'

'I made it my business to find out,' he smiled. 'He fascinated me. He was obviously in love with you. He's a millionaire, manipulative, handsome. A legend in his own time. I discovered that one of the reasons he is such a success, is because he does his homework. He checks people out, puts them under a microscope. I can appreciate that, I do it too.'

Georgia just sat there, watching the road ahead. Was Peter trying to tell her something? This wasn't what she had expected.

'Don't look like that,' he reached across the seats and took her hand. 'I had to work like a dog to stay at university, building sites in the holidays, behind a bar at night. I've seen people who are a darn sight brighter than me end up in some boring job, and people with nothing but sharp wits get out there and make something of themselves. Making a pile of money isn't my goal. But doing something worthwhile, becoming a big person is. Do you understand?'

'I think so,' she smiled weakly. 'But you teach. How does that fit in?'

'Maybe it was Celia who put the germ of the idea in my head,' he said. 'Africa, India. All those people crying out for education. Right now it's Branscombe Road Secondary Modern, but the world doesn't end there.'

Peter's face was a picture as they entered her flat. It was just the way it had been the first time she took him home to tea at Blackheath. Back then, he had stood wiping his feet on the doormat, staring around the hall with its thick carpets, the grandfather clock, the pictures on the wall, sniffing the smell of fresh-baked scones as if he'd entered a new world. Almost like a stray dog being taken into a real home.

'This is the business!' His voice was husky with reverence. He looked up at the Italian lights, the vast expanse of apple-green carpet leading down the long hall. 'Can I be nosy?'

She took his hand in hers and led him first into the lounge, giggling as she put on all the lights.

He was so much bigger than he'd been that day over six years earlier in her parents' home. The child-like wonder was still there, but mixed now with maturity. He stood silently, feet apart, his eyes sweeping over the white settees, the stereo equipment, the antique writing desk and her collection of mementoes from every country she'd sung in.

'It's best by day,' she said, clutching at his arm and taking him over to the window. She pulled on a cord and the long curtains drew back to reveal the small balcony and view over the Thames. To their left was Albert Bridge lit up like a glittering spider's web, to the right Chelsea, the river joining them like a slick of black tar, reflecting back silver lights on the far bank. 'The sun comes in here all day. At night in the summer I sit out there and watch boats going past.'

'How long did it take to put me aside?' he said softly, switching the lights off and joining her at the window.

'I didn't,' she said turning to him, putting one hand on his cheek and stroking it. 'Maybe the pain stopped after joining the band. But you were always there. I used to scan audiences when we did university gigs, hoping against hope you'd be amongst the crowd. Each record I made, I imagined you listening.'

'It was the same for me,' he said softly, running one hand down her back. 'Every time I spotted a dark slender girl in a bar or club I'd rush over to check her out. But then when "No time" reached the charts your face was everywhere. I read everything, kept a box full of reviews, interviews and press pictures. Yet the more famous you became, somehow the more distant you seemed.'

'And now?' she whispered.

'I feel just like I did that night on the heath,' he said,

running one finger down her cheek-bone. 'Wanting you so much, but afraid.'

Nothing compared with that moment. Not singing, applause or driving her Mercedes for the first time. His hands held her face, his lips came down on hers and it was as if Battersea fun fair with all its lights and music were turned on in her head.

All the pent up emotion of the day, all the years of missing one another vanished at his touch. They were back on that landing outside her playroom, the sounds of the Everly Brothers wafting out to them, two bodies and minds as one.

But this time there was no hesitation, no question of holding back. Peter's fingers were already under her sweater, reaching greedily for her small breasts.

Clothes torn off and tossed heedlessly away. Each touch electric. No time for careful foreplay. Just two bodies devouring each other, out of control, possession more important than subtlety.

Not the settee or even the bedroom. Peter lowered her to the floor right there under the window, covering her naked body with his. Georgia wound her legs around him, clawing at his back, demanding his lips. It was animalistic, brutal, yet perfect. She arched her back to draw him into her, tears streaming down her face.

'Georgia,' she heard him shout as he came, and although it had been over too soon, it was enough for the moment.

Above her head Georgia could see the moon shining in on them. Peter's body on hers was hot and sticky with sweat, his face buried in her shoulder and she knew he was crying too.

'I love you Peter,' she said drawing his lips back to hers. 'Nothing's changed has it?'

'I didn't dare even dream this,' his cheek against hers was damp. 'Just to see you was enough. Don't ever go out of my life again.'

They had a bath together later. Lying each end of the big tub. The room was once a bedroom, and the interior designer had pulled out all the stops to make it memorable. A mural of a jungle went right round the walls, and over a shower cubicle. Exotic birds, flowers, even a monkey grinned down at them. Real potted palms and a dark green carpet added to the illusion.

'This is wonderful,' Peter rubbed soap over her breasts. 'The bath where I live you wouldn't take your dog, let alone your girl.'

'I had a dose of places like that,' she said softly and bit by bit the past came out.

Helen. The abortion. Her hopes with the band, the disappointments, Ian, Rod and Max, the men she'd dated, the places she'd seen.

Peter told her about girls. Working on a building site, a summer on a Kibbutz in Israel, hitchhiking over Europe. Brief, vividly-painted sketches of six years packed with experiences so different to hers, yet enabling them to come together now as equals.

The water was getting cold. They climbed out and wrapped themselves in warm towels, moving on to the bedroom.

'No one's ever been here,' she said as she sank down on to the big bed, covered in the Nottingham lace bedspread Max had bought her. 'This is all ours.'

It was a beautiful room, decorated in a very soft pink with cream. Totally feminine, from the soft pink lamps to the ruffled lace at the windows.

Peter stood just looking at her. Dressed only in the white towel round his middle he looked like a Christian slave. His peachy skin, his legs and arms covered with fine blond hair, yet his broad chest as smooth and silky as a child's.

'I think you are the most beautiful man I ever saw,' she said softly, getting up to move towards him. Her heart was racing again. She had that churning in her stomach the way she did when she first met him.

He came towards her slowly, reaching out and taking the band from her hair, then teasing it with his fingers till it fell over her naked shoulders.

'You aren't just beautiful,' he murmured. 'You're exquisite. Can you possibly imagine how much I love you? For six years I've studied your pictures, listened to other men's fantasies about you and all the time I remembered the touch of your lips, the curve of your breasts and kept it to myself. I've told other women I loved them, but until now I didn't know what it meant.'

'Oh Peter,' she stroked his chest lightly. 'I feel so happy.'

'I used to try and imagine your breasts, when we were in the choir,' he said huskily, his fingers tugging at the towel covering them. 'I wondered what colour your nipples were, and whether I'd ever get to touch them.' The towel fell away, and he put one hand on each small pointed breast, running his fingers over her erect nipples. 'So they were dark, like chocolate buttons.' He knelt down on the floor in front of her, burying his head in them.

Georgia couldn't speak. She felt as if she could burst with tenderness and longing. The warmth of his body, gentle sensuous fingers, lips and tongue were driving her wild with desire.

'Let me look at you,' she whispered, unwrapping his towel from round his waist. 'I want to watch it grow big.'

'Men are so ugly next to women,' he said with a hint of embarrassment, but he stood up and let her take his towel away.

'Not you,' she said softly, her hand going down to his penis. 'I used to wonder about this too in choir, it's a wonder we ever sang a note.'

There was no headlong rush now. His tongue and

lips crept down her body, teasing and probing. He knelt in front of her just looking at her, touching, stroking and exploring. Time and time again she pulled him back to her, reaching for his lips, winding her legs around him. But still he made no attempt to enter her. He turned her on to her stomach licking her spine and massaging her back, then more kisses and stroking till she felt she would burst with longing.

He was heavier and stronger than Rod and Ian had been. He had Ian's sensitivity, Rod's passion and understanding of women, yet just enough of the brute in him to eclipse everything that had gone before. One moment so gentle she felt herself slipping away into a dream world. The next he crushed her into his arms as if he wanted to devour her.

Never before had she taken the initiative in love-making, hers had always been the passive role. But now she wanted to please him and she moved down the bed to take him in her mouth.

She watched him as her tongue slid over his penis, his hands just touching her head, his mouth open, breathing heavily, a look of exquisite bliss in his eyes.

'No more,' he groaned, 'It's too much.'

Georgia moved to climb on to him, but he grabbed her, rolling her onto her back and kneeling between her legs, pushing himself into her and enfolding her in his arms.

A roller-coaster of pleasure, a feeling that any moment she would explode like a volcano. Moments of tenderness, more of savagery. Rolling together as if they were one person.

She remembered seeing his face at the moment her orgasm came, his eyes searching hers, a look of adoration more beautiful than anything she'd ever seen before, and his lips found hers at the moment her body erupted like a firework.

Hot and damp they lay entwined, Peter's head on her

breasts. Tears welled up in her eyes and trickled down her cheeks.

'Why the tears?' he whispered, wiping them away with one finger. 'Is it the pain of too much tenderness?'

'That's a lovely way to put it,' she smiled up at him, tracing round his wide mouth with one finger.

'It's not original,' he smiled sheepishly. 'I got it out of a book.'

'Tell me about it?'

'It's quite long and I don't know it all.' He rolled over and pulled her into his arms, nestling her head on his shoulder.

'Go on,' she said softly. 'I want to hear it.'

His voice so deep and warm sent shivers down her spine.

'"Love has no other desire but to fulfil itself.

But if you love and must need have desires, let these be your desires.

To melt and be like a running brook that sings its melody to the night.

To know the pain of too much tenderness".' He looked down at her, wiping away the last of her tears.

'"To be wounded by your own understanding of love, and to bleed willingly and joyfully.

To wake at dawn with a winged heart and give thanks for another day of loving.

To rest at the noon hour and meditate love's ecstasy.

To return home at eventide with gratitude.

And then to sleep with a prayer for the beloved in your heart and a song of praise upon your lips."'

'That's beautiful,' she sighed.

'The whole chapter is even better,' he said softly. 'I used to read it and think of us. No one could ever touch that special place I kept for you.'

'But Peter,' she whispered. 'You do know there are people out there who will try to come between us? My life isn't entirely my own any longer.'

'Is anyone's?' He lifted one perfect eyebrow, turning over on his stomach to look down at her. 'I can't promise to be entirely yours either. I didn't spend all those years studying just to throw it away to be your consort.'

'But will we be strong enough to stand it when people whisper things about our past? Old friends can be tactless.'

'It's good to hear those incidents,' he said running his hand over her shoulders. 'Every person you meet and feel something for, leaves their mark. It's that which makes a well-rounded human being. So we couldn't share the last six years, but other people can put a new perspective to it.'

'You are very wise,' she smiled. 'Is that what studying philosophy does for you?'

'That was never more than a hobby and a second string,' he grinned. 'English is my main subject.'

'There's so much about you I have to catch up on,' she said wistfully.

'We've got the rest of our lives for that.'

'Can we be that sure?'

'Are you sure now?'

'Yes,' she whispered. 'Absolutely!'

'Well, that's all there is to it. Just take it one day at a time. Maybe in six weeks we'll find it was just a mirage. But for now it's real and beautiful. We don't need chains Georgia. The last few years have taught us that if nothing else.'

'I love you,' she said, another tear dripping down her cheek. 'Nothing in my life has ever felt so right.'

All through the night they had to keep touching, as if to check that it was real. If they slept at all it was brief moments, only to wake to kiss again.

As the first rays of sunshine crept through the curtains, Georgia looked down at Peter. Her heart felt as if it could burst.

She was looking for a flaw, but she could see none. From his long knobbly toes, up the golden legs to his tight bottom, slim hips and smooth chest. Even the way he slept was perfection, legs splayed out, one curled up against her, one arm behind him, the other curled around his head. Golden lashes like brushes against peachy cheeks, even the stubble on his chin was blond. His lips were squashed against his arm, childlike and soft.

She knew then just how much power he had over her. If he asked her to give up singing, to live in a terraced house in Manchester as a teacher's wife, to give up her money, her car and never once again step out onto a stage, she would, willingly.

As if sensing her eyes on him, he woke, rubbed his eyes and smiled.

'I love you,' he said, one sleepy hand coming up slowly to reach for her face.

'You're so beautiful,' she said. 'I could watch you for ever.'

'Just think what handsome devils our children will be,' he said pulling her back down to him.

'Let's get up and run away?' she whispered. 'Even now those newspapers are plonking down on doormats everywhere. The phone will start ringing soon. It will be a circus and I've had enough of that.'

'Where could we go?' His eyes lit up.

'Somewhere warm,' she held him tightly against her.

'But my passport's back in Manchester.'

'So much the better,' she sighed. 'London airport is always swarming with press. We'll drive to Manchester now and catch the first flight.'

'I haven't much money,' he retorted.

'I've got lots,' she said. 'Now don't argue, just get in that shower. I'll ring Sam and tell him to keep the dogs off our scent.'

Chapter 26

Sam whistled cheerfully as he made his way up Berwick Street to Bert's café.

Spring sunshine had finally found its way into the narrow streets of Soho. Shopkeepers were out sweeping their pavements. Stallholders were polishing apples, putting sale prices on winter woollies. The handbag stall was bright with pastel and white bags, flower stalls vivid with tulips. Even the pigeons had paused in their constant search for food to preen and coo in the sun.

'She's my girl all right,' he thought to himself. 'Impulsive, hot-headed, but I wouldn't change her one bit.'

Last night he had reluctantly left her to play at Ronnie Scott's. She insisted she didn't mind being alone; now she'd told her story she felt relaxed and secure. But he hadn't been sure. She looked tense and anxious to him, despite her delight that the editor had agreed to find Celia.

'I can't keep you here wet-nursing me,' she laughed at his concern. 'Besides, it will be nice to be alone for a change.'

When she rang him at his flat at seven in the morning, for a moment he thought some new disaster had erupted.

'What is it? Has something happened?'

'Oh yes,' she sort of sighed and he could hear

happiness buzzing down the wire. 'I've found Peter, everything's wonderful.'

He didn't want to admit even to himself that he felt a pang of jealousy. But that was it, whether he liked it or not. His little girl had a man in her life now and maybe she'd never have room for him again.

'That's wonderful, honey,' was all he could think of saying, as she rattled on about the pair of them running off to somewhere warm. Max's conspiracy to keep them apart and her conviction Peter was the love of her life.

'Of course I'll sort things out here. Have a good time. You need time alone together.'

He couldn't go back to sleep again. Every time he shut his eyes, mean thoughts came to him. Suppose he was just another fortune hunter? What if she promised to marry him then regretted it later?

His other children plagued him too. He should get back to them. He had enough money now to bring them back to England and if he put himself about he could get enough work to keep them far more comfortably than they'd ever known. But somehow staying in England rested on admitting the truth to Georgia about himself.

By eight he was too wound up to stay in. He could see the newspaper man across the street waving papers and the caption on his box looked ominous.

'RAPE! Georgia tells all.' It took him just a few minutes to jump into jeans and sneakers, then off across the road to pick up a paper.

He paused only briefly to check they had written her story correctly, then turning to the inside pages a picture of Peter Radcliffe leapt up at him.

It was a face of a real man, not a boy as he'd expected. Square jaw, bright eyes. An honest, open face.

'I should have stayed with her that night,' Sam read. 'Anderson was drunk and in an odd mood, but you don't expect something like that to happen. Next morning when the police took me in for questioning was the worst day in my life. I may have only been seventeen, but I loved her. How could any man do something as animal as that to a child he'd brought up as his own?'

He spoke of the evening he discovered she'd run away.

'Who could blame her? Her world was shattered, she knew the children's department would take her anyway. In her mind it was the only option. She believed that by removing herself from the picture, she could protect us all.'

He spoke of Celia, the beating she took from her husband when he returned home. The humiliation and the anguish of not knowing where her child was. The searching in clubs, bars and hostels.

But it was his final words that cut through all the doubts.

'I never stopped caring. Maybe our worlds are too far apart for there to be anything but friendship between us. But I won't let that sick, tortured man hurt her further.'

Charing Cross Road was heaving with people rushing to work. Traffic honked and snarled, exhaust fumes thick and choking. Yet for a moment Sam could have been standing in a garden.

This wasn't a boy wearing his heart on his sleeve, or some snivelling student with an eye to the main chance. It was a man who had held on to his love at all costs, who had searched for his girl. Someone who didn't give up, crumple under opposition as Sam had done himself. How could he have thought badly of the guy?

He took the paper into Leicester Square, sat on a bench and read and re-read the whole story.

There were a great deal of omissions, some facts bent. But it was written so well Sam could pass over that. It lingered over the horror, created an impression Max

Menzies had been her Svengali, but in the main it was accurate.

As he sat there in spring sunshine he saw office workers flicking through the paper as they walked to work. By lunchtime the whole world would know the truth and with luck Georgia would be far enough away to escape further questions.

Sam knew where he wanted to be now. Up in the market where Georgia's real friends still lived. She had introduced him to so many of them while they were making the recording and he just knew the street would be buzzing with the news. It would be their opinion Georgia would want to know about when she telephoned again. So he'd just get himself up to the café and join in the celebration.

Babs was red-faced and flustered as she poured tea, fried eggs and brushed back her straggly hair all at once. Most of the tables were taken, filled with men in donkey-jackets and flat caps, huge greasy breakfasts in front of them and mugs of steaming tea. Her yellow apron was stained and greasy, a lank lacy collar, half in, half out of a matted blue sweater, yet there was new bounce to her normal shuffling gait.

As she saw Sam her round homely face burst into a wide grin.

'Have you seen the news?' Her voice was squeaky with excitement. Heads turned to him, smiles of recognition on weatherbeaten faces. A sense of anticipation and a desire to know more.

'Just read it,' Sam smiled, waved his paper at her and nodded to the men. 'I knew I could rely on you to be as happy as I am.'

'I don't know why I feel so 'appy,' she wiped a tear away from her eye with the corner of her grubby apron. 'I started crying when I read what that man done to 'er. 'Er mate Janet always claimed that was what made 'er run away. I don't know why I didn't 'suss it out for meself. But it's that old boyfriend that's really got me going. Just look at him!'

Babs held out the paper to Sam, pointing a wet finger at the picture.

'A real movie star,' Sam grinned. 'Mind you, I've heard Georgia tell me how handsome he is for so long it's no surprise.'

Babs gave him one of those long stares, like she was thinking something but didn't quite dare voice it.

'Go on then, ask away!' Sam laughed cheerfully. 'Am I scared I'll lose her?'

Babs blushed. 'Georgia said yous was just mates. Is that all?'

Behind him he knew the men were waiting for his answer. His secret was bubbling inside him, like a child longing to tell a stranger it was his birthday. It would be so easy to tell Babs, she would burst into tears and give him one of those hugs she always gave Georgia. But he couldn't. It wouldn't be right.

'Have you ever known her lie to you?'

'No,' she giggled and blushed again, rushing over to rescue burning toast. 'She leaves things out, but doesn't lie,' she tossed over her shoulder.

'Well she didn't leave anything out this time,' Sam retorted. 'It's true we are just mates. After all I'm – ' he stopped. He'd almost said it, old enough to be her father. 'An old man,' he added quickly.

'I wouldn't say that,' she grinned wickedly, showing her broken front tooth. 'There's plenty round 'ere who wouldn't mind going a few rounds with you.'

'I'm all tied up,' he joked. 'You've had my heart since I met you Babs.'

She giggled, showing more than a hint of the girl hidden beneath the slatternly apron.

'Go on!' she reproved him. 'Me a married woman an' all. So do you think anything will come of it?' She leaned across the counter, her tired grey face alight with romance. 'I mean, he's clever, he's got letters after 'is name.'

'Shall I tell you a secret?' Sam got up and leaned across the counter till his lips were right by her ear. She smelled of bacon and fried fat, a smell that took him right back to his own mother.

'Go on,' she nodded, her eyes twinkling.

'Something has come of it. She met him last night and they've run off together.'

Her face mirrored his own pleasure. She slapped her hands over her mouth, tears sprang to her eyes.

'Oh Sam,' she whispered. 'Really?'

Maybe he should have been more discreet, yet in his heart he knew Georgia would have shouted it from the roof tops.

'She rang me this morning,' Sam felt like a kid himself passing on an overheard secret. 'But don't you go saying anything to anyone, or I shan't tell you anything else.'

He had to go all over it again when Bert came in. What would happen at the studio? Would Anderson be charged with rape? Were Georgia and Peter getting married?

'She ain't ever 'ad anyone to look after her.' Bert's customary gloomy face broke into a wide smile revealing blackened teeth. 'They've all made money out of her, worn her out, then wanted to kick her on the slag heap just because some old weirdo made up a load of lies. He deserves horse whipping.'

Georgia had told him so much about this pair. The frugal way they lived, the endless hours of work. A life that could be made easy by selling up and buying themselves a nice house. Yet he understood now why they stayed, they were the cornerstone of the community. They needed other people, the hustle and bustle. It wasn't money which kept them here, but long roots.

The café had all the cosiness of his mother's kitchen when he was a boy. Gossip and speculation hanging in the air like damp washing. Each and every market trader was urged to look at the paper if they hadn't already seen it and as Sam sat eating eggs and bacon they plonked themselves down to question him.

'What'll happen now? Will she be on the box tonight? When will we get to see her?'

'No wonder Georgia loves it round here,' Sam said as he wiped up his egg with a slice of bread and butter. 'I never saw so many caring people in one place.'

'Well she's our dream come true ain't she.' Babs shuffled round the counter to clear the tables. 'Not many people make it out of 'ere, not unless they're crooks. She's our pride ain't she?'

It was pride Sam's heart filled with too. That same feeling he felt back home in New Orleans when kids pointed to him in the street.

'That's Sam Cameron, he plays a real mean horn.' These people might all be white but it was the same emotion that moved them as moved his folks. Screw the celebrities, the rich, and the tourists, making it was when your own people had that look on their face.

'I bet the girls and Pop aren't doing a stroke of work this morning,' Bert said gleefully. 'They'll be all in 'ere soon, talkin' the hind legs off a donkey.'

'Speaking of work,' Sam got up and felt in his pocket for some money. 'I guess I'd better go up to the studio and see how the land lies there. They say there is no such thing as bad publicity. I'll bet they'll be itching to get this new album out now, and they ain't gonna like it when they find their bird has flown.'

'Stick that back in yer pocket,' Bert said shoving the money back across the counter. 'That's on me today, and if you've got time around six tonight come in and we'll have a few beers. Today we got some'at to celebrate!'

Sam was right. Everyone was in a turmoil at the studio. Phones were ringing, voices raised, teleprinters clattering. Max was in a meeting already with the chiefs and every desk had a copy of the paper spread out on it.

'Do you know where Georgia is?' Ruth one of the secretaries rushed up to him. She had smears of mascara on her cheeks, eyes pink from recent tears, and this was a girl who was normally the blonde ice queen, efficient and unemotional. 'They are all going mad because they can't contact her.'

'Sure,' he grinned. 'She rang me this morning. Shall I go in and put them out of their misery?'

'Give her all our love,' she whispered, laying one cool hand on his arm. 'She deserves happiness after what that swine put her through.'

Once inside the boardroom Sam's elation vanished. His old jeans, grubby sweatshirt and sneakers, stubble on his chin, looked incongruous with their smart business suits. Apart from Jack Levy and Max he knew none of the other five men. All dark and Jewish, navy suits, white shirts and club ties. They cast suspicious glances at him over horn-rimmed glasses. Tight, humourless lips, faces that could have been born middle-aged. Plump, white hands rested on the polished table, water, fountain pens in readiness before them.

Down in the market there had been joy of a wrong righted. Here there was nothing but the smell of money.

He remembered Georgia telling him about the day she signed her contract with them. No wonder she had found it so terrifying.

'Good to see you Sam,' Max frowned as if it wasn't good at all. 'Where's Georgia?'

'She's gone away,' Sam replied, pulling up a chair unasked.

'What on earth does she think she's playing at?' Max exploded. 'She should be down here.'

Seven indignant faces turning to him. Eyes narrowing at plans thwarted.

'Now just one moment,' Sam felt a bubble of anger in his gut. 'Am I hearing right? You guys abandoned her, right at the time when she needed support.'

'We did nothing of the sort.' Jack Levy drew himself up behind the table, dark eyes blinking furiously behind his glasses. 'We had no alternative but to suspend recording.'

'Not one of you called on her, wrote her, sent her flowers,' Sam's eyes flashed from face to face. 'Did anyone of you go to the press and tell them what a nice girl she is? Did you hell!

'You sat on your fat arses, panicking that the golden goose was finally about to be killed off. And probably had a meeting just like this one to decide who would get the carcass.'

'That's not fair Sam,' Max flushed with anger. 'We had to act impartial.' He drew a cigar out of his breast pocket and sniffed it reflectively.

'You acted like cowards,' Sam hissed at them. 'Even if she had done everything that creep said, after all she's given you, you should have stood up for her. I've only known her a few short weeks but it seems I was the only person who truly believed in her.'

'Well, where is she now?' one of the directors said. His face showed no emotion, just irritation that she wasn't here, cap in hand.

'She's doing what she should have done some time ago. Putting her own affairs in order,' Sam said, glaring round at each one of them in turn.

'But the album,' Max said.

'Screw the album,' Sam's voice was rising. 'I'd like

just one of you to express concern for her. To show some emotion. She might find her mother. How ashamed you are that you doubted her? Or even ask about the boyfriend?'

'So that's it,' Max said, a sly look in his eyes, taking out a gold cigar cutter. 'I suppose she's off screwing him.'

Sam leapt out of his chair and caught Max by the collar of his suit jacket, lifting him clean off the floor, scattering cigar and cutter to the floor.

'You motherfucker,' he hissed. 'You stopped that boy from seeing her. You lied to them both. Why Max? Why?'

'How was I to know?' Max's voice whined. 'Countless blokes claim to know her. I was protecting her.'

Sam let go of him, but his fists were clenched. He looked round at all the other men, searching their eyes to see if they had guessed the reason. There was interest, surprise, but no real understanding.

'You wanted her yourself,' Sam snarled. 'I can understand that, but why then if you wanted her so badly didn't you stick up for her? You left the country with some blonde on your arm. What sort of a man are you?'

'You've got it all wrong.' Max pulled at the revers of his jacket, his eyes flashed round the room trying to convey to the other men that Sam was mad. 'Georgia was like my own daughter.'

'Then you,' Sam poked a finger at Max's belly, 'are just like Anderson. Because I've sure as hell heard you describe her as a cockraiser. Did you get to rape her too?'

Max cowered back. Jack Levy leapt to his feet and moved swiftly over to Sam, putting a restraining hand on his arm.

'That's enough, Sam,' he yelled. 'Enough!'

'Enough?' Sam glowered round at the men. 'I ain't even started yet. Georgia is making what promises to be the finest album ever made,' he hissed. 'She's put her heart and soul into it, singing songs of love so beautiful they even move me to tears.' He pushed away Jack's hand, his mouth trembling with anger. 'But all you lot see is money,' he went on glaring at each of the men in turn. 'You don't see a little girl abused by a man she trusted. A girl with guts and fire that made things happen for herself without selling her soul in the process. Don't you know what you've got?'

The atmosphere was charged with electricity. Max shrank back against the wall, even Jack stopped short.

'I'll tell you arseholes what you've got,' Sam yelled, waving his clenched fists at Jack. 'You've got a girl with more heart and guts than all us lot put together. Get off your chairs, get down in the studio and listen to those tapes. Forget how much money they'll make and listen to the message in her voice. When you've done that and found out what Georgia is all about, then maybe I'll tell you where she is!'

He paused. He saw the gaping mouths, sensed that his words had sunk in. Sam turned sharply, pulled open the door, and left, slamming it behind him.

Max turned scarlet. 'I'm sorry about that.' His voice shook nearly as badly as his legs. He couldn't meet their eyes. For once he couldn't think of anything sharp to say. 'He's an artist, he can't help but be emotional.'

Jack Levy took off his glasses and polished them vigorously. He felt something he hadn't felt for years and he knew it was shame.

'We'd better do what the man says.' He replaced his glasses on his nose. 'We'll talk again afterwards.'

Sam paused only long enough in the street to take a few deep breaths. He wasn't going to agonize over whether he'd gone too far, or whether he'd blocked all chances of his own career taking off. Right now he was

going to ring that editor Phillips and make sure everyone was pulling out all the stops.

'It's Sam Cameron,' he said, when they finally put
him through. 'Georgia asked me to phone and find out
the state of play.'

'Where is she?'

Sam wanted to laugh, it was that same frantic
question he'd heard in the boardroom, another would-
be puppet master.

'Why?'

'I just found Peter had gone,' Phillips said. 'I just
hoped they were together. As I see it that pair were
made for each other.'

Sam felt all the anger inside him melt. At last someone had the right idea.

'Between you and me, off to sunny places with Peter.
The recording company is freaking out. They don't
know where she is, so I'd be grateful if you didn't print
that.'

Phillips chuckled. 'Wonderful. That news makes it all
worthwhile. Peter Radcliffe is a real human being. I'm
keeping everything crossed for them.'

'Yup, looks like you might get your big love story
soon. But don't rush it, give them time. Now, about
Mrs Anderson?'

'We've managed to contact the health organization
she is working for. The office is in Nairobi. Apparently
she's way out in the bush running a small clinic and
hospital.'

'You don't say!' Sam's face broke into a broad smile.

'We've got things in hand.' Phillips' voice had a ring
of pure glee. 'It won't be instantaneous. Messages have
to be sent by wire, the last lap will be by jeep over
rough terrain. It could be a couple of weeks before they
can get a replacement out for her.'

'Did you tell them what it was about?'

'Just the bare bones,' Phillips hesitated. 'I was apprehensive about the story being misinterpreted, so I promised to send full details by telex. I've just finished that.'

'Georgia is going to flip,' Sam's voice was breaking with emotion. 'This is all too much. How soon before we know anything positive? I don't want to wind her up and then leave her dangling.'

'I suggest you say nothing, yet,' Phillips' voice was more cautious. 'We don't want her rushing off to Nairobi and then missing her mother. As soon as we know she's on a flight home, that's the time to tell her. The poor kid's had enough grief to last most of us a lifetime.'

'Sounds sensible,' Sam said. 'At least she's got Peter to take her mind off things. I'm very grateful to you.'

'Has she said what action she's going to take about Anderson?' Once again he was just a reporter, wanting to be first with the news.

'I couldn't say,' Sam said. 'If it were up to me I'd go round there and kick seven kinds of shit out of him. But Georgia isn't one for revenge. We'll just have to wait for that.'

'Keep in touch,' Phillips' voice held warmth and sincerity. 'Let me know when your next gig is. I'd like to meet the man Georgia raved about.'

'She spoke of me?'

'Oh yes,' Phillips chuckled. 'You rate in importance along with Celia and Peter, but surely you knew that?'

Down in the recording studio Jack Levy and his team were listening closely to the tapes Georgia had been working on. Heads bent forward, hands on knees, cigars, coffee and even note-making forgotten.

'Sam was right.' Jack twisted his large gold ring around his finger during a pause, looking round at the other men with stunned eyes. 'This is some of the best stuff I've ever heard.'

Georgia's lush, rich voice filled the studio. The complex machinery, the plastic chairs, the glass partitions, the bright lights all softened in the music. With eyes closed, each one of them was transported to a place of beauty, memories and emotions long forgotten were stirred with her special magic.

Every note and instrument on the finished songs was impeccable. Sam's tenor sax sent shivers of delight down their spines, the strings, drums and piano all played their part in creating a masterpiece.

'Sam's one hell of a player too,' one of the men said. 'We ought to get him under contract too, before he floats off back home.'

As the last note died away, Max got up. He felt drained, suddenly old and tired. He'd give anything to have Miriam back home to run to.

Why had he cheated Georgia, lied to her and held her back? Why couldn't he have been like Sam, listened, protected and encouraged? What made a man who had a bright and beautiful butterfly in his hand, crush it and still expect it to fly?

Georgia would merely laugh at the underhand things he'd done in the past. She accepted them all the way a zoo keeper expects the tiger to snarl at him. But by preventing that lad from seeing her, by turning his back on her when she was in trouble, that was when he dug his own grave.

'What's up, Max?' Jack Levy squinted up at him through his glasses. 'Can't stand the heat any longer? She'll re-sign with us. They always do. We'll just have to offer her a better deal.'

'I think I'm through with deals,' Max said. 'Sometimes they leave a nasty taste in your mouth.'

Chapter 27

The newspaper lay crumpled amongst empty sherry bottles, chip papers, cold cups of tea, and congealed greasy plates, hardly an inch of floor exposed from bed to window.

The stained china sink smelled like the lavatory he'd used it as, draining-board groaning with burned saucepans and jagged-edged empty cans.

The frayed brown curtains were no longer opened. The small table in front of the window strewn with pointers to a period of wealth. An empty whiskey bottle, a cigar box, the remains of an Indian takeaway meal thick with mould and a dead potted plant.

Dust, paper and food scraps were everywhere. Vomit lay on the floor just feet from where he lay huddled on his bed. The stench of himself, the vomit and rotting food combined to make the air unbreathable.

Only the wall covered in Georgia's pictures had any semblance of order and light.

He was sweating, so hot he felt he was on fire. But he knew soon the shivering would come back and nothing would warm him.

Drink couldn't help now. Nothing could blot out the misery. No heat, money, drink or food. Trapped, sick and helpless.

Why was it that his mind had cleared now? Ever since that day when he was knocked down and robbed, the grey mist which stopped him hurting and thinking had vanished.

How long ago was it when those newspaper men came here? A week, two, maybe a month. He remembered putting a fiver in Mrs Dooley's hand and persuading her to clean up for him though.

'Fancy her being your daughter,' she kept saying as she swept the floor and changed his bed. 'She should pay to put you in a home, you aren't capable of looking after yourself.'

Mrs Dooley wasn't the only one who treated him like a celebrity then. Someone left a bag of clothes on his doorstep, another neighbour brought him over a pot of stew. Everyday the mail brought letters of sympathy, some with money inside them. Mrs Dooley was glad to clean for him. It gave her an opportunity to ask questions, she even referred to him as her 'poor old gentleman friend.'

So many visitors knocked on his door, offering invitations to their houses, sympathy, help and understanding.

Down at the pub they all wanted to drink with him, they didn't refuse to serve him in the café, everyone said how badly Georgia had treated him.

A taste of what it must be like to be her. A person people wanted to meet. He felt like shaving again, taking baths, eating proper meals, for a while drink hadn't been so necessary.

Church wardens came round and talked of re-housing him in a nice little flat. A lady down the road knitted him a blue pullover. Even the kids along the road began to smile at him.

A hundred pounds seemed fair enough at first. He didn't know he'd been cheated until Adams made off with thousands. In that first week it had been enough to be important and know at last the public had turned against her.

The sickness had started the night he read just a few lines in the *Evening News*. A picture of the bitch standing by a flashy car, wearing a white mini skirt.

'You can read the true story tomorrow,' she said.

That night even whiskey didn't help. A small voice kept whispering in his head, telling him things he didn't like. Later it turned to a gnawing pain in his stomach, just where she stabbed him. The nightmares came back too. Visions of him grabbing her, smooth skin under his hands, a rounded arse in front of him surrounded by harsh net petticoats. An act which until then he'd blotted from his mind.

It was Mrs Dooley that brought in the paper the next morning. The fat slut stood in his doorway, hands on hips, her hair in curlers, mouth like an angry red gash.

'You bastard!' she screamed at him, flinging the paper in disgust. 'You filthy bastard! You'll rot in hell for what you did to her, and I'd gladly get you there a little quicker!'

Funny that Georgia's retaliation didn't make him mad. He just lay there crying, remembering.

Was it that mention of St Joseph's convent that made him think of her tiny, bony back, lacerated and weeping? What prompted the memory of guiding her down the pavement on her first bicycle, holding the saddle and urging her to steer and keep pedalling? Holding her on his shoulders to see penguins at the zoo. One hand under a smooth, soft tummy as he taught her to swim.

Peter too. Sharp, clear pictures of him eating Christmas lunch with them. A red paper hat resting on his blond hair, talking about cricket, laughing at Brian's stories about people in the office. The good feeling at having male company.

Other things wafted back. Georgia coming into the bedroom in her nightdress, with a tray of tea for him and Celia, her stocking under her arm.

591

'I waited as long as I could.' She had that expression on her face that always made them smile. Wide-eyed, mouth trembling, a please-don't-be-cross face that worked everytime. 'Seven o'clock isn't that early?'

Once they'd put sugar mice in her stocking, tiny dolls, pens and pencils. That last year it had been make-up and stockings and a silly false nose and glasses she wore most of the morning.

Why was it now when he needed the grey mist, it didn't return? Sharp memories like Georgia sitting by his knee. The Christmas tree filling the room with the scent of pine, the fire banked up. Celia in a blue costume. Georgia in a tartan dress with a lace collar. He could see that book on photography she gave him. A shiny red and black jacket, the spine two inches thick, one he'd intended to buy for so long.

'Mum didn't give me the money.' He could hear her soft voice shaking with excitement, feel her lips on his cheek, her arms round his neck. 'I saved it up myself.'

He knew when the reporters came back he would get no sympathy. He cowered in his bed listening to them scrabbling round the house, terrified they would burst in. He heard neighbours shout things outside the window.

'Come on out you pervert! We'll show you how we deal with rapists round here.'

Just enough strength to push a chair under the door, then stumble back to bed, hoping they wouldn't hurtle a brick or a fire bomb through his window. His chest, legs and stomach ached, but the worst hurt was inside his head.

How many times was it that he read that newspaper? Twenty, thirty? He lost count.

'I don't know why he changed that night,' he read. 'One moment he was my dad, the sweetest, kindest man alive, the next like an evil stranger. Everything I knew about men came from him. I loved being in the car with him, holding his hand when we went for walks. The way he hugged me when he came home from work. He knew everything. He helped me with my homework, he taught me to swim. He clapped when I danced and sang. My mum and dad were the best parents anyone could have. I had nothing to rebel against. I felt loved. I didn't even mind when he got drunk and came up to the party. Everyone thought it was funny. I told him to go to bed after Peter had gone. But that's when he changed.'

It wasn't a nightmare after all. He really had done those things which haunted him. Soon the police would come for him. They'd lock him up, maybe even beat him. If only he had enough money to put in that meter, to turn the gas on and wait for oblivion.

Someone was insistently ringing the door bell. He heard Mrs Dooley shout to one of her children to answer it. Deep, male voices, too low to hear what they were saying.

'He's in that room,' Mrs Dooley's Irish voice boomed out. 'He hasn't shown his face for nearly two weeks. But he's in there all right, more's the pity. Filthy bastard, you can smell him from the hall.'

'Has anyone got a key?' The male voice was crisp and tough, the sort of voice belonging to someone with authority.

'Don't think so.' Her voice was coming closer as if she was walking down the stairs. 'The landlord was supposed to be coming over to heave him out in a day or two. He hasn't even been out to use the toilet. God knows what you'll find in there.'

He buried his face when the rapping on the door started again. Was it night, or merely the dim light?

'Mr Anderson!' That strong voice again. 'Mr Anderson, open the door or we'll have to break it down!'

He was sure it was the police. Reporters didn't threaten violence. He screwed up his eyes, huddled further under the blanket and waited, too sick and weak to make any protest.

A thump and a splintering noise and they were in.

'Bloody hell.' P.C. Blake clamped one hand over his nose and waved to his partner to open the window as he moved over to the bed. Cautiously he pulled back the thin blanket to find Anderson staring up at him blankly.

'Are you all right mate?' he asked, his stomach churning.

There was no reply. Just those pale frightened eyes looking at him, a haggard, almost shrunken face glistening with sweat, flecks of white foam on his blue lips.

'Get an ambulance,' Blake turned to the younger man standing gasping by the window. 'Warn them about the conditions. Book a fumigator afterwards.'

As the constable rushed back gagging to the door, Blake's professionalism got the better of revulsion. He lifted one scrawny wrist from the sopping bed and felt for a pulse. 'You've got yerself in a right state,' he said. 'It's hospital for you.'

'I'm sorry for what I did,' Brian whimpered. He tried to sit up, but he was too weak. 'Will I go to prison?'

'Don't look that way,' Blake moved away from the man's fetid breath. He glanced up at a picture cut from a glossy magazine. Georgia was sitting astride a cane chair, one arm leaning on the back, drinking a glass of milk wearing shorts and a T-shirt. 'It was her that asked us to check you out. Not a moment too soon I'd say.'

'Georgia asked you?' Brian tried to focus his eyes. All he could see was silver buttons against blue serge as once again his bladder overflowed.

'Welcome home,' Sam threw open the door as he heard the lift.

'Sam!' Georgia launched herself towards him, arms

wide to hug him. Peter was left in the lift with a suitcase.

'I came over to make a meal for you,' Sam said. A lump came up in his throat, making it hard to speak. Her warm body pressed against him, the perfume of her hair, her lips against his neck. 'I felt I had to talk to you before everyone else grabbed you.'

She held him still, looking up at him, nose twitching, like a stray dog hoping for a meal, big eyes dancing.

'It smells wonderful,' she said. 'But I'm being rude. This is Peter, I keep forgetting you haven't met before.'

Peter in the flesh was far more striking than press photographs. Blue eyes alight with laughter, a rugged quality to his features. He seemed to fill the small hall; muscles straining under his thin jacket, blond hair streaked almost white by the sun, the golden tan, all gave the impression it had been achieved by a lifetime in rough country.

'It's great to meet you at last,' Sam put out his hand and Peter gripped it firmly. 'Sorry I had to drag you away from the sun, but the people at Decca were getting frantic.'

'We understood,' Peter grinned. 'I should be back at school anyway.'

They had been in the Canary Islands for nearly two weeks. Georgia looked black now, the whites of her eyes and her teeth flashing against her skin. She wore a red flouncy dress that made him think of gypsy dancers, bare feet in gold sandals.

Rest and love had done wonders for her. Skin glowing, eyes gleaming, she'd even put on a little weight. There was a calmer, softer look in her eyes.

'I still don't understand what the panic is,' Georgia said as she bounced inside, gazing around her in delight. 'But whatever it is, it's nice to be home.'

The lounge was filled with late afternoon sunshine,

lighting up the vivid primary colours of her Spanish rug and turning the white settees to pale gold.

She walked round the room, just reaching out and touching things as if telling them all she was back in charge.

Sam could see her eyes flitting out to the window-boxes on the balcony, her eyes lighting up at the clusters of giant pansies, blue and purple heads nodding at her as if in welcome.

'I kept them watered,' Sam smiled. She was just like Katy, at heart a homemaker. Soon she would be running her fingers over ledges, making mental notes of jobs to be done. 'Now sit down and I'll make us a drink.'

He had to tell her tonight. Everything was moving so fast. He'd removed every possible obstacle to give him a clear field. He just had to hope no one came unexpectedly.

Peter took the glass of beer and sank into a chair, but Georgia flitted in and out of the room looking at things as Peter described their hotel and the beach.

'This is all a bit posh,' Georgia called out from the dining room across the hall. 'Come and see Peter, Sam's laid it all with flowers, and napkins. I didn't know you were so domesticated, Sam!'

'There's lots you don't know about me yet Miss Smartypants,' Sam grinned, as he looked into see her straightening a knife here, a plate there. He too had been surprised to find a sideboard full of white bone china, polished silver cutlery in felt lined boxes and a wealth of starched tablecloths and napkins. Clearly Georgia hadn't rejected Celia Anderson's middle-class values. He wasn't going to admit that he had learned his skills while working as a waiter.

'Now, I don't want you two to think I'm intruding on your last night together. I'll be off later.'

'You don't have to go,' Peter touched Sam's elbow,

his face full of concern that he might feel pushed out. 'We're both pleased to see you.'

Sam heard that deep voice, full of sincerity and knew this was a man he could respect. He wished he had time to get to know him the way he had Georgia, but there wasn't time for that now.

'Thanks,' Sam grinned. 'We'll have lots of opportunities later to dig into each other. But first a drink and I'll dish up. I hope you like spicy food as it's about all I know how to cook.'

'He's got something on his mind,' Peter said as Sam disappeared into the kitchen. He sat down on the settee while Georgia began sifting through records in the corner. 'Do you think he knows something about Celia?'

'No, he would have told us immediately if he did,' she looked reflective. 'I hope there isn't something wrong with his kids. I couldn't bear him to leave England.'

Peter shrugged.

'He'll have to go sometime.'

'Oh Peter,' she jumped up, dropping the record and bounded across the room to him. 'You aren't jealous are you?' She perched next to him, running one hand through his hair.

'I guess so,' he grinned sheepishly. 'No, I'm not jealous of Sam exactly. Just a bit overwhelmed by your life. That welcoming reception at the airport, all those press hanging on to your every word. It makes me wonder about my role in your life.'

He'd read so often about Georgia being mobbed by fans, yet until he was in the thick of it himself it never seemed real. People grabbing his arm, microphones stuck right under his nose, the shouted questions, the flash of cameras, a feeling of terror that they could actually be crushed to death by this crowd.

'You don't have a role in my life,' she smiled. 'You are my life.'

They had spent so much of their time away sounding out each other's ambitions. Georgia's went no further than finishing her album and finding a home out of London, but Peter's ideas were more altruistic. His dreams were filled with education for everyone, decent homes and proper health care and it was apparent to Georgia that the idealistic boy with missionary zeal had grown into a humanitarian.

'Well, sweetness,' Peter put his hands on her neck, lifted her hair, then bent to kiss her ears. 'One thing's certain. Branscombe Road Secondary Modern isn't going to be thrilled at such an infamous teacher in their midst.'

'If they're that small-minded it's the perfect excuse to walk out,' she grinned.

'I don't walk out of anything until I'm ready,' Peter replied sternly. 'And I certainly won't leave them in the lurch just to be one of your acolytes!'

'Well, what do you think of Creole cooking?' Sam said as finally their empty plates were pushed away.

'Superb.' Georgia sat back in her chair, holding her stomach, grinning like a greedy child. Lazily she leaned forward, filling up the wine glasses again. 'If the music world lets you down you can always become my cook/ housekeeper.'

Sam had entertained them during the meal with gossip. The press's speculation about their future together. People from Berwick Street and the club scene too. He said how United Artists had offered the boys a contract, and Norman had written some brilliant music. Rod was taking singing lessons and claimed he was in love with a model called Patti. Speedy was straight still and the others were trying to influence Les to join him.

Sally and Janet had finally been offered new houses in Harlow, and Pop, faced with losing his two most reliable workers, was looking for small factory premises there too. Even Babs and Bert were seriously contemplating retiring.

'You'd better let me meet them all soon,' Peter said. 'Otherwise they'll all be gone.'

'We could throw a party,' Georgia's eyes lit up. 'How about Whitsun when you're on holiday, Peter?'

'We'll talk about that some other time,' Peter groaned. 'I think Sam's got something on his mind.'

It had grown dark outside while they talked and Georgia stood up to draw the red curtains and turn on a small lamp on the sideboard. She'd lived in this flat for nearly two years, but this room was hardly ever used. It gave her a glow of pleasure to see how warm and inviting it could be.

'Is it your kids?' Georgia touched Sam lightly on the shoulder before she sat down. 'Or has someone offered you a contract?'

Sam looked down at his empty plate. Chopin was playing softly from the lounge across the passage, the traffic down below had slowed to a mere purr. He couldn't stay here all night. He had to tell her now.

'Neither of those,' he said. 'It's about you, honey. Hell, I don't exactly know how to put this,' he paused, biting his lip. 'I want you to think about your real background. I mean your natural mother and father.'

Georgia made a face, putting a finger in some sauce and licking it.

'Is this a "let's face the black side of yourself" routine?' she said. 'A warning that mixed-race relationships are doomed from the start?'

Sam chuckled. 'No. There's sure as hell plenty of others will say that for me. I meant don't you ever wonder how you came to be abandoned, orphaned or whatever it was?'

'Of course I do,' she smiled. 'But Celia tried to dig around, didn't she Peter? She didn't find much.'

'All the records were destroyed,' Peter said. 'She was

pretty certain Georgia was in the Billericay war orphans home, but there's not even any real evidence of that. What's made you bring this up?'

He could sense an undercurrent, something Sam had been brooding about for some time.

Sam cleared his throat nervously.

'Before I met you Georgia, when I first arrived in England, I did some digging myself.' He paused looking at Georgia through thick curly lashes. His Southern drawl suddenly seemed more pronounced, or was it he was choosing every word carefully? 'I told you I was here during the war, and somehow it seemed important to just go down to my old haunts and look around.'

'An old flame?' Peter smirked.

'Yeah,' Sam was smiling, yet his eyes were sad. 'She just stopped writing, you see. It happened all the time. One day the girl's crazy about you, the next she's got cold feet.'

Peter reached out and picked up the wine bottle, dividing up the remains between the three of them. He was sure this was leading to a serious warning about mixed marriages whatever Sam had said previously. Perhaps a pep talk to Georgia about accepting that Peter had a career too. He had noticed Sam studying him closely. Was he doubtful they could make it as a couple?

'She was white?' Peter said, raising one eyebrow. 'Come on then, give us the whole story.'

Sam took a deep breath and began. His meeting with Katy at the base, falling in love and her parents' disgust that their only daughter should choose a black G.I. How Katy moved out and found a flat in the East End so they could be together and then on to his departure to France.

'Everything was kinda frantic,' he said, his big lips trembling a little. 'We didn't know where we was goin', if or when we'd be back. I never told Katy just how hard it would be for her if she married me. We just kinda lived for the moment. All we had was letters and trust.'

'Did she write?' Georgia asked.

Sam nodded. 'Every day. Sometimes I didn't get any for weeks, then I got a big bundle. She used to number them. A funny little figure on the back of an envelope with our names written round it. But then they stopped.'

For a moment Georgia thought he was going to cry. No tears, just a twitching in his cheeks as if he were fighting it.

'It nearly broke me. I couldn't eat or sleep. I grew bitter. It kind of sapped all my energy.'

Peter nodded. He knew exactly what Sam had gone through.

'But why didn't you come back?'

'I wanted to,' Sam bit his lip again. 'But everything was crazy in Germany. Then I got wounded, nothing real serious, just a bit of shrapnel in my arm. Just enough for the M.O. to decide I was to go back Stateside instead of staying like the others to clear up the mess.'

'Did you write again?' Georgia asked. 'Did you tell her what was happening?'

'I wrote over and over,' Sam shrugged his shoulders. 'What was I to think? Black guys had enough trouble getting willing girls over. What chance did I have with one who didn't even reply?'

'So that's what you went to dig up?' Peter said.

Sam nodded. 'It had all changed. I found Hughes Mansions where she lived, all right. But something was different. Some people I met there told me about a V.2 dropping on it,' he said, watching Georgia's face. 'Katy was amongst the hundred or so killed.'

'Oh Sam, you never knew?' Georgia's face fell. 'You thought she didn't love you, but all the time she was dead. I don't know which is worse.'

601

'There is something worse,' Sam took Georgia's hand. 'To find the girl I loved didn't tell me she had my child.'

Georgia's hands flew up to her mouth, eyes filling with tears.

'The child died too?'

'No, it was rescued,' Sam said slowly. 'I went to the East End looking to just reminisce. Instead I find I've got another child.'

'Where?' Georgia leaned forward. 'Have you found him?'

'Her,' Sam corrected Georgia. 'That was somethin' else. Blind alleys, disappointment, hundreds of old papers to go through without even a name to help. Finally when I thought I couldn't go no further I found an old social worker who'd taken a child from a foster home, on to a convent.'

Suddenly Peter saw the truth. Not just Sam's words, but the way he was looking at Georgia. The eyes were the same, round and large, two sets of identical dark chocolate, the same delicate eyelids, even the lashes like brushes.

Georgia couldn't see it. She was too immersed in Sam's tale, grieving over a woman she didn't know and the sadness of her child being orphaned.

'What's her name, Sam?' Peter said softly. Someone had to help the man, he could see Sam wanted to blurt it out but couldn't find the right words.

Two weeks ago Peter had only the image the press had painted of this man in his head. A brute who beat his wife and abandoned his children. What would a man in his forties have in common with a girl like Georgia? Wasn't it more likely he was using her to further his own career, building up her trust so one day he could get his hands on her fortune?

Of all the things he feared most about Georgia's life, this man was probably the thing which worried him the most.

602

But on holiday Georgia told him about her Sam. The talented musician, the caring father, the good friend. A man who made no advances to her, asked for nothing. The man who had stayed by her side when everyone else turned away.

Both images had stayed with him, like two pans on a scale. The pans had teetered up and down since meeting him. One moment he was sure Georgia's opinion was right, the next he had his doubts.

But now the pan was thumping down on the table, the image the press had put in his head, flipping out of the window with the force. He could see tears gathering in the man's eyes, feel the emotion in his heart.

'Was it Georgia?' Peter asked.

Sam's eyes closed, a tear trapped by his lashes trickled down his dark cheek.

'Yes,' he whispered. 'Oh yes.'

For a moment Georgia just sat there, stunned.

She rested her elbows on the table, holding her head in her hands. Her eyes moved from Peter to Sam, back to Peter's smiling face, then back to Sam.

'Me?' she questioned. She looked like a frog. Huge bulging eyes and mouth gaping open. 'I don't understand. Are you sure?'

Sam opened his eyes again.

'The nun was Sister Mary from St Joseph's,' he said.

Her chair tipped over and crashed to the floor as she leapt up. She zoomed round the table, flinging her arms round Sam, burying her head in his shoulder, unable to say anything.

'You're glad, ain't you,' Sam whispered against her hair lifting her onto his lap and holding her tightly. 'If I'd knowed I had a little girl I would have come back. There ain't been a day since I knew about the bomb I didn't regret not coming looking for Katy.'

'Oh Sam,' Georgia's deep sigh was buried in his neck. 'It's the most wonderful thing. I knew you were special.

I just knew it.' She cried then, small shoulders heaving, wrapping her arms around him tighter.

'Those had better be happy tears.' Sam disentangled himself, cupping her face in his big hands and lifting it to his.

'She only cries when she's happy,' Peter stood up and moved closer to them both, putting one hand on Sam's shoulder, the other stroking Georgia's hair. 'You should know she grows silent and grim-faced when she's sad. Hell, Sam that is one hell of a story!'

'Why didn't Katy tell you about me?' Georgia's face was a study of glee, curiosity and sadness all at once.

'I guess she didn't know till after I'd gone to France, honey,' Sam explained. 'After Christmas she wrote and said she had a surprise for me, but she never let on what it was. Maybe she was afraid I might go AWOL. I expect I would have too. I guess she knew me only too well.'

They moved into the lounge, leaving the dishes on the table and Sam went on to explain everything.

'Sister Mary!' Georgia was quivering with excitement. 'How is she? Where is she? Did she know who I was?'

'She was the one who led me to you,' Sam smiled, tucking her hand in his big brown one. 'She told me I must get close to you first and win your trust, that God would guide me when the time was right. You were in America then. I got all your records. I used to wallow in them all day. Wonderin' how I could get to meet you.'

'And I came banging on your door,' Georgia laughed. 'No wonder you looked so shocked!'

'Sister Mary's been waitin' for me to tell you, without her to talk to I might have lost my nerve. She's dying to see you, honey.'

'Why did you wait so long to tell her Sam?' Peter frowned. 'I mean there must have been so many opportunities?'

604

'I very nearly told her the day Anderson was plastered across the paper,' Sam half smiled. 'But I was afraid it might make things worse.'

'Why now then, Sam?' Georgia looked round at him, a puzzled expression in her eyes. 'You seemed kind of in a hurry earlier. Are you going back to the States?'

'Not till we've finished that album,' he grinned. 'I've sent Jasmine and Junior your records and said I have a special story about you. They already think you're just about the best thing in the world.'

'My brother and sister,' she said pensively. 'I can hardly believe it.'

'So what is the panic?' Peter asked.

'No panic,' Sam smiled. 'But I knew in the next weeks I'd hardly get a chance to talk to you privately together. You two are so in love you've forgotten what's going on out there,' he paused to look at Peter. 'You've got to get back to Manchester. Georgia's got the album to finish. Your contract with Decca is running out, and there's Max and Anderson's fate hanging in the balance.'

'Why do you lump Max and Anderson together?' Georgia asked. 'What's Max been doing while I was away?'

'Keepin' his head down,' Sam smirked. 'Snakes both of them, and if I had my way I'd do the skinning.'

'You had a fight with Max?' Georgia giggled, her hand over her mouth.

'Me, a Southern gentleman?' Sam said dryly. 'No. I just marked his card.'

Georgia looked at Peter, who nodded as if it was time she too revealed all the things they had discussed.

'I'm going to manage myself in future.'

'Good idea, honey,' Sam grinned showing brilliant white teeth. 'Max'll hate that.'

For a moment she hesitated, looking at Peter for support.

'Not to punish him,' she said softly. 'He's a shark. He can't help taking big bites out of everything. Maybe I don't want to be in the same pool as him any longer, but I can't forget how much he's taught me.'

'He'll see it as the same thing,' Sam said, shrugging his shoulders.

Georgia shook her head.

'No Sam, not once I've talked to him. He'll always have a place in my life.'

'What about Decca?' Sam asked. 'Don't tell me you've gone soft on them too?'

'I'll screw them so hard they may have to wave me goodbye,' she laughed. 'I don't feel any loyalty to them, it's a good deal or goodbye.'

'And I only thought she'd inherited my musical talent,' Sam smirked. 'She's got the brains too!'

'You'd better tell him what you've done about Anderson too,' Peter smiled. 'Maybe he won't be so cocky then.'

'I spoke to the police,' she said in a small voice. 'I told them I wasn't going to press charges, it's all too long ago. But I asked them to check him out, put him on to social workers if he needs help.'

'Shit!' Sam's eyes flashed with anger. 'Georgia, that guy deserves hell, nothing less.'

'Perhaps he's already had that.' Her big dark eyes were full of pity. 'Don't try and bully me, Sam?'

'She's crazy,' Peter put one restraining hand on Sam's arm. 'But it's a good kind of crazy. Phillips did say he reckoned the man had flipped.'

'I've got so much,' Georgia said softly, looking at them both. 'I couldn't bear to see him again. But by the same token I can't pretend he doesn't exist. At least by footing the bill to have him dried out or whatever, I haven't just stood by.'

Sam shook his head and got up.

'You are so very like Katy,' he smiled down at her

where she sat curled up on the settee. 'She was a great one for lame dogs, doubt if she'd have even looked at me if I'd been like Peter. She'd have been so proud of you, honey.'

'Don't go Sam!' she said. 'There's so much more to talk about.'

'Not tonight,' he smiled, moving across the room to her and bending to kiss her forehead. 'We've got years ahead to catch up. You and Peter have only tonight, at least that's the way I remembered separations when I was your age.'

She jumped up then, flinging her arms round him.

'I love you Sam. We're a family now. You get Jasmine and Junior and bring them back. There's plenty of room for them here.'

'All in good time, honey.' He nuzzled his chin against her hair as he held her. 'You're one helluva daughter.'

Sam turned up his jacket collar as he walked along by the Thames. If he lived another twenty years in England he doubted he could get used to the climate. English people talked about this weather as warm, well perhaps they ought to try New Orleans. The smell was kinda the same as walking by the Mississippi, tangy and dirty, darkness turning it into a thing of beauty. But the Thames wasn't his river, just as London wasn't his town.

It was tempting to let Georgia take over his life. He could imagine her finding a house big enough for all of them, playing big sister to Jasmine and Junior, pushing him into the limelight. Perhaps forgetting Peter and herself as she tried to make everyone happy.

He'd learned a great deal about kids from watching Georgia. He had to go back and put all that into practice with Jasmine and Junior, win back their trust and love before he thrust them into a cauldron of new experience.

Georgia had grown up in a white world, learned the hard way how to deal with prejudice, rising above it without losing her deep understanding of human nature. His kids had been born into discrimination and segregation. By replanting them hastily, surrounded by people anxious to make them happy, they might grow up rootless, without that need to achieve anything for themselves.

He stopped for a moment by Albert Bridge. Each strut covered in lights, like a bridge to fairyland.

'Sure is pretty,' he said aloud, looking out over the dark river. At home in New Orleans the place would be jumping now with music and people. Here it was silent and empty, just the odd man, out with his dog, and a pair of lovers further on the bridge, arms around each other. It was a good place to come to terms with his thoughts.

'Finish the album. Then go home. There'll be holidays, time for us all to get acquainted. You've come this far without climbing on someone's back Sam, Jasmine and Junior have to learn that too.'

Maybe he should have told Georgia about Celia. He had planned to. In long telephone conversations he'd come to care deeply for this brave little woman who'd given his daughter so much. But too much emotion in one day didn't make for restful sleep and tomorrow morning would be soon enough to break the good news.

'Only another hour and we'll be landing.' Tania the stewardess stopped by Miss Tutthill's seat to reassure her.

All the crew knew who this lady was and where she was going. Tania just hoped she could get off the plane herself quick enough to see the reunion.

'Maybe I should have waited another day or two?' Celia Tutthill looked up at the tall, willowy redhead, elegant in her cream blouse and skirt. 'I mean suppose she hasn't got back from her holiday yet?'

'But you said her friend would make sure she did?' Tania perched on an empty seat across the aisle.

'I know,' Celia smiled, her greeny-grey eyes wrinkling up with pleasure. In her telephone conversations to Sam Cameron she had heard so much that pleased her. All she could do was hope he did manage to engineer getting her home, and telling Georgia the truth about himself, without giving her daughter more anxiety. 'I'm just being an old worry-guts. I'm even worried Georgia won't recognize me!'

She was two stone lighter than she'd been for much of her life, something that started with African tummy and she never put back on. Her light brown hair was longer too, waving at her neck with streaks of gold from the sun. Gone were the days when she wore tailored suits, now her wardrobe consisted only of shorts and shirts. The green floral dress she wore today was new, bought hastily in Nairobi before flying out.

'Of course she'll recognize you,' Tania chuckled.

Nairobi had been buzzing about this woman.

According to the gossip she had arrived in Africa with only the sketchiest idea of what was ahead of her. Everyone had expected her to last a year at most, before the heat, flies, disease and lack of equipment sent her running home. But Nurse Tutthill took one look at Africa, rolled up her sleeves and adapted.

Tania was surprised to find Celia so small. The image the gossips had created was one of a big fierce woman who scorned bureaucracy, fought tooth and nail for supplies of medicine and almost singlehandedly had vaccinated thousands. When that dark tan faded she would be just another apple-cheeked middle-aged lady, just like her own mother, the sort of woman equally at home in church garden fêtes manning the cake stall.

'I've got a lot more wrinkles,' Celia's eyes twinkled as

she touched her face tentatively. Out in the bush there were no luxuries like mirrors. Faced with herself in a hotel room she had been shocked to see the changes. Crows' feet round her eyes, cheek-bones where once had been pads of flesh. Even her arms and legs seemed to belong to someone else, muscular, sinewy and an indecent dark brown. Yet despite the passing years she liked herself better. Even as a girl she was never pretty, but now at least people described her as striking.

'If I look like you at your age I'll be delighted,' Tania smiled, teeth like an advertisement for dentistry. 'You look ten years younger than that old picture in the paper. But don't you think you should try and sleep for a while? It's going to be a long, emotional day for you.'

'I think I've forgotten how to,' Celia said thoughtfully. 'Since the day that message came I haven't had more than a couple of hours' cat naps.'

'You look good on it,' Tania got up and straightened her uniform. 'Would you like a drink?'

'No thank you,' Celia grinned. 'You can't meet your daughter with alcohol on your breath!'

The message had come third hand. It had been relayed first by telephone, then by radio and the final few miles by a man on a pushbike.

It was early in the morning, already very warm, the sun rising up from behind the mountains when she saw the messenger.

He was young and lanky, wearing nothing but a pair of baggy khaki shorts. His skinny brown legs stood out like paddles as he came blundering down a track to the hospital.

She watched as he put his feet down to stop himself, threw his bike down on the bare earth and disappeared from her view.

It hadn't meant anything. Every day people flocked

to the hospital. When she looked out over the bush for as far as the eye could see there was nothing but waving yellow grass, a few thorn trees, no sign of human habitation, yet day after day an endless procession of the old, the sick, the lame and the blind made their way here for treatment.

She hadn't even finished dressing when she heard feet running on the veranda towards her room.

'What is it?' She hastily buttoned up her shirt and opened the door to see Carmel the Irish nurse coming to a halt, panting. She was fat, her striped dress bursting across her buxom chest, her apron dangling at her waist as if interrupted in her dressing too.

'A message from Nairobi,' she huffed. 'You've got to go there immediately. Something to do with Georgia.'

A wild ride in a beaten-up Landrover to meet her replacement at Buna, then into a mail plane as far as Archer's Post. Two days without sleep, surviving on just adrenalin. Fear and hope mingling like a lethal cocktail.

Urgent messages to her only meant one thing. Death, sickness or disaster. By the time she got to a telephone at Archer's Post every bone in her body screamed for rest, but until someone could reassure her that Georgia wasn't dead she couldn't even pause for refreshment.

'She's fine,' Hilary her old friend in Nairobi said. 'She's a famous singer now and a newspaper has been searching for you. It seems you and I are the only two people in the world who hadn't heard her.'

'But –'

Hilary cut her short. 'It's a long story, love. I can't tell you it all over the phone. Rest up tonight and get someone to drive you here tomorrow. She's safe and healthy. Don't worry anymore. I'll tell you everything soon.'

Another two days before she flopped into a chair in the Nairobi office. Dusty hair, red-rimmed eyes full of grit, bruised from the long hours in a truck, sweat stains covering her old shirt. Yet exhaustion faded as Hilary put a large gin in one hand and the telex in the other.

There, in the same steamy office where she'd started out in Africa, life turned a full circle.

Now she hardly noticed the flies, the cane chairs which stuck in her legs, the bandages and syringes waiting for distribution, or the maddeningly slow fan that only served to churn up papers rather than air.

It was the first time she had cried since leaving England. All those years of uncertainty, all that grief held back came flooding out.

'If you had told anyone but me about her,' Hilary said as she comforted her. 'They might have made the connection. But I'm as bad as you Celia, I don't read the papers or listen to music. Just fancy, your gel a star!'

Tears turned to laughter as Celia saw the absurdity of the situation. Two old nurses, who both fled from England to forget, suddenly aware how out of touch they were.

Hilary with her white cropped hair could have been a man wearing women's clothes. A print dress left over from the mid-forties, its demure lace trim revealing a scraggy, lined neck, and arms like a stevedore. While Celia in her khaki shorts and man's shirt looked more feminine than she ever had at home. No wonder the young girls in the office stared at them as if they were mad, drinking gin in the afternoon, crying and laughing alternately.

Yet those same girls were the ones who found old magazines, copies of Georgia's records and filled her in with everything that had happened in the last few years.

'Why did you stop writing to Peter?' Hilary asked as once again Celia read the telex. 'I keep asking myself why I didn't open them instead of dumping them as you told me to do.'

Even now she couldn't explain that fully, but at the time she got the letter from Mrs Radcliffe it seemed the honourable thing to do. She was just another mother worrying about her son.

What was it she said? 'I am begging you as another mother to let my son forget. He isn't working as he should, each letter from you unsettles him. He has another girl now and they could be happy without reminders of the past. Please let him go, and I promise you if I ever hear of Georgia I will write immediately.'

How could she know then Mrs Radcliffe had no intention of helping? How foolish Celia was to think Peter's integrity had come from her!

'Oh Hilary,' Celia sighed. 'If only you had! But then this whole business is built on "if onlys".'

Celia leaned back in her seat and closed her eyes. She wasn't finished with Africa yet. A long overdue holiday. Time to hear Georgia sing and share in her life. A chance to recharge her batteries and she'd be back. Even Georgia re-entering her life couldn't make her stay in England.

The woman who'd left England five years ago had changed. Drought, famine, malnutrition and disease made the problems she'd encountered in London's East End seem trivial. How could any woman who'd seen people dying for want of clean water, possibly go back to treating verrucae, weighing healthy babies and filling in forms?

'Still can't nod off?' Tania was back, offering her yet another drink.

'Silly, isn't it?' Celia laughed. 'The most comfortable seat I've sat in for five years, all my old worries gone, and yet I'm still wide awake.'

'Do you think she'll marry Peter?'

Celia smiled. It was a bitter irony that people were now so fascinated by Georgia. Six years ago she hadn't

613

even managed to convince the police this same girl was at risk. Was that what fame meant? In Africa people were dying of starvation, yet the rest of the world hung on news of a singer's wedding.

'I hope so,' she said. 'If I could choose any man in the world for her, I'd still pick him.' She could see him so clearly. Those wide, honest blue eyes, his sensitive mouth, floppy blond hair and the proud conviction in his purpose.

Tania hovered, an unspoken question in her eyes. Celia knew she was trying to broach the subject of Brian Anderson, but diplomacy stopped her.

'Speak up girl,' she said, imitating Hilary. 'You want to know about him?'

Tania blushed.

'It's all right,' Celia said in a softer tone. 'Everyone's going to ask me that, why not you? But the answer is I don't know. I guess I'll have to see him at some stage, we are still married after all. Of course I have the advantage over everyone else. I always knew what he did.'

'How do you feel about him now?' Tania said softly.

'I ought to feel anger, I suppose,' Celia said slowly. 'Perhaps I've been exposed to too much horror over the years to feel that any longer. In a way I'm glad he surfaced, at least he brought Georgia back to me.'

'You're a very strong lady,' Tania smiled, touching Celia's hand briefly. 'I can see now who moulded Georgia!'

The sun was warm on her shoulders as she made her way from the aircraft steps to the tarmac. Celia had been expecting, even welcomed, rain. On steamy nights out in the bush she often pictured the garden in Blackheath. Grass cool and damp under her feet, roses twining round the archway to the vegetable garden, the smell of wet soil, the dewy softness of it all. Her heartrate had been gradually quickening as the plane went over London. The vivid green grass, the silver Thames and all the majesty of Windsor Castle somehow embodied everything in England that was dear to her.

The tarmac spread on seemingly forever, surrounded by dark green grass. The air had freshness never felt in Africa. Luggage piled on trucks, men in blue uniforms standing in groups, an orderliness she wasn't used to. The plane behind her disgorged more passengers to add to the stream already making their way to the terminal. She wanted to run now, not wait while Customs men looked in her one small bag.

Looking up at the glass and concrete building ahead of her she saw a figure behind glass. Masses of dark hair, a red dress, brown long legs, jumping up and down, waving with both hands.

A lump came to her throat, tears blinded her. She raised her hand to her lips and blew a kiss.

Quickening her pace, she dodged round an elderly couple and ran the rest of the way.

Dark-suited Customs men waved her through. She felt the smiles though she couldn't see them. All she saw was that finely polished corridor and a glimpse of people waiting beyond.

Hundreds of people pushing and shoving. Cameras flashing, voices shouting out greetings. But all she was aware of was one small voice.

'Mum! Mum!'

A mop of wild black hair, two dancing wet eyes, arms outstretched running towards her.

The longest minute, yet the quickest. She had grown from skinny-legged colt to an Arabian thoroughbred. So beautiful Celia could barely credit it was the same pitiful child she took away from St Joseph's that winter morning. A heart-shaped caramel face. Black curls tossed back, dazzling white teeth and a wide smiling mouth. Her red dress so short and tight it could have

615

been sprayed on, matching tight boots that evoked an image of principal boys in pantomime.

She threw herself at Celia like a puppy, lifting Celia off her feet, crushing her into her arms.

'Mummy,' was all she heard and all the missing years slipped away.

Cameras flashed like lightning. A barrage of shouted questions, an army of people advancing on them. Yet all they felt was two hearts pounding together. Two pairs of streaming eyes, two cheeks pressed against one another's.

Celia felt Georgia take her waist, pushing her back to look at her.

'You've shrunk, Mum! Or is it I've grown?' Georgia looked down at Celia, dark chocolate eyes melting with tears, then pulled her fiercely back to her shoulder, enveloping her in the kind of rocking hug she had once given Georgia.

'My baby,' Celia whispered. 'I thought I'd lost you forever.'

'I was never lost to you,' Georgia whispered back. 'I carried you inside me wherever I went, but let's get home now, away from all this.'

With her arm firmly around Celia's shoulder, Georgia turned to the fans and press.

'I want you all to meet my mother,' she grinned. 'This is the happiest day of my life.'

A mural of grinning faces. Another firing squad of photographs, Celia blinked, her lips trembling.

Georgia held up one hand, the crowd fell silent.

'I know you all want to ask questions,' she said, glancing sideways at Celia. 'But my mother isn't used to this kind of publicity and just now we both want to go home and talk and rediscover one another.'

Another blast of flashing lights. Murmurs of disappointment, a predatory closing in.

'I have just one announcement,' Georgia smiled

round, head held high. 'Today you've seen the reunion with my mother, but last night I also learned who my real father is.'

Silence fell. Two or three hundred people leaning forward to hear.

Georgia grinned, tossing back her hair, using all the timing she'd learned on stage.

'It's a sad, wonderful story,' she said. 'One I'll tell you all in a day or two, but for now you'll all have to be content with just a name. That name is Sam Cameron.'

She didn't appear to hear the tumult that broke around her, or show any concern that she'd merely whetted their appetite for information. Georgia picked up Celia's bag and holding her mother closer to her, walked steadily ahead as if they were alone.

'Well, Mum,' Georgia said as they swept out on to the forecourt where a liveried chauffeur held open the doors of a sleek black limousine. 'How does it feel to be home?'

Celia didn't answer for a moment. She climbed into the back seat and sighed as she sank into the soft leather, waiting for Georgia to sit beside her.

'Do you remember how you felt that first day when I opened the door at Blackheath and led you in?' she asked.

Georgia took her hand and lifted it to her cheek.

'Like I was entering heaven,' she whispered.

'Well, darling, that's just how I feel right now.' She reached out for Georgia and this time it was she who cradled her child against her breast. 'Then it was me taking you to my world, now it's you leading me to yours.'

Ellie

Leslie Pearse

Ellie is a sweet-natured brunette, generous of heart with a sparkling smile and an accent which reveals her East End background. Bonny is beautiful and spoilt, with cascades of blonde hair, the brightest pair of blue eyes and a mouth like Cupid's bow.

The two girls meet in London at the end of the war when, seduced by two American airmen, they pool their wits and resources and set off to make a living on the stage. Set against the hardship and austerity of post-war Britain, and the glamour and ruthlessness of life in variety theatre, their story is one of sacrifice and burning ambition. But most of all a powerful friendship that lasts against all odds . . .

arrow books